# Nightmare

# *Nightmare*

By

Janice Peek

***Nightmare***



---



---

Printed in the United States of America

**Janice Peek**
1603 Capitol Ave, Suite 310 A552,
Cheyenne WY 82001

**ISBN: 979-8-9851336-1-5 (Paperback)**

**ISBN: 979-8-9851336-2-2 (Hardcover)**

**ISBN: 979-8-9851336-0-8 (eBook)**

Oh my gosh! The phone is ringing, and it woke me up from a nightmare. My heart was pounding so hard in my chest, it hurt. I had to catch my breath before I realized I had been dreaming. It is early morning time in San Antonio TX. It is still dark outside at 7:00 am. Me, Casmire (my niece), another girl and two guys (Amanda, Buddy and Lance), we all live in a four-bedroom townhouse together.

The townhouse is part of the old mansion just on the outskirts of San Antonio heading towards 10 West, the mansion is called Blanco Sierra West. The building needs renovations.

Inside the house the pipes and steps squeak, creek and moan, especially at night. The electricity needs rewiring.

The lights are always flickering on and off. We cannot have too many things in the plugs, or we blow the fuses. I hate that, because I gotta go down in the dark, damp basement to put new fuses in. I always imagine someone is waiting for me in the dark corners.

Then out of the blue I hear something scurrying across the floor. I do not want to know what it was. I hurry up, put in the fuse and run upstairs. Then slammed the door and lock it. It is creepy if you are home alone, on your side of the house.

I was in my bedroom, which has two Queen size beds. I am sitting on one of the beds talking to Amanda, when buddy came strolling into the room unannounced. He just politely butted into our conversation like he had been there, all the while we were talking. We had to laugh at him, it was so funny how he did it. Trying to be Mr. Smoothe.

So, we started yacking again, talking about any and everything. When suddenly, the door burst wide open with such a force it almost put a hole in the wall behind it. In walks, Casmire the Tasmanian devil, acting crazy and looking crazy! She was laughing, hollering and talking out loud to no one in particular. Her shoulder length hair was messy, sticking out every which way. Her clothes were too big and wrinkled. She scared the daylights out of us, we all jumped and screamed at the same time. Aaaaaaaaah! I almost wet my pants!

This has also played a big factor in why she displays such erratic behavior. I love her very much, that is why I have taken her into our home. I cannot stand by and see her on the street homeless. Her behavior has recently escalated to the point, that I am considering having her committed to the hospital for evaluation. So, she can get the help she needs.

It was hard, but all of us convinced Casimire to leave the house, so we thought. But before she leaves the room, she left a surprise for us???

Casmir could be a beautiful young lady; she is 21 years old. Her young life was not easy, so many bad things had happened to her. I am afraid it has now scarred her emotionally. The family has shunned her and turned their back on her.

Casmir had left out of the room and all three of us started talking again. Then we heard something making a lot of noise or was somebody talking? At first, we could not make out the words, but we continue to listen, there it was again. We looked around the room and standing in a corner was a kid with no body, just a head. He jumped onto the bed, opened his eyes and started talking to us.

He told us that Casmire was his mother, and his dad was this freaky man that lived in the neighborhood.

We could not believe it, just before our eyes the kids mouth started changing!

All three of us were in shock, we stopped talking and just stood there, staring (our eyes bugging out), our mouths gapped open. We could not believe it, what we were seeing. This kid's mouth was going through a transformation. First, he started out with normal teeth, then suddenly, they started changing, the top and bottom rows of teeth were becoming distorted, twisted and crossing each other. The more he talked, some of the teeth began to change to metal. His voice began to deepen and sounded like growling and snarling as the transformation was taking place.

His face got ugly, then uglier the more he talked. Woah! Then this bodyless headed boys metal teeth are changing again, this time the metal teeth are turning into sharp jagged edges. These metal teeth are sharp enough to gouch big and serious wounds if he starts attacking us, maybe even death, if he is left unchecked.

Me, Amanda, and buddy jumped up, ran out the door and slammed it shut!

We ran into the living room / kitchen area. We could hear the kid crying, screaming, snarling and growling to let him out. I told him noooooooooooo! We do not know how long; the door will contain him before he is able to chew and destroy the door to get out. So, we chilled, turned on the TV and got something to eat, talking about our situation and what we are going to do?

The living room had a little corner section off the kitchen, called the alcove (that had a slanted slope). It was just big enough that we had placed a Queen size bed in there. Buddy goes to the bed and gets under the cover.

I look over where he is at and begin whispering to him to gently move the cover back. Something or someone was in there with him? Oh my God! Who or what is in the bed with buddy??? Me and Amanda are whispering and frantically waving our arms, jesting to buddy to get out of the bed.

Buddy gently pulls the cover back and reveals Casmire. She is lying face down on her stomach, her arms are folded under her head and she is facing the wall. Oh my God! We cannot tell if she heard everything, we said about her or is she really asleep? She is not moving, is this a trap? What is she setting us up for? What are we gonna do now???

Suddenly, the front door bangs open, we all jump and scream at the same time and in walks Lance, talking loudly, said he was tired. He had worked a double shift and all he wanted to do was sleep. He started towards my bedroom and he had placed his hand on the doorknob. And we all scream. Noooooooooo! The phone rings and I wake up.

www.ingramcontent.com/pod-product-compliance
Ingram Content Group UK Ltd.
Pitfield, Milton Keynes, MK11 3LW, UK
UKHW060114300726
14090UKWH00002B/187

* 9 7 9 8 9 8 5 1 3 3 6 1 5 *

# FORCES OF ART

Perspectives
from a Changing World

Contents

## Contents

# PREFACE



Kitty Zijlmans

*Forces of Art* was conceived as an initiative—which included the elaboration of this book—before the Covid-19 pandemic broke loose. But it was finalized right in the middle of the outbreak, or at least during its first wave. Newspapers, the media, experts, and countless others tumble over each other to share their analyses, and comment on taken (or discarded) strategies. Conspiracy theories thrive, international exchange is traded in for nationalist protectionism, but at the same time, people are craving for art, for sharing experiences and feelings, and for connecting with others. We are on the brink of a new world order. Yet, while writing this preface, George Floyd met his awful death literally under the oppression of a racist police force. This 'incident,' as it is euphemistically called, is a spark that has ignited a wave of protest demonstrations—not just in the US, but around the globe—against the never ending discrimination of and violence against black people, against people of colour. Even though, unfortunately, riots and looting sometimes take place, overall the demonstrations are as peaceful as they are persistent. Despite the Corona virus, people of all colours and ages, but especially young people, join in solidarity. Covid-19 plus George Floyd has kindled new waves of camaraderie and concern, a firm call for change.

Yes, we most probably are at the threshold of a new era, one we do not know yet, where the odds for change are towards an increased neoliberalism ruled by multinationals and a deep state; or a recognition of the need for collaboration and fairness, of bottom-up initiatives. This is why this book is so timely. Its driving force is the shared concern and responsibility for societies worldwide, with regards to culture and the well-being of its communities. It alludes to giving free reign to the forces of art and culture. Let us dream a bit. Imagine that for once the world isn't trying to save banks and multinationals, but is turning to the creativity and potentialities of the arts. There it will find forms of lateral thinking able to view things in a different, unusual light. Not a one-size-fits-all solution, but models for a new political imagination stirred by affective movements; not aiming at profit, but prioritising care and driven by concern, not just with the human world but the whole ecology of the human and non-human—of all that matters. Central to this thinking is not what art 'is,' but what it 'does.' This question was the motor of the initiative and book *Forces of Art*.

How did the idea of this massive initiative (and massive it is, covering thirty-eight projects in as many countries by fifteen international research teams) originate? In 2018, motivated to build on their existing knowledge, Prince Claus Fund, Hivos and the European Cultural Foundation invited young and experienced researchers from various disciplines from all over the world to propose approaches for critically investigating the role of arts and culture in societies. The research teams selected chose their research objects from a pool of two hundred cases, based on projects supported through grants by the three foundations over a ten-year period. To arrive at these two hundred cases, a random selection was made from an archive of hundreds of projects supported between 2008 and 2018. The research project aimed at investigating the way in which artists, cultural organizations, and artworks affect people and their social environments, and to explore how, or to what extent, cases of creative practice have been operational in empowering people, communities, and societies in their given contexts. Instead of employing a quantifying methodology, one that is favoured by politics and donor agendas, the three organizations decided for an affective approach: not targeting measurable output, but exploring how art and cultural practices actually work as social praxis.

To encompass the aim of the initiative of researching how arts and culture affect people and their social environment from a global perspective, the working group opted for the working title 'The Force of Art.' This was inspired by Krzysztof Ziarek's book *The Force of Art* (2004),[1] used as a course book in the MA Arts & Culture seminar at Leiden University (2015–2020). Considering the question of how art can be consequential, the book challenges the reader to think beyond art as representation, as merely aesthetical, or as simply an object or commodity. Instead, it stirs thinking of art in terms of a force that has the ability to transform relations and enable alternative configurations and relationalities. Art is thus understood as an event, an act, and as something that 'works' within society and steers away from the unrelenting manipulative drive characteristic of modernity. Many contributions in the book—finally entitled, in consultation with the publisher, *Forces of Art: Perspectives from a Changing World*—reflect how these processes of enabling and becoming function: artworks instantiate an interface between the 'external' social world and the 'internal' artistic space, and this allows art to be embedded in social praxis and yet to remain autonomous. It is this double character, Ziarek contends, that endows art with a critical and performative force.[2]

Art as a force affects people and this does not simply mean unlocking the beholder's emotions, but enabling new relationalities with other people, their surrounding world, nature, the environment—fundamental connections that exceed the subject-object dichotomy. It is this critical potential of art that Chantal Mouffe envisions in her essay 'Artistic Activism and Agonistic Spaces,'[3] exploring the different ways in which artistic practices can contribute to questioning dominant hegemonies. For Mouffe, critical art foments dissensus, making visible what the dominant consensus tends to obscure and obliterate. Such artistic practices aim at giving a voice to all those who are silenced within the frameworks of existing hegemonies. As numerous artistic and cultural practices discussed in this book demonstrate, one needs to go against the grain to be heard; this asks for strong commitment and collaboration of the parties involved to engender systemic change. The book testifies to the ceaseless energy people put into collectively setting up platforms, companies, centres, festivals, archives, projects, workshops, non profit organizations, all driven by the urge to reorganize social reality. It invites the reader on a journey detecting change in dozens of countries around the world, from Central Asia to Meso and Latin America, from Africa to Central Europe, from South and South-East Asia to the Middle East. What a rich panorama of innovative vitality unfolds here!

Woven into this fabric of interrelations, the three funding organizations play their part. In their plea for an affect-driven operation of funding instead of one aiming at ticking the administrative boxes, they mark the shift from ontology to performativity, and from prescribing to stimulating self-empowerment and self-regulation. This shift doesn't come without strong contradictions, as some chapters point out, because funding organizations are embedded by their very nature in a system that is competitive, and within accountability structures that require forms of evaluation (be they less results-oriented). Nonetheless, in making this shift, the

1..........Krzysztof Ziarek, *The Force of Art* (Redwood City, CA: Stanford University Press, 2004).
2..........Ibid., p. 13.
3..........Chantal Mouffe, 'Artistic Activism and Agonistic Spaces,' *Art & Research, A Journal of Ideas, Contexts and Methods* 1, no. 2 (Summer 2007).

three funding organizations in question create the conditions that afford dynamic processes to occur: the emergence of networks of relations that otherwise might not have been possible, intersectional thinking, collaborative and multi-generational peer-learning—because, as Carin Kuoni indicates further on in the book, this is also a pedagogical initiative. Throughout the book, there are many references to the underlying energy and drive encapsulated by the notion of agency, understood as a force between bodies in the process of becoming. By setting up or expanding the dynamics of local cultural infrastructures, generators of creativity can grow. For this, space—literal and metaphysical—is needed. This is another current throughout the fifteen chapters: space to work, to feel safe and free to be who you are, to speak your mind, to work with others, to experiment and discover, to create collectively, to join forces to build and to counter dominant powers—art as a space of political imagination. All these local initiatives and projects connect to the global in their joint strive for bottom-up change driven by artistic, creative, cultural forces.

Lastly, some words of thanks. In terms of enabling, it is the Prince Claus Fund, Hivos, and the European Culture Fund who need to be thanked for this visionary initiative, and this includes all the parties involved: the researchers, artists, enablers. Furthermore, the editorial team, Valiz Publishers, the Advisory Committee with the critical attention of Patrick Flores, Yvette Mutumba and Yudhishthir Raj Isar, and last but not least, the tireless and most committed research coordinator Ilaria Manzini.

Kitty Zijlmans

Leiden University
Chair of the Advisory Committee
Leiden, June 2020

# FORCES OF ART
## Perspectives from a Changing World



Carin Kuoni

Audacious, naïve, ambitious, utopian. These are all qualities that might be ascribed to the *Forces of Art* intiative, and this book in particular. The scope is unprecedented: fifteen international research teams spent the better part of a year investigating thirty-nine projects in majority world countries (artist Shahidul Alam's term to replace 'third world countries') that attribute to art a significant role in advancing civil society. The projects analysed took place in a decade (2008–2018) marked by the global consolidation of neo-liberalism and hypercapitalism, a turn towards populism (and in some Western democracies, authoritarianism), the Syrian, Kyrgyz, and Rojava Revolutions and the Arab Spring, the collapse of climate agreements, the global migration of people on a scale never before seen, and the onset of a global pandemic. And, yet, by sheer force of imagination, determination, and resourcefulness, these projects were launched, and the texts speak to their importance and impact. What you will find in the pages of this book is a dense, multilayered, polyvocal compendium of current thinking about the impact of art on civil society and social change. Utopian, naïve? No, these projects are thriving and animating their communities. Audacious, ambitious? Yes, and also inspiring and wayfinding. I invite you to join us.

The last two decades have seen extraordinary growth in the reach and range of art practices committed to social change, in organizations facilitating this work, and in philanthropic initiatives supporting the field. *Forces of Art* is set to open up the discourse on these art practices, directing sustained observation, providing adjustments and correctives, and shifting perspectives from prevalent approaches. For starters, taking a radical approach, the book only considers case studies from majority population countries. Secondly, in order to move beyond the familiar, the authors were selected from an international call to which they had been invited to apply. They were commissioned to investigate clusters of three to four projects each, based on their personal interests and expertise, regardless of geographical proximity. Accordingly, the projects are seen through highly specialized lenses, but always also in a context that extends beyond local parameters and connects projects beyond geographies. Positioning these projects in larger transnational political, cultural, and economic developments, *Forces of Art* also acknowledges and invites reflection on how the projects are funded, and how the funders—the original commissioners of the research and this book—are implicated in the narratives of projects.

*Forces of Art* makes a commitment to collaborative practices, seeking to nourish and sustain networks of affinities between groups of projects, groups of writers, and publics. It does so by its design, as an ethical imperative, and in response to trends unfolding in contemporary art practices. There is hardly a position represented here that does not derive from partnerships, be it multi-member research teams and their support staff or the projects in and of themselves—many of which are collaborative, entail organizational set-ups, and provide multitiered infrastructures and platforms. Even the editorial process has been a collaborative effort, a lively exchange between my colleagues and myself. In editing this book, we have experienced how these projects sit at the dynamic intersection of different regimes: economic, political, cultural, and financial systems. And we see how the collaborative creation of the projects functions as a form of resistance to hegemonic power constellations, offering opportunities for people to actively and knowingly engage with these forces according to their own inclinations. We invite you—readers—to experience this dynamic intersection for yourselves.

## 'A PLACE OF ENUNCIATION'[1]

The book is our place of enunciation in the present. The projects will live on and change, their affects and effects will multiply and dissipate, people will congregate and depart. At this moment of the book, in the time of coronavirus and social distancing, we can at least inhabit the pages of *Forces of Art* and follow the various narratives that shaped the art projects. These narratives flow in and out of the different sections of the book, at times interweaving with each other and at other times in conflict with each other, delineating different regimes. Here are some more general observations.

Economically and politically, despite looking at vast terrains with very distinct conditions, all projects considered in the book situate themselves within the force fields of hypercapitalism and neoliberalism. Global capitalism is the foil against which they have been conceived. Even the fact that many projects take the form of alternative infrastructures is, in the majority of contributions here, interpreted as a reflection of neoliberalism's entrepreneurial impetus. Humanitarian development initiatives, of which the projects are often the financial beneficiaries, are seen as perpetuating racialized, geopolitical power structures, whether they stem from legacies of colonial nations or the accumulation of extraordinary wealth in private hands. With such transnational capacities come media and information economies that are often considered hegemonic and authoritarian. An ongoing concern is the question of how art escapes these regimes, how it avoids being instrumentalized, and how it provides viable forms of resistance in the face of their overwhelming presence.

In holding a space for distinct and very diverse research methodologies, *Forces of Art* itself serves as a forum for resistance, affords a multisensory experience, and points to a horizon beyond dominant narratives. The vibrant positions unfolding in these pages speak of a triumphant embrace of unique research approaches. While some contributions masterfully conjure theoretical canons—either as a stage from which to examine the projects or as a closing frame to reflect on them—others highlight primary sources, the voices of participants, artists, and/or stakeholders who were instrumental in organizing, participating or witnessing a project. The diversity of applied research methodologies is also informed by how the duration of a project is defined: some are considered terminated, and 'exit interviews' provide the basis of assessment; others are viewed as ongoing because of the stories they inspired, harbouring the possibilities to launch anew. Some of the researchers invite other artists to revisit the site of the original project and commission new artistic interventions. Yet others commission different artists to develop a project elsewhere, based on the original one, to be investigated. In one case, the invisible infrastructure connecting two continents—the deep-ocean internet cables between southern Africa and South America—provide the tenuous connection between the case study in Lima and the newly commissioned project in Johannesburg. The meaning of art as research practice could hardly be taken more literally.

With such vastly different approaches, language becomes a very material medium where frictions, misunderstandings, and divergent interpretations contribute to the reader's appreciation of language's agency. All authors have been invited to submit their texts in English. The fact that some are more comfortable in English as it is an official language in their contexts compared to others where this is not the case, reinforces English—and with it by default a Western approach—as a dominant perspective. On the other hand, this decision also provides evidence of the specificities and incongruities of any one language, and of the frailty, awkwardness, and precariousness of any attempt at translation. Indeed, the possibility of not being understood, of withholding participation, of 'passing' and using codes, is as much an experience as a strategy pursued by some projects. Critical self-reflection of the researchers' own positionality is par for the course, arising within these distinct idioms and regularly alluded to—or explicitly stated—with references to 'desk research.'

The theoretical edifice held up within these contributions still rests primarily on key pillars of the Western canon. This is a serious issue and speaks to the work still ahead of us. It is compounded by prevalent standards of academic validation that continue to favour Western methodologies and accreditation standards and therefore make scholarship of Western theorists globally accessible and available. Among the positions that weave through the majority of chapters are Michael Hardt and Antonio Negri's decisive work on notions of multitude and assemblages; Pierre Bourdieu's analysis of cultural, social and symbolic forms of capital; Bruno Latour's design of actor-network theory, up to his more recent *Compositionist Manifesto*; Jacques Rancière's reformation of political subjectivity through the redistribution of the sensible, starting with *The Ignorant Schoolmaster*. These positions, however, are expanded on in the most welcome manner by less mainstream scholarship, among them Donna J. Haraway's notion of situated knowledge; Suely Rolnik's proposition of the collective body and micropolitics; Stefano Harney and Fred Moten's *Undercommons*; Jack Halberstam's queering of heteronormativity; AbdouMaliq Simone's urbanist research, in particular *Improvised Lives: Rhythms of Endurance*; Doreen Massey's ever-shifting constellation of trajectories as intersecting social relations; Elizabeth Povinelli's radical love; Loïc Wacquant's notion of body capital; and again and again *Pedagogy of the Oppressed* by Paulo Freire. David Gutierrez' redemptive narrative arises in certain contributions, as does Bolivian sociologist Silvia Rivera Cusicanqui's crucial research on *ch'ixi mestizaje*, 'who knows (and recognizes) its internal Indian and is firmly located in the here and now of its land and its landscape.'

What if we listen to what the glacier says? Ways of knowing differ, and perhaps the greatest discrepancies among the contributions to *Forces of Art* arise in the area of epistemology. A small but distinct number of research teams looks at projects that are explicitly considering the agency of non-human beings. Accordingly, such projects propose cosmologies that include human and non-human actors and deliberately embrace a non-anthropocentric polity. For these researchers, such different sensitivities are mapped through transtemporal, heterogeneous, and polysemic logics, and are often pursued through feminist methodologies, notions of situated knowledge, and Indigeneity as centring the quality of relationships between subjects.

Historically, the current decade is bracketed by the Arab Spring at one end and the pandemic fragmentation at the other, with the events mentioned above occurring in between. But the deeper roots that become visible in certain projects entail the two decades at the turn of the century: the dissolution of the USSR in 1989 and the end of South African apartheid in 1994; the Oslo Accords in 1993/1995, and the Israeli reoccupation during the Second Intifada in 2002. In Indonesia, The New Order regime of President Suharto came to a gradual economic and political collapse in 1998, eventually

1 ..........Borrowed from the chapter 'Between Memory and Storage' by Nishant Shah and Maya Indira Ganesh, p. 327ff.

leading to the formation of East Timor as its own country in 2002. This is also the period of various forms of highly publicized courts of international or transitional justice, from Cambodia to Rwanda and the former Yugoslavia among them. Uganda and Kenya's infamous anti-homosexuality legislations took hold in the early twothousands. The terrorist attacks in New York on 11 September 2001 still loom large. More recently, Evo Morales was Bolivia's first Indigenous leader, in power from 2006 to 2019; in the U.S., Occupy Wall Street and its enactment of prefigurative politics, along with the demands to de-colonize cultural institutions, predated the inauguration of the forty-fifth American president. These are just some of the key political events that underlie the chapters that follow.

## 'I AM THE ARCHIVE AND THE INCUBATOR'[2]

Having provided a broad overview of the approaches taken by the researchers who have shaped this book, let's look at the art itself and tease out some of the main qualities that distinguish these practices from other artistic interventions. Key among them is the challenge to notions of linear, chronological time, as suggested by the artist's quote above. There are other core principles that emerge—which I present below as propositions—that impact, each in their own way, civil society and suggest different political formations and subjectivations by offering a look beyond familiar frameworks at alternative sites and forms of discourse, dialogue, and contestation. Like the research teams, the editors have grouped distinct practices according to their own expertise and they in turn also carve out specific and particularly meaningful attributes: Serubiri Moses focuses on temporality and the organizational capacities of art, coalescing around infrastructures and networks. Jordi Baltà Portolés considers how the suggestion of simultaneous realities that may be visible or not activates new forms of political formation. Nora N. Khan in turn expands on artistic research methodologies that embrace modes of abstraction and opacity as part of their place-making impetus, in physical as well as digital space; and I've selected projects that entail peer learning, collectivity, and simultaneity across contexts and time frames. Together, these trends emerge:

### PROPOSITION ONE

History writing is a political act and the narrative holds power. History is present as a life force at every moment. A high degree of specificity must simultaneously afford considerations of larger temporal arcs. Not surprisingly, multi-generational projects abound and the moment of recall is also that of incubating new practices.

### PROPOSITION TWO

There is no single author or subject; every incident is a unique constellation of different intersecting voices and forces. The intensity of these polyvocal gatherings delineates their impact. Polyphony challenges hegemonic structures and identitarian limitations that range from heteronormativity and neoliberalism, to ethnocentrism and ableism.

### PROPOSITION THREE

The successful projects are hyperlocal, and simultaneously intersect with global development and trends. They insert and insinuate themselves into a matrix of political, economic, knowledge, and cultural regimes, but act on a level of micro-politics.

### PROPOSITION FOUR

There is no polity without bodies. The totality of the body in space and as consciousness is the harbinger of everything, the gauge and ultimate sensor, a necessity brought into unexpectedly sharp focus now in times of social distancing.

### PROPOSITION FIVE

Networks are rhizomatic; temporalities are expansive; technology can be modular and flexible.

Each project grows in significance through the exchange with the network. It becomes scalable, which makes it a political project, applicable to other situations.

The forces of art? They attend to contradictions and hold discrepancies and conflicts in place and in time. They are projections but never immaterial, and more intense when materially, historically, and ethically anchored. They afford spaces of intimacy, proximity, vulnerability, and trust. The forces of art have the capacity to speculate on and simultaneously enact possible futures, to open space for the imagination and perform alternative presents. They perform as models or gestures in relation to broader urgencies and society as a whole.

The book *Forces of Art* frames dynamic, collaborative art practices as political because they always also entail an 'other.' With art, we can step outside of ourselves—think of ourselves differently.

At this moment especially, where the Covid-19 pandemic has disrupted economic systems on a planetary scale, an equally radical reorientation of political agency is called for and, perhaps, a new political becoming is possible. As we attempt to get ready for a changing world where conditions of sociality are altered, how do we begin to comprehend and plan the scale and scope of action available to us? How do we organize, navigate, guide, remain relevant, and truthful?

The artistic practices captured in *Forces of Art* point the way. And protocols may serve as a framing device and starting point.

Protocols have moved to the forefront of public life, as the Covid-19 pandemic is making abundantly clear. Disclosed—or not—they determine much of what we do. Like the syntax underlying language, they regulate how we relate to each other, to our cultural, social, and political environments, and to the technologies that create those environments. They are the building blocks of the relationships and power structures between us and the world around us. As such, they favour some and fail others. With recent advances in artificial intelligence and robotics, the controversies surrounding data mining and privacy, the embrace of Indigenous land practices long shunned by extractive industries, and a growing chorus of demands to decolonize our institutions, protocols have emerged as essential tools of empowerment. They are evidence of governmental, political, social, or corporate structures, they speak of power—and thus invite subversion, improvement, and action. Guided by experts, researchers, and artists assembled in this book, we will encounter protocols embedded in different fields. We are invited to consider the inclusive and equitable protocols necessary to conceive of new spaces and opportunities for political empowerment. Protocols emerge as empowering, liberating forces that we can harness to advance social justice in our communities.

Etymologically, a protocol (*proto-collare*, before being glued) is the blank space at the beginning and end of a book, the so-called endpapers that set the conditions for the book's performance, the tone before the content begins. Protocols are actionable, they are structural and offer clarity, transparency, and inclusivity when properly devised. For us, a key protocol was to invite into the pages of this book all who have contributed to its findings. For that reason, the annotated index in the back is key—an invitation for the organizations discussed in the following 380 pages to self-identify and self-represent.

Less space is afforded to other contributors to the book who were crucial to its success. Foremost I would like to thank Ilaria Manzini, research coordinator by title, but in reality the gently powerful force behind the book.

2..........Ibid.

The members of our small editorial team, Nora N. Khan, Serubiri Moses, and Jordi Baltà Portolés have become indispensable companions. I am indebted to the members of the initiative's Advisory Committee as well as copy editor Liana Simmons. My colleagues at the Vera List Center for Art and Politics at The New School, Eriola Pira and Adrienne Umeh, have been extremely supportive. Artists and authors in the Vera List Center's orbit inform much of my thinking; for *Forces of Art*, perhaps most significantly so Robert Sember, who first brought protocols to my awareness, a concept I returned to through Natalie Diaz's writings. I thank John G.H. Oakes for his support and advice; he has been there from the very beginning.

Carin Kuoni
Editor-in-chief

Alta Tecnología Andina (ATA) / Lima, Perú / 6:08am 12°05'49.7"S / 77°03'27.3"W

Fundacion Más Arte Más Acción (MAMA) / Department of Chocó, Colombia / 6:10am 5°15'10.4"N / 76°49'33.6"W

Section One

# WHEN ART OPENS SPACES OF POSSIBILITIES

# WHEN ART OPENS SPACES OF POSSIBILITIES
## Policies, Tensions, and Opportunities

Jordi Baltà Portolés

In his collection of lectures *Facing Gaia*, philosopher, anthropologist and sociologist Bruno Latour suggests that the sciences, the arts, and politics share an ability to 'complicate' approaches to the world, 'involve' those affected by them and thereafter 'compose' new relationships.[1] The ability of the arts to render contexts of complexity more legible, generate terrains of action open to seldom-heard voices—and in doing so open new, more plural political spaces—is one of the ideas that runs through the chapters collected in this section. While, in Latour's view, similar dynamics may be engendered in the sciences and politics, I would argue that the artistic and cultural practices presented here embody distinctive values and meanings which are intrinsic to them,[2] even if they can run in parallel to, and mutually reinforce, the 'composing' of new relationships and the political transformation brought about by processes in other spheres of life.

What gives strength to several of these experiences is their ability to help individuals and communities imagine alternative ways of relating to their environment, to history, to other social groups, or to political institutions and processes. By recognizing that, beyond that which is visible, the space of culture also comprises that which matters but cannot be seen, some of these initiatives open up spaces of possibility[3]—they generate a space where, as Višnja Kisić and Goran Tomka argue in their chapter 'Tickling the Sensible: Art, Politics and Worlding at the Global Margin,' alternative processes of 'living, relating, and creating' may be imagined. Indeed, the political potential of these projects lies also in their uncovering of the many 'minor realities in which we are ... enmeshed,'[4] visualizing the coexistence of stories, meanings, and forms of existence which are often hidden behind the façade of a dominant reality. As anthropologist Ghassan Hage has argued, once we acknowledge that we live in a 'multiplicity of realities' it is also easier to assume that 'we can be other than what we are.'[5] In this respect, recognizing that plurality, and imagining alternatives, may become a step towards effective action.

Indeed, several of the examples analyzed in the following pages can also be identified with the notion of 'civil action' which, as sociologist Pascal Gielen and cultural worker Philipp Dietachmair argue, emerges when 'civilians initiate that which a government or state has not yet thought of (or does not want to think of) and for which there are no interested markets.'[6] Central to this understanding is the collective nature of activities and the conscious effort made to negotiating and designing a specific space for action. Although, as shall be seen, whether or not artistic projects

1..........Bruno Latour, *Face à Gaïa: Huit conférences sur le nouveau régime climatique* (Paris: La Découverte, 2015), p. 325.
2..........Eduard Delgado, 'Planificación cultural contra espacio público,' *Karis* 11 (2001).
3..........Marina Garcés, *Un mundo común* (Barcelona: Bellaterra, 2013), pp. 82–83.
4..........Ghassan Hage, 'Dwelling in the Reality of Utopian Thought,' *Traditional Dwellings and Settlements Review* 23, no. 1 (2011), p. 8.
5..........Hage, 'Dwelling in the Reality of Utopian Thought,' p. 11.
6..........Pascal Gielen and Philipp Dietachmair, 'Introduction: Public, Civil and Civic Spaces,' in *The Art of Civil Action. Political Space and Cultural Dissent*, ed. Philipp Dietachmair and Pascal Gielen (Amsterdam: Valiz, 2017), p. 14.

have tangible consequences in the political realm is often not a relevant concern among project initiators, a reflective approach vis-à-vis broader societal and political matters is, on the other hand, an ever-present concern.

## ART PROJECTS IN INTERNATIONAL DEVELOPMENT CONTEXTS: SOME VISIBLE TENSIONS

The authors of the chapters presented in this section have examined in depth some of the tensions and contradictions that arise in the implementation of art projects in international development programmes and that result from, among others, the complexities of funding, goal-setting, political contexts, and conceptual framing. Drawing from their reflections, I focus on two particular areas of tension.

Firstly, a process of negotiation between local needs and priorities, on the one hand, and the frames of intervention proposed by external funders, on the other, becomes apparent. Both project beneficiaries and the authors of chapters have stressed that, when compared to other funding organizations, support provided by the Prince Claus Fund, Hivos, and European Cultural Foundation (ECF), is notable in its provision of a broad, flexible framework for action. However, a need to 'navigate' the expectations from the diverse set of stakeholders involved remains, as the chapter 'Dissonant Entanglements and Creative Redistributions,' by Judith Naeff, Arnout van Ree, Lenneke Sipkes, Cristiana Strava, Kasper Tromp, and Mark R. Westmoreland, makes obvious. This entails, among other things, combining the managerial skills necessary for securing external support (e.g. using the relevant language to convince funders, and conceptualizing activities in the form of a time-bound project that fits the requirements) and a connection to local communities who will often be diverse and dynamic, and potentially contradictory with the discourse deployed in fundraising strategies. Establishing suitable, ongoing consultation, and participatory mechanisms with grassroots communities, and understanding one's own position and responsibility towards the 'territory' in a broad sense (i.e. the social, economic, environmental, political, cultural implications of a project), emerge as necessary steps in order to retain legitimacy and to be accountable in both directions.

More broadly, the need for organizations to balance skills related to project management in a narrow sense and those of ethical reflection, including the ability to interpret one's own environment in a complex sense, also arises as an important aspect. This is also relevant from the perspective of organizations providing training in areas such as arts management, which should actively engage in these complexities.

Secondly, several authors reflect on the almost-inevitable framing of projects in an instrumental vein, where a narrative connecting causes and consequences, resources, effects and impacts, easily permeates all explanation. They highlight that, in spite of the discourses on autonomy and emancipation enabled by artistic processes, and the critical political reflection that often underpins them, action takes place within the confines of the neoliberal reason. What space exists, then, to open up spaces of possibility, for thinking differently, more exhaustively, about the meaning of one's own actions? In several chapters, authors refer to the ability of arts-based processes to enable 'affective' encounters—that is, more personal, in-depth forms of mutual recognition, solidarity and feeling among participants, which may emerge as an alternative to the 'effect-driven' logic of instrumentalism. Related to this is the emergence of an ethics of caring for one another, and, as philosopher Marina Garcés has suggested, the potential development of an ability to share the fundamental experiences in life such as death, love, commitment, a sense of dignity and care, through the deployment of a receptive, listening attitude.[7]

Another significant response to the instrumental logic lies in challenging the unidimensional, unidirectional explanations based on effect, through more complex explorations of the assemblages of factors and processes that coexist in complex processes. Moving beyond the narrow alleyways of instrumentalism, this implies recognizing plural, multidirectional intersections of diverse intensity, and the potential of each actor to interpret different factors, and their confluences, in their own terms. It also involves moving beyond simple explanations on the power of art, while being open to exploring its many meanings. In their chapter 'Making the Common: Artistic Practices and Social Processes in Latin America,' Nadia Moreno Moya and Fernando Escobar Neira argue that the production of 'the common,' or 'common spaces,' is one of the several possible kinds of assemblage that may emerge in these circumstances. There is indeed a sense that, while the ever-present neoliberal logic may be impossible to escape, by exploring the margins, generating new, locally-rooted processes and expressions, and recognizing the existence of a 'multiplicity of realities,' some alternative forms of meaning may arise.

## A CULTURAL POLICY PERSPECTIVE

From the perspective of cultural policy, where most of my research focuses, the chapters presented in this section raise several important points. An important connection can be established between the challenging of projects based on an instrumental logic and the reflections on the goals and values that should guide cultural policymaking. Whereas goals such as economic impact or social cohesion have played, and continue to play, an important role in the design of public cultural policies, alternative ways of explaining their raison-d'être can also be found. Among them is the placing of cultural rights, including the right of every person to take part in cultural life, at the core of cultural policy, with implications in terms of fostering freedom of expression and promoting access to creative opportunities for everyone, and combatting discrimination and obstacles to participation, among others. Cultural rights, which provide a universal frame but should be underpinned by participatory forms of interpretation and decision-making at the local level, can inspire policies based on values such as universal accessibility, rather than the search for pre-determined goals in the economic or social spheres.[8]

Another important aspect concerns the focus on the provision of an 'enabling environment' for cultural and artistic practices. In this respect, an important emphasis needs to be placed on the existence of legal, financial, political, and social conditions which allow artists, cultural organizations, and other groups to design and develop activities free from external pressure. This is closely linked to the existence of an enabling context for civil society organizations,[9] an aspect which is central in '"The most important thing is to have that space!" The Power of Art and Local Art Communities in Central Asia,' the chapter presented in this section by Diana T. Kudaibergenova. While a focus on the enabling environment involves focusing less on the specific content of activities, public authorities remain important carers of some areas in cultural policy, including, among others, the protection of cultural heritage, the recognition of minority expressions, and the support for innovative practices. There is therefore a need to modulate public authorities' role and the allocation of resources, adapting it to different needs and circumstances—the design of participatory governance mechanisms which recognize and give voice to the multiple agents that contribute to cultural life is a suitable step in this direction.

Partly related to this is the ability of several of the beneficiary organizations presented in the chapters to develop relationships with partners in several fields of action—including education, social transformation, the environment, or political advocacy. In fact, although art remains a central, and generally the main, concern of the organizations analyzed, this is often strongly combined with other areas of activity. From the perspective of cultural policy, public institutions should also increasingly learn to develop 'relational' approaches, which facilitate dialogue and collaboration with other stakeholders, and cultural policies should be better equipped to explore the intersections with other areas of public interest.

Several of the chapters presented in this section address the frequent concern with the time-bound nature of project funding, and the related expectation that projects will lead to specific, tangible outputs. Whereas this remains an ever-present area of negotiation, there is also a sense that approaches promoted by the three funding organizations involved in *The Force of Art* have generally provided sufficient room to manoeuvre, providing flexible space for long-term development and focusing more on the nature of processes than the fulfilment of milestones or the generation of tangible results. This could potentially provide inspiration for funding models elsewhere, including in domestic public funding for culture in many cases. In order to achieve this, suitable institutional capacities to acknowledge and properly assess the complexities encountered by projects on the ground are needed, as is the existence of transparent, accountable frameworks to set priorities and guiding principles.

Finally, by emphasizing the ability of artistic processes to enable alternative ways of making meaning, fostering affect and care, challenging instrumentality, and opening up spaces of possibility, the initiatives presented in this section also serve to stress the important position that the arts and culture have in enabling the development of lives worth living.

While the terms 'sustainability' and 'sustainable development' have been much maligned, it is worth stressing that the discussion on the place of culture in approaches to sustainable development (or, in a less institutional sense, the place of culture in the vision of a life worth living and balanced with the preservation of life on Earth, today and in the future) remains central to this day.[10] Despite the many reflections provided on how cultural aspects inform visions of a desirable life,[11] mainstream approaches to sustainable development have generally failed to give art and culture a significant place. I believe that the reflections presented in the following pages could be seen as evidence of the need for cultural aspects to be given a more central place in strategies and policies concerned with building new relationships and more sustainable ways of living, today and in the future.

7..........Marina Garcés, *Nova il·lustració radical* (Barcelona: Anagrama, 2017), pp. 68–69.

8..........See e.g. Delgado, 'Planificación cultural contra espacio público'; Jordi Baltà Portolés and Milena Dragićevic Šešić, 'Cultural Rights and Their Contribution to Sustainable Development: Implications for Cultural Policy,' *The International Journal of Cultural policy* 23, no. 2 (2017).

9..........See e.g. Andrew Firmin, 'Engaging Civil Society in Cultural Governance,' in *Re|Shaping Cultural Policies: Advancing Creativity for Development*, ed. UNESCO (Paris: UNESCO, 2017).

10........Nancy Duxbury, Anita Kangas, and Christiaan De Beukelaer, 'Cultural Policies for Sustainable Development: Four Strategic Paths,' *The International Journal of Cultural Policy* 23, no. 2 (2017); Joost Dessein et al., *Culture in, for and as Sustainable Development: Conclusions from the COST Action IS1007 Investigating Cultural Sustainability*, ed. Joost Dessein et al. (Jyväskylä: University of Jyväskylä, 2015).

11.........See e.g. Jon Hawkes, *The Fourth Pillar of Sustainability: Culture's Essential Role in Public Planning* (Melbourne: Cultural Development Network (Vic)/Common Ground Publishing, 2001); John Clammer, *Cultures of Transition and Sustainability: Culture after Capitalism* (New York: Palgrave Macmillan, 2016); UCLG, *Culture 21: Actions. Commitments on the Role of Culture in Sustainable Cities* (Barcelona: UCLG, 2015).

← REFERENCES

Baltà Portolés, Jordi, and Milena Dragićevic Šešić. 'Cultural Rights and Their Contribution to Sustainable Development: Implications for Cultural Policy.' *The International Journal of Cultural Policy* 23, no. 2 (2017), pp. 159–73.

Clammer, John. *Cultures of Transition and Sustainability: Culture after Capitalism*. New York: Palgrave Macmillan, 2016.

Delgado, Eduard. 'Planificación Cultural Contra Espacio Público.' *Karis* 11 (2001).

Dessein, Joost, et al. *Culture in, for and as Sustainable Development: Conclusions from the Cost Action Is1007 Investigating Cultural Sustainability*, ed. Joost Dessein et al. Jyväskylä: University of Jyväskylä, 2015.

Duxbury, Nancy, Anita Kangas, and Christiaan De Beukelaer. 'Cultural Policies for Sustainable Development: Four Strategic Paths.' *The International Journal of Cultural Policy* 23, no. 2 (2017), pp 214-30.

Firmin, Andrew. 'Engaging Civil Society in Cultural Governance.' In *Re|Shaping Cultural Policies: Advancing Creativity for Development*, ed. UNESCO, pp. 85–101. Paris: UNESCO, 2017.

Garcés, Marina. *Un Mundo Común*. Barcelona: Bellaterra, 2013.
—. *Nova Il·lustració Radical*. Barcelona: Anagrama, 2017.

Gielen, Pascal, and Philipp Dietachmair. 'Introduction: Public, Civil and Civic Spaces.' In *The Art of Civil Action: Political Space and Cultural Dissent*, ed. Philipp Dietachmair and Pascal Gielen. Amsterdam: Valiz, 2017.

Hage, Ghassan. 'Dwelling in the Reality of Utopian Thought.' *Traditional Dwellings and Settlements Review* 23, no. 1 (2011), pp. 7–13.

Hawkes, Jon. *The Fourth Pillar of Sustainability: Culture's Essential Role in Public Planning*. Melbourne: Cultural Development Network (Vic)/Common Ground Publishing, 2001.

Latour, Bruno. *Face À Gaïa: Huit Conférences Sur Le Nouveau Régime Climatique*. Paris: La Découverte, 2015.

UCLG. *Culture 21: Actions. Commitments on the Role of Culture in Sustainable Cities*. Barcelona: UCLG, 2015.

# MAKING 'THE COMMON'
## Arts Practices and Social Processes in Latin America

Nadia Moreno Moya and
Fernando Escobar Neira

This chapter presents thoughts and findings from a research inquiry exploring the intersections between arts practices and social processes in Latin America through the study of projects led by organizations active in the region: the Museo de Antioquia (Colombia); Proyecto mARTadero (Bolivia); and Fundación 4-18 (Colombia). The authors formulate their arguments from a transdisciplinary perspective that prioritizes spatial registers, the testimonies of those involved, and the paths followed by the organizations. They ask themselves what art can do in the territories where the projects took place, and through that question argue that the synergies between arts practices and social processes allow for the production, resignification, or actualization of 'the common' and common spaces in these territories.

Keywords
→ Arts Practices
→ Social Processes in Latin America
→ the Common
→ Common Spaces
→ Contemporary Art
→ Social Turn
→ Cultural Turn
→ Heritage
→ Territory

## INTRODUCTION

Our research focuses on the study of three projects that were initially chosen due to their resonance with our own research and professional interests—the connections between visual arts and power, issues of cultural policy, and shifts undergone by cities and citizenships in Colombia as well as Latin America in general. Furthermore, we wanted to take a closer look at projects involving arts practices engaged with social processes addressing the particularity of individual territories located in cities that were excluded from dominant narratives of 'Latin American art.' For these reasons, we thought it would be strategically appropriate to include case studies that encompassed large-scale and long-term projects alongside small organizations and short-term endeavours.

With these considerations in mind, we settled on three case studies: the project Museo + Comunidad [Museum + Community], led between 2010 and 2013 by the Museo de Antioquia in Medellín, Colombia; Proyecto mARTadero [Project slaughtARThouse], a physical space and a 'cloud' of organizations and groups that started out in 2004 and that remain active today in Cochabamba, Bolivia; and Visualización de Honda [Visualizing Honda], a set of actions and interventions realized by the 4-18 Foundation in 2014 and 2015 in Honda, Colombia.

Before discussing the individual case studies, we outline our place of enunciation, the methodological path embraced by our research, and its purpose.

In our view, a research project on artistic and cultural practices is more akin to an artisanal process than to a process of instrumental reasoning. It is a mode of inquiry structured like a warp—that is, like a webwork where theories, materialities, and practices come into relation—rather than as a unidirectional process of inductive or deductive analysis based on empirical data. For this reason, we believe that it is off-point to set forth an a priori theoretical framework to display our analysis. Instead, we assemble a toolkit that allows us to approach our case studies through conceptual contributions derived from different disciplines or 'traditions' of thought: theories of art, new art histories, Latin American cultural studies, cultural geography, urban studies, critical theory, and what are known as forms of 'social knowledge.'

We are aware of the degree to which our research is traversed by particular relations of knowledge/power: as researchers and lecturers working in a university, we are in a position of privilege with respect to forms of social knowledge; and the 'book chapter,' as a genre, prioritizes academic knowledge and specialized spaces, more so when it is intended for publication in English, a language that is outside the range of our thought structure (and the same can be said of many of the social agents involved in the projects that we will discuss).[1] For these and other reasons, we felt the need to establish methodological lines of inquiry wherein social agents would not be treated as 'objects' of study, but rather as subjects of thought and knowledge. Accordingly, we decided to recuperate the lived experiences of the people who led and who were participants in the projects by organizing joint journeys, or conversations, at the site where each project took place. Although we were not able to do this in all cases, we conducted a significant number of interviews and conversations; these turned out to be extremely important for us, for the information shared by our interlocutors, as much as for the intensity of their narratives.[2] The latter we embraced as texts and textures that can be brought into the space of memory and which performatively register the effects that these projects have had on their organizers and participants.

What can arts practices achieve within territories? What kind of potency can they deploy? As we advanced in our field work, we found that the concept of 'the common' could help us address these questions: We understand 'the common' as a

> Dynamic form of association that is
> particular and concrete, that is,

1............Spanish was the main language used for research (both for participants and researchers).

2............A list of interviewed participants can be found in the references section at the end of the chapter.

> temporally, geographically, and historically situated, and which, for the most part, targets specific aims, most often having to do with securing or protecting conditions for collective reproduction amidst extreme threats of dispossession or injury.[3]

Since we seek to analyze how artistic practices coproduce and tend towards 'the common,' we should also clearly delineate our understanding of 'common space,' which we take to be a territorial apparatus, at the neighbourhood scale, where the public and the private enter into complex forms of coexistence, and which is subject to a variety of appropriations and identitary strategies.[4]

Considering the limitations in length for the present chapter, measured against the copious amount of information that people shared with us, we find ourselves compelled to focus on key moments where we have found a connection between the tactics of artistic practices and the assemblage (*agencement*, in French) of 'the common' within our three case studies. To this end, we will lay out the historical, political, and spatial circumstances that prefigured the creation of the organizations or projects; the role of the institutions that funded them; the temporality of their organizational processes; and the ways in which the organizations worked with the inhabitants and negotiated with state agencies, or other organizations, in the production of 'the common.'

## THE CASE STUDIES

### Museo + Comunidad

•

Museo de Antioquia (hence MudeA) is a private, non profit institution, whose origins can be traced back to the founding of Museo y Biblioteca de Zea in 1881, initially in commemoration of Francisco Antonio Zea.[5] The museum took on its current name in 1979, when its statutes were drafted anew, and its mission redirected towards the fields of fine arts and culture in the state of Antioquia. In 2000, after taking on a leading role in a plan for urban renewal called 'Ciudad Botero,'[6] the MudeA opened its doors at the former site of the Municipal Palace, in Medellín's historical downtown.

3............Raquel Gutiérrez, *Horizontes comunitario-populares: Producción de lo común más allá de las políticas estado-céntricas* (Madrid: Traficantes de sueños, 2017), p. 73.

4............Natalia Da Representaçao, 'Los espacios comunes como problema: Sociabilidad, gestión y territorio,' in *El retorno de lo político a la cuestión urbana: Territorialidad y acción pública en el Área Metropolitana de Buenos Aires*, ed. Andrea Catenazzi et al. (Buenos Aires: Universidad Nacional de General Sarmiento-Prometeo Libros, 2009).

5............Zea was a botanist and politician born in Medellín who participated in the process by which the territory that is currently Colombia gained independence in the early nineteenth century.

6............So called in honor of artist Fernando Botero, who offered to donate several works from his collection to the museum, including some of his own (by his authorship) public sculptures.

The relocation also brought changes to the museum's management, funding structure, and museological project. All of these changes positioned MudeA as a 'star-museum' representative of Medellín's transformation, along the lines of previous initiatives such as Bilbao's Guggenheim Museum.[7]

The project Museo + Comunidad played a prominent role in the 'social turn' of the museum in 2006: this was a stage during which the practices and discourses of the institution took on a distinct inflection, leading to an encounter between the museum and specific social issues that materialized in particular events as well as in its institutional architecture and profile. An event worth highlighting in this regard was the 'Encuentro Internacional de Medellín 07/Prácticas Artísticas Contemporáneas, Espacios de Hospitalidad' [Medellín International Meeting 07/Contemporary Art Practices, Spaces of Hospitality], a large scale project that reached beyond the exhibition format, encompassing interventions and collective or community projects in different city areas. Likewise, and for the first time in Colombia, for the 2008 project Destierro y Reparación [Exile and Reparation] the museum convened artists, academics, social organizations, and public officials, to debate and reflect on symbolic reparation for populations displaced by the internal armed conflict. As for its institutional architecture, we note that the museum established a section on Museums and Territories, which operated from 2006 to 2015.[8] This section initially carried out a programme for the appropriation of heritage in different towns of the state of Antioquia through exhibitions and collective experiences conceptualized and organized through methodologies of community participation. These events and experiences influenced the Museo + Comunidad project.

This social turn taken by the museum in 2006 should not be regarded exclusively as an intra-institutional project, but rather as a shift rooted in a broader and complex political and territorial fabric, which also foreshadowed the Museo + Comunidad project. Medellín was the city most impacted by the incursion of Colombia's armed conflict into urban spaces since 1995.[9] Starting in 2003, paramilitary groups that had established control over certain areas of the city engaged in a process of collective demobilization, which was legally sanctioned through the 2005 law 975, known as the 'Justice and Peace Law.' Simultaneously, victims' organizations intensified their capacity to organize and have a say in public policy, to a great extent due to the fact that the law granted considerable benefits to the perpetrators of human rights violations and other forms of abuse, while allowing for ineffective measures for unmasking the truth about violent deeds and for the awarding of complete reparations.

For these reasons, Medellín was the first city in Colombia to formally establish a victims' assistance programme (hence PAV, for its initials in Spanish), one of whose sections was devoted to the issue of 'historical

7.............Ascensión Hernández Martínez, 'El efecto Guggenheim-Bilbao en Latinoamérica: *Medellín, Ciudad Botero*, un proyecto cultural para la paz,' *Artigrama* no. 17 (2002), pp. 149–76.

8.............Alejandro Cardona, 'Un museo andariego. La experiencia dialógica de construcción colectiva del patrimonio entre el museo y la comunidad,' *Jangwa Pana* no. 12 (August 2013), p. 152.

9.............Centro Nacional de Memoria Histórica, *Medellín: memorias de una guerra urbana* (Bogotá: CNMH, Corporación Región, Ministerio del Interior, Alcaldía de Medellín, Universidad EAFIT, Universidad de Antioquia, 2017), pp. 84–97.

memory.'[10] Starting in 2004, the PAV programme, led by the office of the city's Secretary of Government, promoted several projects dealing with the issue of symbolic reparation; the PAV was also a crucial participant, alongside the MudeA, in the creation of the Museo Casa de la Memoria de Medellín [Medellín House of Memory Museum], which opened in 2011.

Amidst this context of reflections and actions, and starting in 2008, the MudeA introduced the idea of creating 'community museums for peace,' with a particular emphasis on Communes One and Thirteen. This project was in line with the local government's policies on memory, as explained above; according to several sources its original intent was to encourage the construction of community-based museums in territories that had been impacted by violence and whose populations had been victims in the conflict. Over time, this initial idea was adjusted in response to particular circumstances, as we will explain below. In August 2010, after the project had struggled to procure local funding, the Prince Claus Fund took notice of it and began to formally provide it three years of support.[11]

Broadly speaking, the project may be said to have developed through three stages, which more or less coincide with its operational years. During the first phase—beginning in late 2010 and throughout 2011—the museum, the PAV, and the Con-Vivamos Corporation[12] formed an alliance to join forces and share knowledge. The aim of the alliance was to promote a process of 'community participation around the symbolic representation of local heritage, culture and identities, memory, and territories.'[13] This process was expected to lead to the drafting of a community methodology for the creation of museums. The plan was to move forward with this project in the neighbourhoods of Commune One (Santo Domingo Savio, Popular, and Villa de Guadalupe) and in the Ciudadela Nuevo Occidente (hence CNO), a multifamily development complex located in the village of San Cristobal, to the west of the city.

In its second year (2012), project activities mostly focused in the neighbourhoods of Commune One mentioned above. A survey was conducted with more than four hundred inhabitants of the commune; the questions and methodology of which were arranged and co-constructed by the MudeA and groups of inhabitants from the territories who had been involved in the first stage of the project. The survey was meant to garner wider participation in the process of identifying and conceptualizing locations or features of the neighbourhood to which inhabitants attributed a patrimonial value. Through this stage, and onwards, the museum carried on with the project on its own.

10..........Although it is true that, since then, memory has become a public policy, it is timely to remember that commemorative acts and narratives of the past were already part of the toolkits of resistance of different communities and social organizations in Colombia. Likewise, they played a part in several efforts to bring art into contact with peace initiatives or the restitution of the social fabric. As an example, it is worth recalling the community-based project *La piel de la memoria* [Skin of Memory] carried out in 1998, directed by the artist Suzanne Lacy and the anthropologist Pilar Riaño; and different initiatives of organizations that were formed in Medellín since the late eighties such as Corporación Región, Con-vivamos, Nuestra Gente, Casa Mía, among others.

11..........Carlos Mario Jiménez, interview by the authors.

12..........A community organization long devoted to popular education on the northeastern area of Medellín.

13..........Corporación Con-Vivamos and Museo de Antioquia, 'Propuesta de Museos Comunitarios en la Comuna 1 y la Ciudadela Nuevo Occidente en Medellín,' Final report (Medellín, 2011).

In the third year of the project, the museum invited three collectives who worked in the fields of art and alternative communications to develop collaborative projects with the inhabitants as a way of developing some aspects of the work that had been carried out during the two previous years. The collectives that took part in this third stage of the project were Antena Mutante and Lengüita Producciones, both active in Colombia at the time, and Tranvía Cero from Ecuador.△Figs. 1 & 2.

△ 1
Lengüita Producciones in collaboration with Ratón de Biblioteca, *Love letters*, 2013, artistic action, photographic documentation, courtesy: Museo de Antioquia

△ 2
Tranvía Cero and Vigías del Patrimonio meetings in Santo Domingo Savio neighbourhood, 2013, photographic documentation, courtesy: Museo de Antioquia

As we have pointed out, adjustments were made to the project on different occasions, most significantly during the first year of the project. Several situations led the MudeA to reflect critically on the idea of creating and constructing 'community museums' in the territories. This led them to no longer focus on achieving a particular final product, such as a museological script drafted in collaboration with the communities. The emphasis throughout the three years was to activate encounters, journeys, aesthetic and artistic experiences that could facilitate exercises of collective memory, the self-management of community projects, the acknowledgement of the territory through appropriation, and the resignification of its spaces through the lens of 'heritage.'

To this effect, the museum took on the role of a mediator or companion, which accounts for the name eventually given to the project (Museo + Comunidad), by which the museum meant to underscore a sense of articulation or addition of efforts between the institution and the neighbourhood communities. It should be noted that the Prince Claus Fund continued to support the project in spite of this shift and, according to different sources, proved overall to be remarkably flexible and open to experimentation; this benefited the nature of the project as a process-based endeavour and the adjustments were made in response to territorial situations and dynamics.[14]

14..........Lida Restrepo, interview by Nadia Moreno and Yurilena Velásquez.

Out of the activities and processes carried out within the framework of the project, we highlight the work that was carried out by a group of seniors, mostly women, from the neighbourhood of Santo Domingo Savio who took on the name Vigías del Patrimonio [Guardians of the Heritage]; and that of a group of students from the Fe y Alegría high schools in the neighbourhood 'Popular,' who later came to be known as Caminantes del Popular [Foot Travellers from the Popular neighbourhood]. Both groups were involved in the project throughout its three years of duration, and in collaboration with the MudeA's team they created a set of heritage routes between 2012 and 2013, drawing from legacies of oral memory, subjective experiences, and the information collected through the surveys. These routes singled out meeting places, local characters, or everyday aspects of neighbourhood life, producing narratives where lived spaces and spaces constructed by their own inhabitants take precedence over those built by the state. During our fieldwork, we asked the groups to walk through the routes again with us.

The route traced by Caminantes del Popular went through a bakery, a house where cappuccinos are still sold, and a place where cars and buses were washed, among others. Only two of the sites had been built by state intervention: the Santo Domingo metrocable station, and the UVA

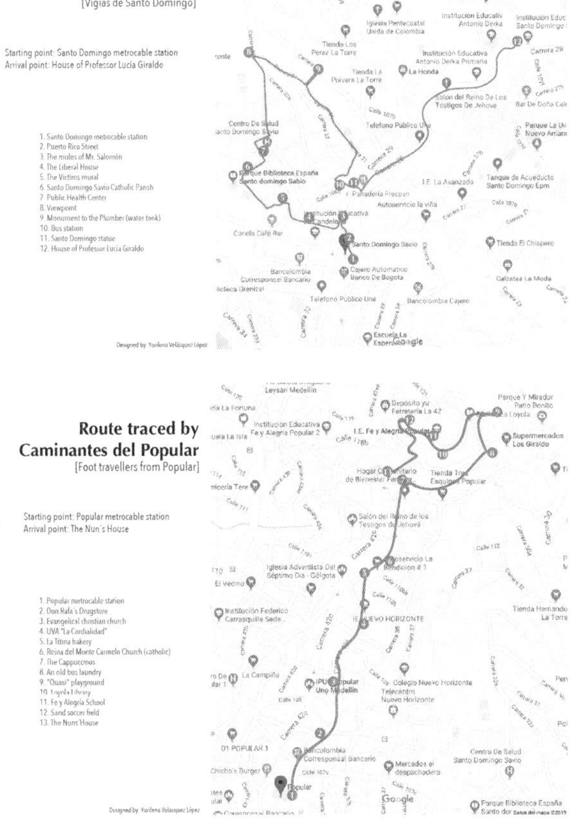


△ 3
Caminantes del Popular, sketch of the route on a map, 2013, graphic design: Yurilena Velásquez, 2019

△ 4
Vigías del Patrimonio, sketch of the route on a map, 2013, graphic design: Yurilena Velásquez, 2019

(a community cultural centre). According to one of the participants, Mónica Giraldo, these places are meaningful because the neighbourhood 'has very few spaces where people can meet and enjoy leisure time. ... [T]here are very few sports courts, parks, and spaces for young people.'[15] △Fig. 3

The route traced by Vigías del Patrimonio is similar, although its spatial narrative privileges places of collective memory associated with the neighbourhood's history of self-construction, or with the armed conflict. △Fig. 4 The latter is due, to a great degree, to the fact that group members directly experienced these events or processes. Their narrative also embodies the long history of social organizing and civil resistance in the neighbourhood.[16] The collective Tranvía Cero proposed the creation of commemorative plaques, in collaboration with Vigías, to be placed in the symbolic locations of their patrimonial route. △Figs. 5–7

At the CNO, on the other hand, the project was only able to move forward during the first year.[17] Unlike the neighbourhoods in Commune One, the CNO was a neighbourhood made up of several recently constructed multifamily building complexes, where the State had relocated a group of people from the Moravia neighbourhood.[18] According to David Henao, a member of the MudeA's team, the people who came to live at the CNO were strongly rooted in rural ways of life, and consequently suffered from cultural shock after moving into the apartment buildings, leading to difficulties in coexistence and an abrupt break from their previous livelihoods. Henao states that 'There was no sense of community there, [as] there were many people who had no social bond.'[19]

At the time, the CNO was also dealing with the presence of groups involved in drug trafficking that fought over control of the territory. This kind of struggle for territory, still present in different areas of Medellín, led to 'non-aggression pacts' between the groups who traffic through 'invisible frontiers' that delimit their areas of economic and social control. Said frontiers also function as limits that prevent inhabitants of different areas of the same neighbourhood to enter other areas, and it may even isolate buildings within the same multi-family complex. In the words of Andrés Arredondo, who at the time led the PAV's Historical Memory section, the CNO was an 'urban archipelago of restrictions, prohibitions, with no passageways.'[20]

Among the project's activities at the CNO, we highlight a process that was put together in collaboration with a group of female residents of the Las Flores housing development, which led to the creation of community gardens. After noting that the women had a deep knowledge of cultivation and gardening, from their rural background, and that they were already engaged in the practice of growing flowers and other plants

15 .......... Mónica Giraldo, interview by the authors.

16 .......... Santo Domingo Savio is one of Medellín's 'historical' neighbourhoods in terms of self-construction and popular organizing.

17 .......... Although the MudeA projected a plan and a budget to further this process in 2012, it interrupted collaboration with the CNO. After cross-checking documentary information with some interviewees, we think that this sector was a priority for the PAV, which at the time pulled out as an institutional ally.

18 .......... There were also inhabitants coming from other neighbourhoods of the city as a result of forced intra-urban migration.

19 .......... David Henao, interview by Nadia Moreno and Yurilena Velázquez.

20 .......... Andrés Arredondo, interview by Fernando Escobar.

7

5

6

8

9

△ 5
Tranvía Cero and Vigías del Patrimonio, commemorative plaques, documentation of the process, 2013, courtesy: Museo de Antioquia

△ 6 & 7
Tranvía Cero and Vigías del Patrimonio, commemorative plaques, 2013, documentation, courtesy: Museo de Antioquia

△ 8 & 9
Museo de Antioquia and residents of the Las Flores housing, wanings for planting, 2011, documentation of the process, courtesy: Museo de Antioquia

△ 10 & 11
Museo de Antioquia and residents of the Las Flores housing, community gardens, 2011, documentation of the workshops, courtesy: Museo de Antioquia

10

11

in the complex, the museum led several workshops, meetings, and exhibitions that focused on these practices and also allowed the women to share their life stories. They jointly programmed days of gardening to produce common spaces in the spaces between the buildings, in the form of *convites* [collective neighbourhood-based action] known as Menguantes para Sembrar [Waning Moons for Planting].[21] At these events, the women shared plant cuttings and exchanged knowledge with the museum's gardener, who also took part in the project. △Figs. 8 & 9

The name 'community gardens' came out of these experiences. It emphasizes the production of common spaces, non-existent until then, but also the strengthening of a common narrative of rootedness and collective memory in that territory. △Figs. 10 & 11

Lastly, the project reached beyond its initial intention, since over time it created a tactical space for overcoming the invisible barriers established by illegal groups. Consuelo Giraldo, an inhabitant who took part in this experience, states that 'The Museum managed to ignite the "spark" of participation. ... Some processes got underway, because we used to shudder at the very idea of going to La Aurora.'[22] The community gardens at the Las Flores complex became exemplary for women from other neighbouring buildings who saw the need to come into contact with them, thus creating possibilities for transit and dialogue among their inhabitants.[23] △Figs. 12–14

△ 12
View of the vegetable plot at Las Flores housing, photo: Fernando Escobar Neira, 2019

△ 13
Partial view of the community gardens at Las Flores housing, photo: Nadia Moreno Moya, 2019

△ 14
View of the bridge that leads to La Aurora housing, photo: Yurilena Velázquez, 2019

## Proyecto mARTadero

• •

The building where Proyecto mARTadero operates was formerly the city slaughterhouse of Cochabamba, Bolivia, built between 1925 and 1926 by the Catalonian architect Miguel Tapias and located in the Organización Territorial de Base (Territorial Base Organization, OTB for its initials in

21 .......... The convite is a traditional practice of community collective action rooted in self-constructed popular neighbourhoods of Medellín. For example, people collaborate in the construction of a neighbour's house while sharing food and drink. In this way, they sow collective feelings of identity and of belonging to the territory.

22 .......... Consuelo Giraldo, interview by the authors.

23 .......... La Aurora is the name of another development at the CNO.

Museo De Antioquia / Medellín, Colombia / 6:15am 6°15'08.8"N / 75°34'08.1"W

Fundación Cuatro Dieciocho 4-18 / Bogotá, Colombia / 6:20am 4°39'01.1"N / 74°03'04.0"W

Spanish) of Villa Coronilla.[24] This was originally the heart of the ancient city (Ranchería de Kanata), on the eastern side of the Rocha River that cuts through the city along the southwest-northeast axis. Nowadays, the location marks the frontier between the historical downtown and the city's southern area, which in the urban imaginary is Cochabamba's poorest district.

In 1992, after rising pressure from local inhabitants concerned with unsanitary public conditions at the Villa Coronilla neighbourhood, the city was forced to shut down the slaughterhouse. From that moment on, the building was put to different uses, among them a sports academy, a warehouse space for the public lightning company, and a deposit for goods confiscated under the Law 1008.[25] Later on, the building fell into complete abandon, which accelerated its deterioration, incidentally causing the decay of the surrounding urban space.

In the early twenty-first century, Bolivia went through a deep social, political, and economic crisis, which provoked what are known as the 'Water' and 'Gas Wars' (2000 and 2003, respectively), two massive social mobilizations that foreshadowed Evo Morales's ascent to power in 2005.[26] Amidst that climate of excitement, the former slaughterhouse building reopened its doors in 2004 to host twenty-nine works by the twenty-five artists who contributed to the second version of the 'Concurso Nacional Bienal de Arte Contemporáneo' [National Biennial Prize for Contemporary Art, or CONART]. With this event, Cochabamba became the first city in Bolivia to launch an open call event for contemporary arts, which incidentally earned it a place within the country's artistic landscape.

That same year, the group of artists in charge of CONART, led by Angélika Heckl and Fernando García, obtained from Cochabamba's City Council a bailment over the slaughterhouse building for thirty years. Immediately after receiving the bailment, they began to work on restoring and reforming the building. △Figs. 15 & 16

△ 15
Partial view of Proyecto mARTadero building, photo: Fernando Escobar Neira, 2019

△ 16
Partial view of Proyecto mARTadero building, photo: Nadia Moreno Moya, 2019

This group of artists had been working under the name Nodo Cultural Asociativo [Cultural Associative Node, or NADA], whose organizational structure was represented as a star with a central point of convergence known as the 'synergetic zone.' This image reinforced the collectivist principle of the mARTadero project as it was taking form. The fact that

24 ........... A Territorial Base Organization is 'the basic unit of a community or neighbourhood type, occupying a specific territorial space, whose population has no distinctions in educational level, occupation, age, sex, or religion, and whose relation to the state is mainly maintained through the city government in the jurisdiction of its location' (Decree 23858 of 9 September 1994).

25 ........... A bill that deals with the confiscation of goods, properties, and other items linked with the coca trade.

26 ........... As of writing, Bolivia was experiencing a new political crisis, produced, above all, by a coup d'etat and the forced resignation of Morales as president of Bolivia in November 2019.

a handful of collectives coming from different art disciplines decided to share a physical space and orient their practice towards a range of social concerns in line with the movements that emerged before 2005, leads us to think that this 'synergetic zone' amounted to a commitment to 'the common.' According to Heckl, this moment signals the rise of the 'contemporary' in local art, as well as its emancipatory and innovative character, being a form of art that encourages and enables connectivity.[27] Along the same lines, 'connecting with others' was perceived, at the time, as linked to the possibility of using the strategic capacity of contemporary art to 'take over' an abandoned building, and to create conditions for synergy among artists, and between art and other dimensions of social and political life.[28]

In our view, Heckl's remarks on the transformative power of contemporary art as the idea underlying the creation of the mARTadero point towards the early emergence of a wager for 'the common' in this project. Although at the time they claimed to be working in defence of the patrimonial value of the building under a traditional framework, we find in their agenda a strategy of political resignification, which perceives the building as a common space for culture and art and as a collective cause, itself encouraged by the exercise of cultural rights on the part of citizens which exerted pressure on diverse political and state authorities.

Since 2010, mARTadero has made more room for the city's cultural diversity, decentring the leading role assigned to contemporary visual arts during its first years. The project began to negotiate, in complex terms, the possibilities of contemporary art practices—such as dance, theatre, music, and the audiovisual arts—within the predominantly urban cultural diversity of Cochabamba, and through the participation of its citizens. We interpret this inflection as a cultural turn, because it exceeds the conventional categories of high culture, using culture as a 'resource' to achieve the defence of minority rights.[29]

Thus, as Fernando García remarks, the mARTadero has stood for a broad and complex view of art and culture, which entails the coexistence of several artistic forms and practices such as those proper to high culture and popular cultural practices.[30] △Fig. 17 Nonetheless, this position has also led to some tensions within Bolivia's cultural field. For instance, mARTadero shares many of the values of Cultura Viva Comunitaria [Living Community Culture, CVC for its initials in Spanish], but they have felt rejection on the part of some members who have questioned the sincerity of their 'social engagement.'[31] As we see it, this is due to divergent political positions regarding the role of art and culture in Latin American societies, with CVC leaning towards supporting traditional forms, and mARTadero having a more open view that does not see a conflict between these values and

27 .......... Heckl was one of the main forces behind CONART, as well as Proyecto mARTadero's first director.
28 .......... Angélika Heckl, interview by the authors.
29 .......... George Yúdice, *El recurso de la cultura: Usos de la cultura en la era global* (Barcelona: Gedisa, 2002).
30 .......... Fernando García, interview by the authors.
31 .......... CVC is a Latin American movement that emerged out of the joint-base of several cultural communities. Grounded on diversity as a founding principle, it promotes the exchange of practices and forms of knowledge. They also seek to influence public policies in their respective countries, in order to respond collectively to the specific needs of their territories.

△ 17
A meeting about the Ollantay Park project in the University of San Simón, Cochabamba, 2019, courtesy: Proyecto mARTadero

those promoted, for example, by Cultura en Red [Networked Culture].[32] The same can be said about contemporary art practices.

However, according to several current members of the team, the cultural turn was made possible by the fact that the mARTadero gained a certain degree of strength as an institution a few years after its foundation. This brought on qualitative changes, such as a conspicuous specialization in its procedures of cultural management, and quantitative changes that entailed a greater reach and forward thrust in mARTadero's actions. Neyda Campos, who is in charge of Project Management, explains these changes as follows: mARTadero 1.0 (2007–2012) initiated a platform for contemporary artists from different disciplines in Cochabamba; mARTadero 2.0 (2012–2014) encouraged a participatory process aimed at the surrounding neighbourhood; and mARTadero 3.0 (2014 onwards) showed that the project had achieved a great capacity for management and gained national and international recognition.[33]

All of this can be said to be grounded in mARTadero's ability to garner sources of support. It is important not to overlook accounts by project members, all of which suggest that international cooperation has for the most part created the financial conditions that have allowed contemporary art to expand during the past few decades in Bolivia.[34]

Currently, several members of Proyecto mARTadero describe it as a 'cloud of organizations,' that is, as an organization of organizations gathering a plurality of artistic and cultural projects within a large physical container. These include, among others, permanent residencies by two theatre companies, a performance duo, several dance groups, the hip hop ensemble Essential Roots, the Workshop for Urban Acupuncture, the breakdance collective Matarifes Villa Coronilla, and the skateboarding group Team Llajta Skate, the Laboratory for Creative Communities (hence CCLAB), Asociación Kuska (focusing on mosaic crafts), the NAM School of Parkour and the Young Artivists project. This cloud-form may well have stemmed from the project's initial organizational structure, which endeavoured to represent a form of collectivist organization within the building as well as within NADA.

According to Susana Obando[35] who coordinates the mARTadero's Social Interaction area, the mARTadero currently fulfils functions for which the city government should be responsible, such as promoting education, experimentation/creation, and the circulation of contemporary art

32 ........... Cultura en Red is an Iberoamerican initiative based on network processes that mix Web 2.0 with collectivist logics in pre-capitalist societies. It is based on principles of cooperation, collaboration, and non-hierarchy, directed at promoting social action, collective creativity, and civil coexistence.

33 ........... Neyda Campos, interview by the authors.

34 ........... Including the support granted by Hivos for four years starting in 2010. This support also took on the form of a dialogue among peers, going beyond the parameters of conventional sponsorship.

35 ........... Susana Obando, interview by the authors.

△ 18
CCLab – Proyecto mARTadero, Ollantay Park, 2019, partial view of the construction, photo: Nadia Moreno Moya

△ 19
CCLab – Proyecto mARTadero, Ollantay Park, 2019, partial view of the final design and murals, courtesy: CCLAB – Proyecto mARTadero

△ 20
Young practitioners of parkour in the opening of Ollantay Park, 2019, courtesy: CCLAB – Proyecto mARTadero, photo: Fabricio Villarroel

△ 21
Detail of the mural painting process in Ollantay Park, 2019, courtesy: Proyecto mARTadero

△ 22
Urban Art Biennal (BAU) poster and view of La Esperanza neighbourhood, 2019, photo: Fernando Escobar Neira

△ 23
Die77 (Diego Vilar), *Untitled*, 2019, mural, mixed media, 'BAU19-Ekos', photo: Fernando Escobar Neira

18

19

23

21

22

20

practices in Cochabamba.[36] Given the absence of public cultural policies in Bolivia, among other circumstances, the mARTadero has taken on the lead role in promoting these practices. In this current stage, the mARTadero is part of the Telartes Network, whose aim is to promulgate a Law of Culture for Bolivia.

When we visited Cochabamba, the group was involved in the last stages of the construction of Ollantay park, a location devoted especially to young practitioners of urban arts like graffiti, hip hop, and parkour. The park, built on a former residual space on the mARTadero's block, is the result of an exercise in participatory design.△Figs. 18 & 19 In our view, this project, resulting from the synergy between the groups and projects that constitute mARTadero, synthesizes a struggle for common spaces. In 2008, mARTadero had envisioned the construction of an 'Arts Square,' and began working on the design and guidelines for the park. This initiative changed over the following years, and critically after 2014, when the collectives of mARTadero's CCLAB. In 2016, the project information was shared and disseminated among different communities living within its area of influence. In 2017, after a long process, the Annual Operational Plan of the city's Office for Tourism approved the project. In 2018, they initiated contracting procedures, and construction finally started in 2019. To put it briefly, the Ollantay urban park is the materialization of a long process, throughout which the mARTadero encouraged these practices and promoted citizenship participation through the lens of cultural rights.△Figs. 20 & 21

We add that the urban rehabilitation plan, in the terms outlined by its proponents, destabilized the traditional understanding of heritage, which focuses on the conservation of buildings invested with patrimonial value by virtue of their connection to colonial or state-formation narratives. Instead, by spatially integrating the slaughterhouse building with a formerly underutilized part of the lot, the project promoted an active integration of the site with the territory from the point of view of the arts. Thus, we see the Ollantay urban park as an expression of the production of 'the common:' a residual space that, like the slaughterhouse, has been resignified as 'everyone's' through the direct impact of emergent artistic and cultural practices in the city.

In a similar vein, the process of the Bienal de Arte Urbano [Urban Art Biennial, BAU for its initials in Spanish], which has completed five editions, one every two years between 2011 and 2019, is another instance of what we have just described. The Biennial has grown, perhaps not in terms of the number of square metres of paintings on the city's walls, or in the presumed artistic 'quality' of its interventions, but in the complexity of the relations that it has been able to foster as a city event, reaching new urban identities and affectivities and connecting with the youth environment of information and communication technologies, and the advance of

36.......... When Obando says 'contemporary arts,' she does not mean visual arts within the global art system, but the broad range of practices mentioned above.

the market, all of which traverse current life conditions and accordingly transform the notion of 'the common.'△Fig. 22

To sum up, Proyecto mARTadero went from being understood as a setting for the circulation of contemporary art, in harmony with the global art system, to becoming an epicentre for art and cultural actions and interventions of a greater scale and complexity—that is, at the territorial scale—which have included expanded practices of different arts such as theatre, music, and dance; a think tank on cultural policies; a lab for urban design analysis; and a common space for the city. Ultimately, all these actions can be understood as necessary to the production of 'the common.'△Fig. 23

## Visualización de Honda

• • •

The city of Honda, Colombia, was established in the seventeenth century, between the rivers Magdalena and Gualí on the northern edge of the state of Tolima; it is known for its historical downtown district and a few civilian constructions that belong to Colombia's cultural heritage.[37] For the past two decades, the city has been hit by an economic slump, caused by the shutting down of a beer brewery that for a long time employed a large segment of the population, and the departure of other manufacturing companies. As a consequence, tourism has become the city's major source of income (or at least the most visible).[38] The current effort to extract value out of its built heritage through cultural tourism has opened the way to processes of gentrification, leading to the appearance of boutique hotels, gourmet restaurants, summer houses for the Bogotá elite, and other services characteristic of a kind of cultural consumption in which the city's inhabitants participate only as workforce. The economic slowdown also froze all funding for culture and cultural education by the city government, since the administration declared bankruptcy in 2010. According to Luz Dary Ariza,[39] who was Honda's Director of Culture and Tourism when Visualización de Honda was in progress, the city had no way of garnering funding for artistic and cultural processes, with the sole exception of traditional events like the 'Festival de la Subienda.'[40] △Fig. 24

Visualización de Honda was a project developed between 2014 and 2015 by Fundación 4-18 (hence 4-18), a foundation created by a collective of professional artists trained and based in Bogotá.[41] During its first years of activity, this collective worked on projects in different abandoned buildings in Bogotá, where they intervened through strategies characteristic of site-specific art. Although these projects were conceived with reference

37...........The historical downtown and the Navarro bridge, which crosses the Magdalena River, were declared national monuments in 1994.

38...........The fact that Honda is perceived as having heritage value, as a tourist destination, has prevented it from being written into established narratives of the armed conflict. It is part of the Middle Magdalena region, controlled by paramilitary groups and drug trafficking organizations in the late twentieth and early twenty-first century. See: 'El DAS y los paras,' Semana, 2 December, 2006, https://verdadabierta.com/guerra-entre-paramilitares-por-el-tolima/ 2006; 'Guerra entre paramilitares por el Tolima,' Verdad abierta, 3 February 2014, https://verdadabierta.com/guerra-entre-paramilitares-por-el-tolima/.

39............Luz Dary Ariza, interview by Fernando Escobar.

40...........The festival takes place in the early months of the year, when fishing is at a maximum. Paradoxically, the city is home to three museums: the Alfonso López Pumarejo museum, the Magdalena River Museum, and the Honda Cultural Center (run by the Bank of the Republic).

41...........The artists from the collective who participated in this project were Nicolás Rodríguez, Felipe Rodríguez, Tomás Silva, Pablo Gómez, and Santiago Rodríguez.

△ 24
Santiago Castro and young locals, bench covered with graffiti, 2014. View of Honda city, courtesy: Fundación 4-18, photo: Santiago Rodríguez, 2014

to local imaginaries, they never engaged in co-creative processes inspired by the tenets of community-based or relational art. Beginning with a project titled 69/71, carried out in Bogotá in 2011, 4-18 factored relationships with other people into their processes, with the particular aim of finding an organic articulation between their projects and the social or cultural uses at play in the spaces where they planned to intervene.[42]

Their first visit to Honda took place in 2014, when Felipe Rodríguez was asked to participate in a six-week residency programme at Flora Ars + Natura's location in this city. Once in Honda, and fearing that he might not be able to complete the residency project as he had intended, Rodríguez invited another member of 4-18 to lend his support for the production of some of his ideas, and to carry out a set of artistic interventions, which they framed under the category of 'expanded art.'[43] They identified the 'absence of the state' as a crucial feature of the city, which became even more prominent at the time since the mayor was in the process of being removed from office. 4-18 then thought that, after Rodriguez's residency, they should try to develop a way of responding to these circumstances in Honda, inspired by an understanding of art as a way of working through social issues.[44]

With this purpose in mind, they applied for support from Arts Collaboratory, which funded a year of work between 2014 and 2015. According to the collective,

> We identified a set of issues upon which we meant to intervene, through a process that we define as urban acupuncture. This process follows three steps: a dialogue with the community, a diagnostic of everyday matters, and the creation of symbols that function as needles, with the intent of having an effect on the everyday life of a location.[45]

42 .......... Felipe Rodríguez, interview by Nadia Moreno.
43 .......... In their website, 4-18 state the point in further detail: 'We are driven by the juxtaposition of artistic, environmental, social, political, scientific, and sportive dynamics. Such intersections are the basis and the philosophy behind 4-18's projects, and this is what we call expanded art.'
44 .......... Nicolás Rodríguez, interview by Fernando Escobar.
45 .......... 'Proyecto Visualización de Honda,' Fundación 4-18, www.4-18.org/honda (accessed 13 November 2019).

Following this methodology, they singled out the following issues: the decay of the Cacao en Pelota hill; pollution in the Magdalena river; a crisis in artisanal fishing practices and contingent economy; and the gentrification of the historic downtown.

They conceived a diverse range of interventions responding to specific locations and involving participants through predominantly artistic premises: a sound booth; a phonograph performance at the cathedral; a workshop on stenopeic photography; three music videos for traditional tunes that refer to the decline of the Magdalena river; a viewing spot for the city; an animated short film on the river's state of pollution, produced with children from the Pacho Mario neighbourhood; a radio programme on a local station; and an artist's book based on cyanotypes portraying the craft of fishing.

Here, we take a closer look at one of these interventions: the sound booth, specifically conceived as a spatial intervention for the Cacao en Pelota hill. To make it possible, 4-18 had to make the site accessible again, in order to make it adequate for a contemplative experience of the landscape. This meant, among other things, constructing a flight of steps leading up to the booth; building and installing trash bins along the path; and working in tandem with young people and other cultural agents involved with the hill. The booth was a way of marking the landscape. It was a cubicle designed for an individual experience through the playback of local natural sounds. It was painted yellow, as the Navarro Bridge, but unlike the bridge it alluded to nature, rather than a building, as the repository of heritage value. To access the booth, one had to climb up two thirds of the hill along a path whose steps were made out of dirt, wood, rebar, and old tires. The sound system was powered by solar energy. Next to the booth, 4-18 built a bench, which was later covered with graffiti

△ 25
Felipe Rodríguez, *Sound Booth*, 2014, intervention, c. 200 × 70 × 60 cm, courtesy: Fundación 4-18, photo: Santiago Rodríguez, 2014

△ 26
Partial view of Cacao en Pelota hill (flight of steps and trash bin), courtesy: Fundación 4-18, photo: Santiago Rodríguez, 2014

by young locals who had participated in a workshop with a guest graffiti artist from Bogotá. △Fig. 25

Although it is located on a privately owned plot of land, the hill is a landmark for many inhabitants, and it is transformed into a common space as people pass through it while engaging in activities of sport or leisure—in fact, many locals think that it is a public space. These ways of using the hill had not entirely disappeared when 4-18 made their intervention, but they had dwindled. In that sense, the sound booth sought to resignify and update these practices: to reiterate the hill's significance within the local imaginary, and to reframe natural resources as a factor in the production and defence of 'the common.' △Fig. 26

Several members of 4-18 now believe that it was only by the time that the project ended that they were in a position to start, because only then had they established close ties to some of Honda's inhabitants and institutions. For this reason, we believe that 4-18's interventions were not based on a conversation with concrete social or community processes, but on artistic operations designed to alter perceptions of existing natural and cultural resources.

## CONCLUDING REMARKS

Throughout our research we observed that the people involved with the case studies' organizations often took a critical and thoughtful stance with respect to 'redemptive narratives'[46] about the capacity of art and culture to intervene in specific social contexts, assistentialist discourses about vulnerable populations, and similar tactics for mobilizing resources of different kinds. The latter was an important point for many of them, for it had to do with their ways of dealing with the need to rely on financial resources obtained through cooperation, private enterprise, or local and national government agencies; as well as political and economic interests—both legal and illegal—established in the territories where their projects were to be carried out.

Given the limitations in length for the present text, we have not delved into these issues in detail. Each project and organization is, of its own accord, a space for debate around the ethical, political, or aesthetic significance of the intersection between artistic practices and social processes; and around the processes, epistemologies, methodologies, or ways of making that these intersections call for and reproduce. Provisionally, we consider it plausible to argue that the discrepant and apparently contradictory positions embraced by participants in all three projects are, precisely, an expression of a productive struggle around the meanings of art and culture. Such struggles are even more acute and relevant when artistic practices intersect with social processes aimed at strengthening

46..........We borrow this category from the work of David Gutiérrez Castañeda (2016), who expands on Elizabeth Povinelli (2006).

citizen participation, social cohesion, cultural diversity, the sense of belonging, and strategies for the care or defence of natural resources and heritage, among other topics that surface in their narratives.

We should also point out that we were not interested in measuring the degree to which these projects were successful, if that entails fixing a criterion for assessing social impact that one could systematically apply and cross-check. When we spoke in terms of 'intersections' between art and social processes, we took it for granted, from the start, that it would not be possible to establish a category that could delimit a specific type of artistic or social event of which our cases would all be examples. In our three case studies, there is no such thing as 'social art,' or the use of art as an instrument for social change. Instead, there are intersections, some of which have a greater or lesser capacity to produce social, cultural, and artistic assemblages.

We have focused on one among many possible kinds of assemblage: the production of 'the common,' or of common spaces, which does not mean that we did not get a glimpse of other possibilities during our inquiries. 'The common,' and common spaces, are simply the categories that, in our view, most accurately captured the way in which certain spaces can be produced or resignified. Some of these arrangements have remained active, as the community gardens in the Las Flores development at the CNO, and the Ollantay urban park. Others were temporary, and only the traces of their spatial markings remain, as with the 'heritage routes' in Medellín's Commune 1, or the sound booth and viewing spot at the Cacao en Pelota hill.

These categories do not figure as such in the narratives of the people we interview, or in their project documents. We have relied on them as a way of representing something concrete, but also as something that comes into view within a narrative, for just as there are common spaces that were produced in the territories, there are others that take place in narratives that have a potential to territorialize. We have used these categories as a way of calling attention to the potentialities of 'artistic practices within a territory,' considering that what they can do lies, above all, in the potency of making. We find their greatest power in the capacity to make and to narrate what can be done. We do not believe that the mere intersection of artistic practices and social processes can transform territorial conflicts, which are spatially configured through a complex web of instances and agents. Such an expectation would amount to an acritical replaying of a 'redemptive narrative' about artistic practices in the territories.

Our analysis should also not be taken as a representation of all of the events constituting each of our cases. Not all of the practices and actions that we encountered through our research struck us as having the same intensity and potency. In spite of the intentions and purposes of their organizers and participants, and even when their planning was adequate, the intersections of artistic practices and social processes are eventful in nature and their unfolding can never be entirely predicted. Moreover, most of the projects in our case studies were themselves moments in a learning process, experiments through trial and error where decisions and adjustments were made along the way. This situation was intensified by the fact that the three organizations in our study were not community-based, or social organizations rooted in the territories where they carried out their key projects.

This is not necessarily a weakness from our point of view. Instead, we find that the possibility of international funding—from Prince Claus Fund, Hivos, and Arts Collaboratory—came at a time when these organizations were in the process of transcending disciplinary, epistemological, and organizational boundaries, engaged in an effort to disrupt their ways of doing and their understanding of the cultural, artistic, or social fields within which they located their practice. In the case of the MudeA and Proyecto mARTadero, we have interpreted these moments as a social and cultural turn, respectively, and we would argue that, for these organizations, these turns led to an unambiguous reorientation towards extra-artistic contexts. In contrast, we do not find such an inflexion in 4-18, and in our view the reason is that such turns can only occur through lasting and sustained interactions with other cultural agents.

To conclude, we note that in all three cases there was an organizational ability to establish alliances with other groups or institutions, or to appeal to or negotiate with government agencies. These we regard as creative and disruptive capacities to promote artistic practices and spaces for dialogue with different communities and inhabitants, for the sake of arranging 'the common.' Undoubtedly, in all cases it could be said that 'a lot of things' had been done, but we sense that, to a great extent, this measure of hyperactivity prevented the projects from settling into a constant regime of writing or archiving that would have allowed for their social reproduction beyond personal testimony. Project members and participants have called attention to the need for systematizing the knowledge that has been collected through these projects, and for a greater degree of critical reflection about them. In a way, during our inquiries we found ourselves playing the part of 'organizational psychologists,' or better yet, as scribes for the projects' memoirs. In that sense, we hope that by writing this text we may be playing a part, as participants, in the unfolding of yet another assemblage.

## ← REFERENCES

Cardona, Alejandro. 'Un museo andariego: La experiencia dialógica de construcción colectiva del patrimonio entre el museo y la comunidad.' *Jangwa Pana* 12 (2013), pp. 150–58, 179.

Centro Nacional de Memoria Histórica. *Medellín: Memorias de una guerra urbana*. Bogotá: CNMH – Corporación Región – Ministerio del Interior – Alcaldía de Medellín – Universidad EAFIT – Universidad de Antioquia, 2017.

Corporación Con-Vivamos and Museo de Antioquia. 'Propuesta de Museos Comunitarios en la Comuna 1 y la Ciudadela Nuevo Occidente en Medellín.' Final report, 2011.

Da Representaçao, Natalia. 'Los espacios comunes como problema. Sociabilidad, gestión y territorio.' In *El retorno de lo político a la cuestión urbana: Territorialidad y acción pública en el Área Metropolitana de Buenos Aires*, ed. Andrea Catenazzi et al. Buenos Aires: Universidad Nacional de General Sarmiento-Prometeo Libros, 2009.

Fundación 4-18. 'Proyecto Visualización de Honda.' www.4-18.org/honda (last updated: 13 November 2019).

García, Fernando. *Proyecto mARTadero vivero de las artes (inter-media-acción)*. Cochabamba: FAUTAPO and Fundación Imagen, 2014.

'Guerra entre paramilitares por el Tolima.' *Verdad abierta*. 3 February 2014. https://verdadabierta.com/guerra-entre-paramilitares-por-el-tolima/.

Gutiérrez Castañeda, David. 'Ejercicios del Cuidado: A propósito de La Piel de la Memoria.' PhD dissertation, Universidad Nacional Autónoma de México, 2013.

Gutiérrez, Raquel. *Horizontes comunitario-populares: Producción de lo común más allá de las políticas estado-céntricas*. Madrid: Traficantes de sueños, 2017.

Hernández Martínez, Ascensión. 'El efecto Guggenheim-Bilbao en Latinoamérica: Medellín, Ciudad Botero, un proyecto cultural para la paz,' Artigrama no. 17 (2002), pp. 149–76.

Povinelli, Elizabeth. *The Empire of Love: Toward a Theory of Intimacy, Genealogy, and Carnality*. Duke: Duke University Press, 2006.

Proyecto mARTadero. 'Bienal de Arte Urbano.' https://bau.martadero.org (last updated: 22 September 2019).
—. 'Laboratorio de Comunidades Creativas mARTadero.' www.cclab.martadero.org (last updated: 4 November 2019).

Riaño, Pilar, Suzanne Lacy, and Olga Agudelo. *Arte, memoria y violencia: Reflexiones sobre la ciudad*. Medellín: Corporación Región, 2003.

Semana. 'El DAS y los paras.' *Semana*. 2 December 2006. www.semana.com/portada/articulo/el-das-paras/75769-3.

Verdad abierta. 'Guerra entre paramilitares por el Tolima.' *Verdad abierta*. 3 February 2014. https://verdadabierta.com/guerra-entre-paramilitares-por-el-tolima/.

Yúdice, George. *El recurso de la cultura: Usos de la cultura en la era global*. Barcelona: Gedisa, 2002.


## ← INTERVIEWS

### MUSEO + COMUNIDAD

Carlos Mario Jiménez, interview by Fernando Escobar and Yurilena Velásquez, 8 April 2019.

Carolina Chacón, interview by Fernando Escobar and Yurilena Velázquez, 10 April 2019.

Elizabeth Echavarría, interview by Fernando Escobar and Yurilena Velázquez, 11 April 2019.

Lida Restrepo, interview by Nadia Moreno and Yurilena Velásquez, 12 April 2019.

Giovanni Correa and Juan Diego Cano, collective interview by Nadia Moreno and Yurilena Velásquez, 15 April 2019.

Carlos Mario Jiménez, interview by Nadia Moreno and Yurilena Velásquez, 30 April 2019.

David Henao, interview by Nadia Moreno, 3 May 2019.

Zinayda Quiñonez, interview by Nadia Moreno, 6 June 2019.

María Cristina Álvarez, interview by Fernando Escobar, 10 June 2019.

Andrés Arredondo, interview by Fernando Escobar, 10 June 2019.

César Cano, interview by Nadia Moreno, 17 June 2019.

Consuelo Giraldo, interview by Nadia Moreno, Fernando Escobar, and Yurilena Velásquez, 20 June 2019.

Edward Niño, interview by Nadia Moreno, Fernando Escobar, and Yurilena Velázquez, 22 June 2019.

Carlos Edwin Rendón, interview by Nadia Moreno, 22 June 2019.

Jader Sánchez, Mónica Giraldo, and Sonia Martínez, collective interview by Nadia Moreno, Fernando Escobar, and Yurilena Velásquez, 22 June 2019.

Lilia Colorado and Silvia Colorado, collective interview by Nadia Moreno, Fernando Escobar, and Yurilena Velásquez, 15 August 2019.

Pablo Ayala, interview by Fernando Escobar, 12 September 2019.

Cristina Vasco, interview by Fernando Escobar, 20 September 2019.

### PROYECTO MARTADERO

Fernando García, interview by Nadia Moreno and Fernando Escobar, 18 November 2018 and 1 August 2019.

Claudia Michel, interview by Nadia Moreno and Fernando Escobar, 8 July 2019.

Marco Marín, interview by Nadia Moreno and Fernando Escobar, 10 July 2019.

Magda Rossi, interview by Nadia Moreno and Fernando Escobar, 10 July 2019.

Angélika Heckel, interview by Nadia Moreno and Fernando Escobar, 11 July 2019.

Fabiola Quiroga, interview by Nadia Moreno and Fernando Escobar, 11 July 2019.

Claudia Silva, interview by Nadia Moreno and Fernando Escobar, 11 July 2019.

Neyda Campos, interview by Nadia Moreno and Fernando Escobar, 12 July 2019.

Susana Obando, interview by Nadia Moreno and Fernando Escobar, 12 July 2019.

Malena Rodríguez, interview by Nadia Moreno and Fernando Escobar, 15 July 2019.

### VISUALIZACIÓN DE HONDA

Marcela Prieto, interview by Nadia Moreno and Fernando Escobar, 21 December 2018.

Felipe Rodríguez, interview by Nadia Moreno, 27 February 2019.

Nicolás Rodríguez, interview by Fernando Escobar, 20 March 2019.

Pablo Gómez, interview by Fernando Escobar, 30 April 2019.

Gonzalo Gamboa, interview by Fernando Escobar, 2 May 2019.

Roberio García, interview by Fernando Escobar, 2 May 2019.

Luz Dary Ariza, interview by Fernando Escobar, 3 May 2019.

# TICKLING THE SENSIBLE
## Art, Politics, and Worlding at the Global Margin

Višnja Kisić and Goran Tomka

In this chapter, we explore the questions of entanglements between arts and politics by looking at the work of the foundation Más Arte Más Acción (MAMA) in the department of Chocó, Colombia, at a global political margin. MAMA's practice is an example of dissenting the global capitalist hegemony and creating spaces where imagination of alternative processes of living, relating, and creating can take place. Our aim has been to conceive politics beyond anthropocentrism, acknowledging ontological interrelatedness of the web of life and agency of a more-than-human world in politics, as well as away from epistemic injustices and modes of coloniality that shape the very conceptions of micro and macro-politics. While questioning the dominant understandings of the relation between art and politics, we claim that it is in the relationship with specific territories, ecosystems, places, beings, and ways of worlding that artistic practice engages in dissenting the policed worlding and in reconfiguring the political. We propose the notion of 'rampant practice' for understanding (artistic) practices that re-engage with the web of life and its interdependencies, uncertainties, and vulnerabilities, thus undisciplining, disturbing, challenging, and 'tickling' the dominant subjectivation of actors, places of existence, processes of becoming, modes of practice, and ways of relating within arts practice.

Keywords
- → Art and Politics
- → Worlding
- → Anthropocentrism
- → Rampant Practice
- → Colombia

## INTRODUCTION

> To the carers of the Dignified, Simple and Solidary life.
> We have gone through all this because of the love
> that we have known in our territories...
> Our land is the place where
> we dream our future with dignity.[1]

The futures we can dream about, desire, and imagine have been saturated by neoliberal capitalism's hegemonic landscape, contaminating spaces and times for questioning the status quo and discussing possible life alternatives. As alternative 'cosmo/visions'[2] pierce through the surface, the growing military, epistemic, and ontological violence is ever harder to hide. In this particular moment, the temptation of quick policy solutions is high. However, radical reimaginings of the political ask for much wider considerations. They require rethinking the very ontological understandings, epistemic injustices, cognitive assumptions, and affective relationships that govern the ways in which life is perceived, politics and its subjects are legitimized, and societies are organized. What do these radical reimaginings of the political mean for arts? How may artistic practices create spaces, encounters, and subjectivities that are shaking the neoliberal capitalist hegemonic order, triggering new imaginations and alternative ways of shaping the world? How can we think about them beyond anthropocentric conceptions of politics and impacts? How can we understand their rampant modes of existence within webs of life?

In this chapter, we explore the questions of entanglements between arts and politics by looking at the work of Más Arte Más Acción (MAMA) in Chocó, Colombia, which takes place in what could be understood as a 'global political margin.' MAMA's practice can be considered a manifestation of dissenting from the neoliberal hegemony and of creating spaces to imagine alternative processes of living, relating, and creating. This is what we call 'tickling the sensible'—referring to practices that play with, poke, divert, and question the ways in which senses, sense and sensibilities are distributed and negotiated. As it will become clearer within this chapter, to tickle the sensible is to challenge the hegemonic order and its attempts to cement life and relations, without desiring to institute a new hegemony. It concerns both micropolitical (intimate) and macropolitical ways of creating wiggle room in which life can take unexpected directions beyond the colonizing grids.

In studying the case of MAMA within the *Force of Art* initiative, we spent seven weeks in Colombia following the organization across the country. This included: participating in their co-organized events visiting and conversing with their collaborators as well as other actors in the independent Colombian art scene; staying in MAMA's Chocó Base residency; and sharing time, conversations, and space with the members of MAMA, other artists and researchers, as well as various communities they relate to in Nuquí, Quibdó, Bogotá, Cali, and Medellín. Our research methodology is based on observation, participation, and group conversations, supplemented by in-depth interviews, and a personal diary in which we have documented our experiences. Before travelling to Colombia, we had explored and analyzed traces of MAMA's work—its website with publications, videos and reflections of people who have been part of residency projects, as well as art interventions, events and writings created throughout their work. Upon our return from Colombia, we conducted additional in-depth interviews via Skype with former residents of the Chocó Base and longterm collaborators proposed by MAMA.

1............Open letter by Francia Márquez in: Arturo Escobar, 'The Colombian Pacific Region: A Dialogue of Cosmo/visions,' in *This Place*, ed. Jonathan Colin (Bogotà: MAMA, 2017), pp. 36–68.

2............Ibid.

Throughout the process, our approach had many traits of participatory research,[3] in that we strived to co-produce data and findings in collaboration with participants as well as exchange and discuss findings and several versions of the final text with them.

The ideas and practices that we have engaged with in this research are part of our interest in geographic, political, economic, and disciplinary marginality, blurriness and liminality, which we understand as possibilities for dissent, rupture and change. We are two researchers (a couple) who conduct research, lecture, and engage in the fields of culture, heritage, and arts—and their political workings and implications. We consciously inhabit various liminal spaces: we live in Serbia, a former colony within Europe and a post-socialist country at the global semi-periphery;[4] we work in often precarious, in-between posts and short-term projects in a transdisciplinary manner; we live at the boundary of the city suburbs and the forested national park where our more-than-human neighbours disrupt our anthropocentric ways of being. △Fig. 1

△ 1
Germaine Acogny and Jóvenes Creadores del Chocó
Photo: Sebastian Bright, 2019

## SETTING THE GRID: POLITICS, SUBJECTIVATION, AND ARTS IN A MORE-THAN-HUMAN WORLD

In setting the theoretical grid of our research, we aim to conceive politics beyond anthropocentrism, acknowledging ontological interrelatedness of the web of life and agency of a 'more-than-human world'[5] in politics, as well as epistemic injustices and modes of coloniality that shape the very conceptions of micro and macro-politics. In doing this, we build upon the political philosophy of Jacques Rancière,[6] which despite being defined by anthropocentrism and Eurocentric assumptions, offers a critical lens

3............Jarg Bergold and Stefan Thomas, 'Participatory Research Methods: A Methodological Approach in Motion,' *Historical Social Research/Historische Sozialforschung* 13, no. 1 (January 2012), pp. 191–222.
4............Ivana Spasić, *Kultura na delu* (Belgrade: Fabrika knjiga, 2013).
5............John Chianchi, *Radical Environmentalism: Nature, Identity and More-than-Human Agency* (London: Palgrave Macmillan UK, 2015).
6............Jacques Rancière, *Disagreement: Politics and Philosophy* (Minneapolis: University of Minnesota Press, 1999); Jacques Rancière, *Dissensus: On Politics and Aesthetics* (London and New York: Continuum, 2010).

for understanding the political in its attempts to ensure a pervasive and all-encompassing arrangement of life, relations, and sensibilities. The notion of 'worlding' that we use underlines the ontological politics of our understanding of the reshaping of worlds as a 'blending of the material and the semiotic that removes the boundaries between subject and environment'[7] and as an accounting for the process of 'human-non-human enmeshment.'[8] Furthermore, Colombian anthropologist and political ecologist Arturo Escobar's notions of pluriverse, plurivisions, and plural ways of worlding (shaping of world), which defy universalists liberal-developmentalist logic,[9] play an important role in understanding the context of Chocó. Moreover, the notion of active micropolitics by Brasilian psychoanalyst, cultural critique and curator Suely Rolnik offers an understanding of subjectivization that tries to defy neoliberal-capitalist-colonial logic.[10]

In Rancière's political philosophy, there is a tripartite division between politics, political, and the police.[11] 'The police'—which Rancière derives from the Greek *polis*—is defined as the arrangement of common life according to a selective, hierarchically privileging accounting of the people. It acts as a hegemonic 'distribution of the sensible,' which defines roles, places, and functions within society, as well as the properties and capabilities linked to them. Police's arrangements pin down ways of being, doing, saying, and relating that are deemed as 'proper' or common-sense—saturating material, ethical, aesthetic, and discursive realms, and making invisible other potential ways of living, understanding, and organizing the commons.

Even though the contemporary context of our research asks for understanding neoliberal global integrated capitalism as today's hegemonic police order, we understand many of its modes of governance and distribution of the sensible as a continuation of colonial-capitalist regimes. We consider the colonial regime as a regime that subdues all life on Earth, as well as the beings, understandings, relations, and senses to one universalizing mode of life. The main subject of the verification of this distribution is a Western European white upper-class heterosexual male, while women, poor, indigenous, coloured, animals, plants, landscapes, and spaces are considered less valid or invalid, and are to be understood as autonomous subjects, suitable to be ruled upon. Anthropocentrism, patriarchy, imperialism, racism, speciesism, ableism, and scientism are all forms of establishing 'coloniality'[12] over life. We consider a capitalist regime as the regime that understands all life and relations as resources for its own growth, and continuously expands the territories and modes of coloniality so as to extract additional life forces that serve the accumulation of capital. We understand global margin of places like Choco as potent places

7............Helen Palmer and Vicky Hunter, 'Worlding,' *New Materialism Almanac*, March 2018, https://newmaterialism.eu/almanac/w/worlding.html.
8............Donna Haraway, *Staying with the Trouble: Making Kin in the Chthulucene* (Durham and London: Duke University Press, 2016).
9............Arturo Escobar, 'The Colombian Pacific Region'; Arturo Escobar, 'Transition Discourses and the Politics of Relationality,' in *Constructing the Pluriverse: The Geopolitics of Knowledge*, ed. Bernd Reiter (Durham: Duke University Press, 2018), pp. 63–89.
10...........Suely Rolnik, 'The Spheres of Insurrection: Suggestions for Combating the Pimping of Life,' E-Flux no. 86 (November 2017), www.e-flux.com/journal/86/163107/the-spheres-of-insurrection-suggestions-for-combating-the-pimping-of-life/; Suely Rolnik, *Esferas de la insurrección* (Ciudad Autónoma de Buenos Aires: Tinta Limón, 2019).
11...........Ibid.
12...........Anibal Quijano, 'Coloniality of Power and Eurocentrism in Latin America,' *International Sociology* 15, no. 2. (June 2000), pp. 215–32.

in which the symbolic and material grip of global neoliberalism is looser, making wiggle room for alternative ways of being. In the global margin, this grip is not present in its glittery version available in the centres of power, but is present through different unwanted spill-overs, extractions and exploitations.

The current neoliberal capitalist world order, according to Rolnik,[13] advances the processes of colonial and capitalist oppression as processes of capturing vital forces by occupying micropolitics with the colonial-capitalist unconscious. In this capture, she says, subjectivity (complexity of experiences of being in this world and relationality of the body with other world forces) is reduced to its experience as a social subject (as an individual that fits into a particular place within a socio-cultural grid). Macropolitics thus saturates subjectivity, flattening it down to the preservation of order and a particular identity within a grid, and resulting in reactive micropolitics. At the same time, reactive micropolitics neutralize complexities of vital life forces and prevent encounters that might give birth to possible alternative worlds. Furthermore, with the global capitalist distribution of the sensible (based on earlier forms of colonial-capitalist regimes), other ways of worlding become increasingly endangered. The hegemonic distribution of the sensible takes itself as the sole and universal point of reference—as the only legitimate way of worlding, knowing, existing, and relating—and in doing so it 'denies any alterity' and 'any other opportunity for inhabiting the relational fabric woven by different modes of existence.'[14] This eats out possibilities of the pluriverse[15] as 'a world in which many worlds fit' in the words of Zapatistas.

However, the police—and its hegemonic manner of worlding—is never left alone. It is always haunted by 'the politics' (*la politique*) that Rancière defines as society's 'absent ground,' and which is characterized by the unconditional ontological equality of 'each and every one of us as speaking (and hence political) beings.'[16] 'The politics' accompanies 'the police' like a shadow, limiting its desired totalization and broadening the actors of politics by making visible those whose sounds (*phōnḗ*) were not heard or understood as speech (*logos*) by the policed distribution of the sensible (the women, the poor, the coloured). Importantly, 'the politics' becomes visible and confronts 'the police' through the act of dissensus, defined as the demonstration (manifestation) of a gap in the sensible itself. As Rancière puts it, dissensus manifests the gap that makes visible that which has no reason to be seen and makes heard those that are not heard or are heard as noise.[17] Dissensus is a type of thinking and activity that produces shocks between worlds, but shocks between worlds in the same world: re-distributions, re-compositions, and re-configurations of elements.[18]

Finally, the meeting ground between 'the politics' and 'the police' is 'the political,' which is created through dissensus. 'The political consists

13 Rolnik, 'The Spheres of Insurrection'; Rolnik, *Esferas de la insurrección*.
14 Rolnik, 'The Spheres of Insurrection.'
15 Escobar, 'Transition Discourses and the Politics of Relationality.'
16 Rancière, *Dissensus: On Politics and Aesthetics*, p. 94.
17 Rancière, *Disagreement*.
18 Rancière, *Dissensus*, p. 212.

in re-configuring the space, that is: what is to be done, to be seen and to be named in it.'[19] It is about changing the cartography of the sensible and thinkable,[20] thereby opening the possibility for other ways of worlding, other ways of distributing the sensible. Dissensus for Rancière is always practiced through new forms of subjectivation that depart from the flattened identity attributed to subjects by 'the police.' The act of dissensus and subjectivation rests on similar terms to that of what Rolnik calls 'active micropolitics':[21] acts of decolonizing subjectivity from the socio-cultural grid that distributes the sensible in its capitalist-colonial frame. For Rolnik, new ways of worlding cannot be achieved solely on a macropolitical level but need to be practiced on an active micropolitics level, which is driven by relational life forces and opposes being put into a grid.

However, even though Rancière's notion of politics posits ontological equality of beings, it reserves that equality only for the speaking subjects, thus reinstituting anthropocentrism rooted in Western European philosophical and scientific thought. Another delineation of the possibility of the political is that dissensus is about the acts that delineate those who can act and take action from those who are passive and who merely exist. This particular distribution of the sensible, which normalizes the distinction between Society and Nature,[22] allows for the exclusion of all 'more-than-human'[23] life as uncountable and ready to be decided upon, ruled, and made sense of by humans.

What we posit is that in challenging 'the police,' 'politics' needs to be expanded beyond the ontological equality of humans. This means expanding the capacity of understanding and communication beyond speech and discourse and towards other ways of worlding and relating. This political field should be a field without the usual sociological divisions, but also without divisions between humans and nature. This is in line with Timothy Morton's 'symbiotic real,'[24] in which all beings are ontologically equal, uncapturable, and interconnected. They are part of an indivisible 'mash' that has no central position that privileges any one form of being over others, and thereby erases definitive interior and exterior boundaries of beings, emphasizing their interdependence.[25] In such borderless, uncontained interdependence of beings, acts of dissensus could be found in what Tupac Cruz philosophizes as a rampant 'form of life,' drawing on the life of non-hierarchical, unpredictable, moving-through, creeping, and meandering existence of procumbent plants.[26]

Such broadening of the political arena widens the concept of agency to non-humans, creating new possibilities of relating, communicating, affecting, and connecting. Strange as it may sound to Western thought traditions (with the exception of object-oriented ontology and post-

19..........Ibid., p. 37.
20..........Ibid., p. 143.
21..........Rolnik, 'The Spheres of Insurrection'; Rolnik, Esferas de la insurrección.
22..........Graham Harvey, *Animism: Respecting the Living World* (London: C. Hurst and Company, 2005).
23..........David Abram, *The Spell of the Sensuous: Perception and Language in a More-than-Human World* (New York: Vintage, 1997).
24..........Timothy Morton, *Human Kind: Solidarity with Non-human People* (London: Verso, 2017).
25..........Timothy Morton, *The Ecological Thought* (Cambridge, MA: Harvard University Press, 2010).
26..........Tupac Cruz, *Rocio en formación* (Bogotá: La Parte Maldita, 2016).

humanism), the understanding of other living and non-living beings as equally legitimate, as well as older brothers or teachers, has its roots in numerous indigenous forms of knowledge across the world, including ones inhabiting the region of Chocó. The cancellation of these forms of knowledge from the field of possibilities is yet another manifestation of coloniality. The broadening of politics to more-than-human life that we suggest here decolonizes hierarchies between diverse forms of living and sensible beings, opening new horizons for being, doing, and knowing the world.

Moments of dissensus are not just those that succeed in instituting a new distribution of the sensible. They are also moments of critical relation towards policed distribution of the sensible and moments of imagining worlding beyond this dominant distribution. The pulsating force of politics is in the attempts, reactions, acts, and beings that unlock the dominant order and offer glimpses into other imaginable futures and worlds. The domain of art is one of many domains in which these challenges, re-articulations, and imaginations beyond the current sensible take place, 'hollowing out the 'real' and multiplying it in a polemical way.'[27] Unlike other domains, in the current police order, the domain of art is instituted with the aura of freedom of expression, political subversion, and the shaking of the status quo. At the same time, the domain of art is shaped to a significant extent by the 'Global Art World'—meaning the art academies, galleries, sources of funding, museums, auction houses, collectors, curators, and artists.[28] Openly 'political' art in a narrow sense, enacted in the gallery space by a trained artist, curated by established experts, and visited by an art audience, does not shake up, but rather further sediments the police order.

To be dissensual, artistic practices and strategies need not only to reconfigure the sensible and aesthetic experience, but also to simultaneously challenge the worlding entangled with artistic practices, and challenge the delineations of arts, politics, and environments. This practice has to 'tickle' and question the subjectivation of actors, places of existence, processes of becoming, modes of practice, and ways of relating deemed as art. It is in this sense that we understand art as the domain of politics and dissensus, as well as the domain of other possible worldings beyond neoliberal global capitalism. This domain is by no means the creator, force, or initiator of dissensus per se, nor is it created by the usual suspects of the arts and the 'Global Art World,' even though some of its actors are the same. It is in the relationship with specific territories, ecosystems, places, beings, and ways of worlding, as well as their struggles for alternatives to the global capitalist order, that artistic practice engages in dissenting the policed worlding and in reconfiguring the political. It is through these lenses that we analyze and understand the practice of MAMA and its relations with multiple communities of practice and the territory of Chocó.

27.......... Rancière, *Dissensus*, p. 149.

28.......... Charlotte Bydler, *The Global Art World Inc.: On the Globalization of Contemporary Art* (Uppsala: Acta Universitatis Upsaliensis, 2004).

## INTRODUCING CHOCÓ— A DIFFERENT WORLDING AT THE GLOBAL MARGIN

Though there is a danger of romanticizing, Chocó is—as our interlocutors consistently said—'a different place.' Covered in hundreds of square miles of impenetrable rainforests, interwoven with numerous rivers, meeting the Pacific Ocean, Chocó is one of the world's biodiversity hotspots. In Chocó, 'nature is overwhelming' and 'wilderness confronts outsiders unused to that environment.'[29] As our interviewees shared, 'everything grows and dies so fast,' 'the body feels different, much more connected,' 'the sense of presence is amazing,' 'you have a special connection, and you don't talk about it because you don't need to speak.' In Chocó, what we call Nature is not absent or passive, it is calling.

Chocoanos, as locals call themselves, speak from their territory from a perspective that is ecological and deeply grounded in the interrelatedness between people, other than human life, and the environment. 'They do not separate social from natural,' says Alejandra Giraldo Rojas, project manager at MAMA, describing the place-based and culturally specific ways of knowing a profoundly aquatic environment—something that Ulrich Oslender, British political and cultural geographer, calls 'relational ontology' and 'local aquatic epistemologies.'[30] These epistemologies are at the centre of a rural Afro-Colombian worldview in the Pacific Coast region, and have underpinned the political organizing process that culminated in *Ley 70* [Law 70] of 1993 that granted Afro-Colombian communities collective titles over the land in the Pacific Coast and over numerous rivers of the region.[31] Their way of relating to the territory and life is genuinely different from the hegemonic, Western ways of knowing, understanding the world, and envisioning development.[32] In fact, Chocó challenges the hegemonic global distribution of the sensible.

Chocó's geographical, cultural, and symbolic remoteness over centuries and decades is what has safeguarded its particular ways of relating and organizing life. What to many visitors seems like a paradise is at the same time challenged by its marginality in Colombian geography, politics, and social imagination. In Chocó, the worlding based on care, inter-existence, communality and relationality of humans, non-humans and territory, has been evaded by the liberal-developmentalist worldview, a worlding based on separation of culture from nature, body from mind, knowledge from spirituality.[33] Being on a margin of Colombia and wider geopolitics, reflects itself not only in richer biodiversity, political vitality and wiggle room from the hegemonic order. On the contrary, Chocó is at the same time a place where the dirty spill-overs of urban centres and global neoliberal exploitative machinery are felt in their worst and most violent extractivist forms. National and multinational companies dream of

29..........Jonathan Colin, ed., Nowhere/Ningun Lugar (Bogotá: Fundación Más Arte Más Acción, 2013), p. 7.

30..........Ulrich Oslender, 'Local Aquatic Epistemologies among Black Communities on Colombia's Pacific Coast and the Pluriverse,' in *Constructing the Pluriverse: The Geopolitics of Knowledge*, ed. Bernd Reiter (Durham: Duke University Press, 2018), p. 137–50.

31..........Ibid.

32..........Escobar, 'The Colombian Pacific Region.'

33..........Ibid., pp. 59–60.

ever-larger extraction of gold, platinum, other rare metals, trees, and fish. Paramilitaries, narco-mafia, guerrillas, and the Colombian state exercise permanent terror, while a newly flourishing tourism industry adds to new forms of coloniality.

Over the last twenty years, Chocó has also become a place of work for numerous NGOs, bringing development aid to the region. With clear-cut project logic, imposing visions of what development means, and translating everything into money and timelines, the practices of development NGOs have become a new face of neo-colonialism. As Paco Gómez, a Spanish journalist and long-term collaborator of MAMA who has spent his life working in Chocó and Colombia, explains: 'Projects are a colonial practice. Territory is more important than time in Chocó ... But development NGOs started translating everything into money and time.' In the act of 'rescuing' local communities, raising their capacities and encouraging development, the power asymmetry between communities and NGOs, as well as between 'underdeveloped' and 'developed' countries, becomes ever larger.

MAMA could have easily become one of the actors that brings and promotes the global hegemonic 'police'—neoliberal capitalist vision of development—to Chocó. It could have also been a destination for solitary artistic work in a lush environment. However, for MAMA, Chocó was not an underdeveloped region in need of foreign aid. For them, Chocó has been a place where it all started and the place that constantly poses new troubling questions. 'Chocó is an ideological place. Chocó connects everything,' says MAMA's director Ana Milena Garzón. In MAMA's beginnings, Chocó was imagined as a place that exposes the disconnection of the urban, 'developed' world from the rest of the web of life, and as a place that inspires imagination of the alternatives to the hegemonic distribution of the sensible. With increased interactions with Chocoano ways of knowing and relating, as well as with their political struggles with the centres of power, MAMA started seeing 'Chocó as a school:' not a typical school subject to the usual power relations between teacher/pupil, but as a learning territory for both those that are visiting and those who are local—a symbolic place of exchange.

Chocó is therefore not only the location within which MAMA's activities happen: it is not a simple backdrop or a vague context for their work, but rather an inspiration for crossing boundaries. It is about 'tentacles that divert and connect,' says Alejandra Rojas Giraldo. The human and more-than-human world in Chocó are active participants in the physical, affective, cognitive, and temporal encounters and relations in the work of MAMA. Chocó is an actor that constantly invites, surprises, and questions—an actor that shakes patterns up to reinvent life beyond the dominant distribution of the sensible.

## INTRODUCING MÁS ARTE MÁS ACCIÓN— WHAT ART AND WHAT ACTION?

Colombian artist Fernando Arias and British arts manager Jonathan Colin have lived and worked as a couple ever since they met at an exhibition in

Scotland in 1995. Three years later, they were invited to cover a magazine story about the sparsely populated Pacific Coast of Colombia, the department of Chocó, a region they had never visited before. Hundreds of miles away from any road or gallery, they found a periphery as far from the white cube as possible. The visit changed them more than they could foresee, and after a decade of returning to Chocó, they ended up buying a patch of land with an abandoned cabin close to the beach. As they explained in our conversation, 'Everything touched [them] there.' These were 'transformative years' for the two. While they kept coming back, they initiated a series of individual and collective art projects, made many local friends, and did several programmes with nearby communities such as the youth community art hub Casa ChocóLate.[34]

As they developed their local knowledge, relationships, and reputation, they also attracted international funding with the reasoning, as they put it, of 'taking from Europe, giving to Chocó.' This is how the foundation Más Arte Más Acción [more art more action] was initiated in 2008 by Arias and Colin, now internationally acclaimed names in the international art scene. The foundation was formally constituted in 2010 to accommodate an incoming grant from the international network Arts Collaboratory,[35] but also to lay a firmer foundation for their evolving work in Chocó. However, MAMA was neither an overly ambitious nor a serious endeavour as the name might suggest. In fact, the name is an ironic reference to a public campaign of the time, and in one of the early versions, it could have been called Menos Art, Más Acción [less art, more action]. 'We hated the mainstream art world,' says Fernando in one of our talks in his typical self-ironic manner.

A starting point for MAMA's work was the Chocó Base. Nestled between the lush and bustling rainforest and the Pacific Ocean, the base is quite an extraordinary residence. Since its construction in 2011, the space has welcomed dozens of artists, academics, researchers, activists, and thinkers in their quest to explore alternatives to current global economic, environmental, and social issues. These residencies have also provided a chance for joint explorations and exchange, some of which have been documented in the *Nuevatopias* book series.[36] The Nuevatopias project (2012–2016) supported by several Dutch funding bodies, was a unique way to frame the residencies in the Chocó Base, referencing Thomas More's *Utopia* and the 500th anniversary since its publication.[37] The project was an invitation to think critically on the global world order and imagine alternative futures and ways to organize societies; the residence ground in Chocó was envisioned as a place to give inspiration

34 'Casa Chocólate,' Más Arte Más Acción, www.masartemasaccion.org/casa-chocolate/ (accessed June 2020).

35 The Arts Collaboratory is a network of twenty-five organizations from Africa, Latin America, Asia, Middle East and the Netherlands, with peculiar ways of self-organizing, supporting and distributing resources, of which MAMA is a part. See more: 'About Arts Collaboratory,' Arts Collaboratory, www.artscollaboratory.org/ (accessed June 2020).

36 Colin, *Nowhere/Ningun Lugar*; Jonathan Colin, ed., *Better Than/Mejor Que* (Bogotá: Fundación Más Arte Más Acción, 2015); Jonathan Colin, ed., *This Place/Este Lugar* (Bogotá: Fundación Más Arte Más Acción, 2017).

37 'Nuevastopias: No Where *Better Than* This Place,' Más Arte Más Acción, www.masartemasaccion.org/nuevatopias-nowhere-better-than-this-place/?lang=en (accessed June 2020).

38 'Base Chocó: Joep van Lieshout,' Más Arte Más Acción, www.masartemasaccion.org/joep-van-lieshout-base-Chocó/?lang=en (accessed June 2020).

for such thinking. The tangible outcomes of the project encompassed the publication of three books that contained articles, photos, drawings, and other expressions of visiting scholars, artists, and performers dealing with contemporary global conditions and local developments.

In the midst of Nuevatopias, MAMA welcomed Ana Milena Garzón, a project manager since 2015, and currently the foundation's director; Alejandra Rojas Giraldo joined in 2018 as programme manager. New projects and collaborations followed, guided by Ana's and Alejandra's commitment to collaborations with local collectives and political struggles in Chocó and elsewhere. Along with this, Fernando and Jonathan became Board members and withdrew from the everyday work.

Common to MAMA's projects and collaborations is the intersection of ecological, social, and political struggles of the territories, peoples, and lives on the margin of the current world order. In them, different forms of arts, sciences, and activism serve as an alternative way to grasp these struggles and create new relationships. From its residency programme through its publications and community activities, MAMA aims to open up spaces for reflection, for extraordinary encounters of ideas, people, plants, and animals. Just as the Chocó Base defies the usual space of residency, the work of MAMA 'tickles' the hegemonic logic of market, competition, business, and exploitation that saturate the 'normal conditions' of Chocó and Colombia as a whole. As a rupture in the fabric of its surrounding normality, but also a rupture in the everydayness of its guests, collaborators, and publics, the work of MAMA streams from Chocó and back in a quest to destabilize, reconnect, and question the current distribution of the sensible.

## TICKLING THE SENSIBLE

### Re-territorializing Existence

•

The Chocó Base is a rather peculiar place. It is built on top of a tree trunk felled over seven decades ago, with hand carved wooden floors that follow the contours of the tree. A few sliding walls expose its heart to the sounds and elements of the forest and the ocean. Going forward and backwards also means going up or down. Gravitation cannot be neglected, just as waves, thunder, rain, and birds resist exclusion. Is it a house or a sensing platform? Like a conquered fortress or an open cave, its protective film is as thin as the silence inside it. It made us question everything; we thought we knew about architecture, and much more. Is the house there to guard or to expose? Where are the lines of separation? Who is on stage and who is watching? Where do we end and where do they begin? Who? △Fig. 2

As there is no external and internal of the house, internal and external of the body and the self of its occupants slowly melt away, just as the urban looks of the house's architect melted away once he reached the site and its notorious humidity. In his mind, Joep van Lieshout[38] brought a sketch of a white concrete cube juxtaposed to the vibrant greenery and life around it. White cube. Popping up around the world as

△ 2
Base Chocó, photo: Más Arte Más Acción, 2011

a McDonald's menu: universal, standardized, familiar, yet slightly 'locally flavoured.' But as the metropolitan capitalist Global Art World behind van Lieshout faded away, so did the white cube.

The problem with juxtaposition is that it requires at least two objects. But the rainforest refuses to be objectified in such a clear-cut manner. As Erna von der Walde, editor of MAMA's many books and former board member said, 'The forest is beyond representation.' The rainforest refuses the juxtaposition game. It's too alive and dynamic to stand still and play the game. What works much better here is pervasion. Just as moss pervades everything fallen, including your leather shoes after two days, the forest knows no boundaries and is very familiar with growing in layers. Finally, the house grew on top; it was made with local wood, by local hands, on a local trunk. No white cube, no Big Mac inside. Just another coat of life that soon received another living layer of greenery on top of itself. Nothing exceptional.

As such, the house is a pedestal of humbleness. 'Nature is always louder,' recalled one of the residents. All the relations that life depends upon are laid bare and demand their attention. 'You always have to negotiate here,' says Fernando. Jonathan adds:

> It is important for people who are used to being in the centre of the art world to go there, to a periphery, and think about their own practice. In some ways, it pulls the rug under your feet and makes you see things from another perspective. For me it has done that, destabilizing our validity: so what?

What suddenly becomes important is the place itself—the territory as 'the collective space of existence, a living space that assures ... survival as a people in profound interdependence with nature, the human, and the spiritual.'[39] Interdependence and territorial boundedness, as well as the struggles to defend it, run against the grain of the dominant order. For decades, neoliberal capitalism has been creating deterritorialized,

39..........Escobar, 'The Colombian Pacific Region: A Dialogue of Cosmo/visions,' p. 57.

uprooted, cosmopolitan subjects that know no borders and no place. They move to the capital's whim, chasing investments, opportunities, and jobs. As Escobar would have it, 'Not only do they push people out of the territory, they push the territory out of the people,' so that exploitation and extraction can go on.[40]

But it is not only coal, gold, or oil that follow this globalized, deterritorialized logic. Art pieces and artistic careers do as well, as Erna states:

> Art became disembodied. We just move symbols around, we move signifiers. ... If you go to the Tate gallery, what you have is the permanent brainstorm of signifiers. ... Tate is not even showing the territory from which the art comes. They collect a particular form of art that could come from anywhere, because it is disembodied. This is the cultural logic of neoliberalism—disembodying experience.

Just like the bodies and experiences of many Chocoanos, MAMA is shaped by Chocó. It is shaped by the place that is, in the founders' view, 'The margin, the edge, the place that is forgotten, underfunded'[41] a place in the periphery that they chose to go to, destabilizing their own position in the Global Art World.

## Unusual Ways of Relating

• •

The 'MAMA Debates' are public events where MAMA connects speakers from different backgrounds to connect divergent perspectives on topics of extractivism, the relationship between rural and urban areas, development narratives, etc. For example, MAMA connects geologists, anti-extractivism activists, and critics of creative industries inviting them to debate and discuss extractivism of both the human creative forces and more-than-human existences. 'I like to see unlikely conversations happen between activists, scientists and artists in diverse fields; these kinds of strange conversations that usually never happen, because they are never invited to the same place,' explains MAMA's director Ana Milena Garzón.

Significant encounters, interdisciplinary reflections, and unexpected relations that develop over time are the backbone of MAMA's work. With no open programme, open calls for residencies, or open spaces for diverse artistic contents, MAMA's work depends on developing relationships.

Different ways of relationality are already present in Chocó, with collectives, collective ownership of land, as well as connections to more-than-human life of the territory. This logic of relating is very different to dominant, urban logic, because the surroundings are much louder, life is

40 .......... Ibid., p. 57.

41 .......... Jonathan Colin, interview by authors, Bogotá, August 2019.

happening everywhere, and everything grows on top of everything. So even though the Chocó Base was imagined as a 'space to reflect in isolation' in the rainforest and by the ocean, at the end of the world, it is a place where one is never alone. The 'space to reflect' turns out to be, in our experience and many others,' a space of radical interrelatedness.

Because Fernando and Jonathan spent more than a decade in Chocó before founding MAMA and the Chocó Base, locals recognize them as neighbours, and do not see MAMA as an NGO. However, residents of the Chocó Base are referred to as 'tourists' by locals. This in itself shakes up the usual relationship in which an NGO comes with its logos, projects, and opportunities for locals. The logic of MAMA is not about changing people's lives there in Chocó or making a certain impact. Residents coming to Chocó are not chosen on the basis of ideas they have for the work with the locals, nor are they required to work in any way with local communities. 'We don't want you to teach them anything,' Erna says; 'We created genuine relations, we are not there to fix problems' explains Jonathan in what is perhaps a more honest position, whereby local communities are not seen as a token for bringing arts and development to the region.

MAMA attracted internationally and nationally recognized artists, scientists, thinkers and activists, offering them time and space to reflect outside of the usual schedules and territories—to reflect on their practice, on Chocó, and possible alternative worlds. However, many residencies have ended up as long-term relations and projects, because, as Ana says, 'Residents became connected with local struggles, with nature here, with the work of MAMA.' With Ana's more permanent engagement as director of MAMA, and Alejandra Rojas Giraldo joining as programme manager, the organization, relations with local struggles, regional collectives and artists from Chocó have became a much stronger focus for MAMA. A number of initiatives have been conducted in Chocó to involve local artists, thinkers and collectives—including 'Postcards from the Future,' seminars for artistic educators, and dance workshops for dancers in the Chocó Base—all of which began with the question 'What kind of art is there in the region?'

> The political is not happening only in terms of narrative, but also in how we connect with these audio-visual collectives and bodies and how they are connecting with their own context and how we can really exchange, so that we all kind of connect agendas and help each other and become stronger.[42]

Unexpected relationships and unlikely connections of diverse geographies, disciplines, professions, and ways of being are forged through MAMA's

42..........Alejandra Rojas Giraldo, interview by authors, Bogotá, August 2019.

activities. This mesh of perspectives grows and develops, affecting and enriching every part of the network. MAMA cannot therefore be easily pinned down as an organization dealing specifically with one thematic issue (such as the environment), providing one type of service (artistic production or residencies), or being an expert in the needs of a particular local community. MAMA does all of these to a certain extent, creating new connections among them.

## Expanding Subjectivation

• • •

Residents of the Chocó Base for a certain period of time inhabit the world in which existence has a different relationality and temporality, as well as spatial and bodily arrangements, than those mediated by a global and dominantly urban sociocultural grid. As Jonathan puts in our group conversation in the Chocó Base:

> The idea of the residency was
> about disrupting artists' careers and
> triggering other ways of thinking.
> [...] There is no escape in the rain.
> This environment is so overwhelming.
> It can rain here for seven days and
> nights. It impacts every part of you.
> It is not just the weather. It absolutely
> impacts how you feel about life.

This disruption of the subjectivation is visible in numerous essays and artworks by residents contributing to Nuevatopias books as well as in our interviews. Accounts of another kind of bodily experience and relationship with a more-than-human world are abundant. There is also a different passing of time in the residency in which one is able to reflect and create in different dynamics and different forms. Julio Fierro, a professor of geology, came to the Chocó Base and wrote a poetic account of human relationships with rocks, sediments, and the 'womb of the Earth,' a text that may be considered unsuitable for many academic journals, conferences, or classrooms.[43] Dissensual subjectivation is also about 'widening the mental map of one's own country' as Charlotte Streck, director of Climate Focus and resident and collaborator of MAMA puts it, and this can also be applied to the world, a map which defies universalist logic of existence. For some, destabilization happens through what Paco Gómez calls the 'experience of a mirror'[44]—from facing the privilege of one's position in the sociocultural grid in relation to life in Chocó. Being in Chocó and interacting with the life there brings new self-awareness and understanding of one's own place in a sociocultural grid and the priveleges therein—an awareness akin to looking at oneself in a mirror. The question of 'How to

43..........Julio Fierro, 'There is Also Mining in Paradise,' in *Better Than/Mejor Que*, ed. Jonathan Colin (Bogotá: MAMA, 2015), pp. 144–63.

44..........Paco Gómez, Skype interview by authors, October 2019.

live with a mirror?' or how to use one's own privilege, stays after Chocó and affects life choices.

In Colombia, creating music, poetry, murals, dance, or movies in the suburbs, poor neighbourhoods or rural areas, and subjectivating oneself as an artist or artistic collective is a powerful source of resistance. Grassroot artistic practices provide a different position from which to engage with the ongoing struggles and the systemic violence. It is a mode of dissensus in places left out of the established Global Art World infrastructure—places where one is meant to subjectify only as a poor, campesino, Indigenous, uneducated, working class, or Afro-Colombian. This is also why being an artist in Chocó and having a wider national and international platform for work defies adaptation to the hegemonic mode of subjectivation. MAMA provides that as a partner to local organizations and collectives in projects that connect the institutional art world in Bogotá, Cali, or Medellín with community collectives and creators under terms that often rework typical institutional logics. Thus, it is not residents of the Chocó Base or MAMA per se that give a voice to communities from Chocó; they provide new spaces and occasions for these voices to be heard. △Fig. 3

△ 3
Postales del Futuro, photo: Más Arte Más Acción, 2019

In the project Postales del Futuro[45] [Postcards from the Future], the communication collective En Puja[46] from the small town of Nuqui and the audio-visual collective Puerto Creativo[47] from Buenaventura engaged in a three-year dialogue to create a series of short artistic movies. These movies address the question of building a massive international port in the small coastal town of Nuqui and the consequences this might have on the territory and life, relating it to the experience of people living in the big coastal port city of Buenaventura. The audio-visual collective En Puja has been showing these films in different kind of spaces including the local congress or local fishermen's meetings. Ana explains that:

> There are moments when we start discussions with a short film and that creates a kind of sensible space for reflecting in a new way. We have seen how the short films from Postales del

45...........'Postcards from the Future,' Más Arte Más Acción, www.masartemasaccion.org/postcards-from-the-future/?lang=en (accessed June 2020).
46...........Collectivo de Communicactiones En PUJA, official Facebook page, www.facebook.com/Colectivo-de-Comunicaciones-En-PU
47...........'¿CUÁL ES LA CINTA?' Puerto Creativo, http://puertocreativo.co/ (accessed June 2020).

> Futuro function in a very institutional discussion about the port, and when we show the films, people are like: Maybe we have to think again about this. It creates another way of talking about alternative ideas, beyond the super rational, more imaginative... And that puts energy into the discussion.

The notion of 'art as a way to talk'[48] involves changing the tone and sensibilities of important conversations (such as how to organize communities' future) and provides different channels for thinking and engaging in dialogue.

## Questioning the Structures of Power

• • • •

In Chocó, global hierarchies of power make themselves extremely evident. Most communities are left without public infrastructure: schools are few and basic, healthcare services barely existent, cultural and artistic infrastructure are absent. If development is offered, it means roads, airports, or ports facilitating the extraction of resources from the territory. In strongholds of paramilitaries and drug traffickers, selling drugs, and prostitution are ways to survive. For urban, national, and global elites, Chocó is an underdeveloped place that should be 'developed.' Tourists, business owners, and aid workers are mostly white, urban 'gringos,' while servants and workers are black locals. One cannot escape structural inequality based on race, coloniality, and peripherality. Even Chocó Base's cook Laura and groundskeeper Chico are both local Afro-Colombians.

Trying to practice alternatives to this situation in organizational work is about reshuffling the sedimented distribution of these structural inequalities. For MAMA, this was done through focused work with local and regional collectives, bringing with it a whole new set of questions regarding art as collective instead of individualist endeavour, how hierarchies within projects are established and challenged, and who the source of knowledge and expertise is. The idea of Chocó as a school, as proposed by local educator Ana Maria Arango, means that no one is a teacher or a student only. Instead of teaching, there is a process of knowledge sharing which decolonizes learning practices and relations.

In Postales del Futuro, many usual working relations were questioned and reworked. For example, during the project the two collectives, defined according to the project logic as 'beneficiaries,' became co-producers involved in joint decision-making. The collectives questioned why the artists, educators, and scientists who come to workshops were not from Chocó, and MAMA made deeper contacts and connections with local teachers and creators. Another example of new working relations is the way the

48 ..........Jonathan Colin, interview by authors, Chocó Base, Chocó, September 2019.

△ 4
La Toma del Mambo, photo: Andrea Gamboa, 2018

En Puja collective's organizational practices influenced the project as a whole. En Puja creates media content and movies in such a way to defy the individualistic logic of artist and artistic authorship. Everything they did in the project had to involve every member and be collectively discussed and created. Furthermore, with transparency regarding the money available, and by putting money in a common pot and discussing how to best spend it, MAMA ceased to be seen as a 'bag of money that should be used,' and local collectives contributed much of their local resources to the project. △Fig. 4

Similar logic was used when 'taking over' the Museum of Modern Art of Bogotá [in 'La Toma del MAMBO']. For three days in February of 2018, twelve local artistic and social collectives joined in an action coordinated by MAMA. Every collective received the same part of the budget and decided jointly how to use and share the space of MAMBO, without curatorship and control on the side of MAMA. 'It is about less control, and more confidence in what others do,' Alejandra says. These experiences and horizontal structure practices by local collectives in Colombia are challenging MAMA's organizational structure as well—posing questions about job titles, roles, responsibilities, and collaborations within the organization—bringing forth new ways of working. So, the questions of horizonal and participative relations with actors outside of the organization trigger questions on internal managing structures and power struggles, as well as organization-based inequalities. The case of MAMA shows that there is an inextorable link between internal organizational practice issues and the external issues that the organization seeks to address. There can be no participatory and empowering relation with target groups without also ensuring non-hierarchical and supportive relations within the organization. And while analyzing and trying to achieve the former, one has to deal with the latter.

## Meandering Processes

• • • • •

'We had the privilege of having flexible funding,'explains Jonathan, remembering how the grants MAMA received from the Arts Collaboratory gave them the freedom to have a rather loosely structured range of actions[49] including constructing the Chocó base, hosting artists and thinkers, publishing books, making exhibitions and so on. Both the type of funding they have received and the way they have directed it left them room to take an evasive, rampant, and negotiation-based approach towards the dominant 'project-logic' and its clear-cut expectations.

> It is our asset that we don't need to comply with this or that format, and we can change and add things in our annual programme ... We are happy to be allowed to do so and we know that others are may not,'

says Fernando.

In the Colombian context, MAMA is a strong and sustainable NGO, a reliable partner with wide international and local networks, and a proven, high-quality track record of project management as well as knowledge and capacity in administering diverse grants. However, ever since their beginning, they have increasingly tried to enable themselves and others (their guests, partners and grantees) to explore relations, territories, and ideas in genuine ways. As programme manager Alejandra puts it, rather tellingly: 'We don't necessarily have a definition of what it is or how to do it, but permanently addressing the tension that life itself poses.' This unorthodox attitude sets MAMA apart from the dominant modus operandi of the international arts foundations, even though a significant part of their financial arrangements come from bigger art foundations. However, it is not an organizational autonomy per se that drives them. It is rather the fact that their attitudes undermine a much wider logic of the capitalist Art World in at least three important ways, all very relevant to the territory that shapes them.

First, most of what they do differs from the strict project logic. Standardized project form is a method that is results-oriented. The method is focused on what is needed for an impact or result to happen and therefore the process is subjected to the result. Meandering, roaming, drifting, failing, are all ways to slow down progress, and yet at the same time they allow for 'learning by practice—evolving vs. planning,' as Alejandra puts it. This is why MAMA always tries to leave ample space and time around processes. Talking of Postales del Futuro, Alejandra notes that 'The three-year project meant we could get to know them, we became good friends, and we can follow someone's growth and evolution.'

49..........The Arts Collaboratory has been sharing available funds not based on project proposals, but based on longer term 'lifelines and future plans' submitted by each member, projecting their interests, needs, vulnerabilities, and priorities. This increases transparency, experimentation and interrogation, and embraces trial and error usually not allowed in the project logic.

This approach gives MAMA an opportunity to reshuffle what matters to them. Instead of planning, they propose evolution, instead of insurance, they accept uncertainty. Instead of impact, MAMA is about 'letting ourselves be affected' as Alejandra puts it. Finally, in terms of a project's goal, it can also be missed, because the ultimate destination might be much more interesting than the planned one. 'We are very open to what comes out. ... Inconsistency is life. "We were not trying to hide it," states Fernando, and somewhat victoriously adding, "We should be allowed to fail."'

While drifting from the project logic and timely planning practices, as mentioned before, MAMA turns to territories, peoples, and events. This is a second very important undisciplining and destabilizing the dominant distributions of the sensible in the work of an organization. Instead of subjecting processes and relations to logic of project interventions, in which timeframes, budgets and outcomes are clearly defined and followed, MAMA balances and experiments with more meandering, rampant, and relational processes of creation within the project boundaries. Thus, group deliberation, questioning, and new encounters can change the course of a project, the hierarchy of structures and roles, and the resources available. There is no hiding from the dominant distribution of the sensible and a place outside of it—but the constant 'staying with the trouble' or 'putting yourself in dissensus,' as Ana proudly says.

Third, the process is loosened from the domination of the final result, and reterritorialized within the very relational ecological context in which the practices are situated. The care for that context and struggles situated in that context is at least as important as the final result. As Ana says, 'The force of art needs to include the complexity and the context of the whole process, it cannot be only about what can be shown.' The struggles in the context are translated into the struggles in the organization and its work, so that what is created, in which contexts, with whom, and through which relations, grows from the complexities of life that always pose troubling questions.

## CONCLUSION: TOWARDS RAMPANT PRACTICES

The entanglement between artistic practice and politics practiced by MAMA is different from what we see as the three dominant discourses on arts and politics that have prevailed for several decades. The first discourse, derived from the notions of 'art for art's sake,' sees art as an autonomous field that should be kept away from politics, politicization, and instrumentalization for diverse social ends.[50] This discourse claims an apolitical position for the arts, as a purely aesthetic domain, understood to be

50..........Eleonora Belfiore and Oliver Bennett, *The Social Impact of the Arts: An Intellectual History* (London: Palgrave Macmillan UK, 2008).

Tsonami / Valparaíso, Chile / 6:31am 33°02'57.1"S / 71°36'42.2"W

Proyecto mARTadero / Cochabamba, Bolivia / 6:52am 17°23'59.7"S / 66°09'57.1"W

outside of politics and ethics.[51] Another discourse understands art as a good, legitimate, and useful means to diverse social and political ends, and normalizes art's instrumentalization for nation building, well-being, education and civic engagement, strengthening democracy, the flourishing of creative industries, social cohesion, sustainable development, city branding, tourism, and other policy goals.[52] This discourse follows the de-politization of art within the cultural policy and arts impacts literature, in which arts and culture have been articulated as consensual tools for social improvement within the neoliberal capitalist instrumentalization. The third discourse relies on the notion of the artist as a disruptive force that questions the dominant order, articulates political and social critique, and resists political and economic domination.[53] Part of this return to politics of artistic practice has been not only embraced, but incorporated and neutralized by the marketed 'Global Art Worlds' and its web of art galleries, biennials, contemporary art museums, art fairs, and auction houses offering aestheticization of rebellion to usual audiences.[54]

Unlike what is suggested by these three discourses, we suggest, through the case of MAMA, that being political in a dissentfull way requires artistic practices and strategies to re-engage with the web of life and its interdependencies, uncertainties, and vulnerabilities. This 'rampant practice'[55] means undisciplining, disturbing, challenging, and tickling the dominant subjectivation of actors, places of existence, processes of becoming, modes of practice, and ways of relating within arts practice. The work of MAMA invites for a rethinking of the dominant ontological understandings, epistemic injustices, cognitive assumptions, and affective relationships that govern the ways in which life is perceived, politics is legitimized, people are subjected, and societies are organized. Their strategies not only reconfigure the sensible and aesthetic experience, but also challenge the borders of art—its existential territories, its modalities of subjectivation of actors, its structures of power, its processes of becoming, and ways of relating. By challenging, displacing, and testing these borders, MAMA is tickling the dominant distribution of the sensible, the very hegemonic policed logic that seeks to organize and contain life within the dominant macropolitical grid. In it, MAMA's practices entail numerous moments and modes of dissensus that offer critical reflection on the hegemonic order, and space to envisage other possible worlds, existences, and relations. Art in MAMA's practice is by no means the creator, force, or initiator of dissensus per se. It is in the relationship with the territories of Chocó, its local creators, communities, and more-than-human world, that the 'Global Art World,' universalist notions of development, modernist science and the Nature/Culture divide get tickled, questioned and destabilized. And it is through the meeting with some of the global artistic

51..........Noël Caroll, 'Art and Ethical Criticism: An Overview of Recent Directions of Research,' *Ethics* 110, no. 2 (January 2000), pp. 350–87.
52..........Belfiore and Bennett, *The Social Impact of the Arts: An Intellectual History*.
53..........Rancière, *Dissensus*, pp. 134, 144, 148.
54..........Robert Morgan, *The End of the Artworld* (New York: Allworth Press, 1998).
55..........The notion of 'rampant' has been triggered and inspired by the work and ideas of Colombian philosopher and artist Tupac Cruz who philosophizes what non-hierarchical, jiggling, rampant forms of life of creeping plants suggest about ways of inhabiting this world, without occupying and owning it. See: *Cruz, Rocio en formación*.

and scientific practices that Chocoanos are tickled and poked to reflect on what kind of future they desire to create.

This means that it is ultimately hard, even impossible, to posit a clear-cut distinction between arts and society or politics, which is needed to theorize the impact or effect of art on the latter two. If our findings express anything, they express that there is a complex and deep and vital entanglement of arts, territories, times, and beings. Art is not a separate field of life, as many would like to suggest with notions of artistic autonomy and independence.[56] By the same token, artists are not clear cut and wholesome identities; artistic practices are mixed, intimately interwoven with other processes of worlding. In fact, to take this argument further, trying to sever the ties that bond all these together in order to make them analyzable and measurable is to lose the very essence of what they are: a living, vibrating ecosystem, a net, a web of life. Life that is much more contingent, uncertain, and evading than most analysts would like to see.[57]

Taking the other path towards them, a path of entanglement and interconnectedness, means to respect their contextuality, their belongings, and their vulnerability. And that respect is an important steppingstone towards imagining and creating a radically different world. As Osneyder Valoy, a young Chocoano and participant of many of MAMA's activities, has told us: 'Revolution is about connection,' implying connections and modes of love and care between not only people, but places and other beings. Thus, other ways of worlding and politics are possible through artistic and organizational practices that leak through the ordered containers of 'the police.' Instead of being pinned to the disembodied and deterritorialized signifiers shown in art galleries, they are rooted in the complexities, connectedness, and troubling questions that life itself bears in the context of their becoming.

56..........Goran Tomka and Višnja Kisić, 'Broken Dreams of Democratic Civilising and the Promise of (Inter)Dependence,' in *Models to Manifestos: A Conceptual Toolkit for Arts and Culture*, ed. Sandy Fitzgerald (Brussels: IETM, 2018), pp. 58–64.

57..........Goran Tomka and Višnja Kisić, 'From Inconsistencies to Contingencies: Understanding Policy Complexities of Novi Sad 2021 European Capital of Culture,' *Croatian International Relations Review*, Special issue on European Union and Challenges of Cultural Policies: Critical Perspectives, 24, no. 1 (2018), pp. 62–89.

ACKNOWLEDGEMENTS

The authors would like to thank the team of Más Arte Más Acción—Ana Milena Garzón, Alejandra Rojas Giraldo, Fernando Arias and Jonathan Colin—for their hospitality, sharing and collaboration during this research; to all the people who have shared their insights with us during interviews and meetings; to Tupac Cruz, Suely Rolnik, Osneyder Valoy and the teams of Lugar a Dudas, Flora, Casa tres Patio, En Puja, Associación para las Investigaciones Culturales del Chocó and Casa Wontanara for inspiring conversations, experiences and learning during our stay in Colombia; to Milena Dragićević Šešić, Irena Ristić, Erna von der Walde and the book editors for their insightful reading of the text and suggestions; and to the Force of Art initiative and Ilaria Manzini for making this learning and research possible.

## ← REFERENCES


Abram, David. *The Spell of the Sensuous: Perception and Language in a More-than-Human World*. New York: Vintage, 1997.

Arts Collaboratory. 'About Arts Collaboratory.' www.artscollaboratory.org/ (accessed June 2020).

Belfiore, Eleonora, and Oliver Bennett. *The Social Impact of the Arts: An Intellectual History*. London: Palgrave Macmillan UK, 2008.

Bergold, Jarg, and Stefan Thomas. 'Participatory Research Methods: A Methodological Approach in Motion.' *Historical Social Research/Historische Sozialforschung* 13, no. 1 (January 2012), pp. 191–222.

Bydler, Charlotte. *The Global Art World Inc.: On the Globalization of Contemporary Art*. Uppsala: Acta Universitatis Upsaliensis, 2004.

Caroll, Noël. 'Art and Ethical Criticism: An Overview of Recent Directions of Research.' *Ethics* 110, no. 2 (January 2000), pp. 350–87.

Chianchi, John. *Radical Environmentalism: Nature, Identity and More-than-Human Agency*. London: Palgrave Macmillan UK, 2015.

Colin, Jonathan, ed. *Nowhere/Ningun Lugar*. Bogotá: Fundación Más Arte Más Acción, 2013.
—. *Better Than/Mejor Que*. Bogotá: Fundación Más Arte Más Acción, 2015.
—. *This Place/Este Lugar*. Bogotá: Fundación Más Arte Más Acción, 2017.

Collectivo de Communicactiones En PUJA. Official Facebook page. www.facebook.com/Colectivo-de-Comunicaciones-En-PUJA-398165833598895/?fref=ts (accessed June 2020).

Cruz, Tupac. *Rocio en formación*. Bogotá: La Parte Maldita, 2016.

Escobar, Arturo. 'The Colombian Pacific Region: A Dialogue of Cosmo/visions.' In *This Place*, ed. Jonathan Colin, pp. 36–68. Bogotá: MAMA, 2017.
—. 'Transition Discourses and the Politics of Relationality.' In *Constructing the Pluriverse: The Geopolitics of Knowledge*, ed. Bernd Reiter, pp. 63–89. Durham: Duke University Press, 2018.

Fierro, Julio. 'There is also Mining in Paradise.' In *Better Than/Mejor Que*, ed. Jonathan Colin, pp. 144–63. Bogotá: MAMA, 2015.

Haraway, Donna. *Staying with the Trouble: Making Kin in the Chthulucene*. Durham and London: Duke University Press, 2016.

Harvey, Graham. *Animism: Respecting the Living World*. London: C. Hurst and Company, 2005.

Más Arte Más Acción. 'Base Chocó: Joep van Lieshout.' www.masartemasaccion.org/joep-van-lieshout-base-Chocó/?lang=en (accessed June 2020).
—. 'Casa Chocólate.' www.masartemasaccion.org/casa-chocolate/ (accessed June 2020).
—. 'Nuevastopias: No Where Better Than This Place.' www.masartemasaccion.org/nuevatopias-nowhere-better-than-this-place/?lang=en (accessed June 2020).
—. 'Postcards from the Future.' www.masartemasaccion.org/postcards-from-the-future/?lang=en (accessed June 2020).

Morgan, Robert. *The End of the Artworld*. New York: Allworth Press, 1998.

Morton, Timothy. *The Ecological Thought*. Cambridge, MA: Harvard University Press, 2010.
—. *Human Kind: Solidarity with Non-human People*. London: Verso, 2017.

Oslender, Ulrich. 'Local Aquatic Epistemologies among Black Communities on Colombia's Pacific Coast and the Pluriverse.' In *Constructing the Pluriverse: The Geopolitics of Knowledge*, ed. Bernd Reiter, pp. 137–50. Durham: Duke University Press, 2018.

Palmer, Helen, and Vicky Hunter. 'Worlding.' *New Materialism Almanac*, March 2018. https://newmaterialism.eu/almanac/w/worlding.html (accessed March 2020).

Puerto Creativo. '¿CUÁL ES LA CINTA?' http://puertocreativo.co/ (accessed June 2020).

Quijano, Anibal. 'Coloniality of Power and Eurocentrism in Latin America.' *International Sociology* 15, no. 2 (June 2000), pp. 215–32.

Rancière, Jacques. *Disagreement: Politics and Philosophy*. Minneapolis: University of Minnesota Press, 1999.
—. *Dissensus: On Politics and Aesthetics*, London and New York: Continuum, 2010.

Rolnik, Suely. 'The Spheres of Insurrection: Suggestions for Combating the Pimping of Life.' *E-Flux* no. 86. November 2017. www.e-flux.com/journal/86/163107/the-spheres-of-insurrection-suggestions-for-combating-the-pimping-of-life/.
—. *Esferas de la insurrección*. Ciudad Autónoma de Buenos Aires: Tinta Limón, 2019.

Spasić, Ivana. *Kultura na delu*. Belgrade: Fabrika knjiga, 2013.

Tomka, Goran, and Višnja Kisić. 'From Inconsistencies to Contingencies: Understanding Policy Complexities of Novi Sad 2021 European Capital of Culture.' *Croatian International Relations Review*, Special issue on European Union and Challenges of Cultural Policies: Critical Perspectives 24, no. 1 (2018), pp. 62–89.
—. 'Broken Dreams of Democratic Civilising and the Promise of (Inter) Dependence.' In *Models to Manifestos: A Conceptual Toolkit for Arts and Culture*, ed. Sandy Fitzgerald, pp. 58–64. Brussels: IETM, 2019.


## ← INTERVIEWS


Alejandra Rojas Giraldo (Colombia), project manager at MAMA and Ana Milena Garzón (Colombia), director of MAMA, interview by authors, Bogotá, 28 August 2019.

Jonathan Colin (UK) and Fernando Arias (Colombia), co-founders of MAMA, interview by authors, Bogotá, 30 August 2019.

Osneyder Valoy (Colombia), law student and collaborator of MAMA from Chocó, interview by authors, Bogotá, 2 September 2019.

Jonathan Colin, Fernando Arias, Alejandra Rojas Giraldo, Ana Milena Garzón and Eugenio Viola (Italy), chief curator of Museum of Modern Art Bogotá (MAMBO), group interview by authors, Choco Base, 8 September 2019.

Alejandra Rojas Giraldo and Ana Milena Garzón, interview by authors, Quibdo, 13 September 2019.

Paco Gómez (Spain), journalist and human rights activist, resident at Chocó Base and collaborator of MAMA, Skype interview by authors, 30 October 2019.

Erna von der Valde (Colombia), literary critic and scholar, resident at Chocó Base, collaborator and Board member of MAMA, Skype interview by authors, 30 October 2019.

Charlotte Streck (Germany), director of Climate Focus and prof. Unibversity of Potsdam, resident at Chocó Base and collaborator of MAMA, Skype interview by authors, 1 November 2019.

Victor Gama (Angola), composer and designer of contemporary musical instruments, resident at Chocó Base and collaborator of MAMA, Skype interview by authors, 8 December 2019. JA-398165833598895/?fref=ts (accessed June 2020).

# 'THE MOST IMPORTANT THING IS TO HAVE THAT SPACE!' The Power of Art and Local Art Communities in Central Asia

Diana T. Kudaibergenova

In this chapter I focus on the ways space is crucial for constructing new environments for artistic communities to explore and promote new values in society. Artistic initiatives play an important role in post-socialist societies through forms of art activism; the study of their existence and work helps shed more light onto the ways in which societies transform. In this chapter, I question how the space for art intervention is formed and how it is able to create different dialogues in local communities. For older generations of local artists in Central Asia, physical spaces such as exhibition halls are key for the development of the contemporary art field: in particular, for promoting educational purposes and facilitating communication and dialogues for the artistic and wider social communities. They see the spatial and tangible institutionalization of art as the only way to ensure its further sustainability. To the younger generation of artists who never experienced the Soviet and strictly institutionalized system of art production and relations between the artist and the state, 'space' is seen more conceptually—echoing a Bourdeusian interpretation of power positions—in the form of autonomy and independence from state institutionalization and censorship. Despite these differences, both groups strive toward the same goal: the creation of a sustainable contemporary art field. This happens because both groups see the social and cultural value in the way art production contributes to education and civil society development on the ground.

Keywords
→ Space
→ Field
→ Contemporary Art
→ State
→ Freedom
→ Institutionalization
→ Power
→ Civil Society

## INTRODUCTION

'It is ironic how history always repeats itself,' says one of my interlocutors; I add: 'often unexpectedly,' as we sit in the warm and small underground space of Bishkek's leading avant-garde Group 705, discussing post-Sovietness, revolutions, and everyday life in Kyrgyzstan and Central Asia.

In this instance, history repeats itself with the story of the group's formation on the eve of the first Kyrgyz post-Soviet revolution in 2005, also known as the Tulip Revolution.[1] Art and social change go hand in hand in Central Asia, conclude the artists.[2] Many of the local artistic initiatives were formed as groups or collectives at the crucial moments of historical changes: right before the collapse of the Soviet Union, in the turbulent nineteen-nineties, and now, in times of revolutions. Group 705 is one of the most well known artistic groups in the region; it was formed in 2005 by a group of like-minded, young, creative individuals in Bishkek to explore theatre of the absurd and the social conditions that fed into their art production. From 2013 to 2015 Group 705's initiatives were funded by Hivos and the Prince Claus Fund, allowing them to create the space and environment for questioning and discussing power through art initiatives. Since 2018, Group 705 is also receiving funding as a NextGen partner of the Prince Claus Fund.

Since 2005, Group 705 has staged a number of theatrical performances and exhibitions and was able to establish itself as a stable collective and a place for public intellectual gatherings in Bishkek. It believes that its contribution to social change in Central Asia is that of working with networks (one of the latest performances was transnational, involving authors and actors from diverse Central Asian backgrounds), exchange of ideas, and the actual physical space for communal engagement on the ground. In light of the post-socialist lack of state support for independent art initiatives that stem away from the institutionalized and stale Artists' Union, the existence of groups and spaces like Group 705 is crucial for further civil society development in the region.

In this chapter, and through the example of Group 705 and similar art initiatives, I focus on the ways space plays an important role in constructing new environments that are able to facilitate new social and cultural values. Artistic initiatives play an important role in post-socialist societies through forms of art activism[3] and the study of their existence and work help to shed more light on the ways in which societies transform. In particular, in this chapter I question how the space for art intervention is formed and how it is able to create different dialogues in local communities. The Bourdieusian understanding of power relations and space are particularly useful for the explanation here.

Much of social theory is devoted to 'space' as the field of interactions and positions. As sociologist Pierre Bourdieu writes,

> The social world can be represented as a space (with several dimensions) constructed on the basis of principles of differentiation or distribution constituted by the set of properties active

1............See Shairbek Juraev, 'Kyrgyz Democracy? The Tulip Revolution and Beyond,' *Central Asian Survey* 27, no. 3–4 (2008), pp. 253–64; Sally N. Cummings and Maxim Ryabkov, 'Situating the "Tulip Revolution",' *Central Asian Survey* 27, no. 3–4 (2008), pp. 241–52.

2............Data for this chapter was collected through numerous interviews with artists from 2017 to 2019 across Central Asia and mainly in Kyrgyzstan and Tajikistan.

3............See Madina Tlostanova, *What Does it Mean to be Post-Soviet? Decolonial Art from the Ruins of the Soviet Empire* (Durham: Duke University Press, 2018); and Valeria Ibrayeva, Iskusstvo Kazakhstana: Post-Sovetskii period [The art of Kazakhstan: Post-Soviet period] (Almaty: Tonkaya gran, 2014).

> within the social universe in question, i.e., capable of conferring strength, and power within that universe, on their holder. Agents and groups of agents are thus defined by their relative position within that space. Each of them is assigned to a position or a precise class of neighbouring positions (i.e., a particular region in this space) and one cannot really—even if one can in thought—occupy two opposite regions of that space. Inasmuch as the properties selected to construct this space are active properties, one can also describe it as a field of forces, i.e., as a set of objective power relations that impose themselves on all who enter the field and that are irreducible to the intentions of the individual agents or even to the direct 'interactions' among agents.[4]

The field of forces is of great importance and focus here when art 'works for the implementation of the future radical changes through altering our thinking and setting our consciousness free from the global neoliberal or jingoistic brainwashing'[5] (Tlostanova 2018:22). Contemporary art initiatives like those of Group 705 and ArtEast in Bishkek that preceded it form special spaces where artists themselves are the actors of change. Through their positions in non-state supported art initiatives, they define their own positions and construct their own spaces within the field of power relations that inevitably involve the state and society.

Contrary to the Soviet model of almost total control and censorship of the cultural production in each of the republics, the collapse of the Soviet Union and the post-Soviet period of independence provide a space of de-institutionalization of art fields but also their further independence from state sponsorship and thus from censorship. The state de-institutionalization of the art field meant the collapse of the infrastructure for cultural production (previously known as *goszakaz*) and financial support for state-sponsored artists. But on the other hand, it meant the creation of the absolutely new system of cultural production without previous frameworks of control and censorships from state institution, metamorphosis of the market and creation of completely independent art spaces.

In this matrix of different positions, free and de-institutionalized artists and the art field do not depend on the state too much but work in parallel to state institutions, including the Ministry of Culture and most of the state museums. Throughout my fieldwork in Kyrgyzstan and Central Asia (Tajikistan, Uzbekistan and Kazakhstan) and through numerous interviews with independent curators, artists, and art communities, I found out that 'space' is seen as the most important feature for the existence of an independent art field. Space is understood both in the form of the physical space for exhibitions, meetings, performances, art schools, and communal dialogues that continuously keep the art field developing as well as in the form of a more Bourdeusian sense of power positions

4............Pierre Bourdieu, 'The Social Space and the Genesis of Groups,' *Information (International Social Science Council)* 24, no. 2 (1985), pp. 195–220.

5............Madina Tlostanova, *What Does it Mean to be Post-Soviet? Decolonial Art from the Ruins of the Soviet Empire* (Durham: Duke University Press, 2018).

and definitions of one's positions within the field. In this chapter I discuss both of these concepts interchangeably through the ways my respondents, independent artists, explain and live through these frameworks of relations. Generational shifts in understanding space are central to these discussions.

I first lay out the ways in which the most recent generation of contemporary artists of Group 705 explain their 'spatial' imagination; I then turn to the efforts to build a wider field of non-state sponsored art of the first generation of contemporary artists Gulnara Kasmalieva and Muratbek Djumaliev with the ArtEast artistic and educational initiative. These two groups and their views are connected in the local contemporary art scene. Group 705 follows the tropes of ArtEast educational initiative run by Gulnara Kasmalieva and Muratbek Djumaliev. However, the shifts in their perceptions of spaces, autonomies, and cultural production differ significantly due to the fact that post-socialist realities in polity and society change rapidly and thus the generational gap between these two initiatives are significant.

This generational shift happens due to the change of attitude in the understanding of artists' own 'space' away from the institutionalized idea of the museum or annual exhibit (in the way it is envisioned by the first generation of post-Soviet artists), towards the individual or communal artistic contribution to society. For the latest generation of artists, such as those in Group 705, this spatial representation changes even the forms in which art can engage with its own society—often without grand exhibitions but through dialogues, meetings, gatherings, and the organization of rallies. Among the most recent rallies in Bishkek, there were the ecological rallies and women's rights rallies (February–March 2020) that were often organized by local artists themselves (e.g. Bermet Borunbayeva or Altyn Kapalova).

## WHY DOES CONTEMPORARY ART MATTER IN EURASIA?

'It was [through] our own initiative [to form the group], we did everything ourselves. [In the beginning] we had to meet right on the street, because back then we didn't have our own space for gatherings,' explains Talgat Berikov, one of the co-founders of Group 705. The discussion inevitably lingers in multiple interpretations of the idea of 'space': from the real walls of the building where the group is able to meet and rehearse their performances (where they invite their audience and those seeking refuge), to the more figurative understanding of space within society. Like other artistic groups all over the world, Group 705 initially sought its own space in the local artistic community, both in the institutionalized or 'official' art scene, and in the non-state and informally institutionalized contemporary art community.[6]

6............Zhanara Nauruzbayeva, 'Portraiture and Proximity: "Official" Artists and the State-ization of the Market in Post-Soviet Kazakhstan,' *Ethnos* 76, no. 3 (2011), pp. 375–97.

In our interview with Group 705, the word 'space' is often pronounced almost subconsciously. Space in these discussions means the physical and tangible place of the theatre. One of the Group's members looks around the white walls and carefully stacked books in the little library and says that things would have worked out differently for Group 705 if funding had not been available for this 'space' to be set up.[7] 'Why is this space so important?' I ask them. 'Because art [and contemporary art specifically] is the solution to so many of the problems of our time,' one member answers.[8] In the conditions of highly challenging political and ideological transformations that affect various societies of the post-communist bloc—but also across the world—art communities remain the independent 'space' for alternative thinking and reinterpretations of the reality around them. Contemporary art allows rethinking some of the most dominant structures of social and political lives. Group 705 uses theatrical performances, films, individual and group art works, and installations—along with conversations that are inevitably entangled in these activities—as ways to see the alternative.

Alternative thinking is even more crucial in contexts where the creeping domination of the state as a totalizing idea, an institutionalized coercive machine, and omnipresent discursive base, appropriates more and more space previously occupied by dissent and freedom. As the decolonial theorist Madina Tlostanova writes in her most recent book on decolonial post-Soviet art, the Soviet tradition of crushing dissent has smoothly travelled to the post-Soviet time.[9] It is thus more surprising that in these conditions, art becomes the new public sphere where:

> [Post-Soviet contemporary] art has more chances to avoid the punishment of repressive systems and offer a wider spectre of interpretations and opinions than purely political and rationalized forms of protests. In contrast with social theory, the immediate and often nonrational affective form of art, is able to better and faster convey the vague and undefined sensibilities of protest and affirmation of another way of being that social theorists cannot formulate.[10]

These examples of art-power relations and artistic communal engagements are applicable in cases beyond the post-Soviet region itself. What is unique about Central Asia though is the complexity of the social and historical contexts on the ground, its incorporation into the colonial space of Russia, followed by state-development under the Soviet Union.

7............Group 705 collective interview by author, December 2019, Bishkek, Kyrgyzstan.
8............Ibid.
9............Tlostanova, *What Does it Mean to be Post-Soviet?*
10..........Ibid., p. 23.

Described in media and scholarship as the Russian 'periphery,' Central Asia has its own powerful artistic discourses to offer.

As such, the following sections focus on the local empirical context and the more conceptual frame of communal engagement through art, performance, and artistic education.

## SPACE

'The most important thing is to have that space!' is the phrase I hear over and over in conversations with local contemporary artists. While there is a very distinct understanding of personal and certainly collective artistic levels of what this space means, there is a growing demand for claiming 'space' to affirm a sense of self-autonomy in the socio-political realm as well as to assert physical space as essential for conducting the dialogues and communication that precede any exhibit or performance. This understanding is distinct from the discussion on having a separate contemporary art space in a form of a museum that could safeguard the genealogy of local art development from the late nineteen-eighties to the present. Many of the artists who speak of a 'contemporary art museum' in Central Asia view it as an institutionalized form of knowledge and an archive first and as a space for discussion and interaction second.

When one speaks of the physical and tangible space with walls, roof and rooms, it is linked to the desire for the stable physical space for gathering and exhibiting. For many artists, the discussion of a potential museum of contemporary art in any of the five states of Central Asia, is indicative of their powerful yet fragile spatial position, which might get lost if it is not preserved in a specialized museum. For example, in Almaty the older generations of contemporary artists, those who started exhibiting in the late nineteen-nineties, have no doubt about the necessity for a formal institutionalization of local and regional (Central Asian) contemporary art, even if this requires an established and (a likely) state-led form of a museum of contemporary art. 'Yes, it would be overpowering but at least it would give us a space for a historical perspective of local independent art development since the collapse of the Soviet Union,' says one female artist in her forties of the possibility of a future museum of contemporary art.[11] In contrast, a younger artist in his thirties states:

> There should be no institutionalization of contemporary art whatsoever! Contemporary art [in Central Asia] exists as an alternative space of self-expression and institutionalizing it would only create more unbearable and overpowering frames for something that requires freedom in its totality.[12]

11 .......... Interview by author, Almaty, November 2017.

12 .......... Group discussion with the author, Astana, August 2018.

'Where is that space where art can live and where the artist can teach younger generations something?' This was a recurring question I heard throughout my time in Uzbekistan. While passing disintegrated Lenin portraits on the walls of old-new buildings—old Soviet buildings now covered with a neoliberal façade—another common question repeated throughout the region was, 'Is there a space for our almost-lost heritage in forms of Soviet murals, mosaics, monuments and other urban artefacts?' During fieldwork in Bishkek a more existential question was asked: 'Is there a need to remember this past at all?' But perhaps an even more pressing question that arose during the fieldwork, and which interviewees often wondered about, was whether there is even a space for the contemporary artists.

I sit in Group 705's warm studio in downtown Bishkek in a circle of its active members who are preparing for their next performance, *White Rhinoceros*—a joint collaboration between transnational actors in Central Asia. 'This contemporary play is about the banking system,' explain the members of Group 705; but in our expanded discussion on this forthcoming performance and their previous works, I see the fragments of our common post-Soviet past. These are the fragments of the collapsed grand infrastructure projects, on the remnants of which most of us grew up, when the number of good schools was shrinking and 'the younger generation no longer found spaces of their own.'[13] These had been spaces just beyond the system of universal schooling, spaces like the creative and intellectual clubs that the Soviet Union used to provide in abundance to our older brothers and sisters. Out of this emptiness and in the aftermath of the collapse, several initiatives built up like Phoenixes out of the ashes.

'I think our Group [705] really started in the [Bishkek] Media Centre; at least, you can say that many of us met there when we were still teenagers,' explains Talgat Berikov, one of the co-founders of the group. 'We were drawn to that space as something that allowed us to create and exist according to our own interests,' continues Marat Raimkulov, the charismatic artistic leader of the group. Berikov and Raimkulov first met in the Media Centre, the local NGO for youngsters where they could learn technical skills of digital editing, broadcasting as well as creative writing and narrating. What is important in their own narration of this past, as well as in what comes after it (their engagement in the artistic school ArtEast created by Gulnara Kasmalieva and Muratbek Djumaliev), is their focus on the institutional grounding of 'spaces' of engagement—meeting points and the further organization of groups such as Group 705 and popular Kyrgyz media resource 'Kloop.' Both Group 705 and Kloop, now widely known in Kyrgyzstan and the region, grew out of these initial NGOs and the physical spaces of the Media Centre and ArtEast school. As one of the Group 705 members remembers it, his first encounter with the artistic scene took place through the network of existing initiatives:

13..........Author's interview with Gulnara Kasmalieva, December 2019, Bishkek, Kyrgyzstan.

> To be fair, this experience in the Media Centre sort of broke me, and not because there were things [there] that were otherwise censored, it wasn't that; it was more like within the frames of my own existence at the time, [the experiences of Media Centre and ArtEast] were considered an underground movement. By the time I came to ArtEast [school] in 2005, I think, by that time they already had the series of their big exhibitions. What was the name of the exhibit when I came in? 'In the Shadows of Heroes.' So, it means that 'and the Others' had already passed [the exhibit that is considered legendary in Central Asian art development and in Kyrgyzstan in particular]. But to be honest I didn't know much about these developments at the time. ArtEast already had the [artistic] school and it already formed a group of young [contemporary] artists. ...What is very interesting is that life really mixed up all these people, and they are now in great dialogues with each other, all of them form this publicly active scene of discussions.[14]

The idea of the ArtEast school for young artists came to Bishkek-based contemporary artists Gulnara Kasmalieva and Muratbek Djumaliev as they saw the need to foster the new generation of artists towards further institutionalization of the local contemporary art scene. The genealogy of this development is rooted in the deeper historical contexts of the pre-Soviet collapse of the late nineteen-eighties, when both Kasmalieva and Djumaliev came back to Bishkek as fresh graduates of the prestigious Soviet art institutions of the Surikov Moscow State Academic Art Institute and the Leningrad Vera Mukhina Higher School of Art and Design respectively. 'We came back home, and we wanted to organize some meetings, artistic discussions and create art locally,' remembers Kasmalieva.[15] They rented an underground space (*podval* in Russian) and started gathering the local artistic community literally under the ground. Quite ironically the couple's further artistic activities became iconic for Central Asian art development and continued to remain spatially underground; as discussed later in the chapter, their biggest exhibits were organized in the underground space of the Ala-Too Square in central Bishkek that hosted both of the country's revolutions in 2005 and 2010.

## INSTITUTION/COMMUNITY

In the late nineteen-eighties and throughout the nineties, Kasmalieva and Djumaliev along with their likeminded colleagues, among them the architect, curator and educator Ulan Djapparov, tirelessly engaged in building the local artistic community. In the context of the total collapse of institutional support for arts and cultural initiatives and during the

14..........Group 705 collective interview by author, December 2019, Bishkek, Kyrgyzstan.

15..........Interview with the author, Bishkek, December 2017.

heightened economic crisis that swept most of the post-communist societies in the nineties, the contemporary art scene in Central Asia thrived.[16] At the time, this first generation of local contemporary artists experimented with new forms and new discourses of art, seeking the freedom from the remaining censorship from the Soviet-era Artists' unions. Contemporary art and the collapse of the Soviet Union provided contemporary artists with the independence from the state and state-sponsored production they were seeking at the end of the eighties.

By 1998 the Soros Centre for Contemporary Art (SCCA) was established in Almaty to become the centre for the whole Central Asian region to 'promote new voices and to encourage artists to experiment with new modes of art-making.'[17] This Centre was the initial attempt to institutionalize local contemporary art and despite it using 'the elements of the Soviet-era language of the social utility of art,'[18] many remember it as a distinct line for creating the necessary 'space' for contemporary art.

'It was a time of almost total freedom,' remembers Valeria Ibrayeva, the founding chair of the SCCA.

> I remember how [Kazakh contemporary artist] Said [Atabekov] brought a painting of the national flag of Kazakhstan to SCCA but it wasn't really the usual flag you expect. The eagle [on the Kazakh flag] was just so predatory. It was so brave, so right into the time and so liberating. This was what art is aimed to do—give you the freedom of your thoughts, your consciousness and your whole being.[19]

However, in 2008 the SCCA was closed down due to the lack of external or internal funding and artists were back to the ground zero, having to self-organize again.

'We needed a community,' remembers Kasmalieva in an interview, 'But in order to build the community, the artists themselves had to engage in literally doing everything—from finding the space for gatherings to getting the nails into the exhibition wall to hang their works.' She remembers that organizing even smaller exhibits and events took much of their efforts, and curatorial experience took away the artistic part of the work.[20] There was a need for communal engagement from a different angle—the community had to grow from people themselves. This is how the ArtEast school for young artists developed as a space that engaged and produced the group of the second generation of contemporary artists in Bishkek. In one of

16...........To name a few of the exceptional artists of the era: Rustam Khalfin and Sergei Maslov in Almaty, Kyzyl Traktor collective and Askhat Akhmediyarov in Shymkent, Gulnara Kasmalieva and Muratbek Djumaliev, and Ulan Djapparov in Bishkek, Vyacheslav Akhunov in Uzbekistan, and, finally, Kanat Ibragimov.

17...........Zhanara Nauruzbayeva, 'Refurbishing Soviet Status: Visual Artists and Marketization in Kazakhstan,' PhD dissertation (Stanford, CA: Stanford University, 2011), p. 41.

18...........Ibid., p. 46.

19...........Series of interviews by author, Almaty, January 2014.

20...........Series of interviews by author, Gulnara Kasmalieva and Muratbek Djumaliev, Bishkek, 2017 and 2019.

the interviews, Kasmalieva and Djumaliev recount this story of communal and institutional space building through ArtEast:

> The idea of the school came spontaneously after being frustrated with the results of the contemporary art exhibitions and workshops that we had previously organized. Of course, we had anticipated educational and cultural results from these events during the nineteen-nineties. But relatively quickly, we realized that these forms of exhibition and education were not really effective. Despite the high level of interest of international artists and curators in contemporary art from Central Asia, the Bishkek, Kyrgyzstan art community still had very few participants represented in international exhibitions. We understood that we needed to create a new contemporary art community, but we did not know how. There were many young people coming to visit ArtEast and among them were some friends of our son. They were curious and we often discussed contemporary art. We saw their interest in this topic and we decided to make an open call for students. Our curricula combined theoretical and practical elements.[21]

Since the start of their first intake, the school has produced four groups of graduates. In early 2020, the first graduates of the school, well-known artistic activists and curators in Bishkek and the region, Bermet Borunbaeva, Oksana Kapishnikova and others announced that they would run the school's new intake and courses. The development of this initiative is exactly what Kasmalieva and Djumaliev envisioned in the beginning of their school, when they wanted someone new to 'follow their steps' and continue to institutionalize the art scene through their own engagement and actions. Group 705 was one of the success stories of ArtEast as it was born out of it and 'grew' along with ArtEast's big exhibitions under the ground of the Ala-Too Square in Bishkek in the two thousands.

The case of the Ala-Too square exhibitions organized by Kasmalieva and Djumaliev is the vivid example of differences in perceptions of contemporary art in different generations of contemporary artists. What Kasmalieva and Djumaliev describe with sadness as the end of big exhibitions and festivals that were held at Ala-Too are not seen as such for Group 705, who invest more in smaller scale but continuous events, interactions and networking. The newest generation of contemporary artists in Central Asia re-organizes its own artistic strategies and interventions into the space. In the recently developed art communities in Kazakhstan, for instance, ongoing but small-scale art interventions in Astana are considered more important by local artists than annual grand exhibits and art festivals.

21 .......... Beth Hinderliter, 'The ArtEast School for Contemporary Art: Interview with Gulnara Kasmalieva and Muratbek Djumaliev,' *Journal of Inquiry and Action in Education* 6, no. 1 (2014), pp. 103–9.

## THE SQUARE

The Ala-Too Square in central Bishkek became a public sphere of its own as the site of both the 2005 and 2010 revolutions. The square continues to serve as the iconic central place for protests, manifestations, activism, and dialogues. It is also a legendary place for Central Asian art development. When I asked local artists and curators about the development of the contemporary art scene in the region, they chronologically go back to the development of the big 'underground' exhibitions—the first Green Triangle group exhibitions in Almaty[22] or the 'Bishkek biennales' that were held under the central Ala-Too square.

In the early two-thousands, Bishkek-based Ulan Djapparov, who serves as a crucial node and link connecting all Central Asian contemporary artists in various different spaces and initiatives,[23] worked on helping the reconstruction of the historical museum. Through this engagement, he found out about the empty space under the Ala-Too Square, a sort of catacomb. 'In the Soviet time this space under the Lenin [statue] on Ala-Too Square was used to deliver the local party leaders to the presidium on top, where they'd give their speeches,' explain Kasmalieva and Djumaliev. The underground space was kept as a 'parking lot' for governmental cars that delivered and dispatched the party leaders after each public event. After the collapse of the Soviet Union, the Lenin monument on the square was removed, the square itself was renamed and the new monument to the Kyrgyz Republic was installed until it was removed after the 2005 revolution[24] and the monument to local historical hero Manas was installed instead. The underground space was left unguarded and many homeless people found refuge there. Since Djapparov found out about the space, he and Kasmalieva and Djumaliev worked hard to establish links with the Ministry of Culture to get hold of this space for future exhibitions. Eventually the Square and its underground played a crucial role in the development of local artistic communities (that of ArtEast, and Group 705), but also had an influence on developing other, neighbouring art initiatives in Kazakhstan, Uzbekistan and Tajikistan.

Gulnara Kasmalieva:

> It all happened with the first Bishkek Exhibition... Oh no, it all started with our grant application for the group work, we wrote that we needed institutional support. We wrote a grant proposal to Hivos...

22..........Diana T. Kudaibergenova, 'Punk Shamanism, Revolt and Break-up of Traditional Linkage: The Waves of Cultural Production in Post-Soviet Kazakhstan,' *European Journal of Cultural Studies* 21, no. 4 (2018), pp. 435–51.

23..........Djapparov curated a number of exhibitions in the nineties in Bishkek and since then established his own group Studio Museum, which supported numerous art-related events and helped a great number of architects and artists to develop their works. Since the nineties he has continuously engaged with Kazakhstan's leading artists and helped the development of Tajikistan's contemporary art scene and has had continuous links to the Uzbek art scene. In Bishkek, he closely collaborates with Kasmalieva and Djumaliev and other local artists and organizes and curates artistic initiatives. Djapparov is a well-known curator in Central Asia but he is also himself an artist, architect, and educator. Every summer he runs the 'Lazy art' initiative in the Issyk-Kul lake in Kyrgyzstan; he also organizes the annual April exhibit in Bishkek and leads the Facebook discussion group on Central Asian art.

24..........Sally N. Cummings, 'Leaving Lenin: Elites, Official Ideology and Monuments in the Kyrgyz Republic,' *Nationalities Papers* 41, no. 4 (2013), pp. 606–21.

Muratbek Djumaliev:

We had to do everything ourselves [independently].

Gulnara Kasmalieva:

We had the initial idea [about forming the group] in 1999; we received the response [from Hivos] in 2004 or 2005. ... They said they wanted to support our initiative and we were very happy. In our application, we wrote that we wanted to organize two exhibitions a year, two big seminars or conferences a year with invitations [to foreign participants, including those of the wider region], we planned it as two big educational events. We really heavily loaded ourselves [with work], someone said we had ambitious plans. When we got the support, we thought it was very important to keep on organizing exhibitions and events, it was important for institutionalization and the creation of that artistic community [that we lacked in the region at the time]. So, our first exhibition "In the Shadow of Heroes" became very big; there were more than 50 participants from all over the world, there were a lot of local artists, and post-Soviet art in general.

But most importantly, [this institutionalization] was combined with the fact that we gained our own space for these exhibitions, our own space—for us it was this sort of improvized, our own Ministry of Culture under the Ala-Too Square.

Muratbek Djumaliev:

You say it like that, and people will think that our [Kyrgyz Republic] Ministry of Culture [the real one] was under the Ala-Too Square. You mean, that our independent artistic initiative gathered there. ... This space was so important to so many young artists and communities, you would know that Group 705, for example, was born there, they literally came up with their name under that Square and formed as an artistic community there.[25]

The transformation of the conception of the 'Ministry of Culture' presented in this excerpt from a dialogue on the genealogy of the Kyrgyz or Central Asian contemporary art scene formation is crucial. At the time of this interview the whole regional artistic community and even further to the post-Soviet and more global art space (with artists in solidarity from Ukraine to Western Europe and US) were going through the shock of the Kyrgyz ministerial attack on the first Feminnale exhibition held in Bishkek from 27 November to 16 December 2019. Intended as a showcase of female artists and a socio-cultural dialogue among engaged feminist artists across the world, the exhibition was first attacked by the Kyrgyz

25..........Series of interviews by author, Gulnara Kasmalieva and Muratbek Djumaliev, Bishkek, 2017 and 2019.

Creating Independent and Artistic Networks (CRIA) / Buenos Aires, Argentina / 7:23am 34°36'12"S / 58°22'54"W

Kër Thiossane / Dakar, Senegal / 10:07am    14°42'54.2"N / 17°27'30.2"W

nationalist groups and then heavily censored by the Kyrgyz Minister of Culture himself for the scenes of nudity and 'amoral' attitudes and values. In the artistic community, it was perceived as a brutal act on the freedom of expression and artists' own positions within the socio-political space of interactions and power relations. However, for many whom I interviewed in the aftermath of the scandal, Feminnale became the 'boiling point' for political and social discussions on censorship, power, control, and growing authoritarianism. Some of my respondents across the region even questioned the necessity of the 'Ministry of Culture' at all if it did not intend to help independent art development, but on the contrary, kill its whole development.

What Kasmalieva alluded to in her remark of the underground 'Ministry of Culture' is specifically this paradoxical urge of the Central Asian art scene to institutionalize and build more initiatives, groups, and educational programmes for young artists: build the museums and spaces of exhibits and dialogues away from censorship and from the politically-controlled agendas of the respective countries' regimes. In her conceptualization and aspiration, she sees that almost two decades of 'underground' artistic activities led by ArtEast, Kasmalieva, and Djumaliev's efforts, as well as numerous initiatives in the region,[26] all directed at 'community-building' activities, have to finalize in a 'solid' and organizational form of an institution. This thought is shared by many first wave contemporary artists in the region as tireless 'builders' of the community.

First-generation contemporary artists believe that if an artistic institution were to appear, it should go beyond just the museum or art gallery where artists finally get a chance to present regular exhibits. Such an institution, more importantly, should become a space for the consolidation of artists, communities, ongoing public dialogues, and the further institutionalization of local contemporary art scenes into a solidified movement with its own institutional history, compartments, and future. In the eyes of these artistic activists, the SCCA largely failed to become this institution or space for further organized dialogues and community engagement. Some share the view that it existed for a rather short period of time to engage fully; others believe that it remained an elitist organization with its own hierarchies and selection of artists. The Central Asian art scene is also far from the Azeri model where the Yarat Foundation was established in 2011 as a space for exhibitions as well as for providing grounded support to the local contemporary art scene through budgets, artistic studios, institutionalizing work for local artists, and instituting a large and engaging educational programme.

The influence of the Bishkek underground Ala-Too Square exhibits on the development of local contemporary art field was as great as the influence of short-term institutionalized initiatives. Many remember it as the comparative effects of the SCCA activities in Almaty. A considerable

26..........Other relevant initiatives have been led by Yulia Sorokina, Valeria Ibrayeva, Almagul Menlibayeva, Elena and Viktor Vorobiev, Georgy Mamedov and the former STAB initiative, Laboratory Ci, Group 705, Djamshed Kholikov, Umida Akhmedova, and Oleg Kaprov, and more recently, by Artcom and ArtCollider, TSE, the Tselinniy Garage initiative and others.

amount of the new cohort of artists from all over the region but mainly from Kyrgyzstan and Kazakhstan was developed;[27] a large number of artistic initiatives, groups and communities were formed; dialogues and networks were built. These exhibitions also went down in history as some of the biggest artistic events in the history of contemporary art development in the region. 'The public who was far from art came and engaged, they left a lot of great comments, once even the whole army squad came and they were very impressed with contemporary art, kept on asking questions,' remembers Kasmalieva.

These trends are still visible in the most recent works of their ArtEast school graduates; for example, activist Bermet Borunbayeva currently runs an ecological-political movement in Bishkek, and Group 705 is building further links with the Tajik and Kazakh artistic communities in their performative works and activism. In this respect there is positive feedback on legacy of the ArtEast school, both Kasmalieva and Djumaliev agree. But the question they raise remains: Is this impact enough, and how much further collective work should be done to keep the artistic movement going in the Central Asian region? Can it bring more contemporary artists to the field?

This is a generational question. In Kazakhstan too, Almagul Menlibayeva, Askhat Akhmediyarov, Saule Suleimenova and others tirelessly engage in local educational initiatives and curating younger artists. A lot of the work happens simultaneously in different spaces—from Almaty to Bishkek and Tashkent, from Dushanbe to Astana and Shymkent. For contemporary artists, borders never formed an obstacle, and country-wide identification only served as one more space for engagement. As one of the cultural experts noted in Dushanbe, Tajikistan:

> Real diplomacy [in the region] is not always done by politicians, but on the ground and through real networks, visible or invisible, it is done by the cultural actors—institutionalized artists, musicians, all that lot of the art world really sticks 'Central Asia' together.[28]

Perhaps Group 705's latest performance *White Rhinoceros*, the production of which spans over several years, cities, and local borders and networks, speaks to that inter-regional development of artistic initiatives and dialogues. Art becomes the language that unites these 'highly interdisciplinary' connections, as Group 705's own composition is made of a kaleidoscope of passports and disciplinary backgrounds (from medicine to journalism). 'We are able to join in together and exist as a group because

27 ........... Responding to an interview question on how much impact these exhibits have had on local communities, Gulnara Kasamalieva states that the local public engaged greatly with the space. Kazakh and Kyrgyz young artists used these exhibitions strategically 'to learn how to organize and run big exhibitions. Kazakh [artists] used to come in full buses just to see the exhibit and used it as a learning practice.'

28 ........... Anonymous interview, in discussion with the author, Dushanbe, March 2019.

we believe in the higher cause of art,' members collectively recount in the interview. 'What is the public good of art for society?' I ask as we speak right before the first full rehearsal of *White Rhinoceros*. The theatre piece is about a contemporary tale of banking corruption schemes, Bishkek is shrouded in smog and public protest against the major corruption scandal over USD 700 million laundering and free media oppression as a result of media reporting of the laundering scheme by former Kyrgyz senior officials. Many of my respondents attended the rally against the oppression of free media and recently have been to another mass-scale rally against air pollution in Bishkek—both held at the Ala-Too Square. In fact, contemporary artists in Central Asia take up a substantial share of the participation in protest movements. The 'Oyan, Qazaqstan' movement in Kazakhstan has a number of leading young contemporary artists who are in charge of changing the visual and creative strategies of protests and rallies. The works of street artist Pasha Cas from Almaty are also a form of protest movement that is new for Central Asia. In Uzbekistan, protest was unthinkable under the late president Karimov, yet art interventions by the local artistic community in the form of independent film festivals took on a creative way to express dissidence by filming the marginality of ordinary citizens and the absurdism of the propaganda in the repressive state. Contemporary artists in these states as well as in Kyrgyzstan are building their work through protest to powerful frameworks and inequalities created by their respective states. Thus, when I asked members of the Group 705 what their main goals were when they were drawn to the December 2019 Bishkek anti-corruption rallies, the answer was to express their civic duty as citizens but also as artists. Art should be reflective of society's problems, they kept on repeating throughout the group interview.

It was true—societal problems were expressed quite clearly in Bishkek during my fieldwork but these problems required more activists and more awareness. As we were leaving the ArtEast studio with Gulnara Kasmalieva and Muratbek Djumaliev, he took out his 'anti-smog' mask. We were standing in an average urban courtyard transformed into another public space with the help of ArtEast's graduates. Djumaliev's black breathing mask looked futuristic and scary and contrasted with the brightly coloured murals behind him. 'Nowadays in Bishkek this [mask] is a necessity,' he uttered; but I felt like the necessity is not only the mask and anti-corruption or ecological rallies where contemporary artists were actively engaged in—it is the whole concept of public art and free art in the region that is simply a necessity. To my respondents, this idea is common sense, as something hidden in every action and in every word they share: exhibits are always free to all and public projects are organized in communal engagement and for the public good. Examples are the reconstruction of the Botanic Garden in Bishkek in 2017 organized by ArtEast or the 'ArtBatFest' public art festival organized in a botanic garden in Almaty in 2016. Both events shared an idea: artists need space for public engagement and art activism. Communities equally need spaces for socialization, engagement, and dialogue. And paradoxically, both of these needs are only satisfied so far by the remnants of the Soviet infrastructure—the surviving parks and botanical gardens as well as rebuilt, restructured yet still Sovietized central squares that active citizens choose for protests and rallies.

## CONCLUSION

This chapter has focused on the artistic initiatives that some authors term as independent—autonomous from the state or not state-sponsored artists.[29] This shift to autonomous and non-state-sponsored art was only possible in the wake of the collapse of the Soviet Union when previous institutions of state support and state censorship over art production diminished in their overarching institutionalization of the artistic field of production. Contemporary art is a very new form and field of cultural production in post-Soviet Eurasia. These are the 'artists who manage to critically and dynamically engage with their national-ethnic elements, with Western and Russian canons, as well as with different subversive traditions within them.'[30]

With every new generational wave of contemporary art producers or even with every new group or community they form, there is an evolution in their thinking, in the ways they problematize the current context of their existence. Inevitably, there is a difference in generational perceptions and actions towards their own representations, autonomies, and positions within the larger field of power relations that many of them term as 'space' within society and state.

In this chapter, I explore how through the post-socialist transformation of societies and with external funding, new forms of communal engagement and self-institutionalization emerge. These processes are not homogeneous or straightforward; most of them are far more complex and often paradoxical. For the first generation of the artistic community, the main goal is to self-organize into a form of a stable institution represented through regular exhibitions, educational programmes and thus a stable, physical space for gatherings and dialogues. In their own discussions and visions of why this is important, they go back to the model of state sponsorship, both Soviet and more contemporary, taken from the Western cases (examples often cited include Sweden and Germany). For this first-generation, the institutionalization of the art field is crucial for its further survival. In contrast, for their followers and successors (like members of Group 705), space is represented more from the point of view of the artist's own position in the field of power relations. For them, having a tangible space is important but not crucial—what is more valuable to them and for their development are the ideas and the engagement with what their art brings to society. They envision a 'space' that can exist within a form of a performance, communication, or a collaborative transnational

29................Nauruzbayeva, 'Refurbishing Soviet Status'; Nauruzbayeva, 'Portraiture and Proximity'; Ibrayeva, *Iskusstvo Kazakhstana;* Tlostanova, *What Does it Mean to be Post-Soviet?*

30................Tlostanova, *What Does it Mean to be Post-Soviet?*, p. 14.

research project. In this way, they believe art becomes more autonomous from state power and censorship and is thus able to deliver more alternatives to society.

Both of these views co-exist in the artistic field and are not in conflict with each other as long as both groups are in agreement about what art development should contribute to society. In the conditions in which contemporary artists have to seek autonomy within the state's institutionalization of the social and political order and within the neoliberal global order, the 'space' of art contributes in its value to generate new ideas, alternative views, protests, and criticisms that are not possible in other forms of social or cultural expressions in their societies.

ACKNOWLEDGEMENTS

This research was facilitated through the NGR.2018.07078 Grant for the research titled 'Contemporary Art in Eurasia: Civil Society, Art Activism and State in a Contemporary Perspective' through the framework of the initiative 'The Force of Art—Research from a Global Perspective' (2018–2020), Prince Claus Fund, Hivos and the European Cultural Foundation that enabled fieldwork and further research in this direction. I also want to thank the art communities and artists I interviewed for this research and the upcoming book manuscript on contemporary art development and civil initiatives in Eurasia. This work was also done under the auspices of the RCUK GCRF COMPASS grant.

## ← REFERENCES


Anderson, John. *Kyrgyzstan: Central Asia's Island of Democracy?* Abingdon: Taylor & Francis, 1999.

Bourdieu, Pierre. 'The Social Space and the Genesis of Groups.' *Information (International Social Science Council)* 24, no. 2 (1985), pp. 195–220.

Buchli, Victor. 'Astana: Materiality and the City.' In *Urban Life in Post-Soviet Asia*, ed. Catherine Alexander, Victor Buchli, and Caroline Humphrey, pp. 52–81. London: UCL Press, 2007.

Cummings, Sally N. 'Leaving Lenin: Elites, Official Ideology and Monuments in the Kyrgyz Republic.' *Nationalities Papers* 41, no. 4 (2013), pp. 606–21.
—, and Maxim Ryabkov. 'Situating the "Tulip Revolution".' *Central Asian Survey* 27, no. 3–4 (2008), pp. 241–52.

Grant, Bruce. 'The Edifice Complex: Architecture and the Political Life of Surplus in the New Baku.' *Public Culture* 26, no. 3 (74) (2014), pp. 501–28.

Heathershaw, John, and Nick Megoran. 'Contesting Danger: A New Agenda for Policy and Scholarship on Central Asia.' *International Affairs* 87, no. 3 (2011), pp. 589–612.

Hinderliter, Beth. 'The ArtEast School for Contemporary Art: Interview with Gulnara Kasmalieva and Muratbek Djumaliev.' *Journal of Inquiry and Action in Education* 6, no. 1 (2014), pp. 103–9.

Ibrayeva, Valeria. *Iskusstvo Kazakhstana: Post-Sovetskii period* [The art of Kazakhstan: Post-Soviet period]. Almaty: Tonkaya gran, 2014.

Isaacs, Rico. *Party System Formation in Kazakhstan: Between Formal and Informal Politics*. Vol. 26. New York: Routledge, 2011.

Juraev, Shairbek. 'Kyrgyz Democracy? The Tulip Revolution and Beyond.' *Central Asian Survey* 27, no. 3–4 (2008), pp. 253–64.

Kudaibergenova, Diana T. 'Contemporary Public Art and Nation: Contesting "Tradition" in Post-Socialist Cultures and Societies.' *Central Asian Affairs* 4, no. 4 (2017), pp. 305–30.
—. 'Punk Shamanism, Revolt and Break-up of Traditional Linkage: The Waves of Cultural Production in Post-Soviet Kazakhstan.' *European Journal of Cultural Studies* 21, no. 4 (2018), pp. 435–51.
—. 'Religion, Power, and Contemporary Art in Central Asia: Visualizing and Performing Islam.' *Central Asian Affairs* 6, no. 2–3 (2019), p. 224–52.
—. 'The Ideology of Development and Legitimation: Beyond "Kazakhstan 2030".' *Central Asian Survey* 34, no. 4 (2015), pp. 440–55.

Laszczkowski, Mateusz. 'Building the Future: Construction, Temporality, and Politics in Astana.' *Focaal* 2011, no. 60 (2011), pp. 77–92.

Lewis, David. 'Blogging Zhanaozen: Hegemonic Discourse and Authoritarian Resilience in Kazakhstan.' *Central Asian Survey* 35, no. 3 (2016), pp. 421–38.

Mamedov, Georgy. 'Sites of Construction: Exhibitions and the Making of Recent Art History in Asia,' 2015, www.aaa.org.hk/en/ideas/ideas/sites-of-construction-and-political-dissent-central-asia-pavilions-in-venice-20052013 (accessed 10 October 2017).

March, Andrew F. 'From Leninism to Karimovism: Hegemony, Ideology, and Authoritarian Legitimation.' *Post-Soviet Affairs* 19, no. 4 (2003), pp. 307–36.

McGlinchey, Eric. *Chaos, Violence, Dynasty: Politics and Islam in Central Asia*. Pittsburgh: University of Pittsburgh Press, 2011.

Nauruzbayeva, Zhanara. 'Portraiture and Proximity: "Official" Artists and the State-ization of the Market in Post-Soviet Kazakhstan.' *Ethnos* 76, no. 3 (2011), pp. 375–97.
—. 'Refurbishing Soviet Status: Visual Artists and Marketization in Kazakhstan,' PhD dissertation, Stanford, CA: Stanford University, 2011.

Sorokina, Yuliya. 'From Evolution to Growth: Central Asian Video Art, 1995–2015.' *Studies in Russian and Soviet Cinema* 10, no. 3 (2016), pp. 238–60.

Tlostanova, Madina. *What Does it Mean to be Post-Soviet? Decolonial Art from the Ruins of the Soviet Empire*. Durham: Duke University Press, 2018.


## ← INTERVIEWS

Gulnara Kasmalieva and Muratbek Djumaliev, series of interviews by author, Bishkek, 2017 and 2019.

Gulnara Kasmalieva, interview by author, Bishkek, December 2019.

Group 705 collective interview by author, Bishkek, December 2019.

# DISSONANT ENTANGLEMENTS AND CREATIVE REDISTRIBUTIONS

Judith Naeff, Arnout van Ree, Lenneke Sipkes, Cristiana Strava, Kasper Tromp, Mark R. Westmoreland

This chapter aims to better understand how international cultural funding shapes opportunities for organizations to grow as generators of creativity able to provide transformative experiences for local audiences. It analyzes the experiences of four cases located in the Middle East and North Africa region, namely L'Atelier de l'Observatoire (Morocco), Clown Me In (Lebanon), Bantmag (Turkey), and Volunteer Palestine (West Bank). Although the Prince Claus Fund, Hivos, and European Cultural Foundation (ECF) have sought alternatives to the neoliberal instrumentalization of their funding measured according to the rubrics of impact, our research shows that organizations still struggle with the need to appeal to international funding bodies while also focusing on their work as embedded in local conditions. To understand these struggles, we draw on the idea that organizations are entangled in a web of relationships and expectations that can undermine the ethical commitment and affective practices of these cultural actors. Furthermore, they are burdened by the way calls for funding are often addressed around frameworks of global concerns that do not always align with the pressing local issues that organizations want to address. Despite these limitations and the need for them to be addressed, these organizations acknowledge that funding offers crucial opportunities to enrich communities marked by a scarcity of creative and communal activities. We propose that the force of art lies in the potentialities activated by these affective encounters, even if they do not always materialize in measurable change.

Keywords
→ Impact
→ Instrumentalization
→ Entanglement
→ Affect
→ Cosmopolitanism

## INTRODUCTION

Research for this chapter has been conducted by a team of diversely trained researchers who share a common concern about the culturally rich and politically complex crossroads that historically define the Middle East and North Africa region—a key site where cultural repertoires of modernity have played out. We collectively aspire to better understand how new aesthetic formations unfold in response to the various forces that constitute a web of affordances and entanglements. The *Force of Art* initiative provided us with an opportunity to bring together concrete case studies to collectively rework our understanding of the way international cultural funding shapes opportunities for these organizations to cultivate affective relationships and grow as generators of creativity able to provide transformative experiences for local audiences in spite of the draining struggles the organizations routinely navigate.

Recognizing the agency of artwork has led many funding agencies to instrumentalize creative practices and expect organizations to demonstrably effect particular ideological and economic pursuits. While the Prince Claus Fund, Hivos, and European Cultural Foundation (ECF) are notable for their efforts to resist employing 'impact' models designed to measure the effectiveness of creative intervention, these neoliberal agendas still dominate the general discussion among organizations in situ. We have learned from our case studies that these organizations struggle with the sometimes-tricky balance between the need to appeal to international funding bodies and the realities on the ground. Common concerns for timely global issues do not always align with local, more urgent challenges. We have found that the way these global logics get reproduced in funding schemes imposes certain conditions onto local applications of this funding: from the writing of applications for funding with exclusionary vernaculars, to their binding agreements, to the practical implementation of the projects linked to the awarded funds.

We have elaborated each case study in its own breakout section where the respective field researcher qualitatively assesses the organization's effort to inspire critical thinking, develop alternative narratives, and create meaningful connections. These cases help us retheorize the dissonant entanglements of the contemporary field of cultural production and the creative redistributions of affective encounters in particular contexts to offer a model based on how cultural organizations themselves imagine successfully cultivating their transformative 'force of art.' But what exactly is the transformative power of art? Noting the object agency of artwork, anthropologist Alfred Gell argues, 'I view art as a system of action, intended to change the world rather than encode symbolic propositions about it.'[1] Rather than viewing art as a universal concept with a common value, we recognize 'the many different factors that influence the ways in which people experience and understand [art].'[2] In addition to the aestheticization of sensorial experiences, Maruška Svašek's anthropological perspective on art emphasizes the transformative processes of transit (situation) and transition (meaning), whereas Patricia Spyer and Mary Steedly follow 'images that move' through both complex processes of 'circulation, imagination, and reception' and their ability to move people to feel and act in significant ways.[3] These affective movements operate within diverse assemblages—networks of multiple actors, organizations, ideas, and ambitions that dynamically interact—in which NGOs and

1............Alfred Gell, *Art and Agency: An Anthropological Theory* (Oxford: Oxford University Press, 1998), p. 6.
2............Alfred Gell, *Art and Agency*, p. 4.
3............Maruška Svašek, *The Anthropology Art and Cultural Production: Histories, Themes, Perspectives* (London: Pluto Press, 2007); Patricia Spyer and Mary Margaret Steedly, *Images that Move* (Santa Fe: SAR Press, 2013), p. 6.

grassroots organizations have become increasingly entangled. Whereas these assemblages may present bottlenecks, delays, and restrictions for organizations, they may also create nodes of possibility for generative initiatives distributed through a complex web of significance. This chapter focuses on how funding agencies can facilitate these possibilities.

In the sections that follow, we argue that several levels of entanglement between funders and recipients, among other actors, produce pressures of professionalization on community initiatives as well as an instrumentalization of culture in the service of so-called universal notions about the developmental power of art. We then advance a theorization of the affective power of aesthetic and performative creations to shift the expectations of art from a tangible impact toward the potential opportunities to redistribute social dispositions and political inter-dependencies. Finally, we adopt the notion of subaltern cosmopolitanism as a way to articulate local strategies for navigating these entanglements. As such, we argue that the transformative power of the cultural initiatives and community practices reside in the affective encounters they enable within marginalized communities and with outsiders.

## DISSONANT ENTANGLEMENTS

The cultural initiatives and grassroots community organizations that form our objects of study have become part of global assemblages as they participate in public-private partnerships or pursue social entrepreneurship. This has been described as NGO-ization, where community organizations are incorporated into neoliberal global assemblages. The initiatives under study are moral actors as they are engaged with 'doing good.' This characteristic defined by a system of morals is visible in their projects, the forms of assistance they provide within their communities, and the causes that they advocate. However, this also leads to a point of friction where these initiatives and organizations must be 'good at doing good.'[4] Community organizations must not only be seen as moral actors but also as skilful and professional actors. In their interactions with donors, navigating bureaucratic language of accountability, and adhering to complicated tax laws, a viable organization needs to appear professionally competent. This professionalism consists of 'holding the requisite trainings, attending the seminars, writing the reports, composing the budget, and tabulating the success statistics.'[5] They must demonstrate a certain 'rationality'—characterized by having a hierarchy, budget, meetings, documentation, offices, and everyday routines—in order to be seen as a legitimate partner able to present policy options and conduct effective policy advocacy.

In this context, organizations operate in several levels of entanglement that profoundly impact them.[6] These entanglements can facilitate,

4.............Steven Sampson, 'Introduction: Engagements and Entanglements in the Anthropology of NGOs,' *in Cultures of Doing Good: Anthropologists and NGOs*, eds. Amanda Lashaw, Christian Vannier, and Steven Sampson (Tuscaloosa: University of Alabama Press, 2017), p. 12.

5.............Sampson, 'Engagements and Entanglements,' p. 13.

6.............Ibid.

alter, or undermine the projects on many different levels. A cultural organization, even if it has global connections, has to operate within state boundaries and limitations. A state may be unwilling or unable to provide certain basic provisions, or may be decidedly antagonistic towards possible foreign influence potentially channelled through these organizations. Larger organizations may also become entangled in neoliberal processes, as they become semi-state actors or even de-facto governments in the local and global realm.[7] The unequal relationship between a recipient and its donors produces another level of entanglement. The donors can offer an organization resources such as funding, expertise, and a local or international network. Despite the best of intentions from donors who use a language of partnership, an organization remains dependent upon the donors for funding,[8] and cultural initiatives must convince their donors of the importance, meaningfulness, and impact of their work.[9] These entanglements further require organizations to adapt new languages, rituals, and practices when communicating with different partners, donors, and target communities. This also means that organizations and activists constantly need to navigate between different identities and language registers, but the level of flexibility to switch between dissonant registers determines which organizations survive and those that disappear in a competitive market.

7.............Chiara De Cesari, *Heritage and the Cultural Struggle for Palestine* (Stanford: Stanford University Press, 2019), p. 117.

8.............Sampson, 'Engagements and Entanglements,' pp. 10–13.

9.............Anika Marschall, 'What Can Theatre Do about the Refugee Crisis? Enacting Commitment and Navigating Complicity in Performative Interventions,' *Research in Drama Education: The Journal of Applied Theatre and Performance* 23, no. 2 (2018), pp. 158–59.

## (1) VOLUNTEER PALESTINE
Lenneke Sipkes

Volunteer Palestine (VP) is a grassroots volunteer organization that strives to assist a local community with limited resources. The organization is situated in the Aida refugee camp in the Palestinian West Bank, home to 5,500 refugees who fled their villages in the Jerusalem area during the Nakba in 1948. VP was founded by a group of camp youth who felt that Aida was lacking many facilities and services for its inhabitants. The programme focuses on engaging the international community with Palestinian culture, while at the same time providing resources to local organizations and families. International volunteers share knowledge and skills in VP projects, and stay with local families. VP's mission is to 'Support socially and economically viable alternative tourism initiatives that positively educate, inspire and create more active global citizens.'[10] This cultural exchange is combined with the development of political consciousness. △Fig. 1

△ 1
VP staff and volunteers sharing home-made knafeh together, photo: Lenneke Sipkes, 2019

△ 2
An international volunteer teaching children of the camp, photo: Lenneke Sipkes, 2019

Volunteer Palestine is a small player in the dense field of the West Bank aid sector, which has mainly been shaped in response to the Oslo Accords in 1993. Political scientist Linda Tabar argues that before Oslo, support for Palestine mainly existed in the shape of solidarity. Solidarity is a practice from below, created in a context of uneven power relationships, which crosses the boundaries of the nation-state and tries to challenge forms of oppression.[11] Tabar states that the dominant meaning shifted to advancing human rights in the last two decades of the twentieth century.[12] Especially in the West Bank, where an 'NGO-ization of the society' took place as part of the Oslo peace process.[13] Many NGOs settled in the West Bank and shaped an aid sector with individual action as its underlying principle instead of collective action.[14] Solidarity with Palestine became largely conditional, based on financial support that can only be given when the donor's demands are being met. △Fig. 2

Nowadays Palestine is home to many big NGOs such as The Red Cross and Doctors Without Borders, which have large professional teams of employees and work internationally. There are, however, many smaller initiatives as well, like VP, often created by locals, to address the specific needs of their own community. Not having access to the same financial resources as the giants of the aid sector, VP has to turn to foundations that support cultural and community building projects to apply for funds. When VP was just founded, they received a start up fund from the European Cultural Foundation, which enabled them to roll out their project. △Fig. 3

△ 3
VP staff telling the story of Aida camp to international volunteers, photo: Lenneke Sipkes, 2019

The following reflections are based on ethnographic material I collected during two visits to the Aida refugee camp in 2019, while doing research in the West Bank for my Master's thesis in Anthropology. During my visits I lived with a host family in the camp, participated in the VP programme, and conducted interviews with both international participants and local members of staff. It became clear that VP has to keep many different actors satisfied: first and foremost, the inhabitants of Aida refugee camp, who they provide services to through educational, creative, and medical programmes. Many inhabitants want their refugee story to be heard, and hope to get more international support for their cause. Secondly, there are the international volunteers who largely carry out VP's programmes and provide a source of income for host families in the camp; these volunteers have their own—often political—motivations for spending time in the West Bank.[15] VP would like to create meaningful, affective encounters between the international volunteers and the camp citizens, facilitating bonds of solidarity. At the same time, cultural foundations often demand a careful, preferably apolitical wording of funding requests, considering the political sensitivity that the Palestinian cause is surrounded with. These international foundations decide whether VP is awarded with funding. Another actor is the State of Israel, which is in control of all West Bank borders. If Israel views VP as a political project, this might have consequences for international volunteers being allowed into the West Bank. Therefore, VP has to continuously balance their narrative.[16]

The volunteers who are able to make it into the West Bank are offered a rich programme in the Aida refugee camp; during the day, they carry out community-building activities, ranging from teaching children or women of the camp to assisting in the local medical clinic. In the evenings and weekends, volunteers are given political tours, Arabic classes, traditional dancing and cooking workshops, and group outings. Free time is often spent with local host families, giving space to in-depth immersion into local Palestinian life and often creating affective bonds.[17]

Just as describing the plans and intended goals of the project asks for a carefully balanced narrative, describing the outcome demands political sensitivity as well. On the one hand, VP presents an effective community-building project, in which international exchange can flourish through international volunteers who offer skills and services to an impoverished community. But if the apolitical aid sector lingo is stripped, another picture can be painted that matches the objectives of camp citizens and international volunteers. International exchange transforms a focus on 'effects' to one valuing the link to 'affect'—from aid to solidarity; the practice from below crosses the boundaries of the nation-state and is created in a context of uneven power relationships, just as Featherstone described it.[18] A stay in Aida refugee camp often teaches volunteers about the political struggle of Palestine, and many residents hope that internationals will leave in solidarity, spreading support for their cause back in their home countries. Ideally, VP can fully combine its two goals of aid and solidarity. Until then, the careful balance continues.

10...........*Volunteer Palestine*, accessed November 2018, http://volunteerpalestine.com.
11...........David Featherstone, *Solidarity: Hidden Histories and Geographies of Internationalism* (London: Zed books, 2012), pp. 5–6.
12...........Linda Tabar, 'From Third World Internationalism to "The Internationals": The Transformation of Solidarity with Palestine,' *Third World Quarterly* 38, no. 2 (2016), pp. 414–35.
13...........Ibid., p. 422.
14...........Ibid., p. 422; Jennifer Kelly, 'Asymmetrical Itineraries: Militarism, Tourism, and Solidarity in Occupied Palestine,' *American Quarterly* 68, no. 3 (2016), pp. 723–45.
15...........Lenneke Sipkes, fieldwork, 2019.
16...........Ibid.
17...........Ibid.
18...........Featherstone, *Solidarity*, pp. 5–6.

In recent decades, funding bodies have increasingly subsumed funding for arts and culture under their developmental goals.[19] This has led to the instrumentalization of arts and culture to address single issue social change, such as creating awareness of social issues or rights, and building socio-political empowerment.[20] This approach has been criticized for ignoring the particular nuances and demands of local contexts,[21] for the false suggestion that quantifiable impact measurement is possible, and for limiting creativity and imagination.[22] In the call for proposals, the *Force of Art* initiative expresses the belief that 'there is a need to critically examine these trends.' With this critical awareness, the donors have been lauded as rare positive exceptions in the field.[23] Polly Stupples' otherwise critical article on the instrumentalization of arts in the development sector for example argues that Hivos and the Prince Claus Fund demonstrate 'a quite distinct conception of the agency of the arts,' valuing 'pleasure, experimentation, curiosity, audacity and intellectual debate' because a thriving cultural sector is seen in and of itself as contributing to peaceful and democratic societies.[24] While aiming to create opportunities for the 'redistribution of the sensible'—a concept developed by Jacques Rancière to theorize the way in which art can put the seemingly self-evident into new light—neither donors nor the recipients can fully escape today's global neoliberal logic. Indeed, the call to conceptualize the force of art demonstrates a desire to capture the elusive contribution of the arts to society in terms of 'transformative power,' itself a form of impact, even if not in conventional developmentalist terms. The aim to stimulate diversity, democracy, and peace in the Middle East is not a neutral universality, but part of a particular paradigm that encourages 'post-nationalist, post-socialist, and anti-Islamist ideals.'[25] Most of the cultural actors in the region have moved away from the traditional left and embraced progressive ideals of emancipation. It is not always easy to disentangle these from the entrepreneurial values of global capitalism. They therefore regularly raise moral suspicion among both conservative and more radically progressive actors in the region. Moreover, our research shows that because funding recipients are entangled in multiple fields, dealing with multiple actors, including other donors, the non-instrumentalist approach of one donor has a limited effect. Given the temporary, project-based nature of the funds we researched, we found that this exceptionalism is on the ground at times perceived as little more than yet another format to adhere to in an endless line of funding applications and reports.

Entanglements also exist between competing cultural organizations, community initiatives, and other activist movements. Community organizations are embedded in networks that influence and facilitate social work, while at the same time these organizations are in competition with each other due to the scarcity of funding and/or resources. The competition for funding leads to an almost Darwinian situation of 'winners' and 'losers' where the inability to effect change, or show relevance, leads to failure to receive funding. This was also confirmed by our interlocutors, who felt that they did not receive funding for certain projects because of their inability to show impact or that funding was not renewed because of a 'perceived' failure. While such conditions can lead to inventive solutions to address the (structural) issues that led to failure as 'a 'launching pad for alternatives' and prompt the questioning of established models,'[26] failure is often seen as an endpoint and not a productive condition. Most artistic interventions will not directly have an impact on the social and political environments in which they are located. However, like 'failure,' art does have the ability to affect the audience, creating productive conditions to imagine and act in new ways. Approaching these artistic interventions as part of such a process would also allow the inclusion of the preparatory phase before the artistic work is produced as relevant and productive in models of change.

Arguably, the most important entanglement is that between an organization and its target community, which provides the reason and rationale for the organization's work, and ultimately its legitimacy. The target communities of our case studies vary greatly but all include subjects that could be considered subaltern, in the sense that they lack access to material resources, cultural capital and/or societal infrastructure and are therefore excluded from political deliberation. The organizational goals of being agents of change overlap with personal motivations for an activist who also has a history of involvement in these community issues. This affective dimension also requires certain practices to be adopted by organizations and activists. Although this emotional component is part of their engagement and possible success, this affective dimension has been overlooked in earlier studies of NGOs.[27] We respond to this oversight by making the affective encounter enabled by cultural community practices central to our conceptualization of the force of art.

19 ........... e.g., Polly Stupples, 'Creative Contributions: The Role of the Arts and the Cultural Sector in Development,' *Progress in Development Studies* 14, no. 2 (2014).

20 ........... João Biehl and Peter Locke, 'Deleuze and the Anthropology of Becoming,' *Current Anthropology* 51, no. 3 (2010), pp. 327–35.

21 ........... Matthew Yoxall, 'At the "Frontiers" of Humanitarian Performance: Refugee Resettlement, Theatre-making and the Geo-politics of Service,' *Research in Drama Education: The Journal of Applied Theatre and Performance* 23, no. 2 (2018), pp. 222–23.

22 ........... Jen Harvie, *Fair Play: Art, Performance and Neoliberalism* (London: Palgrave Macmillan, 2013).

23 ........... e.g. Achille Mbembe, 'African Contemporary Art: Negotiating the Terms of Recognition,' interview by Vivian Paulissen, *Johannesburg Workshop in Theory and Criticism (JWTC)*, 8 September 2009, https://jhbwtc.blogspot.com/2009/09/african-contemporary-art-negotiating.html.

24 ........... Stupples, 'Creative Contributions,' p. 126.

25 ........... Hanan Toukan, 'On Being the Other in Post-Civil War Lebanon: Aid and the Politics of Art in Processes of Contemporary Cultural Production,' *Arab Studies Journal* 18, no. 1 (Spring 2010), p. 142.

26 ........... De Cesari, *Heritage*, p. 158.

27 ........... Sampson, 'Engagements and Entanglements,' p. 16.

## (2) L'ATELIER DE L'OBSERVATOIRE

Cristiana Strava

L'Atelier de l'Observatoire (hereafter Atelier) was established in 2010 by artist Mohamed Fariji and curator and independent researcher Léa Morin. Based in Casablanca, Morocco, it is a unique organization structured and run as an artist collective. Originally located on the semi-rural belt of Casablanca, Atelier focuses on different forms of margins and marginality: be they geographical (urban peripheries, rural areas, neglected territories), historical (occluded or repressed accounts), or social (maligned or criminalized communities). Atelier's approaches are intensely participatory and inclusive, striving to bring together groups and actors that owing to local historical and socio-economic fragmentations are unlikely to meet, interact, or co-create. Their methods include archival and ethnographic research, collaboratively run community workshops, artist-curated pedagogical programmes, and restoration work (of films or citizen archives).

△ 4
The first iteration of La Serre, photo: Atelier, 2014

The production and contestation of discourses on socio-spatial marginality and actual peripheral neighbourhoods are synonymous in Morocco with colonial experimentation with worker housing,[28] post-colonial repression of political and social dissent,[29] and, in the contemporary era of neoliberalization, with anomie, decaying public infrastructures and growing socio-economic precarity.[30] This is the context wherein Atelier, with seed funding from the Heinrich Böll Stiftung (2014) and Prince Claus Fund (2015), began a sustained programme of activities under the umbrella of a project named *La Serre* [The Greenhouse]. △Fig. 4 Originally titled *Eco-Jardin*, the project materialized in response to the complete lack of artistic and ludic spaces for communities on the periphery of Casablanca, where Fariji and Morin owned a studio-space in 2014. What began as a bare-bones structure of metal ribs and green mesh quickly grew into a polysemic space: a platform for helping local youth develop skills alongside their ludic pursuits, an experimental space for 'impossible projects,'[31] a sculpture with [the] function 'of revitalizing public spaces,'[32] and a gesture towards imagining desirable futures from

RAW Material Company / Dakar, Senegal / 10:07am 14°41'54.0"N / 17°27'18.7"W l'atelier de l'observatoire / Casablanca, Morocco / 10:47am 33°34'59.1"N / 7°38'24.2"W

'wounded territories' on the expanding periphery of Casablanca.[33]

As a platform that has given birth to several related preoccupations and projects at the intersection of artistic practice and civic and environmental intervention,[34] La Serre offers a salient angle for reflecting on the role and affordances of art broadly defined. This brief reflection is based on ethnographic material gathered during three field visits to Casablanca carried out at different points during 2019. During these visits, I met with Atelier's core team and several artists whose projects they had supported. Mirroring Atelier's approach to their own work, my interactions with the core team unfolded as a series of open-ended and multivocal conversations held over several days: in their central Casablanca office atop a monumental high-rise from the nineteen-seventies, in *sha'abi* (working-class) lunch rooms,

△ 5
Youth workshop at Initiative Urbaine, photo: Cristiana Strava, 2019

and in the neighbourhood spaces where their activities usually unfold. These conversations were loosely structured by questions on how they envision and understand the consequences and the value of their work at the local and, possibly, national level in Morocco. With Atelier's agreement, I spoke to one of their main collaborators on the periphery of Casablanca, Initiative Urbaine, a neighbourhood association I was already acquainted with and where La Serre had been installed and staged activities twice in recent years. As an anthropologist with several years of fieldwork experience in Morocco, I am both fluent in the local language vernacular as well as familiar with the spaces and networks wherein Atelier moves. At Initiative Urbaine, I also participated in the meetings of a creative workshop on social history and heritage meant for local youth who then generously agreed to speak with me about their encounters with Atelier activities.[△Fig. 5]

Atelier's answer to my questions sketched a picture of thoughtful reflection and repeated self-evaluation undertaken at various stages. 'When setting out on a new project phase we first take stock of ourselves as a collective, of where we are as individuals with our own preconceived ideas, and we attempt to have participants from the local community in which we are entering do the same, through various activities,' explained Sabrina Kamili, Atelier's project manager. 'Then we keep doing that at various points. It's not that we doctor numbers [of beneficiaries] in the reports we submit to funders,' she jestingly went on, 'but we are more concerned with how we might arrive at moving (*toucher*, in French) even just one or two of the youths who participate in our activities.' Kamili pointed out that this was a laborious and often emotionally draining process for both artists and communities with which they work. However, she found that through such reflections and documentation of charged and affective encounters, it became possible to identify meaningful changes resulting from their work.

Several people I spoke with in the communities where *La Serre* had been staged, described their encounters with Atelier's programmeing as unlikely meetings, improbable activities, sometimes challenging in content and form, puzzling yet welcome surprises in a context where, as the youths in Hay Mohammadi put it, 'nothing ever happens' (*makayn walou*, Moroccan Arabic). Given this felt dramatic lack of stimulating cultural activities in impoverished, lower-class areas, inhabitants exposed to and co-opted by *La Serre*'s activities appeared to share an initial sense of scepticism ('what can such activities possibly be doing in their spaces?') that slowly gave way to wonder: amazement that such things could take place in their neighbourhood spaces, puzzled realization from acquiring fresh knowledge of the rich social histories marking these spaces, and as a consequence an altered outlook on their place in all of it (Bakkar).

Alongside such affective encounters, recurring frictions and challenges are also strongly present in the work of Atelier. The latter manifest themselves at various scales and emerge from the intersection of varying assemblages of actors, discourses, and institutions. 'We are not interested in being lumped together with some pan-Arab or Muslim world label,' declares Mohammed Fariji in a vehement tone during our first meeting as I tried to describe the details of the other *Force of Art* case studies my team was working on. Like many of their counterparts in Morocco and elsewhere, Atelier navigates a contemporary field of cultural production in which categories and labels can carry unstable and at times undesirable political valences. Therefore, while their work is informed by, and sometimes responds to, conditions and dynamics that can be found elsewhere, their stated primary concern is with the local in its many manifestations. In this context, several members of Atelier spoke about the delicate balancing act required, at times, vis-à-vis state institutions and their agents, as the limits of what is permissible may shift at any point. In concrete terms this entailed constantly navigating and negotiating across different forms of gatekeeping and censorship that run the gamut from local actors displeased with the 'overly secular' content of an artistic activity, to institutional structures potentially unsettled by the political undertones of a 'cultural' activity.[35] On a different level, the current orthodoxies around funding structures that support cultural actors like Atelier also present their challenges for the work these actors perform. To paraphrase Kamili, operating through project-based funding means 'constantly running on fumes' when it comes to structural costs beyond the lifetime of a single project.

In the context of recent intensified social protests in Morocco, and the repression of many outspoken (cultural) activists, the intensely collaborative and open-ended trajectory of Atelier's project illuminates how vital such critical artistic interventions are for local social and political dynamics. By engaging the imaginations and imaginaries of a broad spectrum of local actors while also interpellating state actors, platforms such as *La Serre* are actively participating in shaping and shifting the distribution of the 'sensible,'[36] from a citizen- and artist-led perspective. While Atelier's experience illustrates some key challenges that are shared transnationally by those engaged in cultural development work—as well as the particular and significant risks of doing this work in authoritarian contexts—it nevertheless testifies to the crucial transformative power of artistic practice and its potential to collectively and collaboratively affect and effect meaningful change.

28..........Paul Rabinow, *French Modern: Norms and Forms of the Social Environment* (Chicago: University of Chicago Press, 1995).

29..........Susan Slyomovics, *The Performance of Human Rights in Morocco* (Philadelphia: University of Pennsylvania Press, 2005).

30..........Koenraad Bogaert, 'The Problem of Slums: Shifting Methods of Neoliberal Urban Government in Morocco,' *Development and Change* 42, no. 3 (2011), pp. 709–31; Cristiana Strava, 'At Home on the Margins: Caregiving and the "Unhomely" among Casablanca's Working Poor,' *City & Society* 29, no. 2 (2017), pp. 329–48.

31..........Sabrina Kamili (project manager) in discussion with the author, Casablanca, April 2019

32..........Fariji, Mohamed. Artist and Founder of Atelier de l'Observatoire. Conversation with Cristiana Strava, Casablanca, April and November 2019.

33..........Cristiana Strava, 'A Tramway Called Atonement: Genealogies of Infrastructure and Emerging Political Imaginaries in Contemporary Casablanca,' *Middle East* 10, no. 8 (2018), pp. 22–29.

34..........The Collective Museum (*Le Musée Collectif* in the original), is the most prominent of these outgrowths in terms of scope, ambition, and resources needed for its realization. Imagined as a citizen-led and co-curated museum dedicated to the public memory of Casablanca, Le Musée (as Atelier members refer to it) is a living and growing archive of traces that the city and its inhabitants have left on each other until the present.

35..........During one visit with Atelier in April 2019 this emerged as a forceful possibility, as a prominent cultural organization had just been tried in court and sentenced to dissolution after being accused of mobilizing a political agenda under the banner of arts and culture. Mohamed Fariji (artist) and Sabrina Kamili (project manager) in discussion with the author, Casablanca, April 2019. See https://pen.org/press-release/dissolution-racines-unacceptable-violation-cultural-rights-morocco/.

36..........Jacques Rancière, *Dissensus: On Politics and Aesthetics*, trans. Steven Corcoran (London: Continuum, 2010).

## CREATIVE REDISTRIBUTIONS

Our approach aligns with James Thompson, a theorist of applied and social theatre, who argues that the ethical commitment and affective practices of cultural actors are not accidental but vital to their projects. Thompson proposes that 'The means and value of socially engaged arts are to be found in a narrative of affect rather than concrete effect ... [which] allows for less-defined, less-constricted encounters of publics with the performing arts.'[37] Philosopher Jacques Rancière, too, has argued 'that there is an assumption that art can change politics because it critiques or mocks unequal power relations, and that in its content it can urge viewers into action,'[38] but that the political potential of arts and culture rather lie in their affective qualities.

There is not a stable definition for the term 'affect' as it is embedded in the sensorium of a specific culture and history, but it is usually associated with words such as feeling, emotion, and direct experience.[39] However, it is useful to differentiate between emotion and affect. While the former refers to named and defined sensations of feeling, the latter suggests visceral intensities that are felt but not yet semiotically mediated.[40] In broad terms, affect refers to an emotive domain, but its scope goes beyond subjectivity or the self, as it does not solely refer to the inner domain of the mind but also to the exterior domain of the body. This exterior domain refers to the encounters with human subjects as well as non-human objects that inform behaviour in everyday life.[41] The nexus between interior and exterior is where Grossberg argues affect should be located as everyday practices are not only about material relationships but also about structures of feeling.[42] For example, hope is an affect as it is something that someone feels but also something that someone does, and something that binds subjects and objects in a collective structure of feeling.

37..........Marschall, 'What Can Theatre Do,' p. 150.
38..........Christine Smith, 'Art as a Diagnostic: Assessing Social and Political Transformation through Public Art in Cairo, Egypt,' *Social & Cultural Geography* 16, no. 1 (2015), p. 26.
39..........Nigel Thrift, 'Intensities of Feeling: Towards a Spatial Politics of Affect,' *Geografiska Annaler. Series B, Human Geography* 86, no. 1 (2004), pp. 58–59.
40..........Mateusz Laszczkowski, 'Rethinking Resistance through and as Affect,' *Anthropological Theory* 19, no. 4 (2019), p. 496.
41..........Yael Navaro-Yashin, 'Affective Spaces, Melancholic Objects: Ruination and the Production of Anthropological Knowledge,' *Journal of the Royal Anthropological Institute* 15 (2009), p. 12.
42..........Lawrence Grossberg, 'Affect's Future: Rediscovering the Virtual in the Actual,' in *The Affect Theory Reader*, ed. Melissa Gregg and Gregory J. Seigworth (Durham: Duke University Press, 2010), p. 313.

## (3)
## CLOWN ME IN
### Arnout van Ree

Clown Me In (CMI) is a Lebanese theatre group that aims 'To use clowning to spread laughter and provide relief to disadvantaged communities while exploring human vulnerabilities and helping individuals to accept them through interactive workshops and performances.'[43] CMI is convinced that issues such as the problems refugees confront in gaining access to healthcare, the rights of children, and the issue of pollution in Lebanon are best confronted through laughter.[44] While I have a background in Middle Eastern Studies with an interest in (online) activism and am familiar with the context of Lebanon, the topic of street theatre was new to me. △Fig. 6

△ 6
Young boy at the VAN12 performance in Tripoli, photo: Arnout van Ree, 2019

The VAN12 street theatre performance is part of CMI's larger Caravan series,

> A project that puts children's voices at the heart of a street theatre performance through the use of recorded storytelling audio. It revolves around a travelling troupe of fantastical persons who present stories that teach twelve of the most fundamental protections from the UN Convention on the Rights of the Child.[45]

Each scene is a comic juxtaposition of reality where the travelling troupe finds the Rights of the Child in the different scenes and shares these with the audience. How can the concept of affect provide insights into the possible impact of these projects? △Fig. 7

△ 7
The end scene of the VAN12 performance, left: Hasbaya; right: Saida, photos: Arnout van Ree, 2019

The performance creates possible affective intensities in several different ways. These affective intensities impact on and open the imaginaries, the perspectives, and subjectivities of audience members.[46] The first element involves the manner in which the stories are collected for the performance. Sabine Choucair, self-described as a humanitarian clown, storyteller, and performer, works with marginalized communities and organizes theatre, social therapy, and storytelling workshops. This creative intervention into marginalized communities allows her to gain the trust of these communities as well as see what issues affect them. She then asks participants if she can record their story. She selects stories based on whether how they may be indicative of issues or themes that the community in question confronts and their potential for breaking down barriers by creating understanding, allowing for a dramatic twist in the performance.[47]

The next element is the creation process of the performance. Sabine organizes the recorded stories in a certain order and approaches the clowns that will perform the show. The clowns, however, are not given the stories but exercises corresponding to feelings and emotions that are evoked by the stories. In this manner, the street performance is constructed through the affective imagination of the clowns. It is only after the performance has a basic structure that they listen to the recorded stories. However, the performance can be adjusted if the clowns feel that this would do more justice to these stories. The affective intensities, with which the recordings confront the audience, add to the performance on stage practices.[48] The décor is also key for creating a certain atmosphere for the audience and adding an artistic layer to the street performance; as shared by Sabine, this exposes (marginalized) communities to new artistic practices.[49]

The location of the performance represents yet another important element contributing to the affective intensity. Performances take place in the communities where the stories were collected, in spaces that are likely to be crowded (such as the corniche in Saida). This enables recognition through affective intensities as communities can recognize themselves, their community, or others in the performance. Furthermore, complex socioeconomic problems and political tensions are taken into consideration in the selection of the location, with an eye to ensuring that pertinent conversations may be opened up. Finally, priority is given to locations where creative initiatives are scarce like in Hasbaya.[50] Audience participation is actively encouraged through either initiating a debate regarding the stories or, in the case of VAN12, through introducing a game show scene on healthcare. In the latter, the audience becomes actively engaged as they shout the

△ 8
Left: the clowns performing the game show scene in the VAN12 performance; right: children laying roses on the 'road' after listening to the flower-selling scene, photos: Arnout van Ree, 2019

correct answers at the contestants and show their disappointment when, for humorous effect, the participants misunderstand them and give the 'wrong' answer. Another instance of audience interaction is when they are asked to put roses on a road on the stage. This scene is based on a boy telling his story of selling roses on Hamra Street.[51] The audience is thus not a passive recipient but an active participant in the performances.[52] △Fig. 8

Humour plays an important role in all the Caravan series. Each performance is a comic juxtaposition of lived realities seeking to make the audience aware of issues through laughter and to encourage them to reflect for themselves on relevant issues. As Marjolein 't Hart argues, humour weakens the defences of the audience and renders them more amenable to listening as well as to persuasion.[53] The humour as well as the drama in each scene makes sense of socio-political issues while entertaining the audience. The stories in VAN12 revolve around children being exposed to violence, abandonment, disease, and child labour. This juxtaposition also enables dialogue as affective bonds and a (temporary) community of feeling are created through mutual participation in the laughter as well as the drama of the street performance.[54] As shared by one interlocutor but echoed by others, 'clowning is about being vulnerable—accepting and laughing about it, a lot is about failures—okay, life is life, but anything gives hope.'[55] It is imagining through comic juxtaposition that another world is possible.

At the closing of the performances, the audience is encouraged to participate in an expression of this other 'possible' world: the end scene is an interactive one between the clowns and the audience whereby audience members, regardless of age, are asked to share their dreams.[56] The clowns write these dreams on red balloons and release them in the air, allowing the audience's dreams to literally fly—reflecting the idea in the show of allowing children to prosper and meet their dreams.[57] The end of the performance creates a space for promises of change to 'blossom.' Though the performance in and of itself does not impact current circumstances, it affects the social imagination and thereby creates the potential for real change.[58] △Figs. 9-11

△ 9
Children sharing their dreams with the clowns at the end of the performance, photos: Arnout van Ree, 2019

△ 10
The travelling troupe watching red balloons with the dreams fly away in the sky, photo: Arnout van Ree, 2019

△ 11
Participating artists Hare Sürel and Imad Habbab, photo: Bantmag, 2016

9

10

11

43..........Clown Me In, 'The Caravan Series,' https://clownmein.com/performances/the-caravan/ (accessed 13 January 2020).
44..........Arnout van Ree, fieldwork, 2019.
45..........Clown Me In, 'The Caravan Series,' https://clownmein.com/performances/the-caravan/ (accessed 13 January 2020)
46..........Mateusz Laszczkowski, 'Rethinking Resistance,' pp. 491–96; Ernst van Alphen and Tomáš Jirsa, 'Introduction: Mapping Affective Operations,' in *How to Do Things with Affects Affective Triggers in Aesthetic Forms*, ed. Ernst van Alphen and Tomáš Jirsa (Leiden: Brill, 2019), pp. 1–4.
47..........Sabine Choucair (co-founder Clown Me In), interview by author, Beirut, June 2019.
48..........Ibid.
49..........Ibid.
50..........Ibid.
51..........Ibid.
52..........James Thompson, *Performance Affects: Applied Theatre and the End of Effect* (Basingstoke: Palgrave Macmillan, 2009), p. 169.
53..........Marjolein 't Hart, 'Humour and Social Protest: An Introduction,' in *Humour and Social Protest*, eds. Marjolein 't Hart and Dennis Bos (Cambridge, MA: Cambridge University Press, 2008), pp. 1–20.
54..........Majken J. Sorensen, 'Radical Clowning: Challenging Militarism through Play and Otherness,' *Humor: International Journal of Humor Research* 28, no. 1 (2015), pp. 25–47.
55..........Van Ree, fieldwork, 2019.
56..........Sabine Choucair (co-founder Clown Me In), interview by author, Anfeh, June 2019.
57..........Van Ree, fieldwork, 2019.
58..........Kathleen Stewart, 'Afterword: Worlding Refrains,' in *The Affect Theory Reader*, ed. Melissa Gregg and Gregory J. Seigworth (Durham: Duke University Press, 2010), pp. 339–54.

Rancière posits that art's affective qualities may result in the (re)formation of political subjectivities. His starting point is art's affective (sensory) quality, in which new perceptions of the world convey a sense of wonder at something strange. Mobilization results from an awareness of the source of this strangeness.[59] James Thompson describes how affective encounters with the 'faces' of performance artists 'binds us to them,' making us 'aware of the limitations of our sovereignty,' which inspires a responsibility for the other and draws us to modes of ethical engagement with each other, and the wider world.[60] According to Rancière, dissensus involves the use of speech by those marginalized from a community in order to emerge as (sensible) subjects recognized as part of a community. Rancière helps conceptualize our interlocutors' creative agency to engage a local community through a redistribution of the sensible. The sensible refers to a shared ethos, or worldview, which is taken for granted as real and self-evident by a community. Dissensus is therefore the 'dispute over the distribution of the sensible' (or a partition of the sensible). As such, dissensus, by colliding two formations of the sensible, 'frames a new fabric of common experience' within a community, placing 'one world in another.'[61]

An affect-oriented, rather than an impact-oriented, perspective would allow more time and room for collaboration and reflection instead of pressuring organizations for a one-sided exchange of finished products. This perspective would provide insights into how affects and emotions are crucial in structuring political fields and how art contributes to inter-dependent social imaginaries. Approaching artistic interventions through the lens of affect highlights the modifications of the mind and the body that can occur during encounters with performative and aesthetic intensities. Such modifications and the concomitant redistribution of the sensible open up the potential to act and to be acted upon.[62] This should be theorized as an open-ended process of potential becoming, given structure through narrativization, culture, and personal and collective memories. Theorizing creative interventions as an open-ended process also acknowledges that outcomes do not necessarily lead to a better 'now' or better 'future.' We also question whether such an actualized political result is even desirable, given the highly politicized context of the MENA region, and its disastrous history of European interventions. Indeed, the call for struggle, rights, protection, or change through the artistic intervention may have a potentially paralyzing effect as these are monumental political challenges. In this case, the benefit of aesthetically beautiful art may simply be that it offers a moment of joy and pleasure.[63] In short, art's ability to affectively reorganize our perception of social reality has incredible political potential by opening up the possibility to act without specifically working towards any concrete political effect.

59 Jacques, Rancière, *Dissensus: On Politics and Aesthetics*, trans. Steven Corcoran (London: Continuum, 2010), p. 142.

60 Thompson, *Performance Affects*, pp. 156, 173.

61 Rancière, *Dissensus*, p. 141, pp. 37–38.

62 Melissa Gregg and Gregory J. Seigworth, 'An Inventory of Shimmers,' in *The Affect Theory Reader*, ed. Melissa Gregg and Gregory J. Seigworth (Durham: Duke University Press, 2010), pp. 1–2.

63 Thompson, *Performance Affects*, pp. 176–77.

## (4) BANTMAG Kasper Tromp

Bantmag (or 'Bant') is a Turkish alternative art magazine and online platform reporting on developments in contemporary art. It was founded in 2004 in the middle class neighbourhood of Kadıköy, Istanbul, where its core audience is based. Bant relies on advertisement for income and generally operates independently of government or private funding. The magazine reports on worldwide issues, interviewing creators behind artistic events, movie releases, and music shows who tend to shun the commercial mainstream and choose to remain independent. Additionally, Bant hosts small exhibitions, performances, and screenings in their gallery space in Kadıköy, and sometimes organizes larger events around the city. Their older readership buys the print version of the magazine and is mostly centred in Istanbul. Bant's younger audience consists of students from across Turkey who follow the magazine online for updates on contemporary art and culture.

In 2015 Bant responded to Prince Claus Fund's open call for organizing cultural projects with refugees, enlisting the help of more experienced acquaintances in writing applications since it was their first application for funding.[64] Using traditional development rhetoric, the resulting proposal pointed to the social marginalization of Syrian refugees among Turkish citizens and emphasized the need to bring the two communities together by creating 'cultural bridges.' With few connections in lower class neighbourhoods, Bant was not acquainted with Syrian artists in Istanbul whatsoever, which posed a major obstacle for realizing their project, proposing collaborative exhibitions between Syrian and Turkish artists, when their application was accepted later on.

Eventually Bant got in touch with Arthere Istanbul allowing them to meet Syrian artists and to share thoughts on how to attain their ambitious project goals. Arthere is a gallery in the Rasimpaşa neighbourhood that was initially founded as a workspace for Syrian artists but later developed into a gallery supporting any artistic expression 'away from war and political rivalries.'[65] Emphasizing artistic creativity over national identity, Arthere had become increasingly disturbed by the media constantly framing their gallery as a space for 'refugee art.' Thus, in order to prevent Bant's initiative from becoming 'a Syrian refugee thing,'[66] several meetings were planned in which Bant's staff and the Arthere gallery director reworked the project with a more manageable scope and in less culturally reductive terms. The two parties chose to utilize their respective social infrastructures, selecting Syrian artists and Turkish illustrators from within their artistic circles, to collaborate at Bant's gallery space in a series of four exhibitions titled 'Mevsimler' [Seasons]. In so doing, Syrian artists were given the chance to interact with experienced art audiences drawn to the exhibitions by the more established illustrators with whom they collaborated. Moreover, by departing from instrumental approaches, the artistic collaboration, exposure to new audiences, and exhibited artworks were now promoted as having value in themselves.[67] Understood within sociologist Pierre Bourdieu's framework of the field of cultural production, Bant and Arthere had organized the 'Mevsimler' exhibitions in such a way that they functioned as an (almost) autonomous artistic field, little burdened by the logic of power or class, and were thus capable of enacting their own logic to the fullest extent possible, having value conferred upon art by other actors operating in the artistic field.[68] △Fig. 12

△ 12
Visitors at the opening of the first edition of the 'Mevsimler' exhibitions, photo: Bantmag, 2016

The Syrian participants in the exhibitions had initially been trained at art academies in Damascus or Aleppo, where they were instructed in art theory and developed their own artistic practice. Some had recently graduated when the civil war broke out and thwarted their career opportunities as artists in their home country. The artist Ali Omar explains that since 2011 he had been doing artistic research in Syria on the intersections between body and soul in his portraits; having migrated to Istanbul did not greatly affect his artistry, but it did secure a safe and inspiring space to continue his work.[69] Indeed, the Syrian participants of the 'Mevsimler' exhibitions went through arduous journeys and lived precarious existences in order to be able to continue to put their artistic practice first.

Not surprisingly, the artists were extremely grateful for Bant's initiative to create an environment in which their artworks took centre stage and where they had the opportunity to interact with interested audiences who kept updated on developments in contemporary art. The artist Imad Habbab found it very meaningful that the audience included many collectors his age that took a genuine interest in his work.[70] Ali Omar, on the other hand, notes that many among the audience had no trained ability for art criticism, 'so they will just say: "it's good".'[71] These observations express appreciation of the opportunity to meet art professionals who respect the artists for their craft, as well as slight disappointment that not everybody was as 'initiated' into the contemporary art world.

The high standards to which the artists held the audience reflect the artists' commitment to performing their artistry on a professional level. Habbab shares his conviction that artists' intrinsic devotion to developing a personal artistic practice involves establishing a genuine connection with audiences—thereby also resisting potential reductive readings pertaining to victimhood, refugee identity, or nationality.[72] Exhibition participants were able to use the artistic habitus which they had long worked to develop (through education, participation in exhibitions, and continual artistic practice), to establish connections with other peers operating in the local field of cultural production through engaging in a common language, or 'horizon of affects,' as Rancière would have it. This interaction with audiences enables artists to challenge common perceptions by the dominant community that subaltern groups are incapable of sensible speech. By partaking in 'aisthesis,' a shared experience of aesthetic art, Rancière contends that subaltern artists become capable of creating alternative formations of the sensible (within this shared aesthetic experience), whereby they become accepted as part of the community.[73] The artworks Habbab exhibited facilitate such a process by depicting the artist's subjective experiences of the various intensities of Istanbul's neighbourhoods which, evoked by the presence of human faces within the intricately painted cityscapes, place alternative modes of 'being in the city' within a horizon of shared urban experiences. The artworks' potential to affect the audience through such common sensibilities, in turn, opened a space for the audience to engage with Habbab. This, he describes as the greatest takeaway from participating in the 'Mevsimler' project, stating that 'there is a warmth to it ... [that] even [in] a new place, human beings feel each other beyond words. These human to human encounters, that's leaving a beautiful trace on oneself.'[74]

63 .......... Thompson, *Performance Affects*, pp. 176–77.
64 .......... Ekin Sanaç (Bantmag art director), interview by author, Istanbul, August 2019.
65 .......... 'About,' Arthere Istanbul, www.arthereistanbul.com/about.html/ (accessed 14 January 2020).
66 .......... Anonymous informant (Arthere Istanbul), in conversation with the author, Istanbul, December 2018.
67 .......... Ironically, Bant's initial use of the ambitious development rhetoric in their proposal may not have been necessary to secure the funding, seeing as Prince Claus Fund has a track record of supporting cultural initiatives 'through clearly non-instrumentalized policies.' See Polly Stupples, 'Creative Contributions: The Role of the Arts and the Cultural Sector in Development,' *Progress in Development Studies* 14 (2014), p. 120.
68 .......... Pierre Bourdieu, '*The Field of Cultural Production* or the Economic World Reversed,' in *The Field of Cultural Production*, ed. Randal Johnson (New York NY: Columbia University Press, 1994), pp. 37–38.
69 .......... Ali Omar (local artist), interview by author, Istanbul, December 2018.
70 .......... Imad Habbab (local artist), interview by author, Istanbul, December 2018.
71 .......... Omar, interview.
72 .......... Habbab, interview.
73 .......... Rancière, *Dissensus*, pp. 38, 2.
74 .......... Habbab, interview.

Although the affective approach is radically open-ended, the four case studies in the inlays of this chapter show that the potentialities provided by the affective encounters and enabled by these cultural initiatives and community practices are all political in their local situatedness. While images and people are constantly on the move, geographer Doreen Massey argues that place becomes 'an ever-shifting constellation of trajectories.'[75] Literary scholar Minhao Zeng takes up Massey's notion of the historical contingency of such 'unexpected throwntogetherness' of people in particular 'material situations,' to argue that this condition underlies multi-cultural social constellations.[76] The local becomes a 'spatial node' tying together a 'multitude of relational networks of varying geographical reach,' despite the 'uneven resource distribution.'[77] Anthropologist Ulf Hannerz's reading of cosmopolitanism involves the will to gain competence in alien systems of meaning, while noting that this competence suggests a sense of mastery: 'Understandings have expanded, [and] a little more of the world is somehow under control.'[78] Accordingly, we adopt the notion of subaltern cosmopolitanism in order to reconceptualize the affective 'force of art' and reveal the creative possibilities for a redistribution of the sensible in these cases.

Zeng discerns two fundamental questions about subaltern cosmopolitanism and the horizontal engagement between individuals or groups of unequal power relations: the first question is about the prospect of living together with difference and the second about living with 'transnational connectivity and solidarity between the disenfranchized.'[79] This form of cosmopolitanism takes into account our interlocutors' subaltern positions within society and local art worlds, while also emphasizing their agency in adopting various habituses and developing various forms of capital in order to gain better positions in the field of cultural production. Tracing our interlocutors' trajectories foregrounds the ways they dynamically responded to the hegemonic structuring of the multiple and oscillating logics of the field of cultural production.[80] By adopting cosmopolitan inclinations to gain competence in the habituses (ethos) of foreign communities, subaltern artists may be valued positively on the basis of artistic quality and consequently gain better access to the field of cultural production. Rancière's attention to artists' agencies in engaging the Other through affect, or through shared affective horizons (aisthesis), helps to effectuate a partition of the sensible (ethos) of the community, and thus gain recognition as a sensible subject within that community.

75 .......... Doreen Massey, *For Space* (London: Sage, 2005), p. 151.

76 .......... Minhao Zeng, 'Subaltern Cosmopolitanism: Concept and Approaches,' *Sociological Review* 62 (2014), p. 144.

77 .......... Doreen Massey, 'Geographies of Responsibility,' *Geografiska Annaler, Series B: Human Geography* 86, no. 1 (2004), p. 44.

78 .......... Ulf Hannerz, 'Cosmopolitans and Locals in World Culture,' in *Global Culture: Nationalism, Globalization and Modernity*, ed. Mike Featherstone (London: Sage Publications, 1990), p. 488.

79 .......... Zeng, 'Subaltern Cosmopolitanism,' p. 144.

80 .......... Pierre Bourdieu, 'The Field of Cultural Production or the Economic World Reversed,' in *The Field of Cultural Production*, ed. Randal Johnson (New York NY: Columbia University Press, 1994), pp. 37–38.

81 .......... Rancière, *Dissensus*, p. 141.

## CONCLUSIONS

Our research indicates that local grassroots organizations enabling affective encounters have to negotiate multiple demands and expectations. Apart from justifying their practices to donors gathered in the *Force of Art* initiative, they often have to deal with other funding bodies each posing different demands and requiring different formats. At the same time, state actors, as well as public opinion on local, regional, or national levels, may look at their practices as well as their European funding with suspicion. Even if the funding bodies never impose political ideology or pose conditions on artistic content, donors and recipients generally align around post-nationalist, post-socialist and anti-Islamist ideals. A term such as 'human rights,' for example, may be perceived as politically neutral by a European donor, but seen as a political threat by an authoritarian regime, or—conversely—as depoliticizing the state of occupation in Palestine; and an overtly secular programme may be seen as advancing a European agenda. Finally, local communities and fellow cultural and community organizations may require yet another set of concerns than those preferred by foreign donors, and communicate them in a discourse with its own set of terms and logic. Our interlocutors show incredible proficiency in navigating the multiple, and sometimes dissonant, registers of these entanglements and perform the delicate balancing act that is required to navigate these entangled fields. By pointing out these tensions, however, we hope to also draw attention to those less fluent in this code switching, who may therefore fail to generate resources, however attuned to local codes and conditions. Moreover, our interlocutors do express fatigue, as the ad hoc and temporary nature of project-based funding can be draining for small organizations.

With this article we have argued that the transformative power of the cultural initiatives and community practices under study reside in the affective encounters they enable among members of marginalized communities or between these communities and outsiders. This is particularly urgent in a region crippled by decades of corruption, authoritarianism, and economic malaise, where the most basic social services are often lacking and where political subjectivity is more often formed by prolonged deprivation than by nurtured critical thinking. The Middle East and North Africa have witnessed a series of unprecedented revolts in the past decade, challenging the political, social, and economic order. Spaces and initiatives that stimulate the imagination and allow for new social relations are vital for such moments of transition. In our case studies, such encounters have helped to shift the distribution of the sensible by weaving 'a new fabric of common experience' within a community.[81]

1. In Palestine, local residents living under occupation and concerned tourists shared meaningful experiences through a grassroots network enabling volunteer aid work.

2. In Morocco, a young man from a criminalized neighbourhood was

granted a moment of wonder, when offered a fresh perspective on his situatedness in a specific social and spatial locality.

3. Lebanese children, parents, and elderly publicly discussed issues of public health and education, opened up by carefully constructed moments of play and laughter.

4. A Turkish arts audience was allowed to appreciate the work of Syrian artists outside of the reductive label of refugee art.

These experiences are particularly enriching for communities marked by a scarcity of creative and communal activities in which most of the initiatives under study operate.

← REFERENCES


Arthere Istanbul. 'Arthere Istanbul.' www.arthereistanbul.com/about.html/ (accessed 14 January 2020).

Biehl, João, and Peter Locke. 'Deleuze and the Anthropology of Becoming.' *Current Anthropology* 51, no. 3 (2010), pp. 317–51.

Bogaert, Koenraad. 'The Problem of Slums: Shifting Methods of Neoliberal Urban Government in Morocco.' *Development and Change* 42, no. 3 (2011), pp. 709–31.

Bourdieu, Pierre. '*The Field of Cultural Production* or the Economic World Reversed.' In *The Field of Cultural Production*, ed. Randal Johnson, pp. 29–73. New York: Columbia University Press, 1994.

Clown Me In (n.d.). 'The Caravan.' https://clownmein.com/performances/the-caravan/ (accessed 13 January 2020).
—. 'About us.' https://clownmein.com/about-us/ (accessed 13 January 2020).
—. 'Main page.' https://clownmein.com/ (accessed 13 January 2020).

De Cesari, Chiara. *Heritage and the Cultural Struggle for Palestine*. Stanford: Stanford University Press, 2019.

Featherstone, David. *Solidarity: Hidden Histories and Geographies of Internationalism*. London: Zed books, 2012.

Gell, Alfred. *Art and Agency: An Anthropological Theory*. Oxford: Oxford University Press, 1998.

Gregg, Melissa, and Gregory J. Seigworth. 'An Inventory of Shimmers.' In *The Affect Theory Reader*, ed. Melissa Gregg and Gregory J. Seigworth, pp. 1–28. Durham: Duke University Press, 2010.

Grossberg, Lawrence. 'Affect's Future: Rediscovering the Virtual in the Actual.' In *The Affect Theory Reader*, ed. Melissa Gregg and Gregory J. Seigworth, pp. 309–38. Durham: Duke University Press, 2010.

Hannerz, Ulf. 'Cosmopolitans and Locals in World Culture.' In *Global Culture: Nationalism, Globalization and Modernity*, ed. Mike Featherstone, pp. 237–51. London: Sage Publications, 1990.

Harvie, Jen. *Fair Play: Art, Performance and Neoliberalism*. London: Palgrave Macmillan, 2013.

Kelly, Jennifer. 'Asymmetrical Itineraries: Militarism, Tourism, and Solidarity in Occupied Palestine.' *American Quarterly* 68, no. 3 (2016), pp. 723–45.

Laszczkowski, Mateusz, and Madeleine Reeves. 'Introduction Affective States: Entanglements, Suspensions, Suspicions.' *Social Analysis* 59, no. 4 (2015), pp. 1–14.

Laszczkowski, Mateusz. 'Rethinking Resistance Through and as Affect.' *Anthropological Theory* 19, no. 4 (2019), pp. 489–509.

Lavender, Andy. 'Viewing and Acting (and Points in Between): The Trouble with Spectating after Rancière.' *Contemporary Theatre Review* 22, no. 3 (2012), pp. 307–26.

Marschall, Anika. 'What Can Theatre Do About the Refugee Crisis? Enacting Commitment and Navigating Complicity in Performative Interventions.' *Research in Drama Education: The Journal of Applied Theatre and Performance* 23, no. 2 (2018), pp. 148–66.

Massey, Doreen. *For Space*. London: Sage, 2005.
—. 'Geographies of Responsibility.' *Geografiska Annaler, Series B: Human Geography* 86, no. 1 (2004), pp. 5–18.

Mbembe, Achille. 'African Contemporary Art: Negotiating the Terms of Recognition.' Interview by Vivan Paulissen. *Johannesburg Workshop in Theory and Criticism (JWTC) blog*. 8 September 2009. https://jhbwtc.blogspot.com/2009/09/african-contemporary-art-negotiating.html (accessed 13 January 2020).

Navaro-Yashin, Yael. 'Affective Spaces, Melancholic Objects: Ruination and the Production of Anthropological Knowledge.' *Journal of the Royal Anthropological Institute* 15 (2009), pp. 1–18.

Rabinow, Paul. *French Modern: Norms and Forms of the Social Environment*. Chicago: University of Chicago Press, 1995.

Rancière, Jacques. *Dissensus: On Politics and Aesthetics*, trans. Steven Corcoran. London: Continuum, 2010.

Sampson, Steven. 'Introduction: Engagements and Entanglements in the Anthropology of NGOs.' In *Cultures of Doing Good: Anthropologists and NGOs*, ed. Amanda Lashaw, Christian Vannier, and Steven Sampson, pp. 1–20. Tuscaloosa: University of Alabama Press, 2017.

Slyomovics, Susan. *The Performance of Human Rights in Morocco*. Philadelphia: University of Pennsylvania Press, 2005.

Smith, Christine. 'Art as a Diagnostic: Assessing Social and Political Transformation through Public Art in Cairo, Egypt.' *Social & Cultural Geography* 16, no. 1 (2015), pp. 22–42.

Sorensen, Majken J. 'Radical Clowning: Challenging Militarism through Play and Otherness.' *Humor: International Journal of Humor Research* 28, no. 1 (2015), pp. 25–47.

Spyer, Patricia, and Mary Margaret Steedly. *Images that Move*. Santa Fe, NM: SAR Press, 2013.

Stewart, Kathleen. 'Afterword: Worlding Refrains.' In *The Affect Theory Reader*, ed. Melissa Gregg and Gregory J. Seigworth, pp. 339–54. Durham: Duke University Press, 2010.

Strava, Cristiana. 'At Home on the Margins: Care Giving and the "Un-homely" among Casablanca's Working Poor.' *City & Society* 29, no. 2 (2017), pp. 329–48.
—. 'A Tramway Called Atonement: Genealogies of Infrastructure and Emerging Political Imaginaries in Contemporary Casablanca.' *Middle East* 10, no. 8 (2018), pp. 22–29.

Stupples, Polly. 'Creative Contributions: The Role of the Arts and the Cultural Sector in Development.' *Progress in Development Studies* 14, no. 2 (2014), pp. 115–30.

Svašek, Maruška. *The Anthropology Art and Cultural Production: Histories, Themes, Perspectives*. London: Pluto Press, 2007.

't Hart, Marjolein. 'Humour and Social Protest: An Introduction.' In *Humour and Social Protest*, ed. Marjolein 't Hart and Dennis Bos, pp. 1–20. Cambridge: Cambridge University Press, 2008.

Tabar, Linda. 'From Third World Internationalism to 'The Internationals': The Transformation of Solidarity with Palestine.' *Third World Quarterly* 38, no. 2 (2016), pp. 414–35.

Thompson, James. *Performance Affects: Applied Theatre and the End of Effect*. Basingstoke: Palgrave Macmillan, 2009.

Toukan, Hanan. 'On Being the Other in Post-Civil War Lebanon: Aid and the Politics of Art in Processes of Contemporary Cultural Production.' *Arab Studies Journal* 18, no. 1 (Spring 2010), pp. 118–61.

Thrift, Nigel. 'Intensities of Feeling: Towards a Spatial Politics of Affect.' *Geografiska Annaler. Series B, Human Geography* 86, no. 1 (2004), pp. 57–78.

Van Alphen, Ernst, and Tomáš Jirsa. 'Introduction: Mapping Affective Operations.' In *How to Do Things with Affects Affective Triggers in Aesthetic Forms*, ed. Ernst van Alphen and Tomáš Jirsa, pp. 1–16. Leiden: Brill, 2019.

Yoxall, Matthew. 'At the 'Frontiers' of Humanitarian Performance: Refugee Resettlement, Theatre-making and the Geo-politics of Service.' *Research in Drama Education: The Journal of Applied Theatre and Performance* 23, no. 2 (2018), pp. 210–27.

Zeng, Minhao. 'Subaltern Cosmopolitanism: Concept and Approaches.' *Sociological Review* 62 (2014), pp. 137–48.

## ← INTERVIEWS

Arthere, conversation with Kasper Tromp, Istanbul, 7 December 2018.

Imad Habbab, interview by Kasper Tromp, Istanbul, 12 December 2018.

Ali Omar, interview by Kasper Tromp, Istanbul, 16 December 2018.

Abdeljalil Bakkar, head of Initiative Urbaine, conversation with Cristiana Strava, Casablanca, April 2019.

Sabrina Kamili, project manager at Atelier, conversation with Cristiana Strava, Casablanca, April and November, 2019.

Sabine Choucair, interview by Arnout van Ree, 20 June 2019.
Bantmag, interview by Kasper Tromp, Istanbul, 18 August 2019.
Mohamed Fariji, artist and founder of Atelier de l'Observatoire, conversation with Cristiana Strava, Casablanca, April and November 2019.

Nubuke Foundation / Accra, Ghana / 11:16am 5°38'14.1"N / 0°10'28.4"W

Jiser Reflexions Mediterrànies / Barcelona, Spain / 11:25am    41°24'26.4"N / 2°12'13.5"E

Section Two

# CONTENT SHARING AND MISTRANSLATION

# CONTENT SHARING AND MISTRANSLATION
## On Global Aspirations and Local Infrastructures

Serubiri Moses

Content, in its characterization as both 'information' made available and as readable material that is distinct from both form and style, is a significant part of recent infrastructure development. Thus, content sharing and the establishment of information standards shape various markets and global economies. Due to the specialization of information in the global arena across Asia, Africa, and the Middle East, emergent economies of art have become subject to such standardization. This begs a question: How are we to address the ongoing relationship between art, content, and economy? Additionally, how can we avoid the tendency towards over-specialized and oversimplified art content in museum discourse?

The chapters that follow in this section of the book reflect, among other contributions, this linguistic challenge. The authors—Mariam Abou Ghazi and Ilka Eickhof; Kobina Ankomah-Graham and Joseph Oduro-Frimpong; Jenny Mbaye and Miranda Iossifidis; Minna Valjakka—are each cognizant of various ethical considerations. For example, Valjakka was particular about her collaborative ethic with the people who informed her, they take on an interpretative role in creating graphic charts that are visual representations of the 'ecosystem' as the object of study. Similarly, Mbaye and Iossifidis borrow from African urban theory taking a critical standpoint in studying their cases in Dakar, Senegal. Rather than focus on content and data generated by individual arts organizations, their study is informed by a critical perspective in which 'collaboration' features as a distinct function through the artistic Dakarois landscape. This study uses urbanist AbdouMaliq Simone's critical theory of 'urban social collaborations.'

The two other contributions to this section of the book also engage with the linguistic problem, either elaborating on new terminologies such as 'post-revolutionary' in Cairo, Egypt, or on the flattening nature of tourist labels for art in Accra, Ghana. Abou Ghazi and Eickhof take the Townhouse Gallery in Cairo as a primary case study. Here a consideration of rapid economic and social decline after the revolution of 2011 in Egypt reveals the challenge of considering art in post-revolutionary contexts. Ankomah-Graham and Oduro-Frimpong equally challenge claims made by the Ghana Tourism Board. Reading the GTB website, an elaborate focus on tourism, the study argues, can be misleading in the sense of mistranslation about what artistic production consists of in Ghana.

Yet, this linguistic problem, and the resulting mistranslation, is equally evident in Eastern Africa. That is, between 1996 and 2006, owing to the lack of communication infrastructure, this phenomenon has led to critical gaps in knowledge about East African artists. In a personal conversation, curator Clémentine Deliss argues that there were no convenient communication channels between Britain and Uganda between 1991 to 1994 (outside of fax machines) through which she could learn about Ugandan artists.[1] Her research was thus limited, and not until her visit to Uganda in those years did she learn about artists such as Pilkington Sengendo and Francis Nnaggenda. In a catalogue essay, the curator describes the paintings she saw at Makerere University Art Gallery as reminiscent of Hieronymus Bosch and Peter Bruegel.[2] A description that has proven divisive: praised by some as accurate, and challenged by other commentators as an example of mistranslation.

Large-scale development of mobile and cable infrastructure during the 1996–2006 decade vastly increased the opportunities for East African artists within the international art field. It increased their visibility, as their artwork could be uploaded onto the internet and they could easily appear in search engines and online databases. As the architect and scholar Keller Easterling has written about Kenya in particular, 'Broadband and ICT Infrastructure are social-technical networks.'[3] This has presented incredible potential for broader forms of development in medical and commercial industrial fields, purely through the availability of data and content.

Thus, if fields of education and banking were impacted by ICT infrastructure and its social-technical networking, what about the field of art? The most central question to the expansion of the field of art has been that of 'visibility.' If ICT infrastructure provided opportunities for content sharing that were virtually limited in the early nineteen-nineties, we need to consider how the art field has been transformed in its globalization, and what the impact of such content-sharing has been on the development of cultural infrastructure on the local scale.

Europe and North America relied on centralized museum and university models, and access to art and artists followed prior models and agendas set by the British Museum. Here, ethnological knowledge as codified in a distinct method of categorization was established. The museums of the nineties and even those of today rely more on this system of centralized knowledge and standardized data to govern access to art. If one wants to find artists, today, they tend to visit the same museums, viewing their archives and databases for information. In the nineties, the biennial international art exhibition presented unique challenges to this centralized model by feeding into the so-called globalization of art.

This came with global 'flows' of art and newer and unexpected 'discoveries' in the art system. Thus, this period could be seen as a time of new 'discoveries' within art through global flows. The global 'artscape' became incredibly diversified in its scope due to the blockbuster exhibitions that were made in the style of the Paris and Venice fairs. The size of exhibitions expanded, in part, due to this new diversity and globalized demand for art at the periphery. While some argued against this centre-periphery discourse by claiming the border as central,[4] little doubt remains about the tendency within the art world to concede to the centralized and standardized model of the museum, and its counterpart—the university. Furthermore, the nineties presented new developments in infrastructure, particularly in the form of the international art biennials: Havana, Johannesburg, Gwangju, Dakar, Dhaka, and Taipei.

The earlier complaints by Octavio Zaya, among other commentators, about the biennialization of art shows posed challenges for new developments in arts infrastructure, and for curators and art critics working in the continually expanding field of art. Yet, complaints about biennialization coincided with

1..........Clémentine Deliss, in discussion with the author, June 2014.

2..........Ibid. '7+7=1: Seven stories, seven stages, one exhibition,' in *Seven Stories About Modern Art in Africa*, ed. Clémentine Deliss and Catherine Lampert (London: Whitechapel, 1995), pp. 19–27.

3..........Keller Easterling, *Extrastatecraft: The Power of Infrastructure Space* (London: Verso Books, 2014), p. 124.

4..........African American author Toni Morrison said to Jana Wendt in a television show, 'I stood at the border, stood at the edge and claimed it as central. I claimed it as central, and let the rest of the world move over to where I was.' *Uncensored*. 'Toni Morrison.' Directed by Gary Deans. Produced by Alan Hall, Jana Wendt. Originally aired 2 September 1998, on Australian Broadcasting Corporation.

calls for art's deterritorialization. Zaya laboured to explain why Latin American Art was in some ways an unstable construct, especially when using the label to describe a large diversity of practices.[5] His use of the anthropological term 'transterritorial' challenged the collection and study of Latin American artists in such broad and undifferentiated strokes. He writes, 'The artistic production of Latin America is the result of confrontations, impositions, assimilations, grafts, and appropriations.'[6]

In calling for the deterritorialization of art, Zaya participated in the process of aesthetic re-naming, while criticizing the ARCO fair committee in Madrid. Latin America could not be simply or merely reduced or aggregated into the international art fair circuit, without critical considerations. His critical reflections were an attempt to dispel the blank assessments of Latin American artists who according to the curator and critic, shared neither a uniform territory, nor 'race, ethnicity.'[7]

This crisis of knowing was evident in the sphere of African art, where the nineties had brought a vibrant interest to contemporary African artists living within and outside of the continent. This same tendency to view African art as 'limited, coherent, and compact'[8] was apparent as Western museums scrambled to collect and present contemporary African arts in a manner that many curators such as Okwui Enwezor and Bisi Silva found questionable. In the debates of the time, Silva called out what she deemed in 1995 to be 'cultural terrorism,'[9] referring to the Benin pillage of the nineteenth century, and museum display of stolen artefacts from West Africa. Enwezor clearly argued against the sentiment pervasive in Western museums that there was no history to speak of in Africa.[10] His exhibitions were meant as a corrective to the misleading projections onto African artists by the centralized museum and university models. Yet, the question of content and meaning which preoccupied Enwezor, Zaya, and others, has re-emerged in recent debates that link infrastructure to content. Thus, South African educator Selby Mvusi's call for 'time consciousness'[11] is important as a call to consider the moment in which we are living; as a directive for an awareness of our contemporary present and future in design and architecture. His questions relate and emphasize awareness, which in turn points to content and design oriented towards now and the future. More so, Mvusi advocates an engagement with recent social history, and a specific kind of technological progress.[12]

Reflecting on current trends in Kenya's progressive ICT infrastructure, Easterling writes of Ushahidi: a 'crowd-sourcing software turned the mobile phone into an instrument of political oversight.'[13] The architect further writes about the ways that Ushahidi has been applied in 'the aftermath of the earthquake in Haiti'[14] and been used to 'track violence in Gaza.'[15] The question of infrastructure appears centrally in the coming four chapters of this book, as specifically related to awareness of art in the present. Infrastructure cited in the chapters includes: libraries, online platforms, exhibition and white-cube spaces, mobile cinemas, and others.

The logic used in the Ankomah-Graham and Oduro-Frimpong chapter is awareness. One of the study's interviewees, arts director Teesa Bahana, says of the conditions of living in and staying afloat in a precarious funding and development setting, 'We are still here.' Considering the experiences of art that are largely removed from the centralized Western museum discourse, the lived experience and awareness of recent times has been crucial in each of these studies. Artists living in places like Cairo and Algiers have demonstrated, in idiosyncratic ways, an awareness of their time, highlighting their engagement with broader social-technical infrastructure. They have adapted to the 'post-revolutionary' times by innovating itinerant structures such as websites and mobile cinemas.

The chapters in this section generously discuss the local infrastructure of art through self-consciousness or self-awareness, focused on central actors within select cultural precincts. Abou Ghazi and Eickhof's chapter reveals an awareness of the difficulties of funding criteria, in which open calls are geared towards 'young' or 'emerging' artists. In cited interviews, the study shows an awareness of the fact that age is a limiting criterion for individual grants.

This begs to ask about voids that are apparent in the study of art and its publics. 'Sensory or perceptual experience,' a prominent methodology by authors of this book, is understood as a form of non-empirical knowledge. What has been left out or unknown runs through as a common thread. In Valjakka's study there is a difficulty both in translating the term 'art ecosystem': a term that entered Indonesian arts through funding structures, and is generally written *ekosistem seni*; as well as the difficulty of finding a corresponding concept for this term 'art ecosystem' in Bahasa Indonesia. Similarly, Mbaye and Iossifidis's study considers para-infrastructure(s) that may form as a result of collaboration. The Biennale 'Dak'Art' and its fringe programming, 'Off,' and Partcours, a self-organized annual, reveal the ways local arts professionals have experienced the biennial over its two decades, and pushed back against the so-called biennialization of art.

For Zaya, art's ontological deterritorialization was a method of push back against the centralized discourse of Latin American art in Western museums. Zaya, like the many interviewees in the forthcoming chapters, understood how Western art fairs and museums drew blanks, in sharp contrast to his lived experiences of Cuban art. I am reminded of Egyptian curator Sarah Rifky's citation of John Searle.[16] Rifky wrote, 'To go back to Searle, a simplistic way of understanding his argument around institutions, is that historically, thinkers have taken language for granted, therefore they have presumed the economy, the institution of economics.'[17] How can we therefore escape this presumption of language? The ontological deterritorialization of art coincides with this attempt to escape 'simplistic' language. Rifky asks, 'When we speak of artists and art, we also speak of language, and here I wonder why, when thinking of institutions, their relations and their future, do we not assume a language that is more akin to art?'

Following Mvusi, an awareness of the decade 1996–2006 reveals problems with content sharing and language. More concretely, the task ahead is to avoid simplistic language about African and Asian contexts, and over-prescriptions of an economic dialectic onto the artists 'discovered' there. Yet, this is no simple lesson to learn. After more than a decade (beyond 2006), we still perceive these limits of knowledge. There is still a problem consisting of lack of content sharing and the problem of mistranslation. It is to be hoped that the strategies used in this section of the book—that is, (1) engage the 'post-revolutionary';

5 ..........'This same essentialist view led to the discriminatory decision of the ARCO Committee. For that Committee, the contemporary artistic production of Latin America is coherent, limited, and compact. In geographical terms, it is also supposedly isolated, and therefore, cannot be contaminated, even when the artistic production of Latin America is the result of confrontations, impositions, assimilations, grafts, and appropriations vis-a-vis the various indigenous and foreign cultures. For the Committee, what is produced outside that territory, even though it is the result of activities by those who were or are its inhabitants or their descendants, is not essentially "Latin American."' In Octavio Zaya, 'Transterritorial: The Spaces of Identity and the Diaspora,' *Art Nexus* 25 (1997), pp. 52–57.

6 ..........Ibid.

7 ..........Ibid.

8 ..........Ibid.

9 ..........Olabisi Silva, 'Africa 95: Cultural Celebration or Colonialism?,' *Nka Journal of Contemporary African Art* no. 4 (1996), pp. 30–35.

10 ........Okwui Enwezor, 'The Short Century: Independence and Liberation Movements in Africa, 1945–1994: An Introduction,' in *The Short Century: Independence and Liberation Movements in Africa 1945–1994* (Munich: Prestel, 2001), p. 10–16.

11 ........See: Daniel Magaziner, 'Designing Knowledge in Postcolonial Africa: A South African abroad,' *Kronos 41*, no. 1 (2015), p. 280; and Selby Mvusi, 'Towards a Contemporary Art in Africa,' in *Proceedings of the First International Congress of African Culture*, ed. Frank McEwen (Salisbury, National Gallery of Art, 1962).

12 ........Ibid.

13 ........Easterling, *Extrastatecraft*, pp. 122–23.

14 ........Ibid.

15 ........Ibid.

16 ........Sarah Rifky, 'On Instituting a New Space for Thought,' in *Condition Report: Symposium on Building Art Institutions in Africa*, ed. Koyo Kouoh (Stuttgart and Berlin: Hatje Cantz Verlag, 2013), pp. 55–57.

17 ........Ibid.

(2) forge collaborative means of interpretation; (3) focus on 'urban social collaborations'; and
(4) push back on art content defined solely through a lens of tourism—will challenge these ontological limits, not merely by reinforcing the blanks, but rather through offering new terms and vocabularies that challenge simplistic language.

← REFERENCES

Deliss, Clémentine, and Catherine Lampert, eds. *Seven Stories About Modern Art in Africa*. London: Whitechapel, 1995.

Easterling, Keller. *Extrastatecraft: The Power of Infrastructure Space*. London: Verso Books, 2014.

Enwezor, Okwui. 'The Short Century: Independence and Liberation Movements in Africa, 1945–1994. An Introduction.' In *The Short Century: Independence and Liberation Movements in Africa 1945–1994*, pp. 10–16. Munich: Prestel, 2001.

Magaziner, Daniel. 'Designing Knowledge in Postcolonial Africa: A South African Abroad.' *Kronos* 41, no. 1 (2015), p. 280.

Mvusi, Selby. 'Towards a Contemporary Art in Africa.' In *Proceedings of the First International Congress of African Culture,* ed. Frank McEwen. Salisbury: National Gallery of Art, 1962.

Rifky, Sarah. 'On Instituting a New Space for Thought.' In *Condition Report: Symposium on Building Art Institutions in Africa*, ed. Koyo Kouoh, pp. 55–57. Stuttgart: Hatje Cantz Verlag, 2013.

Silva, Olabisi. 'Africa 95: Cultural Celebration or Colonialism?' *Nka Journal of Contemporary African Art* no. 4 (1996), pp. 30–35.

*Uncensored*. 'Toni Morrison.' Directed by Gary Deans. Produced by Alan Hall, Jana Wendt. Originally aired 2 September 1998, on Australian Broadcasting Corporation.

Zaya, Octavio. 'Transterritorial: The Spaces of Identity and the Diaspora.' *Art Nexus* 25 (1997), pp. 52–57.

# ARTS AND ECOSYSTEMS
## Building Towards Regeneration of 'Cultural Resilience' in Indonesia

Minna Valjakka

Amid growing interests in the arts and their possible societal impact in the twenty-first century, notions of empowerment, community building, and reinvigoration of villages and urban neighbourhoods are acknowledged across cultural policies, art studies, and redevelopment plans. Such growing attention to the arts and their life-changing potentiality has led to further instrumentalization of artistic practices. This may cause interdependences with financial agencies, and adds urgency to questions of the societal role, autonomy, inclusiveness, and sustainability of arts. A discussion of arts, cultural, and creative ecosystems has also recently emerged in Indonesia to address these challenges. Koalisi Seni Indonesia and ruangrupa are two recognized initiators for public acknowledgement of multidisciplinary art(s) ecosystem(s). By positioning the two actors in a broader socio-political and cultural context, the aim of this chapter is to delineate the main concerns, aspirations, and contingencies related to art(s) ecosystem(s). Through a comparative approach including not only insights by local representatives but also emerging discourses in the region and beyond, I seek to facilitate lateral thinking and further envisionings of more nuanced understandings of 'balanced art(s) ecosystem(s)' and how this can contribute towards the regeneration of 'cultural resilience.' The major objective of this paper is to enable innovative perceptions and help the planning of future theoretical and practical approaches.

Keywords
→ Balanced Art(s) Ecosystem(s)
→ Ecosystem Analysis
→ Multidisciplinarity
→ Sustainability
→ Societal Role of Arts

## INTRODUCTION

> 'I wish there was no more hierarchy in the arts.'
> Rahmadiyah Tria Gayathri[1]

The intricate socio-political environment in Indonesia has meant shifting realities for artists and citizens alike throughout the twentieth century. In the nineteen-seventies, *Gerakan Seni Rupa Baru* (GSRB, New Art Movement) emerged to question the aesthetic and artistic modalities of the predominant notions of 'modern art.' Debates are ongoing about the interconnectedness of the movement and contemporary art in the nineteen-nineties, but the GSRB can nevertheless be regarded as the nascent breakthrough of a strong alignment with socio-political criticism, societal transformation, and community-based works in Indonesian art.[2] Yet the lack of adequate government support and institutional acknowledgement for what has gradually come to be understood as 'contemporary arts' has made some artists reconfigure their own infrastructures, alliances, and spaces. This has happened especially in the nineties within and by local communities but also because of the support and interest of regional and international foundations and art markets.[3] While this unparalleled internationalization and commercialization further reshaped the contemporary art scene in the nineties, it also raised pertinent questions about the role and identity of Indonesian arts. In particular, after the change of regime in 1998, the socio-political and economic transformations led to an unprecedented presence of both Indonesian and international NGOs, which was not always unproblematic.[4]

In the twenty-first century, the particular social, political, and cultural circumstances embedded in the postcolonial and multicultural context of Indonesia continue to build towards contestations of representation and power relations between different ethnicities, institutions, religions, and ideological frameworks. Societal instabilities, growing communal anxieties, and conflicts that in the post-Suharto era shaped the evolving arts scenes across Indonesia, have now embraced new manifestations and ideological departures. This increasingly transnational cultural environment has been shaped by unseen societal transitions, which add new dimensions to the precarious situation of arts. Novel forms of artistic experimentation by artists and (art) collectives continue to meet with parallel forms of cultural production in the fields of urbanization, civil society formation, environmentalism, critical pedagogy, and activism. In this recent wave of interest in the arts and their possible societal impact, notions of empowerment, community building, and reinvigoration of villages and cities have turned to catchphrases commonly employed in cultural policies, art studies, and redevelopment plans. Such growing

1............Rahmadiyah Tria Gayathri (Koalisi Seni member in Palu, Sulawesi), interview by Dara Hanafi, 10 January 2020.

2............Elizabeth Morrell, 'Ethnicity, Art, and Politics away from the Indonesian Centre,' *Sojourn: Journal of Social Issues in Southeast Asia* 15, no. 2 (2000); Grace Samboh, 'Becoming: In Search of the Social Artists, Locating Their Environments, Reorienting the Planet,' in *Making Another World Possible: 10 Creative Time Summits, 10 Global Issues, 100 Art Projects*, ed. Corina L. Apostol and Nato Thompson (London: Routledge, 2019); Yvonne Spielmann, *Contemporary Indonesian Art: Artists, Art Spaces, and Collectors*, expanded and updated English ed. (Singapore: NUS Press, 2017); Helen Spanjaard, *Artists and Their Inspiration: A Guide through Indonesian Art History (1930–2015)* (Volendam: LM Publishers, 2016); Jim Supangkat, *Indonesian Modern Art and Beyond* (Jakarta: Indonesia Fine Arts Foundation, 1997); Jim Supangkat, 'Arts and Politics in Indonesia,' in *Art and Social Change: Contemporary Art in Asia and the Pacific*, ed. Caroline Turner (Canberra: Pandanus Books, 2005); Jim Supangkat, 'Indonesian and Javanese,' *Southeast of Now* 2, no. 2 (2018); H.D. Halim, 'Arts Networks and the Struggle for Democratisation,' in *Reformasi: Crisis and Change in Indonesia*, ed. Arief Budiman, Barbara Hatley, and Damien Kingsbury (Clayton: Monash Asia Institute, 1999); Patrick D. Flores, *Past Peripheral: Curation in Southeast Asia* (Singapore: NUS Museum, 2009), pp. 37–42; Caroline Turner, 'Indonesia: Art, Freedom, Human Rights and Engagement with the West,' in *Art and Social Change: Contemporary Art in Asia and the Pacific*, ed. Caroline Turner (Canberra: Pandanus Books, 2005).

3............Such developments are also mentioned in, e.g., Spielmann, *Contemporary Indonesian Art*, pp. 9–15 and in Flores, *Past Peripheral*, pp. 101–2 and pp. 180–81.

4............Philip Eldridge, 'NGOs and the State in Indonesia,' in *State and Civil Society in Indonesia*, ed. Arief Budiman (Clayton: Centre of Southeast Asian Studies, Monash University, 1990); Bob S. Hadiwinata, *The Politics of NGOs in Indonesia: Developing Democracy and Managing a Movement* (London: Routledge/Curzon, 2003); Verena Beittinger-Lee, *(Un)civil Society and Political Change in Indonesia: A Contested Arena* (London: Routledge, 2009).

attention to the arts and their life-changing potentiality has led to further instrumentalization and NGO-ization of artistic practices.[5] This, in turn, may cause programming dependencies to meet financiers' needs, and adds urgency to the questions on the autonomy, independence, role, and sustainability of arts.

Even though the post-reform era for Indonesian arts is defined by informal collaborations and solidarity, it is not free from intrinsic and international hierarchies premised, for instance, on unequal access to resources and networks, generational differences, Java-centrism, and the growing impact of Islamic traditionalists in certain cities and regions. In addition, a 'localist' cultural policy, focusing on protectionism and the preservation of authentic Indonesian culture, has caused tensions in the circulation and consumption of culture in relation to international markets.[6] As evidenced during this study, such tendencies continue to create tensions on acceptable adaptations of traditions today, in particular for younger-generation artists.

To address these challenges faced by both central and local governments and to reformulate an inclusive cultural policy, the new Law No. 5/2017 on the Advancement of Culture was ratified in May 2017. Detailed discussion on the content of the law, related strategies, policies, programmes, the mapping of regional cultural infrastructure by the local governments in 2018, and the Cultural Endowment Fund is beyond the scope of this study, which discusses the evolving visions on the role of arts and art(s) ecosystem(s) (*ekosistem seni*). Yet, because of an inherent interrelatedness both in practice and in discourse of arts and culture, it is important to acknowledge that the focus of the Law is on culture as 'anything pertaining to human creation, sensibility, motivation, and the work of the community.' It is an 'effort to improve cultural resilience (*ketahanan budaya*) and Indonesian cultural contribution to the development of world civilizations through Cultural Protection, Development, Utilization, and Capacity Building/Empowerment.' Among the central developmental aims is the vitalization of the cultural ecosystems (*ekosistem Kebudayaan*),[7] of which contemporary arts and artists are only one part, as the Director General of Culture, Hilmar Farid, elucidates.[8]

While the analytical research on the implementation and outcomes of the Law with some temporal distance deserves a paper of its own, this art sociological study strives to identify key forms of agency and interpretations regarding the emerging conceptual approach of 'ecosystem' (*ekosistem*). Not only is the concept included in the Law, but initial conversations on arts, cultural, and creative ecosystems have gained written

5............NGO-ization of arts is mentioned, for example, in Raminder Kaur and Parul Dave-Mukherji, 'Introduction,' in *Art and Aesthetics in a Globalizing World*, ed. Raminder Kaur and Parul Dave-Mukherji (New York: Bloomsbury Academic, 2015), p. 15.

6............Tod Jones, *Culture, Power, and Authoritarianism in the Indonesian State: Cultural Policy across the Twentieth Century to the Reform Era* (Leiden: Brill, 2013), p. 278.

7............Law No. 5/2017 on Advancement of Culture (Undang-undang Republic Indonesia Nomor 5 Tahun 2017, Tentang *Pemajuan Kebudayaan*). Available in Indonesian on the Ministry of Education and Culture website https://kebudayaan.kemdikbud.go.id/uu-no-5-tahun-2017-tentang-pemajuan-kebudayaan/ (accessed 15 March 2020). See also Koalisi Seni's website focusing on Development of Culture (Pemajuan Kebudayaan), http://pemajuankebudayaan.id/. An official English translation made by the Ministry is made available by Koalisi Seni (accessed 5 April 2020).

8............Hilmar Farid, interview by author, 18 September 2019.

attention in Indonesia at least since 2015.[9] As two recognized initiators for the public acknowledgement of multidisciplinary art(s) ecosystem(s), ruangrupa and Koalisi Seni Indonesia (hereafter Koalisi Seni) are placed in a broader socio-political and cultural context to help investigate the current aspirations, possibilities, and challenges for enhancing the inter-related roles of arts, culture, and creativity in Indonesia.

By delineating the main concerns and aims related to the emerging discussions on 'art(s) ecosystem(s)' in Indonesia, and by mirroring them against existing discourses in the region and beyond, I seek to facilitate further envisionings on these pragmatic and conceptual processes through multi-layered ecosystem analysis. This comparative approach is employed not to enhance any epistemological hierarchy but rather to encourage lateral thinking, which can open up innovative perceptions of and for future practical and theoretical approaches. In order to directly include local voices and perceptions, and to avoid misrepresentations, diagrams created by local representatives of the arts, culture, and creativity illuminate evolving novel perceptions and hence complement the information derived from interviews. The information gathered throughout this study clearly reveals the significance of more nuanced understandings of 'balanced art(s) ecosystem(s),' which may, in turn, contribute towards the regeneration of 'cultural resilience.'

## METHODOLOGY

Koalisi Seni and ruangrupa represent two originally rather disparate yet closely interrelated positions and roles across the Jakartan, national, and regional arts scenes. Hence, they are chosen as the two key examples to clarify the major transformations in arts in the twenty-first century. In the initial stages of the fieldwork, the concept of 'ecosystem' and the aspirations to further improve the situation of arts as 'an ecosystem(s)' emerged as pertinent issues among different stakeholders. My attention was thus drawn to the role of Koalisi Seni and ruangrupa in these evolving discourses, which provided an apt point of departure for this paper.

In 2000, the young artists' initiative ruangrupa started to work from the perspective of urban youth culture and in the urban context of Jakarta. Over two decades, ruangrupa has gradually grown from an informal collective into an internationally acknowledged non profit organization with around eighty hired staff members along with numerous programmes, platforms, and collaborative components. Changes in focus, aims, and concepts have closely correlated with the spatial changes from a private house to the rented warehouse known as the 'Gudang Sarinah ecosystem' and to the currently owned compound in Jagakarsa in South Jakarta.[10]

9............Djuli Djatiprambudi, 'Saat Menulis Sejarah Seni Rupa Sendiri' ['When Writing Your Own Fine Art History'], in *Biennale Jatim 6: 'Arts Ecosystem: Now!'* (Surabaya: Department of Culture and Tourism, East Java, 2015).

Such remarkable growth and transformation from programmes to audience along with generational changes require new organizational practices, and even though the aim is still to maintain a horizontal structure, ruangrupa's management has inevitably become somewhat hierarchic.[11]

In 2009, Amna Kusumo, founder of Kelola, raised the idea of collaborative advocacy for arts.[12] In the initial meeting in Bogor, West Java, on 5–6 April 2010, twenty-one art practitioners, organizations, and collectives agreed to proceed towards the creation of a new umbrella organization. The need to work together through a particular association to advance the position of arts in general was further endorsed among professionals from all spheres of arts and culture, and resulted in the official establishment of Koalisi Seni Indonesia on 3 May 2012. What used to be forty-one founding members is now a nationally representative organization with 251 members (individuals and organizations) in nineteen provinces.[13] Koalisi Seni defines itself as 'an association which aims to encourage the creation of a healthier arts ecosystem in Indonesia.'[14] Understandably, aspirations for Koalisi Seni's practical efforts and programmes vary among the members, but the clear majority of interviewees (including non-members) acknowledge the significance of its persistence in the development of the Law on the Advancement of Culture and commend the inclusion of people from various geographical and professional positions in the discussions throughout the process.[15]

To situate these two key actors into current arts and cultural scenes, I conducted five fieldwork periods between December 2018 and October 2019 in Jakarta, Jogjakarta, Bandung, Surabaya and Magelang in Java, and in Denpasar in Bali. During these ten intensive weeks, I visited around fifty-five art and/or cultural organizations, institutions, archives, museums, galleries, alternative (art) spaces, art collectives, private art studios, events, and exhibitions. The work and connections of Dara Hanafi, my Indonesian research assistant, were indispensable throughout the study, but I also made many site visits and conducted interviews independently. Besides artists, I reached out to scholars, collectors, curators, art historians, and

10 ........... Information primarily based on seven site visits (including previous locations); informal discussions with members of ruangrupa, Gudskul, Serrum, and Grafis Huru Hara; Ade Darmawan interview by author, 6 December 2018; Ade Darmawan, Reza Afisina, Farid Rakun, and Leonard Barto, interview by author, 6 May 2019; Julia Sarisetiati, interview by author 23 September 2019. For more information, see ruangrupa's website, ruru.ruangrupa.org (accessed 2 February 2020). For a detailed history of ruangrupa, see especially Reinaart Vanhoe, *Also-Space: How Indonesian Art Initiatives Have Reinvented Networking* (Eindhoven: Onomatopee, 2016); ruangrupa, *Expanding the Space and Public: ruangrupa's 10th Anniversary* (Jakarta: Indonesian National Gallery, 2010), and Mirwan Andan, 'All for Jakarta: A Note on the Tenth Anniversary of Ruangrupa: Decompression #10, Expanding the Space and Public,' *Inter-Asia Cultural Studies* 12, no. 4 (2011), pp. 591–602.

11 ........... Darmawan, Afisina, Rakun, and Barto, interview. Cf. with earlier situation discussed in Nuraini Juliastuti, 'Ruangrupa: A Conversation on Horizontal Organisation,' *Afterall: A Journal of Art, Context and Enquiry* 30, no. 1 (2012), pp. 118–25.

12 ........... Amna Kusumo, interview by author, 23 September 2019.

13 ........... Membership as of 30 April 2020. Koalisi Seni secretariat, email message to author, 30 April 2020.

14 ........... Information based on two site visits at the secretariat in Jakarta, with individual and group interviews of board members and the administrative team; participation in a planning meeting and workshop in Yogyakarta on 13–14 December 2018, and informal discussions with participants; complemented with interviews, and informal discussions with board members and members. For more detailed information, see https://koalisiseni.or.id/ (accessed 25 March 2020). 'Koalisi seni adalah perhimpunan yang bertujuan mendorong terwujudnya ekosistem seni yang lebih sehat di Indonesia.' On Koalisi Seni's website, in FAQ section.

15 ........... Already in 2013, Koalisi Seni took an active and public role with an article in a national newspaper about the urgency of revised cultural policies and law corresponding to the contemporary realities and diversity in cultural practices. Linda Hoemar Abidin, Mirwan Andan, and Abduh Aziz, 'Menanggapi RUU Kebudayaan' ['A Respond to the Draft of Cultural Law'], *Kompas*, 26 May 2013.

local and national government officials. The interviewees represent a large spectrum of contemporary and traditional arts, professional backgrounds, and demographics (ages ranging from twenty to eighty, and including six non-Indonesians immersed in Indonesian arts).

Koalisi Seni is a major promoter for the change in legislation and official (national) support for arts and culture, and as such, it is at the frontline of shaping the current discourse. It provides a significant platform for like-minded protagonists with shared interests to improve the current role of arts and culture. Many of the study participants were found among Koalisi Seni's members, but it was essential to also include insights from and site visits to non-members (representing approximately twenty-five per cent of the research data).

Given that Jakarta, Jogjakarta, and Bandung are historically known as the epicentre of Indonesian arts, I visited each of them two to four times. Yet, to build a more comprehensive understanding it was necessary to reach beyond this main triangle. Hence, for instance, my research was extended to Denpasar in Bali, which has gained international acknowledgement for its rich culture since the early twentieth century and is an important centre for arts outside of Java. Because of Indonesia's geographic extensiveness, it was not feasible to include as many visits to outer islands as I originally intended. Instead, Dara Hanafi made six telephone interviews to gather further insights from representatives from Riau in West Sumatra, Kupang in East Nusa Tenggara, Palu and Makassar in Sulawesi, Pontianak in Kalimantan, and from Denpasar in Bali. Altogether fifty-one semi-structured, individual, and group interviews were conducted based on voluntary participation and protection of anonymity with questions provided in advance. Along with my position as an 'outsider,' this approach ensured that people were more comfortable to share critical perceptions and comments that would have not necessarily been told to a person involved in the Indonesian arts scenes. To add to the triangulation of data, around thirty-five to forty informal discussions were held both with the interviewees and people (some of whom were based in Singapore) engaged in Indonesian arts and culture. Notes, transcriptions, and summaries have been cross-checked in personal communication, and permission to publish has been requested from the interviewees for any quotations in this paper.

To further exemplify the differences in perceptions of 'ecosystem(s)' and to demonstrate the potentiality of varied approaches, ten to twelve interested representatives from different cities and positions in arts, culture, and creativity were asked to visualize their current understanding of an 'ecosystem,' or its ideal form. Mainly because of schedules, not all could finalize their contributions, but the six illustrations included here provide a starting point to facilitate more in-depth discussions on existing envisionings.

## FROM NATURE TO ENTREPRENEURSHIP: ECOSYSTEM DISCOURSE

In an effort to inspire lateral thinking and to enhance emerging comparative discussions about arts, culture, creativity, and ecosystems, a short review of the existing approaches can be beneficial, although the scope of this chapter does not permit a detailed assessment of the many usages of 'ecosystems.' It is important to acknowledge that while the concept originates from biology, it has since the nineteen-nineties become an abundant but vaguely defined metaphor not only across academic disciplines but also in varied societal sectors. As Audretsch and colleagues validate, the comprehension of interrelated dynamics and factors of favourable socio-economic conditions has inspired extensive studies on entrepreneurial ecosystems, business ecosystems, and innovative ecosystems in the twenty-first century. They also note that much of the existing literature (in)directly resonates with the understanding of natural ecosystems consistent of living organisms and their environment.[16]

In the fields of contemporary art, interest in ecosystems has gradually expanded from a direct focus on the environment through arts to acknowledging more multiperspective interrelations in and beyond arts. Artists from varied cultural contexts have been keen to develop an 'ecological approach' in their art practices since the nineteen-sixties. In Indonesia, art embedded with and examining aspects of environment and ecology emerged in the nineteen-seventies and eighties.[17] While more in-depth art historical research is still needed for mapping out environmental art forms and their conceptual understandings in Asia, it seems—based on currently available information—that one of the earliest publications concerning the interrelations of art and ecosystem is a Japanese exhibition catalogue published in 1998 on artists examining people's interconnectedness with nature and, in particular, the forest.[18]

Such interest in biological ecosystems in art practices has continued to gain further ground. The different focuses have all contributed to a more elaborate understanding of relationships between people, nature, nonhuman agency, and socio-economic and cultural conditions through interdisciplinary collaborations not limited to the realms of 'art.' One of the most recent examples is the Taipei Biennial 2018, 'Post-Nature—A Museum as an Ecosystem,' and its request for unconventional ecological solutions advocated by people from various professional backgrounds and extending beyond the museum space to interrelate with different social and environmental ecosystems. In their curatorial statement, Mali Wu and Francesco Manacorda emphasize that

> [W]ith this movement away from anthropocentrism, comes an

16..........David B. Audretsch et al., 'Entrepreneurial Ecosystems: Economic, Technological, and Societal Impacts,' *The Journal of Technology Transfer* 44, no. 2 (2019).

17..........See, e.g., Samboh, 'Becoming,' pp. 106–22.

18..........*Āto, seitaikei: bijutsu hyōgen no 'shizen' to 'seisaku.' Art Ecosystem: The Contemporary Japanese Art Scene* (Utsunomiya: Utsunomiya Museum of Art, 1998). 'Ecosystem' is 生態系 (*seitaikei*) in Japanese.

> acceptance of more universal and all-encompassing approaches such as systems thinking, which understands the planet as a collection of interdependent ecosystems, populated by diverse and mutually reliant beings.[19]

Another line of adaptation of 'ecosystem' in arts worldwide examines what constitutes 'an art ecosystem' and how it is made sustainable. Ian David Moss's perceptions on 'ecosystem-based arts research' arose from a practical aim to map out and categorize actors and relationships premised on basic questions of where, how, by and to whom art is made. Such charting of roles, possibilities, and interrelations provides one possible starting point to investigate what Moss understands as a kaleidoscopic complexity of arts.[20] The different approaches and outcomes of what constitutes the arts ecosystems can be further illuminated by two studies available online: the first conducted in the United States in 2005[21] and the other in 2016 in Singapore.[22] While the former focuses on a more holistic understanding of the dynamics built by roles and interrelations through the systems thinking approach, the latter provides detailed quantitative statistics about, for example, art workers' education, motivation, and employment.

Similar aspirations to improve a common understanding of arts and their sustainability are expressed through, among others, arts professionals providing practical guidelines. Mostly emphasizing the importance of a holistic evaluation of the situation, they suggest how to nurture a vivid local art ecosystem premised upon horizontal connections and relationships, and acknowledging the importance of involving the general public.[23] A step further is provided by Moss and his team at Createquity: they shifted the focus from (art) institutions to people and to the collective good shared in equitable ways. In this, several core principles contribute to a healthy arts ecosystem, including the maximizing of 'the arts' capacity to improve the lives of human beings in concrete and meaningful ways.'[24]

Quite different yet illuminating perspectives on the sustainability of arts can be gained by focusing on a specific area, such as the art market as an ecosystem of its own and how 'a process of endorsement by tastemakers within that ecosystem'[25] shapes the dynamics of (economic) value

19...........Mali Wu and Francesco Manacorda, 'Post-Nature: A Museum as an Ecosystem,' curatorial statement online, www.taipeibiennial.org/2018/?lang=en (accessed 10 March 2020). 'Ecosystem' is 生態系統, (*shengtaixitong*) in Chinese.

20...........Ian David Moss, 'An Ecosystem-Based Approach to Arts Research,' *Fractured Atlas Blog*, 17 October 2011, www.fracturedatlas.org/site/blog/an-ecosystem-based-approach-to-arts-research.

21...........'The Cultural Dynamics Map: Exploring the Arts Ecosystem in the United States,' Version 1.0, March 2005, posted on 1 March 2007, www.artstrategies.org/downloads/CulturalMap_v1.pdf.

22...........'The Arts and Culture Employment Study 2016' by the National Art Council of Singapore. The main findings as illuminating statistics and the full study are available online, www.nac.gov.sg/whatwedo/support/research/Research-Main-Page/Arts-Statistics-and-Studies/Arts-Ecosystem/Arts-and-Culture-Employment-Study-.html (accessed 17 November 2019).

23...........Lawrence McCullough, 'Grow Your Own Local Artists: How Any Community Can Cultivate a Robust Arts Ecosystem,' *Public Management* 100, no. 4 (2018), pp. 14–16; Jacqueline O'Neil, 'How to Serve All Parts of the Art Ecosystem, from Artist to Institution,' *Blockchain Art Collective*, 30 October 2018, https://medium.com/blockchain-art-collective/how-to-serve-all-parts-of-the-art-ecosystem-from-artist-to-institution-79e9c532b0b1.

24...........Createquity, 'A Healthy Arts Ecosystem,' https://createquity.com/about/a-healthy-arts-ecosystem/ (accessed 25 October 2019).

creation and risks. Along similar lines, Can-Seng Ooi and Roberta Comunian examine the characteristics of the 'artrepreneurial ecosystem' in Singapore as a part of the creative economy strategy. Through the four main pillars (education; values and social norms; policy and democracy; and markets and competition), 'the often divided perspective of a global city that aims to move forward supporting new creative educational opportunities and new markets, ... is still anchored in established social norms and a narrow definition of freedom of expression.'[26] Adjusted to local specificities, according to them, a similar approach may also be informative in relation to other Asian creative ecosystems.

## ARTS, CULTURAL, AND CREATIVE ECOSYSTEMS IN INDONESIA

In Indonesia, the term 'ecosystem' (*ekosistem*) has gained emerging attention in its relation to arts, culture, and creativity—and their sustainability. It is a recent loanword in this context, and a profound analytical discourse of its adaptation in Indonesia is missing. It is partly because of this that the concept lacks the (post)colonial baggage and tensions carried by, for example, fine arts and/or modern arts.[27] The growing interest in 'ecosystem' can, however, be read in conjunction with the discourses of cultural heritage, creative city policies, and decolonization of arts through practices, representations, and institutional settings. As concepts travel and transform first through oral discussions and practices, and subjective memories may be indecisive, it is quite a challenge to locate empirical evidence for the initial conceptual stages of 'ecosystem' in the Indonesian art world. It is perhaps more important to consider which concepts 'ecosystem' co-exists with and/or replaces and what kind of novel perceptions it may hence bring about.

'Ecosystem,' as denoting arts and their socio-cultural environment, started to emerge in art discussions in Hong Kong, Japan, and Singapore from 2008 to 2011.[28] Taking into consideration the internationality of Indonesian arts, it is likely that 'ecosystem' commenced to orally circulate around the same time or slightly later.

In light of currently available information, the earliest written point

25..........Anders Petterson, 'Value, Risk and the Contemporary Art Ecosystem,' in *Risk and Uncertainty in the Art World*, ed. Anna M. Dempster (London: Bloomsbury Information Ltd, 2014), p. 67. See also Juliet den Oudendammer, 'The Art Ecosystem, and Why Some Artists Are More Successful than Others,' *Art Represent*, 7 December 2015, www.artrepresent.com/blog/the-art-ecosystem.

26..........Can-Seng Ooi and Roberta Comunian, 'The Artrepreneurial Ecosystem in Singapore: Enable and Inhibit the Creative Economy,' in *Routledge Handbook of Cultural and Creative Industries in Asia*, ed. Lorraine Lim and Hye-Kyung Lee (London: Routledge, 2018), p. 68.

27..........It is commonly accepted in global art history studies that the meaning of 'arts' is inevitably a constructed idea and varies remarkably between different languages, cultural contexts, time periods, forms, and movements, among others. For illuminating discussions on the conceptual transformations on and for arts, see especially Supangkat, 'Indonesian and Javanese'; Spanjaard, *Artists and Their Inspiration*, pp. 83–126.

28..........For instance, in Singapore, arts ecosystem is mentioned in relation to the Singapore Art Show 2009, organized by the National Art Council. www.nac.gov.sg/media-resources/press-releases/Singapore-Art-Show-2009.html (accessed 10 December 2019). In Hong Kong, the concept appears, for instance, in a discussion organized by Asian Art Archives in May 2010 and made available on their website, https://aaa.org.hk/en/programmes/programmes/in-the-aftermath-of-the-white-cube-museums-and-other-spaces/ (accessed 10 December 2019). For Japan, it is mentioned in Dōshin Satō, *Modern Japanese Art and the Meiji State: The Politics of Beauty* (Los Angeles: Getty Research Institute, 2011), p. 33.

of departure for 'art(s) ecosystem(s)' in public discussion in Indonesia is the 6th East Java (Jatim) Biennale in 2015, 'Arts Ecosystem: Now!' held in Surabaya on 11–24 November 2015. Through a multi-perspective analysis of an 'arts ecosystem,' the aim was to call for a more nuanced understanding of art practices and how they resonate with and are dependent upon varied micro- and macrosystems of arts and their local historical, formal, and discursive specificities across East Java. As the curator Djuli Djatiprambudi elaborates, this approach indicates that the growth of the art world is not merely driven by artists. Artists are regarded not as autonomous subjects, but are rather positioned as one of the entities in a broader socio-cultural ensemble, yet actively engaged in the field of arts (*medan seni*).[29]

When an arts ecosystem is perceived in the context of cultural capital, as Djatiprambudi further explains, it enables the acknowledgement of the multicultural reality of East Java with specific symbolism, techniques, and mediums along with aesthetic and socio-philosophical concepts. In the context of visual culture, an arts ecosystem reveals the diversity of artefacts (from a temple to tattoo and from batik to graffiti) that can all be understood as having strong, unique, and traditionally maintained local identities and meanings based on conceptual-philosophical relationships. At the level of current art practices, the arts ecosystem refers to new perspectives and methods of artistic creativity in multimedia, multi-aesthetic, multidimensional, and multicultural exploration. It also suggests inter-disciplinary and even multidisciplinary investigations. As a result, an artwork or an artistic practice can be seen as a reinterpretation of the complexity of the technical field, style, cultural capital, and new currents in contemporary art discourse and practice.[30]

The second, a transcultural point of origin for the written formulations of art(s) ecosystem(s) is the Arts Collaboratory (AC) and its Assemblies, the first of which took place in Indonesia in May 2014 and was hosted by ruangrupa in Jakarta and by KUNCI Cultural Studies Center in Yogyakarta.[31] The assembly produced a collaborative drawing, which twice featured the words 'art ecology in Yogyakarta.'[32] A posting after the event stated that participants particularly appreciated learning from 'the diverse art ecology of Jakarta and Yogyakarta.'[33] More insights were gathered from the second Assembly in Senegal in April 2015 to be further formulated by a working group in a future scenario meeting in Utrecht in June 2015. In an internal document of this meeting, ecosystem is mentioned as one of the keywords. Today, the AC defines itself as 'a translocal ecosystem of twenty-five organizations situated in Africa, Asia, Latin America, the Middle East, and the Netherlands that is focused on art practices, processes of social change, and working with communities beyond the field of art.'[34] They clarify this further:

29 Djatiprambudi, 'Saat Menulis Sejarah,' pp. 8–9.
30 Ibid.
31 For more information on KUNCI, see their website, http://kunci.or.id/ (accessed 25 February 2020).
32 Arts Collaboratory, the drawing from Assembly Indonesia, https://artscollaboratory-assembly.tumblr.com/post/90590903257/so-looking-back-to-indonesia-the-drawing (accessed 5 January 2020).
33 Arts Collaboratory, Assembly Indonesia 2014, www.artscollaboratory.org/meetings/assembly/assembly-2014/ (accessed 5 January 2020).

> The use of the word ecosystem suggests that like in nature, our relations are about life cycles, germination and maturation. The ecosystem is the system of connections, relationships and linkages between all the organisations that make up the commonwealth of the Arts Collaboratory.
>
> In the context of the AC the word ecosystem is also understood as it relates to each organization's own context or local ecosystem and the resources that are related specifically to those ecosystems which, by means of the resource map, can also be used to nurture the commonwealth.[35]

While the AC's perception of an ecosystem emphasizes the translocal and international aspects across cultural contexts, the third, a more locally acknowledged point of conceptual departure, and strongly embedded in practice, is represented by ruangrupa.

In their operational plans for 2008–2010, ruangrupa included a Commerce Unit in their organizational structure, which indicates an embryo stage of their current understanding of an ecosystem based on a tripartite structure: self-sustainability, knowledge, and artistic (see Figures 1 and 2 on p. 144). Around 2010, ruangrupa began to develop ideas of 'a collective pot' to enhance sustainability not only for them but also their collaborators. They were initially attracted by the concept of *lumbung*, which refers to a traditional rice barn into which the harvest was collectively stored in a village.[36] Lumbung is also used to protect other valuables and embodies 'a number of indigenous, preventive conservation principles and techniques.' It has been a useful concept, for instance, in translating the Eurocentric model of a modern 'museum' into a less foreign concept more suited to the Indonesian cultural context already in the nineteen-nineties.[37]

In 2011, ruangrupa set up RURU Corps as their internal business unit responsible for finding (non)commercial funding to maintain the growing group of members and activities. Lumbung has since become a key concept, which ruangrupa has continued to develop in their local, national, and international collaborations, and which has gained global awareness through the preparations of the forthcoming Documenta 15 in Kassel, Germany, in 2022. For ruangrupa, lumbung and the concerns of sustainability paved the way for a practical understanding of a multidisciplinary ecosystem in 2015;

34...........Arts Collaboratory, www.artscollaboratory.org/ (accessed 5 January 2020).

35...........Arts Collaboratory, 'Common Language,' www.artscollaboratory.org/about/common-language-index-of-terms/ (accessed 5 January 2020).

36...........Interviews with ruangrupa representatives, see footnote 9 for detailed information.

37...........Christina F. Kreps, *Liberating Culture: Cross-Cultural Perspectives on Museums, Curation, and Heritage Preservation* (London: Routledge, 2003), p. 130.

this was brought into public awareness by the establishment of the Gudang Sarinah Ekosistem in spring 2016. News about the ecosystem was posted on Instagram and Facebook in April 2016.[38]

The fourth, and currently the most prominent local and national trajectory for the 'ecosystem' discourse in the multidisciplinary context of arts (*seni*), derives from the advocation processes of Koalisi Seni through workshops, events, research, discussions, and publications. During the earliest meetings, the deliberations mainly focused on recognizing the key issues faced by Indonesian arts and on improving the material infrastructure of arts, education, and arts management. This also included the question of how to deal with the lack of government support. Gradually this unravelling of the scope of the current situation of arts spurred the acknowledgement of a multitude of inherent elements in an arts ecosystem. Koalisi Seni has investigated a more general, metalevel mapping of the arts ecosystem since 2019, and is now in the process of deciphering detailed ecosystem diagrams regarding, for instance, the music industry, based on the core elements of creation, reproduction, distribution, and consumption. The aim is to understand how government policies could support each core element so they would lead to a healthier music industry ecosystem.[39]

Ecosystem analysis has also emerged in academic research aimed for an international readership. One of the most recent studies in deciphering an 'ecosystem' draws on the creative economy approach. In their detailed account of 'creative ecosystems' in Bandung, Santi Novani, Cici Cintyawati, and Lidia Mayangsari discuss the digital creative ecosystem as 'a place where all of stakeholders are involved in enhancing the digital creative industry development.' They identify at least seven stakeholders: 'digital start-ups, university, government, association/community, customer, industry, and incubator.'[40]

This short review suggests that even though 'ecosystem' can be criticized as a vague and recent catchword compared with some other prevailing concepts (such as *gotong royong*,[41] lumbung, infrastructure, and collectivity), it nonetheless calls for a more nuanced and analytical comprehension reaching beyond existing actors, mutual collaboration, and solidarity. Conceptual approaches through a multi-layered ecosystem analysis carry the possibility of recognizing the importance of intangible elements such as interrelations, their quality and fluidity between actors, along with the socio-political and cultural conditions that inevitably have both a positive and a negative impact on the continuously changing, local, national, regional, and international ecosystems.

38..........An email message about 'ecosystem' on 17 May 2016 and an image of the flyer is included in Vanhoe, *Also-Space*, pp. 67–68.

39..........Information based on interviews and personal communication with the representatives of Koalisi Seni; for detailed information see footnote 12.

40..........Santi Novani, Cici Cintyawati, and Lidia Mayangsari, 'Back to the Future: A Revelation of Conventional Platform Preference of Digital Creative Ecosystem Entities in Bandung,' in *Collaborative Value Co-creation in the Platform Economy*, ed. Anssi Smedlund, Arto Lindblom, and Lasse Mitronen (Singapore: Springer, 2018), pp. 247–48.

41..........*Gotong royong* is an Indonesian concept with slightly varying connotations and usages but indicating mutual collaboration and communal self-help. For an illuminating discussion on the concept and its current relevance through new adaptations among kampung activists and their efforts of cultural commoning, see Melani Budianta, 'Smart Kampung: Doing Cultural Studies in the Global South,' *Communication and Critical/Cultural Studies* 16, no. 3 (2019), pp. 250–51.

## ASPIRATIONS AND ENVISIONINGS FOR THE REFORMULATION OF ECOSYSTEM(S)

Indonesian contemporary arts involve innumerable artists, art collectives, and art spaces across an extensive geographic area. Innovative art practices are often inseparable from varied prevailing forms of arts and culture, as they rely on multimethod approaches and collaborations across fields. This practical interrelatedness reflects the terminological approach in the Indonesian language: *seni* is commonly translated as 'art(s),' but as Jim Supangkat explains, *seni* primarily denotes a skill or a work that is made with great expertise and hence does not differentiate between arts and a craft. Roughly summarized, *seni* pertains to many artistic expressions such as visual arts (*seni rupa*), literature (*seni sastra*), dance art (*seni tari*), and installation art (*seni instalasi*), without implying hierarchical interpretations:

> Visual art is not at all more meaningful in comparison with, for example, dance art, music or literature. This shows that the extraordinary value of artistic creation is not determined by the type of artwork produced, but rather by the artistic sensibility that appears in artistic creation.[42]

A multidisciplinary interrelatedness of arts and culture in relation to the 'ecosystem' discussions is already indicated by Djuli Djatiprambudi's insights above, and was also eminently present throughout my fieldwork. The current realities and richness of arts, culture, and creativity create a multitude of envisionings on what might constitute an ecosystem, or how it might be improved. It is the diversity of these manifold perceptions and departures that the diagrams here further illuminate.

To promote the current decolonialization of arts, and to strengthen emerging local discourses, this section incorporates insights and aspirations of people involved in the Indonesian arts scenes. I consider visualizations of 'an ecosystem' as an elucidating method to include more varied, even just budding, ideas. A useful starting point for many can be to depict their own existing ecosystem to demonstrate the most important aspects and interrelation.

ruangrupa's original notions of an ecosystem, established in practice at the Gudang Sarinah Ekosistem in 2016, have been further developed and expanded with operational and positional changes in and beyond Jakarta. The active role of Gudskul for expanding the understanding of an ecosystem, premised upon knowledge exchange, cannot be overemphasized, as they have further added geographic scope to the previous programs (for example, as seen in the *OK video*), which already reached beyond Jakarta.△Fig. 1 Placing lumbung (the collective pot) in the middle to be governed by *majlis*[43] (roughly translated as a council),

42..........Supangkat, 'Indonesian and Javanese,' p. 191.

43..........Written as *majilis* in Indonesian.

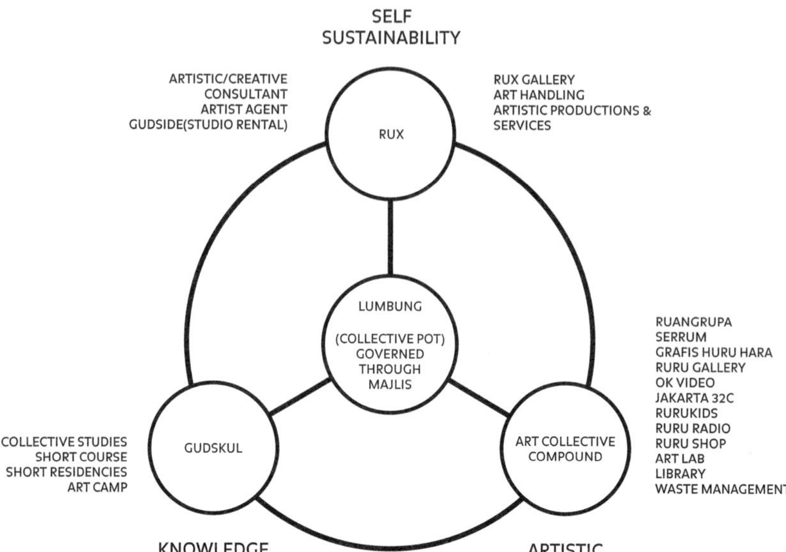


△ 1
ruangrupa's ecosystem in relation to *lumbung*,
© ruangrupa, 2020

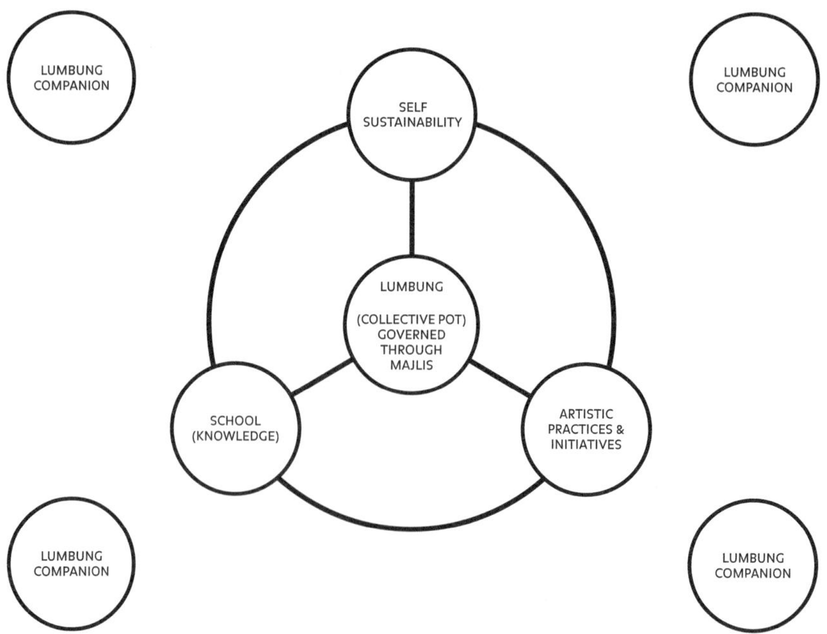


△ 2
ruangrupa's envisioning of a broader and an adaptable
model of an ecosystem, © ruangrupa, 2020

ruangrupa emphasizes the idea of the different components and collaborators working together in order to build up and share im/material resources. This tripartite understanding of an ecosystem can be further modified to include other collaborators (lumbung companions), local or international, who are willing to share their resources with these local initiatives.△Fig. 2 This model of an ecosystem is also meant to be adaptable by anyone.

While these discussions on 'ecosystem' are currently gaining attention across the Indonesian arts scenes, Kelola, a non profit art organization also based in Jakarta, has found it useful to delineate how its programmes activate and support an arts ecosystem. The original diagram was made for Kelola's Arts Grant archive exhibition in October 2019, and all the information was given by Gita Hastarika in an interview when she was still the acting director of Kelola.[44] Here below, a translated and slightly revised version of the diagram to include 'audience'.△Fig. 3

△ 3
Activation of the arts ecosystem by Kelola. ©Kelola, 2019.

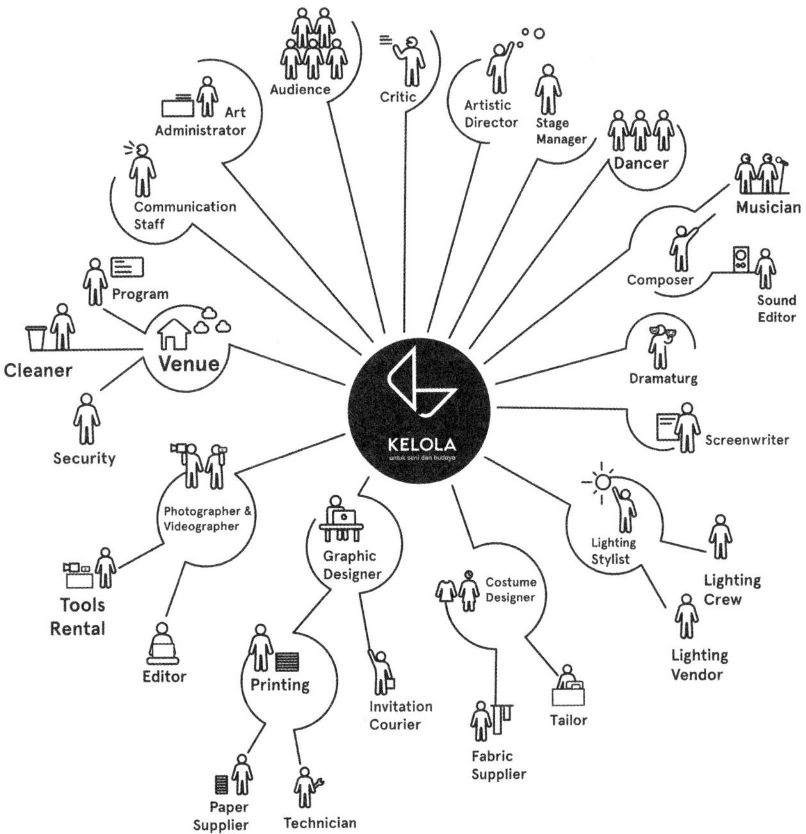


44..........Gita Hastarika, interview by author, 23 September 2019. For more information, see http://kelola.or.id/ (accessed 27 November 2019).

In this diagram, Kelola is placed in the middle, surrounded by the varied professionals and aspects required for producing an art event. Hence, the diagram is to be understood as a multi-layered process, often launched by a grant (of usually IDR 25 million) given, for instance, to an artist, dancer, composer, or a performing group, who then works together with a venue, production, marketing, and practical setting, among others, all required to create the event. Besides demonstrating the intricate interrelations, the diagram makes evident Kelola's aspirations to encourage support for arts: 'By contributing to an Art Grant, you have made a living for the entire arts ecosystem.'[45] Even though not visualized in the diagram itself, it is relevant to acknowledge that the interrelations are not all identical: the audience and the art critic do not have a similar financially beneficial relation to the production as the other forms of agency, yet they too are an inherent part of the arts ecosystem.

In an interview, Gita Hastarika regarded herself and Kelola as cultural brokers. Echoing the common notions in the fields of art, she too was concerned about sustainability, not only for Kelola, but more broadly in these ecosystems of arts and culture. For her, one of the possible survival strategies was to rely on existing and establishing new relationships with transnational and global organizations in Asia and beyond.[46]

Often in visualizations and mappings, what is placed in the centre marks what is considered a significant component or point of departure for the whole ecosystem, while the following layers indicate the supporting systems and their importance. Yet, de-centralized visualizations of an ecosystem can also provide illuminating perspectives, as shown by Arief 'Ayip' Budiman, one of the co-founders of the Rumah Sanur Creative Hub in Denpasar. Since 2014, stimulated by local Balinese knowledge emphasizing the interconnectedness of place (*desa*), time (*kala*) and context (*patra*), and reviving the spirit of the Sanur School, Rumah Sanur has built inclusive creativity mainly by nurturing a creative ecosystem and by fostering social innovation.[47] With a special focus on human-centric place-making, and using the space as 'a living lab,' Rumah Sanur and its programmes are defined by multidisciplinary collaboration, partnerships, and sustainability from music to design and from art to coffee and honey; this approach is also echoed in their understanding of a creative city ecosystem.△Fig. 4

Partially inspired by the internationally known creative city discourses, for Arief Budiman all four stakeholders (academics, community, business, and government) are essential. The core functions of this creative city ecosystem—namely creation, production, conservation, marketing and distribution, consumption, and research and development—are not fractioned according to the stakeholders' roles but are depicted as a resulting reflection from all of them. Even though the 'sustainability' of the local

45..........A slogan included in an earlier version of the diagram.

46..........Ibid.

47..........The richness and depth of the philosophy behind Rumah Sanur's involvement with communities, explained by Arief Budiman (in an interview by author, 11 September 2019) cannot be discussed here in detail. For more information, see Rumah Sanur's website, accessed 25 February 2020, https://rumahsanur.com/.

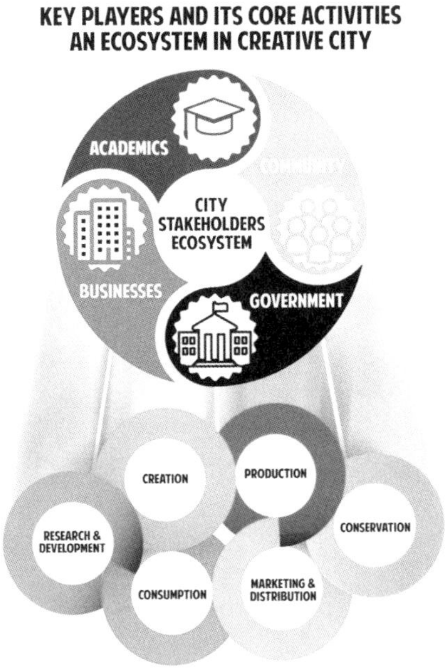

△ 4
A creative city ecosystem, © Arief 'Ayip' Budiman, 2019

communities, artists, producers, and brands is not explicitly mentioned in this diagram, it is the inherent key notion highlighting the interrelatedness of key players and activities as a basis of a vigorous ecosystem in Denpasar and beyond.

While this visualization also indicates flexibility of practices in an ecosystem, more emphasis on the inherent fluidity and informality of an art ecosystem is given in a diagram by Ayos Purwoaji, curator and co-founder of the C20 Library & Collabtive, an independent library and coworking community space established in Surabaya in 2008.[48] With a specific focus on visual arts, Purwoaji seeks to demonstrate how the function, position, and interrelations of varied forms of agency may shift according to the circumstances. The connecting lines are also flexible, indicating mutual ongoing negotiations within Indonesia (the connected ones) and with international agency (partially unattached ones). △Fig. 5

As Purwoaji explains,

> [U]sually, one circle is organically connected with another circle. Maybe this is one of the cultural patterns of Indonesian people who like to gather, help each other (*gotong royong*) and be

48..........Ayos Purwoaji, interview by author, 15 September 2019. For more about the prolific programs for and approach to a sustainable and emancipatory future, see the C20 Library & Collabtive's website, https://c2o-library.net/ (accessed 26 February 2020).

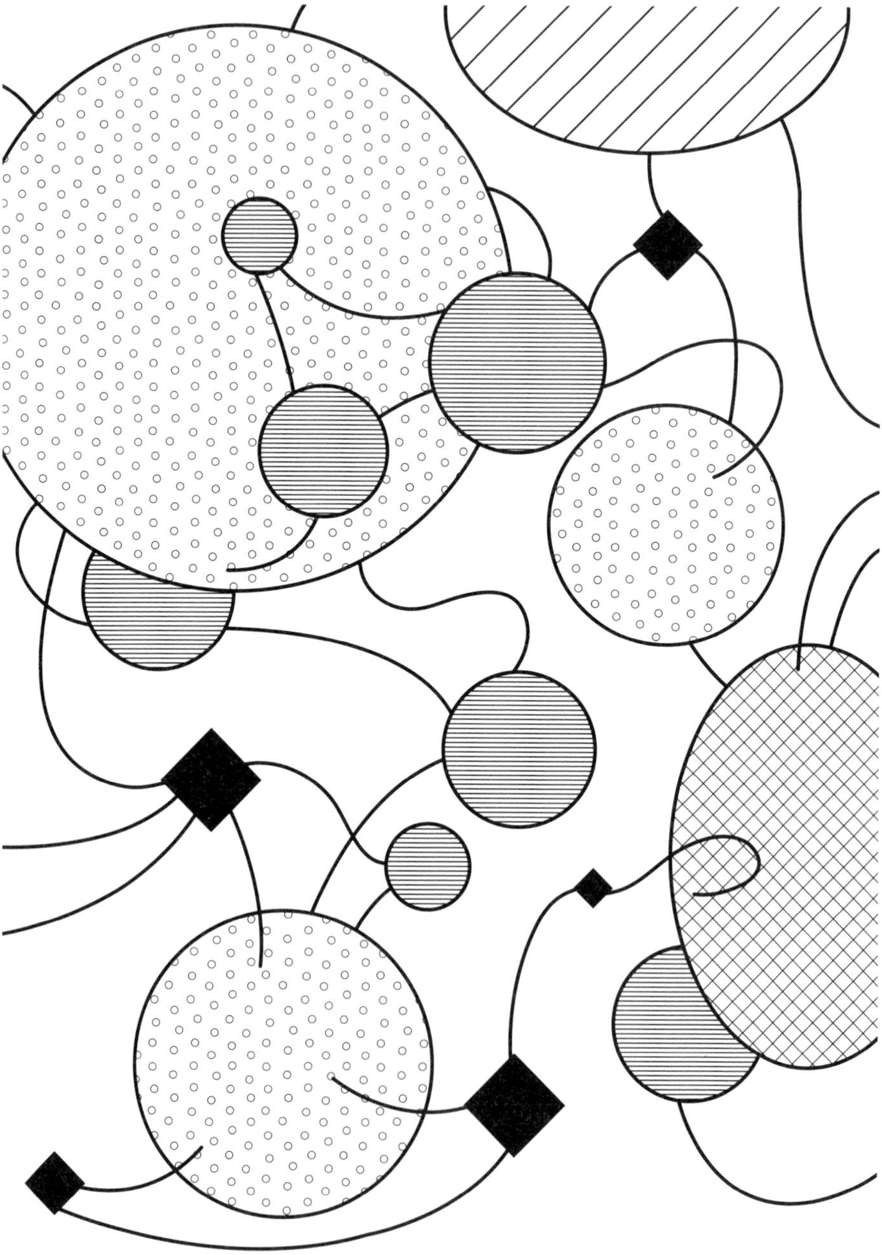

△ 5
Art ecosystem in Indonesia,
© Ayos Purwoaji, 2020

Art schools / Government / State

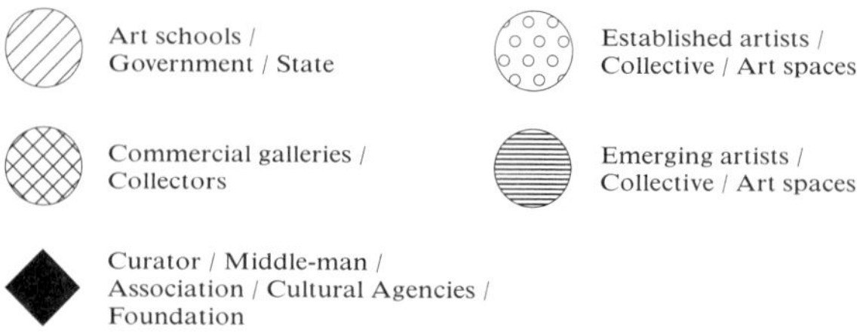

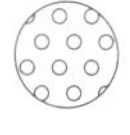
Established artists / Collective / Art spaces

Commercial galleries / Collectors

Emerging artists / Collective / Art spaces

Curator / Middle-man / Association / Cultural Agencies / Foundation

> involved. The larger circles ( ) represent an established artist, collective, or art space. In many cases, they become patrons for smaller (emerging) artists, collectives, or art spaces. Yet, the term patronage needs to be studied further because of its informal nature. These circles are also connected by black diamond shapes that spread around the ecosystem, representing the position of curator, middle-man, cultural agencies (Japan Foundation, Goethe-Institute, IFI), association (Koalisi Seni) or foundation which is a great liaison between actors and supporters of artistic events that occur.[49]

Purwoaji's diagram displays the established artists, spaces, and collectives in a different form, pattern and size from those in the process of emerging and is therefore also an initiative to investigate the existing power relations in the art ecosystem. He however emphasizes how both the emerging and the established ones together are the most important component for the growth of the art ecosystem. The two other stakeholders, art schools, government and state ( ), and commercial galleries and collectors ( ) are somewhat partially depicted because he does not see them as major players in the current arts ecosystem. Due to new forms of knowledge available (the internet for example) and somewhat out-dated curricula, the role of art schools is diminishing. Regardless of numerous new events since the beginning of the twenty-first century and emerging young collectors, the art market still bears elite tones 'and has not yet become a decisive voice for the development of the art ecosystem in the broadest sense.' Yet, for Purwoaji, the crucial question remains, 'Where is the general people in the development of the art ecosystem in Indonesia?'[50]

One possible approach to this question can be envisioned through a more metaphoric comprehension of an ecosystem, as depicted by artist Budi Agung Kuswara from the Ketemu Project. This transnational art collective and social enterprise, which he and Samantha Tio established in 2011, has a keen interest in creating art with people who are socially marginalized because of their disabilities.[51] Placing Ketemu as a node in an organically growing hybrid rose with three sets of roots, the image illustrates Ketemu's existing position in the contemporary cultural ecosystem of Bali.△Fig. 6 For Ketemu, 'contemporary' emphasizes the importance of innovation and sets their aspirations apart from the heritage ecosystem, where one of the key objectives is preservation.

49...........Ayos Purwoaji, email message to author, 10 January 2020.
50...........Ibid.
51...........For more information, see Ketemu's website, http://ketemu.org/ (accessed 15 February 2020).

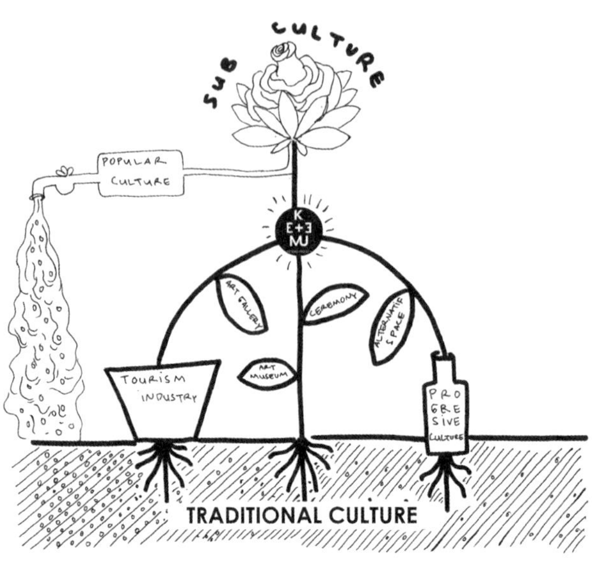


△ 6
Ketemu's existing position in the contemporary cultural ecosystem of Bali, ©Budi Agung Kuswara, 2020

Although in this envisioning Ketemu is positioned in the context of Bali (where the project has its main project space), transnationality is one of the defining characteristics of their programmes and of their understanding of 'ecosystem.' Working in particular between Singapore and Bali, but also in close collaboration with other non profit organizations in the region, especially in smaller cities, Ketemu relies on international intellectual, and financial support. The societal position of disabled people in Indonesia has not yet gained enough official attention, and art made by them is not perceived to be a part of the 'contemporary art' discourse. Hence, Ketemu prefers reducing the social stigma through a change in language and by advocating the acceptance of the 'differently-abled' as a part of the communities.[52]

As these visualizations demonstrate, the understanding of an 'ecosystem' and its key characteristics depends upon a multitude of factors: from professional and institutional background to geographic location, from form of art to age, and from current position (marginality/centrality) to future aspirations. Furthermore, the envisioning of an ecosystem rests on the chosen perspective and emphasis on im/material aspects: a physical space (such as an art collective) or an operational mode (for instance, a non profit foundation) may be taken as an ecosystem of its own and may be expanded to include a network of collaborators. The ecosystem approach can also have a broader geographical scope based on a city, a nation, and/or international relations; it may also shift the focus

52..........Information deriving from a wsite visit on the main project space in Denpasar and interviews of the staff members with the author on 9 September 2019; Samantha Tio and Budi Agung Kuswara, interview by the author, 11 December 2019.

on immaterial modalities that have an impact on the varied ecosystem(s), such as laws and regulations, value structures, and interrelations between traditions and contemporary practices. Additionally, it may include aspects of these different approaches into a multi-layered envisioning.

These diagrams already provide an illuminating summary of the shifting multidimensionalities of an 'ecosystem' and include various facets also mentioned by many other professionals engaged with this study. Still, some key aspects, which are not depicted in these diagrams, deserve to be discussed in more detail—in particular in terms of future developments as seen in the next section. Furthermore, a vital part of the current ecosystem(s) and its/their evolvement, insightfully identified by Abdi Karya, an artist from Makassar, needs to be acknowledged: the increasingly advanced technology that creates unforeseen possibilities for more inclusive and open ecosystems both locally and nationally (for example, for Koalisi Seni) and in particular, regarding distribution and exchange of information.[53] Even though technology and/or (social) media are not explicitly included in these visualizations, they could be understood not only as inherent facilitators for many strengthening processes of ecosystems but also as related elements of power structures which may be employed for multiple purposes.

## TOWARDS ADVANCEMENT IN ECOSYSTEM(S)

During the interviews and informal discussions, it became evident that in addition to the great variety of perceptions on the current conditions of 'ecosystem(s),' there is a concomitant diversity of ideas for how these often-precarious positions could be improved. Even in regards of 'a local art ecosystem,' the insights vary according to regional, professional, and disciplinary lines and hence, bring forward the need for reconciliation of value structures and priorities. Aspirations for further advancement of arts span a range of practical suggestions, from enhancing material infrastructure (for example, spaces and financial support) to developing art education and appreciation (including broader audiences), to advocacy for and about arts (in particular, hopes for and trust in the Koalisi Seni), to ideological aspects (such as rights of artists, freedom of expression).

The majority of the interviewees underlined the role of Koalisi Seni for developing the national art(s) ecosystem(s) through advocacy; in particular, Koalisi Seni's direct involvement in formulating the Law on the Advancement of Culture, and more recently, their efforts in relation to the new Cultural Endowment Fund (CEF, *Dana Abadi Kebudayaan*).[54] Currently, Koalisi Seni is working on a more general, metalevel analysis of

53 .......... Abdi Karya, interview by Dara Hanafi, 12 July 2019.

54 .......... For the latter, Koalisi Seni studied mainly arts practitioners' views on what should be prioritized by the CEF. They did this through a widely distributed questionnaire (and received 1729 replies) and five group discussions in four cities (Jakarta, Yogyakarta, Payakumbuh, and Makassar) from November 2019 to January 2020. Koalisi Seni secretariat, email message to author, 6 February 2020.

arts ecosystem and hence emphasizes that 'a healthier arts ecosystem' is still a working definition that has not yet been tested in the Indonesian context. In an effort to do so, Koalisi Seni will continue to conduct further research. Still, the core characteristics of the ecosystem are to 'be generative and open. It is an organism, not a fixed mechanism, and it should be able to capture not just the economic, but also social and cultural relations between actors.'[55]

Especially in relation to immaterial modalities, the complexities of these emerging understandings of 'ecosystem(s)' can be further investigated by identifying four key issues not yet explicitly illustrated above but raised throughout the site visits and discussions: quality of interrelations, gender, generational differences, and Java-centrism. All of these contribute to the intricate notion of 'balance' in an ecosystem(s). This more inclusive and equality-driven approach is called for by the majority of the participants in this study, and is crystallized in the words of Rahmadiyah Tria Gayathri, a Koalisi Seni member from Palu, Sulawesi, 'I wish there was no more hierarchy in the arts.'[56]

Because 'ecosystem' remains vaguely defined and is often used quite metaphorically in current parlance, it often mirrors the notion of a local natural ecosystem built on a symbiosis between different 'species,' fertile ground, and reciprocal collaboration to maintain a balance. Yet, as Brigitta Isabella, a member of KUNCI insightfully explains, 'The idealistic view of ecosystem as everything works in harmony through "natural law" would sometimes fail to recognize the often exploitative patron-client or master-servant relationship in the art world.' Hence, the possibility of existing predatory relationships should be acknowledged 'because the "organisms" that interact in the "ecosystem" are not always equal in terms of their access and ownership of social and financial capital.' An example is 'gender imbalance and how it influences the quality of relationship in the "ecosystem."'[57]

The importance of gender in the evolving discussions on art(s) ecosystem(s) was similarly highlighted with other interviewed women. Some pointed out how the prevailing patriarchy not only in arts but also in the society at large hinders both female artists and women protagonists in all spheres of the arts scenes. Many women may be actively involved in arts and culture, and hold a great variety of professional positions in society, but they do not share equal visibility, possibilities, and access to resources as men in arts.[58] While the intricate cultural and historical challenges for a feminist approach in arts are far too extensive to be addressed here,[59] improving possibilities for women through parallel ecosystems created and maintained by women (only) can bring new contingencies but also risks in terms of further isolation and marginalization because of gender. One of

55 ........... Ibid.
56 ........... Gayathri, interview.
57 ........... Brigitta Isabella, in a group interview with three representatives of KUNCI by the author, 12 December 2018; email message to author, 14 February 2020.
58 ........... Ruth Onduko, interview by author, 12 September 2019; Naomi Srikandi, interview by author, 17 November 2019.
59 ........... For a detailed and illuminating analysis of the emergence of feminism(s), see Wulan Dirgantoro, *Feminisms and Contemporary Art in Indonesia: Defining Experiences* (Amsterdam: Amsterdam University Press, 2017).

the most important practical questions raised by this study for further discussion is: How can women be included in these emerging multidisciplinary ecosystems of arts, culture, and creativity, and how can they achieve genuine equity?

Apart from gender aspects, notions of an unequal position in art(s) ecosystem(s) can also be based on one's geographical location and/or ethnic/religious identity. In Indonesia, multiple non profit organizations and official programmes on arts, culture, and creativity have aimed to deconstruct Java-centrism in the twenty-first century. And yet, regardless of growing collaborations and practical improvements for more equal appreciation and representation of arts from outer islands, Java-centrism is still widely acknowledged. The realities, such as lack of information, inefficient or non-accessible local government programmes, hierarchies (cultural, intellectual, and aesthetic, among others), and the resulting prejudices in, for instance, the valuation of 'arts from outer islands,' are felt among non-Javanese artists and cultural practitioners including those currently based on Java. The present situation partially stems from the existing mindset of practitioners on outer islands themselves and the tendency to keep art practices in Java in higher esteem.[60] As Rahmadiyah Tria Gayathri from Palu summarizes,

> I think in a healthy arts ecosystem, every art community has the same access to information, both communities in the central and in other regions. This also applies to information from the central government on what kind of programmes they have especially for the arts and culture, and if there is a budget accessible for the local community to run a corresponding programme.[61]

Similarly, because of the internal hierarchies in arts and culture, both younger-generation unestablished artists and other junior protagonists voice their concerns about unequal positions in the existing ecosystems (see also Fig. 5). For example, representatives of the Indonesian Visual Art Archive (IVAA) articulate that

> A healthy art ecosystem gives space for the young generation to grow. Its dynamics are based on healthy competition, openness to criticism, and it has a balanced number of practitioners, critics, collectors, managers, etc., so that it enables us to grow in balance.[62]

60 Information based on six phone interviews of representatives from outer islands by Dara Hanafi.

61 Gayathri, interview.

Similar aspirations of balanced and inclusive art(s) ecosystem(s) are voiced by many, highlighting the importance of having a broader understanding of arts and its audiences to encompass, among others, children, the elderly, villagers in rural areas, and residents of less-privileged urban settlements too. Some would even prefer the primary denominator for art(s) ecosystem(s) to be 'balanced' rather than 'healthy.'

Indeed, one of the aims and challenges in Indonesia is to create balanced circumstances in its abundant cultural environment that will allow the protection and development of arts, culture, and creativity, whilst supporting both the traditional and experimental forms of these to flourish. These intricate realities apply to individual practitioners, communities, local governments, and national cultural policies alike. These policies are a work in progress based on the Principles of Regional Cultural Thoughts (PPKD), gathered and provided by around 300 municipal regencies. One aim of such processes is to gradually contribute to the 'effort to improve cultural resilience (*ketahanan budaya*),' the meaning of which remains to be further discussed during the implementation of the Law. As Hilmar Farid emphasizes, *ketahanan* is about 'keeping the essence' of the cultural form in question (e.g., *wayang*, shadow puppetry), even if it is developed to be more experimental, 'absorbing innovation and technologies without losing the core value.'[63] While such an approach is invaluable, it may come with difficult negotiation processes. For instance, as Melani Budianta insightfully reminds us, Indonesian culture is so rich and diverse that the essential question is not about the concept and its definition, but rather from whose perspective cultural resilience is talked about—resilience against what and whom?[64]

## CONCLUSIONS

The absence of adequate official and national infrastructure supporting arts, culture, and creativity together with the contingencies brought about by transnational collaborations highlight the precarious position of artists and arts in Indonesia. Embedded with socio-political and cultural transitions, the questions of impartial integration and equal opportunities for artists and other cultural professionals alike have become ever more topical along with the emergent discussions on how to develop multidisciplinary and multi-layered ecosystems of arts, culture, and creativity.

The forthcoming move of the capital to East Kalimantan opens up new possibilities and uncertainties to these pertinent questions of the future ecosystems of arts, culture, and creativity and their transitions, emphasizing the potential to further deconstruct Java-centrism—at least to some extent. As Nursalim Yadi Anugerah, musician/composer from Pontianak

62.......... Representatives of IVAA, email message to author, 23 January 2020. For more information about IVAA and its programs, see their website, http://ivaa-online.org/ (accessed 25 January 2020).

63.......... Farid, interview.

64.......... Melani Budianta (professor of literature and cultural studies at the Faculty of Humanities, Universitas Indonesia), interview by the author, 19 September 2020.

65.......... Nursalim Yadi Anugerah, interview by Dara Hanafi, 11 February 2020.

asserts, what is crucial for building local and national arts and cultural ecosystems in the possible future capital is to avoid their simple importation and implementation, and rather to develop them in close collaboration with the already existing structures in Kalimantan.[65]

For a majority of the representatives, the focus of the discourse understandably lies within Indonesia, but for some, sustainable art(s) ecosystem(s) also collaborate on a regional and global scale to ensure that issues not yet fully recognized in Indonesia gain support and acknowledgement. Based on the many insights gathered in this study, a sustainable form of an art(s) ecosystem(s) is most importantly inclusive, collaborative, balanced, equal, supportive, flexible, open and organic, and pays close attention to questions of gender, demographic indicators, geographical locations, and the opportunities of citizens (both in rural and urban areas) to engage with arts. Even though these denominators may appear self-evident, given the pertaining intricate socio-political, economic, and cultural conditions in Indonesia, creating such ecosystem(s) is bound with a multitude of practical and ideological challenges.

As these insights together with the visualizations above indicate, the first step is to delineate what kinds of understandings already exist in order to carry out a nuanced investigation of possible local, national, regional, and global ecosystems and their interrelations. Such a multiperspective and -disciplinary ecosystem analysis approach may then contribute towards improving the current position and role of arts, culture, and creativity. Central to any in-depth characterization of an ecosystem is deep-seated multidimensionality, which extends beyond the core creative process to include a multitude of facilitating forms of agency, production, and audience, but also media, collectors, educators, critics, patronage, and officials, among others. Yet, it is even more important to recognize that deciphering the present and tangible forms of agency and infrastructure is not enough. The intangible modalities that shape the ecosystem(s) (regulations, power relations, gender, cultural traditions, value structures, etc.) need to also be acknowledged and investigated. Only through these gradual multifaceted approaches including both qualitative and quantitative methods along with material and immaterial aspects can the most feasible indicators for further assessment be found.

What emerges in this study is a notion of an 'ecosystem' defined by complexities and fluidity that requires a nuanced combination of perceptions, aspirations, and value structures. Taking into consideration that 'arts,' 'culture,' and 'creativity' are defined by interdependences and continuous renegotiations today in Indonesia, any definite approach to an 'ecosystem' is likely to remain unfeasible. Comprehensions on 'art(s) ecosystem(s)' inevitably vary between geographic locations, institutions, and individual representatives of the related fields and are often seen as inherently part of other cultural and/or creative ecosystem(s). Hence, it is more illuminating for the current discourses and practices to admit that any ecosystem will be premised on continuous transformations and will therefore require repeated acts of translations and mediations between envisionings, partakers, and gatekeepers.

These varied points of departure on 'ecosystem(s)' are all invaluable and useful to anyone working with questions of the sustainability, role, and potential of arts, culture, and creativity—even beyond Indonesia. Acknowledging the great confluence of envisionings on what constitutes an ecosystem not only enriches the discussion but also fosters more nuanced understandings on what is, could, and should be taken into account in an analysis of the current state of ecosystem(s) and, even more importantly, in planning their reformulation. Understanding how the varied interests and power relations are negotiated, mediated, and achieved at local, national, and international levels in the processes of developing more balanced arts, cultural, and/or creative ecosystems can help us further comprehend the challenges in building towards a feasible regeneration of cultural resilience.

ACKNOWLEDGEMENTS

This study has been made possible only by the tremendous generosity and kindness of numerous people involved in Indonesian arts, culture, and creativity. I wish to express my warmest gratitude to every single one of you who have shared your precious time and insights on, among others, arts, ecosystems, policies, and personal aspirations. Every bit of information has enabled me to understand more about the endless intricacies of these issues, although not everything could be included in this paper.

Jiser Reflexions Mediterrànies / Algiers, Algeria / 11:29am     36°45'14"N / 3°3'32"E

Pages Bookstore Amsterdam / Amsterdam, the Netherlands / 11:34am 52°21'56.7"N / 4°53'57.4"E

← REFERENCES


Abidin, Linda Hoemar, Mirwan Andan, and Abduh Aziz. 'Menanggapi RUU Kebudayaan' ['A Response to the Draft of Cultural Law']. *Kompas*, 26 May 2013.

Andan, Mirwan. 'All for Jakarta: A Note on the Tenth Anniversary of Ruangrupa: Decompression #10, Expanding the Space and Public.' *Inter-Asia Cultural Studies* 12, no. 4 (2011), pp. 591–602.

Arts Collaboratory. 'Assembly Indonesia 2014.' www.artscollaboratory.org/meetings/assembly/assembly-2014 (accessed 5 January 2020).
—. 'Common Language.' www.artscollaboratory.org/about/common-language-index-of-terms/ (accessed on 5 January 2020).

Asian Art Archives. 'In the Aftermath of the White Cube: Museums and other Spaces.' https://aaa.org.hk/en/programmes/programmes/in-the-aftermath-of-the-white-cube-museums-and-other-spaces/ (accessed 10 December 2019).

*Āto, seitaikei: bijutsu hyōgen no 'shizen' to 'seisaku.' Art Ecosystem: The Contemporary Japanese Art Scene*. Utsunomiya: Utsunomiya Museum of Art, 1998.

Audretsch, David B., et al. 'Entrepreneurial Ecosystems: Economic, Technological, and Societal Impacts.' *The Journal of Technology Transfer* 44, no. 2 (2019), pp. 313–25.

Beittinger-Lee, Verena. *(Un)civil Society and Political Change in Indonesia: A Contested Arena*. London: Routledge, 2009.

Budianta, Melani. 'Smart Kampung: Doing Cultural Studies in the Global South.' *Communication and Critical/Cultural Studies* 16, no. 3 (2019), pp. 241–56.

C20 Library & Collabtive. https://c2o-library.net/ (accessed 26 February 2020).

Createquity. 'A Healthy Arts Ecosystem.' https://createquity.com/about/a-healthy-arts-ecosystem/ (accessed 25 October 2019).

'The Cultural Dynamics Map: Exploring the Arts Ecosystem in the United States.' Version 1.0, March 2005. www.artstrategies.org/downloads/CulturalMap_v1.pdf (accessed 17 November 2019).

Dirgantoro, Wulan. *Feminisms and Contemporary Art in Indonesia: Defining Experiences*. Amsterdam: Amsterdam University Press, 2017.

Djatiprambudi, Djuli. 'Saat Menulis Sejarah Seni Rupa Sendiri' ['When Writing Your Own Fine Art History']. In *Biennale Jatim 6: 'Arts Ecosystem: Now!,'* pp. 6–22. Surabaya: Department of Culture and Tourism, East Java, 2015.

Eldridge, Philip. 'NGOs and the State in Indonesia.' In *State and Civil Society in Indonesia*, ed. Arief Budiman, pp. 503–38. Clayton: Centre of Southeast Asian Studies, Monash University, 1990.

Flores, Patrick D. *Past Peripheral: Curation in Southeast Asia*. Singapore: NUS Museum, 2009.

Hadiwinata, Bob S. *The Politics of NGOs in Indonesia: Developing Democracy and Managing a Movement*. London: Routledge/Curzon, 2003.

Halim, HD. 'Arts Networks and the Struggle for Democratisation.' In *Reformasi: Crisis and Change in Indonesia*, ed. Arief Budiman, Barbara Hatley, and Damien Kingsbury, pp. 287–98. Clayton: Monash Asia Institute, 1999.

Indonesian Visual Art Archives. http://ivaa-online.org/ (accessed 25 January 2020).

Jones, Tod. *Culture, Power, and Authoritarianism in the Indonesian State: Cultural Policy Across the Twentieth-century to the Reform Era*. Leiden: Brill, 2013.

Juliastuti, Nuraini. 'ruangrupa: A Conversation on Horizontal Organisation.' *Afterall: A Journal of Art, Context and Enquiry* 30, no. 1 (2012), pp. 118–25.

Kaur, Raminder and Parul Dave-Mukherji. 'Introduction.' In *Art and Aesthetics in a Globalizing World*, ed. Raminder Kaur and Parul Dave-Mukherji, pp. 1–19. New York: Bloomsbury Academic, 2015.

Ketemu Project. http://ketemu.org/ (accessed 15 February 2020).

Koalisi Seni Indonesia. https://koalisiseni.or.id/ (accessed 25 March 2020).

Kreps, Christina F. *Liberating Culture: Cross-Cultural Perspectives on Museums, Curation, and Heritage Preservation*. London: Routledge, 2003.

KUNCI. http://kunci.or.id/ (accessed 25 February 2020).

McCullough, Lawrence. 'Grow Your Own Local Artists: How Any Community Can Cultivate a Robust Arts Ecosystem.' *Public Management* 100, no. 4 (2018), pp. 14–16.

Ministry of Education and Culture. Law No. 5/2017 on Advancement of Culture. Undang-undang Republic Indonesia Nomor 5 Tahun 2017, Tentang Pemajuan Kebudayaan. https://kebudayaan.kemdikbud.go.id/uu-no-5-tahun-2017-tentang-pemajuan-kebudayaan/ (accessed 2 January 2020).

Morrell, Elizabeth. 'Ethnicity, Art, and Politics away from the Indonesian Centre.' *Sojourn: Journal of Social Issues in Southeast Asia* 15, no. 2 (2000), pp. 255–72.

Moss, Ian David. 'An Ecosystem-Based Approach to Arts Research,' *Fractured Atlas Blog*, 17 October 2011. www.fracturedatlas.org/site/blog/an-ecosystem-based-approach-to-arts-research.

National Art Council of Singapore. 'The Arts and Culture Employment Study 2016.' www.nac.gov.sg/whatwedo/support/research/Research-Main-Page/Arts-Statistics-and-Studies/Arts-Ecosystem/Arts-and-Culture-Employment-Study-.html (accessed 17 November 2019).
—. 'Singapore Art Show 2009.' www.nac.gov.sg/media-resources/press-releases/Singapore-Art-Show-2009.html (accessed 10 December 2019).

Novani, Santi, Cici Cintyawati, and Lidia Mayangsari. 'Back to the Future: A Revelation of Conventional Platform Preference of Digital Creative Ecosystem Entities in Bandung.' In *Collaborative Value Co-creation in the Platform Economy*, ed. Anssi Smedlund, Arto Lindblom, and Lasse Mitronen, pp. 247–68. Singapore: Springer, 2018.

O'Neil, Jacqueline. 'How to Serve All Parts of the Art Ecosystem, from Artist to Institution.' *Blockchain Art Collective*, 30 October 2018. https://medium.com/blockchain-art-collective/how-to-serve-all-parts-of-the-art-ecosystem-from-artist-to-institution-79e9c532b0b1.

Ooi Can-Seng, and Roberta Comunian. 'The Artrepreneurial Ecosystem in Singapore: Enable and Inhibit the Creative Economy.' In *Routledge Handbook of Cultural and Creative Industries in Asia*, ed. Lorraine Lim and Hye-Kyung Lee, pp. 57–71. London: Routledge, 2018.

Den Oudendammer, Juliet. 'The Art Ecosystem, and Why Some Artists Are More Successful than Others.' In *Art Represent*, 7 December 2015. www.artrepresent.com/blog/the-art-ecosystem.

Petterson, Anders. 'Value, Risk and the Contemporary Art Ecosystem.' In *Risk and Uncertainty in the Art World*, ed. Anna M. Dempster, pp. 67–86. London: Bloomsbury Information Ltd, 2014.

Ruangrupa. *Expanding the Space and Public. Ruangrupa's 10th Anniversary*. Exh. cat. Jakarta: Indonesian National Gallery, 2010.
—. Available at ruru.ruangrupa.org (accessed 2 February 2020).

Rumah Sanur. https://rumahsanur.com/ (accessed 25 February 2020).

Samboh, Grace. 'Becoming: In Search of the Social Artists, Locating Their Environments, Reorienting the Planet.' In *Making Another World Possible: 10 Creative Time Summits, 10 Global Issues, 100 Art Projects*, ed. Corina L. Apostol and Nato Thompson, pp. 106–22. London: Routledge, 2019.

Satō, Dōshin. *Modern Japanese Art and the Meiji State: The Politics of Beauty*. Los Angeles: Getty Research Institute, 2011.

Spanjaard, Helena. *Artists and Their Inspiration: A Guide through Indonesian Art History (1930–2015)*. Volendam: LM Publishers, 2016.

Spielmann, Yvonne. *Contemporary Indonesian Art: Artists, Art Spaces, and Collectors*. Expanded and updated English ed. Singapore: NUS Press, 2017.

Supangkat, Jim. 'Arts and Politics in Indonesia.' In *Art and Social Change: Contemporary Art in Asia and the Pacific*, ed. Caroline Turner, pp. 218–28. Canberra: Pandanus Books, 2005.
—. 'Indonesian and Javanese.' *Southeast of Now* 2, no. 2 (2018), pp. 187–95.
—. *Indonesian Modern Art and Beyond*. Jakarta: Indonesia Fine Arts Foundation, 1997.

Tsui, Denise. 'A Grassroots Perspective on Yogyakarta's Art World.' *Journal of Southeast Asian Studies* 46, no. 3 (2015), pp. 537–45.

Turner, Caroline. 'Indonesia: Art, Freedom, Human Rights and Engagement with the West.' In *Art and Social Change: Contemporary Art in Asia and the Pacific*, ed. Caroline Turner, pp. 196–217. Canberra: Pandanus Books, 2005.

Vanhoe, Reinaart. *Also-Space: How Indonesian Art Initiatives Have Reinvented Networking*. Eindhoven: Onomatopee, 2016.

Wu Mali and Francesco Manacorda. 'Post-Nature: A Museum as an Ecosystem.'www.taipeibiennial.org/2018/?lang=en (accessed 10 March 2020).

## ← INTERVIEWS

Ade Darmawan, member of ruangrupa, interview by author, 6 December 2018.

Brigitta Isabella, member of KUNCI Study Forum & Collective, in a group interview with three representatives of KUNCI by author, 12 December 2018.

Koalisi Seni secretariat, administrative team, and board members, interviews by and discussions with author in a planning meeting and workshop in Yogyakarta on 13–14 December 2018.

Koalisi Seni members, interviews by and discussions with author in a planning meeting and workshop in Yogyakarta on 13–14 December 2018.

Koalisi Seni secretariat, administrative team, and board members, group interviews by author 2 May 2019.

Otty Widasari Rancajale, Hafiz Rancajale, Andang Kelana, and Manshur Zikri, members of Forum Lenteng, a group interview by author, 4 May 2019.

Ade Darmawan, Reza Afisina, Farid Rakun, and Leonard Barto, members of ruangrupa, a group interview by author, 6 May 2019.

Jim Supangkat, interview by author, 8 May 2019.

Abdi Karya, artist in Makassar, interview by Dara Hanafi, 12 July 2019.

Rudolf Dethu, author/music journalist, Koalisi Seni member in Denpasar, interview by Dara Hanafi, 12 July 2019.

Linda Tagie, artist in Kupang, interview by Dara Hanafi, 15 July 2019.

Heri Budiman, artist in Riau, Koalisi Seni member, interview by Dara Hanafi, 27 July 2019.

Members of Gudskul, Serrum and Grafis Huru Hara, interviews by and discussions with author, 4 September 2019.

Ketemu staff members, a group interview by author, 9 September 2019.

Arief 'Ayip' Budiman, co-founder of the Rumah Sanur Creative Hub, interview by author, 11 September 2019.

Ruth Onduko, co-founder of Futuwonder collective, interview by author, 12 September 2019.

Ayos Purwoaji, curator and co-founder of the C20 Library & Collabtive, interview by author, 15 September 2019.

Gustaff Harriman Iskandar, co-founder/managing director of Common Room, interview by author, 17 September 2019.

Hilmar Farid, the Director General of Culture, interview by author, 18 September 2019.

Elisa Sutanudjaja, Executive Director of Rujak Center for Urban Studies, interview by author, 18 September 2019.

Melani Budianta, Professor of Literature and Cultural Studies at the Faculty of Humanities, Universitas Indonesia, interview by author, 19 September 2020.

Amna Kusumo, founder of Kelola, interview by author, 23 September 2019.

Gita Hastarika, director of Kelola, interview by author, 23 September 2019.

Julia Sarisetiati, member of ruangrupa, interview by author, 23 September 2019.

Linda Mayasari, team member of Cemeti - Institute for Art and Society, interview by author, 15 November 2019.

Naomi Srikandi, theatre maker, co-founder of Peretas (Women Across Borders), interview by author, 17 November 2019.

Jeannie Park, Executive Director of Bagong Kussudiardja Foundation, interview by author, 18 November 2019.

Mella Jaarsma, co-counder of Cemeti, interview by author, 19 November 2019.

Samantha Tio (Mintio) and Budi Agung Kuswara (Kabul), founders of Ketemu, interview by author, 11 December 2019.

Ayos Purwoaji, email message to author, 10 January 2020.

Rahmadiyah Tria Gayathri, Koalisi Seni member in Palu, Sulawesi, interview by Dara Hanafi, 10 January 2020.

Representatives of IVAA, email message to author, 23 January 2020.

Koalisi Seni secretariat, email message to author, 6 February 2020.

Nursalim Yadi Anugerah, musician/composer in Pontianak, interview by Dara Hanafi, 11 February 2020.

Brigitta Isabella, email message to author, 14 February 2020.

Koalisi Seni secretariat, email message to author, 30 April 2020.

# THE SUSTAINABILITY OF CONTEMPORARY ARTS SPACES IN GHANA, TANZANIA, AND UGANDA

Kobina Ankomah-Graham and
Joseph Oduro-Frimpong

Recent years have seen the emergence of a number of independent art spaces promoting art and artists from across the African continent. This trend has boosted the visibility of the talent of contemporary African artists to audiences within the continent and beyond. With the burgeoning of such spaces, we investigate and document the successes and challenges of these arts centres. The three centres discussed in this article are The Nubuke Foundation (Ghana), Nafasi Art Space (Tanzania), and 32° East Uganda Arts Trust (Uganda). Based on our interviews with managers and practitioners, we argue that the key to the success of these centres is their community building practices and their creation of art spaces that reach beyond the tourist gaze.

Keywords
→ Contemporary African Art
→ Not-for-Profit Art Spaces
→ African Cities

## INTRODUCTION

Over the last decade, practicing artists across Africa have faced two main challenges: the withdrawal of state support from the art and culture sector and the rise in global attention to and taste for contemporary African art. Artists and art centres across the continent have had to confront the concomitant and ever-present challenge of resolving the tension between supporting locally-informed and locally-networked art spaces and being answerable to international funders. The international press has applauded the establishment of new arts venues like the Savannah Centre for Contemporary Art (SCCA) in Tamale, Ghana, and Zeitz Museum of Contemporary Art Africa (MOCAA) in Cape Town, South Africa, which operate through the support and endowments of private funders. At the other end of this spectrum are smaller and sometimes rather modest not-for-profit art spaces such as the Kuona Trust Arts Centre in Nairobi (Kenya) and privately-owned commercial galleries like Gallery 1957 in Accra (Ghana).[1] This chapter is based on research conducted by the Centre for African Popular Culture at Ashesi University and addresses the following questions: How can scholars and funders support independent art spaces in Africa? How can the Centre for African Popular Culture provide funders and sponsors with useful information to make decisions guided by best practice?

## ON INDEPENDENT ART SPACES IN AFRICA

Most contemporary African countries are characterized by a (near) absence of government interest in providing 'funding and infrastructure, [compelling] individuals and organizations [to step] in to fill the gaps.'[2] As a result, the promotion of African art and artists is led by independent or private art spaces such as GawLab and The Village des Arts (Senegal), First Floor Gallery (Zimbabwe), Centre for Contemporary Art, Lagos (Nigeria), Townhouse Gallery (Egypt), and ANO (Ghana).

Although we currently know more about such independent art spaces in terms of their support and showcasing of both established and emerging artists as well as their ability to 'challenge the white cube that is frequently adopted by commercial art galleries and other exhibition spaces,'[3] not much is known about their successful operation(s) and their focus on 'cultural initiatives to compensate for lack of public cultural institutions.'[4] By examining and sharing key insights regarding these efforts, we aim to provide input for art centres in other African contexts that seek future funding and support. It is in this spirit that this research was undertaken—through a four-week ethnographic research on art scenes in the African cities of Accra (Nubuke Foundation), Dar es Salaam (Nafasi Art Space), and Kampala (32° East Uganda Arts Trust).

This chapter is motivated by two key concerns: to document the work happening in contemporary not-for-profit art spaces in Africa, and understand the challenges such organizations face, as well as the best practices the art spaces espouse in realizing their goals. △Fig. 1

△ 1
*Encounter* brochure cover, courtesy: Nafasi Art Space

1............'Privately-Owned Commercial Galleries,' 2020, www.artscollaboratory.org/participants/.
2............Nana Oforiatta-Ayim, 'Speak Now,' *Frieze: Contemporary Art and Culture* no. 139 (2011).
3............Portia Malatjie, 'Alternative/Experimental Art Spaces in Johannesburg,' *Third Text* 27, no. 3 (2013).
4............Kerstin Pinther and Ugochukwu-Smooth Nwezi, 'On Building New Spaces for Negotiating Art (and) Histories,' in *New Spaces for Negotiating Art and Histories in Africa* (Berlin: LIT Verlag, 2015), p. 8.

## THREE CITIES, THREE SPACES

All three case studies are based on initiatives of members of the Arts Collaboratory, an 'ecosystem' of twenty-five like-minded organizations spread across the world that focus on collective governance, the use of artistic and curatorial practices for social change, and sustainability in their respective contexts.[5] They are also institutions that have previously received funding from Hivos, the European Cultural Foundation, and/or the Prince Claus Fund. In the ensuing discussion, we introduce the three art spaces under observation: the Nubuke Foundation, Nafasi Art Space, and 32° East Uganda Arts Trust. In doing so, our goal is to give readers a grounded experience of the art spaces that moves past cryptic descriptions of who they are as organizations and towards the broader activities that they are involved in, what they stand for, and what they do.

### Nubuke Foundation

•

The Nubuke Foundation (Nubuke) is 'a visual art and cultural institution based in the suburb of East Legon in Accra, Ghana.'[6] Nubuke was founded by Ghanaian bankers, Odile Tevie, Tutu Agyare, and by the acclaimed Ghanaian visual artist, Kofi Setordji. It followed a legacy started by the gallery spaces that emerged in Accra in the years immediately following Ghana's independence from Britain in 1957. In the interview, Tevie describes a dearth of indigenous institutions actively promoting the visual arts and culture of Ghana around the time of Nubuke's launch. She reports that the situation was a motivating factor for its creation, as the role was, at the time, filled by 'foreign-funded missions doing it as public diplomacy.' As a result, the founders were alarmed that 'the lens through which [Ghanaian] art would be selected and promoted was at risk' and that 'it was important for [them] to start promoting ... Ghanaian [artistic] production[s] without being tainted by the lens of an outside entity.'[7]

Since its inception in 2006, Nubuke has been guided by its motto 'Protect. Preserve. Record.' This slogan gives the institution a broad remit for creative interpretation. The space has since served as a venue for the monthly event dubbed, 'Ehalakasa Spoken Word Poetry Series'—a hub for Accra's young performance poets. Nubuke has hosted final-year exhibitions by students from the Department of Fine Arts of the Kwame Nkrumah University of Science and Technology. It has served as a home and springboard for the Accra Theatre Workshop and for the British-Ghanaian fashion brand, 'Ohema Ohene.' Furthermore, it has opened an experimental residency space in Wa in the Upper West region of Ghana to encourage artists in residence to observe and exchange knowledge with local women on traditional artisanry skills such as weaving and open-air firing, in the hopes of fostering innovation.

5............Collaboratory, 'Privately-Owned Commercial Galleries.'

6............'Art Galleries,' 2020, www.nubukefoundation.org/about.php.

7............Odile Tevie (administrator) interview by Kobina Ankomah-Graham, August 2019.

At the time of our research, Nubuke was closed in order to make way for an extensive overhaul and construction of a new two-storey, partially raised, reinforced concrete building. △Fig. 2 The building was designed by Austrian architects Baerbel Mueller and Juergen Strohmayer. The construction is scheduled to be complemented by the opening of new additional spaces for artists, curators, and visitors. The space reopened in November 2019 with a retrospective of the works of world-renowned Ghanaian professional photographer, James Barnor.

△ 2
The new Nubuke Foundation gallery building (under construction), photo: Kobina Ankomah-Graham, 2019

## Nafasi Art Space

As a contemporary art space focused on the visual and performing arts, Nafasi Art Space (Nafasi) is an artist collaborative founded by Tanzanian artists in 2008. The Nafasi Art Space provides independent cultural art spaces for artists to work in. One of its main founding goals is to develop the professionalization of Tanzanian artists and communicate that artists, like other professionals, are equally important in Tanzanian society. From this perspective, Nafasi arguably fills an important void stemming from the Tanzanian government's neglect of former President Nyerere's art initiatives to protect and promote Tanzanian art and artists.[8] The space is located on Eyasi Road in Mikocheni in an industrial area in Dar es Salaam.

Nafasi's official website describes itself as a 'vibrant art centre and platform for artistic exchange in Dar es Salaam, Tanzania, where contemporary visual artists and performing artists come together to create, learn, inspire, exhibit, and perform.'[9] It is only through being actively present in the space and through field visits that it was possible to appreciate the operations of Nafasi. At the time of our visit, Nafasi had thirty-one studios—most of which were renovated shipping containers where Tanzanian artist-members operated from. △Figs. 3 & 4

Maria Kessi explains that the space received funding from the government of Denmark for its first three years.[10] Although Nafasi initially focused only on visual arts, it later expanded to cover technical and applied aspects of the performing arts. The space sits on a fenced plot of approximately three acres.

8 ............Shule Vicensia, 'Mwalimu Nyerere: The artist,' *Pambazuka News*, 13 October, 2009, www.pambazuka.org/pan-africanism/mwalimu-nyerere-artist.

9 ............'Arts Galleries,' 2008, accessed 5 June 2020, 2020, www.nafasiartspace.org/.

10 ..........Maria Kessi (administrator), interview by Joseph Oduro-Frimpong, Dar es Salaam, August 2019.

3

4

5

△ 3 & 4
Nafasi Art Space, renovated shipping studio, photo: Joseph Oduro-Frimpong, 2019

△ 5
Insects, metal artwork on wall, Nafasi Art Space, photo: Joseph Oduro-Frimpong, 2019

△ 6
Mixed media artwork on wall, Nafasi Art Space, photo: Joseph Oduro-Frimpong, 2019

△ 7 & 8
Graffiti art on wall, Nafasi Art Space, photo: Joseph Oduro-Frimpong, 2019

6

7

8

One of the organization's most significant achievements is the implementation of a strong programming and curatorial vision. Such foresight, according to Rebecca Corey, has enabled uninterrupted active programming and a vibrant environment.[11] The evidence of this vital programming is witnessed in the continual stream of artists coming through Nafasi. As a resident artist and the director of the MUDA dance company, Rachel Kessi[12] notes that a distinct feature about Nafasi is its provision of affordable or highly subsidized spaces for artists. This arrangement, in the words of Corey, affords artists 'to create the art that they want and for the general public to experience such art.'[13] Per our observations, the absence of artistic restrictions from Nafasi management manifests itself in the eclectic works produced in the various workshops, in addition to the works that (unofficially) adorn a large area of the open spaces on the walls of the compound including: metal art works,△Fig. 5 mixed media work△Fig. 6 and graffiti art△Figs. 7 & 8.

The variety of art works visibly index the extent to which Nafasi has become, in Corey's words, 'a gravitational location for artists of different orientations and work environments in different media formats.'[14] Nafasi is focused on creating access to the arts and culture in Tanzania as well as promoting experimentation and artistic growth through workshops and exchange activities between artists in Tanzania and other African countries. During our time at Nafasi, we witnessed this special characteristic through its artist residency programme. Nafasi invited artists Bucheta (from Mozambique) and Option (from Zimbabwe) for a six-week period. During their residency, the artists produced works (which were later exhibited) and provided workshops for Nafasi artists and the wider public interested in contemporary art. In these workshops, participants were taken through some of the artists' techniques of generating ideas and materials and were required to apply these knowledges to create their own unique art.△Figs. 9 & 10

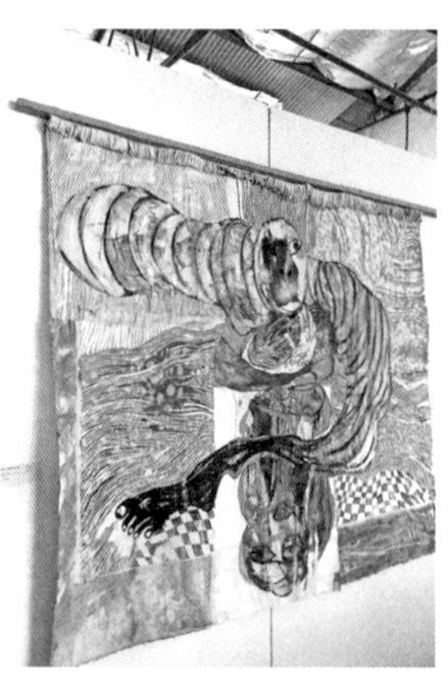

△ 9
Option, *Travelling Intuition*, 2019, mixed media on canvas and paper, photo: Joseph Oduro-Frimpong, 2019

△ 10
Bucheca, Human Time, 2019, acrylic, photo: Joseph Oduro-Frimpong, 2019

11 ........... Rebecca Corey (director), interview by Joseph Oduro-Frimpong, Dar es Salaam, December 2019.
12 ........... Rachel Kessi (creative artist), interview by Joseph Oduro-Frimpong, Dar es Salaam, August 2019.
13 ........... Rebecca Corey (director), interview by Joseph Oduro-Frimpong, Dar es Salaam, August 2019.
14 ........... Rebecca Corey (director), interview by Joseph Oduro-Frimpong, August 2019.

## 32° East Ugandan Arts Trust

• • •

32° East Ugandan Arts Trust (32° East) is a centre for the creation and exploration of contemporary arts in Uganda. Its director, Teesa Bahana explains that 32° East is unique within the Ugandan arts scene;[15] in that, it is a not-for-profit that goes beyond providing artists with structural spaces and facilities by offering its artists resources including daily lunch and per diem for transportation expenses. The justification for providing food and funds for transport ensures that artists already living on slim margins are able to fully focus on their craft and not be rightfully distracted by these issues. △Fig. 11

△ 11
The garden area of 32° East, photo: Kobina Ankomah-Graham, 2019

32° East is a multipurpose resource centre that includes a building that houses a gallery, offices it rents out, studios, accommodation for residency, and a contemporary art library with computers and editing suites. All these are made from shipping containers. Within this space, there is also a garden, a bamboo and thatch-roofed workshop space and meeting area, as well as a restaurant garden/performance venue known as 'The Big Kafunda.' Nadunga Alison who is an artist member, sculptor, and public health specialist, praises 32° East for its mentorship and apprenticeship of artists, pointing out that 'every single person on the [32° East] team is responsible for guiding and checking in on a specific artist.'[16] During our visits, we saw artists working in and out of studio containers as well as making use of the space's container library. We also attended a core-skills training session for artists' professional development. In the session, members were trained in basic skills, which per the conveners' conviction, artists do not get proper guidance on. The 'guidance' included how to make travel and accommodation arrangements for when they receive invitations for international events.

Bahana points out in the interview that with the exception of two Ugandan artists who offer up a room in each of their private homes for residency, and one other space that focuses on sculpture being ran from the UK for visiting British artists, no institution besides 32° East, offers much-needed residency and support to Ugandan artists in the context of a nation where contemporary art is largely ignored by the state authorities.[17]

15..........Teesa Bahana (director), interview by Ankomah-Graham, Kampala, August 2019.
16..........Nadunga Alison (artist), interview by Kobina Ankomah-Graham, Kampala, August 2019.
17..........Teesa Bahana (director), interview by Kobina Ankomah-Graham, Kampala, August 2019.

32° East also offers artists in-residence and members one-on-one drop-in sessions for constructive criticism, professional development workshops for improving practical skills, and a regular discussion series—'Artachat.' The series is aimed at building social engagement with non-artists and introducing artists to some of the professional intricacies of the world of the arts as well as ushering artists into 32° East's space. The objective of connecting members and artists in-residence with lovers of art beyond their walls is expressed through other initiatives including sales of the Uganda Arts Diary,△Fig. 12 a quarterly supper club/pop up exhibition called 'Palate,' and through the 'Kampala Contemporary Art Festival' (KLA ART). The latter is an annual festival celebrating public art that their pamphlet△Fig. 13 describes as 'for and with the city of Kampala...; taking art out of galleries and into the streets to reach non-traditional arts audiences and giving participating contemporary artists new experiences of production and unique platforms for their work.'

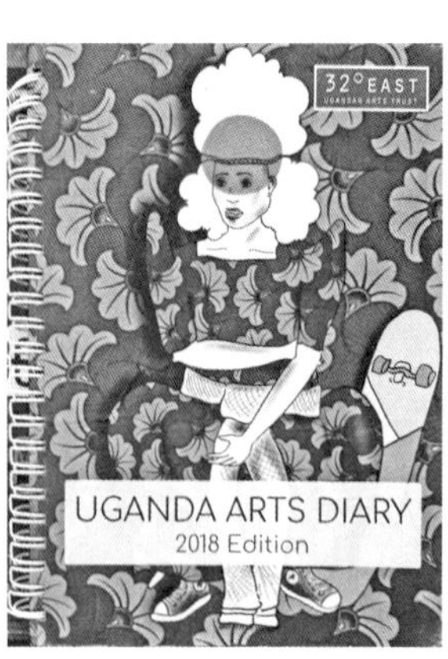

△ 12
The Uganda Arts Diary, photo: Kobina Ankomah-Graham, 2019

△ 13
Programme pamphlet for KLA Art 2018, photo: Kobina Ankomah-Graham, 2019

## ACHIEVEMENT AND AMPLIFICATION

In defining their biggest achievements, all three spaces make mention of their ongoing existence—or, as put by Gloria Kiconco (poet, essayist and Zine maker who self-publishes creative works targeting specific audiences, 32° East beneficiary, while doubling as a sessions facilitator), of merely 'toughing it out for so long.'[18] 'To still be standing after twelve years is a big achievement if we're looking at the terrain of arts in Ghana and the subregion...' says Tevie of Nubuke.[19] Similarily, Bahana points out that 32° East's biggest achievement is 'that we're still around in a place where there is questionable national support for the arts and where they are dealing with the arts as a not-for-profit. Clearly, from these statements, we capture a unique framing and narration of what constitutes 'achievement.' Here, the notion departs from a normative definition highlighting its

18..........Gloria Kiconco (a poet, creative), interview by Ankomah-Graham, Kampala, August 2019.

19..........Odile Tevie (administrator), interview by Ankomah-Graham, Accra, August 2019.

'manifestation in meritocratic principles.'[20] It is understood as 'resilience' and 'persistence' in creative arts environments that do not generally have state support. Such a conception of achievement is really significant as it allows us to grasp one of the unique ways in which the notion is experienced, defined, negotiated, and represented in these creative African spaces.[21] From this standpoint therefore, contrary to Mbembe's[22] version of Afro-radicals who act as victims without any agency, these responses (which index a particular vision of achievement) project the interviewees as self-reflexive individuals capable of reimagining adversities within a positive frame.

Bahana points out that although the arts have a rich African history in which they once were an integral part of people's lives, it is no longer respected on the continent as a whole, especially in Uganda which cannot boast of the reputation held by the likes of Nigeria, Senegal and (to some extent) Kenya in the arts world.[23] She cites as an achievement, the fact that 32° East has hosted sixty artists in residence, many of whom have progressed to achieving international recognition, winning awards, and accomplishing record-breaking sales at auctions. Tevie, similarly, sees as an achievement the fact that as many as sixty per cent of Ghana's most accomplished, internationally touted artists have passed through or worked with Nubuke.[24]

Kessi relates how Nafasi continues to produce graduates (formerly not well known in Tanzanian art circles) whose works collectors eagerly seek to acquire, including those of Cloud Chatanda (painting and illustration), Vita Malulu (a multi-talented artist who is a musician painter and sculptor), and Mwandale Mwanyekwa, a.k.a. Big Mama (sculptor). Furthermore, she notes how Nafasi also defined its success through modest attempts to train various street children to become successful artists and thus become financially independent.[25]

## BEST PRACTICES: COMMUNITY, COLLABORATION, AND GIVING CREDIT

All three art spaces highlight the importance and advantages of forming and being a part of creative communities and working in a community with other artists. Community and collaboration are touted among their biggest achievements. Nadunga sums up the need to practice teamwork and community formations by describing 32° East as being successful on account of the community it has formed (beyond mere social media

20 .......... Eva Ulrike Pirker, 'God [...] expects perfection.' Norms, forms and performance in Chimaman-da Ngozi Adichie's Purple Hibiscus.'

21 .......... Eva Ulrike Pirker, Katja Hericks, and Mandisa Mbali, eds., 'Introduction: Narratives of Achievement in African and Afroeuropean Contexts,' in *Forward, Upward, Onward?: Narratives of Achievement in African and Afroeuropean Contexts* (Düsseldorf: Universitäts- und Landesbibliothek Düsseldorf Publishers, 2020).

22 .......... J.-A. Mbembe and Steven Rendall, 'African modes of self-writing,' *Public Culture* 14, no. 1 (2002).

23 .......... Rachel Kessi (creative artist), interview by Joseph Oduro-Frimpong, Dar es Salaam, August 2019.

24 .......... Odile Tevie (administrator), interview by Kobina Ankomah-Graham, Accra, August 2019.

25 .......... Rachel Kessi (creative artist), interview by Joseph Oduro-Frimpong, Dar es Salaam, August 2019.

followership). She states: 'if you are moving and there is no one behind you, then you are just going for a walk.'

Kessi describes weekly artists' team-building meetings at Nafasi and what they call their 'highs and lows' exercise, explaining how this activity dispels apathy and allows artists to feel valued, take a vested interest in how such a centre functions, and enables 'collegial governance.' Nafasi has a solid base of Tanzanian art audiences not limited to the elite or expatriate crowd, but including different people of varying social classes, a fact we personally observed during the exhibition of Bucheta and Option. In terms of Nubuke, although it was closed for renovation during the period of research, its organized talks at the nearby Basecamp Initiative (a green creative hub and workspace) attracted diverse, primarily, Ghanaian crowds. Our trips to 32° East brought us into contact with Ugandan artists from different social and ethnic backgrounds.

32° East's Bahana points out that despite being 'more ephemeral' and 'less measurable,' community creates prospects for peer validation and relationships, as well as collaborations between artists who may not have otherwise met. She explains that 32° East seeks to be a 'platform for expression and open dialogue with people who are like-minded or not... a space where people can question things, learn and unlearn.'[26] Expounding on this view, she speaks of a philosophy of empathy that results in value being given to credit and recognition, in which members and administrators of the 32° East community are encouraged to actively credit artists with the expectation that artists do the same for each other.[27] 32° East also gives recognition to institutions it collaborates with, particularly through videos on its website. Bahana stresses the importance of this spirit of collaboration and openness: 'It's such hard work being in the arts so why not learn from other people, learn, exchange, and share knowledge. Work hard to treat people well.'[28] Corey also suggests that non-private art organizations should foster meaningful partnerships with public art institutions. Such partnerships ensure complementary exchanges of, for example, creative ways of leveraging ideas and personnel resources.[29] Tevie at Nubuke in Accra, explains:

> It's very important to me that as an institution that we are... working in tandem with different creative people who are contributing to the growth of the arts in Ghana. There's no point being at the top and everyone else is at the bottom.[30]

She further elevates collaboration to best practice, explaining that there are benefits for the entire community in improving collective capacities to the same level. She insists that the resulting bartering of services is

26...........Teesa Bahana (director), interview by Kobina Ankomah-Graham, Kampala, August 2019.
27...........Ibid.
28...........Ibid.
29...........Rebecca Corey (director), interview by Joseph Oduro-Frimpong, Dar es Salaam, August 2019.
30...........Odile Tevie (administrator), interview by Kobina Ankomah-Graham, Accra, August 2019.

something all Ghanaians should be committed to because resources are so scant in the country. An example of an Accra-based group benefitting from this communal approach to artistic practice is the Accra Theatre Workshop (self-styled as 'atw'), founded by the artists Elisabeth Efua Sutherland and Emelia Asiedu. atw initially operated out of Nubuke, renting its grounds and in exchange ran a food outlet programme and workshop sessions for local school children who may not otherwise have thought the space accessible to them, despite the existence of a children's library. As Sutherland puts it, Nubuke showed her a lot of personal support, 'a willingness to collaborate and share space.'[31] She knew of other artists who had also benefited from small cash grants and allowances, general advice, and feedback. atw eventually moved from Nubuke into its own property elsewhere in Accra and has since become an art space of its own, making use of shipping containers to form Accra's first Black Box theatre.[32] Sutherland still praises Nubuke, positioning it within the broader trajectory of growth she has seen in the Accra art scene as a whole over the past five to ten years, particularly in the area of art and museum infrastructures, collections, and programming. She praises the institution for having shown 'consistency and a level of integrity and intention towards arts and cultural work that was absent in many other conversations and spaces, providing platforms and space to so many young people.'[33]

In conclusion, our research findings show that best practices are linked to: the provision of platforms for experimentation; community building practices (such as giving credit and recognition to artists); maintaining a focus on specific artistic practices within small competitive ecosystems. Art spaces that have done this have attracted artists from diverse social backgrounds several of whom go on to international success.

## CHALLENGES: PERSONNEL AND NOT (REALLY) FOR PROFIT

32° East and Nubuke both cited finding the right personnel as one of their biggest challenges. Tevie speaks of the challenge of finding two or three creatives at a time when understanding of the arts and the freedom to support a big vision is rife. Bahana, on the other hand, explains that there is the problem of finding enough people as well as the challenge of finding people with the right level of specialization. Also, the need to actively generate revenue internally (through such practices as selling works in Nubuke's gallery space, participation in international arts fairs, and hosting private events) requires a larger team. The larger team, however, also requires the generation of even more revenue (for salaries,

31 ..........'Funding Black Box Theatre,' 2020 (accessed 5 June 2020), www.indiegogo.com/projects/build-a-black-box-theatre-in-accra-ghana#/ (crowdsourcing to fund the building of a black box theatre in Accra, Ghana).

32 ..........Elisabeth Efua Sutherland (visual artist), interview by Ankomah-Graham, Accra, August 2019.

33 ..........Elisabeth Efua Sutherland (visual artist), interview by Kobina Ankomah-Graham, Accra, August 2019.

for example).[34] Tevie speculates over the possibility of resolving this particular challenge through programmes fostering more loyalty between Nubuke and the artists who pass through its doors. She explains that such arrangements have thus far been 'loose' but ponders as to whether they could be made firmer.[35]

Kessi states that as a not-for-profit, Nafasi considers it an achievement to have been able to sustain itself through accessing donor funding ever since it started operations.[36] Nevertheless, our interviewees reveal that management experiences perennial anxiety over finances needed to sustain ongoing programmes that are linked to donors. This anxiety stems from the fact that such funding is not guaranteed, as there is the possibility of not winning a financial grant when a previous one runs out. Although as of writing, Nafasi had not experienced such a 'funding-drought,' Kessi notes that the thought of this possibility is on the management's mind all the time.[37]

Bahana explains that 32° East's financial model is also a pure not-for-profit model:

> Most funding is from grant applications. Some are core funding, and others are for specific projects. Other activities like the Uganda Arts Diary, subletting our office space, our membership programme, rental for space (currently being used by the Big Kafunda restaurant), and workshops generate income.[38]

In a contrasting light, Tevie is reluctant to describe Nubuke's financial model as being solely not-for-profit, preferring to describe it as leaning more towards 'socially-engaged entrepreneurship.'[39] She elaborates on this phrasing by explaining that Nubuke is

> Not-for-profit, in that the founders are not taking money back in shares and dividends. However, we are not a typical not-for-profit organization that you find... which is being given donor funds. A large chunk of our revenue is internally generated. And that mix is important in Ghana because of the precariousness of the donor terrain: here today and gone tomorrow.[40]

34 ........... Teesa Bahana (director), interview by Kobina Ankomah-Graham. Kampala, August 2019.
35 ........... Odile Tevie (administrator), interview by Kobina Ankomah-Graham. Accra, August 2019.
36 ........... Rachel Kessi (creative artist), interview by Joseph Oduro-Frimpong, Dar es Salaam, August 2019.
37 ........... Maria Kessi (administrator), interview by Joseph Oduro-Frimpong, Dar es Salaam, August 2019.
38 ........... Teesa Bahana (director), interview by Kobina Ankomah-Graham. Kampala, August 2019.
39 ........... Odile Tevie (administrator), interview by Kobina Ankomah-Graham. Accra, August 2019.
40 ........... Ibid.

Corey relates how Nafasi continually sensitizes artists to develop their critical consciousness regarding the demands within global art circles that come with being, in the blunt words of Clark, 'complete unknowns.'[41] Such pressures include artists sourcing funds for projects, balancing funders' requirements with their artistic goals, and the pressure to create 'acceptable' art pieces that run counter to what the artist wants to genuinely create. Kessi stresses the importance of embodying a strong(er), grounded local African identity,[42] a suggestion we suspect is based on the fact that such an identity forces artists to produce unique works that draw inspiration from African indigenous aesthetics. Bahana points out that one of the problems with the Kampala visual arts scene that 32° East has sought to challenge is reorienting many talented artists' focus away from creating work for the tourist audience—which dictate content with tropes like wildlife, gorillas, and boda-bodas with matooke at the back, despite the many other things local art could speak to.

Tevie and her co-founders witnessed a similar problem before establishing Nubuke:

> We didn't see any indigenous
> institution ... actively promoting
> the visual arts and culture of Ghana
> apart from foreign-funded missions ...
> doing it as public diplomacy.
>
> This was precarious ... because
> if a nation decided not to choose
> to promote culture as part of their
> diplomatic mission, that would
> leave Ghana high and dry. The lens
> through which our own art was
> selected and promoted was at risk.
> It was important for us to start off
> promoting Ghanaian production seen,
> appreciated, valued, and welcomed
> without being tainted by the lens
> of an outside entity.[43]

The aforementioned narratives call to mind the work of Alacovska and Gill who (echoing Comaroff and Comaroff) speak of the possibility of 'starting a conversation about what it might mean to displace the empirical locus from the metropolitan creative epi-centres of Euro-America to an ex-centric site of experience and vision situated on the world's peripheries.'[44] In attempting to wrestle the arts away from being purely driven by profit, both Nubuke and 32° East are expanding the possibilities of what art

41 .......... Emily Clark, 'We need to talk: A show of deception exploring millennial engagement at the intersection of exhibition and improv' (The George Washington University, 2015).

42 .......... Rachel Kessi (creative artist), interview by Joseph Oduro-Frimpong, Dar es Salaam, August 2019.

43 .......... Odile Tevie (administrator), interview by Kobina Ankomah-Graham, Accra, August 2019

44 .......... Ana Alacovska and Rosalind Gill, 'De-Westernizing Creative Labour Studies: The Informality of Creative Work from an Ex-Centric Perspective,' *International Journal of Cultural Studies* 22, no. 2 (2019).

can mean within their respective cities and countries. This move not only puts the potential of such art(ists) on equal footing with art(ists) from elsewhere in the world, but it also reconnects to ancient African art practices in which art has purpose beyond profit and even aesthetics: art is about the people, for the people and by the people.

By not pursuing pure profit routes, these spaces open themselves to challenges around funding that requires the kind of creativity expected by the artists they support. As Tevie puts it, '[arts] funding is non-existent in our part of the world, so you have to resort to many innovative ideas ... it is exhausting.[45] She opines that Nubuke reflects Ghana's national character more than it yet affects it, explaining two aspects of that character—tenacity and good humour—in relation to Nubuke's constant need and search for revenue. She states that tenacity is crucial in the arts,

> ... because we have elusive patrons who have to be chased, want to drive a hard bargain, and you have to hold your own. By the time it gets to arts patronage, everyone's budget is running on empty and you have to fight for whatever it is. That's the first thing people say whenever they see me: 'oh we have no money.' Well, we need money... We mean business and we need to keep running and we need to keep open...and so we need the money. That conversation happens a lot.

She reflects the Ghanaian good-humoured nature, adding,

> It's a difficult terrain. There are a lot of actors in the field who are not the people you would choose as your first best friend but you still need to work with them and so you need a bit of it.[46]

Bahana speculates whether it is even possible to become fully self-sustaining as an arts institution and explains how 32° East would have to be creative with its not-for-profit model if it is to ever reduce its reliance on donor funding. This manoeuvre partly involves doubling down on their mission, which is to put premium on the artists as a priority.[47] She also speaks of making sure to recognize whatever strengths and 'institutional power' their space has and wielding it wisely in contexts where the arts are undervalued.[48] She, however, expresses the danger of losing track of one's mission in the quest to survive: 'You can end up doing too much or following the money so much that it diverts from why you got in in the first place.'[49]

45..........Odile Tevie (administrator), interview by Kobina Ankomah-Graham, Accra, August 2019.
46..........Ibid.
47..........Teesa Bahana (director), interview by Kobina Ankomah-Graham, Kampala, August, 2019.
48..........Ibid.
49..........Ibid.

doual'art / Douala, Cameroon / 11:54am     36°51'12.9"N / 10°10'18.6"E

Maison De L'image / Tunis, Tunisia / 11:57am / 36°51'12.9"N / 10°10'18.6"E

As Nadunga puts it from an artist's perspective: 'Most spaces are built to drive you to achieve their goals... so you are a means to an end.'[50]

As a financially dependent organization, Nafasi faces a similar challenge around the politics of respecting donors' agendas or wishes within the context of Nafasi's operations where artists are highly encouraged to be experimental/nonconformist. This situation becomes glaring when donors want to fund conventional art projects. From the financial management side, there is also the ongoing challenge of ensuring that artists are diligent (within an informal economy) to procure and timely turn-in (some form of) receipts to the accounts department to ensure they have an accurate detail of spending.

Tevie hints that some artists at Nubuke had to step outside of their comfort zones on the account of a lucrative museum-like nationwide outreach programme that Nubuke ran for almost five years on behalf of a corporate entity. Artists found themselves having to 'think out of the box'[51] to find ways to accommodate artistic impulses beyond their own and apply their creativity to ends that were not 'art for art's sake.'

The above reflections point to how the management of non-for-profit arts centres are required to invest a substantial effort in, for example, locating grants that match their organization's mission and vision, and in having competent professionals to be able to apply for them. Furthermore, non-for-profit arts centres have to maintain a good financial reputation with donors in order to ensure their trust and continued support. Doing so ensures continued funding for new and existing programmes, as is the case with Nafasi and 32° East.

## LOCAL FUNDING: THE STATE [AND] THE ARTS

Belfiore and Bennett write that 'most nations in the world now have government departments that promote and support the arts.'[52] African governments are paying attention to the cultural and creative industries. Ghana's Ministry of Tourism, Arts and Culture, for example, was briefly renamed the Ministry of Tourism, Culture and Creative Arts, bringing it (at least sonically) into alignment with economic discussions around the arts, framing it as a possible source of revenue and employment. Despite the government's successful sponsorship of Ghana's debut contemporary art-led pavilion at the 58th Venice Biennale, a quick look at the Ministry's website's headline welcoming visitors to 'Your Official Tourism Gateway to Ghana,'[53] suggests that the arts in Ghana fall under tourism and are exclusively historical in perspective and practice. △Fig. 14

50..........Nadunga Alison (artist), interview by Kobina Ankomah-Graham , Kampala, August 2019.

51..........Odile Tevie (administrator), interview by Kobina Ankomah-Graham, Accra, August 2019.

52..........Eleonora Belfiore, '"Impact," "Value" and "Bad Economics": Making Sense of the Problem of Value in the Arts and Humanities,' *Arts and Humanities in Higher Education* 14, no. 1 (2015).

53..........'Tourism, Arts, and Culture in Ghana,' http://motac.gov.gh/ (accessed June, 2020).

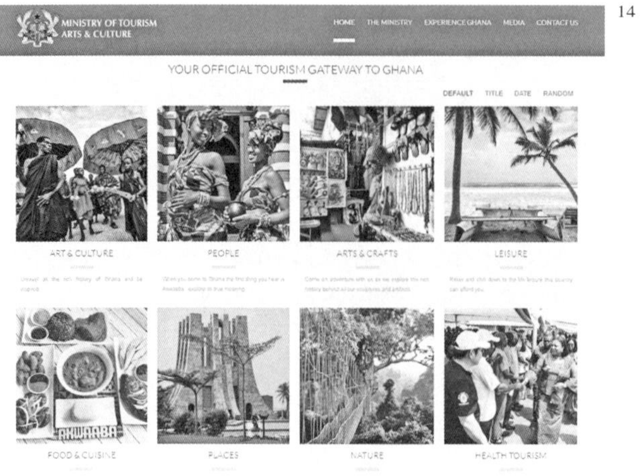


14

15

16

△ 14, 15 & 16
Ghana Ministry of Tourism, Arts & Culture Homepage

Of Uganda, Kiconco says the following:

> There's a national identity given to Uganda which is that we are a very hospitable place—this very particular tourist kind of thing—and I don't think that that's really true. Not that we are not hospitable but ... Uganda is a very nuanced country. We are very nuanced but somehow we manage to make it work.[54]

Nadunga adds that 'tourism is the only part of [Uganda's] governance that allows [Ugandan creatives] to integrate into the system.'[55] But where is room being made within the tourist industry for the contemporary kind of arts being championed by the likes of 32° East, Nafasi and Nubuke?
△Fig. 15 & 16

54..........Gloria Kiconco (poet), interview by Kobina Ankomah-Graham, Kampala, August 2019..

55..........Nadunga Alison (artist), interview by Kobina Ankomah-Graham, Kampala, August 2019.

Belfiore and Bennett point to a growing new awareness of the critical impact of the arts to the economy. However, they also point out that

> even those who argue this case most strongly will usually concede that the economic role is secondary to something much more fundamental [which is] the capacity of the arts to transform the lives not just of individuals but of whole communities.[56]

This statement aptly captures the efforts of institutions like Nubuke, Nafasi Art Space and 32° East. More specifically, they can be described as being on the frontlines of transformative art, contributing towards the building of a viable 'ecosystem' that allows creative artists the possibility of earning a living from their creative talent. They are 'professionalizing the arts' as Nadunga puts it.'[57] Nevertheless, these institutions appear to receive little assistance from their governments. As evidenced in Tevie's observation about the lack of financial support from the state, she says,

> I don't think I remember any arts support ever coming from the state. A lot of it comes from outside entities ... we don't have that recognition that we are contributing much to [anything]. It's always about numbers—isn't it?—regarding national development; so sadly, we are not there.'[58]

Nadunga however wonders if recognition is enough, explaining: 'Government workers ask us, "Does culture put food on your plate?" and thus defining arts as being for the unsuccessful and the sciences for the successful, serious people.' As someone who is a qualified public health specialist, Nadunga's creative activities baffle public officials: 'Art is looked at as a hobby; not a profession... Leaving a profession for a career [in the arts] doesn't make sense to any of them.'[59]

Corey explains how challenging it is to reorient the minds of policy makers about the equally important role of the arts as an opportunity for institutional/national job creation.[60] Unlike Nyerere's era where the arts were respected because of the above-mentioned factors, it seems the post-Nyerere era has witnessed the relegation of the arts into a venue of insignificance. A consequence of this neglect of the arts is witnessed in the dwindling to little or no financial support for arts and culture programmes. In spite of this challenge, there seems to be a gradual government interest in the arts. As Corey made us aware, in the very least, the Minister of Information, Culture Arts and Sports, Professor Ole Gabriel out of his

56..........Belfiore, '"Impact", "Value" and "Bad Economics"'

57..........Nadunga Alison (artist), interview by Kobina Ankomah-Graham, Kampala, August 2019.

58..........Ibid.

59..........Ibid.

60..........Rebecca Corey (director), interview by Joseph Oduro-Frimpong, Dar es Salaam, August 2019.

volition in 2018, visited Nafasi to personally witness how the centre functions. The National Arts Council also offered financial waivers for non-Tanzanian artists who came for art residencies to Nafasi. In trying to overcome the challenge of government near-neglect of the arts, Nafasi management is gradually building close relationships with the government through the National Arts Council and other arts organizations (such as the Alliance Français and Goethe-Institute) to enable such relationship building.

At 32° East, Kiconco points out that despite attending a 2016 government symposium in which she was informed that the government would provide financial support for artists, what she observes is, rather, the rapid dwindling of funds for the arts. She explains that the Ugandan government has been 'cutting arts funding and... not seeing the opportunity there. Currently, they are trying to curb the arts and putting a lot of pressure on us through taxes, [and] bills.'[61] Perhaps the funding cuts result from trust issues. As Bahana puts it, the relationship between the Ugandan state and the arts is 'complicated.'[62] She points out that there are advantages to 'operating under the radar' and 'getting away with things' but these have implications for

> sustainability, for art in schools or for building a national art museum or a national gallery that kids can access, understand arts through and dream of careers in the arts. These are things government can do because they have the resources to do so but I do not know how much I trust government.

Nevertheless, when asked whether or not the government has a duty to support the arts, Tevie says,

> Why not? Where are the state institutions? What's going on with the national museum... the Centres for National Culture... It's important that [the government] recognize the different voices [of] players in the cultural arts scene today in Ghana and let them become your ambassadors. They are ambassadors in spite of the state.[63]

This is not the only time cultural ambassadorship came up in our research. As Nadunga notes, the government owes artists their support 'because we are doing their work. It is their role to preserve heritage... to make it a point that everyone is aware of heritage because it is the heartbeat of

61..........Gloria Kiconco (poet), interview by Kobina Ankomah-Graham, Kamapala, August 2019.
62..........Teesa Bahana (director), interview by Kobina Ankomah-Graham, Kampala, August 2019
63..........Odile Tevie (administrator), interview by Kobina Ankomah-Graham, Accra, August 2019.

the nation.' Bahana concurs, speaking of having attended five events in countries outside Uganda where she was asked about Uganda, its artists, and their arts context: 'Part of the national identity around Ugandan art is tied into 32° East because we are out there talking to and meeting different people in the art networks that we are a part of: the only Ugandan organization.'[64] While Kiconco questions the idea of national identity as being 'very colonial' and 'weird,' she agrees that as an artist, 'you are still an ambassador for your nation and have to answer questions on the country posed by strangers to the state, making artists tied to [the national identity] whether we like it or not.'[65] What is clear from the above discussion relates to how the organizations under discussion, in spite of the lack of financial support from the state, continue to thrive through their resilient practices. We believe international funders should target and fund such arts organizations with such sustainable goals and ethical frameworks. In financially supporting these arts organizations, we suggest that, in as much as possible, such assistance should strike a fine balance with the needs of the donor agencies and that of the initiatives of these art spaces. Furthermore, we also believe that the long-term sustainability of these not-for-profit art spaces will also largely depend on, first a reorientation of policy makers in recognizing that the arts, like other sectors in the economy, have their unique ways of contributing to a nation's development. As well, an enduring sustainability of the art spaces depends on committed and uninterrupted funding from national governments.

## CONCLUSIONS

Kiconco of 32° East encourages artists not to be daunted by challenges in their profession but to think about their impact on the smaller scale of individuals and community, saying that while it may be overconfident of artists to think 'we are going to change the world,'[66] it is also unfair pressure to put on artists. The same can be said of art spaces, given how uphill a struggle it is to run them. Implicit in Kiconco's exhortation is how artists and managers of art arenas should not succumb to the real and present challenges that they encounter but be reflective about how to overcome these obstacles and develop agency and self-determination.

Our research into documenting the successes and challenges of Nubuke Foundation, Nafasi Art Space and 32° East Uganda Arts Trust have convinced us that the not-for-profit arts space approach is worth replicating in other African countries. This position is not to say the manner in which these spaces operate are perfect. Certainly, one can argue that, for example, they have to find creative solutions to source other solid funding streams beyond donor agencies such as liaising with prominent art galleries to sell artists' works. In terms of how these art spaces operate, one can point

64 .......... Teesa Bahana (director), interview by Kobina Ankomah-Graham, Kampala, August 2019

65 .......... Gloria Kiconco (poet), interview by Kobina Ankomah-Graham, Kampala, August 2019.

66 .......... Ibid.

to how they have different variations, ranging from the sheer scale of Nafasi to the elegance of the new Nubuke and the comprehensive 360-degree approach of 32° East. Regardless of the peculiarities via which the above art spaces are managed, however, imaginative practices exist for confronting common challenges faced by such institutions in terms of anxiety over funding, audience, access, state recognition, and moving artists beyond the tourist gaze towards a genuine, expansive African artistic vision. These challenges include having a physical space within which artists can congregate and form community; artist support, ranging from membership to full residencies, either of which should include comprehensive training/mentorship and be mindful of artists' precarious living by providing food and transport; and gallery space within which to exhibit artists' work. In addition to this however, it is also worth noting the movement of the arts out of the centres to the people, through talks and festivals like KLA ART.

ACKNOWLEDGEMENTS

Joseph: My sincerest gratitude to Agnes-Senga Tupper, Rebecca Corey, Maria Kessi, Rachel Kessi, Kwame Mchauru, Jesse Gerard, Option Nyahunzvi and Bucheta for sharing their insights with me about Nafasi Art Space.

Kobina: I deeply appreciate the Semukala family for connecting me with 32° East, to Jessica Horn for encouragement, and most especially, my wife Shari, for keeping our two-year-old during my travels. My thanks to Teesa Bahana, Sandra Suubi, Gloria Kiconco, Alison Nadunga, Aicha, Muhammad Ali as well as Odile Tevie (Nubuke Foundation) and Elisabeth Sutherland (Accra Theatre Workshop).

## ← REFERENCES

Alacovska, Ana, and Rosalind Gill. 'De-Westernizing Creative Labour Studies: The Informality of Creative Work from an Ex-Centric Perspective.' *International Journal of Cultural Studies* 22, no. 2 (2019), pp. 195–212.

'Arts Galleries.' Nafasi Art Space, 2008. www.nafasiartspace.org/ (accessed 5 June 2020).

'Art Galleries.' Nubuke Foundation, 2020, https://www.nubukefoundation.org/about.php.

Belfiore, Eleonora. '"Impact," "Value" and "Bad Economics": Making Sense of the Problem of Value in the Arts and Humanities.' *Arts and Humanities in Higher Education* 14, no. 1 (2015), pp. 95–110.

Clark, Emily. 'We Need to Talk: A Show of Deception Exploring Millennial Engagement at the Intersection of Exhibition and Improv.' The George Washington University, 2015.

'Funding Black Box Theatre.' Crowdsourcing to fund the building of a black box theatre in Accra, Ghana, 2020. www.indiegogo.com/projects/build-a-black-box-theatre-in-accra-ghana#/ (accessed 5 June 2020).

Malatjie, Portia. 'Alternative/Experimental Art Spaces in Johannesburg.' *Third Text* 27, no. 3 (2013), pp. 367–77.

Mbembe, J-A, and Steven Rendall. 'African Modes of Self-Writing.' *Public Culture* 14, no. 1 (2002), pp. 239–73.

Oforiatta-Ayim, Nana. 'Speak Now.' *Frieze: Contemporary Art and Culture* no. 139 (2011): pp. 114–17.

Pinther, Kerstin and Nwezi, Ugochukwu-Smooth, 'On Building New Spaces for Negotiating Art (and) Histories.' In *New Spaces for Negotiating Art and Histories in Africa*, pp. 7–18.Berlin: LIT Verlag, 2015.

Pirker, Eva Ulrike, Katja Hericks, and Mandisa Mbali (eds.). *Forward, Upward,Onward?: Narratives of Achievement in African and Afroeuropean Contexts*. Düsseldorf: Universitäts- und Landesbibliothek Düsseldorf Publishers, 2020.

'Privately-Owned Commercial Galleries.' Arts Collaboratory 2020, http://www.artscollaboratory.org/participants/.

'Tourism, Arts, and Culture in Ghana.' http://motac.gov.gh/ (accessed 5 June 2020).

Vicensia, Shule. 'Mwalimu Nyerere: The Artist.' *Pambazuka News*, 13 October 2009.www.pambazuka.org/pan-africanism/mwalimu-nyerere-artist.

## ← INTERVIEWS

Elisabeth Efua Sutherland (a visual artist and a researcher), interview by Kobina

Ankomah-Graham,'Growth of Accra Art Scene,' Accra, August 2019.

Gloria Kiconco (a poet, essayist, creative), interview by Kobina Ankomah-Graham, 'Arts and Tourism in Uganda,' Kampala, August 2019.

Maria Kessi (creative artist), interview by Joseph Oduro-Frimpong, 'Nafasi Interview,' Dar es Salaam, August 2019.

Nadunga Alison (an artist, sculptor, public health specialist), interview by Kobina Ankomah-Graham, 'Tanzania Art Space,' Kampala, August 2019.

Odile Tevie (an arts curator), interview by Kobina Ankomah-Graham, 'Promoting the Visual Arts and the Ghanaian Culture,' Accra, August 2019.

Teesa Bahana (director of an art space), interview with Kobina Ankomah-Graham, 'Contemporary Arts in Uganda,' Kampala, August 2019.

Rachel Kessi (artist), interview by Joseph Oduro-Frimpong, 'Features of Nafasi,' Dar es Salaam, December 2019.

Rebecca Corey (an artist), interview by Joseph Oduro-Frimpong. 'Nafasi Interview.' 2019.

# CRITICISM IS A LUXURY
## On the Effect of Evaluations

Mariam Abou Ghazi and Ilka Eickhof

This chapter discusses the effect of evaluations on art and culture initiatives by drawing on qualitative research conducted in Tunisia, Algeria, and Egypt, based on interviews with both local practitioners and representatives from European culture institutions funding contemporary art and culture in these countries. The interviews challenge the specific European funding architecture and the role European institutions play as enablers and supporters of the local art and culture field, and question the impact not only of evaluating projects and funding lines, but also of European-supported projects in general. The research highlights how funding programmes and hence their evaluations are structured by neoliberal performance goals and are therefore counterproductive to any form of solidarity or sustainability. The competitive nature of the open calls and the economization of art and culture translate into an evaluation of social relationships based on their usefulness, usability, and the reciprocity of social and economic capital. Key here is not the possible evaluation itself, but the motivation for evaluating.

Keywords
→ Post-colonial Critique
→ European Funding
→ Middle East
→ Art and Culture
→ Evaluation

## INTRODUCTION

> 'The purpose of art is to lay bare the questions that have been hidden by the answers.'[1]

In 2018, the *The Force of Art* (henceforth FoA) initiative commissioned research on 'the role of arts and culture in society,' to analyze projects that were financially supported by the Prince Claus Fund, Hivos, and the European Cultural Foundation. The call included a critical stance on how artists and cultural organizations have to increasingly prove 'the effectiveness of their practice as a tool for intervention and engagement with society,'[2] and warned that the measurement of the 'social and economic 'impact' of arts on society for governments and donors may lead to instrumentalization of artistic practices.'[3] For the FoA initiative, the named foundations specified:

> [W]e will support 15 independent research studies that will carefully

> analyse the role that artists, cultural organizations and artworks/art practices have had, and the ways they have affected people within their respective context ... The aim of the research is to find out the ways in which cultural organizations and artworks can transform people and situations in Africa, Asia, the Caribbean, Eastern Europe, Latin America and the Middle East.[4]

For us, the call seemed to contradict itself. On the one hand, it cautioned against the idea of having to prove the effectiveness and impact of a practice; on the other hand, it aimed to do exactly what it warned against, calling for the analysis of the 'affect' of artists or art practices. To unfold this contradiction and take a look at its source, we focus our research on the evaluation criteria of the FoA initiative, and on how such an initiative is negotiated on the ground, specifically in areas in which European support for contemporary art and culture is prominent. This self-reflexive approach allowed us to include the European funding institutions themselves. The selected case studies for this research include the following art organizations: Jiser Reflexions Mediterrànies in Algeria, the Townhouse Gallery in Egypt, and Maison de l'Image in Tunisia.

In order to determine the European foundations' desire to evaluate the 'effect' of art, artistic projects, or institutions, and whether this is a logical exercise for local practitioners, two lines of thought guided us through this research endeavour: (1) the notion of solidarity and development, as expressed from calls and European institutions supporting arts and culture, in this case in formerly colonized countries in the Global South,[5] and (2) the ongoing financial dependencies that are a product resulting from neoliberal structures, which are partly implemented and supported in a European funding model. The chapter argues that these structures essentially obstruct the aforementioned solidarity.

## METHODOLOGY

The research adopts a sociological perspective combined with cultural analysis inasmuch as it is concerned with the analysis of institutionalized practices of European culture institutions. In this research, we use ethnographic fieldwork methods such as participant observation paired

1............James Baldwin, 'The Creative Process' (New York: Published for the National Cultural Center, The Ridge Press, 1962), pp. 18–19.

2............'The Force of Art: Research from a Global Perspective,' Call for Expression of Interest (CIE), funded by the Prince Claus Fund, Hivos, and the European Cultural Foundation, 2018.

3............Ibid.

4............Ibid.

5............For a critical discussion of the ambiguous term 'Global South,' referring to a complex notion of geographies of power, see Fernando Resende, 'The Global South: Conflicting Narratives and the Invention of Geographies,' *Ibraaz* (6 November 2014), p. 008.

with informal, qualitative interviews with key actors. Most of the local actors are well known and established within the local contemporary art and culture scene. We carried out participant observation in the cities of Cairo and Tunis and conducted interviews via Skype with actors of and around the Algiers case study. Due to political uprisings, we were unable to travel to Algeria to conduct participant observation as planned. The core of the methodological trajectory is thus based on interviews with key actors.

We conducted thirteen qualitative, informal interviews (seven in Tunis, three in Cairo, four with representatives of the European institutions, and two with partners of the Algerian case), and one dinner conversation with eight participants in Cairo for four hours. The interviews were held in the form of open conversations, structured by core questions, and consensually recorded and partly transcribed. Furthermore, an online survey available in Arabic and English was sent to various networks and key individuals, and twenty-seven responses were evaluated in order to frame the research and reflect the information drawn from the qualitative interviews.

Our research recognizes that there are not two binary entities—the European funding institution and their representatives on one side, and the non-European receivers of funding on the other side—standing in front of each other, but people wearing multiple hats, and taking various overlapping and intersecting positions and roles. Employees of the European funding institutions might not necessarily agree with the total rationale of their institutions, respective foreign ministries or other government agencies, and are often friends with actors on the local scene. Furthermore, the contemporary cultural fields in each of these cities are small, partly as a result of the financial limitations they face. Within these fields and detached from any European funding, we find a network with its own structures of power, quarrels, competitions, personal likes and dislikes, interests and experiences in relation to the individual social actors. Keeping these disclaimers in mind and in order to protect individual positions, we anonymized all interviews and quotes. Personal pronouns are also neutralized where necessary in order to protect the identity of an interlocutor.

## CASES AND CONTEXTS

The three cases located in the cities of Cairo, Tunis and Algiers are structured by similar interrelated dynamics. These include a dire socio-political and economic situation (uprisings and a high rate of youth unemployment); an overall tightened governance and state surveillance, and the suppression of civil society; and the emergence of northern European cultural institutions in the field of contemporary art and culture, with funding initiatives specifically geared towards young people.

## Cairo

•

The iconic Townhouse Gallery in Cairo was the host to the Egyptian case study we were supposed to evaluate. By the time we were officially put in contact with the institution (September 2018), its director and founder William Wells was denied entry to Egypt—this situation became emblematic for the dwindling contemporary art scene, and the political harassment many institutions had to endeavour to keep going. Apart from meeting with the Townhouse Gallery, we also organized an informal gathering at the Greek Club in Cairo in order to discuss the topic of this research. Listening again to the recordings of the evening reveals a rather rehearsed conversation about a topic that has been discussed since 2011, with little structural changes overall. Due to the drying up of the general local culture scene, European institutions have become one of the last possibilities when it comes to support for contemporary art. Through these institutions, culture and education has been made available (even if not accessible to everyone); project funding or the participation in any kind of exchange training can possibly lead to travel to Europe, and this has been linked to hopes for a better future—abroad or in the country. The European cultural spaces became spaces in which gatherings or semi-public discussions were still possible, and where people could meet and discuss. But even they have become more and more silent with stricter control by the Egyptian state.

At the end of the research, we were asked why the Cairo case fell short in comparison to the other two cases, which was even more surprising when taking into consideration that we both live and work in this city. We did not have an answer quick at hand, but after further reflection we realized that the all-encompassing bareness of a general contemporary arts/culture scene that was more vibrant even just a couple of years ago, made its imprint on our awareness and thinking. Today, the contemporary art scene in Cairo is almost non-existent; however, this reality has become so normalized that even we, the researchers, fail to take it into consideration.

The sustainability of cultural initiatives in Cairo is constantly challenged by raids, aggravating general working conditions, endless pursuits of legal documents, dealing with bureaucracies and chasing licenses, in addition to general limitations in funding. 'It seems that every time we start to do something, we start to stand up and organize something, something else happens that slaps us so hard, we fall back to the ground, again and again and again. And now we are just tired,' says an interlocutor in a conversation about the dire culture scene these days.[6] 'By now, so many people have left [Egypt], it's bitter for us who are still here,' says another one.[7] Until recently, European institutions often experienced more freedom to manoeuvre within a politically difficult situation because their work was based on diplomatic ties between

6............Anonymous interlocutor, interview by Ilka Eickhof and Alexandra Stock. Group conversation. Cairo, 25 February 2019.

7............Ibid.

European states, their respective foreign ministries, and Egypt. In general, grant-giving cultural institutions that bear promise of improved life in the cultural field undoubtedly execute an element of control over the distribution and reach of knowledge. This is because it is through them that people and projects are selected and invested in—be it in the form of salaries or honorariums, supporting representations in exhibitions, or general artistic productions and discussions that cater to social and symbolic capital. This also applies to personal expenses, such as travel costs, or providing supporting letters for visa applications at embassies, etc. In Cairo, such structures make these institutions key gatekeepers, but also define their disciplinary focus. Cultural practitioners have to assimilate and conform to various anticipated expectations, aesthetically and bureaucratically, in the shape of reports or evaluations of their projects.

After the uprising in 2011, an influx of European funding took place. One of the interviewees explains that

> Now we are at another historical moment, a shift, or wracking, because again the context is changing, Europe has a massive anxiety about the migrant crisis, and it is questioning how it is funding projects in the South. ... Now, as in the nineteen-nineties, we have a similar situation in Egypt where funding and foreign funding becomes more and more difficult. ... I think it's a very interesting moment because I think everybody is tired and sick of this economy and that context, it no longer works for us—what can we do? ... And I think a lot of people are thinking the same way, that there is a way beyond this 1995 moment[8]

of 'let us throw some money at the civil society sector to evolve and make all these autocratic regimes democratic,' and that worked in some ways, but whatever was expected or envisioned in 1995 definitely doesn't measure up to this moment, and I guess we are at this moment of, well, we are still terrified from the migrant crisis, is art the answer?[9]

Cairo's European-supported art and cultural productions are often attached to either quick, hip topics of the moment (like graffiti and street art in the direct aftermath of 2011), or to ongoing fixations such as the West's attempts to fix the Arab Middle East through developing gender

8............Ibid. The reference to the mid-nineteen-nineties signifies the vague feeling of a general opening of the non-state-run contemporary art and culture scene in Egyptian society; it is when the Townhouse Gallery opened its doors in 1998, among other places, followed by the Al-Nitaq arts festival in 2000. Most of the interlocutors were young teenagers at that time, and started becoming interested in arts and culture also through the works and programmes of these spaces.

9............Ibid.

and women's rights. This is the case because these topics are aligned with public discussions in Europe, which in turn mirror current political discourses, such as the Muslim immigrant/migrant debate. Consequently, the conflation of art and politics are linked to the European market because of demand. Together, these dynamics raise questions of how the cultural field in 'the region'[10] is influenced by European foreign cultural politics. Correspondingly, this matter is echoed in the question of what the effect of art could or should be. One interlocutor states:

> There is a gap between proposal talk and actual real life. When I write a proposal I have to find ways to fit my work into the proposal. So all the terms I hate and despise I just had to put them all, and it's interesting because, in no way do I believe in what I wrote ... So, for me, it's very important to be in the head space where I say what they want to read, but I do what I actually think is important.[11]

Another one echoes this sentiment saying, 'There is the proposal talk, and the evaluation talk, and then there is reality.'[12] Other interlocutors agree with this statement, joining in:

> The distance between the writing and the reality bothers me a lot, but in proposal writing that's fine, that is how it works. But when it leaks into the text written about an art work, or when that proposal talk gets outside of proposal land and goes to an audience it eventually affects how we think about our projects, and that is the real danger.[13]

After asking the group about sustainability, one subject replies:

> You write a lie, a dream ... and then a couple of years later you look back and say, well, this isn't working out yet ... but why is that a requirement in the first place, why can't we say we will be funded for three years? So we

10...........In regards to 'the region,' Kirsten Scheid observed that '"here" never requires a map to be found ... occasionally it is replaced by "the local"'; it 'merges with metropolitan, national, regional, and geo-political boundaries ... is taken as spatially fixed references ... [and] not only describes a phenomenon's place but suggests its basis,' but also, it 'will always refer back to the speaker using it to point to a specific setting.' Kirsten Scheid, 'The Everywhere in Here,' *Peeping Tom Digest: A Publication Exploring Contemporary Art Scenes Around the World* 3 (2010), pp. 46-47.

11...........Ibid.

12...........Ibid.

13...........Ibid.

> will work for three years, and then we won't exist anymore, and something else will appear?[14]

Opinions vary regarding the short duration of projects; this is partly linked to different life positions in regard to family/children, health, or general social class background and the availability of different sources of income. The temporality of projects goes hand in hand with the 'illusion of autonomy,'[15] which, in other words, refers to the precarious status of cultural actors—no safety in regard to regular income, health insurance, pension, etc. This is also the case for general European project funding in which honorariums are often symbolic in nature, particularly for younger artists and cultural practitioners. One interlocutor invited the others to completely rethink the social critique of precariousness: 'there is an immense creativity in those temporary, instant responses of projects to certain contexts. ... It is very quick, and it addresses the emergency at hand.'[16] Another adds that European funding invites you to compromise your ideas and thoughts: '[I]t is about how much comfort [you need] that sits with things you compromise. It becomes very comfortable knowing that the money is coming.'[17]

The FoA case study in Cairo, the 'Mobile Hackerspace,' is an example of such short-term projects; it was funded for one year (2015–2016), at a time in which parts of the culture scene were already undermined by the security apparatus of the state. It might be due to this pressure that the description of the project remains unclear:

> ... [T]he Hackerspace ... has pulled in a new community of creative industry and educational programmes that are focusing on economic stability ... offered workshops that produced innovators ... [and] a number of 'makers' have gone on to become entrepreneurs and established their own start-ups.[18]

The Mobile Hackerspace, which by the time of the research occupied an office in an upscale co-working space in the neighbourhood of Maadi, remained sceptical about talking to us about their work, and refused to share information that would help to evaluate the project in regard to its effect. The position is not only understandable in light of its work (which is mainly to provide the physical infrastructure, networks, and tools for members of the group, see website Hackerspace),[19] but also their refusal to give in to the demand for information meant for us that they

14 ........... Ibid.
15 ........... Christina Scharff, 'The Psychic Life of Neoliberalism: Mapping the Contours of Entrepreneurial Subjectivity,' *Theory, Culture & Society* 33, no. 6 (November 2016), p. 109.
16 ........... Group conversation, Cairo, 25 February 2019.
17 ........... Ibid.
18 ........... 'The Force of Art: Research from a Global Perspective,' List of cases for study, 2018.
19 ........... Cairo Hackerspace website, https://cairohackerspace.org/about (accessed 26 April 2020).

were not interested in an evaluation such as we were able to offer, or as the FoA initiative intended. In this sense, the funding is not taken as a 'gift,' thereby reflecting the inherently problematic structure of financial support (which does not demand reciprocity). The idea of a gift carries with it the promise of generosity without self-interest or expectation.[20] However, the structures within which European donors[21] give to non-European receivers, combined with the aforementioned umbrella topics which frame funding lines and grants alongside developmental ideas (such as gender, empowerment of women, resilience, or creative economies), do attach the notion of 'gift' to a clear function. Evaluating the effect of this 'gift' perpetuates the idea that there has to be a function, one that is articulated beforehand within the brackets of the respective funding line. The primacy of function regarding European-funded art and cultural work deconstructs the notion of monetary support as a gift or as an intention-free support because it links culture predominantly to a specific developmental purpose.

However, the concept of the gift (and by extension of cultural funding) does not exclusively indicate something material—it can also be linked to solidarity.[22] The notion of solidarity in this context is important for two reasons: first, in relation to the idea of development aid and giving, as described above; and second, in relation to neoliberalism and structures of competition which actually hinder the possible growth, development, and maintenance of structures of solidarity and sociality.

Creative work makes us all more precarious. It reduces the need for a physical office space, in-work benefits, and long-term contracts, and intrudes into our leisure time, home life, and emotional energies. In this respect, it has inherently neoliberal characteristics because it is actively destroying any form of collectivized, public and social work. Creative work is *anti*social.[23]

One such prominent structure is the field of creative economies, for which European funding in the past years increased in both Egypt as well as Tunisia.

## Tunis

• •

Creative economies are seen as a tool to combat unemployment, and hence make (young) people stay in the country. The Middle East and North Africa (MENA) region has been positioned as a huge growth opportunity for the so-called creative economies with a heightened emphasis on entrepreneurialism as a result of a youthful tech-savvy population experiencing high unemployment.[24] The infrastructures that support the creative economies—co-working spaces, creative economy hubs, and investment

20 .......... Ilan Kapoor, *The Postcolonial Politics of Development* (New York: Routledge, 2008).

21 .......... One interlocutor from the funding institutions' side questioned the description 'European institution,' since not all employees were strictly European. Inasmuch as these descriptive terms should be challenged, what matters in the context of this research is how our interlocutors in Egypt, Tunisia, and Algeria referred to the institutions, and not surprisingly they did so as 'European institutions.'

22 .......... Aafke Komter, *Social Solidarity and the Gift* (Cambridge: Cambridge University Press, 2004).

23 .......... Oli Mould, *Against Creativity* (London: Verso Books, 2018), p. 47.

What, How And For Whom (WHW) / Zagreb, Croatia / 12:18pm 45°49'00.5"N / 15°58'52.8"E

Visual Arts Network Of South Africa (VANSA) / Johannesburg, South Africa / 1:08pm 26°11'13.5'S / 28°02'29.6'E

networks—position themselves as important drivers of economic growth, urban development, and job creation in a context where the government and private sector are failing to generate them.[25]

Short-term development 'fixes' are often problematic in that they do not cater to the specific local context. One interlocutous states,

> There is also something very interesting now, we see that all funding is about cultural entrepreneurship, and trying to push people to be an entrepreneur and to open their own project, but we don't have the cultural market or the structural cultural scene for this, so they [European institutions] are investing money in wrong things.[26]

Another adds:

> One thing is clear now with this new trend and the race for cultural entrepreneurship. ... [N]ow, the same people who were for years doing cultural policies and, cultural art, all come working in incubation and now that the money is in entrepreneurship, they all come working in incubation. They are the same people, and the system is only benefiting those intermediaries. ... Everybody is pushing it, because the donors are funding it. The big calls are all about entrepreneurship and job creation. The whole region, everywhere, is job creation because of youth problems![27]

Whereas the continuous state-led crackdown on civil society in Egypt's case is more or less a well-known fact, Tunisia's revolution has often been declared as successful, with negotiations of cultural expressions less between state and society, and more between different religious groups. With Tunisia's transition from a police state towards a more democratic civil society, it also made the transition to neoliberal authoritarianism, replacing the old regime's military intelligence apparatus with a new system. What is often overlooked though in post-uprising narrations of both Egypt and Tunisia is the way local policies are linked to European politics of migration and immigration. 'Tunisia is often heralded as an

24 ........... See: Timothy Mitchell, *Rule of Experts: Egypt, Techno-Politics, Modernity* (Berkeley: University of California Press, 2002); Julia Elyachar, *Markets of Dispossession: NGOs, Economic Development, and the State in Cairo* (Durham: Duke University Press, 2005).

25 ........... Valentina Primo, 'More than Entrepreneurs: The Rise of the 'Gig Economy,' *Cairo Scene* (2015); Linda Herrera, 'The Precarity of Youth: Entrepreneurship in Not the Solution,' *Mada Masr* (2017).

26 ........... Anonymous interlocutor, interview by Ilka Eickhof and Alexandra Stock, Tunis, 2019.

27 ........... Ibid.

anomaly of the 2011 Arab uprisings, with commentators pointing to the country's political stability and the country's progress on liberalization,' writes historian Edna Bonhomme in November 2019; she reminds of the lesser known facts of legal and extra-legal measures restricting people's freedom of movement and further limiting people's privacy, often similar to Egypt, in the name of preventing terrorism and increasing security.[28] The focus of these measures mostly lies on migration and border surveillance, all too often supported by European surveillance technologies. This is significant because the state's focus on youth (in regards to migration and border politics) is similar to European institutions' focus on youth when it comes to art and culture programmes, specifically when linked to civil society or other developmental notions of societal progress. Evaluating the effect of art is one of the topics that connects these two seemingly different fields, art and migration: 'People cannot live without art, we cannot stop expressing ourselves,' explains one interlocutor when asked about the possible effect of art. 'They [local cultural managers] have a problem to finance art, and they have to prove to the educators that art is growing, and that art is keeping immigrants in their countries.'[29]

In Tunisia, it was only recently that European cultural institutions established themselves more prominently: 'Over the past two or three years, the EU has become the most important funding body. ... After the revolution, ... the Goethe-Institute was the most important cultural operator. We don't like the French though, they want to take our place as an expert, that's for sure,' one interlocutor candidly says at the beginning of the interview, laughing.[30] Another interlocutor explains,

> In Tunisia, it's like from zero to wahhhh [indicating a steep increase with her hands] after the revolution. Before, it was not with the same volume, many other players came in. It is exponential here; don't even compare. Funding has considerably, dangerously increased, but there is no visibility. I can tell you, they are more present, the EU funding has increased in general, but there is a lack of data.[31]

The lack of data is a recurring subject encountered in our interviews. Several point out that, despite evaluations and questionnaires, data has not been made available to local practitioners.

They [European institutions] brought to us some money, but they kept all the information, and they are now trying to have the position of an expert. How can we become a professional if we don't have access to our data?[32]

28 .......... Edna Bonhomme, 'Tunisia's Surveillance State,' *Africa is a Country* (2019), https://africasacountry.com/2019/11/tunisias-surveillance-state

29 .......... Anonymous interlocutor, interview by Ilka Eickhof and Alexandra Stock, Tunis, 2019.

30 .......... Ibid.

31 .......... Ibid.

32 .......... Ibid.

The question of who is seen as an expert, and why, is one that is also linked to the self-sustainability of the art and culture field in general.

The pity is, you think if you understand the system, you will eventually be an influencer, someone who can influence and change it. ... But as with this project [FoA], here you have the people benefiting from the system talking about the problem of the system.

'There is a conflict of interest right there,' says the interlocutor, herself a cultural manager with outstanding experience in the field. She reflects on the idea of expertise,

> The idea should be to transfer skills. ... Come on, if you keep me in the position of a trainee all my life, when are you going to recognize my expertise? The expertise is here. Empower the locals to do it![33]

One of our interlocutors also raises the issue of age that comes with both expertise and European funding: 'You see it in the funding lines, everything now is, there is a lot of age limits to accessing funding; as soon as you are over 40, the message is that you are worthless,' she says, before explaining: 'The Europeans are not investing in knowledge holders ... .'[34]

Similar to Egypt, the question of European funding in general is one that is openly discussed, but not necessarily as politically condemned as in Egypt, where European funding is much more dominating than in Tunis. One Tunisian explains his political position in this regard:

> It's money. People are very comfortable with taking money from foreign institutions. For them, it's their right, they are owed this money. European countries are taking our agriculture, our things for free, so this is our right to have this money.[35]

Another states angrily:

> Europe is involved in five big programme lines in Tunisia. Euromed, Med Culture, a programme for start-up and engineering, two other programmes for waste management, and I don't know. They tick five big boxes. They work with universities, with cultural actors, and with civil society. You get the picture! ... The main website that provides information for funding opportunities,

33 Ibid.
34 Ibid.
35 Ibid.

> jamaity[.org], is financed by Euromed and the Délégation de l'Union Européenne en Tunisie. Not even that is local![36]

The Tunisian FoA case was financially supported by Europe for one year (2015–2016) and is not just a project, but an institution in itself. The Maison de l'Image is an independent visual art space and also functions as a co-working space. The founding director of the institution shares with us his idea of what the effect of art could be, at least for his endeavour:

> Art has to ... affect the life and the quality of life of these young people. With art training we are offering them a job, network, things they did not have and they won't have easily without our institution. We are really seeing this effect on these people, even their way of thinking is changing. When they go back to their community, they are also affecting other people with this new way of thinking. How they can also criticize this community, for us this is very palpable.[37]

The Maison de l'Image has managed to be self-sustainable:

> They [European institutions] are spending money on one project; for me it's not making the institution function and sustainable. I think they want to see the results very quickly, they always ask about how many people are involved, always about quantity, not quality.[38]

Another cultural practitioner shares:

> [M]y impression is that it's all about the showy event. Too much of that, the community, in the name of community involvement, but too much short term, and no structural things, very few, and a lot of money wasted. ... A lot of them [European institutions] are present ... but there is no interest in funding an institution so they can develop their own project.

36 ........... Ibid.
37 ........... Ibid.
38 ........... Ibid.

> They always want to have their word on the project, how it could be done, how you report it. ... We don't like the obligation to report, and you have to justify everything. Sometimes when we have this kind of obligation, it becomes a nightmare to do a project here because you spend a lot of time writing, writing, writing.[39]

Another prominent critique has to do with the quality and faithfulness of reports in general, a critique, which questions the purpose of the funding itself:

> I think they [European institutions] don't spend enough time studying the cultural scene here and identifying the people who are really working in the field, because it's very easy to write something that sounds like a very good report, but I don't think they make some effort to verify this report, and see if its right and if it really shows the reality of the project.[40]

The art festival DJART, which took place in Algeria, was exceptional in regard to specifically this critique for several reasons.

## Algiers

• • •

DJART[41] took place in 2014 and was organized under the umbrella organization JISR (Arabic for bridge), an initiative launched in Barcelona in 2004. 'We were dreaming of another situation that would allow young people to work and develop artistic projects, and how to connect realities that are so close yet so far away,' one of the founders of the project describes their motivation for initiating the organization.[42] 'It was a possibility to create a bridge between these realities.' The initiators started without a budget, and their aim was to gather groups of young artists and researchers in order to debate and exchange experiences. In 2012, JISR collaborated with a number of different initiatives, institutions, artists, and cultural practitioners, who came together under the umbrella of Transcultural Dialogue and started working on DJART.

DJART worked on three levels: the urban scale (the city of Algiers), the national scale (connecting Algiers to other cities like Oran and

39 ........... Ibid.
40 ........... Ibid.
41 ........... 'DJART combines the words *Djazair* and *art* that in Arabic mean respectively "Algeria" and "neighbour." This closeness and complicity will help us explore the Algerian cultural reality open and in relation to the rest of the Mediterranean realm.' Project website, https://transculturaldialogues.noblogs.org/projects/djart/ (accessed 26 April 2020).
42 .......... Anonymous interlocutor, interview by Mariam Aboughazi, Skype interview, 2019.

Constantine), and the regional scale. 'The aim of the project was to connect culture and art with the local scene, to make art accessible for the public, everywhere.'[43] All DJART activities thus took place in the public space. Another important aim was to reinforce the regional connection between Algeria and its neighbours since cultural practitioners in the region (Morocco and Tunisia) were not very well connected. This problem is a consistent one for the Arab Middle East in general: it is often difficult for cultural practitioners from different Arab countries to connect within the region due to Visa restrictions; furthermore, regional South-South cooperation is not the primary focus of European project initiatives, calls, or funding lines.[44]

As aforementioned, there is a general opinion that European cultural institutions fund projects without really knowing the local scene, or that they only fund projects that tick boxes of topics connected to discussions cantered in Europe. One interlocutor explains, 'If [European cultural institutions] decide they will work on women today, then all the projects will work on women.' Another tells us

> When they launch a topic, it's like an annual theme, this year it was immigration. But it's not our problem, we are not facing immigration, ... we are facing economic problems, social problems, social violence. We cannot express our problems because we are obliged to put our idea in their boxes. These boxes are right now resilience, gender, feminism in the Islamic world, you know, these topics.[45]

One of the organizers of DJART describes the 'restrictive topics' that, in his opinion, reflect a limited knowledge about contemporary arts in the Arab-speaking context:

> The calls in general are not innocent, they put forward priorities that are not relevant to the local context. ... The image that people have in Europe about Arab creativity, or art in North Africa or the Middle East, is limited to very few topics, and these are always the same; this is very restrictive, and I don't think that this image was created by the artists of this region, but it was a creation of few curators in Europe—the role

43 ........... Ibid.
44 ........... Ibid.
45 ........... Ibid.

> of women, the covered woman, typography, violence. And these topics are also related to the general image that appears in the media.[46]

As another interlocutor explains the situation in Algeria, she confirms the findings of our broader research. In naming the discord between European cultural institutions and 'local cultural dynamics,' we find that European funded projects are often perceived as irrelevant to the local context, and often seen to feed into a 'neocolonial image' of the region.

Cultural practitioners and artists in the local contexts live in a reality that is so far from the actions of the European cultural institutions. They [the European institutions] have other interests and other priorities than understanding the local dynamics, the local cultural dynamics—how they work, and how they can support them in the right way. They are always trying to impose a point of view that is a European one—how we want to manage your culture. Instead, it would be more interesting if they were conscious of the meaning of their actions, and give out the money in the service of the cultural context, letting locals decide on what they believe is a priority at the moment.[47]

The organizers of DJART took their time to understand the local situation before implementing the project; they were aware that a European artist or curator suddenly appearing and then disappearing again would have very little effect on the local scene. In order to avoid the 'imposed topic-trap,' the DJART organizers did extensive research for over two years, and got in touch with the local scene in Algiers and with already existing projects and initiatives. 'It was really important for all of us not to come with a parachute project from an external point of view, but to develop a project that is giving answers to local needs!' said one of the organizers. In these two years the project participants conducted interviews and collected data from different local entities by walking the streets of Algiers, asking what the perceptions of culture were, and what culture could provide people with in their daily life.[48]

One of the organizers admits,

> We realized that art and culture is conceived as something elitist,' admitted one of the organizers, 'something they think they cannot imagine. At that period no one was interested in going to a cultural space, not even the cinema, or museums. Music seemed to be the only discipline that people interacted with without prejudice.[49]

46..........Ibid.
47..........Ibid.
48..........Ibid.
49..........Ibid.

The presence of European artists in the DJART project was limited. The organizers felt that European work would eventually feel out of context and even more inaccessible to a local audience since the nature of society and the approach to art and culture is very different from main European cultural hubs such as Berlin, London, Amsterdam, Barcelona, or Paris.

The idea was to engage the locals in the sense that they are already doing things that need to be shown, or at least be more visible in the streets. So we were supporting actions that already took place by presenting them on a large scale.[50]

In that regard, the project was considered a success, not only because it made already existing art scenes more accessible to the general public, but most importantly it forged connections between artists from the region that were fostered even after the project came to an end.

The DJART organizers decided not to depend on one funding entity alone, but to keep the power to control content, process, and artistic direction through decentralizing funding processes. Therefore, they created a pool of partners and funders, and kept an equal distance from all of them: 'We felt completely free because we didn't accept any modifications on the programme. The programme was agreed on internally, and no one else had anything to say,' describes the interlocutor.[51] This strategy—to utilize all resources and decentralize efforts and funding—was used for both local state funding as well as European funding.

## Funding Institutions

• • • •

'The response to your work is
symptomatic of what you critique.'[52]

The interventions and cultural programmes of European cultural institutions go beyond the field of art's internal concerns, but produce a hegemonic discourse related to dominant European topics and values. The following section takes a closer look at the European funding institutions through anonymous interviews conducted with employees of the Prince Claus Fund, Hivos, and the European Cultural Fund, and an online questionnaire geared towards artists and cultural practitioners in the MENA region. The interviews with the funders were conducted on the basis of the findings of the survey, and of the evaluations of the project cases.

The online questionnaire developed for this research showed that seventy-six per cent of the respondents felt that the art and culture sector in their country depended on European funding. The responses indicate that the source of funding for artistic projects is important, and the reasons given can be clustered in (1) ethical concerns, (2) other projects funded by these institutions, (3) the intention or the agenda of the funding institution, and (4) the fear of interference of funding institutions with content, aesthetics, or process.

50..........Ibid.
51..........Ibid.
52..........Sara Ahmed, 'A Phenomenology of Whiteness,' *Feminist Theory* 8, no. 2 (August 2007), p. 164.

As one interviewee states, 'Usually the topic is linked to the money.'[53] Another explains that 'Political affiliations dictate agents and reasons behind funding.' While more than fifty per cent of respondents have received funding from European institutions before, eighty per cent of respondents disagree that they influence what is funded by European institutions, and over ninety per cent think that European funding structures are not well connected with local situations. There is a general feeling that European funding entities reiterate a post-colonial attitude toward the recipients of the funds in the region, with the strongest respondent saying that '[t]hey are still trying to 'civilize' the world, trying to impose political agendas on the world, distributing money in ways that are not transparent, not current, and not logical.'[54]

In response to the survey and the evaluational research of three different cases, representatives of funding institutions replied to the two main topic sections that were raised: (1) project calls and their recipients, and (2) the question of the evaluation and impact of art.

'The call for proposals is an ongoing learning experience,' one interviewee mentions.[55] Through the implementation of roundtables and decisions with 'the experts' (often network partners), the institution aims to write calls that are relevant to the local context. Furthermore, collaborations with already existing representations of European institutions on the ground assume a better understanding of the local context, such as the British Council, or one of the Goethe-Institutes; one organization also works with a local committee when assessing the responses to the calls. Another institution divides their calls into two larger sections, one for cultural organizations and institutions, and one for individual artists. One representative explains:

> It's all about language, so we try to create a neutral call, but still have some words in it for people to recognize that this is about challenging hegemonic structures, this is about being critical, this is about addressing topics that are difficult to discuss at the moment, and you want to make that clear to the people applying for this call, but you also don't want to be explicit about it.[56]

Despite these efforts, the vast majority of the survey participants find that European funding structures or projects funded by EU institutions are not well connected with the local situation. One interviewee explains that the European funding structures are not 'connected,' but rather 'in control of aspects of the local situation.'[57] This also nurtures a common trope of

53..........Online questionnaire, by Ilka Eickhof and Mariam Aboughazi, 2019.

54..........Ibid.

55..........Anonymous interlocutor, Skype interview by Ilka Eickhof and Mariam Aboughazi, 2019.

56..........Anonymous interlocutor, Skype interview by Mariam Aboughazi, 2019.

mistrust: 'I feel that a very common and repeated narrative with European funding mechanisms is that there is a lack of trust,' one interlocutor reveals.[58]

On the one hand, there are many funding arms that demonstrate so much effort put forth. They seem to try to guarantee fairness, being ethical stakeholders and impact-driven. Some try very hard to do the most that they can, but it often comes off as rigid, impossible to navigate, and totally disconnected. When bureaucracy and top-down 'thematic areas' linked to certain agendas appear to be more important than the needs of grantees then it can totally be seen how a culture of mistrust is fostered.

The general nature of calls differs from institution to institution. Some are rather lucid and open ended, with no confined topic, while others are more directed and topic based, the latter being criticized by local interlocutors and survey participants, also because such calls perpetuate the problem of 'the network of usual suspects.' As one attendee of the Cairo meeting recounts, 'As a previous recipient of the (redacted)fund, I get calls asking me about new applicants, and whether I know them or not. Which means they end up circling in the same circles.'[59]

In other words, an alternative is needed that builds on local connections without only benefitting the same group of people. One interviewee explains that their institution tries to solve this problem:

> By supporting initiatives outside the capitals, or specifically supporting initiatives and individuals who haven't received funding before. But on the other hand, we are aware that there is not enough funding out there and we don't want to create this illusion that some of these institutions can survive without funding, so sometimes we end up supporting one of the usual suspects again—it's a balancing act![60]

Based on the results of the online questionnaire, over eighty-seven per cent of the respondents disagree that there is diversity in who gets the funds. The majority of the respondents agree that funding is only granted to people within the same circles. In addition, while ninety-five per cent of the respondents believe that people are competing for European funding, over eighty-five per cent of the respondents also feel that European institutions are not trying to reach beyond the usual recipients of funding. On the other hand, the focus on the younger generation is critically mentioned as well, even in cases in which recipients of funding are organizations led by older generations—the project still selectively targets young people.

57..........Online questionnaire, by Ilka Eickhof and Mariam Aboughazi, 2019.
58..........Ibid.
59..........Anonymous interlocutor, interview by Ilka Eickhof and Alexandra Stock. Group conversation. Cairo, 25 February 2019
60..........Anonymous interlocutor, interview by Mariam Aboughazi, Skype interview, 2019.

The funding institutions show a difference in how they try to evaluate art and its impact; one approach focuses on numbers, the other one on stories. The latter tries to break away from more traditional monitoring and evaluation techniques. 'Impact does not equal numbers,' the interviewee explained.[61]

While everything tends to be measured in numbers, culture is one of the places that have the space for us to still be human and express ourselves in a human way. ... You cannot measure certain things, and then hope that there is a change there, development is not a straight line up.

Impact is described as something vague and intangible, something people can 'feel': 'If it has meant something, if it has made them feel something, if there was somehow some transformative value in the projects that we have supported, then I think there was an impact.' It remains unanswered though how this impact can be measured, let alone the question whether it 'should' be measured. 'We are trying to find ways to show how important art and culture are, this is one of the few places where there is no political agenda, no economic agenda, and there is some freedom left there,' one interviewee explains.[62] This also includes a more positive approach to failures.

Funders have a responsibility to show that they understand failures, because otherwise the recipients of funds will feel the need to show the bright and shiny story, therefore we as funders should start by sharing *our* failures. ... It's a long term process and it is not a rapid response like what you see with human rights for instance, but investing in the cultural sector, you harvest its results on the long run.[63]

An evaluative formula that is flexible enough to provide space for change and growth as the institution manages to look more into qualitative results rather than quantitative results seems more adequate and responsive to the given critique.

The FoA initiative comes as an attempt from European funding institutions to find ways that show and evaluate the effect of art, maybe even try to measure it, but also try to show the difficulty, maybe even the 'impossibility' of such endeavour, as one interviewee critically expresses: 'I really hope that this study will really change the way people look at assessing art and culture so that its not only measured the way it is usually measured.' Another interviewee adds, 'One of the main reasons we have commissioned the research is that we wanted to show that there are multiple ways and forms to look at the question of how to measure the impact of art.'[64]

In that sense, the FoA initiative seems to be stuck between a rock and a hard place with representatives knowing that trying to justify why art matters is important within the operating structures, whilst being aware that measuring the impact of art and culture is highly problematic. The impact of art is a long term 'investment' (for the lack of a better,

61 .......... Anonymous interlocutor, interview by Ilka Eickhof and Mariam Aboughazi, Skype interview, 2019.
62 .......... Ibid.
63 .......... Ibid.
64 .......... Ibid.

non-economic word), and we can see in the case of Egypt that an undermined contemporary art scene has severe implications on society and its development. While eighty-four per cent of the online questionnaire respondents agree that art should have an impact on society (without specifying what exactly that could mean), only forty-seven per cent think the 'effect of art' can be measured. As one respondent explains,

> Art has an impact on individuals but we cannot generalize, nor regulate, control, or monitor this impact. As art is not happening in a vacuumed life and we have no real power to make an impact. We as artists or operators cannot claim this power, especially if it is imposed by the European institutions.[65]

## RESEARCH FINDINGS

> 'The question for the evaluation is the why, why is it good to evaluate? [D]o they [FoA] want to compare it with the reality?'[66]

This research is not only an evaluation of different art projects and the way these projects are embedded within their particular scene, but also of the art of evaluation itself, and of the overall FoA initiative. As the interlocutor in the above quote asks, Why is it good to evaluate? What do we do with these evaluations? Do we write about the possible impact of art in order to govern it? Or to structure foreign-funded art in a better, more accessible way? Do we formulate recommendations for structural changes, albeit knowing that within the tight grip of neoliberal structures, only very little can change after all? After years and years of evaluation, what has changed now?

The research shows that both the funder and the funded are well aware of problematic aspects of European funding—its historicity, its effects, and its limits. One major point of critique that funding institutions try to challenge through implementing different expert strategies and boards is the distance and therefore disconnect between the European funders and the specific societal situation. This disconnect is mirrored not only in regard to project calls, but also to the question of who is acknowledged as an expert, general employment structures, accessibility of data and material, and the ability to formulate critique in a self-reflexive rather than defensive way.

65 ..........Online questionnaire, by Ilka Eickhof and Mariam Aboughazi, 2019.

66 ..........Anonymous interlocutor, interview by Ilka Eickhof and Alexandra Stock, Tunis, 2019.

67 ..........Ibid.

68 ..........Ibid.

Based on the research, the main findings are elaborated below in the form of reccomendations.

1. Calls should be more participative.

> These boxes [topics of funding lines such as gender, resilience, migration, etc.] are the market for the funding. We need more people to make advocacy for us for these institutions to change their mindset, and to make their calls more participative,

explains one interlocutor in Tunis.[67] In order to be able to make calls more participative, the institutions need to be connected to the specific local situation, and to engage with the different communities. There are several ways that could improve the calls: long-term engagement with local artists, employing local experts in decision-making positions, or engaging with an inter-generational, interdisciplinary local board. Connecting project calls and funding to local topics would mean possible disengagement from European audiences and European foreign cultural policies. At the same time, it could be seen as a moment to challenge strict hierarchies and entrenched structures within institutions, making them more participatory overall.

2. Acknowledge local experts and nurture their expertise. One interlocutor uses the term empowerment, meaning that financial support should not enforce dependency, but create independence:

> What we want is not that you come to help me, but that you come to empower me. Help me for one year, but after that make sure that I will bring money alone, and that I will write my own policy. We are the experts here, we know what we need.[68]

Using funding to enable local structures to become stable and thrive without said funding is one of the main points of critique raised in almost all the conversations we had. To enable this kind of independence means that local experts have to be involved beyond the usual consultancy or trainee roles, as described by the interlocutor above. Nurturing independence is linked to sustainability, which would shift the focus to a more structural funding of projects and places, and move away from content and topics regulated by specific project funding calls.

3. In accordance with nurturing local expertise, collected data needs to be made available in order to work with it, and to find possible funding gaps or overuses. A cultural manager in Cairo reports:

> I wanted to do an excel sheet of who is funding what, but it is impossible.

> Despite all the proclaimed transparency, programmes, EU structures, and what have you. Third countries, Global South countries, we are supposed to be transparent and good, good students, but when you go to the donors, and you ask can you please send me a list of what are the projects you have funded within this financial year, I just want to make statistics to see, these are the sectors that are overfunded, these are the sectors that are underfunded—no access!

Another interlocutor from Tunis also criticizes the policy of no data sharing: 'We need to influence policies. We have to have the data to tell them, this does not work, this is wrong.'[69] The critique described in this quote is related to the demand to not only acknowledge local expertise, but to assist structures maintained independently, without European funding. In order to achieve sustainability, the vast amount of data collected by those who evaluated in the past decade must be made available to those concerned, and to return the evaluations' focus to project funding and funding apparatus instead of funded projects and reports, hence steering away from furthering dependency by refusing data transparency.

4. Offer expertise-generating activities; for interlocutors this is a key to sustainability and independence. One of the organizers of a larger art institution explains

> The idea is not to say ah, it's bad, European funding is bad. Because to be honest, without that kind of funding in some countries the art and culture scene would not survive. … But, you want to empower me, that is what I want from you. But with your funding, I don't become the product of you. I don't want that. You can help, but then you don't own [me or the project], and I don't owe you.

This part is especially important when taking into consideration that the concept of funding as an unconditioned gift lays the ground for asymmetry within developmental structures and cultural programming.

5. Create focus groups and invite critical thinkers, not just as fig leaves, but rather to introduce possible structural change. 'In the focus groups, they never have critical thinkers. They will talk about the operationality, that's it,' observes one interlocutor.[70] The level of scepticism critical thinkers are met with indicates an unease with obvious and somewhat

acknowledged positions of power, and a silencing of such privileges. Making privilege visible though is only helpful for either side if it engages with a structural change that implies being willing to challenge said privileges.

Both the Maison de l'Image and DJART were good examples of funding in which some of the above findings were met. The funding supported the institutional structure, and not only a short workshop (rent for the space, running costs, equipment), but also preparatory long-time research that guaranteed accessibility for the local audience. Local expertise is recognized, and expertise-generating activities took place. The managing director, defining the space through what it offers and not through who owns it:

> This project, Maison de L'Image, it's not mine. It's the people that come here every day, it's not my space, the idea is also to leave the institution. The success of a space like this is that it can be taken by people here to do things. The space has to be like a real house, open for everybody, a place where people can meet, without having to fit in one box.[71]

The above findings and recommendations are all interconnected: to change project calls, the foci of evaluations, general funding goals and accessibility of data would change the institution's overall aim, and hence the question of what the effect of art would, should or could be. Funding structures would dissolve into the background, giving way to local, 'un-evaluationable' content and connectivity.

## CONCLUSION

Since 2011 and the start of the Arab uprisings, the culture and arts domain has come to be seen by local as well as foreign culture policies as a mobilizer of counter-hegemonic movements, and is perceived as such locally as well as globally, reinforcing the conflation of art and politics.[72] As a result, the contemporary art and culture field in the MENA region has witnessed an exponential growth in the technical and financial support it receives from EU funding bodies.

A neoliberal position in which some sort of competing impact has to be visible and guaranteed on the short run is mirrored in the way evaluations are structured, their key objectives and motivations, and the

69..........Ibid.
70..........Ibid.
71..........Ibid.
72..........See Hisham Aidi, 'The Grand (Hip-Hop) Chessboard,' *Middle East Report* 260 (Fall 2011).

question of art's effect. However, it is exactly this neoliberal structure that allows for authoritarian desires to be nurtured, and that calls for short-term fixes in regard to unemployment, or migration issues. The competitive nature of the open calls and the economization of art and culture mean that social relationships are evaluated mainly in regard to their usefulness, usability, and reciprocity of social and economic capital.

Structures of solidarity are not part of either the calls, or the evaluations, which intensify competitive behaviour, conformity, and performance pressure. Adding to the above-mentioned research findings, if 'the' or 'an' effect of art is supposed to strengthen solidarity, general openness, and a communal sense, then it should target and overcome neoliberal structures which promote competition and othering. It is not the evaluation itself in any way, shape or form that is problematic per se; in fact, evaluations do not seem to matter much at all. What is of significance though is what motivates the evaluation, and what the alleged effect of art is supposed to be—and why there has to be one in the first place. Projects that are uncritically oriented towards an economic output like creative economies, or those which focus only on specific age-limited groups, aiming for quick turnouts without the time or sense for sustainability, will fail to nurture social cohesion, solidarity, or critical anti-hegemonic movements.

Pages Bookstore Istanbul / Istanbul, Turkey / 1:08pm 41°01'56.5"N / 28°56'19.9"E

DEPO / Istanbul, Turkey / 1:10pm    41°01'37.4"N / 28°58'42.0"E

← REFERENCES

Ahmed, Sara. 'A Phenomenology of Whiteness.' *Feminist Theory* 8, no. 2 (August 2007).

Aidi, Hisham. 'The Grand (Hip-Hop) Chessboard.' *Middle East Report* 260 (Fall 2011).

Baldwin, James. *The Creative Process*. New York: Published for the National Cultural Center, The Ridge Press, 1962.

Bonhomme, Edna. 'Tunisia's Surveillance State.' *Africa is a Country*, 2019.

DJART. https://transculturaldialogues.noblogs.org/projects/djart/ (accessed 26 April 2020).

Elyachar, Julia. *Markets of Dispossession: NGOs, Economic Development, and the State in Cairo.* Durham: Duke University Press, 2005.

Hackerspace. https://cairohackerspace.org/about (accessed 26 April 2020).

Herrera, Linda. 'The Precarity of Youth: Entrepreneurship in Not the Solution.' *Mada Masr*, 2017.

Kapoor, Ilan. *The Postcolonial Politics of Development*. New York: Routledge, 2008.

Komter, Aafke. *Social Solidarity and the Gift*. Cambridge: Cambridge University Press, 2004.

Mitchell, Timothy. *Rule of Experts: Egypt, Techno-Politics, Modernity*. Berkeley: University of California Press, 2002.

Mould, Oli. *Against Creativity*. London: Verso Books, 2018.

Primo, Valentina. 'More than Entrepreneurs: The Rise of the "gig economy".' *Cairo Scene*, 2015.

Resende, Fernando. 'The Global South. Conflicting Narratives and the Invention of Geographies.' *Ibraaz*, 6 November 2014.

Scharff, Christina. 'The Psychic Life of Neoliberalism: Mapping the Contours of Entrepreneurial Subjectivity.' *Theory, Culture & Society* 33, no. 6 (November 2016).

Scheid, Kirsten. 'The Everywhere in Here.' In *Peeping Tom Digest: A Publication Exploring Contemporary Art Scenes Around the World* 3. Beirut: 2010.

'The Force of Art: Research from a Global Perspective.' Call for Expression of Interest (CIE), funded by the Prince Claus Fund, Hivos, and the European Cultural Foundation, 2018.

'The Force of Art: Research from a Global Perspective.' List of cases for study, 2018.

← INTERVIEWS

Anonymous interlocutor, interview by Ilka Eickhof and Alexandra Stock, Tunis, 2019.

Anonymous interlocutor, interview by Mariam Aboughazi, Skype interview, 2019.

Anonymous interlocutor, interview by Ilka Eickhof and Alexandra Stock. Group conversation. Cairo, 25 February 2019.

# CURATING DAKAR AS AN 'ART WORLD CITY'

Jenny Mbaye and
Miranda Jeanne Marie Iossifidis

This chapter explores the contours and dynamics that forge Dakar as a contemporary 'art world city,' inquiring into initiatives that operate at the crossroads of art, citizenship and society. In a context marked by a monopolistic role of the state, the chapter interrogates the practices of two independent art organizations, RAW Material Company and Kër Thiossane, and their different engagements with and through the city. Delving into the processes of alternative, independent 'art institution-building,' we draw on AbdouMaliq Simone's notion of 'rhythms of endurance' to explore the ways in which new methods of sharing and producing knowledge are developed and curated. Located at the intersections of creativity, cultural politics, and urban transformation, our contribution focuses on the subjects of such creative and transformative processes. In doing so, we emphasize the capacity of ordinary citizens to engage in the practical and symbolic re-imagining of their city. This chapter demonstrates that curatorial interventions and critical perspectives, through engaging with multiple audiences and investing in 'art as a thinking system,' can create spaces of encounters, of expression, exchange, reflection, and speculation to produce an 'art world city' in constant recreation.

Keywords
→ Dakar
→ Art Institution-Building
→ Urban Transformation
→ Rhythms of Endurance
→ Art World City

## INTRODUCTION

Dakar was recently identified as one of the top five creative cities in the world.[1] The article referenced 'Dak'art,' the Biennale of Contemporary African Arts, and numerous independent organizations thriving in the city. In this chapter, we focus on the rhythms of endurance[2] through which arts practitioners, initiatives, and organizations operate on an everyday basis in Dakar. Specifically focusing on the experiences of Kër Thiossane, Partcours and RAW Material Company, we explore the ways in which these arts initiatives and organizations reaffirm the capacity of 'human infrastructures' to shape the city and its urban life in improvizational and organic ways. As such, this chapter goes beyond 'Dak'Art'—the blockbuster event that has significantly impacted the creative landscape of the capital city—to engage with the day-to-day engagement and artistic commitment of civil society. It highlights the kinds of everyday creative practice that contribute to redefining, and hence transforming, the city, and shifts the focus onto the (extra)ordinary producers of urban spaces. Developing and revisiting new methods of acquiring and sharing knowledge, curating at the crossroads of art, citizenship, and society, these art initiatives are symbolically and practically reinterpreting 'world-class'[3] aesthetics and imaginaries.

This chapter thus provides insights into what has contributed to establishing Dakar as an art world city by first engaging with the contours of the environment: the Biennale 'Dak'Art' and its fringe programming, 'Off.' In a context marked by an omnipresent state within the cultural field, we then introduce the notion of 'art institution building'[4] to understand the ways in which alternative independent art initiatives contribute—on their own terms and conditions—to the curatorial sensibilities of Dakar. We discuss the practices of art initiatives and collectives such as Partcourt and Laboratoire Agit'Art. Such alternative art institutions establish new referents for artistic and curatorial practices and affirm their political responsibility through their engagement with and embeddedness in the dakarois context. We argue that Dakar's art scene is characterized by a diversity of rhythms, and drawing on Simone's concept of 'rhythms of endurance,' we turn to focus in more depth on the experiences of two distinctive art institutions, Kër Thiossane and RAW Material Company. As we shall conclude, albeit with a different approach to curatorial practices, the two art institutions are independent, not-for-profit art organizations which both address a multiplicity of audiences and invest in the notion of 'art as a thinking system' as way to transform the city.

## DAKAR AS AN ART WORLD CITY? THE CONTOURS OF THE ENVIRONMENT: 'DAK'ART' AND ITS 'OFF'

> In the insurgent formulation, ... the residents of the peripheries imagine that their interests derive from their own experiences, not from state plans, and that they are informed and competent to make decisions.[5]

1.............Libby Banks, 'The Five Most Creative Cities in the World?,' BBC, 16 July 2019, www.bbc.com/culture/story/20190715-the-five-most-creative-cities-in-the-world

2.............AbdouMaliq Simone, *Improvised Lives: Rhythms of Endurance in an Urban South* (Cambridge: Polity Press, 2018).

3.............Asher D. Ghertner, 'Rule by Aesthetics: World-Class City Making in Delhi,' *Worlding Cities: Asian Experiments and the Art of Being* Global, ed. Ananya Roy and Aihwa Ong (Malden, and Oxford: Wiley & Sons, 2011), pp. 279–306.

4.............Koyo Kouoh, 'Filling the Voids: The Emergence of Independent Contemporary Art Spaces,' in *Condition Report: Symposium on Building Art Institutions in Africa*, ed. Koyo Kouoh (Stuttgart: Hatje Cantz, 2012).

5.............James Holston, *Insurgent Citizenship: Disjunctions of Democracy and Modernity in Brazil* (Princeton: Princeton University Press, 2009), p. 258.

'Nation' and 'development' were the founding myths of a Senegalese modernity that rested on discourses of identity and unity.[6] In the nineteen-sixties and early nineteen-seventies, acknowledging the power of arts and culture in this process of nation building, the Senegalese government supported visual artists and their work considerably. This support was reflected in the arts education system in place since Senegal's first President Léopold Sédar Senghor: the École des Arts. Founded in 1960, this school paved the way to what came to be known as the École de Dakar, renowned for fine art, sculpture, and textiles. Set up to replace the École des Arts of Mali, the National School of Arts[7] was created to foster and promote young artists carrying forth Senghorian ideas regarding the relationship between modern African identities and the arts, and the President's philosophy of a modern valorization of Negro art: 'Négritude.'

Despite the tyranny of structural adjustments and the consequent withdrawal of the state from the field of cultural production, Dakar's Biennale of Contemporary Art, 'Dak'Art,' a state-sponsored event celebrating African contemporary art, has continued operating since 1992. As a flagship project that affirmed and certified 'a culture of the cultural entrepreneur state,'[8] this 'signature event' was initially thought of in 1990 as a Biennale of Humanities and Arts. Its genealogy, however, can be traced back to President Senghor's World Festival of Negro Arts in 1966. Since its inception, 'Dak'Art' has evolved substantially, most notably with the official incorporation of the fringe programme 'Off' in 2002 in its fifth edition. In this regard, we argue that the organically developed 'Off' and its dramatic growth over the years, as well as its unique contribution to 'monetizing' the exhibited art works, points to the rising and diversified, individual and collective productive participation in the event.[9]

The types of administration perpetuated by the elite and inherited from colonial systems have not placed importance on private and independent initiatives, a general rule considered to be 'especially true in the arts and in the situation of former French colonies.'[10] While in the contemporary landscape 'Dak'Art' remains a notable exception with regards to state support and organization of art events, our argument here is that Senegal's civil society, exceptional on the continent,[11] has nourished the capacity for ordinary citizens to engage in processes of practical and symbolic re-imagining of their city. This has been crucial for sustaining Dakar's position as an art world city, and in establishing the city's 'vibrant and dynamic "art world," a particular site for the production, interpretation, and collection of modern art.'[12]

6............Aminata Diaw, 'Les intellectuels entre mémoire nationaliste et représentations de la modernité,' in *Le Sénégal contemporain* (Paris: Karthala, 2002), p. 550.

7............For more information, see: www.ecolenationaledesarts.sn/articles/general/2/2016/11/17/historique-et-perspectives.html

8............Yacouba Konaté, *La Biennale de Dakar: Pour une esthétique de la création contemporaine africaine: tête à tête avec Adorno* (Paris: L'Harmattan, 2009), p. 34.

9............Joanna Grabski, 'Dakar's Urban Landscapes: Locating Modern Art and Artists in the City,' *African Arts* 36, no. 4 (2003), p. 19.

10..........Kouoh, 'Filling the Voids,' p. 15.

11..........Joan Tilouine, 'Baromètre des sociétés civiles: Sénégal, Niger et RDC sur le podium,' *Paris: Jeune Afrique*, 28 April 2014, www.jeuneafrique.com/164168/politique/barom-tre-des-soci-t-s-civiles-s-n-gal-niger-et-rdc-sur-le-podium/.

12..........Grabski, 'Dakar's Urban Landscapes,' p. 28.

Since the earliest editions of the Biennale in early nineteen-nineties, galleries and artists have been organizing exhibitions and openings on the margins of the official event. These were initiated by ordinary citizens and dedicated creative practitioners, i.e. local residents participating in Dakar's 'art world' who were not programmed in the official 'Dak'Art' selection. These spontaneous initiatives were animated by the 'Ateliers Céramiques Almadies' (Almadies Ceramic Studios), founded and led by artist and curator Mauro Petroni in conversation with public officials around a 'commission for environmental events.'[13] They were soon orchestrated under the banner 'Dak'Art "Off".' The idea was simple: to create maps and signage for private exhibitions without interfering with the autonomy of these parallel events.[14] While the 'Off' gained more visibility, the Biennale gained more curatorial propositions with the 'Off.' As the former General Secretary of 'Dak'Art' put it, by supplementing the official selection with exhibitions located in over one hundred improvised venues, the four official sites of the Biennale have been enriched, benefiting both the official selection and the 'Off':

> In regard to the 'Off,' there was a certain shyness in exhibiting until 2000. What we did was to say out loud that the Biennale needs to recognize the 'Off' as another side of 'Dak'Art.' These are not two oppositional elements, but one and the same event; a part of which is organized under the total responsibility of the General Secretary; and another part, organized by private initiative, but with the support of the Biennale.[15]

Since then, the 'Off' has significantly impacted and contributed to the official programme, while developing avenues of monetization, expanding the structure, propositions and reach of the event. As stressed by the former General Secretary of the Biennale, the 'Off' remains a key component of the Biennale's dynamic:

> Well-known artists manage to get inhabitants of the neighbourhoods to come and visit workshops and exhibitions out of curiosity ... And while there is no sale involved in the Biennale as an international exhibition, in its 'Off,' artists do sell, and sell a lot.[16]

13..........Author's translation for 'Commission pour les manifestations d'environnement,' Dak'Art 'Off,' *Programme* (2012), p. 1.

14..........Ibid.

15..........Ousseynou Wade (former director of Dak'Art), interview by Jenny Mbaye, Dakar, June 2013.

16..........Ibid.

To their credit, this is something that the Senegalese authorities acknowledgement when following the leitmotif of the former Ministry of Culture, to 'accompany and support what already works.'[17] The 'Off' is now organized from the confines of artists' workshops and art galleries, in buildings under construction, in personal homes, car parks, and other improvised exhibition spaces; it allows art aficionados to participate in the larger event, but also to challenge, and at times even contest, the Biennale. Displaying a 'multi-venue configuration [that] results less from a coherent curatorial vision than from the urgency of urban life in Dakar,' this art initiative emerging from civil society demonstrates that contemporary artistic life in the city 'takes place not only within formal spaces designated for the arts, but also between and beyond them.'[18]

For public officials, the 'Off' proposes an alternative use of Dakar's resources, and the geographies of the Biennale, which is 'not necessarily located in the city centre, but is also located inside dwelling places.'[19] This is especially valued by artists who continue to invest time, energy, and capital in contributing to the 'Off.' As such, well-known and successful artists and designers such as Ousmane Mbaye still regularly organize their own personal or collective exhibition in the 'Off' despite being part of the Biennale's official selection. Mobilizing Dakar's residents and transforming urban social space and visual experience, the 'Off' thus reaffirms the relevance of civil society's active participation and involvement in the creation of national and urban cultural spaces, as well as the capacity of informed citizens, as complex human infrastructure, to inform and change their field of practice and its context.[20]

The 'Dak'Art' and its 'Off' are, nevertheless, still inscribed in a context marked by a 'centralistic model of an omnipotent state [adhering to its] constitutional roles as initiator, regulator, controller, promoter, producer and critic.'[21] The state's monopolistic positioning with regards to critical artistic engagement has at times both constrained and limited the critical, dissident voices and alternative narratives. Serious institutional voids can be identified in a paradoxical environment, whereby artists are cultivated to be intellectually and financially dependent on the state. In Dakar, it has notably meant the acute absence of formal spaces to address theoretical concerns around contemporary artistic production, and has given rise to a process of alternative, independent 'art institution-building.'

## ALTERNATIVE INSTITUTION BUILDING

An 'art world city' can be defined as a 'multiscalar, urban site for artistic production, mediation and transaction [a] ... paradigm to account for the imbrication of the creative economy and the urban environment as well

17 ........... Ibid.

18 ........... Grabski, 'Dakar's Urban Landscapes: Locating Modern Art and Artists in the City,' p. 19.

19 ........... Ousseynou Wade (former director of Dak'Art) interview by Jenny Mbaye, Dakar, June 2013.

20 ........... AbdouMaliq Simone, 'The Missing People: Reflections on an Urban Majority in Cities of the South,' in *The Routledge Handbook on Cities of the Global South*, ed. Susan Parnell and Sophie Oldfield (London and New York: Routledge, 2014), pp. 322–36.

21 ........... Kouoh, 'Filling the Voids,' p. 15.

as the interplay of local and global dynamics shaping Dakar's art world.'[22] As such, we argue that the enduring affirmation of Dakar as an 'art world city' is due to the capacity of urban citizens to reconfigure the urban landscape through alternative uses of public spaces, carved through their productive participation. Rescaling the debate between organic and planned developments, i.e. between bottom-up initiatives emerging from an urban community and top-down ones led by state institutions, our focus on urban creativity here is on collectives of participants—akin to the 'Off'—active in the political and material place-making of their city and their creative productivity.[23] To do so, we provide insights into two other art initiatives, both very different and distinctive in their genesis and process, which highlight how insurgent art practitioners have been contributing to the curation of Dakar as an art world city outside the institutionalization of the state: Laboratoire Agit'Art and Partcours. In both instances, though from very different perspectives—the former being an initiated collective and the latter being a collective initiative—are 'an attempt to satisfy personal needs. The need to distribute and disseminate, through a mechanism where decisions, choices and programming did not depend on a committee or an administration.'[24]

The Laboratoire Agit'Art is a collective of intellectuals and activists based in Dakar that has repeatedly criticized the overwhelming monopoly of the state in the field of art, culture, and creative practice, and distanced itself from state-initiated cultural politics. The Laboratoire Agit'Art, which could be understood as a synergetic combination of agency, agitation, and art, was created in 1973 under the leadership of creative practitioners across different artistic disciplines including, amongst others, Issa Samb (aka Joe Ouakam), Youssoupha Done, Mame Less Dia, Djibril Diop Mambéty, and Thierno Seydou Barry. Through its collaborative practices, Agit'Art demonstrates an ethos of 'destroy[ing] current diktats in contemporary art.'[25] Their collective represents 'forms of resistance against the dominant system but also a critique of political and cultural institutions,' which dominate the cultural and creative field in Dakar.[26] Multidisciplinary in nature, the Laboratoire Agit'Art grew out of a counter-discourse to Senghor's utopianism and the manifestation of *Negritude*, opposing the establishment while embodying a conceptually radical, generous, and intellectually stimulating approach to art. The collective has long sought to create a fundamental space of freedom in a tightly regimented artistic scene, with critical thinking and political discourse as key components of its ethos. Indeed, Senghor's École de Dakar rested on a classical, conventional, and monolithic understanding of fine arts, derivative of European Primitivism and dedicating little attention (if any) to alternative paradigms in art practices. In this context, Agit'Art affirmed

22..........Joanna Grabski, *Art World City: The Creative Economy of Artists and Urban Life in Dakar* (Indiana: Indiana University Press, 2017), p. 3.23 Rosalind Fredericks, '"The Old Man is Dead": Hip Hop and the Arts of Citizenship of Senegalese Youth,' in *The Arts of Citizenship in African Cities* (New York: Palgrave Macmillan, 2014), pp. 137–61.

24..........Simon Njami, 'Imagined Communities,' in *Condition Report: Symposium on Building Art Institutions in Africa*, ed. Koyo Kouoh (Stuttgart: Hatje Cantz, 2012), p. 21.

25..........This was recently published in a manifesto of Agit'Art's heirs, as part of their contribution to 2018's Dak'Art 'Off,' *Dismemberment Manifesto*.

26..........Agit'Art, *Dismemberment Manifesto* (Dakar: Khadimou Rassoul, 2018), p. 1.

itself as an institution whose legacy lives on today as a destabilizing and agitating provocation that replenishes the dearth of free expression, production, exhibition, and critical reflection in cultural spaces.

Another alternative art institution of Dakar, we argue, is Partcours. Created in 2012 as a joint initiative of *RAW Material Company* and *Ateliers Céramiques Almadies*, Partcours is an annual event with an itinerary that stretches across the city. It explicitly aims to bring together art and exhibition spaces in Dakar and its peripheries in order to raise the visibility of different kinds of spaces and to allow a larger public to discover artists from Senegal and beyond. Since its creation, Partcours has organized a yearly event (during the month of December) providing a shared space for gallerists, artists and audience to engage, exchange, showcase, and witness the diversity of Dakar's artistic scene. In a spontaneous and autonomous manner, Partcours brings together and unites artists and organizations, with each and every space being able to put forward a curatorial proposal. Contrary to the 'Off' in which anyone can exhibit anywhere, Partcours places emphasis on spaces which offer regular artistic programming throughout the year, as well as individuals and professional art organizations (rather than artists) dedicated to the Dakar art scene on a permanent and longitudinal basis. In other words, an improvised exhibition space cannot register to Partcours; this art *institution* aims, rather, to facilitate the collaboration between already-established spaces that share a sense of collective ownership over the initiative. Although challenging at times, this involves both shared decision-making processes as well as a symbolic financial contribution to support the cost of promotion and communication material. In its content, this event is programmed by neighbourhoods, with each art space in charge of its own programming, curation, and thematic approach. Unique of its kind on the continent, Partcours celebrated its eighth edition in 2019 with twenty art spaces that compose and reflect the dynamic landscape of Dakar's cultural ecosystem, interacting through this exchange-based relationship. △Fig. 1a–c

From the walls of the popular neighbourhood of the Médina to private galleries, from art shops to independent art centres, from conventional cultural institutions to common spaces of high-end hotels, these different cultural sites cultivate art and knowledge through a variety of forms, perspectives, and methods. In doing so, they fertilize the ground of the urban fabric, ensure the germination of its imaginary, and contribute to creating the polyphony that is at the core of the 'cultural polis.'[27] While at times facing 'challenges in terms of decision-making as any kind of collective with a multiplicity of fields of interest and perspectives,' Partcours has 'put its mark on the city of Dakar, a mark that is getting stronger after each edition' as the new director of programmes of RAW explains.[28] Partcours has now become an institution in Dakar's cultural

27 Jenny Mbaye and Cecilia Dinardi, 'Ins and Outs of the Cultural Polis: Informality, Culture and Governance in the Global South,' *Urban Studies* 56, no. 3 (2019), pp. 578–93.

28 Marie Hélène Pereira (director of programmes, RAW Material Company), email interview by Jenny Mbaye, 10 December 2019.

1a

1b

1c

2a

2b

△ 1a–c
Espace Médina during 'Partcours 8', photos: Jenny Mbaye, 2019

△ 2a–b
Ateliers Céramiques Almadies during 'Partcours 8', photos: Jenny Mbaye, 2019

landscape, one in which 'the spirit of independence and conviviality remains the key to shared pleasure, a pleasure which, each year, makes this event a celebration for art throughout the city.'[29]

Exploring the process of alternative art institution-building and knowledge production outside the institutionalization of the state allows us to stress how 'the inventiveness, courage and resilience of these initiatives are testimony to the belief that art and creativity are fundamental parts of humanity.'[30] In a compositional gesture, these institutions claim their intent and desire for 'matters of concern,' and not only 'matters of fact,' thus renewing and making relevant a critical spirit and engagement closer to empiricism.[31] By empiricism, we mean that the knowledge and practice of an institution's curatorial intervention are based on the experience they derive from their senses, the pragmatics of their sensorial appreciation of the cityscape, and the relational affects with and through which they engage in the composition of their urban creative scene. In order to understand the ecosystem of contemporary art in African contexts, one has thus to move away from grand categories (artists, curators, critics, galleries, auctioneers, fairs, museums, grand exhibitions, art centres, collectors) as well as any form of binary logic, and focus on the projects,[32] the initiatives, and the institutions themselves. △Fig. 2a–b

Redefining the institutionalization process through the concept and practice of independent 'art institution-building,' these various art initiatives (Dak'Art Off, Partcours and Laboratoire Agit'Art) have in their own ways developed strategies in the face of an institutional vacuum, elaborating new narratives and modes of curating Dakar as an art world city. Long-time Dakar-based curator Koyo Kouoh explains the importance of claiming and naming these independent organizations as institutions, by stating that it is 'an act to institute something. You're talking about inscribing something, but [it is also a] matter of instituting something that you found, that you *grow*, and that should have a life after you.'[33]

## RHYTHMS OF ENDURANCE IN INSTITUTION-BUILDING

> While it is true that the grand categories [artists, curators, museums, etc.] do represent a part of the art world, the reality is that the majority of the actors and institutions that take part in this sector are, on the contrary, independent and acting alone: a fair amount of cases wrongly considered as exceptions …
> To understand the system according to which [these alternative institutions] … function, one has to move away from the grand categories … as well as the binary logic of centre/periphery,

29 ........... Partcours Programme, 2019, p. 3.

30 Kouoh, 'Filling the Voids,' p. 16.

31 ........... Bruno Latour, 'An Attempt at a "Compositionist Manifesto",' *New Literary History* 41, no. 3 (2010), p. 478.

32 ........... Iolanda Pensa 'The Oeuvre in Progress: The Sud,' in *Public Art in Africa: Art and Urban Transformations in Douala*, eds. Iolenda Pensa et al. (Geneva: Métis Presses, 2017), p. 18.

33 ........... Koyo Kouoh (director of RAW Material Company), interview by Jenny Mbaye, Dakar, December 2019.

> of we/them, in order to concentrate on the project itself. The project is what most deeply characterises all contemporary cultural production.[34]

Following our previous discussion of the political significance of alternative institution-building, we now highlight the ways in which the creation of these independent art initiatives can be considered 'an affirmation, a political gesture that proclaims the primacy of the people over the state apparatus,'[35] and one that has deep pragmatic implications. This section looks at two organizations that deploy and display similar 'rhythms of endurance' in the process of alternative institution building: Kër Thiossane and RAW Material Company. Ingrained in different neighbourhoods, and both positioned in an artistic field marked by a 'state-run postcolonial hangover,' the urban context of Dakar is central to both art spaces as they bring together dakarois and international cultural practitioners, artists, scholars, curators as well as activists around contemporary societal concerns. In fact, while cultivating diverse funding mechanisms beyond the event itself and beyond the white cube, their respective interactions with the city and its inhabitants is essential in both their approaches and practices.[△Fig. 3]

△ 3
RAW Material Company entrance, photo: Jenny Mbaye, 2019

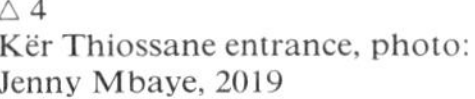
△ 4
Kër Thiossane entrance, photo: Jenny Mbaye, 2019

RAW Material Company (RAW) is a Centre for Art, Knowledge, and Society that was founded in 2011 by Koyo Kouoh after an initial dematerialized version of the space in 2008. RAW is staffed and managed entirely by women and holds exhibitions, residencies, a library, and a bi-annual eight-week academy described as 'an experimental residential programme for the research and study of artistic curatorial practice and thought'[36] and directed different lead faculties. RAW places heterogeneity of practice, knowledge, and cultural background at the forefront of its practice. It was

34........... Pensa 'The Oeuvre in Progress: The Sud,' p. 18.
35........... Njami, 'Imagined Communities,' p. 24.
36........... 'RAW Material Company,' www.rawmaterialcompany.org (accessed 12 January 2020).

borne out of the 'necessity to create a space for the sharing of knowledge. Its core motivation was to establish a space for alternative education and learning.'[37] For Kouoh, the 'roles of art institutions and initiatives are to develop their models in relation to broader artistic urgencies and in relation to society as a whole.' She argues that many recent independent organizations in Africa and beyond have emerged out of necessity and have been founded on similar principles addressing questions of 'action, space, power, control, and quality'[38] △Fig. 4

Kër Thiossane is an independent art and multimedia villa that was established by Marion Louisgrand Sylla and François Sylla in 2002 in the neighbourhood of Sicap. It combines multimedia technology with traditional artistic and creative practices, encouraging interdisciplinary approaches to art. They have created a place where artists can learn to use multimedia tools through training courses, conferences, workshops, as well as residencies. Since 2013, Kër Thiossane has centred its activities on the project *École des Communs* [School of Commons] dedicated to the notion of *vivre-ensemble* [learning to live together], 'urban commons,' and 'shared knowledge' with different axis of intervention. Notably, it includes a monumental garden 'Jet d'Eau,' a fablab, as well as a festival, 'Afropixel,' that explores critical and unconventional ways for people to experiment with media and technology in relation to art and society. The team is comprised of part-time members for each strand of its activities; the fablab, festival programming and garden workers. As Marion explains,

> In 2002, there was a lot of interest and cultural excitement in Dakar at the time ... But in terms of digital it did not have that much, nor a space for experimentation and creation ... So the project was ambitious.[39]

With similar but different ways of instituting, we seek to explore the different engagements of RAW and Kër Thiossane with and through the city by working with Simone's notion of 'rhythms of endurance.' This concept helps us understand the ways in which these initiatives, in the context of Dakar, 'conjoin rhythms of occasions and practices not easily attributed to any single person or thing.'[40] We believe these initiatives are 'shifters in a complex politics that may use the occasion of specific enunciations actualized in particular circumstances to create contexts for bringing provisional collectives to life, ones that don't pin down their constituents to overbearing judgments or histories.'[41]

Simone argues that such contexts—here used to understand the work of alternative art institutions—'enable endurance,' in the sense that endurance is something that is 'felt, where what was aspired to, what

37 Kouoh, 'Filling the Voids,' p. 18.
38 Kouoh, 'Filling the Voids,' p. 17.
39 Marion Louisgrand Sylla (co-founding director of Kër Thiossane), interview by Jenny Mbaye, Dakar, December 2019.
40 Simone, *Improvised Lives*, p. 15.
41 Simone, *Improvised Lives*, pp. 15–16.

was sacrificed for, what was the compelling imagination of all the strivings and hard work of care is not lost.'[42] For Simone, rhythms of endurance involve processes that entail both composition and refusal; he draws upon the Art Ensemble of Chicago as an example to argue that 'it is a matter of composing the conditions that facilitate improvization and dialogue among the players,'[43] similar to Latour's Compositionist Manifesto, to create platforms that 'release an untold energy that propels a different kind of "message for our folks," a different trajectory of historical time.'[44]

Simone's focus on the role of the ensemble, the mechanics of relations in rhythms, and the relationship between the contours of the environment and practices of bricolage, is instructive in our understanding of Kër Thiossane and RAW, two initiatives which are deeply entwined with the shifting ecologies of the city. As Kouoh eloquently outlines:

> Dakar is the protagonist of our work, the main character of our work, the leading character, actually; if you consider RAW as a film, Dakar has the lead role as a city, as a space, real and imagined. The contemporary history of Dakar, if we take it from the festival 66 to today, through the creation of the biennale, shows on the one hand a very strong hand of the government to design the space of arts and culture. On the other hand, this is placed next to or post—or against, if you want—a genealogy of artistic practices in African societies, which reaches way back before 1966 to today.[45]

Put differently, these two independent art institutions remind us of the productive capacity of 'people as infrastructure'[46] whereby the needs of residents 'generate concrete acts and contexts of social collaboration inscribed with multiple identities.'[47] Indeed, both institutions are the results of years of reflection and maturation of their respective founders and artistic directors. These individuals contribute with their knowledge, inspiration, and experience, as well as with the support of their team, in significant and relevant ways to the creative scene of the capital city. Importantly, cities are places from which people, as complex infrastructures, can potentially and profoundly make change. Indeed, many new art centres are 'grappling ever more urgently with the question of what art can accomplish for the emancipation of their citizens in the

42 ........... Ibid.
43 ........... Simone, *Improvised Lives*, p. 20.
44 ........... Ibid.
45 ........... Koyo Kouoh (director of RAW Material Company), interview by Jenny Mbaye, Dakar, December 2019.
46 ........... Simone, 'Reflections on an Urban Majority in Cities of the South,' p. 419.
47 ........... Ibid.

context of strained political relationships.'[48] As Njami stresses, 'there is no centred causal logic, but rather a set of micro-logics which, when shared, constitute the warp and weft of the social fabric.'[49]

Inscribed in the legacy and heritage of politically engaged institutions like Laboratoire Agit'Art, both RAW and Kër Thiossane illustrate the ways in which independent initiatives emerge to 'fill the vacuum left by unfulfilled promises of cultural and artistic programmes led by the governments,' and 'set themselves apart from state-affiliated institutions as well as from commercial (art) markets'; in doing so, they create 'alternative models and platforms for negotiating art and history, and reflect upon the archive, visual culture, and cultural history.'[50] Such independent art initiatives are driven by the desire to share passions, ideals, knowledge, and experience in urban contexts scarred by deep social, political, economic, as well as cultural inequalities. Beyond 'a hierarchical and elitist system that reserves contemporary art for a certain segment of society,' and which highlights and reinforces social divides that 'stand out more starkly on the African continent,' these artistic initiatives explicitly aim to democratize 'culture' and make it more accessible to all.[51]

## MECHANISMS OF RELATIONS IN RHYTHMS

Latour reminds us that '[f]or a compositionist, nothing is beyond dispute. And yet, closure has to be achieved. But it is achieved only by the slow process of composition and compromise, not by the revelation of the world beyond.'[52] While evolving in a similar space, economy, and temporality (Dakar's creative scene and its not-for-profit project-based economy), Kër Thiossane and RAW are two distinctive, independent art initiatives whose complexities are made visible by exploring their orientations, programming, funding mechanisms, and internationalism. The two selected art spaces present different models of artistic interventions and critical perspectives on the transformational power of art, each with their specific focus: Kër Thiossane on the digital technologies and urban commons, and RAW on the development of alternative education and contemporary artistic theory. However different, both organizations are concerned with notions of art as a constellation of cultural practices apart from the commodification of the global art market, operating as part of innovative and collaborative international networks; an enterprise that is not without significant challenges.

Indeed, programming spaces for contemporary art in Dakar is a 'risky and unstable project.'[53] Though Kër Thiossane and RAW are long-term fixtures of Dakar, they are simultaneously fragile. They are concerned with the collective and with changing the urban landscape, diverse sites,

48 .......... Hortensia Völckers and Katharina von Ruckteschell, 'Foreword,' in *Condition Report: Symposium on Building Art Institutions in Africa*, ed. Koyo Kouoh (Stuttgart: Hatje Cantz, 2012), p. 7.

49 .......... Njami, 'Imagined Communities,' p. 24.

50 .......... Kouoh, 'Filling the Void,' p. 16.

51 .......... Njami, 'Imagined Communities,' p. 21.

52 .......... Latour, 'An Attempt at a "Compositionist Manifesto",' p. 478.

53 .......... Kouoh, 'Filling the Voids,' p. 10.

and sources of knowledge production. As not-for-profit initiatives, they operate within different temporalities and perform in a different economy to commercial galleries, purposefully inscribed in a lucrative ecosystem focused on art consumption. Both Kër Thiossane and RAW are critically inscribed in the project-based economy. For Kouoh, it is a 'context or a method of working that fragile-izes anybody that takes part in it, because a project can be big of course—I mean, it's not necessarily the size that that matters—it's really the conditions of work that matter.'[54] This is why alternative institution building, as discussed earlier, is so crucial. Sustaining such rhythms becomes part of the role of the curator. Njami argues that 'In cities such as Dakar, Lagos, Cairo and Douala, the concept of curator has been blurred, echoing the multiplicity of practices encountered in society, which cannot always be reflected in the codified language of contemporary art.'[55] △Fig. 5a–b

△ 5a–b
RAW at Empire Cinéma, 'Partcours 8', photos: Jenny Mbaye, 2019

Artistic rendezvous such as Partcours or 'Dak'art's' 'Off' are composed of spaces dedicated to both cultural production and consumption; as such, some initiatives radically differ from others in their focus on consumer opportunities and citizenship. In Partcours for instance, not-for-profit spaces such as Kër Thiossane or RAW collaborate with commercial galleries such as Galerie Arte or Gallery Fakhoury. This, in turn, suggests that the distinction between public and private initiatives in the production of urban space begs further scrutiny in terms of challenges and potentialities for the greater cityscape. In this regard, both Kër Thiossane and RAW are focused on the 'production side' of the art ecosystem as private organizations with a public ambition: their interests and concerns are about methods of producing, acquiring and sharing knowledge through

54...........Koyo Kouoh (director of RAW Material Company), interview by Jenny Mbaye, Dakar, December 2019.

55...........Njami, 'Imagined Communities,' p. 24.

art. In this regard, the two selected case studies have common grounds in their establishment: 'The need to address an artistic and critical void. They respond to the urgency to create platforms of criticality and production.'[56]

Both initiatives are animated by a desire to curate artistic interventions that contribute to the urban commons, add value to the public culture and sphere, and engage with conversations in the public interest and for collective good. This entails going beyond a 'culture of events,' which is necessary but which doesn't do the 'daily work' of sustaining the practices of arts professionals. As Kouoh affirms: 'It can only happen through solid organizations and institutions that work on a daily basis, that don't wait for an event in order to exist.'[57] Here, building alternative institutions that are alternatives to the project-based economy but not the institutionalization of a project-based economy, is important. Independent art initiatives are focused on longevity, whilst inscribed and dependent on a not-for-profit economy, where long-term sustainable relationships with funding partners need to be nurtured. Considering the precarious and fragile financial working conditions of such independent art institutions, being part of different kinds of international ensembles becomes an important part of their rhythm of endurance.

Both RAW and Kër Thiossane are part of Arts Collaboratory, a self-organized network of twenty-five organizations situated predominantly in Asia, the Middle East, Africa, and Latin America, and joined by their focus on collective governance.

> The network operates as an active ecosystem, where knowledge and strengths are brought together and harvested in processes of collective organization. It is a radical experiment in exploring the potentiality of art and social transformation when the experiences, dreams, and critical reflections of cultural practitioners from across the globe are allowed to meet.[58]

Both institutions refer to the network as an outstanding illustration of how the cultural and artistic field cultivates its own tools, mechanisms, and practices to rethink the world and challenge their imaginations beyond persisting hegemonic borders. Arts Collaboratory has an annual Assembly, includes smaller Banga (face-to-face) meetings, and undertakes collaborative projects. Such South-South cooperation and collaboration are important to Kër Thiossane and RAW, and this network is part of a practice of cultivating a 'transcontinental and transnational imagination,'[59]

56 Kouoh, 'Filling the Voids,' p. 10.

57 Koyo Kouoh (director of RAW Material Company), interview by Jenny Mbaye, Dakar, December 2019.

58 'Arts Collaboratory,' www.artscollaboratory.org (accessed 12 January 2020).

59 Francoise Vergès 'Mapping "invisible lives,"' in *Condition Report: Symposium on Building Art Institutions in Africa*, ed. Koyo Kouoh (Stuttgart: Hatje Cantz, 2012), p. 37.

comprised of spaces which 'question hegemonic viewpoints, canons and narratives of art, and develop and manifest approaches of knowledge production outside state institutionalization.'[60]

The innovative nature of such a network and its funding is not without challenges in terms of the number of institutions working together in different contexts and realities coming together. Since the initiation of the network, the funding is equally divided between the institutions, with an amount that is dedicated to collaborative activities, exchanges, and residencies. Furthermore, involvement in this international ecosystem means that Kër Thiossane and RAW, despite being in the same city and having collaborated before, 'got closer.'[61] The importance of this ensemble, the kinds of strategies and tactics developed and nurtured through these practices, is again a question of composition and refusal: it allows for the possibility to 'go beyond the consensus and existence of established structures, which permits 'in-between' zones, spaces in flux that connect theoretical, visual, practical and local knowledge.'[62] They represent potentialities and conceptions of the world beyond the bare dynamics of economic globalization.

△ 6
Sen Éditions workshop for schoolchildren, Afropixel Festival, photo: Jenny Mbaye, 2019

## TRANSFORMING THE CITY WITH MULTIPLE AUDIENCES THROUGH 'ART AS A THINKING SYSTEM'

Kër Thiossane and RAW employ a diversity of artistic and working practices to animate and articulate different economic, cultural, and social values. However, the two significantly transformative practices are their engage-

60.......... Kouoh, 'Filling the Voids,' p. 17.
61.......... Marie Hélène Pereira (director of programmes, RAW Material Company), interview by Jenny Mbaye, Dakar, December 2019.
62.......... Kouoh, 'Filling the Voids,' p. 16.

ment with multiple audiences and their use of 'art as a thinking system.'[63] As Njami argues, art centres are 'spaces of proximity that know their audiences intimately,' and as such can 'act on their own environment by bringing endogenous and individually-tailored solutions to the problems they have identified.'[64] For both Kër Thiossane and RAW, the different kinds of publics they engage with are central to their orientation; as such, the organizations are sensitive to the diverse ways in which engagement can take place, as well as to the tensions and productive new relations that lie therein. Programmes such as RAW's Parlons Sénégalaiseries or Kër Thiossane's School of Commons demonstrate what is at stake; beyond engaging a diversity of audiences and sharing knowledge, they engage in a redefinition and reflection on identity, and on what it means to be from Dakar, and in the world. As such, these spaces also function as a 'place of building future generations of arts professionals on the continent.'[65] △Fig. 6

People who use Kër Thiossane see it as a 'space to free creativity ... demystify technology and, more importantly, as a space that 'creates vocations'[66] particularly because the organization opens up art and its space to different publics. As the programme/artistic director of Kër Thiossane explains:

> From the very beginning, we addressed ourselves to two kinds of publics: young people at l'USP (engineering department) and forming 'young geeks' who are a bit like hackers, as well as invited European artists, and getting them to work together ... We positioned ourselves as a workshop, a space of dissemination, with the idea of opening a space to support young artists working with the digital.[67]

Opening up the space to different kinds of projects and actors is thus important for Kër Thiossane. One example is welcoming SEN Editions scientific entrepreneurs in a residency during which they further explored ludic approaches to learning STEM subjects in schools, and developed innovative pedagogical games for children using 3D printing facilities. Following their residency at Kër Thiossane, SEN Editions entrepreneurs were invited to animate workshops for a week with school children and pupils using the prototypes of their pedagogical tools in the garden of a public museum as part of 2019's 'Afropixel' festival activities.

RAW and Kër Thiossane's ability to engage with diverse publics and audiences is perhaps partly linked to the way in which they operate

63 Koyo Kouoh (director of RAW), interview by Jenny Mbaye, Dakar, December 2019.
64 Njami, 'Imagined Communities,' p. 22.
65 Koyo Kouoh (director of RAW), interview by Jenny Mbaye, Dakar, December 2019.
66 Essoh (fablab animator), interview by Jenny Mbaye, Dakar, June 2019.
67 Marion Louisgrand Sylla (director, Kër Thiossane), interview by Jenny Mbaye, Dakar, December 2019.

within their initiatives as modular families with extended relatives. RAW is described by the programme director as a space that is both a 'home' and 'family' for the team, as well as a space that creates and gives back. They remark that 'we are in a space which has, over time, enriched a scene and continues to bring a strong, innovative and critical discourse, on what is happening,' informing future interventions in the city's artistic scene.[68] Within the team, there is a level of autonomy and trust that means they feel able to initiate and nurture projects that they want to see happen. Similarly, Kër Thiossane is a space that is actually located within a family home; in fact, *kër* means 'home/house' in Wolof and *thiossane* refers to 'traditional Senegalese culture/heritage.' It operates a 'bit like a family' where 'people who pass through find their place and capability';[69] they are given space and are able to have encounters with people of different professions. This notion of the spaces as loci between different actors is described as 'tentacular' by the project producer/manager of Kër Thiossane, and as a 'passage' by the programme director of RAW: they are spaces created so that 'people can meet, be exposed to each other, exchange, be in contradiction.'[70] As such, a singular form of knowledge sharing here has less to do with what Njami (via Rancière) terms the 'transition from ignorance to knowledge,' and more to do with a 'certain amount of work, both historical and societal,' that is done to cross borders of identities—reconstituting what counts as knowledge production itself.[71] Kouoh explains: 'I've always been interested in art as a thinking system, and not just as a display system. What kind of knowledge can be transmitted, and how to transmit it?'[72]

The experience of both Kër Thiossane and RAW, in their respective and distinctive ways, reveal how the process of the institution itself is grounded as a response to Dakar, both reflective and prospective, and how it is informed by their own spatial literacy and understanding of the Senegalese capital. Resolutely inscribed in the contemporary art scene of the city, in genuine conversation with other art worlds on the continent and beyond, their curation at the crossroads of art, society, people, politics, and the exhibitionary provides an understanding of 'exposure' beyond artworks and towards one that includes exposure to ideas, people, and the connective urban tissue they are embedded in. Drawing on such a refreshing appreciation of artistic and curatorial practices and the role these play within a society, we thus conclude this article focusing on this notion of 'art as a thinking form,' and on the ways in which the different initiatives we have discussed—from Dak'Art Off, Partcours, Agit'Art, RAW Material Company and Kër Thiossane—transform everyday urban and cultural life. More specifically, we stress that actors who change the city profoundly, and who have the potential and capacity to change the

68 Marie Hélène Pereira (director of programmes, RAW Material Company), interview by Jenny Mbaye, Dakar, December 2019.

69 Marion Aidara (production and communication manager, Kër Thiossane), interview by Jenny Mbaye, Dakar, December 2019.

70 Marie Hélène Pereira (director of programmes, RAW Material Company), interview by Jenny Mbaye, Dakar, December 2019.

71 Njami, 'Imagined Communities,' p. 23.

72 Koyo Kouoh (director of RAW Material Company), interview by Jenny Mbaye, Dakar, December 2019.

city deeply, are engaged in everyday practices while inscribing themselves outside of the 'white cube curation.'

As previously discussed, insights into the curatorial practices of both Kër Thiossane and RAW highlight the important ways that their inscription in the city—and in the neighbourhood, in the case of Kër Thiossane—animate their commitments. Their capacity to open up and create spaces where people can converge, to create spaces of proposition, imagination, experimentation, and transcendence requires a continuous presence and engagement.[73] A prerequisite to any transformational practice is the creation of continuous dialogue between artistic practices and their environment in order to reveal how, within their constellations, certain histories are formed or formulated, repeated, universalized, and preserved. As Ngcobo explains,

> These strategies are employed to reveal how artistic and curatorial gestures could perform transformative actions in political spaces, which may not yet be recognized as sites of struggle and may thus be allowed to enter a refreshed political sensibility.[74]

However, and more importantly, we argue that the transformative power of these art institutions lies in their capacity to pragmatically produce new energies and embody a new type of art organization as powerhouses of new, alternative energies.[75] △Fig. 7

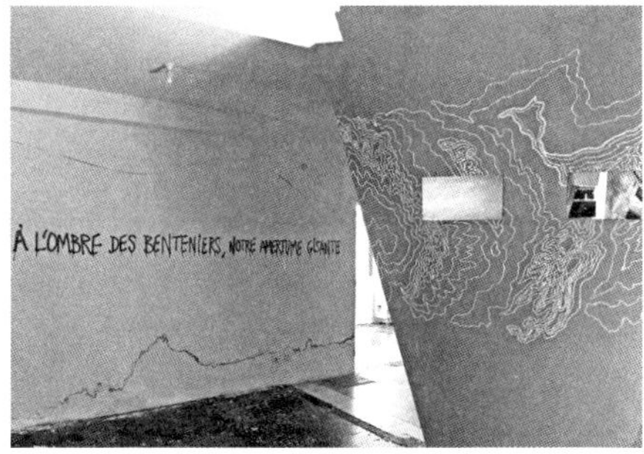


△ 7
Kër Thiossane, *Ruins and Futures*, 'Partcours 8', photo: Jenny Mbaye, 2019

This capacity to invest in 'art as a thinking system' can be illustrated by Kër Thiossane's intervention in the 8th edition of Partcours, 'Ruins and futures,' which continued with its preoccupation with the 'commons' and 'learning to live together.' While there are significant challenges in establishing spaces—both physical and mental—of freedom of artistic, social, and political production that draw on and rely on an understanding

73 .......... This is something that Partcours has clearly institutionalized by including only arts organizations who have programmes throughout the year.

74 .......... Gabi Ngcobo, 'Endnotes: Was it a Question of Power?' in *Condition Report: Symposium on Building Art Institutions in Africa*, ed. Koyo Kouoh (Stuttgart: Hatje Cantz, 2012), p. 66.

75 .......... Völckers and von Ruckteschell, 'Foreword,' p. 7.

of art as a thinking form per se, such an approach shows how 'artists and intellectuals do not work to entertain us nor to decorate our homes. They work to produce food for thought and action and inspiration.'[76] Based on artistic experimentation, open source, and the free-culture movement of shared knowledge, Kër Thiossane's curatorial contribution took place outside of Dakar; it instigated a conversation between its neighbourhood Sicap, the jewel of the West African modern city under President Senghor, and the new satellite/smart city under construction, Diamniadio, which has become a flagship programme of the current presidential plan 'Sénégal Émergent.' Ker Thiossane's curatorial intervention included a popular event, 'Assembly of African Futures' that interrogated the involvement of citizens in the production of their urban territory.[77] Political but not partisan, animated by a collective outlook rather than a pursuit of personal advancement, and anchored in the realities of its urban fabric, Kër Thiossane shows us the conditions of the institutional transformative potential of art. As RAW's founding artistic director put it:

> Independent contemporary art institutions are an important voice in the construction of a strong cultural private sector as well as in forging a critical opinion from an open civil society; ... art institutions are not only products of their environments [but critically] also active agents capable of shaping their societies in return.[78]

## CONCLUSION

This chapter has explored alternative arts institution building in Dakar in terms of the significant contribution to everyday urban cultural life that Kër Thiossane, RAW Material Company, and Partcours make. Taking as a starting point Dakar's status as an 'art world city' we argue that 'Dak'Art' and its 'Off' remain inscribed in a context marked by a monopolistic role of the state, creating institutional voids which generate an imperative towards what can be considered a process of alternative, independent 'art institution-building.' In focusing on Kër Thiossane, RAW Material Company, and Partcours, we have interrogated the specificities and challenges of composing and building alternative art institutions, and the different rhythms of endurance necessary to their everyday sustenance and transformation of and through the city. As Njami argues, 'It is no coincidence that, in most cases, there are women involved; [as such, art initiatives]

76..........Kouoh, 'Filling the Voids,' p. 10.
77..........Partcours *programme*, 2019, p. 9.
78..........Kouoh, 'Filling the Voids,' p. 19.
79..........Njami, 'Imagined Communities,' p. 22.
80..........Kouoh, 'Filling the Voids,' p. 10.
81..........Marilyn Douala Bell, 'Foreword,' in *Public Art in Africa: Art and Urban Transformations in Douala*, ed. Iolanda Pensa et al. (Geneva: Métis Presses, 2017), p. 9.

must have a thorough understanding of their audience.' And it is because of their proximity to the neighbourhoods and communities they are based in and part of that they are 'able to determine the needs to be satisfied to resolve issues raised by community living' and in so doing can act as 'a locus that allows for interactions between several actors.'[79] Through specific mechanisms of relations in rhythms, these independent art institutions are continuously evolving in a not-for-profit project-based economy whereby financial fragility has to be negotiated in order to envisage longer-term programming and the terms and conditions of their survival and sustainability. New alliances are being formed in this process across geographies and histories, and between partners equally engaged in investing in the relationship between arts, citizenship and society—a 'consistent fight against the instrumentalization of art for political purposes and its reduction to the field of leisure.'[80] Their curatorial intervention thus transforms the city by creating spaces of encounters, expression, exchange, reflection, and projection for an 'art world city' in constant recreation. Animated by 'the humanist idea of political generosity that participates in the emancipation of people and of their freedom,' art institutions such as Kër Thiossane and RAW Material Company ultimately show their dedication to 'reflect upon the levers that can accompany transformations of an urban society in search of identity and which are (or could be) contemporary creations or artistic acts.'[81] Through the artistic practices they display, stage and initiate, they institute new and alternative ways of seeing, of being and engaging with Dakar, always in relation with its different publics and audiences.

## ← REFERENCES


Agit'Art. *The Dismemberment Manifesto*. Dakar: Khadimou Rassoul, 2018.

Banks, Libby. 'The Five Most Creative Cities in the World?' *BBC*, 16 July 2019, www.bbc.com/culture/story/20190715-the-five-most-creative-cities-in-the-world.

Diaw, Aminata. 'Les intellectuels entre mémoire nationaliste et représentations de la modernité.' *Le Sénégal contemporain*, ed. Mamadou Diop, pp. 549–74. Paris: Karthala SSP. 2002.

Fredericks, Rosalind. '"The Old Man is Dead": Hip Hop and the Arts of Citizenship of Senegalese Youth.' In *The Arts of Citizenship in African Cities*, pp. 137–61. New York: Palgrave Macmillan, 2014.

Ghertner, D. Asher. 'Rule by Aesthetics: World-class City Making in Delhi.' *Worlding Cities: Asian Experiments and the Art of Being Global*, ed. Ananya Roy and Aihwa Ong, pp. 279–306. Malden, and Oxford: Wiley & Sons, 2011.

Grabski, Joanna L. 'Dakar's Urban Landscapes: Locating Modern Art and Artists in the City.' *African Arts* 36, no. 4 (2003), pp. 28–93.
—. 'Making Fashion in the City: A Case Study of Tailors and Designers in Dakar, Senegal.' *Fashion Theory* 13, no. 2 (2009), pp. 215–42.
—. *Art World City: The Creative Economy of Artists and Urban Life in Dakar*. Bloomington: Indiana University Press, 2017.

Holston, James. *Insurgent Citizenship: Disjunctions of Democracy and Modernity in Brazil*. Princeton: Princeton University Press, 2009.

Konaté, Yacouba. *La Biennale de Dakar, Pour une esthétique de la création contemporaine africaine: tête à tête avec Adorno*. Paris: L'Harmattan, 2009.

Kouoh, Koyo, 'Filling the Voids. The Emergence of Independent Contemporary Art Spaces.' In *Condition Report: Symposium on Building Art Institutions in Africa*, ed. Koyo Kouoh, pp. 15–18. Stuttgart: Hatje Cantz, 2012.

Latour, Bruno. 'An Attempt at a "Compositionist Manifesto".' *New Literary History* 41, no. 3 (2010), pp. 471–90.

Mbaye, Jenny, and Cecilia Dinardi. 'Ins and Outs of the Cultural Polis: Informality, Culture and Governance in the Global South.' *Urban Studies* 56, no. 3 (2019), pp. 578–93.

Ngcobo, Gabi. 'Endnotes: Was It a Question of Power?' In *Condition Report: Symposium on Building Art Institutions in Africa*, ed. Koyo Kouoh. Stuttgart: Hatje Cantz, 2012.

Njami, Simon. 'Imagined Communities.' In *Condition Report: Symposium on Building Art Institutions in Africa*, ed. Koyo Kouoh, pp. 21–24. Stuttgart: Hatje Cantz, 2012.

Partcours 8, *Programme*, 2019.

Pensa, Iolanda, et al. *Public Art in Africa: Art and Urban Transformations in Douala*. Geneva: Métis Presses, 2017.

Simone, AbdouMaliq. *Improvised Lives: Rhythms of Endurance in an Urban South*. Cambridge: Polity Press, 2018.
—. 'People as Infrastructure: Intersecting Fragments in Johannesburg.' *Public Culture* 16, no. 3 (2004), pp. 407–29.
—. 'The Missing People: Reflections on an Urban Majority in Cities of the South.' In *The Routledge Handbook on Cities of the Global South*, ed. Susan Parnell and Sophie Oldfield, pp. 322–36. London: Routledge, 2014.

Tilouine, Joan. *Baromètre des sociétés civiles: Sénégal, Niger et RDC sur le podium*. Paris: Jeune Afrique, 2014. www.jeuneafrique.com/164168/politique/barom-tre-des-soci-t-s-civiles-s-n-gal-niger-et-rdc-sur-le-podium/ (accessed 22 January 2020).

Verges, Françoise. 'Mapping 'Invisible Lives.' In *Condition Report: Symposium on Building Art Institutions in Africa*, ed. Koyo Kouoh, pp. 37–44. Stuttgart: Hatje Cantz, 2012.

Völckers, Hortensia, and Katharina von Ruckteschell. 'Foreword.' In *Condition Report: Symposium on Building Art Institutions in Africa*, ed. Koyo Kouoh, pp. 7–8. Stuttgart: Hatje Cantz, 2012.


## ← INTERVIEWS


Wade, Ousseynou (former director of Dak'Art), interview by Jenny Mbaye, Dakar, June 2013.

Essoh (fablab animator), interview by Jenny Mbaye, Dakar, June 2019.

Aidara, Marion (Production and communication manager, Kër Thiossane), interview by Jenny Mbaye, Dakar, December 2019.

Kouoh, Koyo (director of RAW Material Company), interview by Jenny Mbaye, Dakar, December 2019.

Louisgrand Sylla, Marion (director, Kër Thiossane), interview by Jenny Mbaye, Dakar, December 2019.

Pereira, Marie Hélène (director of programmes, RAW Material Company), email interview by Jenny Mbaye, 10 December 2019.

Section Three

# ARTISTIC RESEARCH AND ITS CAPACITY TO CROSS CONTEXTS

# ARTISTIC RESEARCH AND ITS CAPACITY TO CROSS CONTEXTS
## New Methodologies and Digital Technologies

Nora N. Khan

In 1979, Audre Lorde made a speech in which she famously stated, 'The master's tools will never dismantle the master's house.'[1] In 2018, Jack Halberstam revisited Lorde's address, noting how in the several decades after she spoke, cultural critics and theorists have been entirely laser-focused on diagnosing the master's tools alone. Now, instead, Halberstam writes, 'We should remember [Lorde's] main goal—it was not only to create a debate about which tools to use; it was to argue for the demolition itself with purpose and without a chance of reconstruction.'[2] What would it mean to truly demolish the house of neoliberal capitalism, systemic oppression, and virulent nationalism? Where, and how, could the work of thinking through resistance strategies, through tools besides the master's, take place?

In the extraordinary case studies that follow, I am struck by how art is described as precisely that space, sometimes firmly entrenched within, or just outside of, 'the house.' Art and cultural production create a space for a different kind of study, reflection, discursive thought, memory-construction, and theoretical analysis that is hard-found within the relentless pace of spectacular online discourse, mediating the events of spectacular contemporary life. Art and cultural production make space for precisely the work of imagining other kinds of tools, for creating pockets of temporary resistance, in order to begin the work of dismantling of the master's house. These spaces are havens for unofficial, informal thoughts and learning, for the ideas, concepts, and practices that are otherwise homeless in wider society. Methodologies of artistic research become ways of loosely formalizing these practices. And digital technologies, in all their problematic promise, are ways of archiving, distributing, and making these methodologies known at scale, across time.

The geographic span of the research projects that follow is dizzying: we flow between accounts of arts organizations and public art projects, installations and festivals, residencies and free schools, in Cameroon, Kenya, Uganda, Timor Leste, Cambodia, Myanmar, Bangladesh, Pakistan, and Sri Lanka. In a great number of cases, overwhelming imperial and colonial legacies have left indelible traces on the local social, economic, and cultural landscape. Further, present-day imperatives of authorial states are viscerally felt, exercised through tools of law, exclusion, punishment, censorship, and a slower violence of unequal resource distribution and access to education.[3] Artists—and arts organizations—must navigate and create within these shaping forces. Further, technocratic and market imperatives overdetermine cultural perceptions of the role of art, of what art should look like and what it should do, and whose interests it should serve. As we will find, arts organizations often play with these expectations to their advantage, presenting one story to an outside, while the real work takes place within, illegible to overseeing eyes.

The researchers focus on small arts organizations that often take up informality and looseness as a significant cultural and political strategy, as a way to even build infrastructure, teaching programmes, and learning spaces. It is precisely this aspect of projected and actual informality that allows each organization, through its physical space and programming interventions, to serve as an expansive place-maker. Each, in its loose, discursive functions, creates capacity and affordances for its practitioners, residents, students, and artists to develop serious pedagogical and activist strategies. Young artists and cultural producers learn to navigate challenging social environments by exercising the same strategic flexibility of these organizations, in which they hone their skills and practices. They develop modes of abstraction and opacity for protest that can survive in plain sight, methodologies for archiving histories at risk of being occluded or lost. Informality forms a critical shield for delicate work.

Artistic production and practice is also home for more invisible work, which doesn't always register in the international art world circuit. There is a lovely impulse throughout each research project to honour art and art spaces as lived through, and experienced by, surrounding communities, as much as by artists. Art creates space for literal survival and protection. It forms a gathering space in which children can have an education, one that could not otherwise be attained. It helps citizens have pride in their neighbourhood, their city, and their culture.

Each research group spends an enormous amount of time describing and mapping their own formal research methodologies, along with the more informal artistic research methodologies of the artists and cultural producers they studied and spent time with. A research or design methodology involves a hypothesis, a set of research questions, a deep understanding of surrounding cultural and political context and systems, informing a plan for emerging methods and modes of research to be undertaken. As these projects reveal, the researchers are all keen documentarians and observers, but are also sensitive to artistic methods themselves; their field research involves casual discussions, hanging out sessions, active and passive listening, absorption of information through pithy asides, and details that couldn't be learned in formal conversation.

Artistic research methodologies are even yet more expansive; they emerge and unfold in response to context, either in spite of, or hidden in plain sight of, the demands of dominant hegemonic structures. The research questions may change. Tactics may be abandoned, while others may emerge through off-script discoveries. The artists, through their own methods of prototyping, may come to produce performance, sculpture, teaching, experimental publishing and printing, public art, public forums, archive intervention—any of an infinite number of possible aesthetic and political gestures—to answer their own questions.

The questions that the artistic research methodologies pursue in these chapters are necessarily open and expansive, while expressing a set of beliefs and values, in order to allow for creation of space: How do neocolonial gestures replicate themselves through global artistic efforts, and through platform technologies of expression? What forms of communion and restoration can address the legacies of political

1 .......... Audre Lorde, *The Master's Tools Will Never Dismantle the Master's House* (London: Penguin, 2018). Lorde delivered her rousing address at an NYU Institute for the Humanities-sponsored conference, 'The Second Sex: Thirty Years Later,' which gathered feminist scholars from around the world.

2 .......... Jack Halberstam, 'Vertiginous Capital, or The Master's Toolkit,' in *queer.archive.work*/1, ed. Paul Soulellis (Providence, RI, 2018), https://queer.archive.work/1/, full text at: https://bullybloggers.wordpress.com/2018/07/02/vertiginous-capital-or-the-masters-toolkit-by-jack-halberstam/.

3 .......... The concept of 'slow violence' was theorized by Rob Nixon in his book, *Slow Violence and the Environmentalism of the Poor* (Cambridge: Harvard University Press, 2011). Writer Elvia Wilk elaborates that the 'biggest disasters are the ones that are never identified as such ... those occurrences, like gradual environmental devastation, that disproportionately affect those without a megaphone, and which are not deemed newsworthy because they are not sensational single events.' Elvia Wilk, 'What's Happening? Or: How to Name a Disaster,' *Bookforum* 27, no. 2 (2020), www.bookforum.com/print/2702/or-how-to-name-a-disaster-24019.

erasure that continue on into the present? What freedom and gathering can be found in spaces that aren't articulated or understood as official artistic projects? Such widely framed questions allow for these artists and arts organizations to stress informal space-making and exploration. Artists can avail themselves of these collectives, their energy and community, to co-produce their own critical work of speaking truth to power.

The researchers treat the artists' research methodologies with care and respect, and are also careful to conceptualize frames that allow for elusive intentions and for contradiction. Instead of being a firm set of processes that must be followed to the letter to attain a clear objective, an artistic research methodology is an emergent design process, aimed at developing diverse procedures of inquiry, which necessarily must change. In framing them generously, the researchers argue for more of such flexibility in creating artistic research models, paradigms, and principles, and for best practices to ideally emerge in co-production with the technological and social pressures of one's place and moment. All of the works are critically framed as part of an ongoing process, as expressive of a point in time, and as subject to revision. Tools and methods may switch on the fly, in response to environment, demands, and context.

Briefly, Nuraini Juliastuti theorizes the 'studying-turn' as a co-produced activity, which takes place in the independent arts organizations Tiny Toones (Phnom Penh, Cambodia), and Arte Moris (in Dili, Timor Leste), in which public alternative learning spaces—free schools—are embedded. The studying-turn is a way of informal, free style, learning together, a methodology of collective, inter-relational thinking. The spaces are places of practice, experiments 'in living and thinking together.' Autodidacticism and a loose curriculum allow artists to thrive, despite infrastructural and environmental lacks. Inclusion, collectivity, openness, mutual aid, are made possible in these spaces, allowing for the development of a 'cultural strategy from below,' a long-term collective project.

Rocca Holly-Nambi carefully frames the ways in which queerness is made possible in para-institutional art spaces, within the homophobic contexts of Nairobi, Kenya and Kampala, Uganda. Through strategies of transparency and opacity, Creatives Garage and the Babishai Niwe Poetry Foundation allow for inhabitable safe spaces for queer people, by deploying curatorial tactics of careful editing, publishing, residencies, and festivals that allow for multivalent practices of masking queer expression. Art forms active and evolving spaces for survival, and for physical and psychological relief.

Zayd Minty, Laura Nkula-Wenz, Naomi Roux, Vaughn Sadie, Anna Selmeczi and Rike Sitas assess the doual'art art space in Douala, Cameroon, through the legacy and work of its public art interventions. The city itself is theorized as a potential 'field of experience,' a place in constant flux. Projects become both living gathering places and sites of inter-ethnic debate. Art creates open public space that shapes urban experience in unexpected, productive ways; culture actively shapes the city, creates sustainable development, and answers a need for equitable public spaces that foster a feeling of local belonging.

Finally, Maya Ganesh and Nishant Shah conceptualize the digital turn from memory to storage within arts production in Sri Lanka, Pakistan, Bangladesh, and Myanmar, as it can allow small collectives to take ownership of memory and narrative-making in opposition to state methods. They argue that arts organizations must critically engage with digital technologies and media. However, they are careful to scale back any overly critical, academic, brutal assessment of how these groups don't yet grapple with deeper ethical issues of technology: algorithmic prediction, state and corporations in harmony, advancing surveillance architecture, machine learning compounding profound bias at unimaginable scales. Instead, we read about how these organizations find their way, within the context of local knowledge: they revise databases of their tendency to violent taxonomic identification; they use social media productively as a living archive; they frame and name online hate (fuelled by machine learning, uncorrected by platforms like Facebook) as it has real-world, deadly effects. What is presented is an artistic approach: to locate philosophical issues central to computation through their own active use, to allow for embrace of open data and knowledge circulation, for ground-up critical assessment of platforms in ways that can be taught and shared.

Indeed, one might find that in reading these cases that the beauty of an artistic research methodology is its capacity for pedagogical transfer across contexts. The brave, moving, surprising work of a queer artist in Nairobi is strategic, and that strategy—of intentionally layered curation, of leveraged opacity, of novel methods of double- and triple-coded expression—can be taught and replicated. Brazen informal methods of study, or of reclamation of the archive, can be poetically condensed, replicated, exported. Artists elsewhere can learn from these loose methodologies, can learn to create unexpected space within their own radically different socio-technical contexts.

Art is itself a place where co-production of hybrid knowledges is made possible. The archivist meets the data analyst to discuss taxonomy of knowledge, with the intent of resisting erasure of an ongoing genocide. The publisher meets the arts organization to allow for censurable text to evade radar. The curator meets the local activist to understand that technology must be locally developed, contextualized, and used to avoid neocolonial acts of surveillance and capture. Individuals of divergent technical and creative skillsets collide to think together a bit more freely in art, it would seem, than in other fields. Competing practitioners across the sciences and technology meet artists and writers to open up their respective practices and find a collaborative work that answers the knotty, systemic challenges that face us as a society.

The theoretical underpinnings of these four pieces are crucial foundations, drawing on vital scholarship. They range from critique of techno-solutionism and the politics of algorithms, to histories of black radical thought, to the deeply productive concept of 'study' rendered by poet Fred Moten and Stefano Harney.[4] I find myself returning to the endlessly generative concept of study in each of these projects, past its explicit mention in Juliastuti's article. Study, as an act 'without an end, plan without a pause, rebel without a policy, conserve without a patrimony,' is a powerful counter to neoliberal demands that learning, and art, have a conclusion, an object, a takeaway.[5] Study—and art—are often strange, unwieldy, social, co-produced spaces, in which just the work of gathering and talking, take place.

As each project looks directly or peripherally at the projects of neoliberal capitalism, they necessarily invoke the role of technology and digital networks in accelerating and expressing them globally. Whether mediated through the internet, software, media, or algorithms, we find ourselves enmeshed in acts of co-production with technology. Digital technologies

4..........'Study' is a mode of activity, a way of learning in collective spaces that is unofficial and unordained, akin to the 'notion of a rehearsal—being in a kind of workshop, playing in a band, in a jam session, or old men sitting on a porch, or people working together in a factory.' From Stefano Harney and Fred Moten, *The Undercommons: Fugitive Planning and Black Study* (Wivenhoe: Minor Compositions, 2013), p. 110. Found at: www.minorcompositions.info/wp-content/uploads/2013/04/undercommons-web.pdf. For Fred Moten, the 'point of calling it "study" is to mark that the incessant and irreversible intellectuality of these activities is already present'; study is just 'what you do with other people. It's talking and walking around with other people, working, dancing, suffering, some irreducible convergence of all three, held under the name of speculative practice.' From David Wallace, 'Fred Moten's Radical Critique of the Present,' *New Yorker Magazine*, 30 April 2018, www.newyorker.com/culture/persons-of-interest/fred-motens-radical-critique-of-the-present.

5..........Harney and Moten, *The Undercommons*, p. 67.

are constant mediators, active agents in our understanding of national and global events. The artists and researchers in this section create hybrid methodologies, philosophies of investigation and production. Even as the interfaces, software, and hardware may offer possibility for such small arts organizations to resist and refuse hegemonic structures, the organizations must also account for how these technologies, by design, erase and flatten the long-term possibility of such resistance—through surveillance creep, through violent predictive algorithms that limit conceptions of justice. In the future, arts collectives will need to critically engage with the technological space to ensure that their spaces of informality, free learning, of place- and space-making, can live on in the digital.

In the process of editing and finalizing this section over many months, I have heard a rapidly-changing procession of sounds outside my window: in January 2020, the occasional car, and homeward-bound students chattering, gave way to three months of tomb-like silence, which then gave way to wails of sirens, linked in an unending chain, and the drone of helicopters overhead. During teleconferences with colleagues across the country, I now hear the whistles of trains on their end, carrying National Guard troops. I watch, within the context of a global pandemic, intensifying protests centred on the murders of George Floyd and Breonna Taylor and the crisis of police brutality, mediated through live feeds. I watch a near-instantaneous activation of impassioned responses to systemic oppression across the world. Their focus, in each locale, is a geopolitical system of capitalist, colonial, and racialized power that, though expressed differently at local levels and in ever-colourful ways, share, as systems tend to, similar languages, forms, and strategies.

There is immense potential for art to leverage its informal, place-making capacities in the digital. This work is desperately needed given the flattening of interfaces, the media that shape and formalize thinking in real time, the ongoing predictive capacities shaping immediate action and response. We see acts of sousveillance and counter-surveillance—such as those of filming police brutality that have galvanized the wave of protests—frequently described as creative intervention, a gaze back at the surveilling eye. The digital and the internet are political, and they retain their military-industrial foundations. To dismantle the master's house, artists and art organizations cannot uncritically adopt a decades-old dream of connectivity as a serious way to counter oppression, but instead must take up the centralized, non-egalitarian, and data-driven imperatives of surveillance, predictive policing, simulation science, and modelling as part of the house itself. How can artists and arts organizations continue to make space digitally, to help us imagine roles outside of the paradigms of user, of consumer? What would place-making, free style study, and thinking together be, in the digital? Perhaps, one hopes, platforms, networks, and systems can be a new home for the flexible, changing, strategic artistic methodologies represented on these pages—a home for imagining new tools.

← REFERENCES

Halberstam, Jack. 'Vertiginous Capital, or The Master's Toolkit.' In *queer.archive.work*/1, ed. Paul Soulellis (Providence, RI, 2018). https://queer.archive.work/1/ and full text at: https://bullybloggers.wordpress.com/2018/07/02/vertiginous-capital-or-the-masters-toolkit-by-jack-halberstam/.

Harney, Stefano, and Fred Moten. *The Undercommons: Fugitive Planning & Black Study*. New York: Minor Compositions, 2013.

Lorde, Audre. *The Master's Tools Will Never Dismantle the Master's House*. London: Penguin, 2018.

Wallace, David. 'Fred Moten's Radical Critique of the Present,' *The New Yorker*, 30 April, 2018. www.newyorker.com/culture/persons-of-interest/fred-motens-radical-critique-of-the-present.

Wilk, Elvia. 'What's Happening? Or: How to Name a Disaster,' *Bookforum* 27, no. 2 (2020). www.bookforum.com/print/2702/or-how-to-name-a-disaster-24019.

Bantmag / Istanbul, Turkey / 1:12pm    40°58'52.1"N / 29°01'28.1"E

Townhouse Gallery / Cairo, Egypt / 1:21 pm    30°02'55.3"N / 31°14'15.9"E

# CREATING SPACE FOR QUEERNESS

Rocca Holly-Nambi

There is an urgent need to create space for queerness in Nairobi, Kenya and Kampala, Uganda. Queer communities are silenced, unable to speak due to the threat and reality of violence. At the same time, queerness is hyper-visualized with private lives viciously revealed by the media, government, and religious institutions. This research project focuses on the strategic ways artists and arts organizations are creating space for queerness in Nairobi and Kampala. This takes place through an exploration of two case studies: Creatives Garage's 2016 book project *Femmolution* (in Nairobi) and in Uganda, Babishai Niwe Poetry Foundation's 2012 programme 'Making Poetry Matter.' To understand the current possibilities for creating queer space, this project works with two artists associated with these organizations: a Nairobi-based writer who operates under the pseudonym 'Kins of Spade' and a Kampala-based poet and spoken-word artist, Gloria Kiconco. The project invites and commissions Kins of Spade and Kiconco to produce new artworks through undertaking residencies in each other's cities. In doing so, this Forces of Art project aims, in and of itself, to contribute to the creation of queer space.

Keywords
→ Queerness
→ Community
→ Space
→ Residencies
→ Contemporary Art
→ Abstraction
→ Kampala
→ Uganda
→ Nairobi
→ Kenya
→ Creatives Garage
→ Babishai Niwe Poetry Foundation

## INTRODUCTION

There is an urgent need to create space for queerness in Nairobi, Kenya and Kampala, Uganda. Queer communities are hidden and silenced; unable to speak or be seen due to the threat and reality of arrests and violence. Also, and in paradox, queer communities are hyper-visualized. Queer private lives are viciously revealed—and often distorted—by the media, government figures, and religious leaders with anti-homosexual agendas. This amplified and misrepresented exposure heightens the possibilities of attack and humiliates queer communities. Spaces for queer bodies to feel safe in, spaces for queer people to be seen and heard, and space for queerness to decide how it wants to show itself—how much and to who—are critical for queer communities to survive and thrive in Nairobi and Kampala today.

This chapter focuses on the strategic ways artists and arts organizations are creating space for queerness in Nairobi and Kampala, two cities within countries where homosexuality is fiercely illegal. This is achieved through a critique of two key case studies. The first case study is Creatives Garage in Nairobi and the ways in which the organization gathers, publishes, and distributes content. In particular, the research focuses on their 2016 project *Femmolution* (a book and music album—and a queer Nairobi-based poet who operates under the pseudonym 'Kins of Spade' and whose work is woven throughout the pages of the book. The second case study is a Ugandan artist-in-residence programme run by the Babishai Niwe Poetry Foundation called 'Making Poetry Matter.' The activity enabled artists to detach themselves from their everyday urban environments and to produce new works in unpopulated rural spaces. The impact of this process of removal is understood by highlighting the practice of Ugandan, Kampala-based poet and performance artist Gloria Kiconco, who took part in 'Making Poetry Matter' in 2018. Although not directly aimed at queer artists, 'Making Poetry Matter' allowed for this queer-identifying artist to be momentarily extracted from an exhausting atmosphere of homophobia. It carved out a space for Kiconco to pause, self-reflect, and explore new creative processes that may not have otherwise been possible.

*Femmolution* and 'Making Poetry Matter' serve as starting points to show the impact that creating space for queerness had for Kins of Spade Kiconco, and further, queer Kenyan and Ugandan communities. But the need for queer space remains vital and urgent today. This research project allowed me to reactivate the processes undertaken by *Femmolution* and 'Making Poetry Matter' by inviting and commissioning Kins of Spade and Kiconco to produce new artworks through undertaking residencies in each other's cities. Some of the artworks produced by this process are embedded within this text, with the consent of the artists. The decision to commission new works was made to ensure that this research project would not just talk about a situation but that it would directly contribute to and work within a live moment. In doing so, the research conducted for this chapter contributes in and of itself to the creation of queer space.

The chapter begins by unpacking the anti-homosexual contexts of Nairobi and Kampala. The queer, creative, and caring possibilities between the cities are then considered through desk-research, as well as through drawing on my own familiarities having lived in both spaces, and through interviews with Kiconco and Kins of Spade (recalling experiences of Nairobi and Kampala through their residencies). In section two, I introduce Creatives Garage: their space, team, and artistic programming. I then dive into the project *Femmolution* and its strategies to weave queerness through the book and music album; within this are the works of the poet Kins of Spade.[1] Through the practice-based element of this 'Forces of Art' project, Kins of Spade produced a new anthology of poetry titled *Queer Abstraction*. A close reading of a work from this collection explores the artist's strategies of obscurity and transparency to hide and reveal their queerness. Section two finishes with a walkthrough of the exhibition 'Prosexive' installed at Creatives Garage. Taking place throughout one night, the exhibition creates layers of intimacy by staggering different displays and activities throughout Creatives Garage's building, the queerest of experiences being the hardest to access. It is within the layers of the building and the night of the exhibition that readings of *Femmolution* and *Queer Abstraction* take place.

Section three opens with an overview of the Babishai Niwe Poetry Foundation: its founder, mission, and activities. It follows with an analysis of Babishai's project 'Making Poetry Matter' to understand their process of removal of artists from the frantic space of Kampala to the natural settings of Sipi Falls, Mount Elgon, and Mabira Forest—providing a space for 'queerness to breathe.' It is through Babishai that we get to know Gloria Kiconco and understand the impact a temporary action such as that offered by Babishai can have on a queer artist's practice. This activity of transporting oneself temporarily to a new space is replicated through the residency that Kiconco undertook for this 'Forces of Art' project. In June 2019, the artist travelled from Kampala to an artist-run residency space within the parameters of Nairobi National Park. Whilst at the residency Kiconco began creating four new bodies of creative writing: *Drm sqncs:// <root/s> (Dream Sequences)*, *Lttrs:// (Letters)*, *Pms:// (Poems)* and *Five Lives*. The writings were then shaped into zines. This section offers a close reading of selected works from *Dream Sequences*, and considers the myriad of spaces the artist travelled through to create this work, from Kampala to Nairobi, to the space of their dreams, and then writings on a page transformed into a three-dimensional zine. Finally, here, the zine now travels to the reader—to be read in their own space—and digested in the space of their mind.

*Femmolution*, 'Making Poetry Matter,' and the 'Forces of Art' residencies have ended. But Creatives Garage and Babishai Niwe Poetry Foundation continue to operate today. The organizations continue to provide physical spaces for people to feel safe within, emotional, and psychological space to be heard and to heal, and space for aesthetics to be seen. This project concludes that these organizations must survive. It also discusses ways—summarized in the conclusion—in which the organizations can further their creative and compassionate missions. To continue their work, the organizations must make and receive social and economic resources. The need for such resources takes on an amplified urgency as the world enters into a global pandemic. We are already seeing the impact of this global crisis on creative and cultural industries: resources being diverted into other areas, gig economies crumbling, artists in lockdown connecting to audiences through the limitations of a computer screen. There is a particular worry for queer communities at this time as anti-homosexual authorities take advantage of this moment of fragility to disrupt the few safe spaces queerness has managed to create. Creatives Garage and Babishai must be

1............Despite becoming more intimately known to them, their safety is maintained through the use of their pseudonym.

resourced to continue their work, as it is through their efforts that queer communities have a physical and digital home. And it is within these households that queerness can control its levels of visibility and, where strategic to do so, perform strategies to push back against invisibility.

## Kenya's Anti-Homosexual Context

•

The legal landscape for homosexuality in Kenya is turbulent. The country's anti-homosexual law has its foundations in a British colonial framework. Section 162 of the Penal Code ensures imprisonment for fourteen years for any 'male person to have carnal knowledge of him or her against the order of nature.'[2] Although there have been relatively few arrests that have led to incarcerations, the code creates a dangerously hostile environment for queer people.[3] It is both this hostile legal environment and the discriminatory attitudes and actions of state and society that queer activists are actively working against. In 2011, the Kenya Human Rights Commission published research on the LGBTI community's search for equality and non-discrimination in Kenya. Key findings of the commission showed the ways that queer Kenyan people are unprotected by law, left vulnerable to attacks by the public, and desperately seek safe spaces to live within.[4]

The legal landscape for homosexuality in Kenya is also treacherously contradictory. Article 27 of the Constitution of Kenya, promulgated in 2010, counters the Penal Code, stating, 'The State shall not discriminate directly or indirectly against any person on any ground.'[5] [6] It is this tormenting inconsistency between Kenya's Constitution and Penal Code Act that impelled three activist organizations to take the Kenyan government to court in an attempt to challenge the legal environment and create a safer space for queerness.[7] However, to the disbelief and distress of Kenya's queer community and allies, the high court dismissed the petition, stating there was insufficient evidence to 'convince the court that the (Penal Code) clauses were used to discriminate against sexual and gender minorities.'[8]

2............Kenyan National Council for Law Reporting, *Laws of Kenya: Penal Code*, ch 63, 2012, www.ilo.org/dyn/natlex/docs/ELECTRONIC/28595/115477/F-857725769/KEN28595.pdf (accessed 1 June 2020). Kenya's Penal Code was created in 1930 and re-worked in 2006.

3............See Kenyan activist Jane Wothaya Thirikwa's study confirming how 'the criminalisation of same-sex conduct gives a pretext for stigmatising and discriminatory attitudes, and it radically undermines human rights efforts for sexual minorities.' Jane W. Thirikwa, 'Emergent momentum for equality: LGBT visibility and organizing in Kenya,' in *Envisioning Global LGBT Human Rights: (Neo)colonialism, Neoliberalism, Resistance and Hope*, eds. Nancy Nicol et al. (London: University of London Press, 2018), p. 308.

4............The commission detailed a 'high prevalence of LGBTI persons who are routinely abused, subjected to hate speech, and raped by police, vigilantes and organized criminals' and 'a deliberate failure by the state to protect LGBTI persons from discrimination both in policy and legislation.' See: Kenya Human Rights Commission, *The Outlawed Amongst Us*, Nairobi, Kenya, 2011, www.khrc.or.ke/mobile-publications/equality-and-anti-discrimination/70-the-outlawed-amongst-us/file.html (accessed 1 June 2020).

5............Kenyan National Council for Law Reporting, *Constitution of Kenya*, art 27, 2010, http://kenyalaw.org:8181/exist/kenyalex/actview.xql?actid=Const2010 (accessed 1 June 2020).

6............And yet, also in 2010, former MP Omar Masumbuko, infamously called for 'homosexuality to be stopped,' telling public crowds they should 'not even bother to bring the homosexuals they find to the police station but should take care of the issue themselves.' Rob Tisinai, 'Africa's Gays Increasingly Under Siege,' *The Atlantic*, 22 February 2010, www.theatlantic.com/daily-dish/archive/2010/02/africas-gays-increasingly-under-siege/190118/.

7............The three organizations are the National Gay and Lesbian Human Rights Commission (NGLHRC), The Gay and Lesbian Coalition of Kenya (GALCK), and the Nyanza Rift Valley and Western Kenya Network (NYARWEK). On 24 May 2019–during the time this 'Forces of Art' project was active—Milimani Law Courts in Nairobi heard a ruling to repeal section 162 of the Kenyan Penal Code, the key argument being that the penal code was 'unconstitutional, as it discriminated directly against LGBT people.' (None on Record, 'Criminalization and Colonization,' *AfroQueer*, season 2, podcast audio, 22 May 2019, https://afroqueerpodcast.com/2019/05/22/bonus-episode-criminalization-an-colonization/ (accessed 1 June 2020).

The comments from the three judges stung Nairobi's queer community, especially those that had come to witness the case in person and had been direct victims of vicious homophobic attacks.[9]

## Uganda's Anti-Homosexual Context

• •

The outcome of Kenya's decriminalization case in May 2019 was watched with nervous anticipation in neighbouring Uganda, where anti-homosexual laws are infamous. As the court's ruling was announced, a sigh of relief was heard from the advocates and one of despair, from the queer community.

The criminality of homosexuality in Uganda also has its foundation in the British colonial government's Penal Code Act (1950). Since 2011, the legal structures of homophobia have hazardously evolved and fluctuated.[10] In 2011, Ugandan ministers updated the Act to ensure women who partake in same-sex intimacies receive equal consequences as men. Ministers also added a clause to ban the promotion of homosexuality in any media format. The vagueness of this second clause creates additional problems for queer Ugandan artists. What constitutes the marketing of homosexuality is purposefully undefined, making the censorship of queer culture an authoritarian-driven act.

The ferocity of Uganda's anti-homosexuality laws peaked in 2014 when the reworked Uganda Anti-Homosexuality Act—termed by Western media as the 'Kill the Gays' bill, for its allowance of those convicted of homosexuality to be imprisoned for life—was signed in parliament by President Museveni.[11] Although nulled six months later (upon procedural grounds, and not for moral reasons) in October 2019, Simon Lokodo, Uganda's Minister of Ethics and Integrity, announced that the Act would be reintroduced in parliament within weeks.[12] The statement was later denied amidst an international outcry and threats of aid retraction.[13] In the wake of this precarious fluctuation of legal structures are waves of aggression towards queer people. Just the threat of an intensified anti-homosexual legal structure suggests permission for the public to handle queer people as they see fit.[14] On 1 April 2020, a group of queer homeless people who

8............The National Gay and Lesbian Human Rights Commission, Gay and Lesbian Coalition of Kenya, and Nyanza, Rift Valley & Western Kenya Network, 'Repeal 162.' Online. *Love Is Human*, 2019, www.repeal162.org/about162 (accessed 1 June 2020).

9............See this report which 'documents rights abuses against LGBT people in the coast region, including violence, incitement to violence, and inadequate protection, and identifies ways in which the Kenyan authorities could better address these abuses and uphold their responsibility to protect all Kenyans.' Human Rights Watch, 'The Issue Is Violence: Attacks on LGBT People on Kenya's Coast.' Online. *Human Rights Watch*, 28 September 2015, www.hrw.org/report/2015/09/28/issue-violence/attacks-lgbt-people-kenyas-coast#page (accessed 15 May 2020).

10..........For a timeline of Ugandan LGBT rights, please see the following report: GLAD, 'Uganda Anti-Gay Timeline,' *GLAD*, 6 May 2014, www.glad.org/wp-content/uploads/2014/05/uganda-timeline.pdf (accessed 1 June 2020). For an overview of Kenyan LGBT rights, see information documented on the National Gay and Lesbian Human Rights Commissions' website: 'National Gay and Lesbian Human Rights Commission,' 2019, www.nglhrc.com/litigation/#our-wins (accessed 1 June 2020).

11..........See Amy Fallon, 'Uganda politicians celebrate passing of anti-gay laws,' *The Guardian*, 24 February 2014, www.theguardian.com/world/2014/feb/24/uganda-president-signs-anti-gay-laws.

12..........Nita Bhalla, 'Uganda Plans Bill Imposing Death Penalty for Gay Sex,' Reuters, 10 October 2019, www.reuters.com/article/us-uganda-lgbt-rights/uganda-plans-bill-imposing-death-penalty-for-gay-sex-idUSKBN1WP1GN.

13..........The connection between Uganda's intensified anti-homosexuality laws and pressure from international—government and business—communities to retract aid, is an ongoing tension. This is bitterly ironic as the current and foundational anti-homosexuality laws in both Kenya and Uganda are British Penal Codes established by the British colonial administration. See BBC News, 'Uganda Fury at David Cameron Aid Threat over Gay Rights,' *BBC*, 31 October 2011, www.bbc.co.uk/news/world-africa-15524013.

were self-quarantining from Covid-19 were arrested in a raid on their shelter.[15] A neighbour had tipped off the police, using the excuse of social distancing rules to raise their attention. Ugandans rejected by their families, trying to build new familial structures and finding well-being together, had their safe space torn apart. Despite a global pandemic, there is still a lack of social empathy to respect spaces for queerness in Uganda today.

Adding to these damaging legal frameworks and social interventions is the growing influence and anti-homosexual agendas of the majority of Kenya's and Uganda's religious institutions. Where religion connects with social spaces, through the act of church-going, schools, and groups, it plays an influential role in framing the public discourse on sexuality.[16] Homosexuality is largely seen to be in contradiction to one's religion.[17] Queerness and religion are however not incompatible in Kenya and Uganda. There are Ugandans—such as the charismatic Bishop Christopher Senyonjo[18]—who are strong supporters of Christianity's need to embrace queerness. There are also organizations bridging the painful divide between religion and queerness such as the proactive Cosmopolitan Affirming Community in Kenya.[19] Even within religious structures that have mainly rejected and incited hatred towards queerness, queer Kenyans and Ugandans search for a space of spiritual safety.

## Care, Creativity, and Queerness between Nairobi and Kampala

• • •

The anti-homosexual backdrop of Kenya and Uganda has generated a heightened visual and cultural response. An intense aesthetic conversation is occurring led by the two country's capital cities. The quantity of visual culture being produced—both celebrating and condemning queerness—is increasing. This production is being driven by a myriad of sources: artists, media and press houses, religious figures, governments, schools, universities, and medical institutions. The production of culture lies along-

14..........In an interview conducted in 2016, Ugandan artist and professor, Angelo Kakande recalls a fear that lay not with the legal implementation of Uganda's Anti-Homosexuality Act, but with the public interpretation of the law: 'We knew no court would enforce this law, except one, the court of public opinion. Here, in this country, killing a gay person in front of the police is okay. There's the law and then there's the public law. I knew I could be protected in the law, but not in the people's law.' Angelo Kakande, interview by author, Kampala, June 2016.

15..........Jason Burke, 'Ugandan Police Accused of Abusing Lockdown Laws after LGBT Arrests,' *The Guardian*, 1 April 2020, www.theguardian.com/world/2020/apr/01/ugandan-police-accused-of-abusing-lockdown-laws-after-lgbt-arrests.

16..........David Kuria Mbote, et al., 'Kenyan Religious Leaders' Views on Same-Sex Sexuality and Gender Nonconformity: Religious Freedom versus Constitutional Rights,' *Journal of Sex Research* 55, no. 4–5 (2018), pp. 630–41, doi:10.1080/00224499.2016.1255702.

17..........This present-day view can again be traced to the British colonizing mission. Research by Nancy Baraza highlights how the criminalization of homosexuality in Kenya in 1930 was closely tied to British Judeo-Christian religious beliefs that aimed to replace African customary laws and standardize divergent ethnic sexualities to ease and assist the British colonizing project. (See Eric Mawira Gitari, 'The Gay Debate: Decriminalising Homosexuality in Kenya,' *The Elephant*, 28 February 2019, www.theelephant.info/features/2019/02/28/the-gay-debate-decriminalising-homosexuality-in-kenya/).

In Uganda, queerness played a pivotal role at the birth of its nation. The last Buganda monarch—Kabaka Mwanga II—is a central figure of resistance to the British colonization of Buganda (the Buganda kingdom and the Baganda people are the dominant ethnic group of the region known as Uganda today). Bound together in resistance to British imperialism and Western religious institutions, Mwanga's bi-sexuality was one of the reasons British imperialists proffered to justify intervening in the governance of Uganda. The colonizers believed that the more that could be made homogeneous, the more that could be controlled (See Aida Holly-Nambi, *Against the Order of Ugandan Nature*, presentation, 2015.)

18..........Christopher Senyonjo, 'Bishop Christopher Senyonjo on LGBT rights in Uganda,' interview by Amnesty International, 25 June 2013, www.youtube.com/watch?v=Z-AQmcAU5mk.

19..........CAC Kenya. https://cac-kenya.com/aboutus/ (accessed 1 June 2020).

side both an intensification and fluctuation in homophobic laws—and social stigmas—regarding queer lives. Artists and audiences are in dialogue about queer aesthetics and making art rigorously in response to this evolving social and legal situation. Nairobi and Kampala are therefore strong case studies to witness how shifts in the legal and social landscape of a city affect and shape queer artistic practice and cultural organizations' curatorial strategies.

Between the cities of Nairobi and Kampala, a conversation of queer care and creativity is taking place, which both Creatives Garage and Babishai contribute to. In 2014, queer refugees travelled from Uganda to Kenya to seek refuge from Uganda's Anti-Homosexuality Act. Queer Ugandan refugees continue to make this journey today. Responding to the lack of working opportunities offered to these refugees when arriving to Nairobi, Creatives Garage ran a project within and from their space offering enterprise skills for these individuals to set up micro-businesses.[20] To push against social isolation, Creatives Garage work to connect queer refugees to Nairobi's community through social events and community gatherings. Artists travel between Nairobi and Kampala to undertake residencies and creative exchanges, utilizing the resources of art collectives such as 32° East | Ugandan Arts Trust; Bayimba International Arts Festival; Maisha Film Lab; and the Nest Collective. In 2014, Baishai Niwe Poetry Foundation opened its annual poetry award to writers from across Africa. The 'Babishai Niwe Poetry Award' has been an important platform for Kenyan writers to be read and heard ever since. Consumers of culture travel between the countries to attend cultural festivities like the 'Bayimba Festival' (Kampala) and 'Africa Nouveau Festival' (Nairobi). Kenyan party-goers also—somewhat ironically—travel to Kampala to let loose in city spaces like the infamous red-light district, Kabalagala. Despite its conservativism and anti-homosexual legal structures, Kampala is well known in the East African region for its proudly pleasure-seeking lifestyle practices. Nairobi-based poet Kins of Spade was initially fearful of travelling to Kampala. The residency undertaken during this 'Forces of Art' project was their first opportunity to visit the city. Their experience of Ugandan queerness had been primarily through hearing the experiences of queer Ugandan refugees at Creatives Garage. Upon returning from Kampala, Kins of Spade recalled with admiration that 'despite Kampala being a homophobic city, love continues to thrive.'[21]

Entangled into these knotted associations and creative relationships is a queer dialogue between the two cities. Queerness—the term used preferentially and throughout this text—is a critical term owned by communities in Kenya and Uganda to challenge the binaries of homo- and heterosexuality. A term of expansive possibilities, queerness achieves the work of moving away from historical colonial references of sexuality and opens up communities to plural interpretations of same-sex intimacies. Queerness is an umbrella term, not grounded in any geographical region, around which a myriad of possibilities of gender and sexuality can be debated.

20.......... See the project *Safe Spaces for LGBTI Refugees in Nairobi*, Voice. Global, https://voice.global/grantees/safe-spaces-lgbti-refugees-nairobi-2/#project (accessed 1 June 2020).

21.......... Kins of Spade (poet), interview by author, Nairobi, May 2019.

△ 1
Kins of Spade, *Things I would like to tell my daughter*, 2019, digital print

The plurality of queerness provides a layer of protection to queer communities in Kenya and Uganda as the term itself refuses to offer a concrete definition of sexuality to a watching public. Communities can find a place of safety within the spacious meaning of the word itself. After their Forces of Art residency, Kampala-based Kiconco describes a possible queer dynamic of the two city spaces:

> If there is a queer relationship between Kampala and Nairobi, it is a complicated friendship based on discovery. Where Nairobi has discovered how to define itself and has the vocabulary and scholarship to back up every category and subcategory of queerness it wears, Kampala has discovered how to unravel itself and bypasses vocabulary in favour of euphemisms. If Nairobi is gravitating towards sharp, defined terms, Kampala is gravitating toward umbrella queerness. If Nairobi is pursuing legal freedom, Kampala is beside it pursuing freedom within queerness, trying to expand who fits in the label of queer and how they exist within that label.[22]

Kenyan activists are taking an appeal of May 2019's decriminalization case to the Supreme Court. If the ruling is overturned, a landmark moment for human rights in Kenya will have been achieved. Whilst there have been legal successes in Uganda—most notably, the nulling of the Anti-Homosexuality Act 2014—the queer community is realistic about timescales for seismic legal shifts to occur. Meanwhile, communities are focusing their energies on the creation of safe places to be together. I have had the privilege

22..........Gloria Kiconco (poet), interview by author, Nairobi, June 2019.

of witnessing the careful strategies and curated secrets used to enter such spaces in Kampala. Once inside, the atmosphere is experienced as an expansive feeling—as expansive as queerness itself. △Fig. 1

## CREATIVES GARAGE: THE SPACE, TEAM, AND PROGRAMME

> Art has always been a vehicle of
> expression for the oppressed.
> Censorship has always been about
> silencing voices that go against
> the grain of what mainstream society,
> governments, and oppressive cultures
> insist should be true.
>
> For queer people, poetry, prose
> and visual art that humanizes us has
> always been deemed as rebellious
> despite it being merely a reflection
> of our own lives.
>
> Without art and culture,
> we'd feel very alone in society.
> Without art, it would be easier for
> society to isolate us and dismiss us
> as aberrant members of society.[23]

Creatives Garage is a physical space for artists, audiences, and activists to walk into and feel safe: a six-roomed, two-storied house with an open-air rooftop, in a semi-residential area of Nairobi. Rooms within the house are repurposed: what was once a bedroom is now a recording studio for Creatives Garage's CG Radio station, a platform to push and promote underground African music talent. What used to be a living room is now an artist's studio, where a group of musicians are rehearsing for the forthcoming 'Sondeka Festival,' a cross-artform, three-day celebration of East African art founded by Creatives Garage. Remnants of domesticity are visible throughout the house. Instead of office blinds, there are curtains on the windows. A comfy sofa sits invitingly in the team's office. The aesthetics of home complement Creatives Garage's welcoming and inclusive way of working.

The Creatives Garage team have operated for eight years to build an atmosphere of trust with their community of creatives.[24] The conditions for this environment are deceptively simple. Founder of Creatives Garage,

23..........Kins of Spade, interview by author, Nairobi, May 2019.

24..........As of May 2020, the Creatives Garage team include: Liz Kilili, Muthoni Gathecha, Trish Gitau, Sammy Muriuki, Judith Adurani, Steven Wanaina, Laban Machogu, Martin Karugu, Stephen Odipo, Adam Ahsan, Adam Kiboi, Robert Otieno, Dan Nyadhaya, James Kioko, Lekek Chebii, Duncan Mukide.

Kenyan cultural manager Liz Kilili, describes how 'safe spaces have always been difficult to find in Nairobi. When artists need a place to rant, just sit down, take a moment and re-strategize, we provide a safe haven for them.'[25] Although this tactic of community-building is rooted in simplicity—providing space and a listening ear—it takes substantial effort and courage to create such an environment of care, especially for people who are under intense legal and social scrutiny. Creatives Garage reach out to a diverse but clearly defined set of people: artists practising in all art forms, including musicians, painters, gamers, dancers, and producers; activists using their art and energy to transform social situations with and without government support; audiences of art, both those that turn to art for expression, escapism, and enjoyment, and those that might invest in the industry; and members of communities (Ugandan LGBT refugees, for example) who are drawn to Creatives Garage programming through chance or compulsion.[26] Running across all these types of publics are queer people. Queer artists, activists, audiences, allies, adolescents, and adults.

Creatives Garage programming reflects the diversity of the people they work with. They have produced book projects *Femmolutions*, a video streaming platform Kalabars, creative economy courses 'Cr8 Academy,' social justice art installations *Lebo*, and a shoemaking project called 'Shoejaa.' Their programmes are topical to Nairobi issues, and responsive to global challenges.[27] Perhaps, at times, Creatives Garage take on too much; some projects appear un-finished, dropped in the flurry of starting another. This state reflects the unquestionable urgency of social and creative work that needs to be undertaken in Nairobi, as Creatives Garage's scale of activity matches this pressure. The team's ability to be responsive comes down to their tireless commitment and the skill sets held within the organization. Kilili's nine-strong team holds proficiencies and values—from leadership to humility, administration to enthusiasm—that they share with communities from within their Nairobi space, across the city through public programming, and online with their community of over eighteen thousand (and counting) engaged members.

## Language

Running across Creatives Garage's physical and digital space is a considered use of languages. The team switches fluently between Swahili, English, Sheng, and mother tongue languages from Creatives Garage community's ethnic groups.[28] The choice of which language to use is driven by the impact

25 ..........Liz Kilili (founder of Creatives Garage), interview by author, Nairobi, June 2019.

26 ..........For instance, NGOs might encourage community members to attend a Creatives Garage workshop.

27 ..........Within five weeks of Covid-19 hitting Nairobi, the team brainstormed and produced a response in the form of 'Lock In Festival,' a seven-day online festival filled with podcasts, live streams from musicians, inspirational webinars, online vendor stalls, and a thoughtfully curated children's section.

28 ..........The use of Sheng connects to a Nairobi youth and cuts across socio-economic divides. The language was born from Nairobi street culture (see Aurélia Ferrari, 'Evolution of Sheng During the Last Decade,' *The East African Review* 49 (2014), https://journals.openedition.org/eastafrica/340#tocto1n1.) On *Kalabars—Creatives Garage* streaming platform for African media content—there is a Sheng cooking show: two young men encourage other young men to get cooking, amusingly telling their audience how it is both enjoyable and economic. The use of English ensures translation of Creatives Garage projects across East Africa: the British did an infamously good job of imposing their native tongue on others.

of the project and the people Creatives Garage reach out to.[29] Creatives Garage project 'I Speak,' a digital media storytelling project giving a voice to working women in Taita-Taveta county in south-east Kenya, was undertaken in both Swahili and Taita.[30] Creatives Garage team member Adam Kiboi describes the appreciation from those engaged in the project to have the process and outcomes of the activity—beautifully-crafted documentaries and short videos—delivered in their language. To ensure the work reached an audience across Kenya and online, the media content was translated from Taita, to Swahili, to English. Retaining the same nuance and directness of language originally relayed by the women was an essential part of the translation process.

## Language of Queerness

• •

The term 'queer' can become lost in translation. This makes the use of the word a strategic choice. The lack of meaning of queer to one person provides a level of protection to the queer person standing behind it. The slipperiness of the term, queerness, ensures it is impossible to grasp in the wrong hands. The word 'lesbian' would raise alerts immediately in Nairobi. A space like Creatives Garage could be shut down quickly if their content was seen to be promoting 'lesbianism.'[31] But caution is needed, as some people that need to be included and cared for within queerness become locked out because of linguistics. The word queer in Nairobi speaks mainly to an educated middle class. Creatives Garage continually navigates the line between clarity and danger, opacity and exclusion. When programming queer activities there are methods Creatives Garage uses to widen their audience demographics whilst keeping safety a priority. Creatives Garage hosts discussions, such as 'Sex in Antiquity' exploring sexuality in pre-colonial Africa, which are moderated by someone all sides of the room feel an affinity with. The front cover of Creatives Garage-produced books, *A Look-book on Sex in Modern Kenya* for example, often remove their title and point only slightly to queer intimacies, intriguing some to open the book and others to move on.

## Creating Space for Queerness

• • •

Creatives Garage produces programmes specifically targeted at exploring expressions of gender and sexuality, such as the exhibition 'Prosexive' presented at the end of this section. The team also ensures queerness is welcomed within each strand of their eclectic work. Queer inclusivity is achieved by the team's capability to self-reflect and imagine what reassurance might feel like for someone scared. Kilili expounds, 'We bring conversations down to a personal level, to create an environment where victims of discrimination can be seen as human beings and not just

29..........Adam Kiboi (Creatives Garage team member), interview by author, Nairobi, February 2020.

30..........'I Speak,' *Creatives Garage*, www.creativesgarage.org/i-speak/ (accessed 1 June 2020).

31..........'Lesbianism' is a Nairobism: a term, like 'gayism,' used—with some irony—by anti-gay ambassadors like the director of Kenya's Film Classification Board, Ezekiel Mutua.

as the "other".'[32] The programmes engendered at Creatives Garage ensure victims of discrimination see each other as human beings. As Kins of Spade describes, without art and culture as a vehicle of expression, queer people would be dismissed as aberrant members of society. Within Creatives Garage people are allowed to function in the range of modes that queerness allows, past rigid modes of enforced heterosexuality. The Creatives Garage programmes themselves become a space of queer exploration and queer safety.

## FEMMOLUTION

However careful the team are and however many tactics of opacity they use, a space like Creatives Garage could still be shut down.[33] Today, in 2020, the space has had to close temporarily due to Covid-19. The programmes that come out of Creatives Garage become ever more vital to continue the work of the space. The book and music album *Femmolution* is one such venture. *Femmolution* is a bringing together of female voices; it is a space for women to express themselves without having to show themselves. Kilili, who was Creative Director of the book, invited twenty-eight writers, five artists, and twelve musicians to contribute. Her messaging to the contributors was open: 'You do not have to be a seasoned writer or poet, just a woman ready to talk.'[34] The traditional format of a softback book became a platform for public sharing and intimate interactions. Stitched into the book's two hundred and four pages are stories of self-love, loss, violence, and resilience. There are short essays, visual poems, and one-line statements. Thirty-four images reflect and expand on the ideas within the written works. The music album is accessible through a QR code that transports readers to Creatives Garage's SoundCloud site and twelve eclectic compilations[35] including spoken-word and storytelling (in Swahili, Sheng, and English) and tracks of soul, electronica, hip-hop, and folk. The album is a rich range of sounds and voices for a diversity of listening ears.

*Femmolution* is an ambitious, energy-fuelled project. In Kilili's words: 'I'm amazed by what we each carry within ourselves. The joy, struggles, the pain, hurt, and the need to release. I am glad *Femmolution* was just a tiny ripple in a huge sea.'[36] We might think of this as a ripple in the huge sea of patriarchy perhaps, but a groundswell of creativity in itself.

32 .......... Kilili, interview by author, Nairobi, June 2019.

33 .......... In 2012, the National Gay and Lesbian Human Rights Commission (NGLHRC) sought to register their organization with Kenya's Non-Governmental Organizations Coordination Board. This government body rejected the group's request to register. In denying the application, the board said that the name of the organization was 'unacceptable,' and that it could not register it because Kenya's penal code 'criminalizes gay and lesbian liaisons.' For further information: 'Kenya: High Court Orders LGBT Group Registration.' *Human Rights Watch*. 2015. www.hrw.org/news/2015/04/28/kenya-high-court-orders-lgbt-group-registration.

34 .......... Liz Kilili, 'Behind the Audacious Curtains,' *Creatives Garage*, 5 July 2019, www.creativesgarage.org/2019/07/05/behind-the-audacious-curations/.

35 .......... Creatives Garage, *Femmolution*, Creatives Garage Studios, Soundcloud album, 10 December 2016. https://soundcloud.com/creatives-garage/sets/femmolution.

36 .......... Kilili, interview by author, Nairobi, June 2019.

## Curation as Community Building

•

A reader can move between ideas in *Femmolution* in a non-linear way. Chapters are marked by a focus on feelings: 'Anxiety'; 'Resilience'; 'Self-Love,' and 'Acceptance.' And further, in the editor's note (an editor who remains anonymous to the reader) we are urged to do just this: 'Why follow the straight route when the one that curves through the trees is so much more scenic?'[37] This is a playful suggestion to move away from the normative path and find the queerness between the book's paper pages. Editing is undertaken 'as loosely as possible,' kept to a purposeful minimum in an attempt to ensure the female writers' voices are heard directly throughout the journey of the book.[38] The purpose of the edit is to sharpen the experience of the writer's words, and never to erase. I note here that editing has become synonymous to erasure when it comes to the publishing of queer content in Nairobi.[39] The book *Stories of our Lives*, published by Kenya's Nest Collective and telling personal accounts of people identifying as queer in Kenya, contains words blacked out by the collective to protect the people in the text—self-erasure tactics to ensure the book remains in circulation. *Femmolution* aims to achieve the opposite of erasure. One reader of the book gave Creatives Garage the feedback that it has done just this, it has 'brought women together and given them a platform to speak of their lives and in their terms.' The curatorial process undertaken by Kilili and within *Femmolution* can be seen as a method of community building amongst women and queer people who both share experiences, and who have led divergent lives. The chapter titled 'Violence' offers intense and harrowing examples of shared female pain. And in the work *Reflections* by Stella Nsubuga, which outlines a daughter's tested love of their mother, Nsubuga sets to remind us that every person's grief and every person's loss 'remains uniquely, our loss alone.'[40]

Curation in *Femmolution* harkens back to the etymology of the word: *curatus*, to curate, to take care of. *Femmolution* is a bringing together, an assembling of women—and those that identify as women—with care.

## A Space to See New Futures

• •

Through the curation of shared affiliations within *Femmolution*, new ways of being together are hinted at. The book presents an alternative narrative to the dominant media stories of female oppression in Kenya. There are major struggles in Kenya that cannot be ignored: the anti-homosexual legal framework aforementioned, the under-representation of women in decision-making processes in government, the lack of safe spaces to protect women against gender-based violence. *Femmolution* is a ripple in addressing these fights, but a ripple nonetheless. The space of *Femmolution* builds momentum

37 ..........Creatives Garage, Mwihaki Mundia, and Liz Kilili, *Femmolution* (Nairobi: Creatives Garage, 2016).

38 ..........Ibid.

39 ..........See 'Stories of Our Lives: Queer Kenyan Narratives (2015),' *The Nest Collective*, www.thisisthenest.com/sool-book (accessed 1 June 2020).

40 ..........Stella Nsubuga, 'Reflections,' in *Femmolution*, ed. Oluwademilade Adeniyi (Nairobi: Creatives Garage, 2016), pp. 52–53.

towards female self-acceptance and a glance at what a feminist future could look like. For example, *Twist and Shout* by Kingwa calls for an embrace of our misshapen selves through the visual metaphor of a forest; where some trees grow straight, whilst others bend and curve. The poem reads:

> Straight trees
> Are found in thick forests
> Where, because clustered together
> There's no space
> To lean out, to bend, to reach out.[41]

The poet calls for us not to fret 'when you look upon yourself and find your own trunk partly twisted.' It means you reached for the sun, held the rain, and 'whether by fate or choice,' you stood alone. Kingwa could be calling for self-acceptance of our physical forms, our mental states, our sexual preferences. There is an exciting gap between metaphor and precision, which allows a reader to fill it with their interpretation and their own life's story.

A photographic intervention within the book called 'Common Thread' by Fayth W. takes the reader through a coming out process. The images are self-portraits in black and white portraying one, sometimes two, bodies—it is difficult to tell if they are the same body or two different forms as one body is in focus and the other is blurred. The figures face the camera directly but are partly covered in a white cloth, often obscuring the viewers' gaze and full understanding of where faces are looking. Through accompanying text the artist carries us on a journey from the fear engendered 'when you start leading the lifestyle you want, [and] you [then] realize how misunderstanding your community and family might be, and it can be a risky tale.'[42] To the artist, reaching a state of self-acceptance where they decide 'to live [their] life as [they] want.'[43] The artist does not point directly to a queer coming-out. There are no direct visual signifiers to same-sex intimacies in the photographs. The lighting within the photographs that fall on the body in focus, and the forms out-of-focus, point instead at a queer potential. The combination of text and image leaves the viewer questioning what they are privy to. The works call to mind José Esteban Muñoz's description of queerness: 'A warm illumination on a horizon imbued with potentiality.'[44] We can't fully see queerness in the works, but through the 'anticipatory illumination of art,' a queer viewer can be confident it is there.[45]

Punctuating Kenya's context of unsatisfactory legal frameworks and ignored human rights for women and queer people, *Femmolution* is a space to let out grief, fears, and revelations, as well as celebrate what it is to be femme, female, and queer today. Queerness is visible through the conscious and subconscious experimentations of the works described above and many others within *Femmolution*. Occasionally, the reader may have to squint to see the queerness in the book; as Muñoz describes, 'The visual

41 ........... Kingwa, 'Twist and Shout,' in *Femmolution*, ed. Oluwademilade Adeniyi (Nairobi: Creatives Garage, 2016), p. 70.
42 ........... Fayth W., 'Common Thread,' in *Femmolution*, ed. Oluwademilade Adeniyi (Nairobi: Creatives Garage, 2016), p. 98.
43 ........... Ibid., p. 103.
44 ........... José Esteban Muñoz, *Cruising Utopia: The Then and There of Queer Futurity* (New York: NYU Press, 2009), p. 1.
45 ........... Ibid.

language that emerges is sometimes loud, and sometimes barely seen,' but queerness is very much there.[46] The process of viewing such a project calls for the reader to see how impossible ways of life—such as embracing queerness in Kenya and Uganda—might one day become possible.

KINS OF SPADE

△ 2
Kins of Spade, *Kins of Spade*, 2016, digital print

## KINS OF SPADE

Travelling through *Femmolution*, the reader realizes that although they are witnessing deeply personal stories, there are times they are being kept out of certain narratives. Decisions of what is heard are carefully considered. A prominent absence is the true name of a poet featuring powerfully in *Femmolution*, Kins of Spade. The writer speaks to the reader, deeply, personally, and directly through their work, and yet by using a pseudonym, they become less accessible to the reader. Within their biography, they reveal both a closeness and a mask of who they might be: 'Kins of Spade is a recluse who only comes out to play with her words and is only very rarely seen in public… You might never meet her but you will always feel as if you know her intimately.'[47] △Fig. 2

This 'Forces of Art' project worked with Kins of Spade throughout 2019 to offer time and space to the artist to produce a new body of artwork.

46……….Ibid., p. 7.
47……….Kins of Spade, 'Biography,' in *Femmolution*, ed. Oluwademilade Adeniyi (Nairobi: Creatives Garage, 2016), p. 168.

Kins of Spade produced a poetry anthology entitled *Queer Abstraction*, an intimate exploration into a deeply private individual. Through a series of semi-structured interviews, understandings emerge of the need for strategies, such as a pseudonym, to play between the space of being seen and keeping safe. As they have said in an interview:

> I've been shy all my life. I've not been
> able to place it, but often I prefer
> to communicate remotely, such as
> through my art. Even then I work via
> a pseudonym because I can't stand
> the public eye and being judged
> for what they expect my work to be
> and not what it is on its own merit.[48]

The pseudonym becomes a protective barrier for Kins of Spade to play beneath. This masking of their identity allows the artist to move through a printed space like *Femmolution* with confidence, marking pages with words that would not be able to exist if their true name was revealed.[49]

## Abstraction

•

Within Kins of Spade's poems, in both *Femmolution* and *Queer Abstraction*, the audience witnesses varying levels of queerness, from the confrontational to the obscure. From:

> *Bad decisions*
> His haggard dick tastes
> of bad decisions
> Her pussy, ripe juicy mangoes
> in spring
> To:
> *Cowards*
> Cowards die last in the
> Battlefield of what's, ifs and should

Between the spaces of the comprehensible and the incomprehensible is the poet's varying use of abstraction, referring to the freedom from representational qualities in art.[50] Kins of Spade turns to abstraction to play with levels of queer visibility. Abstraction becomes a way for the artist to steer their sentences away from literal messaging, landing audiences in a space where they must interpret ideas for themselves, removing liabilities—and

48...........Kins of Spade, interview by author, Nairobi, May 2019.

49...........Kins of Spade shares a chronological connection with Black female writers who also used pseudonyms to be heard. The newspapers and journals of apartheid South Africa, for example, had no shortage of pseudonyms due to the racial power dynamics and gatekeeping of white publishers (see Tim Couzens, 'Pseudonyms in Black South African Writing, 1920–1950,' *Research in African Literatures* 6, no. 2 [1975], pp. 226–31). The usual author profile of South African university presses were white males, with an occasional white female author (see Elizabeth Le Roux, 'Black Writers, White Publishers,' *E-Rea* 11 [2013], p. 2). In a patriarchal world hostile to female creativity, women were and still are, obliged to change their name to pass as men to get the attention of publishers.

50...........Oxford English Dictionary online, 'abstract,' https://en.oxforddictionaries.com/definition/abstraction.

32º East | Ugandan Arts Trust / Kampala, Uganda / 1:26pm 0°17'33.5"N / 32°36'22.8"E

BN Poetry Award / Kampala, Uganda / 1:26pm 0°17'33.5"N / 32°36'22.8"E

danger—from the artist. Abstraction enables the artist's work to be heard before questions about their sexuality can be asked. Kins of Spade describes the reason for abstraction contextually:

> Homophobia is pervasive in Nairobi,
> and it's hard for a lot of people to
> take you seriously if you're just 'the
> lesbian poet' or the 'lesbian painter.'
> Abstraction cuts through homophobia,
> in the sense that my message gets
> across much faster than my orientation.
> I'm more likely seen as a person with
> human feelings and desires in life,
> more than the deviant homosexual
> society paints me as.[51]

There is an intimacy experienced by some in knowing the layers of truth embedded within the two publications, while others are shut firmly out. Abstraction, like the use of a pseudonym, becomes a mask for the artist to continue to speak behind.

## Things I Would Like to Tell my Daughter

There is agony to hiding, as well, which one of the works within *Queer Abstraction*, entitled 'Things I would like to tell my daughter' exposes. △Fig. 1 Through a poem of nine stanzas, a mother imagines advising their daughter. A call to love freely leads the poem: 'I would tell her to be herself/ To love deeply, moan freely/ Experiment fail and love while at it.' A request to embrace life, to let love lead the way. The words are as carefree as the choice of the typeface: Luna, a free-to-download 'handwritten' font that represents the feeling of 'joy, and casual.'[52] The second stanza instructs their daughter to be cautious of their own and others' struggles because, as the third stanza warns, 'life isn't always what it seems.' This is the moment when we get a sense that something cannot be said. Why is the title 'Things I would like to tell my daughter,' not 'Things that I am telling my daughter'? This poem is a letter that cannot be sent. A mother is giving advice through their words and not in person. In verse four the mother wants to tell their daughter:

> To listen,
> To understand before
> She jumps to conclusions
> And decide
> To forgive
> To learn to move on
> To fight for what's right
> And trample evil

51..........Kins of Spade, interview by author, Nairobi, May 2019.

52..........'Luna: Free Font,' *Free Design Sources*, 29 October 2019, https://freedesignresources.net/luna-free-font/.

This is a request for their daughter to hear their full truth, and to then take this knowledge, along with her compassion for her mother, to join the struggle in ousting prejudice, judgement, homophobia. These words may bypass a young person, who may be oblivious to their deeper meaning. The age of the child is hinted at in the block-filled graphic accompanying the poem, also created by Kins of Spade. The graphic is the listening face of a child, staring slightly upwards at her mother as she speaks. Innocence and a growing awareness are denoted by a glowing yellow halo, illuminating the back of the child's head. These are also words that might be lost on a reader who may not know who Kins of Spade is. There is no reason why this poem could not potentially be the words of advice by a cisgender heterosexual woman to her daughter. But if this is the case, then why does the writer not reveal their identity? And why is the poet not speaking directly to their daughter, but about them? Verse six wishes the daughter to 'love her imperfections, for there lies great perfection.' Here the larger project of *Femmolution*—self-acceptance—is called upon. It is at verse seven that the poet checks themselves, holds back: 'To trust—and sometimes not.' A reversal of stanza one's imperative 'to love deeply, moan freely.' Kins of Spade is here caught between the impossibility of not giving advice as a mother and the impossibility of speaking their queer truth to their daughter. Here is the anguish of secrecy, even if it is being used to keep one safe. The mother's advice peaks with a sense of urgency and a warning in verse eight: of the disguise of friendship, behind which might hide evil. Although masks can create a space for queerness to survive behind—such as this writers' own use of a pseudonym—masks can also hide vicious agendas. That seemingly friendly and enquiring neighbour might be what leads to an arrest of your space of queer safety. The reader feels a frustrated irony as this mother cautions against two-faced agendas, even while themselves having to talk through a pseudonym to their daughter. The poem ends with a direction of hope: 'Let love always win, let love be her compass in her life journey.' The needle of the compass points away from a present containing poisonous homophobia and guides us towards a queer horizon of future possibilities.

## 'Prosexive' Exhibition

• • •

Publishing queer work has its difficulties and dangers in Nairobi and Kampala. A publishing house might refuse the production of work, or, worse, could raise alarm bells on the content of the work to authorities with homophobic agendas. *Femmolution* was published independently by Creatives Garage. The team then carefully curated the distribution of the book. *Femmolution* was circulated during a private launch attended by people who Creatives Garage were confident could handle the pages with respect. Following this, the team printed three hundred copies, earmarking two hundred for women and female-led institutions and placing the remaining one hundred 'in public spaces such as hotels, pubs, and airports for anyone to pick up.'[53] Distribution methods became wider reaching as the confidence of the team grew in the safety of the book's contributors. Today, four years on from the first printed copy being released, readers can download a PDF version of *Femmolution* from the Creatives Garage website.[54]

Readings from *Femmolution* and *Queer Abstraction* were also undertaken within Creatives Garage's exhibition 'Prosexive.' The exhibition aimed to offer a safe, open space for conversations about sex. And for sex to be challenged and taken apart in the process. Kilili describes:

> Sex has often been described as being concrete, restricted to heteronormative depictions. I feel that sex is too varied and wide to get limited. Sex and our definition of it have always been mutating and will continue to as we move towards a world where sexual liberation is the norm.[55]

'Prosexive' took place throughout one night. Experiencing the exhibition was an impactful moment, displaying Creatives Garage's unique ability to create space for queerness. The following passage offers an account of the event.

> I walk into what I think is an exhibition of photographs about love. I am in Creatives Garage, in the first room of the house-turned-gallery. On the wall are photos of bodies entwined together. The images are serene: a close-up, detailed, and yet semi-abstracted view of couples bound in secure and comforting holds. The bodies' genders are ambiguous: I trace how one person's limbs become melded into others'. Innermost areas are carefully absorbed by both couples, hiding the possibility of revealing same-sex intimacies. Turning away from the photos, I walk through the full gallery. The atmosphere feels animated, more so than what I remember of stiff exhibition opening nights. Above me are party balloons, hanging from the ceiling, a strange addition to what appears to be a photography exhibition. On closer inspection, I see that the balloons are air-filled condoms packed with glitter. By now, the gallery is teeming, full of Kenyan and East African teenagers and twenty-somethings. I feel old and awkward, but I am immediately and warmly smiled at. People are streaming up the stairs; I follow. I enter an empty room—cold tiled floor, whitewashed walls—a shy man stands facing the small group of us that have managed to arrive before the door shuts us away from the sounds of the now humming house. The man humbly tells us he is a sub, that his 'dominant partner [for the BDSM activity] has not turned up, and would anyone mind whipping [him]?' I am queer and seven months pregnant and feel ready to run from the room when we all start laughing. Laughter takes us into a space of

53.......... Kilili, 'Behind the Audacious Curations,' 2019.

54..........A downloadable PDF of *Femmolution* can be found at: www.creativesgarage.org/femmolution/ (accessed 1 June 2020).

55..........Kilili, 'Behind the Audacious Curations,' 2019.

safety and for the next hour, nine strangers become allies in a trustful and playful exploration of intimacy.

In the next packed room, I am taking in information from a Ssenga, a Ugandan practice which sees the aunt of the family tutor young women in a range of sexual matters, including 'pre-menarche practices, pre-marriage preparation, erotics and reproduction.'[56] As the practice is predominantly associated with heterosexual partnerships, I listen with wonder as this Ssenga tells us how to ensure that we as women, as queer people, as trans bodies, are also pleasured.[57] Sex is not just for the straight man's enjoyment. There are awkward giggles, and tears of relief. I think to myself, is this room in the same country where homosexuality is so famously illegal? And where today, in 2020, in neighbouring Uganda, the threat of the Anti-Homosexuality Act, bringing life imprisonment upon two same-gendered people loving each other, still lingers? Within the house, the exhibition, and the space of night readings of *Femmolution* and *Queer Abstraction* take place. People were able to flip intimately between the sheets of the book alone, or join a community to share, laugh, and cry through the pages together. An ideal setting, and space, for the sharing of queer lives.

The first room of photographs in the 'Prosexive' exhibition were powerful in their own right, and yet they also stood as a tactical mask to the depths of queer activity taking place in the house. An audience member who might have threatened the queer space could have been stopped at room one, keeping others safe in the layers of the house beyond. Promotion of the exhibition was carefully planned.[58] In invitations that were distributed, through closed Facebook and Whatsapp groups, the language was both clear and cautious: 'Prosexive welcomes all ways of thinking about sex. People of all genders and sexual preferences are welcome and we ask that you respect that 'Prosexive' will be a safe space free of judgment and hostility.'[59] The language, timing, location, and curation of the exhibition together enabled a queer community to be seen by those they wanted to be seen by, ensuring others—who would have disrupted this careful strengthening of a queer community—were kept out. △Fig. 3

## BABISHAI NIWE POETRY FOUNDATION

Art and culture always offer alternative spaces. Where people might be afraid

56..........Sylvia Tamale, 'Eroticism, Sensuality and "Women's Secrets" Among the Baganda.' *IDS Bulletin* 37, no. 5 (2006), pp. 89–97, doi.org/10.1111/j.1759-5436.2006.tb00308.x.

57..........This Ssenga, through Creatives Garage's curation, has been asked to 'demonstrate some intimate activities to enlighten curious minds on what goes on with the female body during intercourse,' Kilili, 'Behind the Audacious Curations,' 2019, p. 5.

58..........Kilili explains that 'In a society that is constantly policing our sexuality, we had to have minimal publicity for 'Prosexive' to avoid attracting the attention of government censors,' (Kilili, interview by author, Nairobi, June 2019.)

> to hear political vocabulary or confront queerness directly, they are not as afraid to watch someone dance or to enjoy a fashion show. But when queer voices are being silenced, these spaces are less for speaking out to an audience. They are there so queer people don't forget that they have a voice. These are spaces where they speak to each other, share ideas, express the diversity of queerness. These are spaces to enjoy each other as well and remove a lot of the heaviness that comes with queer struggles. These are also often the safe spaces to exist in when everywhere else seems threatening. I think art and culture provide the spaces that sustain queer voices and give them the strength to speak out to a wider audience.[60]

△ 3
Gloria Kiconco,
*Drm sqncs://<root/s> (2)*, 2019, zine

Babishai Niwe Poetry Foundation (Babishai) was founded in 2008 by Beverley Nambozo Nsengiyunva. A Ugandan poet, actress, literary activist, biographer, mother, and teacher, Nsengiyunva believes in the power of poetry to shift landscapes: political, creative, pedagogical, and natural landscapes.[61] Her work as both artist and organizer has undoubtedly raised the profile of contemporary Ugandan poetry. In an interview, Nsengiyunva describes how Babishai allowed Ugandan poetry to 'come out.' She explains, 'You see, Uganda at the time was filled with closeted poets, those who wrote and wove beautiful words together but just crumpled them under their pillows, fearful of gazing eyes.'[62] Through Nsengiyunva's encouragement, Ugandan poets gained the confidence to be seen and heard.

59...........Creatives Garage, 'Invitation to Prosexive,' Digital. July 2019.

60...........Kiconco, interview by author, Nairobi, June 2019.

61...........'Babishai Niwe Poetry's Instagram Post: @Beverlynambozonsengiyunva, Is Proud of Her Association with the Babishai Niwe Poetry Foundation.' Instagram, 7 May 2020, www.instagram.com/p/B_5PmJMFfhB/ (accessed 1 June 2020).

Through Babishai's programmes, Ugandan poetry has a space to play within and a platform to be heard from. The foundation started as an annual 'BN Poetry Award,' giving recognition to new Ugandan literary talent. Babishai has now expanded its portfolio and presence and is instrumental in promoting Ugandan and African creative literary talent. Their programmes include the independent publishing of Ugandan and African poetry; the delivery of an annual poetry award (from 2014, the 'BN Poetry Award' extended across Africa); an annual poetry festival (focused upon in this chapter); and the delivery of school education programmes. Babishai's urgency is driven by the necessity to produce, protect, preserve, and present African poetry.

Babishai's programmes are not explicitly for queer poets and writers. However, the programmatic strategies Babishai undertake have allowed for sub-cultured work to be made that might not have otherwise been. The programme 'Making Poetry Matter' is a case in point. Nsengiyunva's values and beliefs drive the inclusive nature of Babishai. In the foreword to its 2014 poetry anthology *A Thousand Voices Rising*, she states, 'I believe that poetry ultimately frees individuals.'[63] For Nsengiyunva, poetry is a place to unravel ourselves from our constraints—constraints that might be imposed upon us by societies, states, or by ourselves. The process of creating—and consuming—poetry becomes a space to reach new personal freedoms.

I do however find a slight contradiction within the freedoms Nsengiyunva speaks of in *A Thousand Voices*. It is through this anthology that we discover a controversial patron of Babishai: Rebecca Kadaga, speaker of parliament of Uganda (the first woman to hold this position) and a vocal advocate of Uganda's Anti-Homosexual Act. In 2012, Kadaga became well known for announcing that she would pass the Anti-Homosexuality law as a 'Christmas gift to the Ugandan public.'[64] The presence of Kadaga temporarily locks me out of the anthology; I pause at the thought of supporting such a patron by reading the book. And yet, at the same time, her presence spurs me to find the inevitable queerness within the book's pages. Kadaga's words of support for poetry alongside a poet's celebration of queerness is such sweet irony.[65]

## 'Making Poetry Matter'

•

The project 'Making Poetry Matter' (2012–2013) was part of the expansion of Babishai's portfolio and its commitment to creating space for the production of new literary works. It focused on the importance of experimentation and free speech when producing and presenting Ugandan poetry by organizing residential poetry camps. The process began through a partner-

62..........Beverley Nsengiyunva (founder of Babishai), interview by author, Kampala, March 2020.63 Beverley Nambozo Nsengiyunva, ed., *A Thousand Voices Rising: An Anthology of Contemporary African Poetry* (Kampala: Gilgil Media Arts, 2014), p. 1. Funded by Prince Claus Fund.

64..........Elias Biryabarema, 'Uganda says want to pass anti-gay laws as "Christmas Gift",' Reuters, 13 November 2012, www.reuters.com/article/us-uganda-homosexuality/uganda-says-wants-to-pass-anti-gay-law-as-christmas-gift-idUSBRE8AC0V720121113.

65..........Although subtle and secretive the collision is very much present in the anthology and I urge you to read *A Thousand Voices Rising* to discover this entanglement for yourself.

ship between Babishai and Nairobi's 'Storymoja Festival.'[66] The Babishai team travelled to Nairobi and held creative writing workshops with Kenyan and Ugandan poets. This exchange sparked the motivation to continue cross-country collaborations. Babishai then experimented with organizing residential camps for Ugandan and East African poets. The camps took place over one to two days in areas of Uganda known for their natural beauty, such as Mount Elgon and Mabira Forest. The camps combined time for the poets to explore the landscapes they were immersed in, and time for writing, for engaging with other poets, and for presenting their works to each other. The camps were a moment for artists to step away from their everyday and engage with a space of art-making, knowledge-sharing, and community-building with the poets and creatives attending the camps.

The process of removal of artists from Kampala to a natural setting that took place during 'Making Poetry Matter' is what interests me as a researcher of this project. For artists that are dealing with their queerness within the claustrophobia of their family homes, offices, colleges, and neighbourhoods, this journey to another place offers a space for their queerness to breathe. For artists directly confronting harassment, violence, and censorship—against themselves or their work—the process of removal creates space for queerness, through their extraction from such vehement social and legal homophobic contexts.

There is a poignant relationship throughout this narrative: one between removal, extraction, and abstraction. Kins of Spade uses abstraction in their work to free themselves from the representational. Through the use of a pseudonym, they create a mask to obscure their identity, and through strategic choices in the form and content of their poems, they ensure they are not too starkly revealed. Abstraction is 'the process of removing something,' as well as a drive away from realism.[67] For queerness, there is violence in abstraction, which is the violence of removal, the violence of erasure. Queer people in Uganda are abstracted from society; they are excluded from homophobic families, deleted from their living spaces through incarceration and imprisonment. Queer Ugandans are told they do not exist, that they are the imaginings of a Western mode of living, that they are un-African; unaccepted by Uganda's nation-building projects, the very concept of their queerness is denied.

Babishai reverses the process of removal as one of erasure. The removal they offer is to a place of care, to creative abundance. The places the 'Making Poetry Matter' poetry camps are located are not in themselves less homophobic than Kampala. It can be more difficult to be queer in such towns as Kasese (adjacent to the Rwenzori Mountains where a poetry camp took place) due to the lack of a queer community and an increased sense of isolation. However, the process of being transported to an environment that does not know you, as we will see through Gloria Kiconco's experience of Babishai, can lead to opportunities for self-reflection, and space to re-strategize methods and tactics as a queer artist. Through such

66...........See: 'Storymoja Festival,' Storymoja Festival, 14 November 2019, http://storymojafestival.co.ke/.

Oxford English Dictionary online, 'abstract.'

67...........Oxford English Dictionary online, 'abstract.'

spaces, queer artists can become free from the rules that they are usually held to. The temporality of the moment heightens the opportunity for queerness to thrive. Participants can step away from their here and now and enter a transitory utopia.[68] Within this space, a radical imagining can take place of what it might be like to live in a world where anti-queerness does not exist.

## Gloria Kiconco

In 2016, the project 'Making Poetry Matter' transitioned and expanded into the 'Babishai Niwe Poetry Festival.' The festival now takes place every year and like residencies, it offers a juncture of removal. It offers a temporary escape from the everyday, and an opportunity to act differently—or be one's true self.[69] Artists continue to travel from Kampala across Uganda and to scenic rural settings: in 2016, the festival took place around the Rwenzori Mountain range, in 2017 at the Mabira Forest, and in 2019 at Lake Bunyoni. The format of the festival combines nature hikes, poetry performances, group dinners, and visits to schools to promote Ugandan poetry. Through the format of Babishai's three-day festival, Ugandan poets now have the opportunity for a recurring temporary removal, a recurring escapism.

Gloria Kiconco, a Ugandan poet and spoken-word artist, has been connected with 'Babishai Niwe Poetry Festival' since 2014 as an audience-member and most recently as a guest at Babishai's 2018 festival. Kiconco's practice crosses forms of written poetry, spoken-word performances, and experimental visual poetry. Her tussle with a cross-cultural heritage, while dealing with personal and intimate identities, fuels her work. Kiconco's practice stems from the way she plays with double-layered meanings and coded language. Her use of metaphor to speak about one thing, while revealing another—reviewing the different tastes of chilli, for example, to reveal her disdain of dictatorship, (lack of) democracy, and dance-hall music—result in unexpected, often hilarious, moving pieces. Reading one of the layers of Kiconco's work readers witness the poet undertaking a rapid self-education of 'Ugandan-ness.' A furious search for what it is, so that her diaspora-self might fit into it. The poet sits alongside a Ugandan woman cooking traditional food, trying to learn the correct methods for its consumption. But looking between the layers of Kiconco's texts the reader sees that the more Kiconco discovers the less likely she is to fit in. Each stir of the pot made whilst listening to the cook's views on politics, religion, sexuality, the poet is left with a bitter, uncomfortable taste.

In August 2018, Kiconco travelled with poets, writers, and artists to the Babishai festival in Sipi Falls, Eastern Uganda. The most significant experience for Kiconco was building connections with another Ugandan

68 ........... See Angela Jones, *A Critical Inquiry into Queer Utopias* (New York: Pallgrave Macmillan, 2013).
69 ........... Exploring the origins of queer festivals, Konstantinos Eleftheriadis notes, 'The organization committees play particular attention to the creation of safe spaces ... there is the normative assumption that the festivals should function as places where participants would be able to express themselves without fear, threat, or violence based on their gender, sexuality or other characteristics,' Konstantinos Eleftheriadis, 'The Origins of Queer Festivals in Europe,' in *Queer Festivals* (Amsterdam: Amsterdam University Press, 2018), p. 48.
70 ........... Kiconco, interview by author, Nairobi, June 2019.
71 ........... Ibid.

poet who helped her to reflect on what she wanted her work to do. Of the time, she recalls: 'This was a very different experience for me in terms of sharing my work. It made me think a lot about what I'm writing about, who I'm writing for, why I perform, and especially if I should keep performing.'[70] Kiconco realized that when she performed her poetry, she was performing a certain version of herself, a self that was safe for consumption. After the experience, she decided to stop performing and start writing for the audience she wants to affect, namely, queer Ugandan women. During the camp, she recognized her work was hiding herself and pleasing others. Kiconco's practice has since become less self-censored, more confident, more explicit. Still retaining an agile use of code and metaphor, Kiconco flips fluently between the spaces of abstraction and reality. In our interview, she explains, 'I've dug deeper into my experiences to try and keep that connection in my work. More than anything, I'm aware of what I want my writing to do out in the world.'[71]

## Drm sqncs://<root/s>s (Dream Sequences)

• • •

The process we see within Babishai's poetry camps and festivals (of temporary removal from the artists' everyday time and space) was replicated in the residency Kiconco undertook for this 'Forces of Art' project. During her residency, the artist crossed a multitude of different spaces to explore and expand her definitions and experiences of queerness. She travelled from Kampala to the outskirts of Nairobi and an artist-run, residency space in Nairobi national park. She spent three weeks at the residency writing alone and engaging in the company of artists who would come to visit the space

△ 4 & 5
Gloria Kiconco,
*Drm sqncs://<root/s>*, 2019, zine

on day-breaks from the city of Nairobi. Through the residency, Kiconco then travelled to the space of her dreams. *Drm sqncs://<root/s>* (Dream Sequences) is a diary of these dreams and their connection to the artist's day. The entries are written somewhere between sleep and wakefulness. The dreams are then transformed from the mind, to pen, to paper, into a zine.[△Fig. 3-5], an extract below from *Drm sqncs://<root/s>s (Dream Sequences)*, and the following text offer a picture of the work created for this 'Forces of Art' project.

*Drm sqncs://<root/s> (Dream Sequences)*

\\\\
21.05.19

We must wait and we must work. In this dream

there are children, a party train, and a party bus. I am
with my mother, at some point, and also s.k. Nothing bad
happens but a sadness lingers.

I remember how I used to love to sleep, *just to dream*.
Ah, but now I remember. Again, I dream of a.g. Why?
Was she on my mind yesterday? Again,

I am trying to get her attention. There is a child, her cousin,
whose age shifts, but who speaks like an adult. I am with him
in the hopes that she will notice me. (She is on stage—an MC
with a large afro glittering with shea butter and stage lights.
The audience is in the dark). We are in the wings. When she
does ask me something it is not the question I expect.
The power is off. All she wants is for me to pick a number.
My ego imagines she wants me to perform, *but this is not it at all*.

I wonder why she ended up being the one to return to
my dreams. Is my mind so allergic to rejection, it cannot
stop playing her on loop?

And before I sleep, again, it occurs to me that I have no purpose.
Yesterday, I masturbated four times. Desire without direction.
A person cannot be my purpose.

Yes, I am doing something... oh I am doing many things.
All the things. But inside, a vacuum. Zero gravity.

I've just woken up but already I can tell I have nothing
to look forward to.

\\\\
22.05.19

I wake up feeling heavy.

In this dream

I run away from the military, twice. And I am captured, twice. They were doing experiments on us.

At least I slept.

It's been a hard time. Stone in my stomach upon waking.

\\\\

I dream a lot of dreams
none of them dream me back
or slide into my conscious
or, through my hands, work.

I wake to a cascade of falling
planks, heavy reams of wood
like gravity got feathers wrong
or a forest woke on the wrong
side of the riverbed.

The heat is strangling me
again. Wrapping knife hands
around my favourite part
of my body. A burning hug.

I shower in brief kisses.
Touch the tiles but feel
no pulse, no pulse, no pulse.

## Dreams

• • • •

There is vulnerability in sharing dreams. The reader goes with the poet to intimate places of desire and despair. This work is the most uncensored of Kiconco's work to date and yet, also, the dreams are incoherent, unfinished, confusing. Can we interpret this as a purposeful failure to communicate, to keep some of the subconscious private? We are left out of the narratives, as we cannot place reference points for the artist's subconscious. We will never dream what the writer has dreamt. The writer both hints at attraction—'I am with him, in the hopes that she will notice me'—and speaks directly to intimate sexualities, self-gratification, and their discontents. Other people's names in the dream are only known through initials: Kiconco protects their safety through concealment. The dreams are disturbed. In one line: 'The military is doing experiments on us.' The writer uncovers the depths of harassment—both conscious and subconscious—that queer lives in Kampala must navigate.

Kiconco's dreams are then translated onto pages of paper, and the pages are then sculpted into a zine. The zine is both a sketchpad and a carefully crafted sculpture. Lines merge into illustrations throughout the zine, which in turn merge with text. The three components often blur together. Kiconco elucidates, 'Line contours form directly around the text as that is what dreams feel like. Dreams are almost something, but usually nothing.'[72] The artist's dreams almost point to clarity, perhaps answers to the artist's search for queer ways of being. But they fail and fall into insensibility or lost memories. Similarly, queerness within the zine falls in and out of readability, as the text dances between clarity and metaphor and the images wax and wane in and out of legibility.

## Zines

• • • • •

The visuals in the zine are drawings of queer people in Kiconco's life. They are sketched from photos and memories of the artist's friends in their queer safe spaces, at parties, at festivals, in homes and shelters. The artworks are unfinished. Flutters of paper reveal ongoing thoughts, visual stories, and further blank pages. The journey towards queerness is ongoing. The three-dimensional zine resembles an accordion; you can unfurl it to disclose its private messages but you can also fold it away and tie it up with the zine's red thread, the same thread that binds the artwork together. What holds the zine together also has the potential to keep unwanted eyes out. Just one zine, the zine shown in this text, was made from the dream writings. Zines, in general, are not mass-produced, but handcrafted, self-published, and then distributed from person to person. There is as much care in the zine's delivery as in its crafting. Kiconco notes how 'zines create an alternate route to distribution and help queer people navigate formal and possibly homophobic structures of publishing.'[73] The process of publishing *Drm sqncs://<root/s> (Dream Sequences)* is controlled by one person. From creation to circulation, there is command over how the queerness within the zine is seen. The dispersal of zines falls between the cracks of regulated, formalized, and profit-orientated distribution methods. This crack becomes a freeing space to share queer artworks. Kiconco can decide who the zine should reach and deliver it by hand—to the hands, eyes, and minds of a chosen reader to consume in their own queer space.

72..........Kiconco, interview by author, Nairobi, June 2019.

73..........Ibid.

74..........Muñoz, *Cruising Utopia*, p. 4.

## CONCLUDING WITH HOPE FORCES OF ART

Hope is 'a backward glance that enacts a future vision.'[74]

The legal, social, and religious structures in Kenya and Uganda set the stage for relentless homophobia. Nairobi and Kampala also share unconstitutional legal frameworks and growing social violence against queer people. Today's unyielding maltreatment of queer lives has created a critical need for physical, emotional, and spiritual space for queerness to survive and thrive within. The reality of violence has further produced the necessity for strategies of abstraction and identity-shielding to ensure that when queer spaces are created, they can continue to exist. And so, the two cities also share a complex relationship of queerness, care, and creativity. Tactics of abstraction, concealment, and masking are used skilfully by queer artists and by spaces that support queerness. Pseudonyms, metaphor, and code raise the intrigue of queer readers and viewers. Curating layers of queerness in an exhibition ensures the most intimate stories are kept the safest. These manoeuvres allow queerness into a space and keep those who might threaten the space from even knowing the spaces exist. These schemes push back against queer invisibility, ensuring that a visual, aural, and written archive of queerness exists. They allow for methods of precise control over levels of visibility and interpretation of how queerness is seen.

The research conducted for this chapter provided the opportunity to look back at two projects (*Femmolution* by Creatives Garage, and 'Making Poetry Matter' by the Babishai Poetry Foundation) to understand their impact on the creation of space for queerness in Nairobi and Kampala. It also offered the chance to work with artists associated with these organizations, to contribute to the urgent need to create space for queerness today. This helps ensure this research not only looks to the past to understand the importance of creating space for queerness, but also to the present.

Creatives Garage is in a partly residential area of Nairobi. The space is a house-cum-office. This setting, plus the remnants of familial furniture from the previous tenants dotted throughout the building, immediately sets the scene for creativity and care. The technical and emotional talents of the team (their use of language, of social media, of exhibition-making) ensure that all who they work with are seen as human. Programmes that reach beyond their space connect with communities that might not travel to Creatives Garage due to financial restraints, social anxieties, or, right now, Covid-19. Agile explorations of media (radio, websites, podcasts, books, and albums) mean that their work continues, and *Femmolution* is a core example of this. The book and music album is a bringing together of women with the utmost care to ensure voices and images are sent unswervingly to listeners ears and viewers eyes. From the invitation to participate, to the slimline editing process, to curated distribution methods, Creatives Garage created a mobile, transportable space of feminist queer hope. Within both *Femmolution* and this 'Forces of Art' project, we step into the ideas of Kenyan queer poet, Kins of Spade. The use of a pseudonym and tactics of concealment and abstraction demonstrate the artist's continued need for shelter; Creatives Garage helps carve a path to a place where a queer mum can speak truth to their daughter.

Babishai Niwe Poetry Foundation started as an annual award which, according to Gloria Kiconco, 'carved out a space that wasn't there.'[75] It was the first award to recognize female Ugandan poets. Babishai has now stretched to publishing Ugandan and African poetry, working with young people in schools, and undertaking residential poetry camps and an annual festival. Poetry for Babishai—its creation and consumption—is a tool to achieve freedom. Their 2012 programme 'Making Poetry Matter,' contributed to this pursuit of freedom by inviting artists to temporarily remove themselves from Kampala, immerse themselves into Uganda's natural landscapes, and engage with a community of diverse and differing creative minds. The programme was a success and expanded into the 'Babishai Poetry Festival' and it was through this process that Kiconco was able to reflect upon and deepen the connection between her queerness and her writing; the 'Babishai Festival' was a space to consider strategies for creative engagement as a queer poet. Kiconco's 'Forces of Art' residency further pushed this exploration. She travelled between geographical spaces (Kampala to Nairobi) to an intimately internal space (her dreams). The dreams were then transferred to words (in the form of a diary) and into the three-dimensional space of a zine. Distributed, informally, personally, with control, to the safe hands and eyes of queer Ugandans.

It is thanks to Creatives Garage and Babishai that within Nairobi and Kampala lie spaces of queer hope. By investing in such programmatic strategies as 'Making Poetry Matter,' creative community building thrives; through the tireless work of Creatives Garage, queerness is carefully visualized. When such endeavours come together, the queer horizon looks promising. In it, we can see how spaces for queerness ensure queer voices are seen, heard and—one day embraced—into society in Nairobi and Kampala.

75..........Gloria Kiconco, interview by author, Kampala, May 2020.

## ← REFERENCES


Ahmed, Sara. *The Promise of Happiness*. Durham: Duke University Press, 2010.

BBC News. 'Uganda Fury at David Cameron Aid Threat over Gay Rights.' *BBC*, 31 October 2011. www.bbc.co.uk/news/world-africa-15524013.

Bhalla, Nita. 'Uganda Plans Bill Imposing Death Penalty for Gay Sex.' Reuters, 10 October 2019. www.reuters.com/article/us-uganda-lgbt-rights/uganda-plans-bill-imposing-death-penalty-for-gay-sex-idUSKBN1WP1GN.

Biren, Joan E. 'Lesbian Photography: Seeing Through Our Own Eyes.' *The Blatant Image: A Magazine of Feminist Photography* 1 (1981), pp. 81–96.

Biryabarema, Elias. 'Uganda Says Want to Pass Anti-gay Laws as "Christmas Gift."' Reuters, 13 November 2012. www.reuters.com/article/us-uganda-homosexuality/uganda-says-wants-to-pass-anti-gay-law-as-christmas-gift-idUSBRE8AC0V720121113.

Boyd, Lydia. 'What's Driving Homophobia in Uganda?' *The Conversation*, 20 November 2019. https://theconversation.com/whats-driving-homophobia-in-uganda-126071.

Burke, Jason. 'Ugandan Police Accused of Abusing Lockdown Laws after LGBT Arrests.' *The Guardian*, 1 April 2020. www.theguardian.com/world/2020/apr/01/ugandan-police-accused-of-abusing-lockdown-laws-after-lgbt-arrests.

Contemporary And. *Kampala Focus*. 2nd ed. Berlin: Contemporary And. www.contemporaryand.com/cand_print/kampala-focus/.

Couzens, Tim. 'Pseudonyms in Black South African Writing, 1920–1950.' *Research in African Literatures* 6, no. 2 (1975), pp. 226–31. www.jstor.org/stable/3819061 (accessed 13 January 2020).

Creatives Garage, Mwihaki Mundia, and Liz Kilili. *Femmolution*, ed. Oluwademilade Adeniyi (1st ed.). Nairobi: Creatives Garage, 2016.

Creatives Garage. 'Invitation to Prosexive.' Digital. July 2019.

Eleftheriadis, Konstantinos. 'The Origins of Queer Festivals in Europe.' In *Queer Festivals*, pp. 39–52. Amsterdam: Amsterdam University Press, 2018. doi:10.2307/j.ctv5nph43.5 (accessed 11 January 2020).

Halberstam, Jack. *In a Queer Time and Place: Transgender Bodies, Subcultural Lives*. New York: New York University Press, 2005.

Holly-Nambi, Aida. *Against the Order of Ugandan Nature*. Presentation, 2015.

Holly-Nambi, Rocca. 'Queer Abstraction: Visual Strategies to See New Queer Futures.' *Art Journal* 157 (2020, under construction), p. 27.

Human Rights Watch. 'The Issue Is Violence: Attacks on LGBT People on Kenya's Coast.' *Human Rights Watch*, 28 September 2015. www.hrw.org/report/2015/09/28/issue-violence/attacks-lgbt-people-kenyas-coast#page.

Jones, Angela. *A Critical Inquiry into Queer Utopias*. New York: Pallgrave Macmillan, 2013.

Kelly, Owen. *Community, Art, and the State: Storming the Citadels* (1st ed.). London: Comedia Publishing Group, 1984.

Kilili, Liz. 'Behind the Audacious Curations.' *Creatives Garage*, 5 July 2019. www.creativesgarage.org/2019/07/05/behind-the-audacious-curations/.

Lawton, Pamela Harris. 'Hand-in-Hand, Building Community on Common Ground.' *Art Education* 63, no. 6 (2010), pp. 6–12. www.jstor.org/stable/20799848 (accessed 12 January 2020).

Le Roux, Elizabeth. 'Black Writers, White Publishers.' *E-Rea* 11 (2013). http://journals.openedition.org/erea/3515 (accessed 13 January 2020).

Mbote, David Kuria, Theo Sandfort, Esther Waweru and Andrew Zapfel. 'Kenyan Religious Leaders' Views on Same-Sex Sexuality and Gender Nonconformity: Religious Freedom versus Constitutional Rights.' *Journal of Sex Research* 55, no. 4–5 (2018), pp. 630–41. doi:10.1080/00224499.2016.1255702.

Muholi, Zanele. 'Faces and Phases.' *Transition Magazine* 107 (2012), pp. 113–24. http://www.jstor.org/stable/10.2979/transition.107.113.

Muñoz, José Esteban. *Cruising Utopia: The Then and There of Queer Futurity*. New York: NYU Press, 2009. www.jstor.org/stable/j.ctt9qg4nr (accessed 13 January 2020).

National Gay and Lesbian Human Rights Commission, Gay and Lesbian Coalition of Kenya, and Nyanza, Rift Valley & Western Kenya Network. 'Repeal 162.' *Love Is Human*. 2019. www.repeal162.org/about162.

None on Record. Criminalization and Colonization. *AfroQueer*. Season 2. Podcast audio. 22 May 2019. https://afroqueerpodcast.com/2019/05/22/bonus-episode-criminalization-an-colonization/.

Nsengiyunva, Beverley Nambozo. *A Thousand Voices Rising: An Anthology of Contemporary African Poetry*. Kampala: Gilgil Media Arts, 2014.

. 'Babishai Niwe Poetry Foundation.' *Babishai Niwe Poetry Foundation*. 2008. http://babishainiwe.com/.

Pilcher, Alex. *A Queer Little History of Art*. 1st ed. London: Tate Publishing, 2017.

Rycroft, Simon. 'The Artist Placement Group: An Archaeology of Impact.' *Cultural Geographies* 26, no. 3 (2019), pp. 289–304. doi:10.1177/1474474018821860.

Senyonjo, Christopher. 'Bishop Christopher Senyonjo on LGBT rights in Uganda.' Interview by Amnesty International. 25 June 2013. www.youtube.com/watch?v=Z-AQmcAU5mk.

Tamale, Sylvia. 'Eroticism, Sensuality and "Women's Secrets" Among the Baganda.' *IDS Bulletin* 37(2009), pp. 89–97. doi10.1111/j.1759-5436.2006.tb00308.x.

Thirikwa, Jane W. 'Emergent Momentum for Equality: LGBT Visibility and Organising in Kenya.' In *Envisioning Global LGBT Human Rights: (Neo)colonialism, Neoliberalism, Resistance and Hope*, eds. Nancy Nicol et al. London: University of London Press, 2018. www.jstor.org/stable/j.ctv5132j6.1.

Tisinai, Rob. 'Africa's Gays Increasingly Under Siege.' *The Atlantic*, 22 February 2010, www.theatlantic.com/daily-dish/archive/2010/02/africas-gays-increasingly-under-siege/190118/.


## ← INTERVIEWS

Kins of Spade (poet), interview by author, Nairobi, May 2019.

Angelo Kakande (Ugandan artist and professor), interview by author, Kampala, June, 2016.

Gloria Kiconco (poet), interview by author, Nairobi, June 2019.

Liz Kilili (founder of Creatives Garage), interview by author, Nairobi, June 2019.

Beverley Nambozo Nsengiyunva (founder of Babishai Poetry Foundation), interview by author, Kampala, August 2019.

Adam Kiboi (Creatives Garage team member), interview by author, Nairobi, February 2020.

Gloria Kiconco (poet), interview by author, Kampala, May 2020.

Volunteer Palestine / Aida Refugee Camp Bethlehem, Palestine / 1:37pm 31°42'20.1"N / 35°12'09.0"E

Masrah Ensemble / Beirut, Lebanon / 1:37pm 33°54'08.5"N 35°31'25.4"E

# DOUAL'ART: ART, PUBLICS, AND THE CITY AS A 'FIELD OF EXPERIENCE'

Zayd Minty, Laura Nkula-Wenz, Naomi Roux, Vaughn Sadie, Anna Selmeczi and Rike Sitas

This chapter focuses on the power of art in the city of Douala, Cameroon, by drawing on research conducted with doual'art, a cultural non profit organization active since 1991. doual'art has harnessed the power to transform public space across different neighbourhoods by fusing artistic and infrastructural interventions and integrating the places that these interventions create into Douala's everyday urban fabric. Seeing the city through the eyes of doual'art—as a field of experience—this chapter reflects on the organization's interdisciplinary, site-specific, and context-sensitive mode of working. Beyond consistently involving residents in their integrative practice of place-making through art and development, doual'art operates as a key interface between global and local artistic and cultural scenes and is a strong advocate vis-a-vis local authority for recognizing the power of arts-based urbanism. As we show, one of the most powerful effects of supporting the creation of public art in Douala is doual'art's capacity to productively evoke dissent and discord, thus fostering a sense of agency, symbolic ownership and possibility that opens a space for other kinds of democratic engagements and demands beyond conventional frameworks of development.

Keywords
- → Public Space
- → Public Art
- → Southern Urbanism
- → doual'art
- → Cultural Urban Governance
- → Urban Affect

## INTRODUCTION

> '...the city remains a place of dreams, present and past, of bits and pieces of ways of doing things...'[1]

Cities are increasingly being seen not simply as vessels for economic action, but as spaces constantly in flux, caught in processes of becoming. They are 'best thought of not so much as enduring sites but as moments of encounter, not so much as 'presents,' fixed in space and time, but as variable events; twists and fluxes of interrelation.'[2] Experiences and encounters in cities are wildly diverse, and 'African cities simultaneously face countless crises, emergencies and risks, as well as being the hotbeds for creativity and innovation; they are places both of joy and abject desolation and every other state in between.'[3] Within these complex urban contexts, public artists, architects, urban designers, and cultural activists have explored a wide range of art practices—from monuments to murals, community arts programmes to commercial sculptures.

The role of art, and particularly the nexus between public art and cities, has received widespread attention from scholars and practitioners, exploring the relation of public art to site;[4] its impact on city-making;[5] its relationship to development;[6] and the role of participation and power dynamics in its production.[7] Nevertheless, while culture remains globally hailed as the fourth pillar of sustainable development, the manifold ways in which creative and cultural practices simultaneously shape and are profoundly shaped by urban societies remains poorly understood. This is particularly true for African cities, where cultural issues are routinely relegated to the margins of both government and donor priorities.[8] Further, when cultural and artistic practices do receive financial support, they are often pressured into aligning with narrow market or state agendas. We share the view that it is important for us as urban scholars to critically engage with these cultural trends, in order to contribute to a more holistic understanding of the role of arts and culture in the making of contemporary African societies.

This chapter reflects on the relationship between art, publics, and cities in the Global South. As Mabin suggests, 'The city is always suspended as a case of 'here' and 'elsewheres,' connected yet—yet ... and that is why the artists may be doing a better job than southern theorists in 'painting,' 'composing,' 'dancing,' and 'writing' cities into being.'[9] Following doual'art's lead in approaching the 'city as a field of experience' allowed us to better understand how art- and architecture-based practices can enliven the city, and engage with it.[10] Key to this conception of the city as a field of experience is doual'art's insistence on integrating artworks and the spaces that they create into the tangible everyday fabric of the city: the fabric that makes

1 ............ AbdouMaliq Simone, *City Life from Jakarta to Dakar: Movements at the Crossroads* (London: Routledge, 2010), p. 9.
2 ............ Ash Amin and Nigel Thrift, *Cities: Reimagining the Urban* (Cambridge: Wiley, 2002), p. 30.
3 ............ Rike Sitas, 'Cultural Policy and the Power of Place, South Africa,' in *The Routledge Handbook of Global Cultural Policy* (New York and London: Routledge, 2017), pp. 597–614.
4 ............ Nick Kaye, *Site-Specific Art: Performance, Place and Documentation* (London: Psychology Press, 2000); Miwon Kwon, *One Place After Another: Site-Specific Art and Locational Identity* (Cambridge, MA: The MIT Press, 2004); Erika Suderburg, *Space, Site, Intervention: Situating Installation Art* (Minneapolis: University of Minnesota Press, 2000).
5 ............ Jenny Mbaye and Cecilia Dinardi, 'Ins and Outs of the Cultural Polis: Informality, Culture and Governance in the Global South,' *Urban Studies* 56, no. 3 (1 February 2019), pp. 578–93; Malcolm Miles, *Art, Space and the City* (London: Routledge, 1997); David Pinder, 'Arts of Urban Exploration,' *Cultural Geographies* 12, no. 4 (1 October 2005), pp. 383–411; David Pinder, 'Urban Interventions: Art, Politics and Pedagogy,' *International Journal of Urban and Regional Research* 32, no. 3 (2008), pp. 730–36.
6 ............ Nancy Duxbury, Catherine Cullen, and Jordi Pascual, 'Cities, Culture and Sustainable Development,' in *Cultural Policy and Governance in a New Metropolitan Age*, Cultures and Globalization (London: SAGE, 2012), pp. 73–86; Graeme Evans, 'Creative Cities, Creative Spaces and Urban Policy,' *Urban Studies* 46, no. 5–6 (1 May 2009), pp. 1003–40; Frank Moulaert, Hilde Demuynck, and Jacques Nussbaumer, 'Urban Renaissance: From Physical Beautification to Social Empowerment,' *City* 8, no. 2 (1 July 2004), pp. 229–35; Laura Nkula-Wenz, 'Worlding Cape Town by Design: Encounters with Creative Cityness,' *Environment and Planning A: Economy and Space* (29 August 2018).
7 ............ Claire Bishop, *Artificial Hells: Participatory Art and the Politics of Spectatorship* (London and New York: Verso Books, 2012); Nicolas Bourriaud, *Relational Aesthetics* (Dijon: Les Presses du réel, 2002); Grant H. Kester, *Conversation Pieces: Community and Communication in Modern Art* (Berkeley: University of California Press, 2004); Rike Sitas and Edgar Pieterse, 'Democratic Renovations and Affective Political Imaginaries,' *Third Text* 27, no. 3 (1 May 2013), pp. 327–42.
8 ............ Polly Stupples and Katerina Teaiwa, *Contemporary Perspectives on Art and International Development* (London: Taylor & Francis, 2016).
9 ............ Alan Mabin, 'Grounding Southern City Theory in Time and Place,' in *The Routledge Handbook on Cities of the Global South*, ed. Susan Parnell and Sophie Oldfield (New York and London: Routledge, 2014), p. 18.
10 .......... Nadège Ngouegni Ngnoulaye (doual'art's socio-cultural mediator) interview by authors (Minty, Roux, Sadie), Douala, 27 June, 2019.

and is made by Doualans' daily experiences of living in the city. After all, the power of art lies in its ability to shape discursive publics—to reflect complex social processes, including things that would otherwise go unspoken, rendering them visible and opening up other possible ways of being.

Douala is Cameroon's cosmopolitan economic heart, its biggest and most diverse city of 1.9 million inhabitants. It is also a highly challenged city with a difficult heritage, deep ethnic divisions, and a legacy of urban dysfunction. Because of the area's strategic position at an estuary, allowing access inland via the Woori River, it was established as the colonial headquarters under German rule (from 1885) and later, under French rule. In-migration for economic opportunities makes it vibrant, but Douala faces major urban obstacles. These include: high levels of poverty, inequality and unemployment; substance dependency, anti-social behaviour, and crime; underdevelopment of infrastructure (including those for potable water, sewerage, roads and bridges, street lighting, and refuse management); and environmental degradation. Though there are some prestigious neighbourhoods supplied with basic services, many neighbourhoods lack such access, resulting in living conditions that impose an everyday struggle of self-sustenance and stigma on the majority of residents. A considerable part of the city consists of structures that are either erected illegally or are informal in nature. The city often floods because of its geography, with low-lying informal areas bearing the brunt thereof.

Pensa describes Douala as an inhospitable and often unattractive city, which, in addition to high levels of traffic, is difficult to navigate since many areas lack street names or easily identifiable landmarks.[11] The physical lack of legibility is reflected in the fragmentation of its community, holding a plethora of languages, ethnicities, and religions, at times at odds with each other. Complicated by a centralized autocratic national state, it also lacks structures of integrated urban governance necessary for improving its conditions. At the neighbourhood level, the city is governed by chiefs, both traditional and elected, and at the municipal level by a mayor appointed from the capital Yaounde. However, no legislative connection exists between the two. The implications of these challenges for the possible spaces and forms of democratic practice hold considerable weight.[12]

In this context, doual'art, a cultural non profit organization set up in 1991, is a pioneer of working at the intersection of art, development, and urbanism on the continent.[13] The unique non profit was co-founded by Marilyn Douala-Bell, a development economist, and her French partner and curator, the late Didier Schaub. Over the past decades, doual'art has creatively engaged with the urban possibilities and challenges posed by

11 ........... Iolanda Pensa, 'System Error: Art as a Space to Produce What We Would Never Have Thought We Needed,' in *Contemporary Perspectives on Art and International Development* (London: Taylor & Francis, 2016), pp. 124–37. In fact, Pensa's evaluation of the city's aesthetics is unequivocally harsh: she describes it as 'inhospitable... violent and ugly.' We include her characterization here not as a value judgment on the city's aesthetics, but to contextualize some of the complexities of making art and implementing spatial change in Douala. In this context, the work of doul'art is crucial for its ability to use arts-based methods to move beyond the fixed categories and binaries of both the language of development, and the language of aesthetics.

12 ........... Marilyn Douala-Bell (Présidente de doual'art) interview by authors (Minty, Roux and Sadie), Douala, 25 June, 2019; Yves Makongo (project manager and artistic assistant, doual'art), interview by authors (Minty, Roux and Sadie) Douala, 27 June, 2019.

13 ........... Anette Schemmel, *Visual Arts in Cameroon: A Genealogy of Non-Formal Training 1976–2014* (Bamenda and Buea: Langaa RPCIG, 2016).

Douala, a city often referred to as a 'pirate city,' and characterized by high levels of informality and a general lack of quality and equitable public space.[14] The organization's conscious linking of art, development, the built environment and people's lived experiences is particularly important at a time when the continent is urbanizing and city dwellers face complex societal, economic, and environmental challenges in the pursuit of a better future.[15]

Through the 'Salon Urbaine de Douala' (SUD), a quadrennial event, as well as an ongoing 'process of enquiry,' twelve neighbourhoods across the city have been involved in participatory artistic projects working with identity and context to further the local democratic imaginary. Underpinning doual'art's work is the idea that projects produce both contextually respondent artworks as well as knowledge about the city.[16] Since it began its cultural experimentation in public space, SUD has managed to implement over sixty arts-led projects in Douala, asserting its role as an urban laboratory and positioning the city as a 'field of experience.'[17] In this pursuit, the organization expresses a clear vision to foster dialogue, to shape public space and to enable greater expression in the streets, as a way to build a better city from the bottom up and to foster a greater sense of local belonging and identities.[18]

Considering the challenges of sustaining cultural organizations on the continent, doual'art is a long surviving and active cultural implementor, and has catalyzed unique responses to burgeoning development. The non profit has worked to build democratic agency through public interventions by supporting the creation of monumental and non-monumental, permanent and temporary artworks, such as sculptures, performances, murals, and artful forms of urban infrastructures. Working with artists as provocateurs, it has attempted to activate a sense of collective agency in Douala's neighbourhoods, sparking inspiration through participatory processes. Manoeuvring the on going funding precarity plaguing such institutions in Africa,[19] it has remained experimental, innovative, productive, and engaged with its community throughout. Most importantly, its rooted and context-sensitive practice in Douala has made the city—both institutionally and as a place—an important partner in the project.

In light of this, our research posed the question: In what ways has doual'art's arts-based, place-informed approach impacted the city, furthering the democratization process in Douala? How do these artful urban interventions, driven by participation, impact societal change in Douala? In what ways can we evaluate the work of the organization—its aims to further dialogue and foster exchange and creative expression?

14 .......... AbdouMaliq Simone, 'Pirate Towns: Reworking Social and Symbolic Infrastructures in Johannesburg and Douala,' *Urban Studies* 43, no. 2 (February 2006): pp. 357–70, doi.org/10.1080/00420980500146974.

15 .......... AbdouMaliq Simone and Edgar Pieterse, *New Urban Worlds: Inhabiting Dissonant Times* (Hoboken, New Jersey: John Wiley & Sons, 2018).

16 .......... Rike Sitas, 'Becoming Otherwise: Artful Urban Enquiry,' *Urban Forum*, 26 February, 2020, doi.org/10.1007/s12132-020-09387-4.

17 .......... Nadège Ngouegni Ngnoulaye (doual'art's socio-cultural mediator) interview by authors (Minty, Roux, Sadie), Douala, 27 June, 2019.

18 .......... Marilyn Douala-Bell (Présidente de doual'art) interview by authors (Minty, Roux and Sadie), Douala, 25 June 2019.

19 .......... Claudia Fontes, 'The What and the How: Rethinking Evaluation Practice for the Arts and Development,' in *Contemporary Perspectives on Art and International Development* (London: Taylor & Francis, 2016), pp. 238–52.

We begin this chapter by describing the methodology used to explore the impacts and effects of doual'art's work. We also introduce the three neighbourhoods our analysis focuses on. Our main argument is clustered into three themes. First, we focus on doual'art as an organization, exploring its role in cultural governance and cultural action, intermediation, patronage, and networks. Here we hone in on the question of how the organization has managed to sustain itself since 1991 and remain functional throughout. Although doual'art is not solely an arts organization, and does not claim to be, it has realized a wide array of artistic interventions and cultural encounters in the city. As the second analytical section discusses, these processes involve a range of tactics and methods; they leave intended and unintended traces; they transform spaces and have interesting urban afterlives. Third, we turn to a discussion of how the organization's artful processes shape urban design. The effects and affects are not only evident in the physical or tangible manifestations of doual'art's work: through their working processes, different forms of public spaces and publics are created, and different entanglements of the tangible and intangible are produced. Here we also consider how processes, objects, and artworks are appropriated, assimilated, and adapted. We conclude by arguing that doul'art's impact and its sustainability lies in its ability to navigate the complex intersections between art, 'development,' and place-making, and in its abilities to leverage the power of art to generate knowledge, insight, and new urban imaginaries.

## METHODOLOGY

Given the richness of doual'art's work over the past nineteen years, and the complexities of the sites in which the organization is active, we adopted a broadly qualitative research framework. We conducted fieldwork over five days in July 2019, focusing on three neighbourhoods where doual'art has worked. The sites were selected in conversation with doual'art's leadership, based on our interest in understanding the place-specific and time-sensitive dynamics and challenges of the organization's diverse artistic interventions over time. The three neighbourhoods we focused on were Bessengue, Bonamouti-Deido, and N'dogpassi[△Fig. 1], encompassing a range of projects both past and present. Eleven artworks still exist across the three areas, some more well preserved than others.

We observed the sites, spoke to community participants, artists who had worked at the sites, or in other contexts with doual'art, local government officials, and doual'art staff.[20] Our analysis considers the impacts of such place-based artwork in terms of both the tactics and traces that accompany it, and its afterlife in the respective neighbourhoods. We found the typology used in previous work on doual'art, including reviews by Marta Pucciarelli and Iolanda Pensa, useful in establishing and defining our analytical focus.[21]

20..........There were eight individual meetings and four group meetings, reaching twenty-two individuals in total.

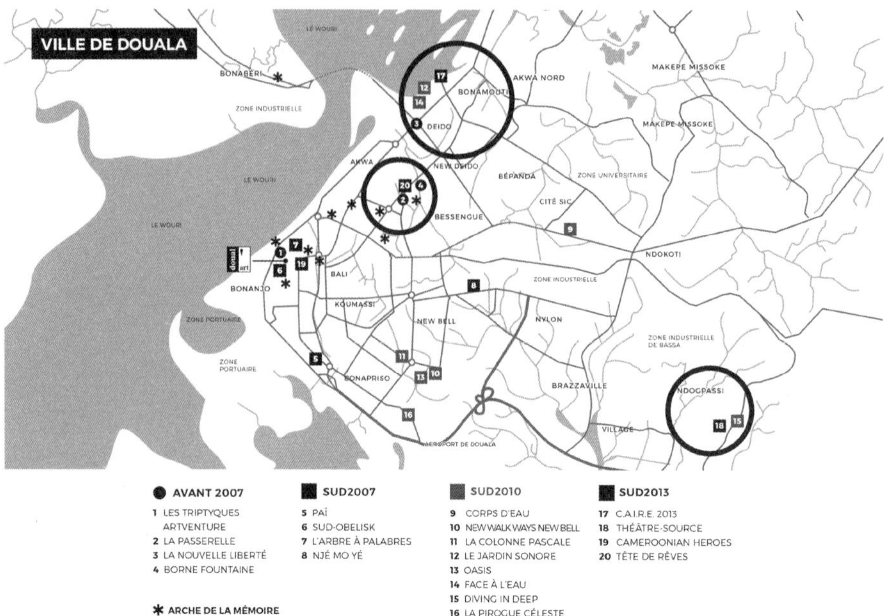


△ 1
Map of Douala produced by doual'art for its SUD 2013 showing the location of major works produced over the years, the three subject areas of this study, and Espace Contemporain.

Particularly helpful are the three categories that Marta Pucciarelli and others mobilize to classify artworks and other interventions in Douala. These include: (1) Proximity artworks: defined as architectural or infrastructural installations with very specific functions located within the everyday lived spaces of marginalized neighbourhoods, (2) Monumental artworks: large scale installations and sculptures predominantly positioned at crossroads and roundabouts, and (3) Passageway installations: murals, small scale sculptures, and ephemeral works located or taking place along the roads of marginalized neighbourhoods.[22] These categories aptly illustrate the diverse scale of doual'art's interventions. They also demonstrate the ways in which approaching the city as a field of experience is critical for these interventions, allowing them to blend artistic and infrastructural projects both in their conceptions and outcomes.

## BESSENGUE

Bessengue is a popular, largely informal settlement, situated between the commercially important Akwa and Deido districts. The neighbourhood, wedged into a valley between two watercourses, is regularly flooded during the rainy season. For a long time, the area had limited access to basic

21 .......... Marta Pucciarelli, 'Douala (Final Report)' (Lugano: SUPSI, 2014); Iolanda Pensa et al., *Public Art in Africa: Art and Urban Transformations in Douala*, ed. Iolanda Pensa et al. (Geneva: Métis Presses, 2017).

22 .......... Pucciarelli, 'Douala (Final Report),' p. 3.

infrastructure and services.[23] In the mid two thousands, the community's needs and aspirations were organized under a development committee. This led to several infrastructure initiatives, including those involving artists discussed below, which transformed the area. Though unplanned as an outcome, the placing of these interventions close to each other resulted in the emergence of a bustling public space, where people meet, drink beers, flirt, relax, and play.[24] Since quality public space is hard to come by in many parts of Douala, its creation—in large part the result of these 'proximity artworks'—has been important for building a more democratic public in the area and allowing residents to engage the city as a complex field of 'experiences.'

Since 2000, doual'art facilitated nine art interventions in Bessengue. One of their earliest projects here, credited with influencing doual'art's later practice,[25] was that of an international collective of three artists led by the late Goddy Leye. The collaboration, called 'Bessengue City,' involved the creation of a temporary shelter, housing a youth-run community radio station. Later, in 2005, doual'art produced two important 'proximity artworks' linked to infrastructure initiatives, which were specifically relevant to those living in the area and integrally involved the community in their making. A bridge, 'La Passerelle,' provides safe passage over the river and connects the area to a busy main road. The work was a partnership between municipal engineers and artist Alioum Moussa, who designed the handrails. 'Borne Fontaine,' designed by architect Diwouto-Kotto, is a water pump providing access to potable water, doubling as a shop and a meeting place. Collectively these three projects identified the importance for doual'art's work in public space making.[26] While doual'art has worked in Bessengue for several years, as of 2019 there are currently no new projects planned for the area.

## BONAMOUTI-DEIDO

doual'arts' involvement in Bonamouti-Deido spanned two iterations of SUD (2010, 2013). Although some of the artworks from these two festivals remain in place, the organization has made the choice not to continue working here, due to local political and interpersonal complexities and some resistance of the area's chief to doula'art's continued involvement.

Bonamouti was originally a traditional fishing village of the Sawa people. Although it retains a strong sense of local identity, it was absorbed, like many such villages, into the city of Douala. A small informal settlement of relative newcomers has formed in the area, further shifting its demographics. doual'art's difficulties of working in Bonamouti-Deido are largely due to the tensions and fragmentations exacerbated in part by this shift from a culturally homogenous village to an extension of the ever-expanding city. As in many other parts of the city, usable public space has been

23 ........... Pensa, 'System Error.'

24 ........... Pucciarelli, 'Douala (Final Report)'; Pensa et al., *Public Art in Africa: Art and Urban Transformations in Douala.*

25 ........... Marilyn Douala-Bell (Présidente de doual'art) interview by authors (Minty, Roux and Sadie), Douala, 25 June 2019.

26 ........... Pensa, 'System Error.'

a casualty of unplanned transformation. Nonetheless, the village's access to the Wouri River beach makes it an unusual space for the cultural life of the city, and alongside its fishing activities, it has become popular with tourists. The area hosts the annual November 'Ngondo' festival; this week-long event is heavily supported by the municipality and includes boating competitions, local gastronomy, and music. The festival has its roots in a traditional ritual feast of the original residents, who venerate the river's spiritual force. A large number of syncretic religious practices take place during the week.

Given the clear importance of the river and of water to the neighbourhood, its identities, and its deep histories, it perhaps makes sense that all three of doual'art's remaining works here are linked to water. The most visible remaining artwork in Bonamouti is *Le Jardin sonore* (Sound Garden) by Lucas Grandin from the 2010 SUD. It is a three-level wooden structure with distinctive yellow awnings on various levels that protect users from sun and rain. While the artwork is a version of Grandin's earlier work in Angers, France, what makes this iteration special is that it is situated in an area that was once a rubbish dump. By reclaiming the site for an art initiative, public space was created. The structure's sociable design in context makes it ideal for small gatherings, card games, and for young lovers seeking romantic viewpoints of the river,[27] while the concrete platform around it is used as an informal soccer pitch. Initially, the piece included a hydroponic botanical garden, with water-gathering barrels and a percussive water dripping system made up of different sized tin cans that emitted a musical score as the garden watered itself. Since its construction, the structure has been renovated twice (commissioned by doul'art), and the sonic water installation has been removed in the course of these reconstructions. Although it was a beautiful and sustainable element of the original work, it proved impossible to maintain in the corrosive and harsh tropical climate conditions.

*Face à l'eau* (2010) by Salifou Lindou was a work of artful dividers, beautiful objects that served to shield fishermen as they changed clothing, and provide a place to hold items for washing. It paid homage to the area's traditional work roles, and reflected on Cameroonians living much of their lives next to water. *Floating Quay* (2013), by the Colombian artist Juan Fernando Herrán, represents another attempt to create a space for the traditional fishermen to dock their canoes, regardless of tide. Its shape reflected that of the traditional canoes used by fisherfolk. These two works no longer exist, the result of adverse community reactions (as we shall see later), and a reflection of some of the challenges doual'art faces in presenting its ground-breaking work.

Deido is home to what is arguably doual'art's most famous commission, *La Nouvelle Liberté* (1996): a monumental public artwork by artist Joseph-Francis Sumégné of Yaoundé. This was the first time a permanent public artwork was ever installed in Cameroon. *La Nouvelle Liberté*,

27 ........... Pucciarelli, 'Douala (Final Report).'

2

4

5

3

△ 2
Alioum Moussa, *La Passerelle de Bessengué*, 2005, documentation, photo: Vaugh Sadie, 2019

△ 3
Danièle Diwouta-Kotto, *Borne Fontaine*, 2003, documentation, photo: Zayd Minty, 2019

△ 4
Lucas Grandin, *'Le Jardin Sonore' de Bonamouti*, 2010, documentation, photo: Vaugh Sadie, 2019

△ 5
Joseph-Francis Sumégné, *La Nouvelle Liberté*, 1996, documentation, photo: Vaughn Sadie, 2019

△ 6
Philip Aguirre y Otegui with Mauro Lugaresi, *Le théâtre Source*, 2010, documentation, photo: Vaughn Sadie, 2019

6

a figure holding the globe in one hand, is made of scrap metal and car parts, and is placed in the centre of a prominent intersection at the district's edge. The statue's initial appearance was controversial: judged negatively because it was made by someone from a tribe outside of Douala, its intervention fed into on going inter-ethnic rivalries. Today, the statue has achieved iconic status and has become a symbol of Douala. The once unpaved roundabout is tarred.

## N'DOGPASSI

N'dogpassi is a relatively young, diverse and largely informal neighbourhood where doual'art has had three SUD iterations (2010 to 2017). This continuity is in no small part due to the area's committed chief, who has been critical in working with doual'art and championing the area's vision of itself. In comparison with the difficulties of working in Bonamouti, it is clear that having supportive local and traditional governance systems is a critical factor in doual'art's ability to sustain relationships and impact. Organized in several 'blocs,' the just over 2,000 households all report to Chief Ndoutou Jean-Marie, the neighbourhood's elected representative. It is the chief who approached doual'art, after recognizing what the organization could bring to his community by building outwards from 'the Source' (the natural spring).

Less than a decade and a half old, situated in a relatively isolated area to the Southeast of the city, and marked by high levels of poverty and informality (both in form and modes of operating), N'dogpassi has not seen many opportunities for development. Set in a fluvial depression, the neighbourhood regularly floods during the rainy season, leaving inhabitants to navigate muddy roads. Its key asset is its natural spring with good quality water, a valuable resource in a city where accessing fresh water remains a challenge.

While doual'art has had several successful projects in the area, the *Théâtre Source* (2013) is arguably its centrepiece. Designed by Philip Aguirre, with support from architect Mauro Lugaresi, the work pays homage to the community's main asset—its natural spring, which has been incorporated into a concrete amphitheatre that also serves as a water filtration system. As a result, this piece of infrastructure has become a managed source of clean water in one of the main parts of the neighbourhood, and thus a central gathering place. Capable of hosting 1,000 people over its six levels, the amphitheatre connects two 'blocs' and supports the natural use of the area as a meeting point for women and children, young and old. It is a key attractor and, with the added charisma of an art project, it has become the symbol of the area.

Other projects, both preceding and following *Théâtre Source*, have worked to support the key strategies developed by the community. *Diving in Deep* (2010) was a series of performances during a six-week residency in Ndogpassi. *Pont Source* by Ties Ten Bosch is a wooden bridge crossing a small river that is subject to flooding. The building of the bridge engaged the community in many smaller interventions around it, to help identify the final piece and its site. *Caravane d'images* (2013) is a set of murals about everyday life in the area, placed along the path leading to the *Théâtre Source*. Developed out of a collaborative painting project for women and children by French artist Leah Touitou and local artist Edwige Ndjeng, it offers artistic representations of the area's people.

## DOUAL'ART, CULTURAL GOVERNANCE AND PROCESSES OF NETWORK BUILDING

In order to understand how doual'art as an organization managed to leverage the power of the city as a field of experience, one has to explore its role in local cultural governance, meaning local cultural action, intermediation, patronage, and network building. doual'art has established itself in the last three decades as one of the most important artistic and cultural nodal points in Cameroon, Africa, and the Global South. Since its humble beginnings, it has not only managed to thrive as an organization but has also established and sustained a multitude of local and international networks.

The role of doual'art as a trailblazer for place-sensitive artistic programming on the continent, boosting the visibility and status of both local and international artists in global networks of cultural value production, has been well documented.[28] Foreign art professionals and researchers regularly move through Douala to touch base with the local scene and numerous Cameroonian curators, art historians, and academics have managed to leverage their work with doual'art as a launching pad for transnational careers. The organization depends largely on international donor agencies for the continuation of their programming, as the support from local authorities remains limited. Although this transnational approach has resulted in financial and epistemic hierarchies with some 'neo-colonial implications,'[29] the organization has been adept at working with these contradictions.[30]

In fact, as doual'art co-founder Marilyn Douala-Bell divulged, pragmatically utilizing general development funding opportunities to further the specific socio-cultural and artistic goals of the organization has been part of its DNA. After all, when it was first founded, the first opportunity for doual'art to work directly with people in different areas of the city came on the back of an EU-funded decentralization project. The organization had no artistic or cultural dimension, but rather focused on strengthening local democratic practices. However, by involving two local artists in the project evaluation for the different localities, the organization managed to 'open the neighbourhoods' and built momentum around

28 Pensa, 'System Error'; Schemmel, *Visual Arts in Cameroon*.
29 Schemmel, *Visual Arts in Cameroon*, p. 204.
30 Pensa, 'System Error'; Schemmel, *Visual Arts in Cameroon*.

the possibilities of art as a socio-spatial and cultural mediator. For Douala-Bell, reflecting on how the nexus of art and development evolved in the institution over time, the dial has now firmly shifted towards art: 'It was development and art, now it's art and development. So, art has the dominance and the question of mediation is very important.'

While the role of art as an important mediator of space and place might seem self-evident to many of doual'art's international partners, building locally supportive networks around this idea—particularly amongst traditional authorities and local government circles—has been a lot more time-consuming and less straight-forward for the organization. Though some of these relationships started out rather tenuous and remain subject to ongoing dialogue, doual'art's local governance networks have nonetheless played an important part in the organization's longevity.

doual'art's relationship with the local city government has been a challenging one but has improved significantly over the years as the organization has grown in stature and influence locally and internationally. In Douala, like in many other African cities, competing developmental needs centred around infrastructure and service delivery regularly push support for arts and culture to the bottom of the political agenda. Consequently, local government's direct financial support to doual'art remains limited, though they still try to assist with in-kind support such as printing, offering city venues, and providing tax breaks.

Over the years, three strategies helped doual'art to firmly establish itself on the local political radar. Firstly, it developed a role as a global platform and transnational meeting point, augmented through the support from the international diplomatic corps based in the city; secondly, its practice effectively blurred the lines between art, infrastructure, and development; and thirdly, the organization demonstrated consistency as, to quote Else Kingue Etame, a city official, 'an actor that gets things done in society.'[31] Though the local government had been involved in the SUDs from the beginning, for many years its role did not extend beyond performing its routine administrative function as the formal custodian of public space. In 2017 however, the city council and doual'art signed their first partnership agreement, appointing doual'art as the official community mediator in one of the city's key urban sustainability projects. While doual'art sees this new partnership as a positive development, they are keenly aware of the tensions and possible political pitfalls. As Douala-Bell notes: 'They [the municipality] want us to be just tools. We want to really empower people in their own area and it's a lot of discussions ... We don't want to be compromised. Art is something which has to be respected as art.'[32]

Promisingly, it appears that doual'art's work has shifted some of the technocratic mindsets within local government towards considering art an important tool for both understanding and shaping people's

31..........Else Kingue Etame (Head of the Department of Decentralised Cooperation and Translation, Douala City Council), Douala, 25 June 2019.

32..........Marilyn Douala-Bell (Présidente de doual'art) interview by authors (Minty, Roux and Sadie), Douala, 25 June 2019

lived urban experiences. We note this without wanting to discount the persistent risk of art being tokenized in urban development processes. As Etame, head of the city's Department of Decentralised Cooperation and Translation remarks: 'When you walk in the city, you see we have many challenges in terms of infrastructure, but we cannot only focus on infrastructure. We also need to target the daily life of the citizens.'[33]

While different editions of the SUD carried the work of doual'art into numerous city neighbourhoods, the role of doual'art's permanent gallery and event space 'Espace Contemporain' has been equally important in building local traction and maintaining visibility for art and artists. First established in 1995 in Bonanjo, the former white colonial nerve centre of the city, it occupies the renovated premises of an old cinema owned by the Bell family. The first exhibitions were mostly frequented by expatriates and artists' families, but nowadays the space receives mostly Cameroonian visitors, especially on opening nights.[34]

For doual'art, engaging local patronage networks, particularly the area-based chieftaincies, has been yet another way to ensure that communities participate in the creation and maintenance of site-specific public artworks. Hence, whenever it embarks on a new round of projects, the organization enters a dialogue with the local chief of the selected neighbourhood. Gaining access to traditional authorities is aided by the fact that doual'art's co-founder is herself a traditional princess, carrying a royal family name which bears considerable clout in the local political ecosystem. At the same time, engaging traditional authorities has always been more than just a performative gesture. As the examples of the *Théâtre Source* in N'dogpassi and *Le Jardin sonore* in Bonamouti-Deido show, the support or opposition of a local chief can be a decisive factor in the question of community ownership beyond the SUD. While the former is described as the 'community's jewel' by the local chief, who sees to its regular cleaning and maintenance, the upkeep of the latter has fallen onto a handful of undeterred local youth.

In sum, despite its contentious relationship with, at times, both traditional authorities and local government, doual'art has successfully evaded political capture and manages to maintain a productive dialogue across a wide spectrum of local and international stakeholders. As the next section shows, this has allowed the organization to develop its locally rooted and globally recognized format of arts-based urbanism.

## TRACES, TACTICS, TRANSFORMATIONS: THE OBJECTS AND AFTERLIVES OF ARTS-BASED URBANISM

Initially, doual'art was established as an architectural and design-based organization interested in creative strategies of urban design. The use of

33 .......... Else Kingue Etame (Head of the Department of Decentralised Cooperation and Translation, Douala City Council), Douala, 25 June, 2019.

34 .......... Marilyn Douala-Bell (Présidente de doual'art) interview by authors (Minty, Roux and Sadie), Douala, 25 June 2019.

arts-based techniques is not new in urban development and has been both valorized and criticized. For example, Florida sees property market potential in fostering bohemian neighbourhoods, while Landry proposes the transformation of cities through creative means as crucial for more integrated and accessible cities.[35] Many neighbourhoods around the world have been invigorated by creative action. But criticisms also abound, from questioning the evaluation methods,[36] to challenging the displacement and erosion of social connections through gentrification processes.[37]

Neither the utopian, nor the dystopian views match the specific realities of African cities, however. Speaking 'from a place off the map'[38]—to use Jennifer Robinson's seminal phrase—inclusionary arts-based practices have been shown to foster more just spaces in cities.[39] Urban spaces continue to bring dynamic opportunities, as well as possibilities for cultural experimentation and expression. These can help build economic potential, social cohesiveness, and diverse modes of cultural exchange, and further, create place.[40] As a result, culture is increasingly being recognized for its role in furthering sustainable urban development,[41] but this recognition has not yet made an impact on patterns of governmental and donor funding. As mentioned above, culture remains marginal in urban policy and is consequently poorly financed. In the Global South, then, it is usually a small pool of international development and diplomacy agencies that see opportunities in linking culture and development and choose to harness the potential of non profit organizations.[42] Thus, it is often these 'informal' arts organizations, not formal arts institutions, which draw on this potential, and become the key innovators in their cities and region. Locally rooted agencies such as doual'art provide us with a glimpse of unique perspectives and approaches to urban change, using culture in complex contexts.

The context of Douala is defined by Cameroon's fraught colonial past, numerous instances of urban dysfunction, and a fractured public sphere. doual'art has aptly managed these multiple contradictions, raising local and international awareness of the city while working, as the rest of Doualans do, by the philosophy of 'System D,' that Douala-Bell describes as surviving or managing with little.[43] The organization employs this method to make the city more liveable and enjoyable, fostering tangible shifts through

35 ........... Richard Florida, *The Rise of the Creative Class: And How It's Transforming Work, Leisure, Community and Everyday Life* (New York: Basic Books, 2003); Charles Landry, *The Creative City: A Toolkit for Urban Innovators* (London: Earthscan, 2000).

36 ........... Graeme Evans, 'Measure for Measure: Evaluating the Evidence of Culture's Contribution to Regeneration,' *Urban Studies*, 1 May 2005; Malcolm Miles, 'Interruptions: Testing the Rhetoric of Culturally Led Urban Development,' *Urban Studies* 42, no. 5–6 (1 May 2005): pp. 889–911.

37 ........... Sharon Zukin, *Loft Living: Culture and Capital in Urban Change* (New Brunswick, New Jersey: Rutgers University Press, 1989).

38 ........... Jennifer Robinson, 'Global and World Cities: A View from off the Map,' *International Journal of Urban and Regional Research* 26, no. 3 (1 September 2002), pp. 531–54.

39 ........... Kim Gurney, *The Art of Public Space: Curating and Re-Imagining the Ephemeral City* (Springer, 2015); Mbaye and Dinardi, 'Ins and Outs of the Cultural Polis'; Miles, *Art, Space and the City*; Pinder, 'Arts of Urban Exploration'; Pinder, 'Urban Interventions'; Joanne Sharp, Venda Pollock, and Ronan Paddison, 'Just Art for a Just City: Public Art and Social Inclusion in Urban Regeneration,' *Urban Studies* 42, no. 5–6 (1 May 2005), pp. 1001–23; Sitas and Pieterse, 'Democratic Renovations and Affective Political Imaginaries,' *Third Text* 27, no. 3 (2013).

40 ........... Evans, 'Creative Cities, Creative Spaces and Urban Policy'; Zayd Minty and Laura Nkula-Wenz, 'Effecting Cultural Change from below? A Comparison of Cape Town and Bandung's Pathways to Urban Cultural Governance,' *Cultural Trends* 28, no. 4 (8 August 2019), pp. 281–93; Octavio Arbeláez Tobón, 'Medellín: Tales of Fear and Hope,' in *Cultures and Globalization: Cities, Cultural Policy and Governance* (New York: SAGE Publications, 2012), pp. 227–34.

41 ........... See e.g., Duxbury, Cullen, and Pascual, 'Cities, Culture and Sustainable Development.'

42 ........... Fontes, 'The What and the How.'

43 ........... Marilyn Douala-Bell (Présidente de doual'art) interview by authors (Minty, Roux and Sadie), Douala, 25 June 2019.

improved public and common spaces, and promoting artworks that speak to post-colonial aspirations and historical challenges, as well as intangible aspirations, such as facilitating residents' changing relationship to their neighbourhoods and the city's heritage.[44]

As such, and very much in line with their conception of the city as a field of experience, doual'art's work poses a serious invitation for us to revise the ways in which we think about the effect of public art, as well as the ways in which we frame projects of infrastructural development. The experiences of work in Bessengue-Akwa, and in particular some of the projects focused on in this chapter, have been crucial in honing this key aspect of doual'art's practice; this practice is defined by a productive blurring of the supposed boundaries of 'artistic' and 'developmental.' It was in Bessengue-Akwa that doual'art first brought art practitioners into an infrastructural intervention, under the auspices of an EU project. More specifically, the project sought to foster decentralized decision-making in processes of urban development initiatives through establishing development committees in twenty neighbourhoods of Douala. doual'art got involved at the stage of evaluating the development committees' work; artists designed and facilitated the dialogical process with the community of residents. As Yves Makongo explains,

> [P]eople have a lot to say but they do not have … any avenue[s] to express themselves. … We saw that the artistic way was the strongest means to express or address some [processual] issues. So, when we are in the neighbourhoods, we address all these issues with art. … art is like a place for negotiation [of] all these issues.[45]

The radical difference that art makes in these dialogical situations—the difference that allows art to become a place—is its potential to create channels for modes and subjects of communication that frames of engagement conventionally attached to development projects, even participatory ones, cannot accommodate. As Marilyn Douala-Bell observes, people 'are ashamed of the conditions of their lives,' and find it hard to talk about these conditions, but arts-based practices allow them to express their concerns meaningfully and with dignity.[46]

On the flip side of doual'art's fusional approach to artistic and infrastructural projects is the evaporation of the artistic aspect from interventions that seek to improve the quality of life in under-serviced areas. This approach suggests another way in which evaluating the impact of public artwork calls for more nuance, especially in the context of cities like Douala. doual'art's involvement in Bessengue-Akwa over almost twenty

44 ……… Pucciarelli, 'Douala (Final Report),' p. 17.

45 ……… Yves Makongo (project manager and artistic assistant, doual'art), interview by authors (Minty, Roux and Sadie) Douala, June 27, 2019

46 ……… Marilyn Douala-Bell (Présidente de doual'art) interview by authors (Minty, Roux and Sadie), Douala, 25 June 2019

years offers many instances of such processes. The organization facilitated various artists' entry into and engagement with the neighbourhood to collectively develop projects that respond to some of the residents' many basic needs. Despite their involvement as artists, however, the artistic element of the projects either remained completely implicit, or had been initially present, but once the community appropriated the artefacts and the spaces around them, continued on only in faint traces.

'La Borne Fontaine' (the water pump that also serves as a public space) and 'La Passerelle' (the bridge that links Bessengue to the rest of the city) both illustrate this implied artistic element. They both invite us to rethink the role of public art in light of residents' expectations and reflections regarding these proximity artworks. La Passerelle's design was developed through a participatory process that included conversations about the ethnic tensions in the neighbourhood, which, in turn, gained symbolic resolution in the bridge's hand-railings that are made up of colourful human figures holding hands.[47] And yet, this symbolism is marginal or completely insignificant compared to the great value that Bessengue residents attribute to the bridge. In contrast, the upside-down buckets of Madiba Square, one of several later works, is neglected and left to deteriorate because they do not intersect with residents' daily life or usage of the place in a meaningful way.

According to Makongo, communities tend to read these interventions as development projects and do not see them as art. But that does not mean that the artworks' impact should be dismissed. It seems to us that in successful cases such as La Passerelle or La Borne Fontaine, urban place-making occurred 'through' art but not 'as' art. And yet, if we take seriously Makongo's point about art as a place, reducing the role of art in these interventions to be merely instrumental would be a mistake. In some cases, art is very much present and works as a significant factor in creating publics (such as in *La Nouvelle Liberté*), in others it is processual (bringing in participatory and creative methods at various stages of the intervention), and in others again it is bracketed or completely discarded after having been a conceptual or practical entry point, with often even the participating artists finding the artistic element irrelevant to how the whole intervention comes to life. What we have to account for, then, are the varied processes through which the material, cultural, and experiential fabric of the city is made and remade through particular installations.

## DECLAMATORY, DOMESTIC, AND DEMOCRATIZING PUBLICNESS

This urban fabric, shaped and reshaped through art and infrastructure installations, constitutes new publics as well as engages with existing ones. The kinds of publics that coalesce in response to artworks and other

47...........Pensa et al., *Public Art in Africa.*

Clown Me In / Beirut, Lebanon / 1:37pm 33°52'41.2"N / 35°32'23.7"E

Creatives Garage / Nairobi, Kenya / 1:42pm     1°17'39.5"S 36°47'10.4"E

interventions differ from context to context, often linked to the kinds of spaces in which these works appear. One useful way of thinking about this is via the idea of a discursive public: in other words, a public that is not necessarily geographically bounded, but that arises in the process of debate, argument, and engagement.[48] As the example of doual'art shows, public art has the potential to act as a powerful catalyst for the formation of discursive publics. In some instances, for example the controversial *La Nouvelle Liberté*, this engagement might be argumentative or acrimonious; in others, it may result in the outright rejection of the artwork, as in the case of *Face à l'eau*.

The differing functions and unexpected effects of public artworks could be related to Gopnik's notion of 'declamatory' and 'domestic' public squares.[49] A declamatory square is a grand public square, the kind often found at the heart of large cities, and often is a space intrinsically linked with authority and national identity.[50] A domestic square is a small, localized, neighbourhood space, where chance meetings and the rhythms of inward-facing everyday life play out. As public squares and public spaces constitute different kinds of publics, so too, do artworks. While a large monumental work like *La Nouvelle Liberté* gestures towards what might be termed a 'declamatory public,' a work like *Le Jardin sonore* or the *Théâtre Source* are inward-facing, addressing and constituting a 'domestic' public rooted in belonging to a particular place in the city.

This framing of declamatory and domestic publics is, of course, not a perfect binary; but is useful for thinking through the different kinds of responses that doul'art's interventions have evoked. Participation is critical to doual'art's programming, both in the gallery and in the SUD; but the meanings and forms of 'participation' are hugely diverse, in part because different works address different types of publics and are situated in a range of spatial (and consequently social) contexts.

Since the establishment of the first SUD in 2007, the organization's work has been strongly shaped by the cycle of a regular event (once a triennial and now a quadrennial). Albeit an event, the festival is also part of a longer and larger set of processes, incorporating the organization and build-up to the festivals, as well as their aftermaths and afterlives. doual'art serves as the key producer, providing conceptual and logistical guidance. Crucially, it employs a full-time socio-cultural mediator, whose primary role is to ensure community buy-in throughout the process. This is, perhaps, one example of quite a direct way in which doual'art works to constitute publics linked to its public art and festival programming. They have been developing profiles of neighbourhoods, through in-depth interviews, participatory surveying to build community knowledge, and understanding the context of the environment, such as the demands for access to water.[51]

48 ........... Michael Warner, 'Publics and Counterpublics,' *Public Culture* 14, no. 1 (1 January 2002): pp. 49–90.

49 ........... Adam Gopnik, 'Place Des Voges, Paris: A Private Place,' in *City Squares: Eighteen Writers on the Spirit and Significance of Squares Around the World* (New York: HarperCollins, 2016), pp. 39–52.

50 ........... Wendy Wilson, 'Living Heritage in the Historic Urban Landscape: The Grand Parade Market' (MPhil Dissertation, University of Cape Town, 2019).

51 ........... Pucciarelli, 'Douala (Final Report),' p. 26.

Through these broad engagements and research-driven processes, doual'art's work has had an important impact on ideas of 'publicness,' belonging, and the possibility of spatial and material transformation in the city as a whole. At the same time, to return to the idea of 'domestic' publics and public spaces, the organization has played a significant role in shaping discourse around public space at the microlevel. At the neighbourhood level, local chiefs and leadership structures bring people together through relationships and longstanding networks. These relationships, close localized connections, and expertise have been critical to doual'art's neighbourhood-facing projects, enabling a sense of consistent presence, dialogue, and local ownership of interventions. These local micro-publics could be thought of both as 'domestic' publics, and as discursive publics who directly shape and influence the kinds of interventions that their neighbourhoods need and want, and either enable or prevent the appropriation, assimilation, and adaptation of public art and space interventions.

While these micropublics are partially constituted by doual'art, this does not necessarily guarantee consensus or smooth processes. The spaces often bring to the surface conflicts and tensions between various participants and the organization, creating an agonistic space for the residents and organization to work through the productive tensions that are present.[52] Contestation, dissonance, and debate are not inherently negative impacts —often, these processes bring to light important insights into power dynamics, desired change, social relationships, and identities.

Though the contestation around *La Nouvelle Liberté* has been mentioned above and written about extensively,[53] here we want to take note of a shift in its reception. Some residents originally rejected the artwork made of scrap metal, for they thought it suggested that the area was garbage, to be used as a dumping ground.[54] This negative response has since shifted for several reasons. Besides an organic growing acceptance of the work's presence over time, doual'art representatives and the artist, Joseph-Francis Sumégné, directly engaged with people in the area, initiating and sustaining discussions and public debates about the meaning and value of the work. Since then, *La Nouvelle Liberté* has been used in several national and international advertising campaigns and is now seen as a symbol of Douala. The impact of this external acknowledgement and unofficial status as a positive symbol has likewise contributed to changing city residents' perception of the work and their own relation to it. As project managerand artistic assistant Yves Makongo notes, 'Even if you're Bamiléké, you're Douala. ... And they recognize themselves in that statue that today is the image of Douala, of this city. Everywhere now, when you see that statue, you know that it's Douala.'[55]

In *La Nouvelle Liberté*, we now see a collective ownership and space-based identity. The value of the work to the place identity of the city goes

52..........Chantal Mouffe, 'Artistic Activism and Agonistic Spaces,' *Arts & Research: A Journal of Ideas, Contexts and Methods* 1, no. 2 (2005), pp. 1–5.

53..........Dominique Malaquais, 'Une nouvelle liberté ? Art et politique urbaine à Douala (Cameroun),' *Afrique histoire* 5, no. 1 (1 July, 2006), pp. 111–34; Pensa, 'System Error'; Schemmel, *Visual Arts in Cameroon*.

54..........Yves Makongo (Project manager and artistic assistant, doual'art), interview by authors (Minty, Roux and Sadie) Douala, 27 June 2019.

55..........Ibid.

a long way to begin creating a positive relation for individuals with the city; most would traditionally not see themselves as from Douala, and rather use their place of birth/origin as a primary identifier. In this way, *La Nouvelle Liberté* has simultaneously provoked public conversations and contestations about art and about the power of public symbols. Further, it has produced a new kind of public, and new ways of seeing and claiming a 'Douala' identity.

The work *Le Jardin sonore*, meanwhile, appears in a very different context and constitutes a smaller, localized public, while also catalyzing a much more bounded, neighbourhood-level sense of public space and spatial identity. Although its original musical and botanical elements no longer function, this does not particularly matter; the work has become something else: a site of gathering, meeting, playing, talking, laughing, shouting. In a fairly literal sense, it has become the focal point of a clearly 'domestic' public space, in contrast to the outward-facing, city-scale impact of *La Nouvelle Liberté*. But it is also a good example of what it means to foster a domestic micro-public, linked to a sense of neighbourhood identity.

For example, a group of four youths (Roger Dipomo, Woo Elie, Cedrick Toube, and Fredéric Mpondo) living in Bonamouti-Deido took responsibility for *Le Jardine sonore*'s maintenance and restoration, as well participated in doual'art's projects outside of the neighbourhood, as foreseen in the original concept presentation for the work. This group of youths describe the project as simultaneously 'crazy' and 'inspiring.'[56] By constituting their group to oversee the maintenance, they form a micropublic where their collective social capital is used to access the organization and to grow their confidence, networks, and skills.[57] The group thus demonstrates that 'claiming ownership' extends beyond new forms of localized publicness and belonging for the neighbourhood. Their initiative also shows that ownership can circumnavigate established hierarchies and power structures, demonstrating the ways in which localized agency is activated through doual'art's work.

The N'dogpassi chief Ndoutou Jean-Marie, who was instrumental in the development and the implementation of the *Théâtre Source* (2013), both leads and is actively involved in its maintenance. As a result, he has fully claimed the project, strategically recognizing the opportunity doual'art brings to help reshape and reposition his neighbourhood physically and symbolically.[58]

The forms of public spaces and publics that are created through doual'art's processes illustrate that to be public, of course, is not necessarily to be democratic; furthermore, artistic interventions, no matter how participatory or how well-intentioned, are not inherently democratizing. However, the work discussed here intersects in a range of ways with the larger projects of building identity, belonging, and a sense of possibility for how space can be made, claimed, and changed—both literally and figuratively. When thinking through the city as a field of experience,

56 .......... Roger Dipomo Mouen, Toube Cédric Edoube Ngongue, and Jean Frédéric Npondo Nkongo, (Community Participants) Focus Group with authors (Minty, Roux and Sadie), Douala, 27 June 2019.

57 .......... Ibid.

58 .......... Jean-Marie Ndoutou (Chief of N'dogpassi), interview by authors (Minty, Roux and Sadie), Douala, 26 June 2019.

we see public art and cultural production as mechanisms with the potential to foster a sense of agency, symbolic ownership, and possibility that become threaded into the material, social, and affective fabric of the city. They open spaces for other kinds of democratic engagements and demands.

## CONCLUSION

doual'art's artistic practices have engaged and enlivened the city of Douala—understood as a field of experience that is complex, diverse, and exhilarating. Since 1991, through both its gallery space and the recurring SUD, doual'art has created an interdisciplinary, site-specific and context-sensitive mode of working in and with the city that surrounds it. It regularly involves residents in the creation of different types of public art, operates as a key interface between global and local artistic and cultural scenes, and is a strong advocate for recognizing the power of arts-based urbanism.

doual'art has been able to work creatively and unusually sustainably between the art and development nexus, often blurring the divisions between these categories. This has required not only pragmatism, but also a high level of organizational agility. Our research shows how doual'art manages to interact with local authorities (both formal and traditional) at arm's length, thereby successfully avoiding any form of political capture. This impartial stance is key to building a rapport with different stakeholders and fostering the organization's role as a key mediator of artistic expression and a fulcrum of local cultural governance. Consequently, the city government has identified doual'art as a key project implementer, one that can work productively with the complexity of different neighbourhoods and engage communities at eye level, acknowledging and working through tensions rather than glossing over them.

The work of doual'art is neither entirely about 'development,' nor entirely about art. In many of the cases discussed in this chapter, the actual objects or images produced are less important than their after effects and the processes through which they came into being. There is something more complex at work here than an instrumental use of 'art as development' or 'art as place-making'; rather, art meets public space, infrastructure, the city, and social process to speak to and to constitute a range of urban identities and spaces of belonging or contestation. As we have argued, there are instances in which the artwork itself serves as a catalyst leading to material change in a neighbourhood. In others, the participatory (and sometimes fraught) processes of making art and engaging with its after-lives have a more intangible but no less crucial effect. The most long-lived and 'successful' of the art interventions driven by doual'art seem to be those that are able to provoke this kind of deep engagement and claiming of ownership, catalysing new forms of creative urban place-making in a way that becomes part of the city's experiential fabric.

We have argued that to be public is not to be democratic. Publicness is also not necessarily shorthand for consensus. One of the most powerful effects of many of the public art installations in Douala has been their capacity to productively evoke dissent and discord. Through both the processes of making and installing art, and via its reception and the way subsequent conversations are handled, doual'art's work has been able to bring to the surface social relations, contestations, and points of tension that would be difficult to access or to speak about openly within a classic 'development' framework.

The works and the processes discussed in this chapter suggest that art, broadly defined, holds unique possibilities in the making of urban spaces and urban publics. The power of art, in this instance, lies in its ability to shape discursive publics: to reflect complex social processes, including things that would otherwise go unspoken, rendering them visible and opening other possible ways of being in and imagining urban life.

← REFERENCES

Amin, Ash, and Nigel Thrift. *Cities: Reimagining the Urban*. Hoboken: Wiley, 2002.

Bishop, Claire. *Artificial Hells: Participatory Art and the Politics of Spectatorship*. London: Verso Books, 2012.

Bourriaud, Nicolas. *Relational Aesthetics*. Dijon: Les Presses du réel, 2002.

Duxbury, Nancy, Catherine Cullen, and Jordi Pascual. 'Cities, Culture and Sustainable Development.' In *Cultural Policy and Governance in a New Metropolitan Age*, pp. 73–86. Cultures and Globalization. London: SAGE, 2012.

Evans, Graeme. 'Creative Cities, Creative Spaces and Urban Policy.' *Urban Studies* 46, no. 5-6 (May 1, 2009), pp. 1003–40. doi.org/10.1177/0042098009103853.

—. 'Measure for Measure: Evaluating the Evidence of Culture's Contribution to Regeneration.' *Urban Studies*, 1 May 2005. doi.org/10.1080/00420980500107102.

Florida, Richard. *The Rise of the Creative Class: And How It's Transforming Work, Leisure, Community and Everyday Life*. New York: Basic Books, 2003.

Fontes, Claudia. 'The What and the How: Rethinking Evaluation Practice for the Arts and Development.' In *Contemporary Perspectives on Art and International Development*, pp. 238–52. London: Taylor & Francis, 2016.

Gopnik, Adam. 'Place des Voges, Paris: A Private Place.' In *City Squares: Eighteen Writers on the Spirit and Significance of Squares Around the World*, pp. 39–52. New York: HarperCollins, 2016.

Gurney, Kim. *The Art of Public Space: Curating and Re-Imagining the Ephemeral City*. New York: Springer, 2015.

Kaye, Nick. *Site-Specific Art: Performance, Place and Documentation*. London: Psychology Press, 2000.

Kester, Grant H. *Conversation Pieces: Community and Communication in Modern Art*. Berkeley: University of California Press, 2004.

Kwon, Miwon. *One Place After Another: Site-Specific Art and Locational Identity*. Cambridge: MIT Press, 2004.

Landry, Charles. *The Creative City: A Toolkit for Urban Innovators*. Earthscan, 2000.

Mabin, Alan. 'Grounding Southern City Theory in Time and Place.' In *The Routledge Handbook on Cities of the Global South*, ed. Susan Parnell and Sophie Oldfield, pp. 43–58. London and New York: Routledge, 2014.

Malaquais, Dominique. 'Une nouvelle liberté? Art et politique urbaine à Douala (Cameroun).' *Afrique histoire* 5, no. 1 (1 July 2006), pp. 111–34.

Mbaye, Jenny, and Cecilia Dinardi. 'Ins and Outs of the Cultural Polis: Informality, Culture and Governance in the Global South.' *Urban Studies* 56, no. 3 (1 February 2019), pp. 578–93. doi.org/10.1177/0042098017744168.

Miles, Malcolm. *Art, Space and the City*. London: Routledge, 1997.

Miles, Malcolm. 'Interruptions: Testing the Rhetoric of Culturally Led Urban Development.' *Urban Studies* 42, no. 5–6 (1 May 2005), pp. 889–911. doi.org/10.1080/00420980500107375.

Minty, Zayd, and Laura Nkula-Wenz. 'Effecting Cultural Change from below? A Comparison of Cape Town and Bandung's Pathways to Urban Cultural Governance.' *Cultural Trends* 28, no. 4 (8 August 2019), pp. 281–93. doi.org/10.1080/09548963.2019.1644785.

Mouffe, Chantal. 'Artistic Activism and Agonistic Spaces.' *Arts & Research: A Journal of Ideas, Contexts and Methods* 1, no. 2 (2005), pp. 1–5.

Moulaert, Frank, Hilde Demuynck, and Jacques Nussbaumer. 'Urban Renaissance: From Physical Beautification to Social Empowerment.' *City* 8, no. 2 (1 July 2004), pp. 229–35. doi.org/10.1080/1360481042000242175.

Nkula-Wenz, Laura. 'Worlding Cape Town by Design: Encounters with Creative Cityness.' *Environment and Planning A: Economy and Space*, 29 August 2018. doi.org/10.1177/0308518X18796503.

Pensa, Iolanda. 'System Error: Art as a Space to Produce What We Would Never Have Thought We Needed.' In *Contemporary Perspectives on Art and International Development*, pp. 124–37. Abingdon-on-Thames: Taylor & Francis, 2016.
—. et al., eds. *Public Art in Africa: Art and Urban Transformations in Douala*. Geneva: Métis Presses, 2017. http://edoc.unibas.ch/54721/.

Pinder, David. 'Arts of Urban Exploration.' *Cultural Geographies* 12, no. 4 (1 October 2005), pp. 383–411. doi.org/10.1191/1474474005eu347oa.
—. 'Urban Interventions: Art, Politics and Pedagogy.' *International Journal of Urban and Regional Research* 32, no. 3 (2008), pp. 730–36. doi.org/10.1111/j.1468-2427.2008.00810.x.

Pucciarelli, Marta. 'Douala (Final Report).' Lugano: SUPSI, 2014. www.mobilea2k.supsi.ch/wp-content/uploads/douala-report.pdf.

Robinson, Jennifer. 'Global and World Cities: A View from off the Map.' *International Journal of Urban and Regional Research* 26, no. 3 (1 September 2002), pp. 531–54. doi.org/10.1111/1468-2427.00397.

Schemmel, Anette. *Visual Arts in Cameroon: A Genealogy of Non-Formal Training 1976–2014*. Langaa: RPCIG, 2016.

Sharp, Joanne, Venda Pollock, and Ronan Paddison. 'Just Art for a Just City: Public Art and Social Inclusion in Urban Regeneration.' *Urban Studies* 42, no. 5–6 (1 May 2005), pp. 1001–23. doi.org/10.1080/00420980500106963.

Simone, AbdouMaliq. *City Life from Jakarta to Dakar: Movements at the Crossroads*. London: Routledge, 2010.
—. 'Pirate Towns: Reworking Social and Symbolic Infrastructures in Johannesburg and Douala.' *Urban Studies* 43, no. 2 (February 2006), pp. 357–70. doi.org/10.1080/00420980500146974.
—, and Edgar Pieterse. *New Urban Worlds: Inhabiting Dissonant Times*. Hoboken: John Wiley & Sons, 2018.

Sitas, Rike. 'Becoming Otherwise: Artful Urban Enquiry.' *Urban Forum*, 26 February 2020. doi.org/10.1007/s12132-020-09387-4.
—. 'Cultural Policy and the Power of Place, South Africa.' In *The Routledge Handbook of Global Cultural Policy*, pp. 597–614. London: Routledge, 2017.
—, and Edgar Pieterse. 'Democratic Renovations and Affective Political Imaginaries.' *Third Text* 27, no. 3 (1 May 2013), pp. 327–42. doi.org/10.1080/09528822.2013.798183.

Stupples, Polly, and Katerina Teaiwa. *Contemporary Perspectives on Art and International Development*. Abingdon-on-Thames: Taylor & Francis, 2016.

Suderburg, Erika. *Space, Site, Intervention: Situating Installation Art*. Minneapolis: University of Minnesota Press, 2000.

Tobón, Octavio Arbeláez. 'Medellín: Tales of Fear and Hope.' In *Cultures and Globalization: Cities, Cultural Policy and Governance*, 227–34. Newbury Park: SAGE Publications, 2012.

Warner, Michael. 'Publics and Counterpublics.' *Public Culture* 14, no. 1 (1 January 2002): pp. 49–90.

Wilson, Wendy. 'Living Heritage in the Historic Urban Landscape: The Grand Parade Market.' MPhil Dissertation, University of Cape Town, 2019.

Zukin, Sharon. *Loft Living: Culture and Capital in Urban Change*. New Jersey: Rutgers University Press, 1989.

## ← INTERVIEWS

Else Kingue Etame (Head of the Department of Decentralised Cooperation and Translation, Douala City Council), Douala, 25 June 2019.

Marilyn Douala-Bell (Présidente de doual'art) interview by authors (Minty, Roux and Sadie), Douala, 25 June 2019.

Jean-Marie Ndoutou (chief of N'dogpassi), interview by authors (Minty, Roux and Sadie), Douala, 26 June 2019.

Nadège Ngouegni Ngnoulaye (doual'art's socio-cultural mediator) interview by authors (Minty, Roux, Sadie), Douala, 27 June 2019.

Roger Dipomo Mouen, Toube Cédric Edoube Ngongue, and Jean Frédéric Npondo Nkongo, (community participants) Focus Group by authors (Minty, Roux and Sadie), Douala, 27 June 2019.

Yves Makongo (project manager and artistic assistant, doual'art), interview by authors (Minty, Roux and Sadie) Douala, 27 June 2019.

# FREE SCHOOLS AS TOOLS FOR INCLUSION
## Tiny Toones and Arte Moris

Nuraini Juliastuti

This chapter explores intersections of the visual arts and education by analysing the development of free school and classes organized by Tiny Toones (Phnom Penh, Cambodia) and Arte Moris Art Centre (Dili, Timor Leste). I argue that Tiny Toones and Arte Moris not only serve as a model for alternative schooling, but emerge as spaces for nurturing local strategies for everyday sustainability. I conceptualize the 'studying-turn' as a method for reimagining the usefulness of an alternative space for a wider social ecosystem. I focus on various layers of teaching and learning practices to understand the vernacular vocabularies of the making of teachers, students, classes, and friendship-based learning methods. As such, I seek to understand the meaning of developing a free school and studying together. My research shows that Tiny Toones and Arte Moris serve as tools for inclusion to access equality in education systems. Tiny Toones creates a structure of freestyle education for children. Arte Moris serves as a free art school which develops into a medium to facilitate the sustainability of an artist community. It functions as practice, in the ethics of living together.

Keywords
→ Free Education
→ Collective Learning
→ Non-Knowledge
→ Sustainability

## INTRODUCTION

This chapter examines the 'free school' practices of Tiny Toones and Arte Moris. Tiny Toones is a Phnom Penh-based organization that focuses on young people in Cambodia. Arte Moris is a free art school based in Dili, Timor Leste. The establishment of Tiny Toones and Arte Moris provides an avenue for exploring the link between art and pedagogy. My research poses direct questions about youth culture, cultural infrastructure, a sense of crisis, and the development of agency that shapes a collective vision. Tiny Toones' and Arte Moris' long-standing practices reveal a relationship between doing art and the creation of collective sustainability mechanisms that intersect with the organization of the spaces. I elaborate the 'studying-turn' and the notion of 'studying together' as both inter-relational thinking, and a mechanism to develop a long-term cultural strategy from below.

Tiny Toones was founded during the post-Khmer Rouge period, when the country had attempted to achieve normalization through the assistance of various international NGOs, UN bodies, and capital investments. The country strives to become a more democratic nation, while still healing from the wounds of internal conflicts and wars. My research provides insights into how the organization of Tiny Toones is also informed by the volunteering culture, and by various workers of these international organizations.

Arte Moris was founded when Timor Leste was in the process of transitioning into a newly independent country. The Indonesian New Order military regime invaded East Timor (or Portuguese Timor) shortly after the Revolutionary Front of an Independent East Timor (Fretilin) gained independence from Portugal in November 1975. During the New Order regime, East Timor was the twenty-seventh province of Indonesia. Following 'Reformation 1998'[1] in Indonesia, seventy-eight and a half per cent of the East Timorese people voted for separation from Indonesia through an Independence Referendum.

The conceptualization of a 'studying-turn' grows from my observations of various independent initiatives and artist collectives that develop various education or learning activities as the basis of their work. These organizations function as both independent art spaces and public learning spaces. The 'studying-turn' involves two ways of doing. First, it attempts to provide learning spaces for the public. Second, it attempts to reframe certain spaces as studying spaces. It shows an intention of going back to studying. Here I use Stefano Harney and Fred Moten's concept of 'study.'[2] Harney and Moten situate the act of 'studying' in between debt and credit; studying is located between what we can do, and what we fail to do. It assumes the readiness to accept the condition in which the future does not always lead to an expected outcome.

This chapter is divided in two parts: the first explores the learning processes in Tiny Toones and the diverse narratives that inform its programme; the second part explores how Arte Moris has emerged as an independent art institution that facilitates the survival process of an artist community. Both these sections include field-work descriptions and reflections which bring to life the spaces and faces in these places.

Free schools, as organized by Tiny Toones and Arte Moris, provide the ground for imagining a pattern of alternative education projects embedded in the formation of independent arts organizations. In the context of Tiny Toones and Arte Moris, my research shows that organizing a school means to perform a new mechanism for caring about local ecosystems. In the context studied, education is both the product of crisis and a way of dealing with the crisis. This research argues that doing education through art is an intuitive act to be performed in a socially challenged context. Further, the studying-turn is inter-relational thinking that can connect art and community.

1............Reformation 1998, or *Reformasi* refers to the political period preceded by authoritarian style of New Order Regime government led by President Soeharto for thirty-two years, characterized by corruption, collusion, and nepotism leadership, combined with heavy-handed military operation. Following the monetary crisis in 1997 and attendant student protests and riots, it culminated in the *Reformasi 1998*, with the fall of Soeharto.

2............Stefano Harney and Fred Moten, *The Undercommons: Fugitive Planning & Black Study* (Wivenhoe and Port Watson: Minor Compositions, 2013), pp. 58–69.

In labelling Tiny Toones and Arte Moris as independent art organizations, I use my definition of alternative spaces. An alternative space, as expounded in my previous research, refers to new cultural spaces—an artist-run space, gallery, performance space, or discussion place—for thoughts that would otherwise be 'homeless' in the cultural spaces formed and designed by established cultural authorities.[3] These spaces are composed of a group of individuals with different backgrounds and trajectories who develop their own attitudes to test their thoughts on arts and culture. Their works range from art production and research and are all conducted with clear interdisciplinary intention: be it for the provision of art and culture that in turn supports wider infrastructure, or to facilitate dialogue with policy makers, or to organize activities that can be classified as community empowerment. An alternative space serves as a model platform for artists and cultural activists to fulfill their visionary ideas.[4]

## TINY TOONES: AN ARCHITECTURE OF FREESTYLE SCHOOLING HELPING CREATE EQUALITY IN EDUCATION SYSTEMS

Tiny Toones' founder, Tuy Sobil (better known as KayKay or KK), was born in a refugee camp on the Thai-Cambodian border in 1977. Like thousands of Khmer people who populated the camp, KK's family fled from the country to escape the Khmer Rouge regime and other internal military conflicts. In 1984, when KK was seven years old, he immigrated to Long Beach, California, with his family. The number of Cambodian refugee communities in Long Beach is reported to be the largest outside Cambodia and the centre of the Cambodian diaspora.[5]

A major event in KK's life led to his deportation from the United States in 2004. He arrived in Phnom Penh later that year: everything felt unfamiliar, as Cambodia was a 'foreign' country for him. KK found himself scraping by with various jobs in the city's foreign and local NGOs. He observed that there were not many activities conducted specifically for children in Phnom Penh's urban landscape. As a skillful breakdancer, KK opened his house to provide free breakdance classes for kids and teenagers in Phnom Penh. Tiny Toones grew from a dance centre to a free school providing, in addition to dance classes, free classes in English, mathematics, and Khmer. △Fig. 1 The need for an actual physical space for education for children elevated Tiny Toones to an important position in the community.

In particular, Tiny Toones became pivotal for children who are excluded from the mainstream education system (because they lack of state-made documents to access school).

3............Nuraini Juliastuti, 'Knowledge Performativity of Alternative Spaces,' paper presented at *Cultural Performance in Post-New Order Indonesia: New Structures, Scenes, Meanings* symposium (Yogyakarta: Sanata Dharma University, 2010); Nuraini Juliastuti, 'A Conversation on Horizontal Organization,' *Afterall: A Journal of Art, Context, and Enquiry* 30 (2012), pp. 118–25.

4............Nuraini Juliastuti, 'Commons People: Managing Music and Culture in Contemporary Yogyakarta' (PhD Dissertation, Leiden University, 2019), pp. 24–25.

5............Susan Needham, Karen Quintiliani, 'Cambodians in Long Beach, California: The Making of a Community,' *Journal of Immigrant and Refugee Studies* 5, no. 1 (2007), pp. 29–53.

△ 1
Students walking down the corridor in Tiny Toones, photo: Gatari Surya Kusuma, 2019

KK explains that the establishment of Tiny Toones originated from his desire to create an alternative for after school care. It was not intended to fulfill the role of a standard school in the national school system. KK described his education trajectory as one full of disruption; for example, he has not yet fully mastered writing in Khmer. He has channeled his personal aspirations for having a sufficient level of Khmer into elements of the school programme, which focus on improving students' skills in reading and writing in Khmer.

Susan Needham's long-term research in the Cambodian community in Long Beach explains that in the nineteen-eighties and nineteen-nineties, many Cambodian parents were concerned that their children were not mastering their native language. This led to the organization of various language classes managed by the local Buddhist temple, churches, colleges, student groups, and other bodies in the community.[6] It suggests that the development of Tiny Toones is based on KK's knowledge and personal history of engaging in this kind of alternative education during his life in Long Beach. Needham's research also asserts that more than a matter of sustaining the connections with the homeland, the need to teach Khmer is based on the respect for the symbolic meanings of the written characters. It is rooted in the religious pagoda-based learning system. The Buddhist temple held an important value in the Cambodian educational institution until it was shifted into a more modern schooling with French influence.[7]

It is beyond the remit of this chapter to explore the personal aspect of KK's education. However, I use his specific story of educational disruption to understand the diverse narratives that inform the idea of schooling in Tiny Toones. Tiny Toones sits at the confluence of principles that value informal schooling and learning practices. In writing about Cambodian authors, Roger Nelson argues that their rejection of narrative linearity stems both from the newness of novel as an artistic format and the character of the national education.[8] Pagoda-based education offered informality, openness, and an unstructured style of teaching. Such a learning style was also part of the disciplining project under French colonial rule. However, Nelson

6.............Susan Needham, 'How Can You Be Cambodian If You Don't Speak Khmer? Language, Literacy, and Education in Cambodian "Rhetoric of Distinction",' *Negotiating Transnationalism: Selected Papers on Refugees and Immigrants* 9 (2001), pp. 123–41.

7.............Ibid; Will Brehm, 'Historical Memory and Educational Privatisation: A Portrait From Cambodia,' *Ethnography and Education* 14, no. 1 (2017), p. 3.

8.............Roger Nelson, 'The Present is a Foreign Country: Some Thoughts on the (Dis)Entanglement of Exploration and Conquest,' in *Fields: An Itinerant Inquiry Across the Kingdom of Cambodia*, eds. Charlotte Huddleston and Roger Nelson (Auckland: ST Paul St Gallery and Sa Sa Bassac, 2015), pp. 58–66.

puts forward the thought that the 'stop-and-start nature of education in Cambodia was, apparently hard to displace.'[9] During my fieldwork, I visited Tuol Sleng Genocide Museum, known as Security Prison 21 (S-21) by the Khmer Rouge regime. The prison formerly functioned as an education institution called Tuol Svay Pray High School. The existence of this prison, in the place of a school, shows the extent of disruption in the Cambodian education process.

In the following sections, I reflect on my field notes to examine how Tiny Toones organizes the learning process for it students; I explore the formal and informal characters involved in the school and their struggles to help frame its existence as a response to the unequal access to education that many children face in the country.

## The Payback Mechanism and Sustainability of the School

•

*Slick's story*

> Slick joined Tiny Toones in 2006. That was 13 years ago; he was 16 years old. He was a drug user at the time. 'Ice has been a big problem for the youths in Cambodia,' said Slick. According to Slick, KK approached him and told him to stop using drugs. That was how Slick's story with Tiny Toones began. As it turns out, he really loved breakdancing. He found it liberating; it made him feel more confident. Slick started to learn about breakdancing from various sources—particularly, bingeing on YouTube. As his dance skills improved, KK began to ask him to share these skills with the younger kids. Today, Slick holds multiple roles in Tiny Toones: besides teaching dance, he also teaches English and works as a kind of operational manager and a mediator in the school. Slick speaks English well. This makes him a reliable partner for some volunteer-teachers who have limited Khmer language abilities. Mimi, another English teacher, says she often felt frustrated when students seemed to not fully understand what she said; this frustration grew when she was not able to convey certain messages to the students in Khmer either. In events like this, Slick often comes to the rescue. The kids like him.
>
> *(Field notes, 2 March 2019)*

Tiny Toones has moved locations on several occasions. Its current location is tucked away in a narrow alley of a *kampong* [urban village] in Chbar Ampov market area in central Phnom Penh. A passage connects the front gate to the small yard at the back of the building. There are two basketball rings in the yard, and both sides of the passage are lined with classrooms. There is another building behind the yard where the office is located. The

9............Roger Nelson, 'The Present is a Foreign Country,' p. 65.

walls of the classrooms and the yard are decorated with murals. If we were to stand right in front of the basketball ring, a mural with KK's face would be facing us.

Tiny Toones does not have a fixed curriculum system. Its daily activities are divided into morning and afternoon sessions. Each session includes three to four classes (English, Khmer, mathematics, and dance).△Fig. 2 Depending on the availability of volunteers or other organizations who are willing to contribute their skills, there are additional classes such as drawing, music, computer, or skateboarding classes. The number of students who attend ranges from fifteen to fifty. There are occasions where the number is smaller.

△ 2
Slick teaching the Hip Hop class, photo: Gatari Surya Kusuma, 2019

△ 3
Slick teaching the English class, photo: Nuraini Juliastuti, 2019

The class organization in Tiny Toones partly depends on the availability of various NGO workers who are willing to serve as volunteers. Tiny Toones has benefitted from the popularity of Cambodia as a site for practicing what Maria Koleth refers to as 'volunteer tourism.'[10] The volunteer tourists pay with their interest in working at various historical conservation sites, orphanages, educational, and health institutions. Their practices function as personal exercises to learn about hope. Koleth's research narrates that such practices are often not accompanied with efforts to contextualize this vonluteer experience within the country's violent history.

International volunteers usually work in Tiny Toones for six to ten months. After their teaching period is done, they go back to their previous employment or embark on a new position in a different organization.

10..........Maria Koleth, 'Hope in the Dark: Geographies of Volunteer and Dark Tourism in Cambodia,' *Cultural Geographies* 21, no. 4 (2014), pp. 681–94.

In some cases, Tiny Toones uses its growing network of successful breakdance performers, 'B Boys' and other artists who visit Phnom Penh for performances, to volunteer to teach the dance class during their stay in the city.

During my research I noticed the frequent use of the word 'outreach' to describe the creation of attractive and relevant activities to involve children from different communities. This term is indicative of the influence of the NGO world on the school; it informs the way that Tiny Toones staff imagines the profile of the students attending the school. Though more research in this area is needed, it is clear that Tiny Toones is situated within the operationalization of various NGOs, and as such it lends and uses certain vocabularies from the NGO world to describe its own activities.

Although Tiny Toones depends on foreign volunteers to fill teacher positions, my research indicates that these foreign volunteers are highly dependent on local staff at Tiny Toones. For example, as my field notes above suggest, a foreign teacher-volunteer like Mimi always depended on the local teachers to mediate the communication with the students. I note this to emphasize the strong role of the local people, something that differentiates Tiny Toones from other organizations that work with children (that are fully dependent on international staff). This factor reveals the potential future sustainability of the organization.

I observe that Tiny Toones employs former students to become its teachers. In conversation, KK talks about this hiring as part of the 'trust system' and 'payback mechanism' in the organization.[△Fig. 3] The system provides job opportunities for former students and creates an established system of transition, from being students to becoming teachers. This can be understood as further creating a mechanism to facilitate ongoing connectivity between the former students and the school.

## Regularity and repetition

• •

> Gatari and I were cramped in a van along with the students who were going home after the morning class session finished. There were fifteen students in the van. Jacky the van driver is a former Tiny Toones student. Occasionally Jacky also helps teach the dance class when Slick is not around.
>
> It took almost an hour to get all the students to their homes. We drove around the sprawling suburbs and slums under the Manivong Bridge. After dropping off the last student in Sangkat Preaek Pra area, Jacky parked the van under the shades of trees in the corner of a quiet neighborhood.
>
> Jacky spent an hour there before he turned on the car engine again, and went to pick up another group of students for the afternoon class. The car followed a slightly different route. In different spots, the students stood in front of their houses, or the alleys where their houses were located, along the route. They waived as Jacky's car approached. The car was a bit more packed than it was in the morning. I recognized

> some students who attended the morning session came again to the school for the afternoon session.
>
> *(Field notes, 5 March 2019)*

Tiny Toones provides free transportation for the students. There are two Tuk-Tuks and a van that operate as a kind of school bus system for the students. The availability of free transport is not only intended to create ease for the students, but it also ensures the students' regular participation.

There is a sense of regularity mixed with formality in the organization of Tiny Toones. For example, before the learning sessions start, the students congregate in the yard for an assembly.△Fig. 4 The students address the teachers as *krou* [teacher]. The classes are arranged by specific subjects, and programmed at a designated time. I assume that the formality is intended to create an impression—that Tiny Toones be perceived as a real school. But as my field notes suggest, Tiny Toones indeed does perform as a real school for many students. It is the only kind of school that they can access. The flexible curriculum system allows the teachers to improvise with the teaching materials. There is potential for repetition in the class. There is also freedom, as this flexibility does not entail any schoolwork. There is no limitation to the duration of study. Tiny Toones allows the students to be students as long as they want to be. Just like those who study in a pagoda, Tiny Toones' students are also allowed to leave the education any time. The students attend Tiny Toones everyday to learn together, but also to play with their friends. Tiny Toones accommodates all these various needs.

△ 4
Students lining up in a school assembly, photo: Gatari Surya Kusuma, 2019

## ARTE MORIS: HOW TO BECOME AN ARTIST AND THE MAKING OF ETHICS ON HOW TO LIVE TOGETHER

The emergence of various *sanggar* [informal education institutions] in post-independence Timor Leste plays an important role, within the context of artist collectives, in nurturing the development of young artists.[11] In the Indonesian context, a sanggar refers to a space where a group of people learn to practice a certain kind of art under the auspices of a mentor. Leonor Veiga's research suggests that the use of the term sanggar in Timor Leste might stem from the active roles of the Indonesian-speaking Timor Leste artists in the local art scene. Language skills usually provide insights into the personal history of people's education. Those who were born in the nineteen-ninties usually do not posses Indonesian language skills unless they learn it from the *sinetron* [Indonesian telenovela] broadcasted by Indonesian television stations.

During the early development of modern Indonesian art, when the country was still in the early stages of developing a national consciousness, art associations played an important role not only in defining the relation between art and politics, but also in defining the meaning of 'doing art.'[12] A sanggar is considered an informal education institution; teaching methods are informal and students and teachers often live and work together. The communal dimension of a sanggar is similar to what can be found in Arte Moris in post-independence Timor Leste, particularly in regards to its functioning as a collective. I use this aspect of commonality to discuss the kinds of mechanisms that the members have created to manage their shared goals as a community.

Luca and Gabi Gansser, the founders of Arte Moris, left Timor Leste in 2012. Their departure serves as a starting point to explore the new phase of a collective learning process in the organization. My writing narrates the transformation that Arte Moris has gone through from a sanggar into an artist collective. It entails the changes inherent in the learning process of an aspiring artist. The process changes from learning from a teacher, or a mentor, to learning together, to become an artist. I dedicate some parts of this chapter to discuss different teacher figures that inform Arte Moris—from the founders Luca and Gabi Gansser, to the volunteers, to the peers-turned-study partners. I show how the aspiration of the members to become artists is interlinked with the idea and ambition to sustain the existence of Arte Moris as a space. Arte Moris emerged as a new artist collective in the process.

I consider Loïc Wacquant's concept of teaching as a collective enterprise to elucidate the learning context of Arte Moris.[13] In Wacquant's research about a boxing gym in the Woodlawn area in Chicago in the mid-nineteen-eighties, he describes the workings of the transmission of a kind of 'pugilistic knowledge.' He observed that boxing skills, both in tacit and explicit forms, were handed down from the trainers to the boxers in a collective manner. The boxing gym appeared as a family where the members took care of each other. This created a condition whereby the progress of a boxer becomes part of the collective responsibility.

Some studies and reports on Arte Moris define the school as a 'free school' and the teaching method of Luca and Gabi Gansser as 'free style.'[14]

11 .......... Leonor Veiga, 'Movimentu Kultura: Making Timor Leste,' in *Routledge Handbook of Contemporary Timor Leste*, eds. Andrew McWilliam and Michael Leach (London and New York: Routledge, 2019), pp. 256–70.

12 .......... Nuraini Juliastuti, '*Sanggar* as a Model for Practicing Art in Communal Life,' in *Made in Commons*, ed. Ferdiansyah Thajib and Kerstin Winking (Amsterdam: KUNCI Cultural Studies Centre; Stedelijk Museum Bureau Amsterdam, 2013), pp. 9–17.

13 .......... Loïc Wacquant, *Body & Soul: Notebooks of An Apprentice Boxer* (Oxford and New York: Oxford University Press, 2004), pp. 118–27.

14 .......... Khoo Ying Hooi, 'How Arts Heal and Galvanise the Youth of Timor Leste?,' *The Conversation*, 12 June 2017, https://theconversation.com/how-arts-heal-and-galvanise-the-youth-of-timor-leste-73927; Leonor Veiga, 'Movimentu Kultura in Timor Leste: Maria Madeira's Agency,' *Cadernos de Arte e Antropologia* 4, no. 1 (2015), pp. 85–101.

The meaning of 'free style' here refers to the fact that both founders did not create a specific curriculum on which to base their teaching practices. I connect these observations to the notion of teaching as a collective enterprise, forwarded by Wacquant. We can use this to investigate and understand what kinds of knowledge and non-knowledge circulate in Arte Moris. What kind of capacities do the members need to have to intuit that a certain learning activity can lead to useful knowledge?

Many studies of contemporary art history in Timor Leste focus on the narratives of traditional art[15] and the revival of traditional elements,[16] the rise of mural artists and the role of the walls as 'public forums'[17] and as a space to rewrite national identity,[18] and the power of art as the driving force for social change,[19] and art's healing, therapeutic, and uniting energies.[20] I propose that the study of contemporary art in Timor Leste will be enriched by taking into account the condition of cultural production and the well-being of cultural producers. J.K. Gibson-Graham, Jenny Cameron, and Stephen Healy propose the idea of well-being, which encapsulates the interaction between five elements: 'material well-being, occupational well-being, social well-being, community well-being, and physical well-being.'[21]

My definition of well-being concerns itself not only with the existence of Arte Moris as a space, but also with the people who activate the space. And my study further shifts a common perspective from seeing the visual performance as the ultimate form of cultural expression, to a mode of viewing art as a collective project. To view Arte Moris as a collective project means to move away from emphasizing the works of the members of the organization, and instead to understand this work as one part of long-term cultural strategy.

Most of the people that I met in Arte Moris are in the seventeen to thirty-five age range. The population below age thirty-five constitutes seventy-four percent of the total population in Timor Leste.[22] According to the recent Timor Leste government report, the fast growing working age population 'requires strong investment in skills and the creation of decent jobs'—one of the key areas in the country that needs to be strengthened.[23] The sustainability of an independent art school intersects with this young demographic's sense of vulnerability, and with the survival strategy of the youth generation, navigating the post-Indonesian New Order regime of Timor Leste.

15 ........... David Hicks, 'Glimpses of Alternatives: The Uma Lulik of East Timor,' *Social Analysis* 52 (2008), pp. 166–80; Andrew McWilliam, Lisa Palmer, and Christopher Shepherd, 'Lulik Encounters and Cultural Frictions in East Timor: Past and Present,' *The Australian Journal of Anthropology* 25, no. 3 (2014), pp. 304–20.

16 ........... Veiga, 'Movimentu Kultura.'

17 ........... Chris Parkinson, *Peace of Wall* (Melbourne: Affirm Press, 2010).

18 ........... Catherine Elizabeth Arthur, 'Writing National Identity on the Wall: The Geracao Foun, Street Art and Language Choices in Timor Leste,' *Cadernos de Arte e Antropologia* 4, no. 1 (2015), pp. 41–63.

19 ........... Kim Dunphy, 'The Role of Participatory Arts in Social Change in Timor Leste' (PhD Dissertation, Deakin University, 2013).

20 ........... Hooi, 'How Arts Heal and Galvanise the Youth of Timor Leste?'; Danielle Udjvari, 'Children's Peace Education in Post-Conflict Timor Leste,' *Development Bulletin* 68 (October 2005), pp. 121–24.

21 ........... J.K. Gibson-Graham, Jenny Cameron, and Stephen Healy, *Take Back the Economy: An Ethical Guide for Transforming Our Communities* (Minneapolis: University of Minnesota Press, 2013), pp. 21–22.

22 ........... Government of Timor Leste, *Report on the Implementation of the Sustainable Development Goals: From Ashes to Reconciliation, Reconstruction, and Sustainable Development, Voluntary National Review of Timor Leste* (Dili: Timor Leste, 2019), p. 25.

23 ........... Ibid.

Arte Moris set up various ways for managing their living and working space: collective cleaning, collective gardening, and collective cooking. Such cooperative housekeeping can be traced to the habits of many artist communities in managing their dual-function studio and living spaces, and transforming them into a productive working space and a liveable place.

The term 'cooperative housekeeping' here is inspired from the materialist feminist tradition, which focused its works on creating feminist homes aiming for equality for women. The proponents of this movement had created various design inventions and forms of domestic reforms revolved around public houses, socialized housework, and child care.[24] I find it useful to employ 'cooperative housekeeping' as a lens through which I can explore how an artist community like Arte Moris directs the aspiration of the members to become artists, through management of their space. To be an artist embodies personal aspirations. When the process of achieving these is conducted through living together with other aspiring individuals, it becomes a collective endeavour.

I consider Marie Mies and Veronika Bennholdt-Thomsen's view on 'housework' in the context of cultural production.[25] Mies and Bennholdt-Thomsen assert that in order to promote a just perspective of the contemporary social movement, one needs to renew a perspective of women in cultural production. They propose a subsistence, or 'life production' perspective, as opposed to 'commodity production.' I use this concept to develop a connection between collective responsibility and support systems in contemporary art. To talk about support means to talk about a certain kind of organizing and caring work that is often gendered, or discoursed in certain ways.

In the following passages, I reflect on my field notes to explore how Arte Moris emerged to become a space where the members not only train themselves to become artists but more importantly to survive together as an artist community.

## A Free Art School, Productivity, and Opportunities through Art

•

> Iliwatu, or Ili for short, took us to see the Arte Moris gallery this afternoon. We had been chatting away at the porch of the pavilion at the back part of the building complex. This pavilion is used as the office of the organization. Some parts of this pavilion are allocated as the library and the art supply shop. Ili said that they intend to create a cafe in the future. Next to the pavilion is the garden, the pond, and the favourite hang-out spot for everyone here.
>
> The gallery is located in the main building of the complex. The artworks displayed in the gallery are mainly paintings.

24 .......... Dolores Hayden, *The Grand Domestic Revolution: A History of Feminist Designs for American Homes, Neighbourhoods, and Cities* (Cambridge: MIT Press, 1982).

25 .......... Marie Mies and Veronika Bennholdt-Thomsen, *The Subsistence Perspective: Beyond the Globalised Economy* (London: Zed Books, 2000).

> The themes of these paintings are predominantly personal expressions, Timor Leste culture, and the struggle of Timor Leste people during the Indonesian occupation. There are many three dimensional objects lying on the floor—various figurines made of wood sculpture, indicating the strong wood-carving and sculptural tradition in Timor Leste.
>
> There is a classroom situated at the back part of the gallery. The classroom is big and can be used as a multipurpose space. The structure of the class seems to follow the conventional rules: a set of chairs and wooden benches are arranged next to each other. There are easels on top of the benches. The walls around the room are filled with charcoal and watercolour sketches, portraits of the members made during a portrait workshop. The class sessions are usually conducted twice a week, for approximately two hours (but last longer depending on class dynamics). But the class can also be cancelled for various reasons.
>
> As we walked back to the pavilion, I looked around the surroundings. The walls of the building are all adorned with huge murals. These murals are of various themes, and made by the members. The number of the sculptures outside the gallery room is a lot more than inside. They are everywhere. Some of them are made from wood, depicting traditional mermaid figures or crocodiles—known locally as the ancestors of the people. What strikes me is that a lot of these sculptures are made from various waste materials—food packages, used tires, plastic bottles, glass bottles, and flip-flops. Everywhere I look there is art.
>
> *(Field notes, 18 June 2019)*
>
> Arte Moris is an independent art school located in the former art museum of East Timor province that was built by the Indonesian New Order regime. After Timor Leste gained independence, the building was gifted by then Prime Minister Jose Ramos Horta to Arte Moris, to be repurposed as their headquarters.

This building complex not only serves as the headquarters for Arte Moris. The site is also used to host a theatre group, a music group, and has been frequented by various artists, activists, researchers, and writers. It has become an important part of public art infrastructure, meant to nurture the development of contemporary art and culture in the city. △Fig. 5

The 'first generation' of Arte Moris refers to those who experienced the transition from the organization's location in Luca and Gabi's rented house (some of them lived together in this house), to its current location in the former art museum of East Timor province.

When I conducted my fieldwork in Timor Leste in June 2019, the strong reputation of Arte Moris as a free school to study art had earned the institution popularity among young people. △Fig. 6 I met many new members who came from various districts in Timor Leste. These members are often regarded as the new generation of Arte Moris since they do not have first-hand experience of learning directly from Luca and Gabi Gansser. They come from various education backgrounds including fine arts, architecture, community health, and sports education. Some of these new generation students were still in university, while others were either graduates from university, or did not go to university at all. They all had different starting points in their trajectory of becoming artists.

△ 5
Arte Moris Free Art School, photo: Nuraini Juliastuti, 2019

△ 6
The gallery, photo: Nuraini Juliastuti, 2019

In the early years of Arte Moris, the Ganssers proposed that doing art and making good quality works of art were part of a useful pathway for healing from trauma and moving towards economic independence; the members kept a certain percentage of the sales and used it to fulfill their basic needs.[26] The gallery served and continues to serve as the display room for all the artworks created by all members. It has became a source of pride for the organization. Many tourists often made impromptu visits to the gallery. This created the possibility to purchase the artworks, which boosted the sense of confidence of the members.

Many city residents come to Arte Moris every afternoon to enjoy it as a public park. This opens up another possibility to earn revenue from

26...........Dunphy, 'The Role of Participatory Arts in Social Change in Timor Leste,' p. 93.

△ 7
A group of high school students wanted to take a picture with Brigitta Isabela (research assistant). Iliwatu Danubere was asked to take a picture with the student's camera, photo: Nuraini Juliastuti, 2019

the building. There is a group of Arte Moris' members who are in charge of guarding the gate everyday. Their task is to greet the visitors—high school students and other types of young people – who mainly come here to enjoy the green scenery, socialize, and to take selfies. △Fig. 7 There is a suggested donation to be able to come inside the building, ranging from twenty cents to fifty cents per visitor.

Being a member of Arte Moris often leads to opportunities to advance one's artistic skills. According to Iliwatu, residency, scholarship opportunities, and cultural exchanges are important for deepening autodidactic learning methods. Such opportunities also come in the forms of book illustrations, advertisements, mural painting, or art workshop jobs. These do not always come often. Evan, the current programme manager, is confident that the reputation of Arte Moris will pave the way for these opportunities to keep coming.

## An Intermittent Teaching System

• •

> We had a long conversation with Kiki ze Lara yesterday afternoon in the studio. Kiki works in the logistics department of the army. The room is located right next to the art supply shop. Working in the army has provided Kiki income stability. But he often feels that the military uniform limits his creative expression. That is why he likes to spend his lunch hour in Arte Moris. All around us are Kiki's paintings. I have seen some of his paintings in the gallery too. We talk about how he idolizes Pramoedya Ananta Toer, about Loriku the mythical bird, about the spirit of Timor Leste people. Kiki told me a story about the years when he joined Arte Moris for the first time. Luca always said that there are three aspects to learn in painting a still life—shadow, lighting, darkness. Throughout the conversation, Acacio, a guest from Rekreativ, an art space for photography, was there. Abe came, made us coffee, and listened to the conversation.
>
> Luca passed away last night. The news of his passing quickly reached Dili from Rome where he currently lived with Gabi. When I came to Arte Moris this afternoon, Arte Moris organized the ceremony to pay homage to Luca. Many

> local artists and former students of Arte Moris came from far and near to pay their last homage. They gathered in the hanging-out spot next to the pond in the garden. Everyone talked about memories, about Luca, and how they felt connected to him and the space. There was a big fish being grilled. There were bottles of local wine on the table. As they were engaging in a conversation, they were nibbling on grilled fish and circulating a glass of local wine. The newer members of the space were there too. Sometimes they chipped in during the conversation. But often they were just there, quietly observing, and being attentive to what the older members were talking about. The ceremony and other fringe activities around it serve as an occasion for younger students of Arte Moris to learn about Luca and how he impacted the lives of other people.
>
> *(Field notes, 23 June 2019)*

△ 8
Some Arte Moris' members were making frames for the paintings together, photo: Nuraini Juliastuti, 2019

Arte Moris does not have a fixed structure or rigid teaching system.△Fig. 8 Teachers in the organization work on an intermittent basis. The knowledge facilitators reach Arte Moris through networks, friendships, and generosity. Volunteers have played an important role in the learning process in Arte Moris. The existence of the volunteers emerged from the reciprocal gesture due to the opportunities given to them to stay at Arte Moris. The generosity of the organization generated a group of volunteer-teachers. However these volunteers often stay only for a short period of time. It makes it difficult to trace various skills circulated and to establish them formally as part of the institutional memory of the organization.

During my fieldwork, I observed that the planned classes were often cancelled for various reasons. Arte Moris is a school in which the class organization is based on the agreement of the people. In Wacquant's research, the learning process becomes a collective teaching project because the pugilistic knowledge transfer in the boxing gym follows a more or less fixed teaching system—from the trainer, to the assistant trainer, to the boxers. Further, it is structured around the regularity of the training schedule.

Similarly, there is no clear learning process pattern in Arte Moris. Since its inception, there is a relaxed approach to how the learning process should be conducted. Rather than perceiving this as a shortfall, Kiki ze Lara, one of the members, suggests that we see practice as a more important dimension. Kiki explains: 'Doing art is all about practice. Practice is the criteria of truth.' He suggests that even without the rigid structure of class organization, many members of Arte Moris produce good art and organize an independent style of visual art exhibitions.

Further, the practice of hanging out performs a role as a regular event in Arte Moris. Hanging out was one of the regular activities through which I mined valuable information. It serves as a useful activity to observe how one learns from others through conversation, taking cues from everyone's stories and experiences, forming plans and executing them into actions.

Antariksa's research on *nyantrik* [learning from the master] offers an inroad for understanding how this hang out practice leads to useful knowledge. He reveals that learning resembles a soul-searching process. *Nyantrik* is a learning process to acquire certain craftsmanship or to learn about art from a master. Learning about art does not necessarily lead to the mastery of a specific knowledge. Rather it might lead to another process—'to understand the universe, and the meaning and secret of the growth of the human soul towards perfection.'[27]

The learning habits in Arte Moris can be seen as part of a process of creating the character of an artist. Such character is rooted in a strong autodidactic culture. The autodidactic culture stems from the combination of having to make do with what is available, of growing in a limited infrastructure, and of attempting to fill in what is lacking in the wider social environment.[28] A keen awareness of the lack of infrastructure informs the way Arte Moris members view opportunities and the future. In order to value the knowledge produced in the space, they needed to create their own ways of remembering, storing, and transforming this knowledge into practice.

## On regularity:<br>Cooking and Surviving Together

• • •

Arte Moris organizes collective meals for its members everyday. These are prepared by a group of members who are in charge of chores each day of the week. There are vegetables growing in the garden in the back part of the building. These include spinach, chillies, cassava, corn, banana, papaya, and coconut. The crops will be used for the daily cooking, in addition to the ingredients bought at a nearby market.

The menu is usually humble—*nasi* [cooked rice], a vegetable dish, and a dollop of *sambal* [hot relish]. The menu will change

27...........Antariksa, 'Nyantrik as Commoning,' in *Qalqalah: A Reader*, ed. Virginie Bobin et al. (Paris: Betonsalon, Villa Vassilieff; Kadist Art Foundation, 2016), p. 10.

28...........Nuraini Juliastuti, 'Some Explanation about the Birth of an Autodidactic Culture,' in *Beyond the Dutch: Indonesia, the Netherlands, and the Visual Arts, from 1900 until Now*, ed. Meta Knol, Remco Raben, and Kitty Zijlmans (Amsterdam: KIT Publishers, 2009).

daily, depending on the available ingredients and the creativity of the cooks in charge. At around 12pm or 1pm, or when the meal is ready, a 'lunch is ready' call is made through the *karau dikur* [flute made of a cow horn]. There is a painting of a giant pumpkin, with corn, eggplants, and tomatoes dangling around it and hung on the wall next to the dining table. The text on the painting reads *mai ita han* [let's have a meal together] in Tetum.

Guo was in charge of cooking the vegetable dish today. Today's menu was nasi, stir-fry cabbages and *tempeh* [fermented soybean cake], and sambal. We had started eating and chatting away, when Abe came. Apparently there was no more food available for him. I was feeling guilty because I thought I had taken his food. If I had not joined the lunch, there would have been enough food for everyone. *'Aduh maaf ya. Ini pasti karena aku ikut makan di sini, jadi jatah makan kalian berkurang'* [Oh dear. This must be because I am having lunch here. Now there is not enough food for everyone] I said in Indonesian. Abe replied, *'Oh tidak, kakak jangan khawatir. Bagi kami orang Timor, kalau ada tamu datang, mereka harus ikut makan.'* [Oh please sister, don't worry about that. For us Timorese people, if there is a guest, they have to eat together with us].

*(Field notes, 22 June 2019)*

△ 9
Lunch is in progress, photo: Nuraini Juliastuti, 2019

A series of housework activities function to regulate the time in Arte Moris. These activities are gardening, taking care of the gallery space, cooking together, having lunch and dinner together, and hanging-out together. They serve as the daily routine to create order in living together. △Fig. 9

During my conversation with Evan, I learned that doing chores collectively is based on the notion that they have the space to manage and to care for. What is the role of cooking and sharing meals together in sustaining the artistic career of Arte Moris' members? There is a sense of certainty that emerges from the daily ritual of preparing the food and eating together. The sound of the *karau dikur* always feels assuring. It means that there will always be food available for everyone. The act of cooking, to follow Luce Giard, is 'the nourishing art.'[29] Cooking also provides another sense of certainty in managing time in collective practices. I often felt how time moved in a meandering manner while staying in Arte Moris. At 8 am, many members were already awake. Breakfast and coffee sessions that followed seemed to be able to continue on without end, until some people needed to leave to go to the university or to do other activities. Cooking is a task which holds clarity of purpose, a sure sense that this is what, at least, needs to be done today.

Cooking together and sharing meals with other people outside the family unit are often new skills and experiences for many members of Arte Moris. Being in Arte Moris has given members the opportunity to do 'an apprenticeship in communal meals,'[30] appreciate different tastes, and find different values in food. Arte Moris serves as a space to learn cooking skills and other domestic skills. Guo was forced to learn how to cook from seeing what the others usually did while in the kitchen. At first, it seemed like an obligation because cooking is part of living together in Arte Moris. Eventually, because he needed to eat, cooking felt like a necessity; Guo needed to learn how to cook and prepare food for himself and the others, so that he could access the system of food provision in the organization. Some parts of the apprenticeship in communal meals also include learning how to deal with various food technologies. Guo told me that he did not know how to operate a rice cooker until he arrived to Arte Moris.

My field notes highlights the connection between cooking practices and the tradition of Timorese hospitality marked by Abe. Cooking a meal demonstrates generosity, and helps to regulate the relation between the host and the guest. Within the Arte Moris community, cooking and eating together emerges as a performance of care. Giard states that 'the art of nourishing has to do with the art of loving, thus also with the art of dying.'[31] In Giard's writing, the art of dying refers to the practice of sharing food and having a family reunion during a situation of mourning. Food represents the sustenance for the bodies, and for the soul. When Luca passed away, we also sat together around food. △Fig. 10

△ 10
Eating together on the next day after Luca Gansser died, photo: Nuraini Juliastuti, 2019

29..........Luce Giard, 'The Nourishing Arts,' in *The Practice of Everyday Life: Volume 2: Living and Cooking*, ed. Michel de Certeau, Luce Giard, and Pierre Mayol, trans. Timothy J. Tomasik (Minneapolis: University of Minnesota Press, 1998), pp. 151–69.

30..........Ibid., p. 152.

31..........Ibid., p. 169.

Collective cooking provides an assurance that there will be food on the table. On a more practical level, it helps to assure the members that they do not need to worry about the food, and to focus on their art practices. This provides insights into the development of art making as a collective endeavor. Cooking together serves as a means to achieve this goal.

## CONCLUSION

Tiny Toones and Arte Moris are both born from the necessity of providing an urgent space of education for their respective social ecosystems. They are both part of responsive activism efforts to tackle disruptions in education systems caused by political and social turmoil. Tiny Toones and Arte Moris started out as organizations that provided free art classes. They both developed into deeper, broader efforts that go beyond this original ambit. Their informal character has given them more freedom in organizing their schools. Here, 'informality' is a critical tool for fostering inclusion in education: 'free school' emerges as the means to facilitate a learning process with the ultimate goal of learning together.

In Arte Moris, collective housework creates a familial condition in which the members rehearse potentially shared ethics of living together. It replaces the intermittent condition of art classes. When my fieldwork was almost finished, Iliwatu told me that he had been negotiating the status of the land of the Arte Moris building with the government. Iliwatu said that if the government would like to take over the building, they needed to consider the fact that the cooperative housekeeping is a key point in keeping the Arte Moris' premises in good conditions. The members took great pride in how they managed to transform the bare and dry land around the building into a green environment full of trees and vegetable patches. The ability to maintain collective housework gives more power to the bargaining position of the organization.

My research in Arte Moris suggests that studying together provides an avenue for learning about how to live together. Developing a free art school paves the way for creating mechanisms for living together. Arte Moris students are trained to be productive through doing art. The most important lesson, it seems, for being an artist, is to learn how to survive.

ACKNOWLEDGEMENTS

In conducting this research, I worked with my two colleagues from KUNCI Study Forum & Collective—Gatari Surya Kusuma and Brigitta Isabella. I would like to thank them and express my appreciation for their work in assisting me to conduct my fieldwork in Phnom Penh and Dili. I also would like to thank the Tiny Toones and Arte Moris communities for their generosity and support.

← REFERENCES


Antariksa. 'Nyantrik as Commoning.' In *Qalqalah: A Reader*, ed. Virginie Bobin et al. San Francisco: Kadist Art Foundation, 2016.

Arthur, Catherine Elizabeth. 'Writing National Identity on the Wall: the Geracao Foun, Street Art and Language Choices in Timor Leste.' *Cadernos de Arte e Antropologia* 4, no. 1 (2015), pp. 41–63.

Brehm, Will. 'Historical Memory and Educational Privatisation: A Portrait From Cambodia.' *Ethnography and Education* 14, no. 1 (2017), p. 3.

Dunphy, Kim. 'The Role of Participatory Arts in Social Change in Timor Leste.' PhD Dissertation. Melbourne: Deakin University, 2013.

Giard, Luce. 'The Nourishing Arts.' In *The Practice of Everyday Life: Volume 2: Living and Cooking*, ed. Michel de Certeau, Luce Giard, and Pierre Mayol. Minneapolis: University of Minnesota Press, 1998.

Gibson-Graham, J.K., Jenny Cameron, and Stephen Healy. *Take Back the Economy: An Ethical Guide for Transforming Our Communities*. Minneapolis: University of Minnesota Press, 2013.

Government of Timor Leste. *Report on the Implementation of the Sustainable Development Goals: From Ashes to Reconciliation, Reconstruction, and Sustainable Development, Voluntary National Review of Timor Leste*. Dili: Timor Leste, 2019.

Harney, Stefano, and Fred Moten. *The Undercommons: Fugitive Planning & Black Study*. Wivenhoe, New York: Minor Compositions, 2013.

Hayden, Dolores. *The Grand Domestic Revolution: A History of Feminist Designs for American Homes, Neighbourhoods, and Cities*. Cambridge: MIT Press, 1982.

Hicks, David. 'Glimpses of Alternatives: The Uma Lulik of East Timor.' *Social Analysis* 52, (2008), pp. 166–80.

Hooi, Khoo Ying. 'How Arts Heal and Galvanise the Youth of Timor Leste?' *The Conversation*, 12 June 2017. https://theconversation.com/how-arts-heal-and-galvanise-the-youth-of-timor-leste-73927.

Juliastuti, Nuraini. 'A Conversation on Horizontal Organization.' *Afterall: A Journal of Art, Context, and Enquiry* 30 (2012), pp. 118–25.
—. 'Commons People: Managing Music and Culture in Contemporary Yogyakarta.' PhD Dissertation. Leiden University, 2019.
—. 'Knowledge Performativity of Alternative Spaces.' Paper presented at *Cultural Performance in Post-New Order Indonesia: New Structures, Scenes, Meanings* symposium. Yogyakarta: Sanata Dharma University, 2010.
—. '*Sanggar* as a Model for Practicing Art in Communal Life.' In *Made in Commons*, ed. Ferdiansyah Thajib and Kerstin Winking, pp. 9–17. Amsterdam: KUNCI Cultural Studies Centre; Stedelijk Museum Bureau Amsterdam, 2013.
—. 'Some Explanation about the Birth of an Autodidactic Culture.' In *Beyond the Dutch: Indonesia, the Netherlands, and the Visual Arts, from 1900 until Now*, ed. Meta Knol, Remco Raben, and Kitty Zijlmans. Amsterdam: KIT Publishers, 2009.

Koleth, Maria. 'Hope in the Dark: Geographies of Volunteer and Dark Tourism in Cambodia.' *Cultural Geographies* 21, no. 4 (2014), pp. 681–94.

McWilliam, Andrew, Lisa Palmer, and Christopher Shepherd. 'Lulik Encounters and Cultural Frictions in East Timor: Past and present.' *The Australian Journal of Anthropology* 25, no. 3 (2014), pp. 304–20.

Mies, Marie, and Veronika Bennholdt-Thomsen. *The Subsistence Perspective: Beyond the Globalised Economy*. London: Zed Books, 2000.

Needham, Susan, and Karen Quintiliani. 'Cambodians in Long Beach, California: The Making of a Community.' *Journal of Immigrant and Refugee Studies* 5, no. 1 (2007), pp. 29–53.

Needham, Susan. 'How Can You Be Cambodian If You Don't Speak Khmer? Language, Literacy, and Education in Cambodian "Rhetoric of Distinction".' *Negotiating Transnationalism: Selected Papers on Refugees and Immigrants* 9 (2001).

Nelson, Roger. 'The Present is a Foreign Country: Some Thoughts on the (Dis)Entanglement of Exploration and Conquest.' In *Fields: An Itinerant Inquiry Across the Kingdom of Cambodia*, ed. Charlotte Huddleston and Roger Nelson, pp. 58–66. Auckland: ST Paul St Gallery and Sa Sa Bassac, 2015.

Parkinson, Chris. *Peace of Wall*. Melbourne: Affirm Press, 2010.

Udjvari, Danielle. 'Children's Peace Education in Post-Conflict Timor Leste.' *Development Bulletin* 68 (October 2005), pp. 121–24.

Veiga, Leonor. 'Movimentu Kultura in Timor Leste: Maria Madeira's Agency.' *Cadernos de Arte e Antropologia* 4, no. 1 (2015), pp. 85–101.
—. 'Movimentu Kultura: Making Timor Leste.' In *Routledge Handbook of Contemporary Timor Leste*, ed. Andrew McWilliam and Michael Leach, pp. 256–70. London: Routledge, 2019.

Wacquant, Loïc. *Body & Soul: Notebooks of An Apprentice Boxer*. Oxford: Oxford University Press, 2004.

# BETWEEN MEMORY AND STORAGE
## Digital Transitions for Art Organizations

Maya Indira Ganesh and Nishant Shah

This chapter reflects on the dynamics of memory-as-storage, and memory-making in the digital practices of arts and cultural producers in Bangladesh, Myanmar, Pakistan and Sri Lanka. These cultural producers' resistance to the violence, fascism, and intolerance in their countries takes place through their own re-working of memory-making within the conditions of the digital afforded to them. They create narratives and memories in the context of a fixation with counting and collecting data in algorithmic networks, the elision and inclusion of bodies, and the imperatives of spectacularization. They keep themselves firmly inside circuits of media production: staking their security, opening themselves up to the possible fortunes of amplification online, and making content openly available. However, the digital can also be just a platform, or business card. Drawing on the work of four organizations and their programming, we argue that the digital is embodied, situated, that it requires tacit knowledge to navigate, and is affective, material, and political—these elements represent what we propose are a set of 'touchstones' for the digital. This interpretative framework ('ESTAMP' for the elements aforementioned) presents a lens, rather than metrics for the digital turn. What might future memory-making in the digital be through this framework?

Keywords
- → South Asia
- → Arts
- → Cultural Production
- → Digital
- → Material
- → Internet
- → Politics
- → Civil Society

## INTRODUCTION

This chapter reflects on the affordances of and opportunities in the digital (the internet, mobile phones, and social media) for small arts and cultural organizations that have stepped away from mainstream, status quo-ist, state-driven art patronage. We also discuss the pitfalls in digital practices in the current political milieu of authoritarian governments, militarization, economic inequality, neo-colonialisms, platformization, and a clamping down on civil liberties.[1] Across the post-colonial context of South Asia, it is the state that has typically taken on the task of storage—of identities, histories, narratives, and entire populations.[2] Now, the 'digital turn' has issued a substantial challenge to the authorial state and makes possible new kinds of narratives and memory-making by individuals and collectives, like the ones that will be profiled in this chapter. Yet, the 'digital' also includes the peculiarities of software, the limits of hardware, the logics of databases, and algorithms. The digital is further controlled by for-profit corporations that can operate as states do, in setting up the terms of storage, memory-making, access, legibility, interfaces, and retrieval. This constellation of factors introduces unique tensions in the digital that echo through its promises. This chapter draws on both digital studies and theories of aesthetics to mark and frame this significant transition. We organize the chapter in terms of the following themes related to 'making memory': memory as a counting exercise, memory-making through the entwining of bodies with technology, memory-making through algorithmic logics, and the spectacle of sharing in digital memory-making. We look at the paradigm shift from storage to memory through stories of cultural producers and activists from four countries in the region. These include: the feminist organizing, research, and activist Women and Media Collective (WMC) in Sri Lanka; the Burmese performance artist, Moe Satt; arts and cultural programming by 'The Second Floor' (T2F)/Peace Niche in Pakistan; and artist residencies and programming by Britto Arts Trust, Bangladesh. These organizations, varied in scale, size, context, and history, exemplify resistance to structural political challenges, as well as the loose and tight relationships between technology and publics.[3] As academics, activists, and researchers working with arts and cultural institutions, and anchored in South Asia whilst living in Northern Europe, we have been witness to a shift in the role and position of art institutions in the region. 'Arts and Cultural Management' is a relatively new phenomenon in South Asia, through which the focus of public art organizations has been to preserve and produce archives, galleries, and museums that further canonical legacies. This work of enshrining the canon persists despite many diverse, independent, disruptive, and transformative practices and spaces, undeterred by artistic and curatorial voices from the region that harness the force of art towards critical and radical transformation. The discrepancy between the older keepers of archives and gatekeepers of gallery-based artwork and the new artistic interventions has often been

1............Following a definition proposed by Anita Gurumurthy, 'platformization' refers to what social media platforms, as corporations, do: how they re-shape conditions of labor, economics, citizenship, commerce, geopolitics, and the new relationalities produced therein.

2............Every country in South Asia—roughly including the landmass from west to east, Afghanistan to Myanmar, and from north to south Nepal to Sri Lanka, though exact geography can be tricky—has been shaped by centuries of British colonialism and the history of Partition. Partition is still the largest mass migration of people in human history. We cannot do justice to its history here and suggest the reader refer to the following resources to better understand the context of this chapter: Vazira Fazila-Yacoobali Zamindar, *The Long Partition and the Making of Modern South Asia: Refugees, Boundaries, Histories* (New York: Columbia University, 2010); Urvashi Butalia, *The Other Side of Silence: Voices from the Partition of India* (Durham: Duke University, 2000); a *New Yorker* article by William Dalrymple, 'The Great Divide: The Violent Legacy of Indian Partition,' 2015, www.newyorker.com/magazine/2015/06/29/the-great-divide-books-dalrymple; and the collectively-authored blog Chapati Mystery, founded in 2004, which remains an excellent source of commentary on South Asian history, culture, and politics.

3............These four organizations were selected out of a total of seven from South Asia that received funding from the European Cultural Foundation, Prince Claus Fund, and Hivos. They responded to our invitation for interviews to share their work; the other three were not available for different reasons. All interviews took place in 2019. The organizations were funded between 2008–2016 for either a one-off event, or for a year-long (at most) project.

perceived as generational and infrastructural. In this chapter, we propose that this distance is also transitional, both enabled by the digital turn that produces systemic shifts in the national and regional policy and politics, and shaped by the global material economies of digitization.[4]

## FROM STORAGE TO MEMORY

The 'database nation' counts, accounts for, holds accountable, and discounts its populations based on the ledger-keeping of the erstwhile empire and national censuses.[5] This extends to the censuses establishing themselves as the central storage system safeguarding and safekeeping the political agenda and the cultural status quo alike. National archives, museums, and galleries are devoted to championing a homogeneous cultural ethos, and preserving indigenous arts and crafts as a way of controlling national narratives. The tight control over the narrative of the nation through a closed infrastructure of access and circulation has been the cornerstone of nation-building exercises across the region.[6] Practices of storage—where cultural material is stored, how it is stored, what meanings are attributed to the stored, and who gets to access and interpret it—are determined by proximity to power, and an affinity with dominant narratives. The second half of the twentieth century has seen meaning made in this way—through storage and its capacity to control stories—and has shaped the milieu within which the arts have developed. We particularly understand these conditions of storage as wedded to the logic of counting, algorithmic spread, a separation of the technological infrastructure from the embodied experience, and a flattening through interface. Digital technologies have been introduced as a way of strengthening these conditions of storage.[7] We weave this understanding into our discussion of memory-making, showing how new players emerge with the spread of digital networks: not as custodians of data, but as 'makers of memory.' With movement towards open information and data, and the production of easily accessible, shareable, and circulating digital archives and knowledges, there is a new ethos of working within the arts. It has destabilized the state-driven patronage and narrative, and allowed for a new body of art and cultural organizations who have harnessed the power of arts in order to excavate histories, to unearth resistant narratives, to perform alternative 'presents,' and to speculate possible futures.

We draw on the work of four organizations addressing a diverse range of themes such as gender and sexuality rights, migration, freedom

4............Vivek Menezes, 'The Indian Art World is Dead: Long Live the New Indian Art World,' *The Hindustan Times*, 29 December 2018, www.hindustantimes.com/analysis/the-indian-art-world-is-dead-long-live-the-new-indian-art-world/story-MMFURyQy8K3ZPmtotFtNXL.html.

5............Simon Garfinkel, *Database Nation* (Sebastopol, CA: O'Reilly Media, 2000); Simon A. Cole, 'Review of Imprint of the Raj: How Fingerprinting was Born in Colonial India,' *Technology and Culture* 46 no. 1 (2005), p. 252–53.

6............For example, the Hindu nationalist BJP government in India is erasing the legacy of the Mughal dynasty on Indian culture. See: Audrey Truschke, 'The Great Mughal Whitewash,' *India Today*, 21 March 2016, www.indiatoday.in/magazine/up-front/story/20160321-the-great-mughal-whitewash-audrey-truschke-south-asian-history-828594-2016-03-10.

7............Biometrics storage databases as the basis for identification infrastructures—such as the Aadhar scheme in India—are a significant new example of this.

of speech and expression, religious freedom and tolerance. Not all of them are engaged in digital practices, producing digital art or incubating technological practices. We do not create portraits of these organizations nor compile exhaustive case studies of their practice, but detail their programming through the lens of our interpretative framework. We examine the techno-spheres within which these organizations operate, and the elements of their practice that use digital tools to record, amplify, and circulate marginal and threatened voices and communities of resistance. In doing so, we hope to produce a refracted story of what happens when we move into the domains of the digital. This transition into the digital is not just about mere logistics and operations, but the contexts within which arts and cultural organizations develop positionality, and make space.

## MAKING MEMORY IN TIMES OF COUNTING

Tayeba Begum Lipi is a memory keeper, and she is a far more reliable one than the internet.[8] She tells me an elaborate story of how the website of the Britto Arts Trust—the arts residency and collective she co-founded in Dhaka—was hacked. Speaking with her on a WhatsApp call, I can hear her hesitate, even struggle with the right words for the story's technical details. She says that maybe because I 'know technology,' I may understand how it happened, and to forgive her if she gets it wrong. Lipi says that the web domain the collective bought in 2002 was available for ten years, the 'highest timeframe' offered for a website. A decade later, in 2012, they were told that their freedom had expired. There was no opportunity for renewal. Apparently, a 'company' based in Hong Kong was demanding that they pay for the domain, because it now belonged to them. According to the 'rules,' they learned, the domain would be available after forty days so Britto could have access to their website. However, 'it was on Hong Kong time,' she told me, 'and we had to be sitting at the computer early in the morning and click a button before someone else did.' They could not best whoever was behind this extortionate scheme, and they ultimately lost their domain. As a result, the Britto Arts Trust lost its archives, because they had not been backed up offline, and the staff did not know how to access their web-hosted data. Yet, in our hour-long conversation, Lipi shows no skip or delay in recalling every event their organization has executed, every biennale they have exhibited at, every artist they've hosted as a resident, and every date of artists' visits. She says she has been keeping a list over the years of everyone they have worked with.

8............Begum Tayeba Lipi (co-founder and director, Britto Arts Trust), interview by author, September 2019.

> Did they ever get around to building a new website? 'It's coming, it's coming,' says Lipi; but the story gets darker: 'We hired someone to design and build a new site for us, but then he died quite unexpectedly.' They have to find a new person to take on the legacy of turning organizational memory into storage. Lipi and her list are, for the time being, always there.

One of the primary assurances of information storage was its capacity to keep things forever. Once stored, information becomes robust, subject to protocols of retrieval and access. Information storage would ostensibly be both more exhaustive and reliable than human memory and remembrance. This particular binary of infallible technology versus the limited human has been a propelling force towards full digitization. Hence, even in the face of 'planned obsolescence,' the digital was foregrounded as more reliable. This resulted in what Erwin Alampay calls 'quantiphilia.'[9] This is a focus on quantification, metrics, and quantity, which reduces lived reality and practice to collecting, storing, analyzing, transmitting, re-purposing, circulating and amplifying information. There is little attention to the impulses and ambitions of the communities and people who the information comes from. The end point of quantiphilia is quantification. We draw on what Wendy Chun refers to as an'opaque metaphor': here, the measure of measurement is that which can be measured.[10] Quantiphilia has informed the extraordinary investments in digital infrastructure through state and private partnerships, as well as any kind of 'monitoring and evaluation' activity that donors engage in. It has led to the dismissal of analogue memory-making, and the human capacity to forget as regretful. Who is the figure of a Tayeba Lipi, then, a human who doesn't just record events but has the uncanny ability to remember details over time?

The promise of the digital is to turn memory into storage. If our old information systems (books, archives, lists) were about the quest to remember that which gets forgotten with time, our new digital information systems store things that will never be remembered, creating datasets for algorithms to trawl for patterns. Here, the digital emerges as a point of departure in how we conceptualize our lived, informational realities: it transforms us from subjects who are afraid of losing memory, into subjects who now concede that non-human actors remember more about us than we can ever know. We have gone from subjects worrying about information scarcity, to subjects either struggling to survive in the midst of an information overload, or figuring out how to leverage it for profit.

Focusing on these shifts between memory and storage simultaneously performs two functions: a possible move away from the quantiphilia of digital technologies in arts and culture, and an inroads into the role of arts and culture in a critical framework that frees it from the logic of statistics, circulation, and amplification. Consider Google's Art Selfie app that

9............Alampay, Edwin, 'Introduction,' in *Living the Information Society in Asia*, ed. Edwin Alampay (Singapore: Institute of South East Asian Studies), pp. 10–14.

10..........Wendy Chun, *Programmed Visions: Software and Memory* (Cambridge, MA: MIT Press, 2011).

searches for the likeness of a selfie from a database of the canon of Western visual art.[11] The app appears as a light-hearted exploration of European and North American art and culture through a contemporary digital practice that is fuelled by facial recognition technology and machine learning. However, it does not invite critical reflection on the ethnocentric biases in this canon; and what it does with the face data it collects for its statistical sorting exercise is most likely buried in its Byzantine 'Terms & Conditions' that no one reads.[12] Quantiphilia is neither a naturalized nor a preferred mode of thinking about the contexts that the art and cultural organizations shape and are shaped by. While we do not seek to glorify the humanist over the computational, as if they were discrete and separable models or value systems, we do want to emphasize that digitization is only one of the many different impulses of technology development and deployment.

## What Does it Mean to Make Memories in the Age of Quantiphilia?

•

This is a question that Karachi's legendary and much-loved arts and cultural venue, The Second Floor (T2F), has been contemplating (though, with different phrasing). T2F is a favoured spot for intellectuals, cultural pioneers, and everyday people in Karachi. It was founded by Sabeen Mahmud who was assassinated on 24 April 2015 for hosting a public discussion about the 'disappeared' in the federal region of Balochistan.[13] This was not the first time there had been a threat to her safety, because this was not the first time that T2F had pushed the boundaries of what was deemed appropriate for public discussion in Pakistani civil society.

In interviews, Mahmud states that T2F and the organization that manages it, Peace Niche, are 'not NGOs, but are social platforms where goodness can be launched.' The bustling café has become a de facto hub where anybody 'without a membership, without a club exclusivity can freely enter, sit, enjoy a coffee, look around and chat and meet people in comfort.' Mahmud's ethics, critical interest in building a movement of social conscience, and her capacity to weave together diverse social networks made the café an epicentre for progressive change. It was not a space of dramatic revolutions but a slow movement towards a 'more tolerant, aware and egalitarian Pakistan.' In the same interview, she vouched for the 'organic growth' of people pulling in people, the 'friend of a friend' effect, of weak ties in human networks as the key to the success of T2F. It was a physical space for serendipitous solidarity—a space where memories were made.

In his interview with the authors, Arieb Azhar, then the new manager of T2F and member of the Peace Niche board, describes Mahmud, a technologist, curator, and cultural producer as 'One of the first people in Pakistan

11 ........... The Google Art Selfie Project, https://artsandculture.google.com/camera/selfie.
12 ........... Noopur Raval, 'Google Arts App has a Data Problem,' *Factor Daily*, 2 February 2018, https://factordaily.com/google-art-app-data-problem/.
13 ........... Kamila Shamsie, 'Murdered on the Streets of Karachi: My Friend Who Dared to Believe in Free Speech,' *The Guardian*, 27 April 2015, www.theguardian.com/commentisfree/2015/apr/27/murdered-karachi-free-speech-sabeen-mahmud; Declan Walsh, 'Pakistan's Secret Dirty War,' *The Guardian*, 29 March 2011, www.theguardian.com/world/2011/mar/29/balochistan-pakistans-secret-dirty-war.

Nafasi Art Space / Dar Es Salaam, Tanzania / 1:53pm 6°45'47.1"S / 39°14'30.3"E

The Second Floor (T2F) / Karachi, Pakistan / 3:44pm 24°49'55.1"N / 67°03'55.5"E

△ Muhammad Zarar and Hassan Ali, Events at The 2nd Floor, 2015, courtesy: The 2nd Floor, Karachi

to realize the future lay with technology and the internet.'[14] Along with Zaheer Kidvai, Mahmud worked to ensure that everything that could be, was digitized. T2F started going live on Facebook and archiving all the events as soon as they could. They wanted to 'Connect people across Pakistan through arts and cultural events through social media.' They aimed to expand memory-making to more people through their secular cultural space (secular meaning 'Not anti-religion, but respecting the right to practice whatever you believe in,' clarifies Azhar) to create a commons, a society, a future. The last image Mahmud posted on Instagram is of the meeting with Balochi activists.[15]

Digital memory-making is an uncontrolled space. If inclusion, engagement, resistance, and the creation of a commons are foundational to programming, and thresholds of participation and access are low, the potentials for abuse, violence, and backlash are manifold. Mahmud's assassination echoes in a region where writers, cultural curators, artists, and performers have been persecuted, sometimes fatally, for speaking truth to power. The small, situated discussion that entered the state of quantiphilic sharing presented a clear and present threat to both the existence and the future activities of T2F.

14..........Arieb Azhar (Manager, Board Member, The Second Floor), interview with the author, September 2019. Azhar is no longer with T2F in this role.

15..........Sabeen Mahmud's Instagram feed: www.instagram.com/p/13RnOLnFzq/.

Yet, the organization has a clear choice to carry on as Mahmud would have wanted them to. Refusing to shutter or invest more in physical security, T2F carries on its work of hosting and curating arts and cultural work in Karachi. The possibility of exposure in digital networks and the experiences of violence are real. It might have been possible for them to use their visibility to pivot into a more 'acceptable,' meaning depoliticized, venue that was more in tune with nationalist narratives. 'We did not want to convert T2F into a shrine to Sabeen, or fold in fear,' says Azhar. 'She never would have wanted that. She would have wanted us to carry on.' So they continue to hold themselves accountable to her legacy, even as they struggle with financial uncertainty.

T2F is now considering radical openness. They are putting all their content online to develop their crowdfunding campaign. Peace Niche has accounts on all the popular channels: YouTube, Facebook, Instagram, Vimeo, and Twitter. Digital content rendered as podcasts, recorded talks, and videos of events hosted at T2F were always intended for 'free and open' access, and not just for people who have the economic and cultural capital to participate and consume. Azhar and his team think through how content metrics might translate into a revenue stream: their Facebook page has 85,000 followers, and they have five events a week. As more people share and distribute their content, the more their ideas spread. If they populate their followers' feeds with their content, they might be likely to share it and potentially attract potential new donors. They have launched a crowdfunding campaign through Facebook to target people who would make subscription-based regular donations for a year. They see this game of metrics as a way to bolster their revenue stream.

However, they also recognize that the only way by which memories can be built in an unstable regime, in conditions of persistent internet censorship in the country, is to make every member of the community a custodian and a maker of these memories.[16] The digital allows content to be 'owned' individually and collectively, even as it translates into income (hopefully). The immediacy of digital technologies, the ubiquity of information-gathering devices, and the ease of publishing this information on aggregating social media platforms, all favour speed in artistic practice and knowledge production. Timelines shrink, and institutions are encouraged to use social media platforms as their living archives. This is especially true for groups operating in hostile environments.

However, this easy relationship between the information producers and intended audiences is a false one. Closely guarded, proprietary, and black-boxed algorithms highlight or downplay content circulating online. Moreover, there is a political and cultural context around information-sharing to consider. In focusing on speed and scale, there are dangers, harms, and material consequences for these new forms of memory making. Fake news and disinformation is one of them; surveillance is another, as is the inability to control visibility and narratives online. The algorithms are in charge.

We did not find these discussions at the forefront at T2F. They believe that their financial future hinges on leveraging the arresting headline, the fast skim, and bite-sized information delivered to the right audiences.

## MEMORIES = BODIES + TECHNOLOGIES

Moe Satt is easy to find on the internet but not easy to get in touch with. The first email addressed to him remains unanswered despite multiple follow-ups.[17] Email is not the medium of preferred communication; it can be too formal to build solidarity, as it might require a computer rather than a mobile phone. I eventually reach out to Hivos to get Satt's phone number. I can't cold call, but I buzz him on WhatsApp.

We have a conversation; it is smooth, invigorating, fragmented. Satt travels across the world and is temporally and geographically distributed. He presents his work at arts and cultural events across the globe. In most instances, WhatsApp works, and the exchange is detailed and rich. I ask him for some photographs of his work to be included in this chapter.

There is another bout of radio silence. He said he would send them on WhatsApp but nothing arrives. 'Just get them from Facebook, become my friend,' Satt says. I have been averse to Facebook, but it seems that the only way of getting the images is to be his personal friend. I do it. The images arrive.

In countries where censorship, state-mandated cracking of devices, internet lock-downs, and policing are commonplace, artists and cultural producers should be wary of local archives and stand-alone infrastructure. Much as corporations like Facebook and Google might be critiqued for their data sharing practices, they do serve as archives that governments cannot directly censor or control. However, the life of information on these platforms is also subject to algorithmic curation, and erasure.

As the task of memory-making was coded into technologies of storage, it also led to a dissociation of technologies and bodies. Protocols of sharing that govern our digital networks haunt and shape the material practices and bodies involved in that infrastructure. Yet, the digital, with its emphasis on engagement, virality, scale, and amplitude, is often understood as dissociated from bodies. Metaphors of the cloud as above us, 'up there,' and the internet as pure information and signals all floating through the air, suggest a benign atmospheric layer that is free and open, and not tethered to bodies.[18] The reality is different; the cloud is anchored to server farms that are strategically located, physically highly secured, and policed by particular jurisdictions.[19]

16..........The history of internet censorship in Pakistan has its own Wikipedia entry: https://en.wikipedia.org/wiki/internet_censorship_in_Pakistan.

17..........Moe Satt (Artist), interview by author, October 2019.

18..........Tim Hwang and Karen Levy, '"The Cloud" and Other Dangerous Metaphors,' *The Atlantic*, 20 January 2015, www.theatlantic.com/technology/archive/2015/01/the-cloud-and-other-dangerous-metaphors/384518/.

The focus on digital storage in the cloud promotes scale: endless replication, repetition, and regurgitation. Memories persist not because of storage but because of embodied experience, affective solidarity, and investment of care and collective action, which cannot be measured merely by numbers. Memories are functions of intensity, not scale. Memory requires acts of remembrance and witnessing many times past the occurrence of an event. It is thus both the chronicle of history as well as its verifying measure. To make memories is a political act. To defend them, is activism. In regimes where historical revisionism and erasure are strategically used against people, as well as arts and cultural organizations, it is vital to be attentive to the implications of digital technology infrastructures being dissociated from bodies.

## How Do you Make Memories with Bodies and Technologies Entwined?

•

The Women and Media Collective (WMC) was formed by a group of Sri Lankan feminists in the aftermath of the 1983 pogrom that resulted in the deaths of 3000 Tamils. WMC has adopted, and adapted to, different kinds of old and new media to bring a gendered perspective to the impact of militarized conflict, the economy, political participation, sexuality, and sexual health and rights. They are 'actively engaged in bringing about change based on feminist principles in creating a just society that does not discriminate based on gender.'[20] Making memories, so that bodies and technologies remain connected, has been central to their impact and transformative presence in the region.

The development of indigenous, tacit knowledge through art and cultural production has been key to WMC's history, and to the history of feminist organizing in the region. WMC has worked with community radio, graphic design, performance arts, a range of visual arts from screen-printing to filmmaking, email and listservs, blogs, and now social media. The organization has always had a deep relationship with technologies of production and communication, and realized very early on that in order for them to be in control of their content and practice, they needed to weave technological infrastructure into their programming.

Subha Wijersiriwardene narrates the story of a landmark meeting of progressive, urban, feminist activists from across South Asia in 1984.[21] Here—for the first time for many in a generation of women—connections were forged across boundaries, and diverging yet interlinked histories of colonialism, partition, war, gender, and ethnicity were shared as readily as skills were. Lala Rukh, the renowned feminist activist and artist from Pakistan, travelled to Sri Lanka and taught WMC and its members screen-printing and poster-making; this remains a cherished marker in the

19...........Maya Indira Ganesh and Johannes Bruder, 'Cloud Cosmogram' on Data Farms: Circuits, Labour, Territory, 2019, www.datafarms.org/2019/12/16/cloud-cosmogram/.

20...........Women and Media Collective website, https://womenandmedia.org/.

21...........Subha Wijeseriwardene (Gender & Sexuality programs coordinator, Women and Media Collective), interview with author, August 2019. Wijeseriwardene is no longer with WMC in this role.

organization's history of doing across the region. Curator Natasha Ginwala writes in her tribute at Rukh's passing that the artist's work with the Pakistani feminist organization she co-founded, Women's Action Forum, and its partners, resulted in a trove of posters, calendar prints, and screen-printing manuals that 'Are not to be read as nostalgic documents of a movement that once was, but rather remind that such struggles continue to simmer, challenge, and awaken, so we must doggedly keep going.'[22]

Talking about their media practice and political positions over time, Wijeseriwardene says that the WMC has always been ahead of the curve, ever reflexive about its role and place in Sri Lankan civil society and feminist movements. It has picked up media and technology to experiment with, learn about, and use for its own ends, in keeping with the organization's mission. 'We are doing it, but not thinking about it,' she says about WMC's 'natural' and fearless history of doing with and through media technologies. 'We are both the archive and the incubator. ...We carry both the tangible and intangible histories of the women's movement in Sri Lanka.' WMC is an archivist organization, and their practice of media use has allowed them to develop their own approaches to how they want to use the media of the moment. In this sense, they are both generating and developing their own knowledge and use and applications of technology; however, they are also aware that this happens within the dominant frame of international aid and development.

Recently, WMC organized HerSpace, which was an online portal to showcase Sri Lankan women's writing about multiple aspects of their lives, from memorializing the anniversary of the 1983 pogrom against Tamils, to responding to the government's regressive laws on rape. HerSpace also included training programmes for feminist groups to learn more about how to work with 'new' internet platforms.

Training programmes to learn about technology are a continuing legacy of 'Information and Communication Technologies for Development' (ICT4D), often part of international donor-funded projects in the Global South.[23] The 'media training programme' emerges at the intersection of multiple conditions related to access: new media is not always 'personal' and women primarily do not necessarily have access to digital technologies. Plus, there is an inherent assumption that people in the South will learn through supervized training rather than a holistic education, and by top-down instruction, rather than discovery through play and experimentation.[24] And this all takes place within the frame of 'development,' which must be in and of itself critically unpacked as perpetuating geopolitical, racialized, and colonial power.

Popular policy narratives suggest that crossing the 'digital divide' through access to technology will narrow socio-economic gaps in developing societies. However, ethnographic studies of tech trainings for low

22 Natasha Ginwala's blog, 'In Memoriam: Lala Rukh (1948–2017),' 27 December 2017, https://natashaginwala.wordpress.com/2017/12/27/in-memoriam-lala-rukh-1948-2017/.

23 Sergio Garcia, 'Why ICT for Development,' official website of the European Union, 7 December 2015, https://europa.eu/capacity4dev/public-ict/wiki/why-ict-development-ict4d.

24 Sreela Sarkar, 'From the Maistry to the Computer Operator: The Colonial Legacy of "Skilling India" through ICT Training,' *Perspectives on Global Development and Technology* 18 (2019), pp. 343–62.

income women show that access to these trainings reproduce gendered, class, caste and religious differences; they do not necessarily enable women to escape structural disempowerment.[25] In the same vein, the function of digitally mediated arts and cultural practices is defined by the developmental agenda of ICT4D, often ignoring the affective, experiential, and creative but rather favouring the empirical, probable, and predictable deployments of the digital.

The practices of the WMC and their stitching-together of the technological context with the embodied experiences of their communities are exemplary and rare. Perhaps the longevity of the collective is also predicated on how they re-calibrate their practice with every technological shift. They recognize that these transitions toward storage and scale need to be not just countered by memory and intensity, but also adopted and adapted to fit the goals and ambitions of the larger movement they find themselves in.

## FRAMING MEMORY IN AN ALGORITHMIC NETWORK

Once upon a time, one of us was invited to an event at a globally renowned arts and culture organization in Northern Europe, where a digital arts curator was telling us about her recent trip to Mumbai, India. She was surprised and disappointed by the dearth of 'software art' there and asked us about who we thought were 'diamonds' buried somewhere in the earth, just waiting to be launched at a European show. She believed that being from India, we would know something about the digital art scene that was unavailable to her as an outsider.

We mentioned the names of some artists and collectives who are already well-known names, having exhibited their work globally over the years. She already knew of them. She was even more disappointed now: 'So there is really no culture or practice of digital and software art in India,' she declared.

We had to disagree; but we understood what she meant by 'software art.' She was referring to interventions that demonstrate both delight in and fluency with computational tools and practices, an understanding of computation's prehistories, ordering logics, and gaze; and the application of this fluency to create works that critique the entanglements of capitalism, militarism, bodies, mathematics and science that birthed the computer and the internet. Basically, works from

25 Sreela Sarkar, 'Beyond the "Digital Divide": The "Computer Girls" of Seelampur,' *Feminist Media Studies* (2016), pp. 1–16.

> India that would also look like works from North America and Europe that she was familiar with.
>
> We didn't contribute more to that conversation, but we came back from it thinking of other trajectories and contexts: electricity, identity cards, pirate cinema, local cable networks, virtual pilgrimages, and information code switching, none of which lend themselves to the taxonomy that the curator had naturalized.

The digital backend is an unglamorous space. Despite the fantastic rendering of a binary stream visualized in sci-fi imagery, when boiled down to digital brass tacks, all that remains is a database. It can be overwhelming to realize that what powers all our seemingly human, intuitive, connected interactions is a numerical transaction of data arranged in different arrays across the vast mathematical landscape of computation. For anybody who has designed computational systems (even simple websites), this is a common sense observation. But we find it particularly useful to emphasize this because a database is a system of taxonomy. Taxonomy is a practice of giving names. Names have power.

Indeed, the advanced engineer, especially one focused on variable and adaptive databases and creating relational and object-oriented databases, would contest this simplification. Databases, they would argue, are human forms, and they can be amended, upgraded, evolved, verified, and corrected. With machine learning, they are not even awaiting human verification, but are instead continually self-correcting. And yet, databases are systems of organizing that naturalize the principles, logics, and patterns that define the limits and controls of our systems. Database manipulations can bring new things into reality, erase existing records, invalidate specific truths, and create disinformation.

There is a history of processes of identification in databases: who gets called what, how they are identified, and how they are represented, and in what form, within the digital. This is not just a rehashing of the older debates of representation and authenticity. Initially, the digital emerged as a space of self-determination. John Perry Barlow's manifesto, *A Declaration of the Independence of Cyberspace*, claimed that the internet was shaped as a medium where 'weary titans of flesh and steel were not welcome.' For Barlow, the hegemonies of the embodied and material offline worlds, ruled by governments and corporations, with their power to name, blame, shame, and tame those who were the least privileged, were to be dissolved in cyberspace. He writes:

> Cyberspace consists of transactions,
> relationships, and thought itself,
> arrayed like a standing wave in the
> web of our communications. Ours
> is a world that is both everywhere
> and nowhere, but it is not where
> bodies live. We are creating a world

> that all may enter without privilege
> or prejudice accorded by race,
> economic power, military force,
> or station of birth.[26]

To our post-Cambridge Analytica, post-Snowden-revelation, intersectional gaze, Barlow's sentiment might seem naïve or hopelessly romantic. But it still holds within itself the emphasis that the guiding principle of digital networks is taxonomy, and that the democratization of the web was supposed to usher in a new age of 'folksonomy' where 'everything is miscellaneous' and thus, we can recreate the world in a new image. Cyberspace, for Barlow, was not just an action but also the creation of a new language that escapes the confines of power and punishment. However, when it comes to the digital shift in South Asia, things are complicated by two main prospects: one, the state exercises extreme control over the physical infrastructure of internet access, often partnering with corporations to create massive surveillance apparatuses. Two, the vector and velocity of big data collection makes it impossible for an individual human to counteract the claims and proposals made by algorithmic consolidation at scale.

A famous 1993 cartoon in *The New Yorker* magazine reads, 'On the internet, nobody knows you're a dog,' suggesting the anonymizing and flattening infrastructures of the web where you can be anybody you want to be, as Barlow promised.[27]

The current scenario of 'surveillance capitalism'[28] and big data mapping leads to a new proposition: on the internet, if one database verifies you as a dog, it might be easier to just become a dog than try to change information about yourself online. It is not as catchy as the original, but it is perhaps more true. The cartoon has also been updated to reflect our present awareness of the internet.[29] And nobody has faced this particular problem of being named, mobbed, punished and lynched, more than the political activists and artists who have used online spaces to question the status quo.

## How do you Make Human Memories in a Language Shaped by Algorithmic Databases?

•

Moe Satt is a performance artist based in Yangon, Myanmar, and the initiator of the 2008 performance art festival, 'Beyond Pressure.' 'Politics is the poisoned fruit,' he says, referring to the imprisonment of comedians who critiqued the ruling military junta in their jokes. Three topics were off limits in any kind of media at that time: nudity, criticisms of Buddhism (the national

26 ........... John Perry Barlow, 'A Declaration of the Independence of Cyberspace,' The Electronic Frontier Foundation blog, 8 February 1996, www.eff.org/cyberspace-independence.

27 ........... Wikipedia entry for *The New Yorker* cartoon: https://en.wikipedia.org/wiki/On_the_Internet,_nobody_knows_you%27re_a_dog.

28 ........... Shoshanna Zuboff, *The Age of Surveillance Capitalism: The Fight for the Human Future at the New Frontier of Power* (New York: Public Affairs Books, 2019).

29 ........... An update on the New Yorker cartoon: https://newyorker.tumblr.com/post/111446912131/a-cartoon-by-kaamran-hafeez-from-this-weeks.

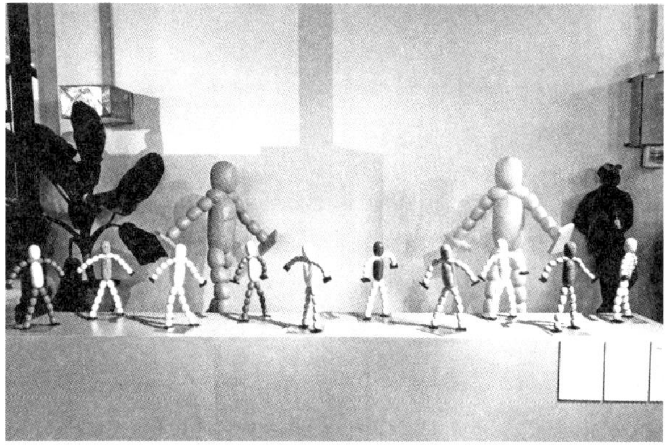

△ Moe Satt, *Balloon babies*, 'A gar ahla ku htone', 2019, sculpture, courtesy: artist

religion), and of the military government. Art events required a formal permit from the government. Satt relates the story of comedians in the nineteen-eighties who were jailed for making fun of the government. Now, Myanmar has a democratic electoral process in place, and restrictions on speech and expression have been lifted. Facebook has rapidly become central to communications, but not without its casualties. Satt recounts multiple instances at the intersection of a lack of digital literacy, and people emerging, almost overnight, into being nominally free to speak: a filmmaker arrested for saying 'fuck the military' in a Facebook post; a street vendor committing suicide for being bullied online.

At a cursory glance, this seems like a continuation of the dialogues on free and hateful speech and expression in the region, where acts of censorship and censure are not just plenty but seem to find easy execution. However, Satt's laconic recounting of this violence signals the role that digital technologies play in developing taxonomies and identifications. For instance, Facebook has become the de facto internet in Myanmar and presents itself as a champion of free speech, expression, and artistic practice. Simultaneously, the ongoing Rohingya genocide is fuelled by fake news and digital organization of lynch mobs by different hate groups on Facebook, which continue to go unchecked.[30] Racist slurs in Burmese are not effectively apprehended by the platform's automated content moderation, because it is not calibrated for Burmese. The platform relies on a small team of Burmese language content moderators—stretched thin and contracted by a Malaysian firm—who were either unable, or unwilling, to curb these hateful excesses.[31]

Satt's new work is set against this backdrop of online violence. As a part of the 'Sa Gar Ahla Ku Htone (Beauty Word Therapy)' exhibition held in collaboration with Facebook and co-sponsored by Love Frankie and Pyinsa Rasa, Satt created twelve clay sculptures that resemble human

30 Steve Stecklow, 'Why Facebook is Losing the War on Hate Speech in Myanmar,' Reuters, 15 February 2018, www.reuters.com/investigates/special-report/myanmar-facebook-hate/.

31 Ibid.

forms not unlike 'balloon animals.' Each of these sculptures is giving voice to cyber-bullying experienced by those who were victims of ethnic cleansing, amplified by Facebook. His collection of ten miniatures and two life-size fiberglass and clay sculptures are meant to represent ' The fragility of the ego online, and perhaps the inflated nature of the self in the online Facebook feed.'[32] Satt interviewed people on Facebook to explore how people felt about being harassed and bullied online, with his sculptures accompanying their quotes.

The end-point of digital storage is taxonomy. Taxonomy is also its starting point. The creation of databases where information can be cleanly categorized, named, sorted, assigned a value and a purpose is the default; any inquiry made of the database must eventually fit this default. Not getting a result to your search does not mean that the item you want does not exist in the database, only that you have phrased your search incorrectly. Hence, even when measuring critical and nuanced practices, the shape of the question is determined by the intention of storage. Thus, a critical question of online violence gets positioned as a 'fight against hate speech.' The nature of correlative algorithms would expect some clearly-defined objects: words that are hate speech, and those that are not. But as we know, language is infinitely slippery and words are not always what they mean—until they are. But the database has no way of knowing this.

Neither in Satt's own work, nor in the other art works in this exhibition hosted by Facebook, is there any mention of the role that the platform performs in the escalation and perpetuation of hate speech and online abuse. The emphasis was on Facebook-ers as victims and villains, a lack of digital literacy, and the responsibility of users to cultivate appropriate speech online. In an interview reported on in a local newspaper, the Facebook spokesperson said that their approach is to generate 'positive thinking, [since] empathy and kindness [can be] a more significant part of the solution [to hate speech].'[33] Satt's work was eventually about of Facebook's fight against bullying and abuse, thus reframing the debate by giving different values to particular actors and by identifying a different straw man: the user.

## MEMORY AS SHARING IN THE SPECTACLE

Subha Wijesiriwardene mixes memory with politics, bearing witness to how technologies frame the work that emerges from WMC's practice. 'Because technologies are often thought of as originating in the West and applied in the East, how our work gets documented by that technological gaze needs to be examined. There is a long legacy of us being watched. We wanted to document

32..........Lae Phyu Pya Myo Myint and Saw Yi Nanda, 'Art Exhibition to Fight Hate Speech on Facebook,' *Myanmar Times*, 28 October 2019, www.mmtimes.com/news/art-exhibition-fight-hate-speech-facebook.html.

33..........Ibid.

34..........Subha Wijeseriwardene (Gender & Sexuality programs coordinator, Women and Media Collective), interview with author, August 2019. Wijeseriwardene is no longer with WMC in this role.

> ourselves as doing the seeing.'[34] When the images arrive from WMC, they are not just portfolios of the artefacts (the books, posters, T-shirts or campaign materials). They are almost all images of the people—mostly women—looking at things that they are engaging with, things that they, their people, might have produced. Digitization usually tends to remove the artist and emphasize the work; this trend works differently here. At WMC, who is looking at the work of art is perhaps more important than the artwork itself.

The digital depends on a visual culture and overwhelming value placed on it as the default way we access reality. The Covid-19 pandemic has been a telling crash course in visual data literacy as we learn to read graphs about 'flattening the curve.' The visual is how we delight in ourselves and each other; our lives are lived as tiny snatches of banal, decontextualized, yet absorbing online performances, stitched together into larger narratives that perhaps can only be registered and followed by algorithms of personalization, storage, distribution, and curation. From ubiquitous cameras to satellites and drones, surveillance systems in our phones tracking our moves and desires, to our aunties and uncles on Facebook doing the same—there is a continuation of a culture of watching and being watched in the digital. This overriding value and place of the visual is what we call a 'spectacular imperative': visualization on a screen has become the default way by which we now access reality. The paradox of the spectacular imperative is that visual-ization is human work, sense, and meaning-making, with no correlation to what is made of it in the networked operation of our devices.

One of the outcomes of this spectacular imperative is that many artistic practices are reduced to flattened forms of documentation that can be accessed on a screen. The process, politics, materiality, and intention all get hidden under the overarching need for making things visible, visual, and accessible to particular forms of looking. Hence, for many arts and cultural organizations, the digital becomes the space where they 'exhibit' their final products. Collections of video archives, live streaming of events, and publishing of information about various programmes remains the extent of their interaction with the digital shifts. Even when their artists and curators might be engaged in critically understanding the digital, their own institutional practices seem detached from these technologies, which appear only as tools, rather than as existential forms of expression and transformation.

## How do you Make Memories in the Face of Spectacular Imperatives?

•

Most arts and cultural organizations' interaction with the digital spaces have, at their heart, a focus on being online, SEO-compatible, and available on social media. They must have accessible archives, show some form of community outreach, and create new forms of documentation.[35] The digital shift that they are a part of, which is often a part of their content-based practice, does not manifest in their online strategies and tactics. This is compounded by three particular factors: (1) That the work might be socially and geographically marginalized with communities that do not have access to the digital and thus do not develop a fluent practice; (2) Funding and monitoring practices might fetishize the visual outcomes so strongly, that the organization does not develop the capacity to re-imagine itself in the wake of digital emergency(ies); (3) Digital literacy is a generational practice and for many cultural spaces still establishing themselves as physical hubs, there might not be enough inter-generational leadership to facilitate a transition into the digital.

Our conversations with Britto Arts Trust brought some of these questions to the fore. An autonomous, artist led organization that started in 2002 in Dhaka, Bangladesh, Britto is the first of its kind: an alternative space for emerging, contemporary artists set up to encourage experimentation in the visual arts, for dialogue and exchange between artists from the region and internationally, and activities in and with local communities.

Britto is firmly located in the aftermath of Partition; however, the scars of history and Partition's legacy of geographic uncertainty are not just the backdrop, but the actual business of Britto's work. For example, No Man's Land (2015) was an open research studio located on the border between India and Bangladesh with artists from both countries, who engaged with local, rural communities of people who have no passports or bureaucratically determined citizenship. Since the Indian artists could not get permission to cross over to Bangladesh, this meant that the studio was stretched across the empty landscape between the two countries, involving large scale visualizations, photographs printed at a very large scale, and performances that had to be heard and seen across the distance. Artists worked on performances, installations, video, and photography projects. And so, across the space of No Man's Land, the artists could see each other and interact—albeit across physical distance between the two countries—without passports and visas.

The question of connection, migration, situated-ness, political dialogue, and aesthetic expression are central to the various communities that Britto addresses, particularly focusing on those who are displaced, fragile, and lacking in political autonomy.

Since 2009, Britto has organized small artist residencies in the countryside between India and Bangladesh where a number of groups with a shared language (Bengali) live, but with no allegiance to either country by way of formal citizenship. By encouraging artists to live the hardscrabble lives of the villagers for a week, Britto hopes to inspire their practice. Sometimes, it is just about being there, even if it does not spark a specific 'output,' says Tayeba Begum Lipi, who is the director and co-founder of Britto Arts. Their ambition is to provide a transformative and profound experience to their artists.

35.......... 'SEO' (search engine optimization) is the manipulation of the presentation (such as the use of particular words and phrases 'read' by search technologies) of digital material online in order to be appropriately identified by search engines.

◁ Yasmin Jahan Nupur, *No Man's Land*, 2014, durational performance still, courtesy: Britto Arts Trust, Dhaka

▽ Mahbubur Rahman, *No Man's Land*, 2014, performance still, courtesy: Britto Arts Trust, Dhaka

▽ Subir Paul, *No Man's Land*, 2014, performance still, courtesy: Britto Arts Trust, Dhaka

Britto's work is relevant, urgent, and stitches into some critical narratives of migration, belonging, state-sponsored border violence, and increasing xenophobia in the region. However, the digital remains strangely removed from these articulations. A number of critical facts do not feature in their narratives: that India launched a biometric identity system to re-verify citizens' rights to remain in the country (engineered also to limit alleged 'infiltrators' from Bangladesh); that India has massive drone surveillance projects on borders with Bangladesh; that Chinese-made mobile phones connect communities in no-man's lands between India and Pakistan and Bangladesh. Even when faced with a problem of physical distance, there are no digital responses that emerge such as a web residency, a digital third space, a de-territorialized infrastructure, or the like. To reiterate, digital literacy, a fetishization of the visual, and legacy approaches to the arts might have something to do with these gaps—beyond an embrace of the ubiquitous Facebook Group.

When it comes to the digital, the emphasis is on documentation for the spectacular imperative: to attract artists and gallerists, readers and benefactors, for them to do the seeing, the meaning-making, and the determination of value and worth. With the important cultural and political space that Britto occupies, it is telling that it also represents a sector that needs a huge impetus and investment to engage with the digital and move out of the conditions of storage into the new contexts and interventions of making memory.

## FROM STORAGE TO MEMORY

This chapter has toured through four South Asian organizations' encounters with the digital in their arts and cultural practices, framed as shifts from storage to memory to storage. In doing so, we wanted to present the digital as: a mode, a scape, a set of situated practices and promises, and as affordances of interfaces imbricated in social, political, and cultural milieus. This goes beyond the use of a device, the inhabitation of a platform, or programming skills. We unpacked these conditions of storage and memory in terms of a fixation with counting and collecting data in algorithmic networks, the elision and inclusion of bodies, and the imperatives of spectacularization. We found that each organization's resistance to the violence, fascism, and intolerance in their countries, emerging from a shared history, took place through their own re-working of memory-making within the conditions of the digital afforded to them. They did this by keeping their bodies firmly inside circuits of media production; opening themselves up to the possible fortunes of amplification online; making content as openly available as possible. However, the digital can also remain, sometimes, just a tool, a platform, a business card.

We conclude by proposing a set of 'touchstones' for the digital 'ESTAMP' that we describe in the following way. The digital turn is an 'embodied' phenomenon; it directly affects different kinds of bodies, their practices, identities, transactions, and livelihoods. Furthermore, digital practices are 'situated': they challenge flattened narratives of globality and instead try and grapple with situated-ness in both geography and in temporal contexts. Turning with the torque of the digital requires 'tacit' knowledge for survival, which cannot always be explicitly written down, verbalized, and transmitted. Those who are not 'in the know' are often excluded, and made invisible in those narratives, but they are also the ones who need the most care. The touchstones question the claims of rationality and predictability in the digital turn; within this is a valorization of 'affect' as a condition through which expressions and actions find space. New frameworks of measurement challenge the narrative of virtuality, and remind us of the 'materiality' of the digital turn; critical to our understanding of the turn is a focused attention on its affordances, including hardware, regulation, and the infrastructure of code and its materiality.

And lastly, the touchstones insist that the digital turn is not merely a technological transformation but a 'political' paradigm. We recognize the covert and explicit politics embedded in technological devices and apparatuses, and how these politics shape the world within which human and social practices exist.

The touchstones work as a lens and a map, a framework and a narrative to think through the digital in arts and culture. However, we do not intend for this to become a new scale for measurement and data collection. We want to resist the universalization of these touchstones through templates, and focus more on what they open up when put into a dialogue with art practices. Instead, we propose seeing how we might think about the digital differently now, through the realities of people, publics, and their relationships.

## ← REFERENCES


Alampay, Edwin. 'Introduction.' In *Living the Information Society in Asia*, ed. Edwin Alampay, pp. 10–14. Singapore: Institute of South East Asian Studies, 2009.

Barlow, John Perry. 'A Declaration of the Independence of Cyberspace,' The Electronic Frontier Foundation blog, 8 February 1996. www.eff.org/cyberspace-independence.

Chun, Wendy. *Programmed Visions: Software and Memory*. Cambridge, MA: MIT Press, 2011.

Cole, Simon A. 'Review of Imprint of the Raj: How Fingerprinting was Born in Colonial India.' *Technology and Culture* 46, no. 1 (2005), pp. 252–53. doi:10.1353/tech.2005.0010.

Ganesh, Maya Indira, and Johannes Bruder. 'Cloud Cosmogram' on Data Farms: Circuits, Labour, Territory, 2019. www.datafarms.org/2019/12/16/cloud-cosmogram/.

Garcia, Sergio. 'Why ICT for Development,' official website of the European Union, 7 December 2015. https://europa.eu/capacity4dev/public-ict/wiki/why-ict-development-ict4d.

Garfinkel, Simon. *Database Nation*. Sebastopol, CA: O'Reilly Media, 2000.

Ginwala, Natasha (blog). 'In Memoriam: Lala Rukh (1948–2017),' 27 December 2017. https://natashaginwala.wordpress.com/2017/12/27/in-memoriam-lala-rukh-1948-2017/.

Google Art Selfie Project, https://artsandculture.google.com/camera/selfie.

Hwang, Tim, and Karen Levy. '"The Cloud" and Other Dangerous Metaphors.' *The Atlantic*, 20 January 2015. www.theatlantic.com/technology/archive/2015/01/the-cloud-and-other-dangerous-metaphors/384518/.

Menezes, Vivek. 'The Indian Art World is Dead: Long Live the New Indian Art World.' *The Hindustan Times*, 29 December 2018. www.hindustantimes.com/analysis/the-indian-art-world-is-dead-long-live-the-new-indian-art-world/story-MMFURyQy8K3ZPmtotFtNXL.html.

Myint, Lae Phyu Pya Myo, and Saw Yi Nanda. 'Art Exhibition to Fight Hate Speech on Facebook,' *Myanmar Times*, 28 October 2019. www.mmtimes.com/news/art-exhibition-fight-hate-speech-facebook.html.

Raval, Noopur. 'Google Arts App has a Data Problem.' *Factor Daily*, 2 February 2018. https://factordaily.com/google-art-app-data-problem/.

Sarkar, Sreela. 'Beyond the "Digital Divide": The "Computer Girls" of Seelampur.' *Feminist Media Studies* (2016), pp. 1–16. doi: 10.1080/14680777.2016.1169207.

—. 'From the Maistry to the Computer Operator: The Colonial Legacy of "Skilling India" through ICT Training.' *Perspectives on Global Development and Technology* 18 (2019), pp. 343–62. doi: 10.1163/15691497-12341523.

Shamsie, Kamila. 'Murdered on the Streets of Karachi: My Friend Who Dared to Believe in Free Speech.' *The Guardian*, 27 April 2015. www.theguardian.com/commentisfree/2015/apr/27/murdered-karachi-free-speech-sabeen-mahmud.

Stecklow, Steve. 'Why Facebook is Losing the War on Hate Speech in Myanmar.' Reuters, 15 February 2018. www.reuters.com/investigates/special-report/myanmar-facebook-hate/.

Truschke, Audrey. 'The Great Mughal Whitewash.' *India Today*, 21 March 2016. www.indiatoday.in/magazine/up-front/story/20160321-the-great-mughal-whitewash-audrey-truschke-south-asian-history-828594-2016-03-10.

Walsh, Declan. 'Pakistan's Secret Dirty War.' *The Guardian*, 29 March 2011. www.theguardian.com/world/2011/mar/29/balochistan-pakistans-secret-dirty-war.

Wikipedia Entry, 'On the internet no one knows you're a dog.' *Wikipedia* https://en.wikipedia.org/wiki/On_the_Internet,_nobody_knows_you%27re_a_dog.

Women and Media Collective (website). https://womenandmedia.org/.

Zaidi, Meher. 'T2F: A Pursuit of the Heart.' *The Express Tribune*, 7 August 2010. https://blogs.tribune.com.pk/story/985/t2f-a-pursuit-of-the-heart/.

Zuboff, Shoshanna. *The Age of Surveillance Capitalism: The Fight for the Human Future at the New Frontier of Power*. New York: Public Affairs Books, 2019.


## ← INTERVIEWS

Subha Wijeseriwardene (Gender & Sexuality programs coordinator, Women and Media Collective), interview by author, August 2019.

Arieb Azhar (manager, board member, The Second Floor), interview by author, September 2019.

Begum Tayeba Lipi (co-founder and director, Britto Arts Trust), interview by author, September 2019.

Moe Satt (artist), interview by author, October 2019.

Dushanbe Art Ground/ Dushanbe, Tajikistan / 3:50pm 38°34'03.1"N 68°46'59.5"E

ArtEast / Bishkek, Kyrgyz Republic / 4:14pm     42°51'17.3"N / 74°35'13.1"E

Section Four

# HISTORIES OF THE PRESENT

# HISTORIES OF THE PRESENT
## On the Political Agency of Art

Carin Kuoni

> I carry a river. It is who I am:
> 'Aha Makav. This is not
> a metaphor.
>
> When a Mojave says, *Inyech*
> *'Aha Makavchithuum,*
> we are saying our name.
>
> We are telling a story of our
> existence. *The river runs*
> *through the middle of my body.*[1]
>
> Natalie Diaz

Like currents pulsing through bioluminescent waters, a set of core qualities animates the visionary projects captured in this book. The case studies put forward in this section display characteristics that are present in other projects as well but are particularly forceful in those assembled here. By and large, despite the immense difference of site, scale, and orientation, the projects that follow are intentional collaborations. They deliberately engage with notions of time. And as they enact a prefigurative politics, they provide educational experiences. Taken together, such qualities amount to various shades of the same proposition: art can be a political project that opens new perspectives on collaboration, time, and pedagogy, contributing to building and expanding civic societies throughout the world.

The researchers in this next section—Fatin Farhat, Kabelo Malatsie, Paulina E. Varas—approach the projects they have chosen to analyze from very different points of view. I offer the considerations below as evidence of my ongoing thinking on the intersection of art and politics of which I found, to my great delight, resonances in the art projects discussed by my peers here.

### THREE PRINCIPLES—COLLABORATION, TIME, PEDAGOGY

Collaborative practices are of course well established in contemporary art. Whether it is anonymous craft circles, artist collectives, or community-generated work, the notion of the singular author has been disproven long ago. What we find in the examples here, however, are forms of collaboration that demand systemic change, whether explicitly so or by virtue of performing them within a clearly identified system.[2] The contours of these systems and their scale vary and, accordingly, the actors collaborating within them do as well. They range from groups that act in solidarity within a constellation of like-minded groups, to the individual human body that is defined as a porous crossing point of human and non-human life forces, from networks of experts with a particular skill set, to those defining themselves in relation to a historical event. They all conceive of themselves, however, as constituents of a meaningful system. Such awareness of their positionality within a larger system leads to an understanding of the system's performative nature. It empowers the actors within these systems or networks, and unleashes the potential for systematic change.

Take the example of collaborative media platforms: research from a historical project on one continent fuels a contemporary investigation using a newer generation of similar technical devices an ocean away, thus paying tribute to the earlier manifestation. The new project—discussed by Kabelo Malatsie in her chapter 'Network(ing) from Lima to Johannesburg'—is conceived in solidarity with those that came before and now re-emerge here.[3] Think of the artist who partners with a glacier, listens to, and makes available what it has to 'say,' in an affirmation of Indigenous cosmologies; here I'm referring to an example in Paulina E. Varas' chapter 'Collective Creations: Art and Politics for the Present.'[4] Collaborations also happen around shared political experiences, as acts of defiance against forced displacement that result in exile, nomadic existences, refugee realities, or diasporic communities, as exemplified in Fatin Farhat's chapter 'Syrian Artists Outside Syria: Conflicts, Challenges, and Possibilities for Artists Working in Displacement.'[5] As part of a system, all this highly localized work is always conceived of in reference to these systems. Far from schizophrenic waffling, the art practices brought forward by researchers Malatsie, Varas and Farhat are always also elsewhere, and embrace such distributed authorship or 'collaboration.'

Mojave poet Natalie Diaz—who is not part of these studies—speaks of such alignments in a recent poem, *The First Body is the Water*:

> In Mojave thinking, body and land are the same. The words are separated only by letters 'ii and 'a: 'iimat for body, 'amat for land. In conversation, we often use a shortened form for each: *mat*-. Unless you know the context of a conversation, you might not know if we are speaking about our body or our land. You might not know which has been injured, which is remembering, which is alive, which was dreamed, which needs care. You might not know we mean both.[6]

While chronological time underpins Western epistemology, in the examples the researchers offer here, such a linear approach to understanding causality comes off as inadequate and irrelevant. In this section, several projects incorporate historical events into a practice as active agents or partners, with impacts in the now. The legacy of fascism in World War II, for instance, appears in one of the examples as 'minor fascism.' It is not just a referent; through performances, readings, and exhibitions it is also an enacted presence. Unfolding at the periphery of contemporary political life in Central Europe, the project excavates and lifts to the centre incidents of minor fascism to be acted on.[7] The project works in different time frames simultaneously and, to borrow Diaz's words from above, it is injured, remembering, alive, dreaming, and in need of care. Elsewhere, the Syrian Revolution of 2011 is the through line of several projects,[8] both memory and promise at once, and the substance that binds people as recollection and as aspiration.

Other projects apply time as a metric for solidarity. In the political project of establishing a network of cultural organizers and producers across different geographies in South Africa, for instance, time marks presence and facilitates the appreciation and perhaps even learning of a local vernacular.[9] In this case, time is a constituent of the network itself, not a means to it. It is continuously required, and when it is withdrawn, the network collapses. If different time spans are embraced, on the other hand, a millennia-old Native forest that moans and a person today who is listening, can join in an

1..........Natalie Diaz, excerpt from 'The First Water Is the Body,' in *Postcolonial Love Poem* (New York: Graywolf Press, 2020), p. 46. Diaz's poem has been my companion ever since she presented an early version of it at the Vera List Center for Art and Politics, The New School, on 11 March 2019, as part of 'Say It Like You Mean It: Translation, Communication, and Languages' (VLC Seminar IV of Freedom of Speech: A Curriculum for Studies Into Darkness), www.veralistcenter.org.

2..........This is different from German American artist Hans Haacke's *Condensation Cube* (1963–1965) and his other early systemcentric work that function as metaphors for the artworld's implication in economic and political systems.

3..........Rf. p. 340ff, for VANSA's complex and multi-tentacled project 'Performance Code/MCL100,' connecting Lima, Peru, with Johannesburg, South Africa.

4..........Rf. p. 418ff, for Tsonami's Automapa project, 'Disappearing,' across Latin America.

5..........Rf. p. 359ff, for Fatin Farhat's texts on Syrian artists in exile.

6..........Diaz, *Postcolonial Love Poem*, p. 48.

7..........Rf. p. 410ff, for WHW's 'Beginning As Well As We Can,' spanning Zagreb, Croatia; Budapest, Hungary; and Utrecht and Antwerp, the Netherlands.

8..........Rf. p. 359ff, for Fatin Farhat's texts on Syrian artists in exile.

9..........Rf. p. 392ff, and Kabelo Malatsie's exposé on the origins of VANSA, especially the challenges of becoming familiar with local vernaculars, what she also refers to as local 'language.'

empathetic relationship. The emerging expressive action—art—can then be politically harnessed.

The third characteristic I would like to highlight in the projects of this section concerns a commitment to what American political scientist Carl Boggs terms 'prefigurative politics,' 'embody[ing] within the ongoing political practice of a movement ... those forms of social relations, decision-making, culture, and human experience that are the ultimate goal.'[10] Among the early examples of prefigurative movements are the Paris Commune of 1871 and its efforts to unionize labourers at the onset of industrialization. Boggs' concept of prefigurative politics is also informed by a particular strand of American utopian communities on the West Coast in the nineteen-sixties, which acquired new relevance during recent movements such as Occupy Wall Street. For Boggs, political order is a process that is collectively shaped and constantly shifting, a means to instantiate radical change with the participation of all constituents.

Prefigurative politics provides a useful intersection between Indigenous approaches to personhood and media materialism. From an Indigenous point of view, evoked by some of the projects as well as by Natalie Diaz above, the body is often considered a gathering of different forces that encompass history, present, and future. In the case of some of the technology-driven projects, infrastructures facilitate networks and collaborations but also significantly shape them.[11] Paraphrasing Marshall McLuhan, the media theoretician who figures prominently in one of the projects discussed, technology is the message but also the medium—but not exclusively so. As anthropologist David Graeber mused on prefigurative politics, the term he said is meant ' ... literally. It is not a metaphor.'[12] Similarly, it is not so much an alignment of means and ends, but a simultaneous embodiment of both.

## STRATEGIES

As art opens new perspectives on collaboration, time, and prefigurative politics, what are some of the strategies developed in the projects examined in this section of the book that lead to an expansion of civic societies?

First among them, and related to the notion of collaboration, is the desire to go public—to create platforms that make the projects and their stakeholders visible to each other and the public. The platforms have very different manifestations, from bookstores to cultural festivals, from distribution sites to plays, but they all perform in recognition of how they are implicated within a larger system. And sometimes they come with protocols to structure participation.

The position that the contemporary, the now, is always also the past and the future allows for considerations and caregiving to be offered to unexpected participants. It, too, results in an expansion of our sense of subjectivity and of how our individual subjectivity is always a composite of other agents. By making these agents visible, providing them with space, the artists here bestow on them agency. Political scientist Jane Bennett, building on Bruno Latour's notion of the 'actant,' proposes 'vibrant materiality' to account for different temporalities and agencies, with the goal to

> Encourage more intelligent and sustainable engagements with vibrant matter and lively things. ... By vitality I mean the capacity of things—edibles, commodities, storms, metals—not only to impede or block the will and designs of humans but also to act as quasi

10........Carl Boggs, 'Marxism, Prefigurative Communism, and the Problem of Workers' Control,' *Radical America* 11 (November 1977), p. 100.
11........This is recognized in VANSA's network and Audiomapa's projects.
12........David Graeber, *Fragments of an Anarchist Anthropology* (Chicago: Prickly Paradigm Press, 2004), p. 84.
13........Jane Bennett, *Vibrant Matter* (Durham: Duke University Press, 2010), p. vii.
14........Ibid., p. 13.
15........Diaz, *Postcolonial Love Poem*, p. 49.

> agents or forces with trajectories, propensities, or tendencies of their own.[13]

In this scenario, the political subject far exceeds humans. Bennett concludes that,

> Such a newfound attentiveness to matter and its powers ... can inspire a greater sense of the extent to which all bodies are kin in the sense of inextricably enmeshed in a dense network of relations. And in a knotted world of vibrant matter, to harm one section of the web may very well be to harm oneself.[14]

Lastly, prefigurative politics in our examples here is educational in motivation. The projects that follow entail situations of multi-generational peer learning that are established in theatres, schools, streets, cultural centres, or just among participants. And as collaboration and temporality in the expanded sense discussed above get incorporated into this pedagogical project, expansive, inclusive, and politically more effective epistemologies can emerge. To close with Natalie Diaz,

> We must go until we smell the black root-wet anchoring the river's mud banks. We must go beyond beyond to a place where we have never been the center, where there is no center—beyond, toward what does not need us yet makes us.[15]

← REFERENCES

Bennett, Jane. *Vibrant Matter*. Durham: Duke University Press, 2010.

Boggs, Carl. 'Marxism, Prefigurative Communism, and the Problem of Workers' Control.' *Radical America* 11 (November 1977).

Diaz, Natalie. *Postcolonial Love Poem*. New York: Graywolf Press, 2020.

Graeber, David. *Fragments of an Anarchist Anthropology*. Chicago: Prickly Paradigm Press, 2004.

# SYRIAN ARTISTS OUTSIDE SYRIA
## Conflicts, Challenges, and Possibilities for Artists Working in Displacement

Fatin Farhat

This chapter explores the rise to visibility of Syrian art that was unleashed by the Syrian Revolution. Since 2011, new waves of Syrian independent artists, artistic collectives, and organizations have emerged and spread across the Arab region and beyond; at the same time, new funding mechanisms and donors have developed. The chapter takes Syrian artists and initiatives as its main subject of investigation, drawing parallels, synergies, and contrasts between three chosen case studies. It shows how the rise to visibility of Syrian art outside Syria has come at a price. Persistently labelled as 'political agents' or 'refugees,' Syrian artists and practitioners find themselves at risk of seeing their creative identity 'flattened.' Whereas one should not underestimate the positive role that funding agencies have played in support of these new artistic movements, it is also important to recognize how project-based support can limit the work of these artists due to its short-term vision and institutional pre-requisites. The chapter offers a fresh look at how a strong, sturdy, and independent Syrian artistic is being formed outside of Syria, and calls for bridges to be built back into the country.

Keywords
→ Syria
→ Revolution
→ Creativity
→ Displaced Artists

## INTRODUCTION

Focusing on three art projects—'Family Ti-Jean' by Masrah Ensemble (Beirut, 2015–2016), the Pages Bookstore Café (Istanbul/Amsterdam, 2013–2018), and the Visual Arts Festival Damascus @DEPO Istanbul (2013)—this chapter outlines some of the political and social contexts that have influenced Syrian artists' works and practices from 2011 onward. In particular, it discusses how displacement to Lebanon and Turkey and other geographies has informed narratives and artistic frameworks in the practice of Syrian artists, and shaped their engagement with various communities. The impact of funding trends on displaced Syrian artists' creative processes is also discussed.

To situate the three case studies, the chapter offers a brief overview of the creative fervour contemporaneous with or unleashed by the Syrian

Revolution. After 2011, new waves of Syrian independent artists, artistic collectives, and organizations were born and spread across the Arab region and beyond. These included special programmes designed to support Syrian artists and Syrian artistic initiatives.[1] Syrian artists' visibility increased, and their tools and practices were altered and enhanced.

However, as the three case studies will show, the rise to visibility of Syrian art outside Syria has come at a price. Persistently labelled as 'political agents' or 'refugees,' Syrian artists and practitioners find themselves at risk of seeing their creative identity 'flattened.' The vast majority of Syrian artists interviewed stated that 'revolution,' 'alienation,' 'home' and 'trauma' remain central motifs in their work. The examination of their artworks and essays confirms that these themes dominate recent Syrian cultural production. For many, it is a way of keeping the revolution alive and Syria close. Syrian artists continue to feel in 'transit,' as they have not yet found closure and catharsis. Syrian artists and practitioners are also confronted with complicated concerns with regard to the sustainability and continuity of their artworks and practices as individuals and as institutions.

Whereas one should not underestimate the positive role that funding agencies have played in support of these new artistic movements, some limitations and challenges must be addressed with regard to their work. While useful in the short term, their project-based support hinders the long-term and comprehensive development of Syrian artists and art organizations. Funding agencies support Syrian artists in accordance with their own priorities rather than with Syrian artists' immediate and long-term needs.

The chapter concludes with an acknowledgement, shared by all the artists and practitioners interviewed, that more time is needed to understand the impact of the new artistic narratives, frameworks, opportunities, and funding trends uncovered in this research, on the broader Syrian cultural landscape.

## RESEARCH METHODOLOGY

This chapter was written in the context of my ongoing artistic research practice which examines the conditions, realities, and social and political contexts that affect displaced artists, art initiatives, and collectives immediately post-displacement and in the years that follow. This interest developed as a result of almost twenty years of professional experience working in the cultural field in Palestine and in the neighbouring Arab region, confronting questions of creativity and displacement during politically turbulent times, out of a necessity flowing from the Israeli occupation of Palestine.

A qualitative methodology is adopted in this research in order to draw parallels, synergies, and contrasts between the three chosen case studies. Research data is based on one-on-one conversations held in person with

1............Hassan Abbas (researcher), interview by author, Beirut, 8 January 2020.

artists and arts administrators in Beirut, Istanbul, and Amsterdam, as well as over Skype with many others across the globe following the main research questions. My interlocutors were not limited to the cohort of artists, art managers, participants, and audience members who are directly involved with the three projects under study. I also spoke with key artists, curators, and practitioners from Syria, Palestine, and Lebanon, among other countries. Moreover, the methodology relied heavily on the study of first-hand accounts of the situation, whether in the form of essays and testimonies, or artworks by Syrian artists working around the world. These sources supplanted my readings of traditional academic literature, including a select number of academic articles, essays, and books.

The analysis of the input from these interviews was conducted along three broad thematic lines: (1) Content and form—exploring how the narratives of displaced Syrian artists has changed, with particular attention given to recurring themes and motifs and their choice of artistic forms; (2) Community engagement—focusing on Syrian artists' engagement with their own community (how they represent the plight of others and perceive a personal moral responsibilities towards Syria) and on their engagement with new publics/communities, including having to deal with the possibility of being typecast as spokespeople for their compatriots; (3) Funding and continuity—analyzing how funding trends affect the narratives produced by Syrian artists outside of Syria (whether they facilitate or hamper the creation of new initiatives, connect them to Syria or pressure them to produce works that mirror the political context).[2]

I encountered substantial challenges over the course of my research. Syrian artists are dispersed all over the world, engage with a vast kaleidoscope of communities, and use numerous tools and artistic disciplines in their work. Thus, proposing focused and concise research questions, while using the three case studies as a recurrent theme, proved to be a challenging task, especially since each case study represents a distinct and unique experience in and of itself. On another note, the projects under review were implemented years ago, and on many occasions, insights and details were lost over time. In the case of the 'Family Ti-Jean' project, the children actors who participated in the play had dispersed by the time I began my research. Meanwhile, the partner organization, Basmeh & Zeitooneh, had experienced a high staff turnover. The founder of the Pages Bookstore Café project had been forced to leave Turkey by the authorities; consequently, many of his business associates in Istanbul were reluctant to speak

2............Despite the substantial volume of literature already available, a consensus among my interlocutors emerged that only time will make it possible to understand the impact these new artistic expressions will have on Syrian cultural history. Among the titles I consulted, is the book *Yet to Come*, edited by theatre director Wael Qaddour (Syria), which presents a remarkable collection of the testimonies of eighty-three Syrian and Syrian-Palestinian artists, writers, journalists, and practitioners on their practices as well as on the question of the artists' role(s), representation and responsibility post-2011. It includes the testimonies of several of the practitioners and artists involved in the three case studies presented here. *On Syrian Cultural Work During the Years of Ember* (Beirut: Mamdouh Adwan Publishing House, 2016) is another essential book. It comprises three studies: 'Cultural Mechanisms and Cultural Production During the Crisis' by Mary Elias; 'The Role of Culture and Art in Achieving Reconciliation and Peace in Countries of Violent Conflicts,' by Rama Najmeh; and 'Toward the Development of Cultural Structures in Syria,' by the Syrian Center for Policy Studies. Another critical paper, titled *Syrian Art Production: Support Models and Sustainability Challenges*, by researcher and theatre critic Mona Merhi, explores the nature and form of donor responses to Syrian artists and cultural organizations post-2011.

about the project publicly. And since the project's space no longer existed, it was not possible to observe the community's direct interaction with the artistic programme. The festival at DEPO Istanbul took place at a particularly difficult political moment with sudden political unrest that compromised the Turkish artists' involvement in the festival. In my interview, it became clear that the participating artists were not substantially invested in the festival: due to funding constraints, they had not produced their work specifically for the art show nor had they been able to attend the festival. As a result, their feedback on the event was limited .

## POLITICAL AND CULTURAL CONTEXTS

In March 2011, as anti-government protests swept accross many Arab countries in what later came to be known as the Arab Spring, Syrians started a peaceful protest demanding political change after decades of oppressive rule. After the kidnapping, torture, and killing of boys in Daraa for anti-government graffiti writing, the protests expanded and spread across Syria. A few days into the demonstrations, Syrian president Bashar Assad ordered the military to attack the protestors, and the violence escalated. Since the onset of the 2011 Syrian Revolution, nine years of armed conflict have left hundreds of thousands dead and wounded. Moreover, of the estimated 22 million Syrians living in the country in 2011, more than 5.5 million have become refugees in Lebanon, Jordan, Turkey and other neighbouring Arab countries, in Europe and Canada, and the crisis has displaced a further 6 million within the country's borders.[3]

It should be noted that there is an intense debate on the terminology that describes the 'events' in Syria since 2011. Terms like 'revolution,' 'crisis,' 'civil war,' and others are used differently by politicians, artists, researchers, and civilians depending on their political views. The term 'revolution' will be used in this chapter as it is used by the overwhelming majority of the artists and practitioners involved in the research process.

The destruction of Syria's cultural infrastructure, the dispersal of thousands of emerging and established artists, and the increased censorship have all negatively affected the cultural ecosystem in the country, forcing yet more to flee. The fear caused by the control of the Islamic State and other 'political Islamic parties' cannot be underestimated. Syrian cities that underwent heavy shelling have lost many of their cultural facilities, as well as their architectural and archaeological sites. The impact of the resulting migration of artists and art initiatives is significant in Syrian cities. There are as of yet no exact statistics for the number of Syrian artists, writers, cultural managers, and producers who left Syria between 2011 and 2019. However, it must be high if one looks at the vast number of Syrian plays, films, publications, and concerts that have been produced, organized, and showcased outside Syria since 2011.[4]

3............Please note that the above statistics vary from one source to another as statistics are perceived as a political tool, OTCHA being the most 'neutral' reference, www.unocha.org/syrian-arab-republic/about-ocha-syria.

Initially, Syrian artists took refuge in neighbouring countries such as Jordan, Lebanon, the Arab Gulf, Egypt, and Turkey, assuming that their departure was temporary. Due to the limited work opportunities in these countries and sometimes with long-term residency plans in place, many Syrian artists dispersed across the rest of the world, including Europe. Researcher and arts manager Jumana Al Yasiri has detailed the challenges that awaited Syrian artists in their exile:

> Geographical distance from Syria and the events raging within; the stigma of helplessness in the wake of disaster; a complete restructuring of the social and professional dynamic to which they were accustomed; bureaucratic complexities to receive permanent residencies and work permits; foreign languages and different cultural backgrounds, and many more.[5]

While the dispersal of Syrian artists outside the country has repositioned Syria in the international art scene, it has also exposed these artists to significant vulnerability. Indeed, separated from their usual networks and work environments, these artists must rebuild their careers with little to no formal support.

## OVERVIEW OF CASE STUDIES

The three case studies chosen to anchor this chapter offer compelling points of departure with which to understand the trajectories of Syrian art practice since 2011. Rooted in distinct but often interconnected artistic disciplines and practices, the projects represent different responses to a shared context of dispersal and displacement. As they adapted to new living and working conditions, the practitioners driving these projects have piloted new forms of collaboration, production, and artistic practice, in turn generating new narratives, frameworks, and forms of community involvement and new publics. Syrian curator and art manager Alma Salem, who is currently based in Canada, compellingly summarizes the thrust of this new movement in the following terms:

> Syrian artists and initiatives have moved from a stillness of ideas to perplexing new zones of exploration. From the evident to the doubtful. From a set of clearly narrowed

4.............Basma Husseini, *The Status of the Arts: Current Issues in Artistic Creation in the Arab Region* (Beirut: Jadaliyaa, 2018), p. 6.

5.............Jumana Yasiri, *The World as a Battlefield: The Migration of Contemporary Syrian Art and the Prospects of Continuity* (Beirut: Creative Memory, 2015), p. 2.

answers imposed by hideous regime
dogmas to an open space of new
questioning, openness to new
global trends, genuine solidarity
a new friendships circles in the arts.[6]

## Masrah Ensemble, 'Family Ti-Jean,' Beirut (2015–2016)

•

Masrah Ensemble is a Beirut-based non profit theatre organization that fosters critical discourse and research around theatre, with a particular focus on the Arab region. Established in 2009 by Syrian artist and theatre director Eyad Houssami, the ensemble brings together an eclectic mix of professionals and amateurs of diverse backgrounds. Their audiences are equally diverse; performing for citizens, youth, refugees, and migrant workers, the ensemble aims to challenge prevailing ideas of what theatre should be, where it should take place, and to whom it belongs.

Launched in 2015, the 'Family Ti-Jean' project was specifically designed to encourage social cohesion between refugee and immigrant youth and Beirut society at large. From the outset, the Ensemble's idea was to create a theatrical adaptation in which refugee and immigrant youth could join the cast as actors and perform in public settings throughout Beirut. Based on a West Indian folktale about brothers who seek to overpower the devil, the classic play 'Ti-Jean and his Brothers' by poet Saint Lucian and playwright Derek Walcott was chosen for how strongly its themes of political adversity, survival, and resistance resonate with the reality of young people in Beirut. Indeed, the children and the play's protagonist share similar stories of leaving home and standing up against adults. △Fig. 4

△ 4
Masrah Ensemble Rehearsal, Family T- Jean Project, 2016. Jad Safar/Ettijahat for Independent Culture.

Collaboration with the residents of the Shatila refugee camps was central to the development of the production. Established in 1948 in the aftermath of the Palestinian Nakbeh, the camps are currently home to Palestinian refugees, impoverished Lebanese and Syrian immigrants as well as other immigrants from the Middle East and South Asia. This diversity

6............Alma Salem, 'The Avant-garde Movement in Syrian Art was it a Creative Revaluation?,' in Prince Claus Catalogue (Amsterdam 2018), p. 22.

of backgrounds was one of the main reasons the camp was chosen as a backdrop for the 'Family Ti-Jean' production. In order to ensure the project's success and the community's 'ownership' over it, Masrah Ensemble partnered with the non profit Basmeh & Zeitooneh and the 'Create Syria' project, led by Ettijahat for Independent Culture, two local organizations working on the ground with refugees in Lebanon and with displaced Syrian artists around the world, respectively.[7] The mission of the latter is specifically to build leadership capacity among artists to direct high-quality community arts initiatives.

As a social theatre for which process is of central concern, the Masrah Ensemble team worked over a long period of time: the children actors were chosen through a process that lasted six months in total. Towards the end of the process, seven young refugees were selected to participate in the play along with a few migrant workers, with the purpose of building links between the two communities in recognition of their common struggles.

The Ensemble conducted the rehearsals for the project in the Shatila camp, as well as in different public spaces around Beirut and on the American University of Beirut campus. The performances were held in six different open spaces throughout the capital, with the intention of blurring the rigid lines of spatial segregation. A total audience of three thousand people attended the different performances, including parents, family members, local communities as well as a broader audience.

## Pages Bookshop Café, Istanbul (2013–2017) and Amsterdam (2017–2018)

• •

Pages is an independent cultural institution committed to publishing, theatre, cinema, music, children's literature, education, and e-learning. It was founded by Syrian publisher Samir Kadri, who had directed Smart Fingers Press in Damascus until the onset of the revolution, and Syrian visual artist and children's book illustrator Gulnar Hajo. The project was implemented in two phases, first in Istanbul (2013–2017) and then in Amsterdam (2017–2018). The project involved bookshops and cafés operating also as publishing houses: introducing novels by young Syrian and Arab writers, all the while creating spaces of interaction between Syrian refugees and local communities.

The project was born from and shaped by Kadri and Hajo's story of forced displacements over the course of seven years. While attending a book fair in Abu Dhabi in 2012, Kadri learned that security forces had raided his publishing house in Damascus, accusing him of supporting terrorist activities. After a first move to Amman, the couple settled in Istanbul in 2013. Pages started as a private entrepreneurial venture, driven

7............Launched in 2012, Basmeh & Zeitooneh is an organization that conducts field visits to the most marginalized and desperate Syrian refugees inside Lebanon. The aim of the visits is to assess the needs of the local refugee communities and to propose action in areas that are being neglected by local, regional, and international aid organizations. Early in 2014, Basmeh & Zeitooneh became an officially registered NGO. Currently, the organization serves approximately 18,000 Syrians in Lebanon. Source: www.basmeh-zeitooneh.org/about-us/history.

by a need to survive but also by the couple's dedication to their vocation as artists and publishers. Working with extremely limited funds, Kadri and Hajo were able to get started in Istanbul through crucial collaborations with local friends and partners.

According to Kadri, Pages was a necessity, especially in 2013, when the number of Syrian people living in Istanbul was still not so high and Turkish people had little knowledge of Syrian culture and art. It was created to bridge this gap, but also with an eye to the great number of students from across the world living in Istanbul at the time. Indeed, the project's critical aim was to foster understanding between people coming from different countries and cultures.

Within two years, Pages organized more than one hundred and fifty art workshops for children and more than two hundred musical events. The space also had its own theatre, called 'Tabasheer/Chalks,' where visitors were taught to write and produce plays in which they could also act. Guitar and oud classes were provided to young people and more than sixty literary events were organized. All public activities and workshops were free, and Pages became very well known in Istanbul, garnering significant media attention. △Fig. 7

△ 7
A Book Fair, Pages Café Istanbul, 2017. Courtesy Pages Café.

The Amsterdam branch was opened in June 2017 as the result of a sequence of unplanned events. In 2016, Kadri had been invited by the Prince Claus Fund to attend their annual awards ceremony in the Netherlands. While he was in the Netherlands, Kadri was denied his visa to re-enter Turkey.[8] The same week, Hajo was arrested by the Turkish authorities. She was only released on condition of leaving Turkey within the month. Kadri applied for political asylum in the Netherlands and was granted refugee status. The Prince Claus Fund offered him a space on its premises to establish a branch of Pages Bookstore Café. Just four months after the opening, seven thousand people had visited the bookstore to attend or participate in its rich offering of workshops, activities, and events. The project ended in 2018.

8............I personally transported some of Samir Kadri's belongings from the Pages Bookstore Café project from Istanbul to Amsterdam in the context of this research project.

## Visual Arts Festival Damascus @DEPOIstanbul, Istanbul (2013)

• • •

The 'Visual Arts Festival Damascus' is a festival that was implemented in three editions in three different cities between 2010 and 2013. It was launched in Damascus in 2010 by curators Charlotte Blake and Delphine Leccasto to provide a platform for meetings and debates focusing on contemporary visual practices in the Middle East. It was intended to encourage and facilitate exchange between young artists in Syria and neighbouring Arab countries, as well as their international peers. The festival had to become nomadic as early as 2011, as the revolution made its continuation in Damascus impossible. In 2012, it was hosted by the 'International Film Festival Rotterdam,' as part of the 'Power Cut Middle East' convening.

The 2013 edition was hosted in Istanbul by local arts organization DEPO Istanbul. The programme consisted of exhibitions, screenings, talks, and workshops. Istanbul was chosen to host the festival for several reasons: the physical proximity to Damascus, the desire to raise awareness about Syrian culture following the surge of Syrian refugees to Turkey, and the readiness of DEPO to support the event administratively and logistically. DEPO also acted as the intermediary for the festival's fundraising initiatives.

Charlotte Blake and Delphine Leccas are two experienced curators who are not only knowledgeable about the contemporary Arab scene, but also share a deep commitment to the Arab region and to Arab and Syrian artists in particular. In launching the festival and organizing it in different cities, they were responding to the heightened visibility of the ongoing upheavals in many artists' recent works and to the questions this visibility generated. A number of threads seemed to run through the works being produced: a search for new definitions of social and geographical identities and roles, a need to create new notions of belonging, and a general tendency to center the human experience. Many of the works selected for the festival addressed important social issues and many had a distinctive activist character.

Due to funding constraints, the festival was not organized around a specific theme but rather around digital artworks by artists from Arab countries and Turkey, selected from an open call. The festival budget did not allow for new commissions. Of the three hundred submissions received, the festival showcased works by twenty-six artists: five Syrians, twelve Arabs (from Lebanon, Palestine, Tunisia, Algeria, Egypt, Iraq, Kuwait), six Turkish artists, and three artists from Europe (France and Hungary). Some of the digital art installations and exhibitions were shown for the first time.[9]

The 2013 festival took place at a particularly difficult time in the history of Turkey. Only a few days before the opening, protests had

9............Names of participating artists: Madonna Adib, Amer Al Chalati, Akram Al Halabi, Sama Al Shaibi, Basma Al Sharif, Wastedworks, Anynous Syrian Exhibition, Artikisler, Mouna Abou Assali, Collective No, Rosa El Hassan, Khaled Jarrar, Bariz Evis, Ozden Dimer, Sireince Fattouh, Paul Haj Botrous, Ipek Hamzaoglu, Nadia Kabbi Linke, Katia Kameli, Mazen Kerbaj, Elif Kose, Massasit Matti, Amina Minia, Belit Sag, Maryam Samaan, Salah Saouli, Sharif Sehnaoui, Denis Uster, and Mayye Zayid.

erupted throughout Turkey in response to the government's plans to replace Taksim Gezi Park with a shopping mall. What started as a rally against yet another 'development' project in Istanbul, which would deprive the city's inhabitants of a favorite gathering place, quickly developed into a statement against the repression of civil rights nationwide. The people of Istanbul guarded Taksim Square, with its park and its memories of civic engagement and communal life. Much like their colleagues in the ongoing fights for freedom and civil rights in the Arab world, many artists in Turkey were engaged in this movement, including the artists who were showcased in the festival.

The demonstrations entailed important modifications to the festival's programme, as well as an unfortunate drop in attendance. The live music performance by Lebanese duo Kerbaj-Sehnaoui that had been planned as the closing event had to be cancelled at the last minute, due to the high level of violence and attacks surrounding the venue.

## THE REVOLUTION AS CONTENT AND FORM

The concept of revolution permeated the Visual Arts Festival Damascus @DEPO Istanbul. To be sure, all the pieces presented by Syrian artists dealt with revolution and displacement—even though the curators had not chosen this specific theme for the festival. For example, Madonna Adib's *Love in time of war* was presented as 'A revolt against fear, anger, perturbation, and the presence of death.'[10] Another example is Masasit Mati, who showcased episodes from the *Top Goon Diaries*, a web-based series of finger puppet theatre. The episodes express the collective's criticism of the Syrian regime and its violence towards the population. This thematic consistency amongst the featured Syrian artists can be attributed to the fact that the Istanbul edition happened only two years after the revolution.

The theme of revolution was also present in the works of the Turkish artists, albeit rooted in different realities. For instance, the festival showcased 'An Ankra Resistance,' a project by Wastedworks Video Collective that captures the resistance by the people of the Dikmen Valley in Ankara to the urban transformation and gentrification taking place in their neighbourhood.

But revolution also made its way into the fabric of the festival itself, as the Istanbul riots exploded just as the festival was about to open. Immediately, the Turkish artists involved in the festival took to the streets, as did many of the publics who would likely have attended. Not surprisingly, artists and publics were equally haunted by concerns for civic space. However, their absence inevitably left a mark on the festival, in a way drawing the revolution into the hollowed exhibition halls in the form of an echo, an invisible presence.

The Pages Bookstore Café project is slightly different, as the project was implemented over two distinct time spans and in two different cities.

10.......... Visual Arts Festival Damascus @DEPO Istanbul Catalogue, p. 28.

Art Group ‘705’ / Bishkek, Kyrgyz Republic / 4:14pm 42°52'06.1"N / 74°35'24.3"E

Women And Media Collective (WMC) / Colombo, Sri Lanka / 4:34pm     6°54'34.0"N / 79°53'11.5"E

The project's evolution illustrates a shift in how the revolution was viewed. When Kadri and Hajo opened Pages in Istanbul in 2013, the revolution was still underway and as such, it consumed their thoughts and concerns. This sense of urgency was reflected in Pages' initial artistic programming: the multiple art shows, literary readings, roundtables, and events all addressed the revolution and the status of Syrian refugees in Turkey. Later in Amsterdam in 2017, the programming took a different direction in response to the changed circumstances: a greater physical distance from Syria, more time had elapsed since the start of the revolution, and of course, a new public. While it maintained its focus on Syria, the programme also involved artists from non-Syrian backgrounds working on a variety of themes. It was also more inclusive in terms of its publics, reaching out to people who knew only very little about Syria. The forced move to Amsterdam became an opportunity for Kadri and Hajo to pause and reflect, and to start considering new means of addressing Syria through universal themes and perhaps with less anguish.

## Trauma and Loss

On the other side of the spectrum of revolution are trauma and loss. Artists have depicted the trauma that still haunts them in several ways, both through the visual arts and theatre: some have collected stories of survival, while others have chosen to address war, destruction, and loss directly. Regardless of the means used, for artists, these works represent a channel of reflection and deliberation on painful lived experience.[11]

The 'Family Ti-Jean' project mobilized participants around a literary text whose themes could resonate with their life experiences, rather than demanding that they tell their own stories or create new ones. The children

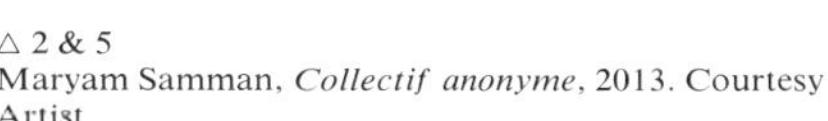

△ 2 & 5
Maryam Samman, *Collectif anonyme*, 2013. Courtesy Artist.

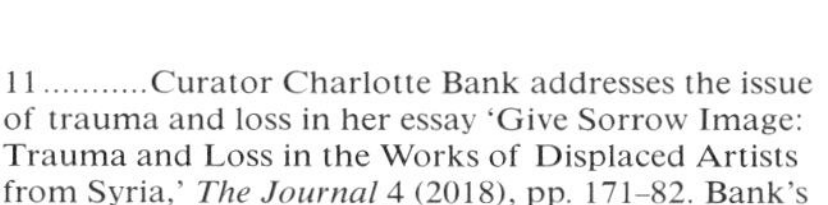

11 ..........Curator Charlotte Bank addresses the issue of trauma and loss in her essay 'Give Sorrow Image: Trauma and Loss in the Works of Displaced Artists from Syria,' *The Journal* 4 (2018), pp. 171–82. Bank's involvement and work with Syrian artists started long before 2011 and continues to this day in her self-managed space in Berlin.

were encouraged to contemplate questions such as 'What is the story about for you?' Some of the main themes that emerged were the love of a mother for her children and the experience of forced displacement. Like the characters of 'Family Ti-Jean,' some of the actors had been confronted with the loss of their homes, family members, and country, with exile, fear, violence, and the loss of hope. The theatre project created a safe space in which to deal with these feelings and painful memories, channelling them through the characters of the play.△Figs. 2 & 5

Sadly, loss worked its way into the artistic process itself: while rehearsals were underway, Alaa Eldin Mohammad Mohammad, the twenty-five-year-old production manager from Syria, drowned in the sea of Byblos. While the distance from Syria and the immersion into the world of acting had been helping them to heal, the sudden death of Alaa brought trauma back to the young actors' lives, sharply and vividly. As the anguish they felt might point to the limits of creating a distance from the everyday afforded by theatre, the story that follows also shows the extent of theatre's cathartic potential. At the gathering they organized in Alaa's memory, one of the actors began reciting lines from 'Ti-Jean': 'I think nothing dies. My brothers are dead, but they live in the memory of our mother.' This entrance of fiction into reality became a magical moment of consolation. As Hossami recalls, 'Smiles broke out, the initial shock of grief lifted. We were alive again.'[12] They performed the play in Shatila that day, as planned.

Pages Bookstore Café's artistic programme aimed to create a community that could collectively help Syrian refugees find catharsis and reconciliation with the past. For example, Kadri established a special theatre group for youth, teaching them professional acting techniques as a way of helping them to channel their personal trauma and intense feelings of loss. However, trauma has continued to shape the project's trajectory, as Kadri and Hajo were forced to close the Istanbul bookshop and relocate to Amsterdam. After running the project at the Amsterdam location for two years, the space was returned to the Prince Claus Fund due to a pre-contractual agreement and the founders decided to pause and not look for a new location. Now they are focused on their own personal healing and survival.

## Home and Alienation

• •

Places, spaces, and their stories emerge as core elements in most of the artworks reviewed in this research. Masrah Ensemble chose to work with the text of 'Family Ti-Jean' in recognition of the potency of these themes: with its focus on family stories, the play could help the participating community of artists to articulate their own definitions of home, both as physical space and symbol. The production process gave the community of displaced actors the opportunity to reflect on their perceptions of

12.......... Eyad Houssami told the story in an interview for this chapter. It can also be found in several articles and testimonies by Houssami.

home, from their vantage point in Shatila refugee camp. Ali, one of the young actors, expresses his feelings in the following terms: 'The play took me back to my grandparents' house in Syria. It created a 'temporary' home for me that made being away more tolerable.'[13] Ali's description resonates with the project's goals. As Milia Ayache, one of the actors from the Ensemble, explains, the team worked hard to build trust amongst the different participating communities so that the project could become a safe haven for all.[14] But they also aimed to foster a more long-lasting sense of home in the city space. While they were working in public spaces, Ayache recalls, a young Syrian girl said that being outside, in the open air outside the refugee camps 'reminded [her] of being at home in Syria.' According to Ayache, the young actors needed to feel that they belonged to Beirut, beyond their confined life in the camp.

The concept of home was also vivid in the artistic programme of the Visual Arts Festival Damascus @DEPO. In the distance between an old home and a new one, stories of conflict, nostalgia, and adaptation are born. Soudade Kaadan, a Syrian Kurdish filmmaker, describes this conflict in the following way:

> As a filmmaker, my main occupation remains Syria, now lost to me. How do you do a project on Damascus when you no longer have access to the city? Are there cities and streets that resemble Damascus? Suddenly one is obliged to [...] recreate Syria as a compromise.[15]

At DEPO, the artworks from Turkish artists also addressed alienation in relation to modernization, while the works from Lebanon spoke to the ever-present hegemony of the private sector over cities, especially Beirut.

## Nomadic Artists

• • •

In tandem with Syrian artists' dispersal across the globe, the term 'nomadic artists' has proliferated in the discourse on Syrian art. It is used both by the artists themselves as well as by practitioners, curators, and researchers—Syrian and non-Syrian alike. The artists who call themselves 'nomadic' generally consider their new dwellings as 'temporary homes.' As Samir Qadiri elaborates in our interview, Syrian artists still seem to think of themselves as being in 'transit,' even though they are working and living in other cities and countries. They are not yet comfortable with their new social environments or new artistic tools. The notion of ephemerality seems to be central to their work and their practice: their

13.......... Eyad Houssami (theatre director/Masrah Ensemble), interview by author, Beirut, 8 January 2020.

14.......... Milia Ayache (theatre director/Masrah Ensemble), interview by author, Beirut, 27 October 2018 and 27 January 2020.

15.......... Wael Qaddour, *Now Then: Testimonials on Independent Syrian Cultural Work* (Beirut: Mamdouh Adwan Publishing House & Ettijahat for Independent Culture, 2017), p. 180.

△ 1
Maryam Samman, *La Ville Amoureuse*, 2013. Courtesy Artist.

projects are never long-term, the funding is temporary, and for the most part, artists remain receptive rather than proactive in their approach to their work. △Fig. 1

The Visual Arts Festival Damascus @DEPO Istanbul itself is a nomadic event. The festival originated in Damascus but moved to Rotterdam and then to Istanbul. When one compares the participating artists' locations at the time of the festival with their original places of birth, it is notable that all the Syrian artists were living outside Syria in 2013—whether it was in Europe or Canada, or in one of the Arab countries that were politically stable at the time. As for the other participating artists, they had either settled outside their countries or were in regular transit between their cities and other cities around the world. Maryam Samman, for example, sees herself as a nomad. As a Syrian-Palestinian artist, she says she has had to 'master the art of survival' to live her life between Beirut and Paris.

The Pages Bookstore Café can also be seen as a nomadic project. Established in Istanbul after Kadri and Hajo's forced exit from Syria, the project had to relocate temporarily to Amsterdam, only to eventually move to a purely virtual presence on social media outlets in the last two years after the Amsterdam café shut down. Kadri says that even though the café created a 'home' for him and many Syrian artists in Istanbul, he always knew that one day, the project would end. On a more hopeful note, he also says that the project has not yet found its final destination.

Masrah Ensemble was founded by a Syrian artist who was born and raised in the U.S. but who now lives in Berlin, along with a cohort of artists who come from different corners of the world. The project's direct circle of immediate beneficiaries, 'the young artists,' are also displaced youngsters. Most live in refugee camps in Lebanon, are still not completely settled in their new homes, and are living in transit in the hope of either getting out of the camp and going to Europe, or eventually going back to Syria.

It is worth mentioning the many of the artists/researchers/curators (including Khaled Barakeh, Ghayath Madhmoun, Hassan Abbas) interviewed in the context of this research (in 2019 and early 2020) expressed concern about the pressure placed on them by their host communities, gallerists and exhibition spaces regarding the themes and questions to be addressed in their work. While many of the artists actively took part in the surge of creative activity surrounding the revolution, their questions and artistic concerns have in most cases evolved since then. With manifold funding schemes and opportunities specifically for Syrian artists now available to them, and with their own sense of personal and moral responsibility towards their country always alive, displaced Syrian artists are pressured to produce works that mirror the political context back home. As such, they can feel a level of discomfort or frustration, not to say pain, at the idea of having to continue address the same questions as before. As Jumana Al-Yasiri argued, Syrian artists' capabilities are not limited to representing the plight of the people (in the homeland and outside); these artists also possess the artistic and intellectual capacities to address topics and questions that transcend their immediate conditions or the political context in their home country. They are eager to escape the condition of 'professional Syrians' and to have their works be considered beyond the political parameters of the struggle in Syria.

## ARTISTS, COMMUNITIES, AND THEIR PUBLICS

### Artists as Social Change Agents

•

Living in undemocratic political systems, artists and intellectuals in the Arab region have not traditionally been catalysts of change in their societies. With the independent cultural scene having little to no space to flourish,

△ 3
Masrah Ensemble Performance, Family T-Jean Project, 2016. Jad Safar/Ettijahat for Independent Culture.

artistic work has had little impact on communities.[16] In addition, Syrian artists have been faced with another complexity: the pressure of aligning themselves along the secular vs. Islamist divide. According to Basma El Husseini, founder of Action for Hope: 'Artists find themselves in the middle of this conflict, siding consciously, or marked as so by the media, with the secular side. Consequently, they are considered hostile to conservative Islam.' Popular perceptions of artists and intellectuals as belonging to 'the elite' also contribute to their stigmatization. Indeed, as Husseini argues, 'This image promulgates a class divide by suggesting that artists and cultural activists do not understand the hardships of the common man.'[17]

These trends changed significantly after 2011. The Arab Spring carried the hope that it would be possible to create pluralistic and inclusive, political and cultural systems, thereby motivating societies to reorganize. In the case of Syria, this discussion around the social and political role of the artist occurred mostly outside the country, among displaced artists. Almost all the artists interviewed in the context of this research view themselves as agents of social change, with strong ethical responsibilities towards their communities and towards other Syrian artists and art organizations.△Fig. 3

## New Publics

Another significant change that must be considered is the displacement of Syrian 'publics.' The majority of displaced Syrians live in isolated refugee camps or in small communities outside major urban centres. With few exceptions, most migrant communities have been isolated from the services and cultural activities provided by their host countries and/or fellow migrants. The situation in Lebanon is perhaps the only exception, as many Syrian artists, academics, and researchers are active agents of Lebanon's cultural scene.

The 'Family Ti-Jean' project was precisely designed to cater to these 'new publics' of Syrian immigrant communities living in Lebanon. It also aimed to strengthen the links between Syrian artists and Lebanon's immigrant communities at large. Early on, Masrah Ensemble realized that the project would need the support of local organizations to meet these objectives. The partnership with 'Create Syria' created a space for Masrah Ensemble to convene with other artists working locally to discuss their methods and practices, especially in terms of community engagement. Meanwhile, the partnership with Basmeh & Zeitooneh facilitated the Ensemble's connection with the immigrant community and ensured that the participants felt ownership of the project.

The Pages Bookstore Café also fashioned several of its activities to cater to the needs of the Syrian refugees in Istanbul. However, it did so with a precise focus on artistic and cultural programming. Unlike the 'Family Ti-Jean' project, the Pages Bookstore Café did not design specific

16..........Ibid., p. 30.

17..........Merhi, *Syrian Art Production*, p. 39.

activities to involve a broader public of Syrian immigrants. Its public was far more inclusive, embracing tourists, students, and Istanbul residents of all walks of life. The fact that it had autonomy over its physical space was crucial in this regard, enabling more regular and intimate relationships with the public to emerge.△Fig. 6

△ 6
Opening, Pages Café Amsterdam, 2019.
Courtesy Pages Café.

It is not easy to identify the audiences that were reached by the Visual Arts Festival Damascus @DEPO. Initially, the project was designed to provide a platform for Turkish, Syrian, and other audiences in Turkey to discover Syrian and Arab artists. However, the sudden disruption of life during the festival seems to have hindered this process. Indeed, several events were cancelled as the city's residents and visitors were preoccupied with the sudden political upheaval at Taksim Square.

Unfortunately, the three projects did not create direct or strong links with artists inside Syria. This can be attributed to several factors, the most obvious being the fact that large numbers of emerging as well as well-established Syrian artists left Syria in the years of the revolution. In addition, there exists a great polarization between the inside and the outside of Syria (including among Syrian artists and intellectuals) that escalates day after day, leading to severe divisions that often amount to accusations of treason and estrangement, and leave a kind of isolation from both sides. This is reinforced by funders' tendency to divide their financial support between the inside and the outside of Syria.[18]

## New Institutional Structures vs. Contextualized Projects

• • •

In their new locations, displaced Syrian artists have faced new challenges: besides the practical tasks of organizing life in an unfamiliar environment, they have also needed to adjust to new institutional structures. Expectations from audiences, curators, and exhibition spaces often no longer correspond to their previous experiences as artists. This leaves them with the triple challenge of having to reconsider their media, their professional position, as well as their self-perception as 'Syrian artists.'[19]

18...........Ibid., p. 39.
19...........Charlotte Bank, *Remaking a World: Recently Displaced Artists from Syria in Berlin* (Berlin: Mobile Culture Studies, 2018), p. 171.

When they lived in Syria, visual artists exhibited solely in galleries. Many artists, especially those who are emerging, often find it extremely difficult to adjust to the contemporary arts scene in their host countries. This puts some at risk of losing their practice. According to most of the artists interviewed, well-established artists have faced fewer challenges in adjusting to new institutional, artistic, and aesthetic norms. Emerging artists suffer far more, as they are often forced to make compromises that often entail being portrayed as refugee artists. Well-established artists, while not immune to the challenges that face the artists in most host countries, tend to be able to sustain themselves financially. Emerging and lesser-known artists struggle.

These observations underscore the timeliness and relevance of the three case studies. As displaced Syrian artists were adjusting to their new environments, the opportunity to participate in projects that were especially tailored to their tools and practices, in an open and understanding environment, came as a relief. The Visual Arts Festival Damascus @DEPO Istanbul was particularly successful in this regard. Having worked with Syrian artists in Damascus prior to the revolution, the project's curators created a non-judgmental platform that was open to Syrian and non-Syrian artists alike. In my interviews, the artists confirmed that they had never felt judged nor pushed to present one image over another. They felt at ease to simply 'be.'

## Use of Social Media

• • • •

After the revolution, the artistic mediums and tools used by displaced artists changed immensely, especially in the visual arts. A new generation of Syrian artists has been using the internet and social networks to speak to the situation in Syria, posting videos, drawings, etchings, paintings, and photos on a variety of channels to reach ever broader audiences. As Charlotte Blake has observed, 'the Internet has become an important platform to distribute works and to comment on the news.'[20] It has also created a safe space for artists to express themselves freely, without fear of persecution. Notwithstanding, many of the projects that started on social media immediately after the revolution were run by artists who chose to remain anonymous. This period led to the creation of several collectives and projects, such and the Foundland Collective and 'Emergency Cinéma' by the filmmakers collective Abounaddara (a collective formed just before the onset of the revolution), which were both showcased at the Visual Arts Damascus Festival @DEPO. As the festival's catalogue explains, 'In the last year [2012], the collective's focus has shifted to considering virtual environments (such as Facebook and YouTube) as public space environments with a political function.'[21]

20..........Charlotte Blake (curator/researcher),interview by author, Berlin, 18 January 2020.

21..........Visual Arts Festival – Damascus @DEPO Istanbul Catalogue, p. 28.

22..........Merhi, *Syrian Art Production*, p. 35.

## FUNDING TRENDS FOR INDEPENDENT SYRIAN ARTISTS AND INITIATIVES

In Syria, before 2011, funding for independent artists and independent artistic initiatives was limited. Syrian artists and organizations working in Syria relied on four central schemes to support their practices: government support, which provided limited direct support for independent artists; corporate responsibility funding, which supported TV productions and entertainment festivals; funding from multinational organizations like UNESCO/UN, channelled through governmental platforms; and finally, support from foreign cultural centres. Until late 2011, the latter—centres such as the Institut Français, the Goethe-Institut and the British Council—played the most significant role in supporting independent artists and art initiatives, laying the ground for the creation of an independent cultural scene in Syria.[22] Regional and international funding agencies also provided important support to independent artists in Syria. Organizations such as Al Mawred Al Thaqafy, the Arab Fund for Arts and Culture (AFAC), and the Young Arab Theatre Fund supported independent contemporary artists through capacity-building, mobility, and production funds.

### Funding Trends Post-2011

Funding trends for Syrian artists and art initiatives changed significantly after 2011.[23] In Syria, foreign cultural offices began to put their operations within the country on hold. The British Council moved its staff and the Syria programme to Lebanon, while Goethe-Institut continued to support Syrian artists through its branches in Beirut and Istanbul.[24] However, outside Syria and especially in nearby Lebanon, Turkey, and Jordan, a new scenario emerged. Regional and international funding organizations started to direct parts of their funding to Syrian artists and Syrian cultural organizations there. The regional Arab organizations cited above increased their funding for Syrian artists and initiatives. International organizations specialized in art and culture, such as the European Cultural Foundation and the Prince Claus Fund, also supported numerous projects that had either been initiated by Syrian artists, targeted Syrian artists, or featured Syria as a central motif.[25]

In the aftermath of the Arab Spring, the Ford Foundation especially redirected significant parts of its funding in the region to support Syrian cultural initiatives such as Action for Hope, Ettijahat–Independent Culture, and the Syrian Cultural Index. Ettijahat-Independent Culture, an NGO that grew out of Al Mawred Al Thaqafy's project Abbara, is currently the leading player in supporting Syrian artists (and a funder of the 'Family Ti-Jean' project). The Arab Fund for Art and Culture (AFAC) was launched in

23 .......... It is impossible to map and survey all the funding trends and support opportunities that exist at present for Syrian artists and art initiatives, as they are scattered all around the world and each country and region, cultural space and gallery has its own specificity. Thus, the analysis here revolves around the three case studies and focuses on the Arab region, as the three projects originated and developed there.

24 .......... Stephanie Twigg (coordinator of culture program at British Council Syria), interview by author, Beirut, 13 February 2019.

25 .......... Merhi, *Syrian Art Production*, p. 35.

2011 to support artists and initiatives that are directly affected by the Arab Intifadas. From 2012 to 2016, the Young Arab Theatre Fund (YATF, now Mophradat) offered support to eight Syrian artists living outside Syria. The Prince Claus Fund launched its support for Syrian art initiatives in 2012, with funding for Pages Bookstore Café in Istanbul, the Visual Arts Festival Damacus @DEPO, and artist group Massasit Mati (who, incidentally, participated in the 2013 edition of the festival). In 2013, the British Council launched 'Arts and Beyond,' followed by the 'Third Space' initiative, which has provided grants to almost seventy Syrian artists living outside the country.

There are several humanitarian agencies that continue to provide psychosocial support in refugee camps through the involvement of artists. While some artists are sceptical of the long-term effects of these interventions, the projects do offer 'free spaces' of relief. For many artists, these projects also provide an income. Other artists engage in these activities out of a sense of ethical responsibility towards their communities, while cultivating their own practice.

It is worth highlighting three interesting characteristics that are common to all funding trends for dispersed Syrian artists, and especially relevant to the three case studies. Almost all funding agencies offer their financial support on the condition that the recipient provide matching funds. It is extremely rare to find a funding agency that will fund a project from inception to conclusion. As a result, artists and art organizations are pressured to stay on a constant lookout for new partnerships and funders to support their projects. In addition, most of the support comes in the form of one-time grants for specific projects or productions, which leaves artists and cultural organizations uncertain about the future of their work and stifles their chances of continuity.

The 'Family Ti-Jean' project was supported by seven different organizations, namely the Prince Claus Fund, International Alert, Create Syria (supported by Ettijahat and the British Council), Al Mawred Al Thaqafy, the French Cultural Center, and the Violet Jabra Charitable Trust. This case illustrates how funding agencies are opting to work within a network of supporting partners rather than as sole funders. Masrah Ensemble had to present the project under different angles (artistic and social) to be able to secure its funding. The 'project-based' nature of the support hampers the fulfilment of the Ensemble's long-term objectives, and the expectations of its different beneficiaries, especially the youth. Some of the youth who participated in the 'Family T-Jean' project frequently checked in with Masrah Ensemble for continuity as the project did not only trigger an interest in theatre as an art form, but also allowed the youth to be integrated within a safe community. This involvement with youth and investment in their talent and emotions demands long-term and stable interventions that must also be institutionally sustained by the theatre itself as Eyad Houssami argues. Charlotte Blake voices the same concern as the project based funding scheme has also hampered the continuity of the Visual Arts Festival.

Finally, a common trend amongst foreign funders is to divide funding between artists working inside and outside of Syria thus hampering continuity between Syrian artists in the homeland and in the exile. This characteristic displaced itself in the three case studies, as the artists who were involved in the projects were only displaced artists.

The Visual Arts Festival Damascus @DEPO Istanbul also suffered from a lack of financial resources, not least because it had partnered with a Turkish cultural organization, depriving it of the coveted 'associative status' that would have made it eligible for other European funding. For the 2013 edition, this meant that it had to be executed on a much more modest scale than initially planned, for instance no longer commissioning new work. With the lack of financial and organizational resources, the festival's long-term sustainability was jeopardized, and it speaks to the curators' ingenuity that they were able to organize the funding of another edition.

The Pages Bookstore Café is a unique case. While the project in Istanbul was supported by the Prince Claus Fund and other organizations, the publishing house that Samir Qadri had founded and run prior to 2011 served as an income-generating project keeping the family afloat since leaving Damascus. Being located in a permanent space in Istanbul, the project garnered much media attention over the years, which in turn inspired several funders to contribute to its program and activities.

## CONCLUDING REMARKS

The longevity, impact, and creativity of the three projects examined in this chapter can be attributed to the strong dedication and determination of the people who directed them—artists acting as curators acting as managers who found ways to overcome limited resources and institutional support. 'Family Ti-Jean' was made possible by professional theatre makers who are dedicated to social change and to working with immigrant and marginalized communities. For the founders of the Pages Bookstore Café, personal and professional trajectories intersected, shaping the course of the project and its development. The insistence of the curators of the Visual Arts Damascus Festival @DEPO Istanbul to go forward with the 2013 edition similarly mirrors an ongoing dedication to Syrian and Arab artists.

The three case studies further make clear that these art initiatives have the intellectual capacity and strategic ambition to do far more than represent the plight of Syrian people: they are evidence of a high degree of resilience and adaptability to new environments, of a sophisticated sense of aesthetics, and of access to professional networks and solidarity movements. All of these skills are called on to ensure that the artists are recognized for their own merits and on their own terms, not because they perform as 'professional Syrians' who can be reduced to the political parameters of the struggle in Syria. The risk of becoming 'professional Syrians' will remain as long as the conflict continues, and surely beyond that time as well, but many artists and art practitioners are already aware of it. As the value of their cultural contributions to their new (host) cities are being recognized, they will be able to better negotiate the terms and conditions of their work.

What matters now is having platforms continue this passionate, vital, and highly sophisticated debate among Syrians and the artists, hosting communities, and funders associated with them. It is imperative that Syrian artists and arts practitioners embark on an 'inner Syrian dialogue,' and that they develop their projects with a fine ear to the needs and desires of Syrian artists, practitioners, and organizations. I am talking about an 'internal' dialogue that includes Syrian artists and researchers who have chosen to remain in Syria. Some possibilities may reside with long-term, careful, and multidimensional collaborations between support organizations from Syria, the Middle East, and Europe and Syrian artists and European art professionals. Together, and in response to the priorities identified by the Syrian artists and publics, they could invent and imagine new tools, different activities, and courageous strategies to help sustain and cultivate the attention currently given to displaced Syrian in order to cultivate a fertile field of art practitioners inside Syria. The artistic movement that is being formed outside the country is creating a strong, sturdy, and independent artistic scene, one that embodies the spirit of civic movement all the while drawing on the strength of regional and international partnerships. This movement could very well be instrumental to future reconciliation processes within Syria.

## ← REFERENCES


Ada, Serhan. 'New Concepts for a New Set of Actions.' August 2018. www.ettijahat.org/page/744.

Al-Yasiri, Jumana. n.d. 'Exiled Scene(s): Anchors and Displacements of the Syrian Theatre since 2011.' www.academia.edu/16958185/Exiled_Scene_s_Anchors_and_Displacements_of_the_Syrian_Theatre_since_2011 (accessed 8 March 2020).

Al-Yasiri, Jumana. n.d. 'The World as a Battlefield: The Migration of Contemporary Syrian Art and the Prospects of Continuity in Hosting Countries.' www.academia.edu/16959108/The_World_as_a_Battlefield_The_Migration_of_Contemporary_Syrian_Art_and_the_Prospects_of_Continuity_in_Hosting_Countries (accessed 8 March 2020).

Appelt, Nicolas. 2017. 'The Syrian Documentary: An Aesthetic Dictated by Ethic.' October 2017. www.ettijahat.org/page/540.

Bank, Charlotte. 'Give Sorrow Images: Memory and Trauma in the Works of Recently Displaced Artists from Syria.' *Contemporary Art, Migration, Studies* (2018).
—. 'Remaking a World: Recently Displaced Artists from Syria in Berlin: Mobile Culture Studies.' *The Journal* 4 (2018), pp. 171–82.

Cusenza, Cristina. 'Artists from Syria in the International Art World: Mediators of a Universal Humanism.' *Arts* 8, no. 45 (2019).

Delphine, Leccas. 2018. 'Dis-Organ-Ised: The Body as a Conflict Zone in Syrian Contemporary Art.' March 2018. www.ettijahat.org/page/629.

DeVlieg, Mary Ann. *Ettijahat-Independent Culture*. https://ettijahat.org/page/553 (accessed 8 March 2020).
—. *Ettijahat-Independent Culture*. www.ettijahat.org/page/574 (accessed 8 March 2020).

Farhat, Fatin. 2017. 'Palestine as a "Profession": Syria Also? By Fatin Farhat, Palestine.' السياسات الثقافية في المنطقة العربية August 2017. www.arabcp.org/page/859.

Gorman, Daniel. 'Ettijahat: Independent Culture.' November 2018. www.ettijahat.org/page/784.

Graan, Mike. 'Forms of Establishing and Structuring Syrian Arts Groups.' *Arab Region Database of Cultural Policy*, August 2018. www.arabcp.org/page/1020.

Griswold, Eliza. 'Mapping the Journeys of Syria's Artists.' *The New Yorker*, 2018. www.newyorker.com/culture/culture-desk/mapping-the-journeys-of-syrias-artists.

Halasa, Malu, Zaher Omareen, and Nawara Mahfoud, eds. *Syria Speaks: Art and Culture from the Frontline*. London: Saqi Books, 2014.

Hamadeh, Dima. 'Bridges, Hearts, Cash: Neoliberal Markets of Cultural Understanding.' *The Contemporary Journal* no. 2 (February 2018).

Hussein, Haitham. 'الأفلام الوثائقية السورية.. ذاكرة الثورة.' *News Agency Al Jazeera*, 2013. www.aljazeera.net/news/cultureandart/2013/9/16/الأفلام-الوثائقية-السورية-ذاكرة-الثورة.
—. 'The Status of the Arts: Current Issues in Artistic Creation in the Arab Region. Jadaliyya,' February 2018. www.jadaliyya.com/Details/35206.

Ilic, Milicia. 'The Necessary Element: Working with the Syrian Arts Scene.' October 2018. www.ettijahat.org/page/771.

Imady, Omar. *The Syrian Uprising*, ed. Raymond Hinnebusch, first ed. London and New York: Routledge, 2018.

Kawakibi, Salam. *On Syrian Cultural Working the Years of Ember*. Beirut: MamdouhAdwan Publishing House, Ettijahat-Independent, 2016.

Mahmoud, Zuhour. 'The Revolutionary Art at the Heart Of Syria's Uprising.' *HuffPost*, 2016. www.huffpost.com/entry/artwork-syrian-war_n_56eafa60e-4b03a640a69e3df.

Naddaf, A.J. 'Do Syrian Artists Lose Their Identity Abroad? SyriaUntold,' 2017 | حكاية ما انحكت.' https://syriauntold.com/2017/08/04/do-syrian-artists-lose-their-identity-abroad/.

News Deeply. 'The Youngsters Turning the Crisis in Lebanon into Living Theater.' 1 August 2016. www.newsdeeply.com/refugees/community/2016/08/01/the-youngsters-turning-the-crisis-in-lebanon-into-living-theatre.

Pearlman, Wendy. *We Crossed a Bridge and It Trembled: Voices from Syria*. New York, NY: Custom House, 2017.

Qaddour, Wael. *Now Then: Testimonials on Independent Syrian Cultural Work*. Beirut: Mamdouh Adwan Publishing House, Ettijahat-Independent, 2017.

Richard, Ferdinand. 'Article Number One.' *Ettijahat*, July 2017. www.ettijahat.org/page/508?_lang=1.

Salem, Alma. 'The Avant-garde Movement in Syrian Art was it a Creative Revaluation?' *Prince Claus Catalogue*, Amsterdam, 2018.

Saih, Ruba, and Sophie Richter-Devroe. 'Cultures of Resistance in Palestine and Beyond: On the Politics of Art, Aesthetics, and Affect.' *ARAB STUDIES JOURNAL* (2014), pp. 8–27.

Yazigi, Rana. 'Syria's Cultural Priorities: Culture as a Component of the Syrian Transition.' *Arab Reform Initiative* (2014). https://archives.arab-reform.net/en/node/468.

Young, James O. *Cultural Appropriation and the Arts*. Hoboken, NJ: Wiley-Blackwell, 2008.


## ← INTERVIEWS

Milia Alyosh (theatre director/Masrah Ensemble), interview by author, Beirut, 27 October 2018 and 27 January 2020.

Asena Gunal (coordinator/DEPO), interview by author, Istanbul, 2 November 2018.

Delphine Leccas (curator/researcher), interview by author, Athens, 10 November 2018.

Racha Nasreddine (director of culture programme at British Council Syria), interview by author, Beirut, 13 February 2019.

Stephanie Twigg (coordinator of culture programme at British Council Syria), interview by author, Beirut, 13 February 2019.

Chadi Makrach (actor), interview by author, Beirut, 14 February 2019.

Fadi Hawashi (actor), interview by author, Beirut, 14 February 2019.

Grace Al Ahmar (actor), interview by author, Beirut, 14 February 2019.

Hamzeh Hamadeh (actor), interview by author, Beirut, 14 February 2019.

Hassan AlMalla (actor), interview by author, Beirut, 14 February 2019.

Seba Kourani (actor), interview by author, Beirut, 14 February 2019.

Anas Yunes (actor), interview by author, Beirut, 14 February 2019.

Abdallah Kafri (director of Ettijahat), interview by author, Beirut, 15 February 2019.

Hanane Haj Ali (actress/researcher), interview by author, Beirut, 14 March 2019.

Mann Hasbani (filmmaker), interview by author, Brussels, 6 June 2019.

Samir Kadri (founder of Pages Café), personal interview, Amsterdam, 10 August 2019.

Ghaiyath Madhoun (writer), interview by author, Berlin, 6 January 2020.

Eyad Houssami (theatre director/Masrah Ensemble), interview by author, Beirut, 8 January 2020.

Hassan Abbas (researcher), interview by author, Beirut, 8 January 2020.

Khaled Barakeh (visual artist), interview by author, Berlin, 10 January 2020.

Charlotte Blake (curator/researcher), interview by author, Berlin, 18 January 2020.

Khaled Jarrar (visual artist), interview by author, Ramallah, 20 January 2020.

Maryam Samman (scenography/ visual artist). Personal Interview, 20 January 2020.

Deniz Uster (visual artist), email to author, Vienna, 22 January 2020.

Ipek Ozden (visual artist), email to author, 30 January 2020.

# NETWORK(ING) FROM LIMA TO JOHANNESBURG

Kabelo Malatsie

If the medium has an impact on our thought patterns and behaviour, how do we network without succumbing to the organizing logic of the technology we use to network?

This chapter interrogates the notion of a network, defined as 'an arrangement of intersecting horizontal and vertical lines' or 'a group or system of interconnected people or things.'[1] In taking Alta Tecnología Andina (ATA), a non profit organization in Lima, Peru, as the case study and examining their project 'MMcL100 Communications, Art and Thought,' (2011) this chapter interrogates the notions of both 'network' and 'networking.' ATA's project took place in Lima and included exhibitions, a seminar, lectures, and workshops celebrating Canadian philosopher Marshall McLuhan's ideas of 'the medium is the message,' 'the global village,' and the 'hybridization of the media.' Pursuing a practice-focused approach Visual Arts Network of South Africa (VANSA), a non profit organization operating from Johannesburg, is put in dialogue with ATA to examine the repercussions of their 'MMcL100 Communications, Art and Thought' project across the South Atlantic Ocean in South Africa. The chapter argues for a vigilant awareness of the social and political impact of the mediums we use as we organize in solidarity with social formations that are working in diverse and often difficult conditions producing multi-axial networks. It concludes that to arrive at true decentralization, there is a need for networks that are rhizomatic, temporalities that are expansive, and technology that is modular and flexible using languages that acknowledge incongruencies of the Majority World.

Keywords
→ Alta Tecnología Andina
→ Visual Arts Network of South Africa
→ Global South
→ Networks

## INTRODUCTION

If the medium has an impact on our thought patterns and behaviour, how do we network without succumbing to the organizing logic of the technology we use to network?

'Network(ing) from Lima to Johannesburg' interrogates the notion of a network, which has been defined as 'an arrangement of intersecting horizontal and vertical lines' or 'a group or system of interconnected people or things.'[2] In choosing as a case study the non profit organization

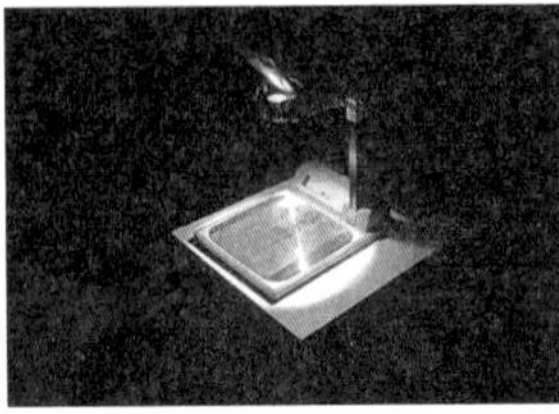

▷ Installation views of *MMcLuhan 100, communication, art and thought*, 2009, courtesy: Fundación Telefónica del Perú

Alta Tecnología Andina (ATA) in Lima, Peru, and examining in particular their project 'MMcL100 Communications, Art and Thought,' (MMcL100) this chapter interrogates the notions of both 'network' and 'networking.' 'MMcL100' took place in Lima in 2011 and included exhibitions, a seminar, lectures, and workshops celebrating Canadian philosopher Marshall McLuhan's ideas of 'the medium is the message,' 'the global village,' and the 'hybridization of the media.' This examines this project across the South Atlantic Ocean in South Africa.

This chapter draws in particular on the examination of textual resources related to ATA and interviews with ATA's José-Carlos Mariátegui, philosopher Victor J. Krebs, and curator Daphne Dragona who curated exhibitions as part of the 'MMcL100' project. Mariátegui was a crucial source for insight into ATA's programmes. I also draw on my personal experience at the arts organization Visual Arts Network of South Africa (VANSA), which I directed from June 2018 to September 2019.

In September 2019, Johannesburg-based VANSA was put into conversation with ATA through a two-day workshop entitled 'Performance Code' that was conceptualized by South African artist Phumulani Ntuli's collective, Pre-empt Group. The workshop connected the cities and people of Lima and Johannesburg through an exploration of networks and networking in the South. The 'Performance Code' workshop was proposed as the methodology to research ATA rather than have the researcher of this article visit ATA in Lima. Such a practice-focused methodology sought to plug VANSA's network to ATA's, thus multiplying both networks. Through the workshop, networking as an interpersonal tool met coding as a technological tool, implicating the city of Johannesburg both as a site and as another form of network. This was a moment in which the theoretical understanding of what a network is was given complexity, as it played itself out within the contextually located workshop—which in itself was speaking back to ATA's 'MMcL100' project.

1............*Oxford English Dictionary* (Oxford: Oxford University Press, 2004), s.v. 'network.'

2............Ibid.

Britto Arts Trust / Dhaka, Bangladesh / 5:17pm 23°44'49.3"N / 90°23'08.6"E

Beyond Pressure / Yangon, Myanmar / 5:41 pm 16°46'37.2"N / 96°10'10.9"E

This chapter further reflects on the nature and function of networks and notions of temporality within the current capitalist technological sphere, and the shifting of national power blocks globally. In their 2009 article 'Social Formations of Global Media Art,' José-Carlos Mariátegui, Sean Cubitt, and Gunalan Nadarajan conclude that, 'the best new media artefacts are not necessarily websites or installations: they may well be the artefacts of new organizational forms, linking local to global struggles, building solidarities.'[3] In this chapter, the term 'social formations' is used to constitute contributions of collective work done by formally registered arts organizations, collectives, and collaborative work on once-off projects. The chapter has three sections; the first section is an introduction to ATA and its 'MMcL100' where key ideas that inspire VANSA's research are discussed. Secondly, the infrastructure that underpins and facilitates networks is unpacked through looking at the discourse that situates networking in the South. Marshall McLuhan wrote that technology would lead to rhizomatic temporality. The last section speaks of the rhizomatic temporality that McLuhan points to and the disconnect between this thinking and how technology in the South is seen by the global north as linear.

This chapter argues for a vigilant awareness of the social and political impact of the mediums we use as we organize in solidarity with social formations that are working in diverse and often difficult conditions producing multi-axial networks.

## NETWORK(ING)

◁ *Performance Code*, workshop at Johannesburg Art Gallery, 2019, courtesy: Visual Arts Network of South Africa and Pre-empt Group

3 José-Carlos Mariátegui, Sean Cubitt, and Gunalan Nadarajan, 'Social Formations of Global Media Art,' *Third Text* 23, no. 3 (2009), pp. 217–28.

Network is a broad term: it can refer to people being connected socially, culturally, and politically; or to biological networks that can be ecological or neurological. It involves technical infrastructure—a network of submarine cables and computer systems that facilitates human interaction. It also involves a network of national and global legal conventions (such as trade agreements) that underpin how accessible infrastructures and people are to each other. And underlying all of these is the capitalist economic system that pushes and pulls many of these forces—enabling, but also undermining and often determining, what is accessible and inaccessible in terms of financial profitability.

The research in this chapter is about the complexity and intersectionality of all these networks. The text oscillates between references to the social and the technological, taking to heart the definition of the term 'technology' as the 'application of scientific knowledge for practical purposes'[4] to deal with the infrastructure or hardware that mediates our connections.

## Alta Tecnología Andina (ATA)

•

ATA was founded in 1995 in Lima (Peru) by scientist, curator, and scholar José-Carlos Mariátegui and economist César Zevallos Heudebert. For over twenty-five years, ATA has been working at the intersection of art, science, and technology. The organization supports and hosts art exhibitions and runs a rich variety of programmes including the annual 'International Video Art Festival;' the 'First National Contest of Video and Electronic Arts,' an Art and Science Creation Laboratory (ATALab) which supports young artists in the creation of their artworks; the MideaTeka video art archive; and Escuelab, a public and production platform (supported by the Prince Claus Fund) that encourages the creation of art through technology.

In 2011, ATA launched the project 'MMcL100' in celebration of McLuhan's significant contribution to media theory and communication. It did so in collaboration with Professor Victor J. Krebs, working on the philosophy and psychoanalysis of technology at the Pontifical Catholic University of Peru, and the Fundación Telefónica, the Peruvian telecommunication company's foundation that has partnered with ATA since 2005 when Fundación Telefónica opened the exhibition space Espacio Fundación Telefónica. 'MMcL100' included an exhibition curated by Daphne Dragona entitled 'Data Bodies: Networked Portraits: Critical Reflections on Today's Interconnected Self.'[5] The show explored identities on social media networks through the perspectives of selected artists, and explored the way in which information technology companies amass personal data provided by unassuming users. Dragona explains that at the time, there

4............Oxford English Dictionary (Oxford: Oxford University Press, 2004), s.v. 'technology.'

5............There are two titles in circulation for the exhibition, 'Data Bodies and Shared Portraits, from the Global Village to Social Networks' as used by ATA in its communication and 'Data Bodies – Networked Portraits: Critical Reflections on Today's Interconnected Self' as used by Daphne Dragona on her website. I use the latter. The following artists participated: Christopher Baker (USA); Heath Bunting (UK); Paolo Cirio and Alessandro Ludovico (Italy); Gabriela Flores del Poso (Peru); Matthias Fritsch (Germany); Aaron Koblin and Daniel Massey (USA); Men In Grey with Julian Oliver (New Zealand) and Danja Vasiliev (Russia); MIT Sociable Media Group with Alex Dragulescu, Aaron Zinman, Fernanda Viegas, and Scott Golder (USA); and Jon Rafman (Canada).

was an air of optimism about the enormous social and political possibilities opened up by information technology.[6] In her exhibition essay, she describes the internet as:

> ... heterogeneous, polyphonic and multicultural. This charming networked condition is based on two fundamental elements: on the growing wealth of data being provided, controlled and exchanged on one hand and on the multitude of users contributing this data on the other.[7]

The artists in the exhibition, however, provided a critical framework for such an optimistic outlook. Artists Paolo Cirio and Alessandro Ludovico's *Face to Facebook* demonstrated the vulnerability of large social networks from which personal information can easily be accessed, stolen, and re-used or even abused. For their project, the artists extracted one million Facebook profile pictures by applying what they call 'a simple algorithm.' They then categorized these pictures into six groups based on the facial expressions ('climber,' 'easy going,' 'funny,' 'mild,' 'sly,' and 'smug') and placed them onto a custom-built dating website. Through their exhibit they critique large social networks that use surveillance techniques for 'crowdsourced targeting,' thus getting users to reveal their own and their friends' desires and then using this information for marketing purposes.[8] While the *Face to Facebook* exhibit revealed the ease of extracting personal data from social media, it was still far from anticipating the abuse such activities would unleash, such as the data breach perpetrated by Cambridge Analytica five years later in order to manipulate the United States' presidential elections of 2016 in favour of Donald Trump.[9] It was only in May 2018 that the European Union finally implemented data protection laws to ensure online privacy.[10] It is this misuse of users' trust by big corporations that Dragona reflects upon in our interview nine years after her exhibition.[11]

Another part of Dragona's 2011 exhibition was the workshop 'NETworkshop: Lightning in the Age of Cloud-Computing' in which artists Julian Oliver and Danja Vasiliev demonstrated the infrastructural and political implications of the increasing dependency on technology and how it could be easily manipulated. The five-day workshop unpacked the inner workings of the internet, from its infrastructure to software (algorithms and code), and mapped where most of the infrastructure that sustains the internet is based. The workshop taught a low-level understanding of

6............Daphne Dragona, Skype interview by author, 10 February 2020.
7............Daphne Dragona, 'Data Bodies – Networked Portraits: Critical Reflections on Today's Interconnected Self.' *Daphne Dragona Curator & Writer*, 2011, https://daphnedragona.net/projects/data-bodies-networked-portraits.
8............Face to Facebook, 'Home,' *Face to Facebook*, www.face-to-facebook.net/.
9............Carole Cadwalladr, '"I made Steve Bannon's Psychological Warfare Tool": Meet the Data War Whistleblower,' *The Guardian*, 17 March 2018, www.theguardian.com/news/2018/mar/17/data-war-whistleblower-christopher-wylie faceook-nix-bannon-trump.
10...........European Commission, 'Data Protection in the EU,' *European Commission*, https://ec.europa.eu/info/law/law-topic/data-protection/data-protection-eu_en.
11...........Daphne Dragona, Skype interview by author, 10 February 2020.

coding exposing its propensity for easy manipulation. It was this workshop that inspired VANSA to invite the Pre-empt Group to host the 'Performance Code' workshop in 2019 as a contextually situated link to 'MMcL100' (as discussed below).

The artists who participated in 'MMcL100' had been predicting the types of scenarios described above as foreseeable consequences of the internet and social networks. José-Carlos Mariátegui fervently argues that the 'MMcL100' artists, as he put it, 'saw into the future,' since many of the works presented there foretold our current interaction with information technology.[12] This was exactly in line with McLuhan who had described the effects of the media on the public in similar terms, and argued that 'the serious artist is the only person able to encounter technology with impunity, just because he [sic] is an expert aware of the changes in sense perception.'[13]

## Visual Arts Network of South Africa (VANSA)

VANSA was founded in 2003 when several artists decided to call on fellow artists to form a lobby and advocacy group throughout South Africa with regional representation in each of the country's nine provinces. Its aim is to support art practices in South Africa by developing industry knowledge, resources, networks, and projects concerned with opening up new social, cultural, and economic possibilities for artists. VANSA aims to be a decentralized network with bases in each of the country's nine provinces. Yet challenges with access to financial resources and to capacity, driven by regional economic disparities, resulted in the collapse of the network's regional representations, leaving a single office that operates from Johannesburg. VANSA is part of the Arts Collaboratory, a network of twenty-five arts organizations from all over the world (including Palestine, Costa Rica, Kyrgyzstan, and Cameroon, to name but a few) mostly located in the Global South.[14] VANSA's emphasis on networking with other art organizations around the world by sharing strategies and support reflects their translocal solidarity with social formations operating in economic and/or political precarity.

As of 2020, VANSA has over 6,300 members, made up of artists, curators, writers, administrators, gallerists, arts organizations, and art enthusiasts spread throughout the country. It is rather unfathomable that one organization would represent such a vast number of practitioners and support them by providing industry research, offering workshops, staging exhibitions and, importantly, lobbying governments on behalf of the visual arts. Importantly, by defining itself as a network, VANSA embraces decentralization as the guiding strategy for its work, and therefore works with practitioners in their various locales within a horizontal leadership

12 José-Carlos Mariátegui and Victor Krebs, Skype interview by author, 4 February 2020.

13 Marshall McLuhan, *Understanding Media: The Extension of Man* (Berkeley: Gingko Press, 2017), p. 31.

14 I reflect on terms such as 'Global South' and their value in today's landscape later in this article.

15 Pre-empt Group 2018 workshop document.

system that, as a network, formally and conceptually challenges the familiar asymmetrical power relationships between urban and rural. Two elements are central to using decentralization as a methodological approach: a focus on power dynamics (as already stated) and a focus on language. Language here is understood not in terms of linguistic understanding but rather in the sense of culture-specificity where every place has its own way of working, its own pace and rhythm. Many provinces communicate in their own language (such as isiXhosa in the Eastern Cape or isiZulu in KwaZulu Natal) while others use several languages (Tshivenda, Xitsonga, and Sepedi are all spoken, for example, in Limpopo). Each of these languages has its own cultural code and artistic heritage. In addition, a focus on language means taking seriously cultural readings of factors such as age, gender, and economic capacity as well as thinking about rural, peri-urban, and urban differences in terms of pace and rhythms. Decentralization thus means accepting that there is no one-size-fits-all model that can be used, even within one province. While VANSA is unable to respond to all the issues that its members have in their different locales in a speedy manner, there is a desire on VANSA's part to be sensitive to and understand these multiple dynamics, which results in very engaged interactions and includes the need to fill in gaps of varying degrees amongst and between the members of the network.

It is important to VANSA to be a plug for arts practitioners and foster networks amongst members while being vigilant that networking as a practice needs constant reflection. This chapter and the workshop are other instances where these principles applied. The Performance Code workshop was held at the Johannesburg Art Gallery in September 2011, which boasts one of the country's best art collections but struggles to survive in a now largely rundown part of the inner city. At this workshop Phumulani Ntuli and his colleagues from the Pre-empt Group facilitated discussions of the same concepts that Oliver and Vasiliev had raised in Lima in 2011. The Pre-empt Group is a Johannesburg-based collective of artists that come together to work collaboratively and host the Pre-make Workshop Series with Performance Code as one of many. They describe these workshops in the following manner:

> [The] Pre-make Workshop Series is a constellation of workshops composed of [a] different process of critical thinking, exchange, reflection, pedagogy, storytelling, and problem solving to foster the notion of collaboration amongst youth as a space of resisting dominant cultural spectrums. The workshop series attempts to diversify content, or create content from the perspective of marginality in order to enhance new artistic voices within the Performance/Visual/Sonic Landscape. The important vista of radical artistic thesis comes from the place of disfranchisement where various vistas are proposed in an open and dynamic environment. As such the workshop encourages interaction and/or collaboration with participants as active agents within disparate spaces of culture, knowledge, and conflict (sexual/religious/traditional).[15]

At its Performance Code workshop, the Pre-empt Group uses a small Raspberry Pi computer system that can be built to do almost anything and, as it comes with no proprietary software, is immune to the risks of data mining. The group applies to its practice philosopher Jacques Rancière's concept of non-hierarchical learning, drawn from his book *The Ignorant Schoolmaster: Five Lessons in Intellectual Emancipation*.[16] Participants alternate between being teacher or learner—a method that flattens out the hierarchies prevalent in most learning conditions.

The Performance Code workshop held at the Johannesburg Art Gallery established a network of peers right at the beginning, having invited participants to explain to each other their distinct and varied practices. All participants were art practitioners working in theatre, dance, design, music, and the visual arts. Film was used as a theme and vehicle to inform the entire workshop: Mishal Husain's 2011 documentary *How Facebook Changed the World: The Arab Spring* (Part 1 of 4) led to a discussion on the roles of social media within sociopolitical protest and of social networks in social formations. John Akomfrah's 1996 sci-fi film, *The Last Angel of History*, followed on that same day. On day two, José-Carlos Mariátegui spoke via Skype about how his curatorial work navigates the intersection between art, technology, and science and engaged in a question-and-answer session with the participants. The Pre-empt Group then introduced participants to the Raspberry Pi computer and its many uses, introducing them to open source and modular technologies. The modularity of the Raspberry Pi and the increasing surveillance through technology can stifle dissenting voices which is ever more important as we see the increasing polarization and right wing sentiments in the world. Open source technology can provide relative autonomy for people imagining ways of being in the world without falling into the traps that most existing technological mediums impose. These traps have been seen in artificial intelligence algorithms that have been critiqued for perpetuating stereotypes and cultural prejudices. This is because the pre-selected datasets that are used for the initial pattern recognition carry the programmers' prejudice. The effects of this are visible in the prejudiced profiling in facial recognition software. As McLuhan writes, 'Any medium has the power of imposing its own assumption on the unwary.'[17]

The success of the workshop thus lay particularly in this introduction of art practitioners to a technology that allows the building of networks outside of the purview of the technological systems widely provided (seemingly for free) by capitalist companies.

Arts organizations in most parts of the world often get their funding from development agencies whose monitoring and evaluation metrics are based on quantity and ever faster delivery timelines, rather than programming that considers the complexities I have mentioned above, or providing interventions that have a longer lasting impact. The question then is, how do we continue to build social formations that add complexity to our understanding of the world in the face of these challenges?

16.......... Jacques Rancière, *The Ignorant Schoolmaster: Five Lessons in Intellectual Emancipation* (Palo Alto: Stanford University Press, 1991); Phumulani Ntuli of Pre-empt Group, conversation with author July 2019.

17.......... McLuhan, *Understanding Media*, p. 28.

## Lima to Johannesburg and Back: Attempts at Topography

• • •

In this section, I explore the conditions that underpin networks in and between cities such as Lima and Johannesburg where ATA and VANSA operate from respectively. Chief among them is the technological infrastructure of endless submarine cables, connecting Africa and South America, which provide connectivity to the internet. These cables are in themselves a network of relations between countries, resources, and capital, and mostly owned by global commercial corporations. Often these networks point to complex webs of relations that cascade and ripple through societies and the world until they reach the individual user who, while being the most visible aspect of those networks, is hardly their initiator.

Another element of this topography is linguistic conventions. Lima is the capital city of Peru. It is 10,872 km away from Johannesburg, South Africa's largest city. These two cities have few similarities: Lima lies on the Pacific coast and is surrounded by mountains and rivers; Johannesburg is landlocked with a man-made urban forest and gold mine dumps marking its founding history. Both are economic hubs of their respective countries. Yet both countries are often spoken about as belonging to the 'Global South.' This has become the accepted term replacing earlier descriptions of them as 'developing' or 'Third World' countries. Access to technology is part of the drive of development agencies working in these countries, where the promise of technology is championed as tool to usher in progress.[18]

Sociologist Sophia Olivia Sanan argues that 'Global South' is a binary term coined in response to the terms 'Global North,' 'Euro-America' and 'the West.'[19] In recent years, especially with the rise of China as international leader in technological advancement, the term has acquired more complexity. The argument for a 'Global South' is based on the assumption of a geographically defined dichotomy between 'centre and periphery,' but for quite some time now it has been apparent that what counts as the centre is shifting. The New Delhi-based artist collective Raqs Media Collective, for instance, in response to a question on centre and periphery, highlighted the complexity of cities in the South: while they have a great capacity for growth, this is also often accompanied by an equal tendency towards volatility.[20] The language that describes cities in the South must convey this complexity and perpetual shifting. And yet, the notion that power is invariably based in the Global North remains the proffered logic of development agencies when they operate in the South, thus imposing this on the cultural organizations they work with.

Bangladeshi photographer Shahidul Alam feels it is important to own the lexicon being used when speaking about developing countries or the Global South, for which he coined the term 'Majority World,' also the

18..........Mariátegui, Cubitt, and Nadarajan, 'Social Formations,' pp. 217–28; McLuhan, *Understanding Media*, p. 28.

19..........Sophia Olivia Sanan, 'Voices from the Global South,' *ArtAfrica*, December 2015, https://artafricamagazine.org/voices-from-the-global-south-by-sophia-sanan/.

20..........Francesca Ceccherini and Noriko Yamakoshi, 'An Interview with Raqs Media Collective,' *Oncurating* no. 41 (June 2019), pp. 90–96.

name of the photo agency he founded that represents photographers from the South.[21] His practice is commendable as it not only incorporates the means of production by representing photographers and questioning documentary photography and its role beyond selling images, but since it also demands an understanding of the power the medium of photography wields, even when the photographer is not from the Global North.

As a member of the Arts Collaboratory,[22] VANSA shares the commitment to translocal solidarity by investing in local networks. Similar to Alam, the Arts Collaboratory has developed its own language, that is to say its own ethical codes, vocabulary, and tools based on common interests. For example, it uses the term *banga*—meaning 'tide' in Lithuanian and 'time and space' in Luganda—to 'call for gathering' when it asks for reciprocal support or collective study of a specific subject. Such a vocabulary that uses more than one linguistic reference and framework not only relates to the multiple frameworks that are at work within the Arts Collaboratory but also adds to the awareness of inherited hierarchical and violent ways of working that need constant interrogation and of other forms of working that must be tested and changed or even discarded. These codes and forms of navigating organizational modes of working are harder to translate to local networks because of the differing cultural codes that pervade territories.

However, for the same reasons I mentioned earlier when discussing VANSA's multi-layered approach, it is an intentional provision to extend these ethics and modes of working into each member organization's local network. As demonstrated above, context requires a localization of ethics in the VANSA network. Similarly, the Arts Collaboratory network intersects multiple languages, cultures, time zones, and networks within networks. For example, to draw on VANSA's experience, the province of Kwazulu-Natal in South Africa is very hierarchical. The translation of some of VANSA's codes, such as horizontal structures of working, needs to be done here in ways that can be understood culturally, without stepping on toes by ignoring ingrained ways of working as these codes may lead to conflict within the local community. Often the time it takes for such a translation is lengthy, because in so many ways it is a practice-based 'language.' Arts Collaboratory's invention of language and terms of engagement speaks to Alam's demand that we must dismantle and create terms that are more suited to ourselves, the Majority World, rather than rely on terms that have been used to define 'Developing Countries.'

A more satisfying framework that seeks to go beyond geography is 'South as a State of Mind.' Not coincidentally this is also the name of a magazine that was established in Athens in 2012 by Marina Fokidis and the Kunsthalle Athena team after the Greek financial crisis. While the term is not yet widely used, it offers an opportunity to include cities that are

21..........Shahidul Alam, 'With Photography as My Guide,' *World Literature Today* 87, no. 2 (March/April 2013), pp. 132–37.

22..........The organizations that belong to the Arts Collaboratory operate from the following cities: Santa Cruz (Bolivia), Cali, Bogotá and Medellín (Colombia), San José (Costa Rica), Mexico D.F. (Mexico), Yogyakarta and Jakarta Selatan (Indonesia), Athurugiriya (Sri Lanka), Beirut (Lebanon), Ramallah and Jerusalem (Palestine), Douala (Cameroon), Lubumbashi (Democratic Republic of Congo), Cairo (Egypt), Accra (Ghana), Bamako (Mali), Dakar (Senegal), Johannesburg (South Africa), Kampala (Uganda), Amsterdam and Utrecht (The Netherlands), and Bishkek (Kyrgyzstan).

located within the geographical space of the Global North, such as New Orleans in the south of the United States of America, but that experience similar forms of othering as cities like Lima or Johannesburg. The reasoning behind this is found in the journal's mission:

> *South as a State of Mind* is a bi-annual arts and culture journal published in Greece and distributed internationally. Possessed by a spirit of absurd authority, we try to contaminate the prevailing culture with ideas that derive from southern mythologies such as the 'perfect climate,' 'easy living,' 'chaos,' 'corruption,' and the 'dramatic temperament,' among others. Through our twisted—and 'southern'—attitude, expressed through critical essays, artist projects, interviews, and features, we would like to give form to the concept of the South as a 'state of mind' rather than a set of fixed places on the map. People from different—literal or metaphorical—'Souths' renegotiate the southern attitude, partly to define it and partly to invent it, within the post-crisis world. Opening up an unexpected dialogue among neighbourhoods, cities, regions, and approaches, *South as a State of Mind* is both a publication and a meeting point for shared intensities.[23]

In line with Alam's thoughts on owning language and the means of production, writer and artist Raimi Gbadamosi, in his text 'Of Wastelands and Landfills,' bemoans Africa's position as 'passive end user' when it comes to the use of technology. He argues that, 'What is crucial is who designs the technology and has legitimate sense of ownership.'[24] Gbadamosi thus points to an additional level of ownership of the manufacturing of technology that needs to be considered and has not been in Africa.[25] The sharp increase in internet traffic and the need for cybersecurity has seen more submarine cables being laid down throughout the world. African governments and private corporations own a few of the submarine cables connecting Africa and South America. While the modest level of ownership especially for cables co-owned by Chinese private corporations[26] does not exactly rectify the issues raised by Gbadamosi, it is a small step towards a more direct connection in the South. The recent rise in ownership of submarine cables by Google, Amazon, and Facebook[27] has raised concern over the loss of freedom that this may bring to end-users. However, filmmaker Wanuri Kahiu argued that, although Africans may not own the means of production through the manufacturing of technology, but are rather the dumping ground for e-waste, they are nevertheless adept at creating objects that work outside of their initial use, a status he has termed,

23 ........... South as a State of Mind, 'About,' *South as a State of Mind*, 2020, https://southasastateofmind.com/about/.

24 ........... Raimi Gbadamosi, 'Of Wastelands and Landfills,' *African Futures: Thinking About the Future Through Word and Image*, ed. Lien Heidenreich-Seleme and Sean O'Toole, pp. 183–99 (Bielefeld: Kerber, 2016).

25 ........... Ibid.

26 ........... Jeremy Page, Kate O'Keefe, and Rob Taylor, 'Explained: US, China's Undersea Battle for Control of Global Internet Grid,' *Business Standard*, July 2019, www.business-standard.com/article/international/explained-us-china-s-undersea-battle-for-control-of-global-internet-grid-119031300168_1.html.

27 ........... Jameson Zimmer, 'Google Owns 63,605 Miles and 8.5% of Submarine Cables Worldwide,' *Broadband Now*, September 2018, https://broadbandnow.com/report/google-content-providers-submarine-cable-ownership/.

'waste-product user.'[28] This is in itself an ownership albeit at a different scale. The slight detour in discussing another lay of ownership reveals the many layers of infrastructural networks that can be discussed even though this chapter only touches on a small part of it.

Last in this section, I touch on the concept of globalism. Invariably, ideas of globalization or universalism arise in association with the internet and technology. Access to technology conjures up ideas of the seeming universal access to information almost in real time. A similar form of universalism is present in the art world. In his essay 'From Medium to Message: The Art Exhibition as Model of a New World Order,' art historian Boris Groys writes about contemporary art's aspiration to present the universal, especially in biennales and mega shows:

> So every biennial can be seen as a model of such a new world order because every biennial tries to negotiate between national and international, cultural identities and global trends, the economically successful. ... And today, the biennials are again the spaces where two closely interconnected nostalgias are installed: nostalgia of universal art and nostalgia of universal political order and the politically relevant.[29]

Yet globalization has been critiqued for creating 'homogenous citizens' and erasing local specificity. In response, anthropologist Aihwa Ong proposed the term 'global assemblage' as a possible alternative. It sidesteps the critique against globalization and instead focuses on the specificities of the diverse localized knowledge within the Majority World:

> I propose a 'global assemblage' concept for framing particular globalized milieus emerging out of complex mediations between global forms and situated political and ethical forces.The concept of 'assemblage' configures a space of inquiry that brings analytical and reflexive precision to our investigation of novel contexts of change. By identifying the specific interaction of disparate variables—global and situated—in a particular site, we account for the crystallization of conditions of possibility within which reflexive practices are exercised. The goal is to investigate how a particular correlation of technologies, institutions, and material resources constitutes a space of intervention that is simultaneously global and distinctive.[30]

While we do not live in a universal world, access to similar information through the internet is a given. The notion of 'global assemblage' allows for this information to be processed locally, precisely in the ways José-Carlos Mariátegui, Sean Cubitt, and Gunalan Nadarajan describe in their essay 'Social Formations.' Their demand for 'localization' of

28 ........... Wanuri Kahiu, 'Technology is Our Mirror,' *African Futures: Thinking About the Future Through Word and Image* (Bielefeld: Kerber, 2016), pp. 227–42.

29 ........... Boris Groys, 'From Medium to Message: The Art Exhibition as Model of a New World Order,' *Open: The Art Biennial as a Global Phenomenon* 8, no. 16 (2009), p. 65.

30 ........... Armen Avanessian and Suhail Malik, 'Situating Global Forms: Aihwa Ong, Interviewed by Armen Avanessian and Suhail Malik,' *9th Berlin Biennale for Contemporary Art*, 2016, https://bb9.berlinbiennale.de/situating-global-forms/.

knowledge is similar to Ong's call for 'situated political and ethical forces.' Ong's 'global assemblage' sidesteps Gbadamosi's notion of 'passive end user' and goes beyond Kahiu's argument to propose that ownership happens when universal information or technology made elsewhere is localized and made distinct.

## Futurity: Time within Art and Technology

• • • •

Lastly, technology often conjures up notions of futurity and progress. Networks and networking operate within this temporality where technology acts as a bridge between social formations from all over the world. It is also a vehicle for sharing of strategies and capacities in the 'Majority World' where there are varying degrees of economic and political disparity. It is important to discuss this for a couple of reasons: for one, by studying ATA's 2011 'McML100' project, this chapter looks backwards in time at an event that in itself operated as a form of time capsule of a famed philosopher and social theorist who worked in the 1960s. For another, time matters when considering the future that is often conjured at the intersection of art and technology. And lastly, time refers to McLuhan's own proposition that technology introduces a temporal shift from linearity to the rhizomatic.

To examine time in greater detail, let's look at 'Expanded Citizen: The Future is Today,' the exhibition and accompanying seminar that formed part of the 'MMcL100' project.[31] Curated by philosopher Victor J. Krebs, 'Expanded Citizen' worked on two levels: first, as a historical account of media and technology and, second, as a projection of the potential of technology for the future. The works in the 'MMcL100' project intimated future scenarios of heavy reliance on technology in daily life, eerily anticipating the writing of this article, eight years later, for which I have relied heavily on e-books, search engines, and Google translations from Spanish to English. Offline and online is no longer separated by a clear boundary, as it may have been in 2011 when the exhibition was shown and already suggested such a blending of existences. The artists and creators who participated in 'Expanded Citizen' presented possible futures for the radio, telephone, television, computer, book, clock, cinema, photography, clothing, and digital manufacturing, that reality has now caught up with. These artistic propositions were offered at a time when the obsolescence of some of these technologies, such as the printing press, was not yet imaginable in Peru.[32] One of the participating artists, Elena Damiani, for example, presented a work that imagined the obsolescence of printed matter and pointed towards the use of e-books.

Technology in particular has created contradictions in our understanding of the concept of time: on the one hand, technology saves time by accelerating and increasing capacity but it also transplants us into

31 ........... Participating artists were: José Aburto and Sebastián Burga (Peru), Gustavo Bockos (Peru) , Elena Damiani (Peru), Clifford Day (Peru), Valeria Ghezzi (Peru), Clara Huárniz (Peru), Beno Juárez (Peru), Gabriel Lama and Jab Lemur (Peru). Lastly, there were master lectures by Norberto Cambiasso (Argentina), Jorge La Ferla (Argentina), Derrick de Kerckhove (Canada) and Bob Stein (USA).

32 ........... Jośe-Carlos Mariátegui and Victor Krebs, Skype interview by author, 4 February 2020.

the future, be it colloquially or in terms of such concepts as Afrofuturism or the many art exhibitions that include future in their premise, such as Krebs' 'Expanded Citizen: The Future is Today.' In an article introducing her SIGGRAPH 2017 exhibition 'Unsettled Artifacts: Technological Speculations from Latin America,' visual artist and educator Paula Gaetano Adi argues that, 'technological artefacts ... help us recognize that we all make the choices that create the future.'[33] In Adi's text, artefacts also project alternative futures. Groys approached it differently: in his 2017 essay 'Art, Technology, and Humanism' when citing Heidegger that 'technology is for him [Heidegger] primarily the interruption of the flow of time, the production of reservoirs of time in which time ceases to flow towards the future – so that a return to previous moments of time becomes possible.'[34] Groys continues to say that the reservoir of time holds true for museums where a return to seeing an artwork that was seen in previous time is possible. This, of course, applies not just to the museum but also to the printing press, photography, video documentaries, and other technologies that allow for the storage of time. José-Carlos Mariátegui argues that technology's storage capacity holds great potential for countries such as Peru where Indigenous knowledge and languages are being shared across communities that have lost their own ways of speaking. He emphasizes the importance of the recovery or storing of time and memory.[35]

In my experience, Phumulani Ntuli's Pre-empt Group and numerous other artists and autodidacts pull apart technology in order to open up other possibilities beyond the technology's intended use, situating their practice within anthropologist Ong's 'global assemblage.' Artists who work with technology on the African continent and its diaspora are often termed Afrofuturists—it is, however, a term that has met a fair amount of resistance, particularly on the continent. Critics comment that it is a reflection of African American perspectives, and they consider that it focuses on diasporic exile in order to then create the alienation that Afrofuturism explores.[36] 'African futurism' has been proposed as alternative term to distinguish futurism from the continent from diasporic futurism. Krebs reflects on time as being rhizomatic:

> ... we live in a society which is rhizomatic, we exist in a network of synchronicities, and so this future that has come with the web, with media, is more compatible with a way of living and thinking in Latin America.[37]

The notion of the rhizomatic time of Latin America and Africa speaks to the non-linearity of Lima and Johannesburg as temporal spaces. Krebs'

33 Paula Gaetano Adi, 'Unsettled Artifacts: Technological Speculations from Latin America: Introduction,' *Leonardo* 50, no. 4 (2017), pp. 410–13.
34 Boris Groys, 'Art, Technology, and Humanism,' *E-flux Journal*, no. 82 (May 2017).
35 Jośe-Carlos Mariátegui and Victor Krebs, Skype interview by author, 4 February 2020.
36 Kodwo Eshun, 'Further Considerations of Afrofuturism,' *The New Centennial Review* 3, no. 2 (Summer 2003), pp. 287–302.
37 Skype interview with Jośe-Carlos Mariátegui and Victor Krebs, 4 February 2020.

sentiments are also in line with McLuhan's projection in the 1960s that the Global North would also ultimately exist in rhizomatic time because of the use of technology that occupies simultaneous timelines, and that this would be a radical shift from the linearity produced by the printed book introduced in the fifteenth century. That said, there is still linearity in the way the Global North defines progress when it comes to the Majority World: it is expected to be linear not rhizomatic. Technology in the Majority World would only create more synchronicities, because of its rhizomatic nature of life coupled with the rhizomatic temporality that McLuhan pointed to.

## CONCLUSION

This chapter points to networks and network(ing) in the Majority World and highlights the geopolitics that underpin how we relate to one another. The reflections on ATA's 2011 'MMcL100 Communications, Art and Thought' project and the enacted, practice-focused networking of young artists and organizations through the 2019 'Performance Code' workshop show the importance of what Mariátegui, Cubitt, and Nadarajan describe as 'linking local to global struggles, building solidarities.'[38] As the exploration demonstrates, however, the need remains paramount to develop modular technologies that enable multicultural, multi-axial, and rhizomatic temporalities, even within powerful nation states. It is the experimental space of artistic practice—and the critical nature of artists themselves—that offers possibilities for the polyphony that curator Daphne Dragona evoked in her 2011 exhibition 'Data Bodies—Networked Portraits: Critical Reflections on Today's Interconnected Self.' If we arrive at true decentralization, we will have achieved networks that are rhizomatic, temporalities that are expansive, and technology that is modular and flexible using languages that acknowledge incongruencies of the Majority World. In this line of thinking, artist Kodwo Eshun's article 'Further Considerations on Afrofuturism' is apt:[39]

Afrofuturism, then, is concerned with the possibilities for intervention within the dimension of the predictive, the projected, the proleptic, the envisioned, the virtual, the anticipatory and the future conditional.

38..........Mariátegui, Cubitt, and Nadarajan, 'Social Formations,' p. 228.

39..........Kodwo Eshun, 'Further Considerations of Afrofuturism,' p. 293.

## ← REFERENCES

Alta Tecnología Andina. 'Sobre ATA.' *Alta Tecnología Andina*. http://ata.org.pe/sobre-ata/.

Bestia, Bastian. 'Archivo de la Etiqueta: Lima.' *Bastian Bestia Wordpress*, 2013. https://bastianbestia.wordpress.com/tag/lima/.

Bristow, Tegan. 'Introductory Essay: Post African Futures.' In *Post African Futures*, pp. 4–7. Johannesburg: Goodman Gallery, 2015.

Fundación Telefónica. 'Fundación Telefónica y Alta Tecnología Andina presentan la exposición "Ciudadano expandido: El futuro es hoy."' *Fundación Telefónica*, 9 September 2011. www.fundaciontelefonica.com/noticias/17_01_2014_esp_6370-2389///9/.

Groys, Boris. 'Cosmic Anxiety.' *9th Berlin Biennale for Contemporary Art*, 2016. http://bb9.berlinbiennale.de/cosmic-anxiety/.

Hernández Calvo, Max, José-Carlos Mariátegui, and Jorge Villacorta, eds. *El mañana fue hoy: 21 años de videocreación y arte electrónico en el Perú = The Future was Now: 21 Years of Video and Electronic Art in Peru*, trans. Nicolás del Castillo and Stephanie Rendell-Dunn. Lima: Alta Tecnología Andina, 2018.

Kahiu, Wanuri. 'Ancestors of the Future.' In *African Futures: Thinking About the Future Through Word and Image*, ed. Lien Heidenreich-Seleme and Sean O'Toole, pp. 165–75. Bielefeld: Kerber, 2016.

Lemur, Jab. 'Jab Lemur– AVATARES, Princesita Pop en busca del amor (excerpt).' *Vimeo*, 1 August 2016. https://vimeo.com/177103990.

Mariátegui, José-Carlos. 'Techno-Revolution: False Evolution?' *Third Text* 13, no. 47 (1999), pp. 71–76.

Martinez, Chuz. 'The Complex Answer.' *9th Berlin Biennale for Contemporary Art*, 2016. https://bb9.berlinbiennale.de/the-complex-answer/.

Mbembe, Achille. 'Africa in the New Century.' In *African Futures: Thinking About the Future Through Word and Image*, ed. Lien Heidenreich-Seleme and Sean O'Toole, pp. 315–37. Bielefeld: Kerber, 2016.

McLuhan, Marshall. *Understanding Media: The Extensions of Man*. Reprint edition. Cambridge, MA: MIT Press, [1964] 1994.
—, and Bruce R. Powers. *The Global Village: Transformations in World Life and Media in the 21st Century*. Reprint edition. Oxford: Oxford University Press, 1992.

Nkosi, Thenjiwe Niki. 'Radical Sharing.' In *African Futures: Thinking About the Future Through Word and Image*, ed. Lien Heidenreich-Seleme and Sean O'Toole, pp. 255–73. Bielefeld: Kerber, 2016.

Playboy Magazine. 'The Playboy Interview: Marshall McLuhan.' *Playboy Magazine*, March 1969.

Steyerl, Hito. 'Too Much World: Is the Internet Dead?' *E-flux Journal* no. 49 (November 2013). www.e-flux.com/journal/49/60004/too-much-world-is-the-internet-dead/.

Synchronicity23. 'MMcLuhan 100: Comunicacion, arte y pensamiento.' *Synchronicity23's Blog*, 31 July 2011. https://synchronicity23.wordpress.com/2011/07/31/mmcluhan-100-comunicacion-arte-y-pensamiento/.

## ← INTERVIEWS

Jośe-Carlos Mariátegui and Victor Krebs, Skype interview by author, 4 February 2020.

Daphne Dragona, Skype interview by author, 10 February 2020.

# COLLECTIVE CREATIONS
## Art and Politics for the Present

Paulina E. Varas

This chapter captures useful ideas to think about current-day socio-political dynamics and their intersection with art and politics. I analyze three different examples of practices of collective creation including exhibiting practices, public events, and sound records, and propose thinking of them, to use Gilles Deleuze's term, as 'Common Notions,' that help us resist oppressive politics of the present and imagine futures.

The three case studies analyzed in this chapter include the exhibition and project 'Beginning As Well As We Can (How Do We Talk About Fascism Today?)' by What, How & for Whom (WHW), a group of curators based in Zagreb, Croatia; the group Civil Association for Creating Independent and Artistic Networks (CRIA) and their project 'LA CRIATURA' developed in Buenos Aires; and the Audiomapa project of artist group Tsonami in Valparaíso, Chile. The chapter draws on theories of social change that offer various approaches to mitigate forms of fascism that are re-emerging in societies that we understand as democratic; to follow the urgent demand for new emancipatory pedagogies that allow us to freely access new knowledge and value our own; and to address the appropriation and devastation of nature by capitalist societies—conditions encountered and addressed by the three projects respectively. I use key texts by Suely Rolnik, Félix Guattari, Silvia Rivera Cusicanqui, Isabelle Stengers, and others who accompany some of the ideas in this text, concluding with a call to think about how we can reactivate our neutralized sensitivity and learn from cultural experiences that contribute to a re-sensitization of our lives through art and politics.

Keywords
→ Art and Politics
→ Collectives
→ Critical Pedagogy
→ Ecosophy

### THEORETICAL FRAMEWORK

'All the old ways of life are devastated', said Félix Guattari (1930–1992) at an environmental conference[1] in Chile in May 1991.[2] As the French philosopher made clear, traditional forms of production have been expropriated by new forms of technological development; as a result, some cultures have been destroyed and many centres of production have been destabilized by general uncertainty and lack of direction.

By 2020, he went on to say, the number of inhabitants on the planet would be unmanageable, with urban ghettos pervasive and life in the big cities entirely unsustainable. He wondered how to counter such forms of neoliberalism—what he described as a 'delusional mythology that consists in believing that problems can solve themselves.'[3] For Guattari, environmental devastation—visible or not—could not be separated from the personal, internalized devastation experienced by individual people, because social, technical, and personal ecosystems are always intertwined. Guattari thus proposed what he called 'Ecosophy,' an expansion of the concept of ecology in order to move beyond exclusively rationalist or Western scientific assessments of ecological problems. As he pointed out: 'If at the heart of the ecological object we introduce problems of ecosystems, not only of social life, but also of art, of incorporeal mathematical universes, we will be introducing personal dimensions, dimensions of the unconscious, of subjectivity and, more importantly, dimensions that I would call ethical-political.'[4]

Ecosophy is thus a path that appeals to a conception of the earth as finite, where human and non-human beings must cooperate to ensure survival of the entire planet. Protecting plants, according to Guattari, also means protecting human culture, since both are being threatened. In the same essay, he speaks of multiple treasures of subjectivity, such as poetry, that are in danger of disappearing and are vital to psychic life. And he demands the embrace of, 'new political and social micro-practices, psychoanalytic and aesthetic micro-practices.'[5] Twenty-five years later, this approach seems as valid as it was then: if we want to pursue ecological justice with ambition and a long-term perspective, we must take into account the registers of different sensitivities mapped through trans-temporal, heterogeneous, and polysemic logics that consider different forms of life, and dispense of the limiting categories of identity that are so common today.

The Guattarian notion of ecosophy can be updated, however, by the powerful work of Brazilian psychoanalyst and cultural critic Suely Rolnik. Born in 1948, Rolnik collaborated closely with Guattari during her exile in Paris during the military dictatorship in Brazil; she has since worked intensively on the production of subjectivity in contemporary politics. In her recent book, *Esferas da insurreição: Notas para uma vida não cafetinada* [Spheres of Insurrection: notes for a non-pimped life], Rolnik addresses the notions of micro and macro politics in the present: 'The planet is now suffering the impact of voraciously destructive forces—and so are we. An unease is spreading everywhere: several sensations are driving us towards this state.'[6] As Rolnik elaborates, such destructive forces emerge

1............The conference, held by Renace Foundation in May 1991 in Santiago de Chile, was entitled 'The Three Ecologies,' inspired by Guattari's eponymous book, published in 1989.

2............This trip came at the invitation of Chilean social psychologist Miguel D. Norambuena, a friend of Guattari's, who introduced the French philosopher to Chilean psychologists, ecologists, intellectuals, artists, Mapuche communities and other, during his visits to the cities of Santiago and Valparaíso. Paulina Varas, 'Transversal Polyphonies: A Reflection with Miguel D. Norambuena on Félix Guattari's Trip to Chile,' *Deleuze and Guattari Studies* 13, no. 3 (2019).

3............Félix Guattari, *El devenir de la subjetividad* (Santiago de Chile: Dolmen editores, 1998), p. 42.

4............Ibid., p. 43.

5............Ibid., p. 49.

6............Suely Rolnik, *Esferas de Insurrección: Apuntes para descolonizar el inconsciente*, trans. Cecilia Palmeiro, Marcia Cabrero, and Damian Kraus (Buenos Aires: Tinta Limón y Traficantes de Sueños editores, 2018), p. 89.

Tiny Toones / Phnom Penh, Cambodia / 6:14pm    11°31'26.1"N 104°56'23.3"E

Ruangrupa / Jakarta, Indonesia / 6:22pm 6°19'06.6"S / 106°48'54.9"E

as world power is controlled by financial capitalism and political (neo)-liberalism. These forces are, in turn, called on to justify fascism; this includes the structural violence that asphyxiates emerging alternatives to these regimes, such as decolonial micropolitics in Brazil. In the same study, Rolnik proposes to, 'develop appropriate tools for work that is committed to decolonizing the unconscious,' and describes seven points, two of which are useful for this study. The first of these tools is to 'identify evaluation criteria for collective situations.' In the context of macropolitics, these are usually moral criteria, that are rational and point towards value systems. On the scale of micropolitics, however, the subject uses a criterion of pulses and an ethical compass, whose needle, as Rolnik posits, points towards 'what life asks as a condition to preserve every time it is weakened.'[7] This micropolitical criterion is guided by affections. The second point from Rolnik's toolkit that I'd like to emphasize here involves 'modes of cooperation.' If groupings in the macropolitical sphere are based on forms of identity created by organized movements and/or political parties, in micropolitics the groupings are formed through resonance between frequencies of affections for the construction of the common. As Rolnik points out: 'It is about weaving multiple networks of connections between subjectivities and groups that live in different situations, with unique experiences and languages.'[8] Rolnik's proposal is nothing less than to liberate the creative vital forces within us, and to form an individual and collective body that may resist the dispossession of life, so that a 'construction of the common' can be unleashed.

The current effects of the neoliberal system are unfathomable. I am writing this text from Chile, where we have experienced several months of a popular social upheaval of unimaginable intensity, the exuberance of which—and its repression—have been witnessed by the world over.[9] Endless rallies, graffiti on the walls of our cities, graphics on the Internet, and collective performances all speak to the deep dissatisfaction of the great majority of Chilean citizens with the system we are living in. In response, collective creativity on the streets has exploded, in the face of horrific state violence that is deaf to the demands of its citizens. How is this situation affecting our practices and reflections, especially those created in direct relation to what we are experiencing? In these episodes of insurgency, we touch on our fragility and vulnerability, and previously hidden strengths reverberate throughout our individual and collective bodies. After decades of subjective repression, the bodies on the streets march together, touching each other, in the great mobilizations organized every day. These are spaces of subjective composition and recomposition, where practices of collective creation acquire new urgency. In the collective practices I discuss below, art and politics are reconfigured to provide new spaces of collective being.

7............Ibid., p. 122.

8............Ibid.

9............In January 2020, the government of Sebastian Piñera was impacted by a strong social demand called 'social outbreak' where citizens demanded, along with other things, a change in the Political Constitution inherited from the military dictatorship of Pinochet.

## METHODOLOGY

In order to situate the three case studies within a larger theoretical framework but also make them actionable, I present this chapter as a thought exercise that aims to produce knowledge and understanding that is connected to very specific contexts. In this, I follow American philosopher Donna Haraway's notion of 'situated knowledges,' aligned with the feminist-informed production of critical thinking. But just as importantly, such an approach is also closely linked to traditions of thinking that are essential to the South. Specifically, I am referring to Bolivian sociologist Silvia Rivera Cusicanqui, and what she calls 'a practice and an ethos, typical of *Ch'ixi*,[10] which knows (and recognizes) its internal Indian and is firmly located in the here and now of its land and its landscape.'[11] The demand for such an ethos is especially important when considering that colonialism does not account for heterogeneity and kaleidoscopic differences, nor equitable citizenships and democratic public spheres. Such an ethos, practice, and situated thinking favour heterogeneous reflections, which allow us to situate ourselves precisely in our motley practices, and to value such divergent forms for the construction of the common. Cusicanqui has rigorously developed the notion that the *Ch'ixi* 'like many others (*allqa*, *ayni*), obey the Aymara idea of something that is and is not at the same time, that is, the logic of the included third.'[12] It is an approach that encompasses a series of possibilities for confronting the notions of *mestizaje* present in our modern societies, where the Ch'ixi as a heterogeneous society, in Cusicanqui's words, 'propose the parallel coexistence of multiple cultural differences that do not merge, but rather antagonize or complement each other.'[13]

In the spirit of the propositions above, this text focuses on collective creations as forms of resistance. Such actions provide for aesthetic-political experiences that open up new ways of thinking and creating in the current global political context. While the artists who developed the experiences examined here are located in the cities of Valparaíso, Chile, Buenos Aires, Argentina, and Zagreb, Croatia, it is important to emphasize that they are in constant dialogue with local and global collaborative networks of other creators and agents of critical thinking. In the cases that I explore in this text, we articulate a position of transversality between subjectivity, society, and the environment. Some experiences are focused on spaces of collective or deep listening, others on the configuration of meeting spaces for sharing emancipatory pedagogies, others still are discursive spaces to collectively address how fascism can be represented in our societies. Above all, these projects are analyzed with the commitment

10..........'The word ch'ixi has many connotations: it is a colour that is the product of the juxtaposition, in small points or spots, of opposed or contrasting colours: black and white, red and green, and so on. It is this heather gray that comes from the imperceptible mixing of black and white, which are confused by perception, without ever being completely mixed. The notion of ch'ixi, like many others (allqa, ayni), reflects the Aymara idea of something that is and is not at the same time. It is the logic of the included third.' Silvia Rivera Cusicanqui, *Un mundo ch'ixi es posible: Ensayos desde un presente en crisis* (Buenos Aires: Tinta Limón ediciones, 2018), p. 69.

11..........Cusicanqui, *Un mundo ch'ixi es posible*, p. 36.

12..........Ibid., p. 69.

13..........Ibid., p. 70.

14..........Gilles Deleuze, *Spinoza: Filosofía práctica* (Barcelona: Tusquets, 2009), p. 58.

to collective knowledge that can only be arrived at and safeguarded when individual bodies and communities are one.

In addition to an analysis of publications referenced in the bibliography, I have conducted extensive interviews with as many of the people who implemented these three projects as possible. I relate some of the ideas of European philosophers or thinkers such as Félix Guattari, Gilles Deleuze, and David Lapoujade with intellectuals whose scholarship is informed by their South American perspectives, among them Suely Rolnik and Rivera Cusicanqui. Such an intercultural theoretical framework accommodates the very different territories where the case studies are developed. Desk research complements these sources. Given that the collective creations studied here bring together artists and cultural organizations affected by their specific cultural environments, it is important to consider the individual, subjective experience. This experience is often recorded in the body of the person who lives it as a series of memories, sensations, emotions, and ideas. Speaking to those who started these three projects allowed me to trace those shared conditions of their distinct experiences.

A crucial role of artistic and cultural practices often consists of critiquing hegemonic structures of society in various ways, in particular the effects of neoliberalism. Hand in hand with this comes the proposition—and enactment—of collective creations to establish networks of solidarity that respond to the effects of neoliberal regimes on society. The three examples presented here—the exhibition 'Beginning As Well As We Can,' the meeting space 'LA CRIATURA,' and the discursive site of the project 'Disappeared'—demonstrate viable forms of intersecting art and politics for the present. Cultural critic and activist Brian Holmes refers to this form as 'immanent critique,' the capacity of some artistic projects to address what is currently in dispute, debate, or danger. This capacity outlines a movement in two directions: one is to occupy a societal field with potential for social agitation in order to radiate out from it the exclusive domain of the artistic discipline and enact social change. The other direction is to propose and implement new paradigms and new reflexivity. Such a dual movement, according to Holmes, requires the work of artists, theorists, and activists who are involved in this transformative spiral of the present with new critical tools.

The relationship between these practices and immanence can also be thought of as 'Common Notions,' a term first coined by French philosopher Gilles Deleuze in his studies on the legacy of the philosopher Baruch Spinoza. Common Notions are opposed to abstract ideas; rather, they incite us to imagine something instead of understanding it. It is something that is common to two or more bodies, 'which convene, that is, which compose their respective relationships according to laws and are affected according to this intrinsic convenience or composition.'[14] Thus, we can observe that these are active affections that depend on the subjects' power to act; they are not at all theoretical things, but have a dimension that is above all practical and ethical. This is why it is possible to think of Common Notions as points of intersection between bodies and historical time, involving the material and also the immaterial that shake up and agitate the present.

To organize the main body of this text I analyze the three case studies based on three Common Notions each of which emerges from one of them: 1 Certain Details, 2 Pedagogies of Doing, 3 Disappearance as a Possibility. These three different Common Notions address the following questions: first, what are the forms of contemporary fascism and how do we discuss them, while addressing both historical and contemporary forms of representation of fascism and fascism itself? Secondly, how are we going to sustain and safeguard our shared lives and collective knowledge in the face of radical neoliberal systems that benefit from keeping us separate? How can we regain strength and build strong bonds after traumatic experiences? And thirdly, how can we listen to what is in danger, beyond a metaphor? Many environmental activists across the world, from Indigenous communities to young Europeans, are denouncing the current and future effects of the devastation of our territories through extractivism and other forms of excessive exploitation of Pachamama or Gaia, consider the earth as a living system. Generating ways of listening for what is on the verge of disappearing is crucial. As the case studies make clear, this type of listening involves collective creations whose aesthetic-political tools provide us—for the present, for this cycle of global struggles—with ways of identifying possible paths to establishing conditions for a truly collective way of life.

## CERTAIN DETAILS. EXHIBITION AND PROJECT: 'BEGINNING AS WELL AS WE CAN (HOW DO WE TALK ABOUT FASCISM?)'

Over the course of several years, the Croatian curators' collective What, How & for Whom (WHW)[15] developed different forms of knowledge and dissemination for their project 'Beginning As Well As We Can (How Do We Talk About Fascism?).' This project explored the advance of the extreme right across Europe, contemporary forms of fascism more broadly, and potential forms of resistance and intervention. It is noteworthy that the term fascism is central to their project and thus moves the contemporary art project towards an urgent analysis of the current forms of repression and resistance. Key to WHW's investigation was the historicity of the term fascism, its associations with the lead-up to World War II, and its subsequent disappearance in the moment we are currently living. Is it, they asked, that the term has deliberately been hidden by its historical associations? They set about to observe very specific details of the current moment to be able to see how fascism is manifest today.

The project was conducted over five years and included exhibitions,[16] seminars,[17] and public dissemination activities in several cities including Bergen, Budapest, and Utrecht. One of the exhibitions, 'Details,' was held

15..........What, How & for Whom/WHW is a curatorial collective formed in 1999. Its members are Ivet Ćurlin, Ana Dević, Nataša Ilić, and Sabina Sabolović, and designer and publicist Dejan Kršić. They are based in Zagreb and Vienna.

16..........'Details' (Kunsthall, Bergen, 2011) and 'How Much Fascism?' (BAK, Utrecht and Extra City, Antwerp; 2012 and Gallery Nova, Zagreb, 2013).

at the Kunsthall in Bergen in 2011. 'Details'[18] as well as other parts of the larger project, was informed by a series of texts by Slovenian sociologist, psychoanalyst, and political activist Rastko Močnik, entitled 'How Much Fascism?' (1995), which starts with the assumption that fascism is everywhere. Given his background and experience, Močnik focuses on the breakup of Yugoslavia and established relationships between these conflicts and the emergence of fascist forces with the introduction of what he calls 'peripheral capitalism in the midst of the disintegration of Yugoslavia.'[19] Močnik relates the conflicts and the rise of fascist forces in geographies 'from the Adriatic to Siberia' to the structural consequences of the introduction and reconstruction of peripheral capitalism. Močnik describes the establishment of several new state entities based on nationalistic ideologies and outlines the social conjunctures crucial to such a process, commenting on the racist undertones of their 'anti-antifascism' and cultural policies.[20] For WHW's proposal, the alarming rise of the right in Europe meant not only focusing on the peripheries, but also on the centre of liberal democracy.

WHW's project used art as a tool for reflection and socialization on contemporary forms of fascism and modes of resistance and intervention. They point out: 'Obviously, open manifestations of fascism are fairly easy to recognize (just as more and more of them are appearing); but we need to turn our attention to the silent fascism that is becoming normalized through the systematic violence that seeps into the laws and everyday administration practices of the nation-states, and to assess the mechanisms of oppression and the various symptoms of contemporary fascism that are being presented as unavoidable, pragmatic necessities.'[21] As such, they call on looking into the seemingly normalized details of life post-World War II where the phenomena of contemporary fascism appear within the negative sides of democracies. The project involved artists and collectives from different countries as well as scholars who were invited to rethink certain staid concepts in public events. The latter included, for instance, 'Talk About Fascism' (with Hito Steyerl from Berlin), 'The Collective Hatred' (with Mikkel Bolt Rasmussen from Denmark) or 'Post-Fascism' (with G.M. Tamás from Hungary).

The exhibition 'Details' aimed to transmit the potential of artistic agency to change the way we perceive the world, where art would have a responsibility to support a more egalitarian society based on the construction of knowledge, to enhance the critical political imagination, and to contribute to a better understanding of social processes and their hidden

17..........The seminar 'How Much Fascism?' of the tranzit.hu Free School for Art Theory and Practice was realized in the framework of 'Art Under a Dangerous Star,' a three-part event and exhibition series at tranzit.hu between April and June 2014. 'Art Under a Dangerous Star' was part of the international collaborative project 'Beginning As Well As We Can (How Do We Talk About Fascism?),' with WHW and Alerta–Centre for Monitoring of Right-Wing Extremism and Anti-Democratic Tendencies in Zagreb.

18..........The exhibition 'Details' took its name from the work of the same name developed between 2003 and 2011 by the Israeli filmmaker Avi Mograbi, whose films highlight systemic violence by inquiring about its personal and collective effects.

19.......... 'Extravagantia II: Koliko Fašizma? [Extravagantia II: How much fascism?],' a selection from the book by Rastko Močnik (p. 11) published at *Red Thread* (e-journal), in WHW, *Details*, Bergen Kunsthall, 2011, www.red-thread.org/en/article.asp?a=19.

20..........WHW, 2012.

21..........WHW, 2011, p. 7.

facets. The exhibition created a base of theoretical contribution and input that WHW further developed and consistently uses in order problematize the field of contemporary art and develop its collaborative approach.

Another example of WHW's collaborative approach is the seminar, 'Free School for Art Theory And Practice,' organized by Tranzit.hu in May 2014. The goal of the seminar was 'to discuss dangers of political apathy that breeds forms of 'soft fascism' embedded in everyday life in different manifestations of administration of life and governing, looking into the role and potentials of cultural production and artistic interventions against a backdrop of 'case studies,' also by the participants, whose 'local' particularity is tested against broader social changes.'[22] The considerable contribution of this exercise in collective conversation involved specifically addressing the singularities that can be identified in local spaces, where the debate on fascism and representations of national identities seems to have been 'overcome' and focus on the free market and liberal democracy. The goal of the seminar was to reflect upon art projects that consider contradictions, seeking to elaborate representative strategies, actions in the public space, and discuss the role/identity of the curator and the artist in an international context. Among the participants in these public events were Barbara Steiner, members of WHW, Branislav Dimitrijevic, and Jens Hoffmann.

Performing across various contexts and platforms, always with a shifting set of participants and actors, and disregarding the dictate of marketability or efficiency, WHW's extensive project brought out key questions that must inform collaborative art practices in order to be meaningful to different audiences: Are there differences in the current political cycles from previous eras? Or is it a continuity of events that, although not visible at that time, were already present in the oppressive climate of global fascism? In this sense, the artistic agency that WHW points to through their project is a way of perceiving the world, with the ambition of contributing to a more egalitarian world.

The notion of 'Details' also speaks of scale, and raises the question of whether art can play a significant role in times of democracy. Art that proposes an ethics of research is a fundamental individual and collective responsibility; as indicated by the curators, it

> examines how specific developments that used to be associated with peripheral regions of Europe 'in transition' to democracy, have shifted and moved to the core of Europe, and examines their relationships with the 'structural changes' that go under the name of neo-liberalism and the consequent rise of certain manifestations of 'fascism.'[23]

22..........http://hu.tranzit.org/en/free_school/0/2014-05-16/how-much-fascism.

23..........WHW, 2011, p. 10.

◁ Civil Association for Creating Independent and Artistic Networks (CRIA), Argentina, 'LA CRIATURA', 2018, courtesy: artist collective

According to WHW, the aesthetic experience has the potential to question reality in the face of political resignation and can pave the way toward a necessary social transformation in our current political contexts. WHW's project 'Beginning As Well As We Can' reveals how this is possible and makes visible the necessary social transformation of the political contexts we live in.

## PEDAGOGIES OF DOING: 'LA CRIATURA'

The Civil Association for Creating Independent and Artistic Networks (CRIA), located in Buenos Aires, Argentina, was established in 2011 but really began in 2009. It is a platform that makes visible the work of its members (art and culture collectives and networks) and showcases their work within the cultural realm. CRIA operates from an ethics of collectivity and does so through collaborations of mutual support networks. As such, it is a 'collective of collectives'[24] that experiments with various formats, such as interventions in public spaces, colloquiums, websites, exhibitions,

24..........Among the members of CRIA are: Hekht Libros; Grupo Etcétera; E-HIEDRA; the Independent Book Museum (MULI); Milena Caserola; SUB Photographers' Cooperative and Cumbiemos el Mundo; Milena Paris; and Fe en la Errata.

workshops, publications, audiovisual works, spaces for economies without intermediaries, and more.

CRIA tapped precisely into this wealth of approaches, proposing to bring these practices together, and including many initiatives that take place in Buenos Aires by groups that are not part of CRIA. Loreto Garin describes the framework for this kind of 'pedagogy of doing': 'The question we asked ourselves was, how can we function as a kind of reservoir, to examine how these educational experiences are working?'[25] This 'pedagogy of doing' implies a critical review of how conventional educational institutions work and presents alternatives that are located in other spaces outside the institutions, but in dialogue with them. One of the foundational motives is to explore how to build knowledge together and how to value what each participant brings.

Most of the members of the collectives that form CRIA met in the context of the 2001 social crisis in Argentina.[26] Assemblies were held, for example, in the Argentine headquarters of the Indymedia[27] global information network (a building previously owned and then abandoned by a bank). In this hot and passionate political context, affections and friendships were born and connections established. CRIA was developed to ensure a sustainable, long-term political strategy for promoting autonomous cultural processes. Two of its members, Loreto Garin and Marilina Wilkins, describe the origin and the impulse that eventually led to the creation of CRIA in the following manner:

> The experience of 2001 was pedagogical, it changed our viewpoint, it changed the way we perceived the world. One could say that much of the feminist movement today was nurtured during 2001, many of the activists who are now the visible faces of that movement come from that experience.[28]

It is important to note here that in December 2001, Argentina faced an economic, social, and institutional crisis, with a general popular revolt led by the slogan 'All of them must go!' It was a period of political instability, featuring multiple strikes and the formation of various popular assemblies to ensure citizen participation. Reflecting on this time, Argentinian philosopher Diego Sztulwark comments, '[2001] was seen as the irruption of an untimely temporality: curse or miracle. The task of thinking about

25..........Interview with the author in Buenos Aires, July 2019.

26..........The social crisis in Argentina in December 2001 was a political, economic, social, and institutional crisis fuelled by a social revolt that lasted for several months, causing 'an unprecedented institutional instability and continuous turmoil, where the new social movements played a leading role. Many groups of artists felt summoned and got involved by the appearance of these collective subjects who were demanding resounding changes to the political system.' Ana Longoni, 'Encrucijadas del arte activista en la Argentina,' *Ramona* no. 74 (2007), p. 31.

27..........The Independent Media Center, or Indymedia, is a global network of independent communicators who report on political and social issues. It was created in 1999 in Seattle, US, to cover the protests that took place in that city. It has had versions in different cities all over the world which accompany social processes. More info at: https://indymedia.org/.

28..........Interview with the author in Buenos Aires, July 2019. The interview with Loreto Garín and Marilina Wilkins was made on the day that former president Fernando de la Rúa died.

disruption and inhabiting the discontinuous presupposed a certain disposition to not give up on the restorations.'[29] In this sense, the social crisis was understood as a learning space to be reclaimed in the present, which is one of the foundations of the proposal made by CRIA. Many of the activities developed by CRIA and supported by international funding mechanisms[30] have been devoted to critical pedagogy projects.[31]

'LA CRIATURA' (2018) (the creature), is a project inscribed in this field that was designed to bring together different groups in the association that focus on education and pedagogy. The first iteration[32] of 'LA CRIATURA' took place just before the G20 Summit that was held in Buenos Aires in 2018; other versions are planned for the future. One CRIA member explains the context of the event: 'There was a lot of fear prior to the G20 Summit, a lot of violence by the police and the media. The media were shielding things, they could not provide any information about this summit until after the event.'[33] In addition to performances, vegetable markets and a book fair 'LA CRIATURA' featured what was ironically referred to as its own 'Summit,' a reference to the G20 Summit, where a different set of thinkers and activists gathered. The presentations covered: art and education, environment, indigenous peoples, alternative economies, gender, feminisms and sexualities, neo-extractivism and human rights. It was a summit in the style of CRIA:

> We mock-ordered the guests to do as we told them, that 'this is a performance, so you are all characters.' That produced a kind of tension, since it was very clearly not part of the academic discourse, but it was a bit more popular, you see? One of the guests at our summit was the feminist researcher Mabel Bellucci, who made a powerful observation: 'There is a climate very similar to 2001 here, something that makes me very nostalgic, because it has been years since I have experienced this kind of open, experimental climate.' That was exactly what we had wanted to

29 Diego Sztulwark, *La ofensiva sensible: Neoliberalismo, populismo y el reverso de lo político* (Buenos Aires: Caja Negra, 2019), p. 19.

30 Some were from international sources, such as the Prince Claus Foundation.

31 It is worth noting that the Etcétera group, an active member of CRIA, developed over many years a pedagogical project called 'Errasmus Mundus,' defined as a programme of 'errorist (des)education' based on a specific moment in recent history. 'With the rise of movements and so-called alter-global resistance, we were complicit in new collective experiences of action, both on the streets and in the international sphere, discovering other artists and intellectuals who were engaged in multiple ways. This led to an amplification of these types of artistic practices in the field of art and activism.' See: interview with Garín, Loreto; Federico Zukerfeld, Erramus Mundus. Programa de (des)educación errorista, autoedición (Buenos Aires, 2017).

32 'LA CRIATURA' also featured an event called 'Performative Summit' which consisted of transdisciplinary poetry laboratories, hip hop, DJ and VJ, photography workshops and the central event called 'The Summit', They were presentations divided into three blocks where different people participated, from academics, feminists, teachers, artists and activists, raising different topics related to civil rights, human rights, urban gentrification, sexual diversity, struggles for land, educational projects, among others.

33 Ibid.

> reproduce, that sensation of subjects that are connected.[34]

LA CRIATURA's 'Summit' was an event that produced content at the local level. In this sense, the organizers point out that since it was not a conventional seminar, it was a stage for collective education and the creation of solidarity networks in times of crisis. For example, after the event was over, podcasts were shared on community radios with content from some sessions that continued to be transmitted afterwards, some people invited to the event were later part of the organization of activities in other spaces. In this sense, 'LA CRIATURA' impact multiplied and continues to reverberate in the Argentinian cultural context of today. This happened because CRIA members proposed to do a collaborative project with different organizations in Buenos Aires whom they invited to co-produce the different activities: conferences, laboratories, film and documentary screenings, speeches, music, live drawing, poetry readings, performances and artistic actions, independent publishers fair and vegetable fair that provided the Union of Land Workers of Argentina.

CRIA states its intent: 'to create a record of the 'LA CRIATURA' is focused on 'pedagogies of doing': a system of contemporary art producing a series of initiatives and experiences through schools, workshops, and small educational projects. By and large, these are all focused on what can be called an 'educational shift' that in recent years has addressed issues in the cultural field, particularly in relation to collaborative practices and collective pedagogies.[35]

Such an approach has produced significant exchanges and dialogues among ecologists, environmentalists, and feminists, where through listening and sharing everyone reaches beyond their own academic disciplinary register. As always, they privilege those who 'do' over those who 'talk about something.'

For CRIA, Argentina's current political landscape provides the fertile context for such collective pedagogies to provide a critical perspective for Argentinian cultural context, along with all other experiences of education and pedagogy that have recently emerged outside of conventional institutions. As the members of CRIA Loreto Garín and Marilina Wilkins observe:

> There is something about formal education which is not attractive to those of us who were producing pedagogy years ago. Many of us provided much content to our professors who spoke about our practices, but then we had no voice in that field, either because we don't have

34 Ibid.

35 Antonio Collados and Javier Rodrigo, 'Retos y complejidades de las prácticas artísticas colaborativas y las pedagogías colectivas,' *Pulso: Revista de educación* 38 (2015), pp. 57–72.

△ Tsonami group, Chile, *Audiomapa*, 2013, courtesy: artist collective

△ Tsonami group, *Audiomapa*, 2013, courtesy: artist collective

> college degrees or because of the competition, because the same people always get the positions as professors. It seems to me that formal education is fundamental, but this proliferation of schools is a reality.[36]

## DISAPPEARANCE AS A POSSIBILITY: 'AUDIOMAPA'

The third example of collective art practices is 'Audiomapa,' a project by Chilean sound festival and artist collective Tsonami. Santiago-based artist Fernando Godoy, a member of the group, had wanted to create a website that could host what he referred to as 'a sound landscape archive,' with recordings of the specific sounds of cities as well as natural environments being produced through geography. A 2012 grant from the Ministry of Culture from the Chilean government for cultural producers named FONDART made this project a reality. 'Audiomapa' is designed as a collaborative map that features the sound landscape of different sites in Latin America, and where those who wish to collaborate may easily upload their audio files. Today, the 'Audiomapa' archive features contributions from more than three hundred and fifty people from different countries in Latin America and beyond. A collective archive has emerged that registers the sound of entire territories and is not divided into nation states. 'Audiomapa' visitors and website users are invited to download the recordings for any use they wish. For that reason, when uploading an audio file, each collaborator must choose the type of license they wish to grant for their recording, selecting from three different Creative Commons license options.

'Disappearing' is the title of a particularly significant 'Audiomapa' project produced by Fernando Godoy and Rodrigo Ríos in 2013. The artists chose this name to refer to sound landscapes that are in danger of disappearing due to extractivist industries and environmental exploitation. They developed a collective way to track such devastation using sound technology to produce a living sound archive. The beginning was a survey of the sound landscape of three places that were at risk of being radically modified or even disappearing. Godoy and Ríos made recordings in these three places and uploaded them to the 'Audiomapa' website. The first place was in the Lluta Valley[37] near Arica, because of plans to install a manganese mine called 'Los Pumas' close to the source of the Lluta River; the river feeds the entire valley and was in danger of becoming severely polluted. The second place was in the territory of Chilean Patagonia, the site where the HydroAysén[38] hydroelectric project was being devised. In this case, the artists mapped much more than the sounds of the contested area,

36...........Interview with the author in Buenos Aires, July 2019.

37...........This is a valley whose name is derived from the river of the same name, whose waters flow from the mountains to the sea throughout the year. It is located in the Arica y Parinacota Region, in the extreme north of Chile.

and included recordings from the territory around it. The third place was the Grey Glacier in the area of Torres del Paine National Park.[39] As Fernando Godoy recalls, this trip was very special because, 'capturing the sound of the glacier is very difficult to begin with. As guests of a scientific expedition dedicated to other purposes, we had all but twenty minutes to record the entire Glacier and its surroundings.' The hydrophones they used could be submerged underwater, allowing for the recording of micro-sounds, vibrations, and other natural phenomena like small tremors of the earth.

The impact of 'Disappearing' is visceral and shocking. As the artists had intended, it serves both as a wake-up call and as a sound bank capturing what no longer exists. Or, as Fernando Godoy says, 'this may be the last time we have the possibility of recording this sound landscape, and of registering these sounds.'[40]

'Audiomapa,' and in particular this project of recording natural phenomena in danger of disappearing, has successfully invited reflection on how we care for the contemporary world. What is often referred to as minor existences because of their limited economic impact constitutes a virtual space full of possibilities. 'Disappearing' is about fragile, evanescent, spectral existences, feeling their presence is rare; it is a breeze, a halo, a mist. This follows the analysis by French philosopher David Lapoujade of Etienne Souriau's work on virtual existences, and it is a helpful referent here. These existences remain separate, they await art projects such as 'Disappearing' that can make them visible, and when they do emerge, they speak to all the arts we know—the visual arts, philosophy, and the natural sciences as well. These existences are immanent to the world we inhabit, and are like pointers in the air, present for anyone who can feel them. They are fragile and it is impossible to grasp their importance without perceiving them. As Souriau demands from us, before we consider an act of creation that would make them visible, we need to ask ourselves what would entitle us to perceive them.

The idea, then, is to recognize the multiple life forms that resist or disappear in order to reinvent themselves in different manifestations, so that they can overcome a hostile context that is trying to eradicate them—the different, the vulnerable, the fragile, or those who are yet unimaginable. Caring for these forms implies protecting modes of existence that are not part of the dominant, hegemonic, logocentric, and patriarchal regimes. This parallel universe embraces the existence of the tenuous, of the unfinished, of what is happening at the moment that we perceive it. We must seek possibilities of resistance and composite subjects sensitive to our multi-layered present. The sounds of a landscape at risk of disappearing or being radically altered represent such persistence of the tenuous. The resulting ecology of listening is a form of resistance.

38..........This was a project that included the construction and operation of five hydroelectric plants, two on the Baker River and three on the Pascua River, located in the Aysén Region, in southern Chile. In November 2017 the final cancellation of the project was announced.

39..........Torres del Paine National Park is a protected wildlife area in Chile, located in the province of Ultima Esperanza. It features valleys, rivers, lakes and glaciers.

40..........Fernando Godoy in an interview with the author, June 2019.

## COLLECTIVE AND COLLABORATIVE CREATIONS IN THIS WORLD

In different contexts and geographies during the different crises of the capitalist system of the twentieth century, the economic viability of cultural projects has been sustained by collaborative networks between artists, theorists, and activists as they lead to new forms of solidarity and mutual support. A model of such collective networks is mail art, active in Latin America and Europe since the nineteen-sixties, creating long-lasting effects of transnational solidarity up to the nineteen-eighties—especially, in later years, between countries of South America and Eastern Europe[41] that were living under dictatorships or totalitarian regimes. Although some international mail art networks are still active, it is worth asking ourselves what other types of collaborative networks from that period are still alive today.

This study analyzed three contemporary projects with a particular emphasis on collaborative networks that in different ways have carried into the present this historical legacy: 'As Well As We Can' by WHW, 'LA CRIATURA' by CRIA, and 'Disappearing' by 'Audiomapa.'

Of these three, WHW reactivated transversal ways of making visible what is present in our societies in collaboration with institutions, artists, theorists, and activists, in recognition that such 'details'—nascent fascist tendencies currently on the rise throughout the world—can be neither named nor addressed except when done collectively. 'LA CRIATURA' functions through collaboration and support networks within the city of Buenos Aires, but extends to other groups and individuals in an internationalist collaboration network. In developing projects such as 'LA CRIATURA,' CRIA's strategy is to enhance pre-existing networks and facilitate collective collaboration in specific activities in order to nurture an ecology of related practices that in turn sustains those who contributed to it. 'Audiomapa' by Tsonami, on the other hand, expands the notion of caring to include not only territories threatened by extractivist industries and environmental destruction, but registers their impact on the individual body, the listener. It conditions us to be sensitive, in order to begin thinking about other forms of caring for an expanded notion of territories, including those 'subjective' territories that map how we relate to the world.

Aside from collaborative processes and the expanded notion of subjectivities, another focus of this study has been the question of the imaginary. From where may we imagine the relationships and networks between art and politics described above as alternatives to the world capitalist order? Belgian philosopher Isabelle Stengers has provided useful conceptual tools to consider such a prompting when she speaks of the vital force that imagines other worlds and other ways of life. In her book

41 ..........Some recent studies have been devoted to the close relationships between artists from South America, especially Chile, Argentina and Uruguay, and artists from different countries in Eastern Europe, most notably: *Art & Margins* 1, no. 2–3 (June 2012); and *Desbordes de la Red Conceptualismos del Sur*, https://des-bor-des.net/2019/12/27/des-bordes-editorial/.

42 ..........Isabelle Stengers and Philippe Pignarre, *La sorcellerie capitaliste: Pratiques de désenvoûtement* (Paris: La Découverte, 2005), p. 137.

with Pignarre, Stengers explains how it may be possible to 'once again inhabit[ing] the devastated zones of experience,'[42] as opposed to and different from those offered by a world 'bewitched by capitalism,' as they call it. This would perform as a way of capturing our subjectivity, sensitivity, and freedom to feel the world and imagine future worlds. These conditions of 'bewitching capitalism' also affect our forms of cultural production. They affect how we relate to one another, relying on the use value of things rather than their exchange value, a proposition enacted by many independent art initiatives in various parts of the world. Capitalism produces sad truths. Thus, to break its spell is to give life to one's soul, and always to return to oneself. To love and desire the other, to remain open to otherness and to create new paths means we maintain a subjective dimension and help create emancipatory forms of connection with each other.

Some of the topics addressed by the groups and individuals who were part of this study are the challenge of hegemonic structures of society; the empowerment of collaborative networks as forms of resistance to prevailing individualism; the need to make visible current forms of oppression, especially stemming from neoliberal politics. Although collective practice can be understood as micropolitical power that is connected to the present through 'immanent critique,' it is necessary to take into account that this process of critique is heterogeneous, discontinuous, and variable. It can take the form of common flow channels that occur transversally and generate ties and collective forms. This means that subjectivity is understood as positioning us in relation to this world; that social and institutional connections are a question of living together and living alone; and that environmental attentiveness demands that we are equally aware of what endures and what disappears. In analysing these dynamics, we must consider fluctuations and variations that continuously affect geographical, political, social, and cultural specificities.

I would like to end with an open question. What if we conceived of art as a political insurgency in the world we live in? This question is situated within the current political and social systems of the so-called Global South, but it is also connected to civil uprisings that are taking place in other countries. The tactics and strategies of WHW, CRIA and 'Audiomapa' discussed above are a critical legacy and provide a crucial roadmap for current social and subjective movements. In situating them intensely aligned with the past and the present we can identify 'Common Notions' within each of them, thus connecting these three projects with presents yet to come, yet to be imagined, yet to be configured from their roots with their place, their time, and all the times and worlds that coexist with their own. 🌎🌍

## ← REFERENCES

Balasch, Marcel and Marisela Montenegro. 'Una propuesta metodológica desde la epistemología de los conocimientos situados: Las producciones narrativas.' *Encuentros en Psicología Social* 1, no. 3 (2017), pp. 44–48.

Collados, Antonio, and Rodrigo, Javier. 'Retos y complejidades de las prácticas artísticas colaborativas y las pedagogías colectivas.' *Pulso: Revista de educación* 38 (2015), pp. 57–72.

Deleuze, Gilles. *Spinoza: Filosofía práctica*. Barcelona: Tusquets, 2009.

Guattari, Félix. *El devenir de la subjetividad*. Santiago de Chile: Dolmen editores, 1998.

Haraway, Donna. *Simians, Cyborgs and Women: The Reinvention of Nature*. New York: Routledge, 1991.

Holmes, Brian. *Extradisciplinary Investigations: Towards a New Critique of Institutions*. https://eipcp.net/transversal/0106/holmes/en.html, 2007.

Lapoujade, David. *Las existencias menores*. Buenos Aires: editorial Cactus, 2018.

Longoni, Ana. 'Encrucijadas del arte activista en la Argentina.' *Ramona* no. 74 (2007), pp. 31–43.

Martínez-Guzmán, Antar and Marisela Montenegro. 'La producción de narrativas como herramienta de investigación y acción sobre el dispositivo de sexo/género: Construyendo nuevos relatos.' *Quaderns de Psicologia* 16, no. 1 (31 May 2014). pp. 111–25. doi:10.5565/rev/qpsicologia.1206.

Rivera Cusicanqui, Silvia. *Ch'ixinakak Utxiwa: Una reflexión sobre prácticas y discursos descoloniales*. Buenos Aires: Tinta limón ediciones, 2014.
—. *Un mundo ch'ixi es posible: Ensayos desde un presente en crisis*. Buenos Aires: Tinta Limón ediciones, 2018.

Rolnik, Suely. *Micropolítica: Cartografías del deseo*. Buenos Aires: Tinta Limón y Traficantes de Sueños editores, 1999.
—. *Esferas de Insurrección. Apuntes para descolonizar el inconsciente*, trans. Cecilia Palmeiro, Marcia Cabrero y Damian Kraus Buenos Aires: Tinta Limón y Traficantes de Sueños editores, 2018.

Stengers, Isabelle and Philippe Pignarre. *La sorcellerie capitaliste: Pratiques de désenvoûtement*. Paris: La Découverte, 2005.

Sztulwark, Diego. *La ofensiva sensible: Neoliberalismo, populismo y el reverso de lo político*. Buenos Aires: Caja Negra, 2019.

What, How & for Whom, eds. *Details*. Bergen: Kunsthall, 2012. www.bakonline.org/how-much-fascism/2011.

Varas, Paulina. 'Transversal Polyphonies: A Reflection with Miguel D. Norambuena on Félix Guattari's Trip to Chile.' *Deleuze and Guattari Studies* 13, no. 3 (2019), pp. 377–94.

## ← INTERVIEWS

Fernando Godoy, Valparaíso, June 2018

Loreto Garín and Marilina Wilkins, Buenos Aires, July 2018

Koalisi Seni Indonesia / Jakarta, Indonesia / 6:22pm    6°16'24.0"S / 106°50'00.6"E

Arte Moris Arts Centre / Dili. Timor Leste / 7:37pm     8°33'10.8"S / 125°31'57.9"E

# REFLECTIONS ON A CHANGING WORLD



The chapters collected in this book represent the outcome of over two years of collaborative work by the Prince Claus Fund, Hivos, and the European Cultural Foundation, three organizations working for and with artists and cultural practitioners around the world. Our support over the decades to a global movement of artists, creatives, and cultural organizations has made us witnesses and firm believers in the transformative forces of art. Art and culture have a unique power, a capacity to critically reflect on our realities and imagine alternative ones, to shape their social surroundings, and to propose new ways of relating with each other and with the world.

We jointly launched the *Forces of Art* initiative in order to explore diverse paths to understanding the role of art and artistic work in different contexts, as well as the passion motivating the creators of the inspiring projects featured here. Our shared starting point was the need to avoid reifying 'success' as a quality of arts projects—an all-too-common trend in the field of international funders. We wanted to critically examine the increasing pressure on artists to demonstrate the worth of their work through quantifiable methodologies that are unsuited to the work they do. Our goal was to understand, without attempting to categorize or to evaluate, the ways in which art reveals its transformative force for and within societies.

As experienced international organizations, we understood that the real effects of art and culture are not easy to capture by any single methodology. Instead, we were looking for a diversity of approaches and perspectives to provide fresh insights into how arts and culture not only impact the lived experiences of individuals, but also the wider societies in which they work. How do artists and cultural practitioners interact with their audiences, communities, networks or institutions, and what is the legacy of their interventions beyond the end of their projects? These are complex questions that can hardly be answered through rigid, one-size-fits-all evaluation frameworks and methods.

More than two years later, we are proud to see how researchers from different disciplines have come together to propose new, sometimes unconventional, ways of looking at the question of how art contributes to shaping our world. The studies in this book employ vastly different methodologies—ranging from trans-national artistic research on, and by, queer voices that defy government repression in Uganda and Kenya, to a workshop connecting participants from Lima and Johannesburg in an exploration of networks and networking, to participant observation of life in a residency in the depths of the Colombian rainforest. Together, these chapters make it clear that it is crucial to work towards the development of a balanced, diverse, and inclusive cultural field—local as well as international—that embraces the institutionalized as well as the improvised, the individual as well as the collective. In such a field, arts and cultural spaces can act as meeting and exchange points. They can provide an enabling environment for new ideas and endeavours, as well as to catalyze change.

In order to contribute to building and expanding this kind of field, we have to be able to honestly assess our role as grant-giving organizations. For organizations in our position, it is easy to assume an artificially neutral view. Instead, our aim has been, and will continue to be, to adopt a critical view that acknowledges our work as an element in an international art support infrastructure marked by the same power imbalances that characterize the world outside the arts. The process of working on the *Forces of Art* initiative has allowed us to consider our own position. We must be able to see ourselves as non-neutral nodes within this field. This entails coming to terms with the power imbalances we're enmeshed in, and trying, wherever possible, to reach across them by listening and recognizing the traps we may fall into.

Much of the research collected here is marked by a tension between what may be called 'a universal story' and the multiplicity of the particular. There are real commonalities to be seen between the experiences of cultural practitioners described in the research, including the importance of the community and self-expression that culture can provide. However, the range of these particular experiences is immense, with each practice shaped by wildly diverse conditions. While being linked to others across the world through funding, collaboration, and influence, the art initiatives and research methodologies represented here are deeply and definitely rooted in specific times and places.

Despite this particularity, we often feel the pressure to justify our work with reference to oversimplified 'universal' stories about the power of culture, which erode the specific details that are vital on the ground. The research collected here reminds us how important it is to resist this tendency. Rather than seeing art as an expression of 'universal' humanity, we would like to see it as a commons, something shared by diverse and interconnected actors. We hope to be able to stand for a kind of solidarity in multiplicity—to defend the individual and the particular against the push to flatten them into marketable stories that can be reproduced halfway across the world.

The research presented in this book was initiated in what today feels like a very different world. The final stages of the *Forces of Art* initiative are taking place in 2020, in a moment when a global pandemic crisis has affected not only us, our partners, and the contributors to this book, but the entire cultural sector. The persistence of the lock down, the restrictions to travel and public gathering, mean present and future challenges and insecurity for artists and cultural organizations.

The goal of the *Forces of Art* initiative was always to allow us to take stock of our pasts, examine our practices, and look towards the future. The impression that we are living through the end of an era makes this concern even weightier. We believe that artists will continue to play a vital role in investigating, critically reflecting, imagining, and building alternative realities. Artists and cultural professionals are resourceful, resilient, and inventive. At the present time more than ever, we are all reminded of the capacity of art and culture to provide hope, meaningful connections, solidarity, and to generate more open societies.

We consider this research as a milestone that marks a new phase in our work as foundations. Knowing our strengths and limitations better, we will try to admit our illusions and mistakes from the past, and embrace a new culture of thoughtful solidarity, as a means to overcome inherited stereotypes and power relations. We will listen more carefully to the multitude of voices and approaches that local cultural ecosystems contribute to global trends. We will enable more stories and voices to be heard in order for the diversity of the forces of art to be made visible.

Prince Claus Fund
Hivos
European Cultural Foundation

Amsterdam, June 2020

Mapping Without Borders
An Account of all Art Projects

P.49 5°15'10.4"N / 76°49'33.6"W

## FUNDACION MÁS ARTE MÁS ACCIÓN (MAMA)

Guachalito, Nuquí and Quibdoó
in the Department of Chocó, Colombia.

Más Arte Más Acción (MAMA) has been a platform for interdisciplinary projects since 2008. It was created following several years of art practice and community engagement in Colombia. In 2011, MAMA built the Chocó Base near Nuquí, on Colombia's remote Pacific coast. Since then, this space to reflect has enabled artists, scientists, activists, and writers to consider the construction of other possible worlds. The ideas and processes of critical thinking have been examined deeply in the framework of territorial struggles with MAMA's networks, which include universities, festivals, art institutions, and local communities of Afro-Colombian and indigenous Embera. Struggles facing the region include the possible construction of the Port of Tribugá and gold mining in the Atratoregion.

Ana Garzón, Alejandra Rojas, Fernando Arias and Jonathan Colin form MAMA's core team and are starting a journey to evaluate the foundation's processes, narratives, and ways of organizing in the coming years. Although the destination is unclear, this process will form part of lumbung documenta 15. As we look around we see shared interests, we engage, we relate, we find empathy, we embrace differences, we act through art, we gather others to join our fights to activate artistic processes. We imagine art through action and action through art.

△ Experience of immersion in the underwater listening station, a vibrant and multi-sensory journey into the depths of the Gulf of Tribuga and the diversity of its voices.
Photo: Leonel Vasquez

△ Seed. Photo: Más Arte Más Acción (archive)

△ Fly. Photo: Fernando Arias

P.385 12°05'49.7"S / 77°03'27.3"W

## ALTA TECNOLOGÍA ANDINA (ATA)

Alberto del Campo 411, Magdalena del Mar,
Lima 17, Perú

Alta Tecnología Andina (ATA) is a non-government, nonprofit international cultural organization working on the intersection of art, science, technology, and society, with a focus on Peru and Latin America. Our work involves the production, promotion, and support of projects and transdisciplinary research and exhibitions, as well as a specialized archive and a library, available both online and onsite.

Founded with the mission of contributing to the development of a new culture based on the use and expansion of electronic media in the region, ATA began its activities in 1995. The members of the organization are Jorge Villacorta (President), José-Carlos Mariátegui (founder/director and a coordinator/researcher).

Some of the main projects developed by ATA are, 'Videografías in(visibles),' 'Insulares/Divergentes,' 'Laboratory of Creation in Art and Science,' 'ATALab,' and the exhibitions 'Poetronico,' 'metadATA. 20 years of culture, art and technology' and 'VIDEO-TRANSLATIONS.' In 2019 the book *The Future Was Now: 21 Years of Video Creation and Electronic Art in Peru* was published, an important research effort that seeks to present an overview of video and electronic art in Peru during the last two decades and thus to contribute to the adequate documentation of the histories of the visual and media arts, the moving image and technology in Peru.

◁ *The Future Was Now: 21 Years of Video Creation and Electronic Art in Peru*, a compilation of essays on the past two decades of Peruvian video and electronic art, edited by Max Hernández-Calvo, José-Carlos Mariátegui and Jorge Villacorta.
© Alta Tecnología Andina (ATA)

△ Project 112/59 intervention process: connecting two independent houses. © 4-18

△ Colombian Artistic Research Magazine research trip Goðafoss, Iceland. © 4-18

FUNDACIÓN CUATRO DIECIOCHO 4-18
Bogotá, Colombia, ZipCode: 110231, Carrera 1 Este # 70 – 47, Apt 301

Fundación Cuatro Dieciocho 4-18 was started in 2008 and named after the address of its first artistic project in an abandoned house in Bogotá, Colombia. The collective was conformed by Sebastián Carrasco, Pablo Gómez, and Felipe Rodríguez. In 2011 they became an established nonprofit organization with a management team conformed by Felipe Rodríguez, Santiago Rodríguez, and Nicolás R. Melo; they were accompanied in the creation and development of projects by Fernando Barrera, Luis González, Pablo Gómez, Hernán Pérez, Tomás Silva and Luisa Valderrama. 4-18 presents a model of itinerant headquarters considering that all their projects are located in different areas of Colombia and the world. So far, they have developed projects in Barranquilla, Bogotá, Bucaramanga, Chicago, Medellín, Honda, Leticia, London, Maní, New York, Popayán, Pore, Sarajevo, Shanghai, Subotica, Valparaiso, Zagreb. They are an undefined research platform and network in constant expansion that supports community initiatives and art projects; their research magazine, created in 2017 and entitled Colombia's Artistic Research Magazine, affirms this idea. For them, Expanded Art is a meeting point between collaborative processes, interdisciplinary relationships and horizontal languages, intermediated through creative tactics and educational activities, seeking to create alternatives through sustainable economic and environmental artistic proposals, and promoting collective mobilization.

www.4-18.org/
www.carmajournal.com/



MUSEO DE ANTIOQUIA
52 Calle 52 43, Medellín, Antioquia, Colombia

The Museo de Antioquia—located in the heart of what was once one of the most violence-prone cities of Colombia—is a contemporary art museum that works to position culture as a key issue for development. Understanding and fully embracing the difficult and complex context in which it works, the museum has made the active choice to go beyond the aesthetic dimension and include the ethical, political, and social dimensions in an urgent drive to stimulate multicultural dialogue and critical thinking. Apart from its extensive art collection that focuses on Colombian history (from pre-Colombian to Contemporary art), the Museum's tools consist of dynamic activities, programmes, and projects that reflect this vision of working for social inclusion. The principles of the museum are: critically reviewing the notion of territory and history, with an emphasis on diversity, to give a voice to those who were excluded from the dominant narrative; promoting the appropriation of art; being a sustainable museum that is constantly, critically, and vitally connected to the present, and with its surroundings in the centre of Medellín.

The concept that 'The museum is the community' has been the principle animating the participation of the Museo de Antioquia in the Network Partnership programme of the Prince Claus Fund for three years (2010–2013, and later for three more years as a non-funded participant).

△ Inauguration of *La consentida* 2019: *La familia negra* (16 March 2019). A work from the Museum collection was selected by people from the local community as part of the project 'Cundinamarca Residence: A case of reparacion' by Liliana Angulo. The project works on archives and anti-racism, and investigates the historical presence of the Afro-descendant population in Medellín and Antioquia, as well as their forms of representation.
Photo: courtesy Museo de Antioquia

△ Inauguration of Polis, towards political reconstruction. This exhibition wants to contribute to the strengthening of practices that make the city. It aims to make visible the actions of those who seek the production of the common good, in processes that have emerged from their own narratives of life and have formed a community fabric, which have been intelligently inserted into current social and economic dynamics through creative resources.
Photo: courtesy Museo de Antioquia

◁ *The corner*, 2019, is an activation nourished by the Museum's bibliographic collection and made up of images, fragments, author's visions, staging and unconventional formats, where the 'leitmotif' was sexual diversity and inclusion.
It began with a literary Bacchanal, by aniG La Libronauta and Severina.
Photo: courtesy Museo de Antioquia

P.403 33°02'57.1"S / 71°36'42.2"W

## TSONAMI

B.A.S.E. Tsonami, Av. Colón 2390, Valparaíso, Chile

Tsonami is a nonprofit organization based in Valparaiso, Chile, dedicated to promoting the culture of sound and the exploration of the soundscape in Chile and South America. Since 2007, Tsonami organizes an international festival once a year, where people who research the intersection of sound, music, and technology meet to experiment and share their experiences and projects. The festival also includes sound installations and street performances, and provides streamed radio plays, concerts, lectures, and workshops in different places and locations in the city of Valparaiso, Chile.

Since 2018, Tsonami has also established a domestic space called B.A.S.E. (Base de Artes Sonoras y Experimentales—Base of Sound and Experimental Arts), which hosts a residency programme, the School of Sound art for children, and Radio Tsonami, a collaborative radio experimentation project focused on using sound and speech as tools for social communication and artistic exploration.

One of Tsonami's projects is Audiomapa, a collaborative sound mapping dedicated to sharing, exploring, and archiving the soundscape of Latin America; this was later broadened to other parts of the world thanks to contributions from its community of users. All the audios on the platform are Creative Commons licensed and can be employed for creative uses, research, and education.

△△ Recording sounds for the project 'Audiomapa' by Tsonami, 2013. Photo: Paola Ruz

P.25 17°23'59.7"S / 66°09'57.1"W

## PROYECTO MARTADERO

Calle 27 de Agosto y Ollantay, Cochabamba, Bolivia

Proyecto mARTadero is a space for social development through art and culture. It is a comprehensive and multidimensional project located in the Villa Coronilla area of Cochabamba (Bolivia), which for fourteen years has been focusing on responsible advocacy through artistic-cultural mechanisms. It has the vocation of a prototype, an irradiating focus of creativity and of producing improvements for the environment. Its strategy is based on three fundamental pillars:

its space, a former slaughterhouse architectural complex built in 1924, which with its 3,000 m2 constitutes a unique, flexible, decentralized, socially and geographically strategic space, suited to the logic and needs of the emerging arts;

the autonomy and collective vocation of its multidisciplinary team, which is highly qualified in intercultural promotion at local, national and international levels; its principles that animate the project: innovation, research, experimentation, conceptual and formal rigor, integration, exchange and interculturality.

P.403 34°36'12"S / 58°22'54"W

## CREATING INDEPENDENT AND ARTISTIC NETWORKS (CRIA)

CABA, Buenos Aires, Argentina
Location of event: Club Cultural Matienzo, Pringles 1249, 1183, CABA, Buenos Aires, Argentina

Creating Independent and Artistic Networks (CRIA) is a transdisciplinary nonprofit association based in Buenos Aires. It is composed of individuals, groups, and cultural spaces that promote projects aimed at transforming society.
Since our foundation in 2011, we have produced many events in cultural and social spaces, including museums, festivals, book fairs, and exhibitions. We organize workshops, seminars, talks, and other activities that encourage exchange. Our work is based on building platforms that are organized into networks in order to enrich research, knowledge, and experimentation in various formats such as performances in public spaces, colloquiums, exhibitions, workshops, publications, videos, etc.

La Criatura is CRIA's intersectional pedagogical platform, centred around four transversal contemporary issues:

1. Defence of the environment
2. Sexual diversity and gender equality
3. Defence of human rights
4. Defence of artistic education as a basic necessity.

The programme invites important actors from the cultural, activist, and artistic communities to come together and participate in a pedagogical experiment. La Criatura is a transdisciplinary programme that centers concrete experiences and new forms of social imagination (and action). It seeks to shift the limits of hegemonic culture, visibilize and empower communities and individuals at risk of censorship or marginalization, and disseminate the practices and alternative pedagogies constructed through action (be they rooted in activism, academia, the arts, or other).

△ Participatory art installation, Banderazo, featuring flags made by over sixty Argentine and international artists. Flags were designed and printed during La Criatura 2018, and later brought to the Congress building during G20 protests. Photo: Loreto Garín

△ Carolina Bracco speaking about feminism in the Muslim world in La Criatura 2018. Photo: Quilomba Collective

△ Facade of RAW Material Company ©Antoine Tempe.jpg

△ Exhibition opening of 'Toutes les fautes qu'il y avait dans le mondeje les ai ramassées,' RAW Material Company © Anna Karima Wane_2.jpg

◁ Site visit to Gad Gomene with participants of interdisciplinary workshops on environmental activism in Senegal organized at RAW as part of the exhibition 'PO4 (Blackout)' with artist Christian Danielewitz, 2019.



## RAW MATERIAL COMPANY

Zone B villa 2A, Dakar, Senegal

RAW Material Company is a centre for art, knowledge, and society founded in 2008. It is an initiative involved with curatorial practice, artistic education, residencies, knowledge production, and archiving of theory and criticism on art.

It works to foster appreciation and growth of artistic and intellectual creativity in Africa. The programme is trans-disciplinary and is equally informed by literature, film, architecture, politics, fashion, cuisine, and diaspora.

We are a team of twelve inspired and dedicated women who thrive to keep our values and ideology alive on a day-to-day basis. Due to a strong belief in hospitality, we succeeded into building a community of art practitioners and art lovers who have become very important members of the RAW family. Our public is very diverse going from artists, curators, art historians and critics, students, political activists, journalists, writers etc.
Our main programmes include:

- RAW Académie, our study programme
- Fridays @RAW, our weekly talks programme
- Condition Report, our biennial symposium on artistic and curatorial practice in Africa
- Ker Issa, the RAW residency programme
- We also conduct exhibition making and publishing.



## KËR THIOSSANE

Villa n°1695 Sicap Liberté 2, Dakar—Senegal

Kër Thiossane, a resource centre for digital creation and citizen artistic practices in Senegal and West Africa since 2002, works for the democratization of multimedia tools, particularly in their creative dimension, with artists as well as with the local public.

Through workshops, residencies, meetings, as well as its Afropixel festival, the seventh edition of which was held in June 2020, Kër Thiossane tries to create relationships with art and multimedia of another kind.

Kër Thiossane links the development of artistic digital practices to other domains of society: education and training, creative industries, citizenship, ecology, and town development.

In 2014, Kër Thiossane initiated a School of Commons in its neighbourhood—an open transdisciplinary research and experimentation space combining art, open source technologies, urban ecology, economy, and neighbourhood practice.

This school is situated around an artistic garden, created on a neighbouring plot of land, which until now had been abandoned to plastic waste and insalubrity. It also holds a fablab *Defko Ak Niep* (Do it with others), a space for the mutualization of digital manufacturing machines, part of a process of spreading free culture where the notion of sharing and enriching common goods prevails.

▷▷▷ © Creative Commons CC-BY-SA_Ker Thiossane

P.95 33°34'59.1"N / 7°38'24.2"W

## L'ATELIER DE L'OBSERVATOIRE

168 Résidence Khouribga. Quartier Maarif. Casablanca. 20100. Morocco.

l'Atelier de l'Observatoire strives to create conditions for projects that do not meet the criteria of the classical artistic and academic production systems in Morocco and in the region.

Its six participatory programmes are lines of work, thought, and research, and seek to allow a better circulation of non-dominant visions, knowledge, and ideas:

1. The Musée Collectif: citizen project of a museum of the collective memory of cities, taking the form of participatory workshops, meetings, and exhibitions in different Casablanca neighbourhoods. The aim of these activities is to create a shared process of writing the history of the city by its inhabitants.

2. Madrassa is a regional programme (MENA) for research, meetings, and training in contemporary curatorial practices. Two training sessions have been carried out, and a third session is in preparation with our partners ARIA (Algeria), NASS (Alexandria, Egypt), and Spring Sessions (Jordan).

3. La Ruche is a production and support programme for emerging Moroccan artists.

4. Les Invisibles is a research and archiving programme for a possible Moroccan artistic and cultural history based on what is forgotten and disappeared. The restoration of the film *De quelques événements sans significations* by Moroccan director Mostapha Derkaoui was carried out within the framework of this programme, and has gained worldwide recognition—notably thanks to its selection at the Berlinale as part of the Archival Constellations programme.

5. The Aquarium is a collective reflection for the possible reactivation of public, educational, and heritage places in Casablanca.

6. The Greenhouse is a mobile ephemeral cultural space that is installed in public spaces (especially on the outskirts of large cities) for a programme—carried out in consultation with the inhabitants —of screenings, meetings, interventions, games, and publications, in a Greenhouse specially designed and open to all.

△ La Serre, Hay Mohammadi, Atelier de l'Observatoire, 2018

△ Mohamed Fariji (ancien Aquarium de Casablanca)

△ Vitrine Madrassa, Musée Collectif de Casablanca, Mohamed Fariji, Thinkart, Atelier de l'Observatoire, 2015

P.161 5°38'14.1"N / 0°10'28.4"W

## NUBUKE FOUNDATION

7 Lome Close, Accra, Ghana, and Loho, near Wa, Ghana

Founded in 2006 by three individuals (Kofi Setordji, Tutu Agyare, and Odile Tevie), the Nubuke Foundation's mission is to record, preserve, and promote the visual arts and culture of Ghana.

Nubuke Foundation serves as a nexus for arts and culture across the country while supporting the artistic practice of young, mid-career, and experienced Ghanaians:. Career development programmes are tailored for young artists and female artisans who weave or work with clay pottery.

Nubuke Foundation's programming calendar includes exhibitions, talks, screenings, music concerts, drama productions, workshops, and seminars, and span the field of visual arts, culture, history, and science. Artistic programmes are devised with audience engagement strategies to suit the needs of all strata and educational backgrounds of Ghanaian society: low income, urban poor, affluent, and rural communities nationwide.

We have managed several multi-year nationwide travelling exhibitions, lasting up to five years. Nubuke Foundation collaborates with the University of Ghana, KNUST, and Takoradi Technical University, offering experiential learning opportunities for students and in co-operation with the Ghana Museums and Monuments Board, Centres for National Culture, and similar arts institutions worldwide.

Nubuke Foundation is part of the Arts Collaboratory Network.

◁◁◁ Nubuke Reading Club. Drama Workshop. Charcoal workshop with Gideon Appah. Photos: courtesy Nubuke Foundation

△ Samer Al Kadri at Pages Bookstore Amsterdam, 2017. Courtesy Prince Claus Fund

△ Performance by CocoNaff at Pages Bookstore Amsterdam, 2017. © Maarten van Haaff

△ Pages Bookstore Amsterdam, opening, 2017. Courtesy Prince Claus Fund

P.359

41°01'56.5"N / 28°56'19.9"E
52°21'56.7"N / 4°53'57.4"E

## PAGES BOOKSTORE

Pages Bookstore Café Istanbul, Kariye Çk.
No: 5 Ayvansaray Mh.34087 Fatih/Istanbul, Turkey

–

Pages Bookstore Amsterdam, Herengracht 603, 1017 CE Amsterdam

–

Pages Bookstore Muscat, 121 Al Inshirah Street,
Madinat Al Sultan Qaboos, Bawshar, Oman

'We are Syrian. We have culture. We lost everything, but we have our culture. Culture gives us the opportunity to know each other before we judge each other.'
– Founder of Pages Bookstore Café Samer Al-Kadri

As simple as it is, Pages was created by Samer Al-Kadri to bring people together around books, music, art, and coffee. Initially established in Istanbul (2015), Pages aimed to provide a place where Syrian refugees could read books in Arabic as long as they liked, and where they could also borrow unlimited books for a small fee. But, more than that, the place presented them an atmosphere they missed, a place that looked like their home country.

Pages also dreamed of bringing people from different backgrounds together, to bridge the gap between cultures using nothing but their humane interest in literature and art. In Amsterdam (2017), and with the support from the Prince Claus Fund, Pages opened its doors not only to customers looking to buy Arabic books, but it also established itself as a cross-cultural platform where people from various countries and cultures came together for exchange and dialogue. By organizing creative workshops, music nights, literary events, language courses, and exhibitions, Pages Amsterdam grew into a well-known and valued meeting space where open dialogue was welcomed and encouraged.

From Istanbul to Amsterdam (2017) and Muscat (2019), and with hundreds of workshops, music nights, art exhibitions, and activities, Pages carries on the dream.

P.186

41°24'26.4"N / 2°12'13.5"E
36°45'14"N / 3°3'32"E

## JISER REFLEXIONS MEDITERRÀNIES

Algeria, Algiers (various locations within the city);
Avinguda Diagonal 105, C2, E-08005 Barcelona

Jiser Reflexions Mediterrànies (bridge in Arabic) is a nonprofit association created in Tunisia in 2004 and based in Barcelona since 2005; it promotes the artistic creation and the use of art as a means of social transformation in the Mediterranean area, through joint activities favouring the exchange and the reconciliation of the various artistic and cultural realities of the region.

During the period 2012–2017, Jiser actively collaborated in the platform TransCultural Dialogues (TCD), along with other associations and cultural workers of the Mediterranean. In November 2014, this platform organized the multidisciplinary festival DJART '14 that took place in the city of Algiers and in September 2016. TCD organized 'el Medreb,' a project diving into a research of abandoned buildings in Algiers (starting from the district of El Hamma) by investigating its social, architectural, and historical context.

Since 2017, Jiser has had a physical space in the Poblenou neighbourhood of Barcelona, where its public activities take place, gathering artists and cultural actors from the local scene with Mediterranean guests through programmes such as Taula/طاولة or MURAL/LOCAL.

△ Abandoned building visits in Algiers. Photo: Hichem Merouche, 2014

△ Abandoned building visits in Algiers with Houssem Mokeddem. Photo: Hichem Merouche, 2014

△ eL Seed mural in Didouche Mourad avenue, Algiers. Photo: Hichem Merouche, 2014

P.186 36°51'12.9"N / 10°10'18.6"E

## MAISON DE L'IMAGE
40, rue Tarek Ibn Zied, Mutuellevielle, Tunis, Tunisia

Maison de l'Image (MDI) is a cultural institution federating artistic talents linked to contemporary visual art and established in Grand Tunis since 2014. It has patiently forged links between the population and the visual arts by organizing cultural meetings, creating projects that reveal talents, and by continually working to integrate young people into the professional world. Through its network of professionals and affiliated organizations, MDI works to bring together differences, to create a dialogue, and to ensure that the moment of the work takes on its full meaning for everyone with passion and enthusiasm.

Through its programmes the MDI:

1. Contributes to the professionalization of the sector and helps young people from disadvantaged neighbourhoods and regions to create their own future (https://www.visionsolidaire.com and www.oasiscreatives.com).

2. Promotes tolerance and fights against stereotypes through its exhibitions, film screenings, and debates.

3. Contributes to enriching the entrepreneurial ecosystem of the Tunisian cultural and creative sector through its spaces of co-learning, photo studio, projection room, etc.

4. Produces communication content at affordable prices for the benefit of artists and Social and Solidarity Enterprises.

△ Oasis Creatives. Photo: courtesy Maison de l'Image

△ Vision Solidaire. Photo: courtesy Maison de l'Image

P.283 4°02'37.2"N / 9°41'13.4"E

## DOUAL'ART
370 place du gouvernement, Bonanjo – Douala, Cameroon

doual'art is a contemporary art centre born in June 1991, in the aftermath of the street riots called *Villes Mortes* (Dead Cities) in Douala (Cameroon), a period of popular demand for more democracy.

For twenty-nine years, doual'art's has been concerned with involving contemporary creators in urban issues such as: citizenship and city management, new urban cultures and the urban condition, the ergonomics of development projects, etc.

Indeed, doual'art is a laboratory that creates information and activates artistic action in the public space in order to enhance free speech, create platforms for dialogue, and give the inhabitants the right to live in the city.

doual'art brings poetry within everyone's reach, participates in popular education on various themes including the question of aesthetics, and offers inhabitants of the city a representation of themselves and their practices. In doing so, doual'art participates in the city's identity and defuses the disenchantment that inhabitants have of themselves and for their urban environment.

Through the international festival Salon Urbain de Douala (SUD) the permanent team of six people positions art as a mediation between inhabitants, between inhabitants and local authorities, and between local residents and foreigners.

△ L'homme de Boue, performance Eric Delphin Kwegoue, SUD2010

△ Espace doual'art, Bonanjo-Douala, entrance

P.403 45°49'00.5"N / 15°58'52.8"E

## WHAT, HOW AND FOR WHOM/WHW
Ribnjak 16, 10 000, Zagreb, Croatia

WHW is a nonprofit organization for visual culture and a curators' collective formed in 1999 (legally established in 2001). Since May 2003, WHW has been directing the programme of Gallery Nova—a nonprofit, city owned gallery in Zagreb. The mission of WHW is to open up discussions on relevant social issues through art, theory, and media, by supporting contemporary art production, organizing art projects, and developing models for collaboration and exchange of knowledge among organizations from different cultural fields.

WHW is the first recipient of the Igor Zabel Award for Culture and Theory in 2008, awarded by Erste Stiftung.

In March 2019, members of WHW Ivet Ćurlin, Nataša Ilić, and Sabina Sabolović were appointed as artistic directors of Kunsthalle Wien in Vienna. WHW as a collective will continue working in Zagreb with collective activities coordinated by WHW member Ana Dević.

In 2018, WHW started the WHW Akademija, a new international art study programme in Zagreb for emerging artists. It is an intervention in the field of art education, aiming to enable new forms of self-determination for the participants, based on modes of critical reflection, curiosity and encounters among artists, artworks, arts professionals, scholars, and practitioners in various disciplines. WHW Akademija is a seven-month tuition-free study programme for ten to twelve international students. It is open to individuals who are at the beginning of developing an independent artistic practice and are seeking to deepen their formal, theoretical, and critical skills in art.

△ Oscar Murillo, *Institute for Reconciliation*, 2018, Augustus Temple, *Pula*, part of the exhibition 'On the Shoulders of Fallen Giants,' 2nd Biennial of Industrial Art, 2018. Photo: Marko Ercegović

◁ Oscar Murillo, *Institute for Reconciliation*, 2018; Augustus Temple, *Pula*, part of the exhibition 'On the Shoulders of Fallen Giants,' 2nd Biennial of Industrial Art, 2018. Photo: Marko Ercegović

△ Ana Dević, Ivet Ćurlin, Nataša Ilić, Sabina Sabolović/WHW. Photo: Damir Žižić

P.385 26°11'13.5'S / 28°02'29.6'E

## VISUAL ARTS NETWORK OF SOUTH AFRICA (VANSA)
Transwerke Building, Constitution Hill, Sam Hancock Street Braampark, Johannesburg, South Africa

Visual Arts Network of South Africa (VANSA)operates as a support point and development agency for contemporary art practice in South Africa. We develop industry knowledge, resources, networks, and projects that are concerned with realizing new social, cultural, and economic possibilities for contemporary art practice in the South African—and the wider African —context.

VANSA aspires to be a dynamic and resilient network-based organization committed to innovation, transparency, social justice, and fairness; it operates as a key support point for contemporary art practice through the promotion of growth, transformation, and opportunities in the contemporary art field in South Africa and the development of projects and services shaped by and delivering benefit to our network of 8,000 members.

The organization works with and through a local, continental, and international network of visual arts professionals, business, organizations, institutions, and agencies on initiatives and projects across five key areas:

- strengthening informational networks,
- promoting better professional and business practice
- facilitating opportunities for new approaches to contemporary art practice, in new contexts with new audiences and publics
- opening up new market opportunities for contemporary art in South Africa
- lobbying and advocacy in all of the above areas, informed by research and evidence

**VANSA did not receive support from Prince Claus Fund, Hivos, or the European Cultural Foundation.*

▽ Michaela Yearwood-Dan's Open Studio. Photo: Tokologo Mphaki

▽ Talent Unlocked Workshop. Photo: Gemma Garman

◁ Chanelle Adams' Open Studio. Photo: Norma Moropodi

P.359 41°01'37.4"N / 28°58'42.0"E

## DEPO

Depo/Tütün Deposu, Lüleci Hendek Caddesi No.12 Tophane 34425
Istanbul, Turkey

Depo is a space for culture, arts, and critical debate located in a four-storey, former tobacco warehouse (Tütün Deposu) in Tophane, Istanbul. It is an initiative of Anadolu Kültür, a not-for-profit organization working in the field of culture since its establishment in 2002 by Osman Kavala. In 2008, following mild renovation works at its premises, the Depo team started working on their first exhibition, held in January 2009. Currently the team is comprised of five people.

Depo hosts and organizes events that deal with historical and contemporary social issues. Its programme includes exhibitions, screenings, panel discussions, workshops, and presentations; it publishes an online journal entitled 'Red Thread.' Depo aims to become a hub where politically and socially engaged projects are realized, and to provide artists, curators, cultural operators, academics, researchers, and a wide audience with a platform for the exchange of ideas and experiences. For developing its programme, Depo often collaborates with initiatives, experts, and cultural institutions from Turkey and abroad.

With its accessible and flexible structure, Depo aims to meet the needs in Istanbul's culture and art scene for non-commercial, independent spaces open to critical voices.

△ Depo: ground floor. Photo: courtesy Depo

△ Depo: entrance. Photo: courtesy Depo

P.95 40°58'52.1"N / 29°01'28.1"E

## BANTMAG

Moda Mektebi Sokak No. 26 Caferaga Kadikoy Istanbul, Turkey

Bantmag is a music, art, culture, and cinema publication and organization company based in Istanbul. We have been an online and print media since 2004. Our main team consists of seven people and we work with many contributing writers and artists. Since 2004, one of our main goals has been to create a platform for young and upcoming artists and musicians in Turkey. Besides being a daily news platform and a magazine, we organize concerts, exhibitions, panels, and screenings giving space to many local and foreign acts. The age of Bantmag's audience ranges from sixteen to forty-five.

In 2015, with the Prince Claus Fund, we created the year-long exhibition project 'Mevsimler/Seasons.' The project's goal was to create a platform for Syrian artists who were living in Turkey. Four exhibitions were organized, with each hosting one Syrian artist and one local Turkish artist. As such, besides helping the Syrian artist reach a broader audience, we helped them connect with local artists.

▷ Imad Habbab and Hare Sürel at the inauguration of the exhibition 'Mevsimler/Seasons,' 2015.

▽▽ Inauguration of the exhibition 'Mevsimler/Seasons,' 2015.

P.186 30°02'55.3"N / 31°14'15.9"E

## TOWNHOUSE GALLERY

3 Hussein Basha Al Meamari, Marouf, Qasr El Nil, Cairo Governorate, Egypt

Townhouse is a nonprofit art space situated in the heart of downtown Cairo. It holds an iconic position in the story of contemporary art in the Middle East; a key driver behind what has become a culturally rich, regional art scene.

Established in 1998, Townhouse has initiated a breadth of activities in its various spaces: key regional symposia, meaningful community outreach, landmark exhibitions, and international residencies for artists, curators, writers, and filmmakers. It has also incubated several important art spaces within Cairo that have gone on to impact the cultural landscape. On an individual level, the gallery has played a pivotal role in the careers of internationally renowned artists and hosted a number of influential practitioners and curators from abroad.

Although Townhouse remains a crucial platform for the visual art scene, over time it has evolved far beyond this linear mission. Between 2006 and 2019, the Rawabet space offered a platform to independent performers and artists of all genres through its own programming, but also acting as a venue to host programmes curated by other institutions.

The Townhouse Library is home to cultural salons for conversation, curated film screenings, and a growing archive emphasizing the significance of discourse dissemination and the documentation of the undertakings of contemporary art in Cairo.

An open-door policy has allowed cultural activists across all creative media to find an avenue of support for their projects, ideas, and experiments. The institution collaborates with a range of artists and institutions in every aspect of their work, aiming to contribute to a comprehensive network in the local, regional, and international arts community.

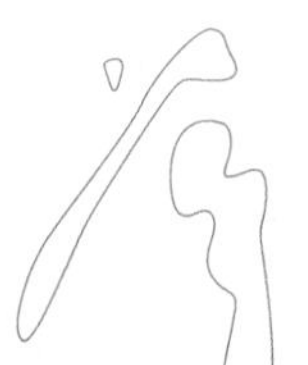

P.167 0°17'33.5"N / 32°36'22.8"E

## 32° EAST | UGANDAN ARTS TRUST

Plot 2239, Ggaba Road, Kansanga, Kampala, Uganda

32° East | Ugandan Arts Trust is an independent nonprofit organization focused on the creation and exploration of contemporary art in Uganda.

Our multi-purpose resource centre is based in the capital city Kampala and includes studios, accommodation for artists in residence, a contemporary art library, computers and editing suites, meeting areas and outdoor workshop space.

Our activities include KLA ART Labs (supported by the Prince Claus Fund, Newcastle University, and Arts Collaboratory), an immersive experiential programme designed to provide creative professionals with the tools and opportunities for in-depth research and critical thinking through public practice, and experience-based collaborative learning.

Through our annual residency programme, we offer both graduate and professional Ugandan artists (approximately ten per year) the space, time, and resources to explore their practice as well as the opportunity to interact and exchange ideas with regional and international artists. We encourage artists in residence and members to take advantage of our gallery and outdoor spaces to showcase and exhibit their work, and to explore and experiment with audiences.

We also believe that professional development is crucial to sustaining a career in the arts, so we invite both local and international experts to facilitate both thematic and practical workshops with our members. We also offer our members weekly one-on-one drop-in sessions for portfolio and application reviews as well as technical training in graphics, photo, and video editing.

With Artachat, we aim to foster an environment for the exchange of ideas and debate between artists and audiences, and a starting platform for further research. Artachat's set up is informal but informative. Each discussion session is driven by engaging speakers, curated topics, and an active curious audience.

P.270 0°17'33.5"N 32°36'22.8"E

## BN POETRY AWARD

Uganda, Kampala, with meetings held in Ntinda on Factory Road, Kampala, to Nairobi Kenya Museums, Kigali spoken word event in Kigali, and discussions in Remera, Kigali.

BN Poetry Award has been promoting poetry by Ugandan women and poetry by Africans since 2009. Our vision is a society immersed in poetry. Our main activities include annual poetry competitions, poetry camps/workshops, annual poetry festivals, and editing and publishing African poetry. Our primary audience is African poets from twenty to sixty years of age.

In 2012, workshops/camps were held at the Storymoja Hay Festival in Nairobi, during which the BN Poetry Award winners participated. During that time, we conducted workshops with fellow poets, and attended master classes. Being the first Ugandan poets at the Storymoja Hay Festival, we used this space of poetry workshops and camps to share the idea of an anthology. These poems were woven into editorial spaces, and were expanded by the day as the poetry camps enlarged through visits to Kigali and connections with Dar es Salaam.

Here, the anthology *A Thousand Voices Rising* was birthed. It was the creative expression of African poets mainly based in East Africa, who had largely participated in poetry workshops and camps. Since 2016, we progressed to annual poetry performances; poetry excursions to Mt. Rwenzori, Mabira Forest, Sipi Falls, and Lake Bunyonyi were initiated to illustrate how scenic environments enhance the poetic nature of words.

△ Poets gathered at 32 Degrees EAST, after a reading of A Thousand Voices Rising anthology.

△ Travelling to Remera, Kigali for a discussion with poets.

△ Babishai poets at Mabira Forest/ poetry camp

## VOLUNTEER PALESTINE

Aida Refugee Camp Bethlehem, Palestine

Volunteer Palestine was founded in 2016 by a small group of friends living and working in the Aida Refugee camp in Bethlehem. Volunteer Palestine considers development as a course of social, political, and economic transformation that empowers the excluded and exploited. Successful development must create conditions for transformation that ends the systematic exclusion and exploitation of the Palestinian people and reverses measures that prevent the rights they are entitled to. Our approach is based on a model in which the root causes of social issues and the continued marginalization, disintegration, and forced displacement of Palestinians are recognized and addressed. Volunteer Palestine pursues these developments by placing Palestinian refugees, women, youth, and other disempowered community members at centre stage in our projects and by promoting them as legitimate holders of rights. We seek to enable all Palestinians to meaningfully engage with the processes that reflect the contours and outcomes of these rights, and as an organization, struggle for their realization.

△ Volunteers' trip to Jaffa. Photo: Romane Devresse.

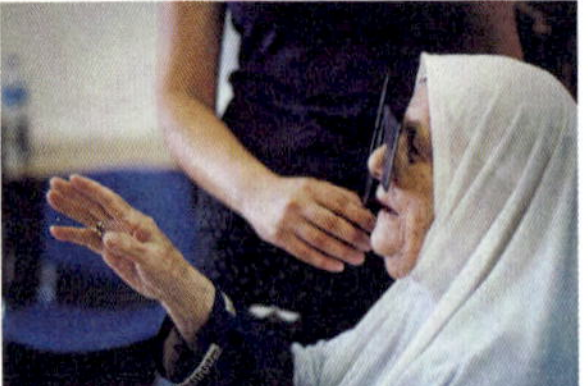

△ Medical day for the refugees from Beit Jabreen & Aida refugee camp, Bethlehem. Photo: Marian Gidi

△ Hike at Battir Village, Bethlehem as part of the weekly activities for volunteers. Photo: Akram Al Warah



## MASRAH ENSEMBLE

Mar Mikhaël Annahr, Beirut 00000, Lebanon

Masrah Ensemble is a nonprofit organization that makes, develops, and fosters research and criticism of theatre with a focus on the Arab stage. Based in Beirut (Lebanon), the Ensemble aims to reconfigure audiences and to encourage transcendent, riveting theatre.

Since 2009, we have been staging performances, cultivating new talent, and championing artistic and cultural exchange.

Our projects have been supported by the Prince Claus Fund, Hivos, Arab Fund for Arts and Culture, Violet Jabara Charitable Trust, Ettijahat—Independent Culture, Theatre Communications Group, Young Arab Theatre Fund, and Culture Resource.

The project featured in this book, Family Ti-Jean (FTJ), was a double-bill musical street theatre project performed in public spaces, an educational programme, and a *cultural* initiative confronting the divisive repercussions of post-colonial warfare. It was developed and presented by amateur teenage and professional adult actors and musicians representing various communities. The plays, *Family Stories* (1998) by Biljana Srbljanovic and Ti-Jean and *His Brothers* (1958) by Derek Walcott, together convey tangled narratives about the postcolonial experience and traumatic aftermath of warfare. Preteen Syrian and Palestinian refugees performed alongside actors and musicians, some from the migrant labour community, for audiences including refugees in Lebanon, in three languages: Arabic, English, and French. The attempt was to build audiences across Lebanon that intermingled theatregoers, refugees, migrant workers, and preteens, as well as young adults and students. These choices not only integrated the voices and movements of a generation currently inhabiting a moment of vicious warfare, but also invited a younger generation to read, think about, and interpret, a play about a society that has emerged from and reflects on a bloody history of civil war and foreign intervention.

△△ Public performance of Family Ti-Jean, 2016. Photo: Jad Safar/ Ettijahat-Independent Culture

△ Masrah Ensemble collaborators at Mansion in Beirut, Lebanon (not pictured: Hanadi Shabta and Christine Youakim), 2015. Courtesy Masrah Ensemble

P.95 33°52'41.2"N / 35°32'23.7"E

## CLOWN ME IN

Lebanon, HQ:
La Pinede Bldg., Beirut Hall Street, Sin El Fil, Beirut, Lebanon.
-
Clown Me In the House (training/rehearsal space):
VG7V+G5 Jisr El Bacha, Jisr El Bacha

Since 2008, Clown Me In's main objective has been to provide relief to disadvantaged communities in remote areas in Lebanon and abroad. We are a team of eight part-time staffers and twenty-five volunteers, who believe in using humour, clowning, street theatre, and social therapy to shed light on important social, environmental, and humanitarian issues. We aim to create direct and lasting social impact through our projects (whether they are immersive street theatre performances or intensive workshops), by addressing difficult themes like migration, human rights, and social responsibility. We also create viral video and social media campaigns on topics like consumption, waste, anti-discrimination and racism (among others), to reach a wider audience. Within Lebanon, we aim to make arts and culture accessible to a wider public by taking our projects outside the capital to rural and/or disadvantaged communities and building bridges between communities through them. There are no age limits for our performances, as they are meant to be accessible to anyone and everyone. Clown Me In has also worked around the world, in Mexican, Lebanese, Palestinian, Indian, Brazilian, Moroccan, Jordanian, Syrian, Greek and British communities.

▷▷ Clown Me In: performances and team. Photos: Amar Sokhen (above), Ali J. Dalloul (right).

P.247 1°17'39.5"S / 36°47'10.4"E

## CREATIVES GARAGE

Kenya, Address: 31 Wood Ave, Nairobi, PQ3P+QH Nairobi

Creatives Garage is an Arts Trust that works with artists and innovators from East Africa. It was founded in 2012 and officially registered in 2013. While the Trust is governed by a board, the day to day running is handled by thirty permanent staff working either remotely or from the Nairobi office.

Our mission is 'to build cultural networks, engage in cultural activism, and seek out social innovation'.

We work with artists in East Africa to facilitate collaboration, networking, market access, and to help them add their voice to calls for social change.

Our core projects include:

- Sondeka Festival, the first arts and innovation festival in Eastern Africa.
- Sondeka Awards, created to recognize artists from various fields for their work.
- Kalabars, a purpose built content-distribution platform helping filmmakers and musicians earn from their content.
- Femmolution, a collection of music, art, poetry, and prose by African women.
- Prosexive, a series of events providing safe spaces for conversations on sex and sexuality.

We work with individuals and collectives from the creative community including visual artists, poets, writers, filmmakers, and performing artists. Furthermore, we work with social activists in mental health awareness and the LGBTIQ+ community.

▽ 3D Printer by one of the creatives. Photo: Creatives Garage

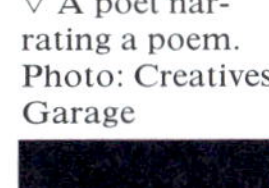

▽ A poet narrating a poem. Photo: Creatives Garage

▽ Nurturing talent in children to help identify their potential. Photo: Creatives Garage

◁ Acting Directing. Photo: Creatives Garage

△ Performance during one evening of the Sur ka Safar series at The 2nd Floor (T2F) in Karachi, 2018. Photo: courtesy T2F

△ Yeh Watan Hamara Hai; Cafe sessions. Photos: courtesy The Second Floor (T2F)

## THE SECOND FLOOR (T2F)

10-C Sunset Lane 5, D.H.A Phase II Extension Phase 2 Ext Defence Housing Authority, Karachi, Karachi City, Sindh 75500, Pakistan

The Second Floor, abbreviated conveniently as T2F as it then occupied the second floor of a nondescript office building, opened its doors in 2007 as part of the NGO Peace Niche. Since its inception in 2007, T2F—whichconsists of an art gallery, a bookshop, and a coffeehouse—has sported an open-door policy for every one willing to explore, create, and ruminate on their capacities and creative ideas. Ranging from poetry readings and film screenings to vibrant debates on critical issues, anything that falls under the four 'Cs' of T2F (Creativity, Community, Culture and Curiosity), is welcomed and channelled through T2F. Although small, its doors are open to all: students, artists, writers, poets, musicians, and anyone with an interest in social change through democracy, cultural activities, or public discourse. In April 2015, T2F was nominated by the Dutch Ministry of Foreign Affairs for The Human Rights Tulip Award, for 'Creating an oasis of free thought in Pakistan.' Since then, T2F has established various projects under which events are hosted: notably, Creative Karachi Festival, Science ka Adda, Urdu Preservation Project, Sur ka Safar, Qavvaali Mahfil, and Haftaltvar Art Bazaar, etc. T2F's audience has never been limited to one—it is an open space for all those who seek to approach us to be a part of our community.

P.161 6°45'47.1"S / 39°14'30.3"E

## NAFASI ART SPACE

Plot 41, Eyasi Road, Light Industrial Area, Mikocheni B, Dar es Salaam, United Republic of Tanzania

Nafasi Art Space is a multidisciplinary contemporary art centre in Dar es Salaam that was founded by a group of Tanzanian artists in 2008. 'Nafasi' means both 'space' and 'opportunity,' and the organization's artistic and strategic orientation emphasizes the interconnections between these terms. Through artist residencies, exhibitions, workshops, working studios, meeting spaces, community art outreach, and dedicated mentoring and artist development programmes for Tanzanian artists, Nafasi aims to further and enrich human potential through contemporary arts.

Nafasi is located on a large plot in an industrial area of Dar es Salaam. The thirty artist studios on the grounds are constructed from recycled shipping containers from the port. Nafasi Art Space also has a large exhibition hall, two permanent gallery spaces, a children's art workshop, an art resource library, two production workshops, a film amphitheatre, and other spaces for performance, meeting, and creation.

Nafasi is an inclusive space founded on a belief in the importance of artistic community, with emphasis placed on creativity, generosity, integrity, cooperation, and consciousness. The space takes an active and critical position in interrogating contemporary life and society and is built on a model of collective decision-making and artistic experimentation. By supporting the creativity, professionalism, and visibility of Tanzanian and African artists, Nafasi sparks cross-cultural dialogue and encourages collaborative artistic endeavours.

Nafasi Art Space has provided a space where successive generations of Tanzanian artists from diverse backgrounds have gained the skills, knowledge, resources, and networks they have needed to develop their artistic practices and succeed professionally. It has become the main space in Tanzania where the public regularly comes to participate in cultural activities and where people have come to expect and anticipate the discovery of new and innovative artistic expressions. Nafasi also works to support emerging art organizations and initiatives, and to collaborate with independent artists, curators, and institutions around the country, continent, and world.

△ Chap Chap Collage Workshop, 2018. Photo: courtesy Nafasi Art Space

△ Nafasi Public Art Workshop. Photo: courtesy Nafasi Art Space

42°51'17.3"N 74°35'13.1"E

## ARTEAST

32, ChingizAytmatovavenue (formerMira), app.3. Bishkek, Kyrgyz Republic,

ArtEast is a non-governmental organization that was founded by artists Gulnara Kasmalieva and Muratbek Djumaliev in 2002. ArtEast supports the development of contemporary art as part of the civil society movement in Kyrgyzstan. During its eighteen years of activity, it has created quite a strong local community of contemporary artists and curators who already work independently or are organized as institutions. Members and leaders of such institutions and independent groups, such as Art Group '705,' Laboratoria CI and Inside Out Group, were involved in ArtEast's educational and artistic projects. In a context where there are a lack of contemporary art institutions in Central Asia, the organization provides a wide spectrum of activities including an educational programme for younger generation of artists, art managers and curators, art residency programme for international and national artists and curators, organization and curatorship of international art exhibitions, and public art festivals. ArtEast uses contemporary art as a platform for examining the social and economic dynamics of the region in Central Asia and more specifically in Kyrgyzstan. The organization has also engaged with projects that address wider audience inviting them to discover contemporary art as a space for development the sense of otherness, originality, non-conformism and an atmosphere of creativity and unity.

◁◁◁ Photos: courtesy ArtEast



38°34'03.1"N 68°46'59.5"E

## DUSHANBE ART GROUND/ 'SANATI MUOSIR' PUBLIC FOUNDATION

Republic of Tajikistan, Dushanbe, Sino Street No 12

Dushanbe Art Ground (DAG)/'Sanati Muosir' is a non-governmental organization that was founded by Jamshed Kholikov in 2012. The organization's strategy is to achieve long-term sustainable development for new media arts and new platforms where creative and civic communities can collaboratively invent alternative avenues for social development and change. DAG's mission is to advocate for the development of contemporary art practices in Tajikistan. Its team seeks to redefine the role of the artist in contemporary society and shift the function of the artist from mere producer to engaged researcher and critic. The projects, programmes, and public events developed by DAG are addressed to students and young artists. DAG serves as a platform for invited artists, lecturers, theorists, media researchers, art managers, and curators who want to gain knowledge and skills in theory and practice of contemporary art, to interact more deeply with the media space, and who want to be participants in the global art process. The Media Archive and Media Art Laboratory are the main formats for professional (theoretical and practical) development for students and young artists. The premises and equipment of the DAG are actively used for Master's classes, presentations, seminars as a part of projects, art residences, and for other creative initiatives.

△ Lecture at Dushanbe Art Ground space. Photo: Jamshed Kholikov. Courtesy Dushanbe Art Ground

△ Dushanbe Art Ground team. Photo: Jamshed Kholikov. Courtesy Dushanbe Art Ground

△ Jamshed Kholikov with workshop participants. Photo: Alisher Primkulov. Courtesy Dushanbe Art Ground

P.75 42°52'06.1"N / 74°35'24.3"E

## ART GROUP '705'

Kyrgyz Republic, Bishkek city, Bokonbaeva 149 street,

The Art Group '705' was formed in 2005 on the basis of the Children's media centre with the assistance of ArtEast. Since 2014, it has been part of translocal network Arts Collaboratory. And from the end of 2018, the collective become part of the NextGen network supported by Prince Claus Fund.

Group 705 represents a group of young artists working as a part of the modern art, theatre, street action, animation, and cinema. Collective practicians, naive and poor art, children's creativity, cross-disciplinary approach, etc. are the main interests of the group.

The number of group members changes periodically; at the moment there are ten full-time participants in the group and about twenty volunteers (actors, designers, artists, curators, activists).

Art is considered a language for judgment of social and political processes and personal experiences. Sometimes, at the workplace meetings with artists, workshops on drawing, animation and woodworks, festivals of experimental cinema and performances all take place.

△ Children's workshop, comics drawing, 2018

△ Film festival Olgoi-Khorkhon, 2018

△ Annual 1 April competiton 2019

P.328 6°54'34.0"N / 79°53'11.5"E

## WOMEN AND MEDIA COLLECTIVE (WMC)

No. 56/1, Sarasavi Lane, Castle Street, Colombo 08, Sri Lanka

The Women and Media Collective (WMC) is a woman's organization formed in 1984 by a group of Sri Lankan feminists interested in exploring ideological and practical issues of concern to women in Sri Lanka.

Our aim is to bring about change based on feminist principles for a society free from violence, which would pave the way for a balanced representation of women in decision-making and governance, and advocate for non-discriminatory laws and politics.

Our work has contributed at different moments in time to social and political change; the inclusion of women and gender concerns in the peace process; increased state recognition of women's rights; the enactment of new legislation or legislative and policy reform promoting and protecting women's rights; and recognition for the need to increase women's representation in politics.

We have helped initiate women's networks and continue to work with a range of organizations from the grassroots level (local women's organizations) to national level institutions, which have a direct voice in policy formulation and implementation. Thus, we act as a bridge that closes the gap between high-level policymaking and the marginalized in the work for promoting and protecting women's rights. WMC structures its work under three broad thematic areas: State and Politics, Gender Identities, and Sexuality and Media. We also use the strategic approaches of Mobilization; Dialogue and Advocacy; Networking and Events; Media and Publications; and Documentation & Research to intersect our three main themes.

P.342 16°46'37.2"N / 96°10'10.9"E

## BEYOND PRESSURE

Multiple locations in Yangon, Myanmar (2008 edition: YMCA, Thamada Art Gallery, M3 and Queen Park Hotel, Yangon, Myanmar)

Beyond Pressure was an independent art organization created to contribute to the expanding of Myanmar art boundaries. It was initiated and run by local artists who worked in their communities to create projects opening up spaces for self-expression and discourse.

Its main activity was the organization of the Beyond Pressure International Performance Art Festival (first edition: 2008, under the artistic direction of Moe Satt), which had a twofold mission: firstly, to create from within Myanmar spaces and forums in which people could take part in the representation of themselves, thus reaffirming their place in the global community. Secondly, through the global power of assembly that art provides, to present critical alternatives to the image of Myanmar to the outside world. The hope was to nurture youths and newcomers alike to the possibilities of art as a social force. The festival brought together artists and artworks from across the world to Myanmar, facilitating exchange between them and introducing them to the Myanmar art scene and vice versa.
In order to reach an audience that was not familiar with art, the activities took place in unexpected public spaces and popular hangouts close to major junctions, in order to be more accessible for locals. Each event included the showcase of art works, street performances, projections of videos on buses, teashop symposiums and workshops.

The organization ceased to exist in 2015.

P.328 23°44'49.3"N / 90°23'08.6"E

## BRITTO ARTS TRUST

33, 33/1 Green Mart, 1st floor, Space no 208-210, Green Road, Dhaka-1205 Bangladesh,

Britto Arts Trust is an artists' run nonprofit network officially founded in 2002 in Dhaka (Bangladesh) with a global reach. It is permanently spaced in Green Road, Dhaka, but works extensively in different locations across the country. Britto Arts Trust is part of the worldwide Triangle Network.

The spirit of Britto lies in innovation, dedication, collaboration, and commitment. Britto works as catalyst for supporting and promoting new ideas.

It seeds and promotes multiple interdisciplinary practitioners, groups, and networks; it provides an international and local forum for the development of professional art practitioners, a place where they can meet, discuss, experiment, and upgrade their abilities on their own terms.

A team of six trustees and seventeen members (as per 2020) commits their time and energy towards the platform in an intermittent way; not everyone is engaged throughout the process of Britto's activities though.

Currently, since there are several new groups and collectives that are launched each year, we have shifted our strategies and programmes in a new direction. Over the last few years, we have emphasized large scale long-term projects focusing on socio-political issues engaging a number of participants from various walks.

Presently, due to the pandemic, Britto is undertaking another long-term project in various locations entitled 'Zero Waste-Food Art.'

www.brittoartstrust.org

△ Photo: courtesy Britto Arts Trust

△ Shohor Nama, Graffiti on garbage containers, 2018. Photo: courtesy Britto Arts Trust

P.131 6°19'06.6"S / 106°48'54.9"E

RUANGRUPA
Jl. Durian Raya No.30, RT.4/RW.4, Jagakarsa, Kec. Jagakarsa, Kota Jakarta Selatan, Daerah Khusus Ibukota Jakarta 12620, Indonesia

ruangrupa is a Jakarta-based collective established in 2000. It is a nonprofit organization that strives to support the idea of art within urban and cultural contexts by involving artists and other disciplines such as social sciences, politics, technology, and media, to give critical observation and views towards Indonesian urban contemporary issues. ruangrupa also produces collaborative works in the form of art projects such as exhibitions, festivals, art labs, workshops, research, as well as book, magazine and online-journal publications.

As an artists' collective, ruangrupa has been involved in many collaborative and exchange projects, including participating in big exhibitions such as Gwangju Biennale (2002 and 2018), Istanbul Biennial (2005), Asia Pacific Triennial of Contemporary Art (Brisbane, 2012), Singapore Biennale (2011), São Paulo Biennial (2014), Aichi Triennale (Nagoya, 2016) and 'Cosmopolis' at Centre Pompidou (Paris, 2017). In 2016, ruangrupa curated 'transACTION' (Sonsbeek '16) in Arnhem, NL.

From 2015 to 2018, together with several artists' collectives in Jakarta, ruangrupa co-developed the cultural platform Gudang Sarinah Ekosistem, located at Gudang Sarinah warehouse, Pancoran, South Jakarta. It is a cross-disciplinary space that aims to maintain, cultivate, and establish an integrated support system for creative talents, diverse communities, and various institutions. It also aspires to be able to make connections and collaborate, to share knowledge and ideas, as well as to encourage critical thinking, creativity, and innovations. The results of these joint collaborations are open for public access.

In 2018, together with Serrum and Grafis Huru Hara, ruangrupa co-initiated Gudskul: a contemporary art collective and ecosystem studies (or Gudskul, in short, pronounced similarly like 'good school' in English). It is a public learning space established to practice an expanded understanding of collective values, such as equality, sharing, solidarity, friendship, and togetherness.

In 2019, ruangrupa was appointed as the artistic director of documenta 15 (Kassel, 18 June–22 September 2022). The appointment marks the first time that an artist collective curates the international art exhibition.

P.307 11°31'26.1"N / 104°56'23.3"E

TINY TOONES
Tiny Toones, #154,
Street 369,Sangkat Chbar Ampov,
Phnom Penh, Cambodia

Since 2005, Tiny Toones has been inspiring and educating children and young people from the poorest neighbourhoods of Phnom Penh. Tiny Toones channels their energy and creativity into hip-hop arts and a range of education opportunities—from English and computer skills to healthy living and HIV awareness—building their self-confidence and developing skills that will help them to continue their education and improve their opportunities in life. Tiny Toones reaches circa 2,400 children and young people annually. Tiny Toones' students are aged five to twenty-four. Tiny Toones provides a safe environment in which these children and young people can enjoy learning, exploring their creativity, and developing a positive sense of identity and community.

△ Pupils of Tiny Toones' break dance school in Phnom Penh during a class and performance in 2008. Photo: Stuart Isett, courtesy Tiny Toones

P.131 6°16'24.0"S / 106°50'00.6"E

## KOALISI SENI INDONESIA

Jalan Amil Raya no 7A, Pejaten Barat,
Pasar Minggu, Jakarta Selatan 12510, Indonesia

Koalisi Seni Indonesia (the Indonesia Arts Coalition) is an association of individuals and organizations established in 2012 by arts practitioners envisioning a healthier arts ecosystem in Indonesia. To reach this goal, Koalisi Seni conducts policy advocacy in the arts sector, promotes the establishment of arts endowment funds in Indonesia, and strengthens management of knowledge and network among members.

Koalisi Seni is the only civil society organization in Indonesia that engages with policies for the arts. Until June 2020, Koalisi Seni had an extensive network of 260 members in twenty provinces from various art sectors such as visual arts, music, film, literature, and performance arts.

Koalisi Seni helped to redraft the initially problematic and xenophobic Cultural Bill into Law No.5/2017 on the Advancement of Culture, which puts the Indonesian government as a facilitator in empowering communities, the driving force of culture. To advocate for a fairer music industry, Koalisi Seni co-prepared the first and second Indonesian Music Conference in 2018 and 2019. Along with Indonesian musicians, Koalisi Seni facilitated the dismissal of a repressive Music Draft Bill in 2019. Koalisi Seni also advocates for policies that can help artists and art workers who are highly affected by the Covid-19 pandemic.

△ Koalisi Seni's Annual Members Meeting in Yogyakarta, 2019. Photo: Yuventius Nicky

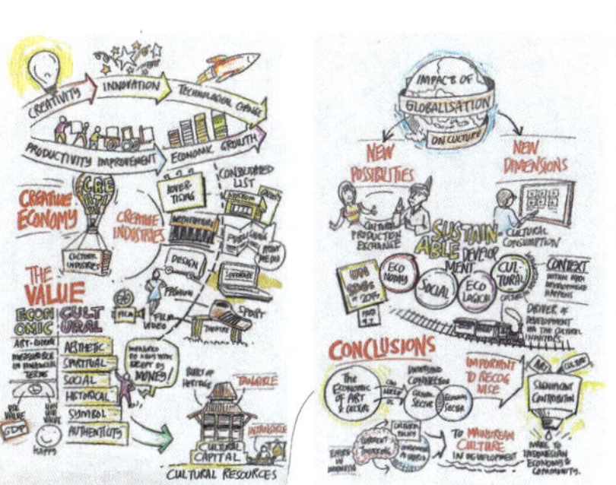



◁ Graphic recording of the Cultural Economics Public Lecture. Prof. David Throsby, cultural economist from Macquarie University, Sydney, spoke in the lecture. Graphic recorder: Deni Rodendo

P.307 8°33'10.8"S / 125°31'57.9"E

## ARTE MORIS ARTS CENTRE

Arte Moris, Dili, Timor Leste

Arte Moris is the first Fine Arts school, Cultural Centre, and Artists Association in Timor-Leste. The project emerged in the aftermath of twenty-five years of Indonesian military occupation and its primary aim was to use art as a building block in the psychological and social reconstruction of a country devastated by violence and oppression, with special emphasis on helping young people. Now one of the most enduring and sustainable youth projects and platforms in East Timor, Arte Moris provides talented young people with a direct means to creative exploration of their world—their unique history and heritage, their personal experiences, and their dreams for the future. Crucially, it also provides the skills and experience for these young people to become future teachers, full-time artists, community arts leaders, and/or key producers in a future Timorese creative industry sector.

Arte Moris is a grassroots project initiated by a group of disenfranchised young people, in collaboration with two Swiss Fine Arts professionals, and grew in response to the needs and actions of its community. It provides basic human needs to its members (most of whom live, work and study at the complex), who experience non-discriminatory guidance and direction, and provides continuous and diverse vocational training to its artists and participants. It seeks to contribute to the consolidation of lasting peace through its on-site and outreach activities and collaborations throughout the country.

△ Photo courtesy Arte Moris Arts Centre

PARTNERS

The Prince Claus Fund supports, connects, and celebrates artists and cultural practitioners where culture is under pressure. The Fund was established on 6 September 1996 as a tribute to His Royal Highness Prince Claus's dedication to culture and development. Since then, the Fund has supported cultural expression primarily in Latin America, Asia, Africa, the Caribbean and Eastern Europe. As part of its mission, the Fund stands with those who create, who believe in the transformative power of culture, who advance new ideas and explore new perspectives. The initiatives highlighted in this book demonstrate a wide range of artistic disciplines and vary from one-time grants for specific projects to longer-term collaborations.

Hivos is an international social justice organization seeking new and creative solutions to persistent global problems; solutions created by people taking their lives into their own hands. Together with our partners, we are building a positive counterbalancing force against discrimination, inequality, abuse of power, and the unsustainable use of our planet's resources.
For twenty-five years, Hivos has supported the arts and cultural sector because we believe art has the power to question hegemonic structures in society, create alternative narratives, imagine new realities, and bring about progressive social change. *Forces of Art* specifically helps in building Hivos' current R.O.O.M. programme, in which we support the creative work of a new generation of artists, musicians, filmmakers and content creators who investigate and challenge the status quo in the societies in which they live.

The European Cultural Foundation (ECF) (founded 1954) is the first foundation with a European mission and vision. ECF believes in the power of culture to achieve a united Europe of diversity, democracy, and freedoms, where solidarity, mutual respect, and collaboration contribute to a shared sense of belonging. ECF's current work focuses on three programmatic areas: Sharing, Experiencing, and Imagining Europe, which respectively contribute to a European public space, enable cross-border cultural exchanges, and support initiatives that tell the stories of Europe through culture. Since 2020, the Culture of Solidarity Fund started supporting imaginative cultural initiatives, which reinforce solidarity and European public space amid the Covid-19 crisis. ECF advocates for more substantial and inclusive cultural policies of the EU, as well as for citizens' engagement in policymaking.

## EDITOR-IN-CHIEF

Carin Kuoni (born 1961) is a curator and writer whose work examines how contemporary artistic practices reflect and inform social, political, and cultural conditions. She is senior director/chief curator of the Vera List Center for Art and Politics at The New School, New York, and assistant professor of Visual Studies. She has curated numerous trans-disciplinary exhibitions, and is editor/co-editor of *Energy Plan for the Western Man: Joseph Beuys in America* (1996); *Considering Forgiveness* (2009); *Entry Points: The Vera List Center Field Guide on Art and Social Justice* (2015); *Assuming Boycott: Resistance, Agency, and Cultural Production* (2017); *Freedom of Speech: A Curriculum for Studies Into Darkness* (2021), and several other books.

## EDITORS

Jordi Baltà Portolés (born 1976) is a researcher, consultant, and trainer at TrànsitProjectes. His work focuses on cultural policy and international affairs, including cultural rights, cultural diversity, the relation between culture and sustainable development, and local cultural policies. He has authored several articles and reports and contributed to international and local conferences and seminars on these matters. He is an expert for the Committee on Culture of United Cities and Local Governments (UCLG/Agenda 21 for culture) and the UNESCO 2005 Convention on the Diversity of Cultural Expressions. He lives and works in Barcelona.

Nora N. Khan (born 1983) is a writer, curator, editor, and professor at Rhode Island School of Design, where she teaches critical theory and artistic research, writing for artists and designers, and technological criticism. Her research focuses on digital visual culture, philosophy of emerging technology, and art and music that make arguments through software. Recent exhibitions include: 'Manual Override, The Shed,' New York City, 2020. She recently published *Seeing, Naming, Knowing* (2019).

Serubiri Moses (born 1989) is an independent writer and curator, and is currently Adjunct Assistant Professor in the Art Department at Hunter College, New York. He is co-curator of MoMA PS1's survey of contemporary art, Greater New York, and previously was on the curatorial team of the 10th Berlin Biennale of Contemporary Art. His current research focuses on theories of African art. Recent publications and conference talks include: 'Violent Dreaming,' *e-flux journal* 107 (March 2020); 'Death as a Premonitory Sign,' Singapore Biennial Symposium (February 2020). He lives and works in New York City.

## AUTHORS

Mariam Abou Ghazi (born 1990) is a Cairo-based researcher, game designer, and anthropologist with a particular interest in oral history, documentation, archiving, and sound. She holds a BA in cultural anthropology from the American University in Cairo, and an MA in Anthropology and Cultural Politics from Goldsmiths, University of London, in 2014. In 2016, Mariam was a fellow as part of the Alliance for Historical Dialogue and Accountability fellowship programme at Columbia University. She has previously worked on different archiving and documenting projects, including Cimatheque's 'Revisiting Memory' and 'The Memory and Consciousness' programme launched by the Association of Freedom of Thought and Expression, part of the organization's attempt to document various events of the Egyptian revolution.

Kobina Ankomah-Graham (born 1977) holds degrees in Law and International Studies and Diplomacy from the School of Oriental and African Studies (SOAS). He is a writer and DJ in Ghana's creative arts scene, and has an endless fascination with African counterculture and creativity. He is pursuing his doctoral degree in contemporary creative industries at the Department of Sociology, University of Ghana. Before full-time immersion in his doctoral studies, he was a faculty member at Ashesi University where he taught classes including African Philosophical Thought, Social Theory, and Text and Meaning. He currently teaches at Webster University Ghana.

Ilka Eickhof (born 1981) is Assistant Professor of Sociology at the American University in Cairo. She holds a PhD in Cultural Anthropology (University of Amsterdam) with a Dissertation on European Cultural Institutions in Cairo after 2011. Her work focuses on social class, postcolonial theory, and politics of representation. Recent publications include: *Class and Creative Economies: The Culture Field in Cairo* (2019); *Producing Inequality: Creative Economies in Cairo* (2017); *All that is Banned is Desired: 'Rebel Documentaries' and the Representation of Egyptian Revolutionaries* (2016); *Situations Arise because of the Weather: On a Happening led by Artist Mahmoud Khaled* (2015). Ilka lives and works in Cairo, Egypt.

Fernando Escobar Neira (born 1973) is professor and researcher at the School of Arts of the Universidad Nacional de Colombia, Medellín headquarters. He holds a PhD in Design and Urban Studies from the Universidad Autónoma Metropolitana (Mexico City). Since the beginning of the nineties, he has centred his work on city-related topics such as the production of public spaces, cultural cartographies and mappings, art-politics relationships, site-specific art, and collaborative and participatory art projects. His artistic and research work has gained him recognition and grants from various cultural and academic institutions, both national and international. Fernando lives and works in Medellín.

An experienced arts manager, researcher, and policy maker, Fatin Farhat (born 1975) is the founding director of the Palestine Observatory for Cultural Policy, where she curates and manages projects that foster community participation through the arts. Fatin has overseen a broad spectrum of cultural initiatives and artistic programmes from street festivals to national and municipal cultural policies. She is a member of the Expert Facility for the implementation of the 2005 Convention on the Protection and Promotion of the diversity of cultural expression, a research fellow of CEC ArtsLink 2019. Currently she is working on her PhD from Hildesheim University (Germany).

Maya Indira Ganesh (born 1975) studies and writes about digital technology, data politics, and society. She is completing a PhD on the social and cultural aspects of machines thought to be 'intelligent' and 'autonomous' and what this means for the category 'human.' She has worked as an information-activist for over a decade, supporting human rights defenders and activists to be safe both online and off. Her recent projects include 'A is for Another: A Dictionary of AI' (https://aisforanother.net, 2020); 'Between Flesh: Tech Degrees of Separation' edited by Ayas, Ginwala, Winder, the 13th Gwangju Biennale 2021 (https://13thgwangjubiennale.org/journal/between-flesh-tech-degrees-ofseparation/). Maya lives and works in Germany.

Rocca Holly-Nambi (born 1983) is an artist and cultural producer. She is a PhD candidate in Visual Cultures at Goldsmiths, University of London, and the British Council's Head of Arts, East Africa. She holds an MA in Contemporary Art Theory from Edinburgh College of Art. Rocca co-founded 32° East | Ugandan Arts Trust, a centre for contemporary art in Kampala, Uganda, and KLA ART, Kampala's biennial public art festival. An ISPA global fellow, Rocca has delivered projects for Edinburgh International Art Festival, Glasgow International Festival, and the Mela Festival of World Music and Dance. She lives and works in Nairobi, Kenya.

Miranda Iossifidis (born 1985) is an urban sociologist based in the Global Urban Research Unit at Newcastle University. Her work focuses broadly on everyday culture and urban imaginaries. Recent work includes research on speculative fiction and ambiguous hopefulness with online reading communities, and on children's exploration of urban public space through magical realism and augmented reality. Miranda lives and works in London.

Nuraini Juliastuti (born 1975) is a researcher and co-founder of Kunci Study Forum and Collective in Yogyakarta, Indonesia. Kunci's long-term project includes a School of Improper Education. Nuraini holds a PhD from Leiden University with a dissertation titled 'Commons People: Managing Music and Culture in Contemporary Yogyakarta.' Her recent essays include: 'Care, Practice, Art Communities in Indonesia,' *un Magazine* 14.1 (May 2020); 'Indonesian Migrant Workers' Writings as a Performance of Self-Care and Embodied Archives,' *PARSE Journal issue on Migration* 10 (June 2020). Her forthcoming book, written collectively with other Kunci members, is entitled *This Country is Burning, Let's Dream about a School of Improper Education* (2020). Other projects include running an independent Reading Sideways Press and *Domestic Notes*, a publication-based project on domestic, migrant spaces, and politics of productivity.

Višnja Kisić (born 1986) is a researcher and lecturer at UNESCO Chair for Cultural Policy and Management. She holds a BA in Art History, MA in Cultural Policy and Management and PhD in Heritage Studies. In her research, teaching, practice and activism she explores entanglements between heritage, politics, and ecology. She is the author of 'Heritage research in the 21st century: departing from the useful futures of sustainable development' (2020); 'Shaking the Solid: Heritage in the Era of Plurality' (2018); *Governing Heritage Dissonance: Promises and Realities of selected Cultural Policies* (2016). She lives in Serbia and works internationally.

Diana T. Kudaibergenova (born 1996) is a political and cultural sociologist. Currently she is a Postdoctoral Research Associate on UKRI Global Challenges Research Fund COMPASS, a project dealing with capacity-building in wider Eurasia. Diana studies different intersections of power relations through the realms of political sociology dealing with concepts of state, nationalising regimes, and ideologies. She received her PhD in 2015 from the Department of Sociology at the University of Cambridge. Her first book, *Rewriting the Nation in Modern Kazakh Literature* (2017) deals with the study of nationalism, modernization, and cultural development in modern Kazakhstan. Her second book, *Toward Nationalizing Regimes*, is based on her doctoral research and focuses on the rise of nationalising regimes in post-Soviet spaces after 1991, with a prime focus on power struggles among the political and cultural elites in democratic and non-democratic states (2020). Currently, she is completing her third book manuscript on power, state, and resistance in contemporary art scenes of the post-Soviet Eurasia and is working on a new project dealing with empowerment.

Kabelo Malatsie (born 1987) is a curator and organizer. She holds an MA in Art History from the University of Witwatersrand. She was recently director of Visual Arts Network of South Africa (2018–2019). Her ongoing curatorial research project explores the exhibitionary mode as unlikely starting points that place incongruous practices together, to instigate other ways of making and reading the world we inhabit. As an organizer, she is preoccupied with the notion of autonomy, specifically of temporary autonomous zones within the African context. Kabelo lives in Cape Town, South Africa.

Jenny Mbaye (born 1981) is a Senior Lecturer at the Centre for Culture and the Creative Industries (University London). Her work focuses on urban popular music and cultural economies in Sub-Saharan Africa, with a specific interest in urban creativity, cultural policy, and governance. She is a research and policy consultant (UNESCO, OSIWA, British Council), member of the group of experts on the UNESCO Convention 2005, as well as independent auditor for its Creative Cities Network. She is also a member of the working group on cultural policy for the Pan-African Arterial Network. Jenny lives and works in London.

Zayd Minty (born 1966), the director of Creative City South, is a cultural management professional and researcher. He has an interest in culture and its implications for diversity governance, infrastructure, and sustainable development in cities of the Global South. He previously developed the first local cultural policy in Africa for the City of Cape Town and its successful bid to become World Design Capital 2014. Before that, he curated a number of contemporary arts projects and facilitated networks. He is currently developing a national research and advocacy initiative on urban cultural governance in South Africa. Zayd lives in Johannesburg.

Nadia Moreno Moya (born 1977) is professor and researcher at the School of Arts of the Universidad Nacional de Colombia, Medellín headquarters. She is a PhD candidate in Art History at the Universidad Nacional Autónoma de México. Her research and publications explore artistic practices in Colombia and Latin America involving topics such as art, power, and subjectivity; art institutions, history of exhibitions, and curatorial and museological practices. Among her publications is the book *Arte y juventud: El Salón Esso de artistas jóvenes en Colombia* (2013) [Art and Youth: The Esso Salon of Young Artists in Colombia]. Nadia lives and works in Medellín.

Judith Naeff (born 1982) is assistant professor in Cultures of the Middle East, Leiden University. She was trained in Arabic Studies and Literary Studies and completed her PhD at the Amsterdam School for Cultural Analysis (ASCA) in 2016. Her main interest is in the way contemporary visual and literary cultures express and reimagine the complex socio-political realities of the modern and contemporary Arab world. Recent publications include 'Precarious Chronotopes in Beirut' in *Contemporary Levant* (2020), 'Writing Shame in Asads Syria' in *The Arab Studies Journal* (2018), *Precarious Imaginaries of Beirut: A City's Suspended Now* (2018) and *Visualizing the Street*, co-edited with Pedram Dibazar (2018).

Laura Nkula-Wenz (born 1984) is a researcher at the African Centre for Cities and lecturer for the MA in Critical Urbanisms, a joint programme between the Universities of Cape Town and Basel. She holds a PhD in Geography from the University of Muenster, Germany, and has a keen interest in postcolonial urban theory, African urbanism, and public culture. Her research focuses on understanding the nexus between design, local governance, and the politics of urban experimentation. Her work has appeared in *Cultural Trends, Journal of Urban Cultural Studies* and *EPA: Society & Space*. Laura lives and works in Cape Town.

Joseph Oduro-Frimpong (born 1975) is a trained media anthropologist. He directs the newly created Centre for African Popular Culture, Ashesi University. His current research explores local understandings of 'pleasure' in Ghanaian satirical works. Recent curations include 'Almost True,' Accra, Ghana, 2018; 'Ghanaian Hand-Painted Book Covers in African (Cultural) Studies,' Birmingham, 2018. His recent publications appear in: *Forward, Upward, Onward? Narratives of Achievement in African and Afroeuropean Contexts* (2020); *Taking African Cartoons Seriously: Politics, Satire and Culture* (2018); *African Popular Culture: The Episteme of Everyday Life* (2014).

Arnout van Ree (born 1985) is a lecturer at International Studies, Leiden University. He holds an RMA in Middle Eastern Studies, Leiden University. His main interest is in the way radical politics in the Middle East and North Africa express and reimagine new socio-political subjectivities with a particular interest in the visual culture produced during these episodes of contentious politics. Arnout lives and works in the Netherlands.

Naomi Roux (born 1982) is a Senior Lecturer in the Department of Architecture, Planning and Geomatics at the University of Cape Town, where she convenes the MPhil in Conservation of the Built Environment. She holds a PhD in History of Art from Birkbeck, University of London, and has held teaching and research posts at the University of the Witwatersrand and the London School of Economics and Political Science. Naomi's research focuses on urban heritage, memory, and spatial transformations. Her first book, *Remaking The Urban: Heritage and Spatial Transformation in Nelson Mandela Bay* will be published by Manchester University Press in 2021.

Vaughn Sadie (born 1978) is a conceptual artist and educator, completing his PhD at the Urban Futures Centre and working as a researcher at the Africa Centre for Cities in Cape Town. He is interested in participatory art practice as a tool to understand social contexts, with a specific focus on the governance arrangements formed during the implementation of projects. Recent curatorial projects include: 'Spier Lights Art' (co-curated with Jay Pather, Spier, Stellenbosch, 2019/2018); 'APPROACH: Cultural Production in a Social Context' (2016). He recently published *Revolution Room* (co-edited with Sari Middernacht, Molemo Moiloa, Patrick Mudekereza, 2017). Vaughn lives and works in Cape Town.

Anna Selmeczi (born 1978) is a political theorist and lecturer currently convening the MA programme in Southern Urbanism at the African Centre for Cities in Cape Town. Her work focuses on the epistemics and aesthetics of urban popular politics. She recently published *Critical Methods in Studying World Politics: Creativity and Transformation* (co-edited with shine choi and Erzsébet Strausz, 2019). Anna lives and works in Cape Town.

Nishant Shah (born 1980) is a feminist, humanist, and technologist working in digital cultures, and the Professor of Aesthetics and Cultures of Technology at ArtEZ University of the Arts. His work is at the intersections of body, identity, digital technologies, artistic practice, and activism. His forthcoming book is entitled *Really Fake* (co-authored with Alexandra Juhasz) (2020). Recent projects include the Digital Earth Fellowship, Hivos, the Netherlands (2019–2021) and the Feminist Internet Research Network, Association of Progressive Communication (2019–2021). Nishant lives and works in the Netherlands.

Lenneke Sipkes (born 1993) is an anthropologist who holds an MA in Middle Eastern Studies (University of Amsterdam) and an MSc in Cultural Anthropology (Leiden University). She specializes in contemporary politics and culture of the Bilad al-Sham. Her MA theses are about solidarity with the Palestinian cause through music (UvA) and through political tourism (LU). Lenneke lives and works in the Netherlands.

Straddling the academic world of urban studies and creative practice, Dr. Rike Sitas (born 1978) is fascinated by the intersection of culture and cities, and more specifically on the role of art, culture, and heritage in urban life. She is based at the African Centre for Cities at the University of Cape Town, researching the role of cultural policy and civic practice in realizing more just and sustainable cities. Recent publications include *Becoming Otherwise: Artful Urban Enquiry* (2020); *Cultural Policy and Just Cities in Africa* (2020). Relevant research projects include *Whose Heritage Matters* and *Public Art and the Power of Place*.

Cristiana Strava (born 1986) is a social anthropologist, trained at Harvard (BA, 2009) and SOAS, University of London (PhD, 2016). She is assistant professor in the School of Middle Eastern Studies at Leiden University, where her work broadly examines urban socio-spatial transformations in North Africa. Recent publications include: 'Losing or Gaining Home? Experiences of Resettlement from Casablanca's Slums' with Raffael Beier in *The Everyday Life of Urban Inequality* (2020); 'A Tramway Called Atonement' in *Middle East Topics & Arguments* (2018), and 'At Home on the Margins' in *City and Society* (2017). Cristiana lives and works between the Netherlands and Morocco.

Goran Tomka (born 1984) is a lecturer and researcher at UNESCO Chair for Cultural Policy and Management. He holds a BA in Culture and Media Studies, MA in Cultural Policy and Management, and a PhD in Culture and Media Studies. In his research and practice on the intersection between politics, culture, and ecology, he is studying as well as crossing social, ecological, disciplinary, and cultural boundaries. Outside of academia, he is active as a trainer, critic, and activist. He is the author of 'Escaping the imaginary of engaged arts' (2019); *Audience Explorations: Guidebook for Hopefully Seeking the Audience* (2016). He lives in Serbia and works internationally.

Kasper Tromp (born 1992) is an art historian, trained at Leiden University (MA, 2018). He specializes in contemporary art from the MENA region, with a particular interest in artistic engagements with Islamic philosophical and mystical traditions in the formation of political subjectivities and the navigation of intercultural encounters. After graduating, he published 'Ayman Yossri's Artistic Interrogation of the Saudi Self Image' in *Zemzem* (2018). Kasper lives and works in the Netherlands.

Minna Valjakka (born 1975) is Senior Lecturer of Art History in the University of Helsinki. In her interdisciplinary research project, *Shades of Green* (funded by the Academy of Finland, 2020–2024), she focuses on artistic and creative practices at the nexus of environmental issues, translocal mediations, and transformations in arts and cultural policies. Her recent publications include journal articles in, among others, *City, Culture and Society*; *Cultural Studies*; and *Urban Design International*, along with *Visual Arts, Representations, and Interventions in Contemporary China*. She co-edited the book *Urbanized Interface* with Meiqin Wang in 2018. Minna lives and works in between Finland and East and South East Asia.

Paulina E. Varas (born 1975) is a researcher and independent curator. She studied at Universidad de Playa Ancha and Universidad de Barcelona. She is a professor and researcher in Universidad Andrés Bello and member of Southern Conceptualism Network. She recently published *Luz Donoso: El arte y la acción en el presente* (2018), and coedited *Archivo CADA. Astuciapráctica y potencias de lo común* (2018). She writes about art and politics in Chile in relation to the current issues addressed by social movements and political memories. She takes care of her son Borja and their cat Cuchita.

Mark Westmoreland (born 1971) coordinates the Visual Ethnography specialization at Leiden University. He has expertise in contemporary Arab visual culture, with particular interests in the interface between sensory embodiment and media aesthetics in ongoing legacies of contentious politics. Recent publications include: 'Time Capsules of Catastrophic Times' in *The Arab Archive: Mediated Memories and Digital Flows* (2020); 'Against the Archive' in *Akram Zaatari: Against Photography* (2018); 'Street Scenes: The Politics of Revolutionary Video in Egypt,' in *Visual Anthropology* (2016); 'Mish Mabsoota: On Teaching with a Camera in Revolutionary Cairo,' in *Journal of Aesthetics & Culture* (2015). Westmoreland lives and works in the Netherlands.

Kitty Zijlmans (born 1955) is an art historian. She studied at Leiden University and was appointed Professor of Contemporary Art History and Theory/World Art Studies at Leiden University in 2000. Her fields of interest are contemporary art, art theory, and methodology. She is especially interested in the ongoing intercultural processes and the globalization of the (art) world, and increasingly collaborates and exchanges with artists in the context of the field of artistic research. Her recent publication is entitled *Sustainable Art Communities. Contemporary Creativity and Policy in the Transnational Caribbean* (eds. Kitty Zijlmans and Leon Wainwright, Manchester, 2017). Kitty lives and works in Leiden, the Netherlands.

# Acknowledgements

This book is the result of a myriad of extraordinary voices coming together, each with its own passion, knowledge, experience, and commitment, to offer an answer to the question of how art and culture contribute to shaping our world. The fifteen chapters in this book have been authored by a remarkable ensemble of thirty-one authors: Mariam Abou Ghazi, Kobina Ankomah-Graham, Ilka Eickhof, Fernando Escobar Neira, Fatin Farhat, Maya Indira Ganesh, Rocca Holly-Nambi, Miranda Jeanne Marie Iossifidis, Nuraini Juliastuti, Višnja Kisić, Diana T. Kudaibergenova, Kabelo Malatsie, Jenny Mbaye, Zayd Minty, Nadia Moreno Moya, Judith Naeff, Laura Nkula-Wenz, Joseph Oduro-Frimpong, Arnout van Ree, Naomi Roux, Vaughn Sadie, Anna Selmeczi, Nishant Shah, Lenneke Sipkes, Rike Sitas, Cristiana Strava, Goran Tomka, Kasper Tromp, Minna Valjakka, Paulina E. Varas, and Mark Westmoreland—working either individually, or in self-organized teams. Each author has brought a distinctly personal and unique contribution to the collective result. We are grateful for the energy and continued dedication with which they have embraced this complex and experimental initiative. The authors have demonstrated profound knowledge, insatiable curiosity, a critical attitude, and deep respect towards the projects and organizations involved in their research—this has been evident not only throughout the writing process, but also in the numerous conversations we have held with them over the past two years. It has been a pleasure to work with each and every one of them and also to reflect and learn about our own work by looking at it through their eyes.

We would like to thank the team of editors. Our deepest appreciation goes to Carin Kuoni, the editorial director, for her truly irreplaceable work over the past year in shaping, bringing into focus, and fine-tuning the book, from its general concept down to the single lines of text. We were lucky to find in her, as well as in Jordi Baltà Portolés, Nora N. Khan, and Serubiri Moses, an astonishing mixture of wisdom, expertise, and earnest openness to discussing and learning with, and from, the authors. They have embraced the essence and spirit of *Forces of Art* in a way that went well beyond our expectations and that enriched the final result immensely.

The research that constitutes the backbone and soul of this book would simply have not existed without the thirty-eight projects and organizations that generously opened their doors to the authors and shared with them their knowledge, experiences, struggles, and visions for the present and the future. Our gratitude goes to many individuals within the teams of 32° East | Ugandan Arts Trust, Alta Tecnologia Andina (ATA), ArtEast, Arte Moris Arts Centre, Art Group '705', Bantmag, Beyond Pressure, BN Poetry Award, Britto Arts Trust, Clown Me In, Creating Independent and Artistic Networks (CRIA), Creatives Garage, Depo, doual'art, Dushanbe Art Ground / 'Sanati Muosir' Public Foundation, Fundación Cuatro Dieciocho 4-18, Fundación Más Arte Más Acción (MAMA), Jiser Reflexions Mediterranies, Këer Thiossane, Koalisi Seni Indonesia, l'Atelier de l'Observatoire, Maison de l'Image, Masrah Ensemble, Museo de Antioquia, Nafasi Art Space, Nubuke Foundation, Pages Bookstore, Proyecto mARTadero, RAW Material Company, ruangrupa, The Second Floor (T2F), Tiny Toones, Townhouse Gallery, Tsonami, Visual Arts Network of South Africa (VANSA), Volunteer Palestine, What, How and for Whom (WHW), and Women and Media Collective (WMC).This book is first and foremost a celebration of the incredible work that they have done and continue to do in spite of sometimes challenging circumstances.

In Valiz, we found a knowledgeable, attentive, and passionate publisher. Pia Pol and Astrid Vorstermans have been fundamental in bringing this complex project to its completion in record time and without losing sight of the centrality of the content and its quality. Our gratitude also goes to Liana Simmons for the care with which she has copy edited an impressive amount of pages with an accurate and gentle touch. We are amazed by the contribution that Lu Liang has brought to the project with the design element. Her concept and the way she developed it throughout these pages are both an act of poetic imagination and the result of a rigorous reflection firmly grounded in the content of the book. We would like to wholeheartedly thank the members of the Advisory Committee, who supported us from the very first months of the *Forces of Art* initiative: Kitty Zijlmans, Chair of the Committee, and Patrick Flores, Yudhishthir Raj Isar, and Yvette Mutumba. We are indebted to them for their advice, continued support, and rigorous—yet caring—guidance throughout the whole process.

Finally, we would also like to thank our colleagues in the teams of the Prince Claus Fund, Hivos, and the European Cultural Foundation for their thoughtful support and for the enriching discussions they have initiated, or contributed to, since the beginning of this initiative. Sharing with them a passionate belief in the transformative force of art and culture has been a fundamental driver for us. We would like to highlight here the strategic role played by the director of the Prince Claus Fund, Joumana El Zein Khoury. It was her vision of a world where the role of artists and cultural practitioners is widely and firmly recognized that provided the initial impetus for the research in this book. This book and the research behind it have been made possible by different funding sources: the Next Generation Programme of the Prince Claus Fund, which is funded by the Dutch Ministry of Foreign Affairs; the Resource of Open Minds (R.O.O.M.) Programme of Hivos, funded by the Swedish International Development Cooperation Agency (Sida); and the European Cultural Foundation, receiving annual funding from BankGiro Loterij and Nederlandse Loterij through the partnership with the Prins Bernhard Cultuurfonds.

Laura Alexander
Tsveta Andreeva
Ilaria Manzini
Mechtild van den Hombergh
Arthur Steiner
Myriam Vandenbroucke

*Forces of Art* Working Group
(Prince Claus Fund, Hivos, and European Cultural Foundation)
Amsterdam, June 2020

Editors
Carin Kuoni (editor-in-chief)
Jordi Baltà Portolés
Nora N. Khan
Moses Serubiri

Contributors
Mariam Abou Ghazi
Kobina Ankomah-Graham
Jordi Baltà Portolés
Ilka Eickhof
Fernando Escobar Neira
Fatin Farhat
Maya Indira Ganesh
Rocca Holly-Nambi
Miranda Jeanne Marie Iossifidis
Nuraini Juliastuti
Nora N. Khan
Višnja Kisić
Diana T. Kudaibergenova
Carin Kuoni
Kabelo Malatsie
Jenny Mbaye
Zayd Minty
Nadia Moreno Moya
Serubiri Moses
Judith Naeff
Laura Nkula-Wenz
Joseph Oduro-Frimpong
Arnout van Ree
Naomi Roux
Vaughn Sadie
Anna Selmeczi
Nishant Shah
Lenneke Sipkes
Rike Sitas
Cristiana Strava
Goran Tomka
Kasper Tromp
Minna Valjakka
Paulina E. Varas
Mark R. Westmoreland
Kitty Zijlmans

Translation
Tupac Cruz / Spanish-English (text by Nadia Moreno Moya & Fernando Escobar Neira)

Copy editor
Liana Simmons
Proofreading
Els Brinkman
Index
Elke Stevens
Nic de Jong

Graphic Design
Lu Liang, The Exercises
Design Assistance
Jungeun Lee
Design Intern
Kexin Hao

Typefaces
Balance
Times Small

Production
Ilaria Manzini, Pia Pol, Astrid Vorstermans

Paper Inside
Amber Graphic
Paper Cover
Brossulin XT

Lithography
Mariska Bijl, Wilco Art Books, Amsterdam

Printing and Binding
Wilco Art Books, Meppel / Amersfoort

Publisher
Valiz, Amsterdam, Pia Pol & Astrid Vorstermans, www.valiz.nl

Partners
Prince Claus Fund for Culture and Development, Amsterdam, www.princeclausfund.org

C
Fonds

Hivos, 's-Gravenhage, www.hivos.org

European Cultural Foundation, Amsterdam, www.culturalfoundation.eu

European Cultural Foundation



Distribution
NL/BE/LU: Centraal Boekhuis, www.cb.nl

GB/IE: Anagram Books, www.anagrambooks.com

Europe/Asia: Idea Books, www.ideabooks.nl

USA, Canada, Latin America: D.A.P., www.artbook.com

Australia: Perimeter, www.perimeterdistribution.com

Individual orders: www.valiz.nl

ISBN 978-94-92095-89-3
Printed and bound in the EU
Valiz, Amsterdam, 2020

A Note on the Design of this Book:
Mapping without Borders

'People only know where one country ends
and another begins because people have said it is so.'
Emma Wolukau-Wanambwa, *Promised Lands*

The land between you and I may be divided by walls and borders, but the land is unaware of this. The land probably doesn't care. When I look up, there is only distance. My clouds travel thousands of miles to you, and turn into rain. The sun hides under my ocean, and rises up behind your mountain. This is the magic of being spherical. When you look up, remember, I am with you under the same borderless sky.

All inserted sky images were taken at or around the location of the projects mentioned in this book, according to the same solar moment; conducted in August, 2020.

Lu Liang / The Exercises